READER'S DIGEST CONDENSED BOOKS

Parrot Tulips
by Charlene Tarbox

READER'S DIGEST CONDENSED BOOKS

Volume 1
1986

THE READER'S DIGEST ASSOCIATION
Pleasantville, New York

READER'S DIGEST CONDENSED BOOKS
Editor: John S. Zinsser, Jr.
Executive Editor: Barbara J. Morgan

Managing Editors: Anne H. Atwater, Ann Berryman, Tanis H. Erdmann,
Thomas Froncek, Marjorie Palmer
Senior Staff Editors: Jean E. Aptakin, Angela Weldon
Senior Editors: Linn Carl, Angela C. Gibbs,
Virginia Rice (Rights), Ray Sipherd, Margery D. Thorndike
Associate Editors: Thomas S. Clemmons, Alice Jones-Miller,
Mary Kirby, Joseph P. McGrath, Maureen A. Mackey, James J. Menick
Senior Copy Editors: Claire A. Bedolis, Jeane Garment
Associate Copy Editors: Maxine Bartow, Rosalind H. Campbell, Jean G. Cornell,
Jean S. Friedman, Diana Marsh, Jane F. Neighbors
Art Director: William Gregory
Executive Art Editor: Soren Noring
Senior Art Editor: Angelo Perrone
Associate Art Editors, Research: George Calas, Jr., Katherine Kelleher

CB PROJECTS
Executive Editor: Herbert H. Lieberman
Senior Editors: Catherine T. Brown, John R. Roberson
Associate Editor: Dana Adkins

CB INTERNATIONAL EDITIONS
Executive Editor: Francis Schell
Senior Staff Editor: Sigrid MacRae
Senior Editor: Istar H. Dole
Associate Editor: Gary Q. Arpin

Reader's Digest Condensed Books are published every two to three months at Pleasantville, N.Y.

The condensations in this volume have been created by The Reader's Digest
Association, Inc., and are used by permission of and special arrangement with
the publishers and the holders of the respective copyrights.

The original editions of the books in this volume are published and copyrighted as follows:
Mrs. Pollifax and the Hong Kong Buddha, published at $14.95 by Doubleday & Company, Inc.
© 1985 by Dorothy Gilman Butters
Wildfire, published at $15.95 by W. W. Norton & Company, Inc.
© 1985 by Richard Martin Stern
Arnie and a House Full of Company, published at $11.95 by Houghton Mifflin Company
© 1985 by Margarete Sigl Corbo and Diane Marie Barras
Take Away One, published at $15.95 by St. Martin's Press/Marek
© 1985 by Thomas Froncek
The Two Farms, published at $12.95 by St. Martin's Press
© 1985 by Mary E. Pearce

CONTENTS

Mrs. Pollifax and the Hong Kong Buddha

A CONDENSATION OF THE NOVEL BY

Dorothy Gilman

ILLUSTRATED BY RAY YELDHAM

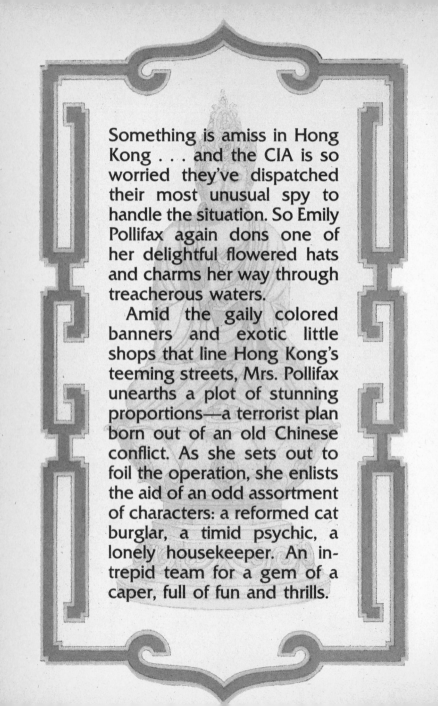

Something is amiss in Hong Kong . . . and the CIA is so worried they've dispatched their most unusual spy to handle the situation. So Emily Pollifax again dons one of her delightful flowered hats and charms her way through treacherous waters.

Amid the gaily colored banners and exotic little shops that line Hong Kong's teeming streets, Mrs. Pollifax unearths a plot of stunning proportions—a terrorist plan born out of an old Chinese conflict. As she sets out to foil the operation, she enlists the aid of an odd assortment of characters: a reformed cat burglar, a timid psychic, a lonely housekeeper. An intrepid team for a gem of a caper, full of fun and thrills.

Prologue

It was raining—a driving spring rain that slashed at the windows—and Mrs. Pollifax hoped that it was not raining in the wilds of Vermont, where Cyrus had gone for a ten-day bird-watching expedition that would find him crouching for hours in the shrubbery or ensconced in a tree with field glasses. She had remained behind in New Jersey—quite wisely, she thought now—to deal with the carpenters swarming over the old house they'd bought, and to which they were adding a greenhouse for her geraniums, a bird-watching balcony for Cyrus and a bay window that was to be placed slightly off center, a decision that deeply pained Mr. Lupalak, the contractor, a man for whom symmetry was a passion.

Standing at the window and staring out at the very green, very wet May landscape, Mrs. Pollifax wondered for the first time if she was really going to *like* the country after years of a more suburban life. Yes, she could admire the sweep of lawn, the curve of road beyond, the spire of a church visible above a dripping willow tree. But when the carpenters left she wondered if it were not going to seem a trifle unoccupied. She knew that out there in the grass and among the hollows the land was teeming with wildlife—mice, toads and even a rumor of a porcupine—but what the scene plainly lacked, she thought, was *people*. Mrs. Pollifax enjoyed people of all shapes, sizes, types and temperaments.

And then quite suddenly there was movement in that placid landscape as a car drove down Route 2, stopped, turned and raced

9

toward her, sending plumes of water into the air as it hurtled through puddles to come to a stop near her front door.

"Now, who . . ." murmured Mrs. Pollifax.

From the car emerged a pleasant-looking young man wearing a boisterous plaid suit and carrying an attaché case: a man very familiar and dear to her, who reminded her at once that her past included not only the growing of prizewinning geraniums, but a great deal of drama, excitement and danger, stemming from certain assignments she had undertaken for the CIA.

She opened the door to him even before he reached it. "Bishop!" she cried. "What a surprise! How on earth—"

"Devil of a time finding you," he said, giving her a hug.

"If you'd only called first, I could have given you terribly efficient directions." She laughed. "I'll put on some coffee. Oh, it's good to see you. Come in and look at our house."

"Love to," he said. "Where's Cyrus?"

"He left three days ago; he's in Vermont."

"Uh-oh," said Bishop.

Mrs. Pollifax gave him a quick glance. *Not* a social call, she thought, and felt a stirring of anticipation. "Now, that's a strange reaction," she told him.

He ignored this. "Put the coffee on and show me around. I've not much time," he added as he dropped his attaché case on the pink-and-red flowered couch.

Mrs. Pollifax led him up to the gabled bedrooms, down through the kitchen into the dining room, with its flagstoned terrace beyond, and into the greenhouse, which as yet lacked glass. She took him into the basement and introduced him to Mr. Lupalak, who regarded Bishop's suit with something approaching awe.

They arrived back in the dining room at last, where Mrs. Pollifax poured coffee for them both, brought out a plate of macaroons and sat down to face him across the polished trestle table.

"And how is Carstairs?" she inquired, nibbling on a macaroon.

"Fine," said Bishop of his superior. "Considering the sedentary life he leads, full of stress and tension. I regard him as a medical phenomenon. He resists running, jogging, even walking, and in effect defies every known law of health. And how is Cyrus?"

"Bird-watching."

He nodded. "And you're still Mrs. *Reed*-Pollifax?"

"Defying every known law of convention, yes," she responded. "Cyrus insisted I keep the name Pollifax, I insisted on including his. A hyphen solved it all."

A silence fell between them as Bishop sipped his coffee. "All right," she said at last, smiling. "You can't possibly expect me to believe that you just happened to be in the neighborhood."

"No, I didn't happen to be in the neighborhood," Bishop admitted cheerfully. "It needed a plane, a taxi, a limousine and a rented car to reach you. Except I'd expected Cyrus to be here."

"He isn't," she pointed out.

"No, but we thought this time he'd want to go with you—now that you're married and all—however, it can't be helped. The thing is," he said, "we need you badly, and at once."

"For what?" she asked. "And what does 'at once' mean?"

He put down his cup of coffee. "If you can help us," he said quietly, "it means now. No time to collect Cyrus, no time for anything. You'd leave here within the hour, by twelve noon."

Mrs. Pollifax glanced at her watch: exactly five minutes after eleven. It was quite impossible, she told herself. There was the bay window, and Cyrus. . . . "Why me?" she asked. "And where?"

"Hong Kong," said Bishop.

Hong Kong. The sun shone in Hong Kong, she recalled. Brilliantly.

"You remember Sheng Ti?" asked Bishop.

She did indeed remember Sheng Ti. A year or so ago—on assignment from Carstairs' department of the CIA—she had met him in a Chinese town called Turfan. After hearing how he was *hai ren*, or a "black person," in Communist China—living without papers or home or identity—she had persuaded her co-agent to smuggle him out of the country along with an imprisoned defense expert whom they'd been sent to rescue.

She nodded. "Of course. A very intelligent young man, his talents absolutely wasted as an outcast."

"You're aware that he's in Hong Kong?"

"So you told me. It sounded," she added tartly, "as if you didn't know what to do with him and he was simply *dumped* there."

Bishop said dryly, "Well, he wasn't exactly dumped, as you phrase it. He was *placed* there. With one of our agents. And to put it in a nutshell, my dear Mrs. Pollifax, we are growing very worried about that agent, and your friend Sheng Ti is the only person in a position to give us some clues."

"What would he know?" she asked doubtfully.

"Sheng Ti works for the agent. His name is Detwiler, he's a Eurasian, and his cover is a business called Feng Imports, Limited, a small business dealing in gems and art pieces. Old Feng runs the shop, Detwiler handles the importing, and Sheng Ti is one of two employees."

"And you're worried about Detwiler?"

"I can't tell you how worried," said Bishop. "The information he sent the department in his last report was so patently false that we went back over his previous reports and discovered that, beginning about two months ago, he's been feeding us doctored information. In a word, something's up. We suspect he's double-crossing us; certainly he's of no use anymore. But we have every intention of finding out why, who he's working for now, and what's going on. What's more," he added, "someone's put the fear of God—or Satan, perhaps—into your friend Sheng Ti."

Startled, she said, "How do you know that?"

"We sent two people into Feng Imports to approach Sheng Ti, but no dice. The verdict was, 'This is a guy who's terrified.' Which, I might add, only confirms our suspicions of something *very* wrong at Feng Imports."

"And you feel that Sheng Ti might talk to me," she said.

Bishop nodded. "He knows you. He trusts you. You're the only person who can get through to him."

"Yes," said Mrs. Pollifax.

Bishop looked at her and said gravely, "It could, of course, be dangerous—there's that too—if you can't find Sheng Ti and have to sniff around Feng Imports."

Mrs. Pollifax considered his words for a moment and then stood up and carried the pot of coffee into the kitchen. "It's just eleven twenty-five," she told Bishop. "If you'll rinse out these cups—"

"You'll go!" cried Bishop joyously.

She smiled. "Yes, I'll go, and now if you'll excuse me . . ."

She hurried upstairs, snatched her suitcase from the closet and crammed into it slacks, skirts and blouses, toothbrush, walking shoes and pajamas. Into her purse she tucked her passport, quickly changed into a purple suit, chose a pink blouse and placed on her head a hat that was a garden of brilliant red and pink roses. She then sat down at the desk to write Cyrus a hasty note. "There's no way to reach you," she wrote, wishing the remote lodge where he was staying had a phone. "This is all terribly unexpected. Bishop is here—he hoped you would be too—I'm off to Hong Kong in fifteen minutes, and I'll be . . ."

"Bishop—" she called. "Where will I stay, and for how long?"

"Give it a week," Bishop shouted back. "And we've booked you in the Hong Kong Hilton."

". . . at the Hong Kong Hilton, back in a week, don't forget how dear you are, love love love, Emily."

She read it over and added, "P.S. Do not allow Mr. Lupalak to center bay window!" and then for just a moment she allowed herself to contemplate Cyrus' reaction when he found her gone and read the note. She had promised never again to work for Carstairs without Cyrus' going with her; on the other hand, Cyrus had insisted that she never forfeit an assignment because of him.

"Won't have you caged, m'dear," he'd said. "Waited too many years for someone as full of surprises as you. Don't want to change anything about you."

Dear Cyrus, she thought. How fortunate she'd been to meet him in Zambia, where he had been traveling with his daughter, Lisa, and where she had been looking for an assassin. He was a judge, retired now, and before their trip was over, he had saved her life, and then she had saved his, which provided grounds for a warm friendship. Except that from the beginning Cyrus made it clear that he had much more than friendship in mind.

Her reverie was interrupted when she thought of Bishop's words, "It could be dangerous—there's that too," and she nodded. Yes, there was always that. Talking with Sheng Ti seemed a relatively small assignment, but so had her trip to mainland China a year ago. No one had envisioned murder or the long hours of interrogation she'd undergone by the Chinese security police. Still, it had all ended well. And out of that adventure had come the realization that Cyrus Reed was absolutely vital to her future.

Now, after years of being a widow, she had been married to Cyrus for ten months. She smiled as she looked around a room that was filled with a sense of his presence. She could only hope that he would understand that she was needed.

"I'm needed," she said aloud, and resolutely folded the note, after which she checked the tilt of her hat in a mirror that reflected back a cheerful face glowing with anticipation.

It was ten minutes to the hour when she carried her suitcase downstairs, and seeing her, Bishop whistled.

"Do you water those roses every night? What a hat," he marveled. "What a *hat!*"

"Thank you," she said demurely, and proceeded down into the basement to explain to an astonished Mr. Lupalak that she was leaving and would not be back that afternoon, or for quite a few afternoons; that he must tell Mr. Reed there was a note for him in the usual place, and would he please not fail her about the bay window, it was to be slightly *off center*. She returned to Bishop. "I'm sure he thinks I'm leaving Cyrus," she said, sighing. "For that matter, I don't think anyone in the neighborhood believes that we're married, what with me being Mrs. Reed-Pollifax."

Bishop grinned. "I could tell him I was at your wedding."

Mrs. Pollifax gave him a mischievous smile. "No. Everyone needs a bit of mystery in their lives, don't you think? Let Mr. Lupalak believe what he likes." With this, she tucked the note for Cyrus in the refrigerator, and walked out to the car with Bishop.

Monday

BOARDING the plane in San Francisco for the second leg of her trip, Mrs. Pollifax found herself astonished by the crowds of people hurrying from point A to point B with such enormous fixity of purpose. As she made her way to her seat, she wondered if there was any other world like this, outside ordinary life, so urgent and capsulated. Perhaps a hospital, she mused, where people also shared a great fixity of purpose and . . .

"Oh, I beg your pardon!" she said, treading on the heel of the man in front of her. He turned and gave her a chilling look. Refusing intimidation, she said, "You did stop very suddenly."

The man's glance was like an assault. Tall, thin, immaculately dressed, a lean face with pockmarked cheeks and cold eyes—not a pleasant young man, she decided. She proceeded down the aisle to 48-B, relieved to see that 48-A was already occupied, and by a far more pleasant-looking gentleman.

She soon exchanged names with her seatmate—his was Albert Hitchens—and shortly after dinner they settled down to a long talk about psychic phenomena, for Mr. Hitchens, it turned out, was a psychic.

"It's my dharma," he said simply.

He was not a prepossessing man; he was scarcely taller than her own five feet five. His features were nondescript, and for a man in his forties his clothes were casual in the extreme—faded jeans, a knit shirt and sneakers—but his eyes were penetrating and a curious silver in color, almost translucent.

Mrs. Pollifax, adept at karate, experienced in Yoga, merely nodded at the word dharma. "Although," she admitted, "I do have trouble with the difference between karma and dharma."

"Ah yes," he said. "Dharma, you know, is the essence of one's individual existence—one's work, you might say—whereas karma, of course, is the force generated from past lives that determines our destiny in this one."

The slightly pedantic tone apparently came from the many lectures he gave; he was a professional psychic, having written several books on the subject and having done considerable work for the police in finding missing persons.

"Which," he explained three hours into their flight, "is why I'm going to Hong Kong. One of my former students, a delightful young man of Chinese origin, telephoned from Hong Kong several days ago, pleading for help in finding a missing relative."

"And do you think you can?" Mrs. Pollifax asked with interest.

He said firmly, "There will be something."

Mrs. Pollifax, glancing into those unusual eyes, conceded that he was probably right. "But how do you do it?"

"It's a matter of impressions," he explained. "I can hold an object belonging to the missing person, and it will tell me whether he's alive or dead. Sometimes I go into a trance and receive impressions of where he can be found."

"Impressions," she murmured, and as a movement down the aisle caught her glance she said, "Tell me your impression of that man, the one returning from the men's room." It was the man on whose heel she'd stepped.

Mr. Hitchens obligingly followed her glance, narrowing his eyes. "Now that," he said distastefully, "is as black an aura as I've

15

seen for a long time." He shook his head. "A great deal of violence surrounds that man."

"Inside or outside?" asked Mrs. Pollifax curiously.

"If a man is a killer of life," said Mr. Hitchens with even more distaste, "does it matter how?"

Mrs. Pollifax considered. "No, I don't suppose it does."

They settled down then to an enthusiastic discussion of out-of-body experiences, precognition and predestination, during which she learned that he too was to stay at the Hong Kong Hilton.

"Perhaps we could breakfast together when we reach the hotel," he suggested.

"You're not being met by your young friend?" she asked.

"I chose not to be," he said. "I want to gather impressions—"

"That word again," said Mrs. Pollifax, smiling.

"Rest for several hours, meditate and clear my head. My friend is to call for me at noon. We'll lunch and then get to work. But I find your vibrations quite energizing and not at all distracting," he told her. "Unless, of course, you have other plans?"

Mrs. Pollifax assured him that she would be delighted to have breakfast with him, and following this they each fell into naps, sleeping through a perpetual dawn and several time zones, until some hours later, reeling with jet lag, they walked off the plane at Kai Tak Airport.

At passport control the man with the violent aura stood ahead of Mrs. Pollifax, and she saw that it was a Canadian passport that he offered to the officer; at the luggage carousel he went off with one very expensive-looking pigskin bag. After that she lost interest in him, and following an interminable wait at customs she and Mr. Hitchens walked out into a clear, fresh morning.

"Sunshine," breathed Mrs. Pollifax happily. Not yet the gold of a tropical noon, but a thin, radiant silver light that ricocheted down and across the sides of gleaming buildings and scattered rhinestones across a blue harbor. "And there's Hong Kong," she told Mr. Hitchens, pointing across a mile of water to rows of sleek buildings encircling the precipitous slopes of Victoria Peak.

"Aren't we already in Hong Kong?" he said, surprised.

"Yes and no," she said. "Hong Kong itself is an island, and it's so crowded and mountainous that I don't think they could ever squeeze in an airport. We're across the bay on Kowloon Peninsula, which has belonged to Hong Kong for at least a hundred years."

Presently a taxi was whisking them out of Kowloon, through a tunnel, and when they emerged they were on the Hong Kong side of the harbor. "Which," Mrs. Pollifax reminded Mr. Hitchens, "is all that Britain will have left when mainland China takes back Kowloon and the New Territories in 1997."

"Takes back!" he repeated. "I'm not aware—"

"Well—they've only been leased to Great Britain," she explained. "I believe Hong Kong was settled back in the early 1800s—it all had something to do with the opium trade—and then, being a very small island, less than thirty miles square and prospering mightily, it leaked over into Kowloon. Later a lease was negotiated with mainland China for the New Territories. They tell me the Hong Kong dollar plunges every time Britain and China meet to discuss the changeover."

"So it's all quite temporary—one might say like life itself," mused Mr. Hitchens.

She smiled, finding him comfortable to be with, and feeling that his presence helped her to adjust to Cyrus' absence. Really, she thought, she had grown quite spoiled without realizing it.

"But we could almost be in Manhattan," protested Mr. Hitchens, glancing at the modern banks and office buildings and hotels. "Except for the faces on the street."

She nodded. "Yes, they're different. Hong Kong is ninety-eight percent Chinese, but the attaché cases are the same, aren't they?"

"You're certainly very well informed," he told her.

She did not mention that she had been briefed by Bishop on the long drive to the airport. "Actually I've told you all I know. I was here last year, just overnight."

"I've never been out of the United States before."

Mr. Hitchens' confession touched her as well as surprised her; she remembered her own first trip abroad, how dazzled and yet oddly insecure she'd felt in the beginning, and she was suddenly very glad that she was breakfasting with him.

Their taxi swept up to the entrance of the Hong Kong Hilton, and they made their way into the huge lobby, where Mr. Hitchens, registering, was given room 601, and Mrs. Pollifax, taking her turn, was given the key to room 614.

"Practically neighbors," said Mrs. Pollifax. "Why don't we

17

meet for breakfast thirty minutes from now. I think, remembering my first visit here, it's in the Golden Lotus room, a buffet, with wonderful papayas and melons."

"I can hardly wait," said Mr. Hitchens.

Mrs. Pollifax found room 614 enormous and filled with light. She peered into the small, well-stocked refrigerator, removed her hat and then sat down on the bed to study the street map of Hong Kong that Bishop had given her. Feng Imports, he'd told her, was in the city's West Point district, at number 31 Dragon Alley. Its location had been lightly circled in pencil, and now Mrs. Pollifax lined it up with the hotel. Obviously a taxi, she realized, as she measured distances, her eye meeting exotic names like Ice House Street, Jardine's Bazaar and Yee Wo Street. Definitely not New Jersey, she thought, and decided that she must reach Dragon Alley before the shop opened so that she could intercept Sheng Ti on the street, before he began work.

Some minutes later Mrs. Pollifax was seated in the Golden Lotus room, sipping coffee while she waited for Mr. Hitchens. When he finally slid into the chair beside her he had changed into slacks and a jacket. His sober face was animated by excitement.

"You won't believe who I just passed in the lobby," he told her boyishly. "The third richest man in the world!"

"Now you're the well-informed one," she told him. "Who on earth is the third richest man in the world?"

"His name is Lars Pettersen." Hitchens grinned. "I turned on my TV as soon as I got into my room, and he was being interviewed on Hong Kong television."

"I suppose I have a TV too," she said doubtfully.

He laughed. "I'm addicted to it, very partial to reruns, especially *I Love Lucy* and Mary Tyler Moore." Positively enlivened now, he added, "I've been married three times, and each wife thought a psychic would live an exciting life."

"They didn't expect TV reruns?" said Mrs. Pollifax.

"No. Oh, thank you," he told the waiter who was pouring him coffee, and then, his glance wandering, he said eagerly, "There he is now! Just walking into the restaurant."

"Who?" said Mrs. Pollifax.

"Mr. Pettersen, the man I was telling you about."

Mrs. Pollifax turned. By the door stood a very attractive young man, tanned and blond, whose slightly bent nose was all that prevented him from being outrageously handsome. Seeing him, she drew in her breath sharply. "*Who* did you say he is?"

"Lars Pettersen. Danish, I think, although he talked with an English accent." His glance returned to Mrs. Pollifax, and he said, "Is something wrong?"

Mrs. Pollifax, considerably jolted, had begun to smile. "No, nothing. Nothing at all," she told him.

But past and present worlds were colliding as she recovered from the shock of recognizing Mr. Lars Pettersen, the third richest man in the world, because the man entering the Golden Lotus she knew much better as Robin Burke-Jones, whom she'd first met in Switzerland, where he had been a very successful cat burglar, discreetly relieving sheiks of their prized gems. For a brief moment a kaleidoscope of vignettes flashed through Mrs. Pollifax's head: Of Robin, discovered with her jewelry case, saying, "You're not going to inform?" Of Robin, lowering her on a rope from a balcony to escape a murderer searching for her in the halls; of a long night spent in the Castle Chillon with a small boy and, upon their finding an escape route, Robin's voice in the darkness, "Over here in a rowboat. What took you so long?"

Dear Robin, she thought, relishing the jest of seeing him here, for she had also been matron of honor at his wedding, and only five months ago there had been the usual Christmas card from him and his bride, Court.

Except that following his wedding—as she ought to have remembered at once—Robin had abandoned the hazards of cat burglary to become an honest man. He had been invited to use his considerable talents to solve crimes instead of commit them. He had joined Interpol.

I wonder, she thought now with intense curiosity and considerable amusement, what he's up to here in Hong Kong.

"I BELIEVE I'll linger over my coffee," Mrs. Pollifax told her breakfast companion half an hour later as he prepared to leave.

"Oh!" said Mr. Hitchens. "Yes, of course." For just a moment he looked a little anxious. Then he smiled and extended his hand. "Yes. Well. It's been a real pleasure meeting you. Perhaps we'll meet again."

She stood up to shake his hand. "I wouldn't mind hearing if you successfully locate your missing person," she told him with a smile. "Give me a call if you've time. Happy hunting!"

Once he was gone, she gathered up her purse and headed for the buffet island, behind which Robin had vanished. She had reached a decision. Robin could not possibly have seen her, and it was infinitely kinder that he become aware of her presence now rather than be surprised by it later, since heaven only knew what he might be up to here. Rounding the buffet's southern end, she sought Robin and found him. He was seated facing her, talking animatedly to a plump Chinese man. As she appeared beside the pineapples the sudden movement caught his eye.

For just the fraction of a second he stopped talking. She allowed her gaze to move past him with the indifference of a stranger; then Robin resumed his conversation. But he had seen her. Good, she thought, and having established that she was here, and that she would not betray him, she continued past the ham and the chafing dishes of omelets, and then made her exit.

Now for Sheng Ti, she thought, and continued out of the hotel to find a cab.

As she was driven through the streets of Hong Kong she thought back to her earlier meetings with this young man. She could concede that China had performed miracles for its billion people, but to her Sheng Ti represented the cost of those miracles, for he was—she struggled to remember her impressions—*different* . . . not because his parents had been rich farmers, but because of what this had denied him in Mao's China. There had been no chance for him to use his considerable intelligence. There had been first of all the primitive commune to which he'd been sent at the age of sixteen and from which he'd run away when he was nineteen. For this he'd been sent deep into the country to work building roads, and here too he'd found it difficult to conform. Eventually he had acquired a dossier, until at twenty-six, when she'd met him, he had become a nonperson, completely without hope and living by his wits.

In America, she thought, he would have become by now a teacher or a lawyer, for he'd been born curious, and Mrs. Pollifax measured intelligence by curiosity, feeling sorry for people who never asked questions. One had not asked questions in Mao's

China, and Mao's influence still lingered. One had to conform.

And so it was she who had urged that Sheng Ti be smuggled out of China. But if he was not happy in Hong Kong, as Bishop had suggested, she wondered if she had done him much good.

Some minutes later she was deposited at the foot of a street too narrow for cars, and told by her driver that she would find Dragon Alley halfway up that street. With a feeling of excitement Mrs. Pollifax stepped out of the cab, to be deliciously assaulted, nearly overwhelmed, by noise, people and color. She had found China again, in a corner of Hong Kong far away in ambiance from the district of polite commerce that she'd just left.

Now this, she thought with pleasure, is more like it. And she stood very still, letting the smells and sounds sweep over her. The narrow street was crammed with buildings from which hung signs of every size and shape. TAILOR! SHOES! SILKS! GEMS! COLOR TV! From balconies protruded bamboo poles hung with laundry of every color, but mostly the eye-shattering scarlet that also blazed from suspended banners and lanterns. The street was filled with people, and the sidewalks with street stalls heaped with plastic flowers, fresh flowers, sandals, herbs, dried seafood and fresh fruit. The predominant smells were of incense, ginger and fried noodles; the sounds were a cacophony of voices competing with blaring radios.

"Lovely," murmured Mrs. Pollifax, and began strolling through the crowds, stopping to peer at jars of pickled snakes, roots of ginseng and souvenir mugs. Eventually she found Dragon Alley, little more than a broad staircase leading up to another street beyond it. She entered and began to climb.

Number 31 lay on her right, a shabby, narrow store with a sign overhead announcing in both Chinese and English the existence of Feng Imports. The door was not open, and drawing abreast of it, Mrs. Pollifax shifted her gaze straight ahead and then—very casually—glanced at the store window, hesitated and stopped to examine its contents, a display of carved jade and ivory objects.

Very nice, she decided, and certainly more attractive than the exterior of the shop. Lifting her eyes, she looked into the interior and found it empty. A sign on the door said the shop opened at ten a.m. It was now nine forty.

Mrs. Pollifax continued up the alley. On her right were more shops. The opposite side, except for a nightclub, appeared to be narrow wooden houses with balconies and gates, one of them with a sign that said ROOMS. This latter building, number 40, she noticed, had a bench beside the gate, and Mrs. Pollifax sat down on it to wait for Sheng Ti.

At nine forty-five a man walked out of Feng Imports, startling Mrs. Pollifax, because she had seen no one enter the shop, and strode at a fast pace up the alley toward her. He carried a pigskin bag and was tall and lean, not Chinese, his cheeks pockmarked, and his eyes—but she knew what his eyes would look like, because she had seen him before. It was the man she had bumped into on the plane, the man with the black aura.

He passed her without a glance and disappeared into the street above the alley, leaving Mrs. Pollifax to speculate on the coincidence of his seeking out Feng Imports too, and obviously before he had stopped anywhere else to deposit his luggage.

At nine fifty-five a young girl hurried up Dragon Alley, stopped at the shop, unlocked the door and entered—a lovely Chinese girl wearing a cheongsam of blue cotton, her hair very black, her skin very pale. Employee number one, decided Mrs. Pollifax.

At ten fifteen, no one else having entered, Mrs. Pollifax strolled down the alley again, trying her best to resemble a wandering tourist. Once again she paused at the window of Feng Imports to look inside. The shop was occupied only by the girl, who was flicking a feathered duster over a display of figurines, and Mrs. Pollifax sighed, feeling a large yawn coming.

I'll try again at noon, she told herself, and took a taxi back to the hotel to unpack and surrender briefly to jet lag.

Promptly at noon, however, she set out, her hat a shade less squarely on her head and one rose listing slightly in spite of efforts to discipline it; it too suffered from travel fatigue, she guessed. Once again she made her way up Dragon Alley and stopped to look into the window. This time she could see two people in the shop, an elderly Chinese gentleman seated behind the counter, and the girl, now rearranging objects on a tray.

There was no Sheng Ti.

At this point Mrs. Pollifax realized that she lacked the patience of a professional spy. She was by nature very direct, and the thought of visiting the shop at hourly intervals all week appalled her. In any case, the whole point of her being here was to talk with Sheng Ti. Carstairs might not approve, but she would go in.

Calmly Mrs. Pollifax entered Feng Imports.

The man seated behind the counter had the face of an ancient Manchu, with skin wrinkled like crepe paper and the ghost of a goatee at his chin; but his eyes were shrewd as they moved over the roses on her hat and then dropped to her face. She thought he looked tired, like a man who had expected a great deal more from life and had not yet resigned himself to having less.

"Good afternoon," she said cheerfully.

"Good afternoon," he responded, bowing.

"I've come to see Sheng Ti," she announced.

The girl looked up quickly and just as quickly looked away. The man—Mr. Feng, she supposed—stiffened only slightly. "I do not understand," he said politely. "Shangchi?"

"Sheng Ti," repeated Mrs. Pollifax.

To the girl he murmured, his eyes on Mrs. Pollifax, "You may go, Lotus." The girl walked to the back of the room, parted the long lines of beads that curtained the doorway, and disappeared. "But," said the man, "there is no one here by that name."

Oh, dear, thought Mrs. Pollifax. They're going to be difficult. "Nonsense," she said cordially. "Of course he's here. I've been told on excellent authority that he works here, and if he no longer works here, perhaps you can tell me where he does. Because," she added breathlessly, "I'm here on holiday for a week and really must say hello to him before I leave."

"Told he works here?" repeated the man, blinking.

Mrs. Pollifax brought out the memo Bishop had scribbled, and read from it in a clear, loud voice. " 'Sheng Ti, care of Feng Imports, 31 Dragon Alley.' You are Mr. Feng?"

He stared at the paper. "If I may see—" With astonishing speed he reached out and grasped it before she could pull back.

"Who gave you this?" he said sharply.

"A friend of Sheng Ti's."

"Friend?" His voice was cool. "How do you know Sheng Ti?"

Even more coolly she said, "I fail to see how it's any concern of yours, Mr. Feng, but since you insist on an inquisition, I met him in mainland China, near Turfan. Really," she said sternly, "that young man was in the most appalling situation. It was a shock to

23

an American tourist, I can assure you. We had a long talk, and—"

He said dryly, "You speak Chinese?"

She waved this aside impatiently. "A companion did. And then learning Sheng Ti had the opportunity to leave China—but so illicitly, so dangerously . . ." She allowed her voice to falter dramatically. "I have since made every effort to find out what happened to him." She added in an aggrieved voice, "Knocking on many doors and writing a great many letters, and not taking no for an answer. And I *will* not take no for an answer now."

He returned the paper to her. "But you have been misinformed, Mrs.—er—"

"Pollifax."

"We are importers here, Mrs. Pollifax. There is no Sheng Ti."

She looked at him squarely. "Then why have you asked so many questions? Frankly, sir, I don't believe you."

Behind the beaded curtain she heard an amused voice say, "Bring our stubborn friend in, Feng."

Mr. Feng's lips thinned. "I don't think—"

"Bring her in." There was a sharpness in the voice that startled Mr. Feng, who shrugged, turned toward the curtain and gestured Mrs. Pollifax to precede him.

The multicolored beads slithered and whispered. Mrs. Pollifax entered a tiny office, where the girl, Lotus, was stringing what looked to be pearls. The man who had eavesdropped from behind the curtain led Mrs. Pollifax through this room, presenting only his back to her, but she could see that he was a large man and that he limped slightly.

The room they entered made her blink, its brightness startling after the dimness of the shop. A huge window had been set very high into one wall to catch the north light; two walls were lined with shelves of exquisite jade and ivory figurines, and under the window ran a bench and long table on which she saw a pile of glittering stones.

But the stranger interested her more, and she turned back quickly to him.

He bowed slightly. "Pray sit down," he said, and to the man behind her, "That will be all, Mr. Feng." He moved to a small desk and gestured her to a nearby chair.

Mrs. Pollifax guessed that he was Eurasian, and therefore Mr.

Detwiler. His face was broad, his nose flat and his mouth very wide, the thin lips turning upward at each corner, giving him a Buddha-like smile. His suit was black silk, his shirt a gleaming white, and she noticed gold cuff links at the wrists.

She told him firmly, "I'm looking for Sheng Ti—"

"Yes, indeed," he said, his smile deepening slightly. "But what do you want of this Sheng Ti?"

"To make sure that he's well and happy," she said promptly, "but—if I may be frank?"

"But of course," he said with an encouraging nod.

Without a twinge of conscience Mrs. Pollifax produced her *pièce de résistance*. "Well," she said, "I went to a great deal of trouble to find him, because he weighed terribly on my mind. I went back to the States, where I am president of my garden club, and I told them about Sheng Ti, and," she finished in triumph, "they have voted to sponsor his entry into the United States!"

"You have indeed been busy," he said. "May I see the paper with its directions to Sheng Ti?"

"Of course," she said, handing over the memo. "Is he here?"

The man studied the memo. "How did you get this?"

Mrs. Pollifax drew a deep breath and sailed in. "Well, I knew the name of the American with whom Sheng Ti left China, you see, and so I tracked him down, and he told me that Sheng Ti was in Hong Kong, and he gave me an address—in Washington, of all places! And finally—after *many* calls—I was given this."

The man stared at the memo. "You could have received this from only one source. No one else could possibly know of Sheng Ti's presence here."

"He is here, then!"

"Oh yes," he said smoothly, handing her back the memo with a smile. "But it is, of course, mysterious to us, your knowing of his presence. You are visiting Hong Kong for how long?"

"A week. To see the flowers. I myself have won a number of prizes for my geraniums and—"

"Yes," he said, leaning forward. "But you must drop the idea of seeing Sheng Ti, if you please. He is quite well—working hard— and I really have to insist that he not be distracted."

"Not see him!" cried Mrs. Pollifax in her best shocked voice. "But I've come so far, and I thought—my garden club thought—"

"But he is very happy here," Detwiler assured her. "Perhaps later, another year—but he is useful to me, and once he has learned more English, he will be even more useful."

Mrs. Pollifax said darkly, "He hoped to go to school. Are you sending him to school? And to learn a trade, and—"

He said gently, "He is being taught English, yes, and also something of jade and diamonds. Come and see," he said, rising and pointing to the workbench. "There are perhaps a hundred thousand U.S. dollars' worth of diamonds here."

Mrs. Pollifax, feeling that she had at least entered the dragons' den and met the head dragon, allowed the diversion. "May I inquire your name?" she asked sweetly. "I believe you already know mine."

He said absently, "Detwiler. But just look at this stone, will you? Five carats—beautifully cut and polished."

"You sell them here in your shop?" she asked.

"Oh no. They're sent all over the world. These particular stones were cut in Antwerp and sent here to be polished. Hong Kong imports millions of dollars' worth of diamonds to be finished." He smiled. "But allow me to give you a small souvenir of your visit. Not a diamond, of course, but still something special. I insist."

He moved to the shelves of ivory and jade objects and selected a figurine. "Ivory," he said softly. "Is it not beautiful?"

"A Buddha!" she gasped. "How lovely!" The figure was roughly twelve inches tall and a masterpiece of intricate carving, the Buddha seated in the traditional lotus position. On its head was an unusual headdress that rose to a peak, while the folds of its robe fell in simple lines. The face was utterly serene.

"Please—it is yours," he told her. "It is as valuable as Sheng Ti is to me. In appreciation of your concern for him."

"How very disarming of you," said Mrs. Pollifax, feeling not at all disarmed and already wondering what she would do next to find Sheng Ti.

"Lotus," he called. "Come and take this to Mr. Feng to wrap for the lady."

The girl came at once and left the room, carrying the Buddha.

"Well," said Mrs. Pollifax, "I mustn't take up any more of your time, but my garden club is going to be heartbroken. I do wonder," she added, feeling that her act needed one last touch, "if

you would have any objections if some of the members wrote to Sheng Ti from the United States. He could become"—she swallowed her dismay at the expression—"a pen pal."

"No objections at all," said Detwiler, looking relieved. "A most auspicious way for him to practice his English."

Mrs. Pollifax composed her face into an agreeable mask, murmured her gratitude at the gift, and moved through the beaded curtains. Here a man stood waiting, a young Chinese wearing a flawlessly cut dark business suit and carrying an attaché case. At the sight of Detwiler he brightened, bowed, and brushed past Mrs. Pollifax to enter the inner sanctum.

Mr. Feng held out her package wrapped in white paper. "Your gift, Mrs. Pollifax," he said, his face impassive.

"Thank you," she said, and walked out, glad to relax her own mask that, she knew, concealed resentment, frustration and anger.

But if Mrs. Pollifax left Feng Imports feeling ruffled, she did not concede defeat. The fact that she had no idea of how to contact Sheng Ti only proved that a brief period of gestation was needed; she would forget the problem for the moment and do some sight-seeing.

She could not, however, forget either Mr. Feng or Mr. Detwiler. As she walked, it struck her as extremely odd that Mr. Detwiler had intervened following Mr. Feng's flat denial of knowing Sheng Ti. She wondered what he'd hoped to gain by making a liar out of Mr. Feng, since the result was the same: she was not to see Sheng Ti. It certainly implied a few interesting conflicts at Feng Imports, but since any such conflicts were not her assignment, she decided that these too had better be put aside.

Or so she had decided until she realized that she was being followed. . . .

At first the streets had been too crowded for this suspicion to dawn on her, but as the crowds thinned she became increasingly aware that someone strolling behind her stopped each time that she did. When she stopped for the fourth time, it was to steal a glance behind her. She was surprised to recognize her surveillant: it was the young man with the attaché case who had been waiting for Detwiler when she emerged from the beaded curtains.

The realization that Detwiler had put a tail on her pleased her. Good, she thought. I've worried them. They want to be sure that

I'm a simple American tourist made happy by the promise that Sheng Ti can have pen pals. Her lip curled—as if they'd allow him that—and then she realized something else: Sheng Ti was as much a captive at Feng Imports as if he'd been placed in a prison.

Mrs. Pollifax silently vowed that she would return to haunt Feng Imports. First, however, she must play out her role as innocent tourist, and exhaust the man behind her.

Hours later Mrs. Pollifax had succeeded only in exhausting herself. She had done a great deal of walking, all of it without lunch; she had bought Cyrus a silk tie that she might just as well have bought for him at home; she had explored the Zoological and Botanical Gardens, making notes for Cyrus in her memo pad. Eventually she had found her way to the Victoria Peak Tram, where she had been happy to sit in the cable car and watch the city drop slowly away as she rode to the top of the peak.

Now, at nearly six o'clock in the evening, she sat on a bench 1809 feet above Hong Kong and rested. The Victoria Peak Tower stood behind her, seeming to float like a space capsule mounted on a broad stem. She supposed that when she was rested she would walk up the path to it and stop for a bite at the coffee shop, or be whisked by elevator to the restaurant at the top, with its magnificent view of Hong Kong. But for now she was content to look down at the city, at buildings crowded into what looked to be an incredibly narrow strip of land between the peak and the water. She admired the great expanse of intensely blue harbor, with its ferries scooting about like water bugs. Presently she leaned over to remove her shoes and blissfully wriggle her toes. Glancing off to her right, she saw that the man with the attaché case had also found a bench, and she was about to concede victory to him when she saw him lean over and remove his shoes too. Human after all, she thought, and at once both her tired feet and her hunger seemed small sacrifices to have made. She sat contentedly, allowing herself to think ahead to a very good dinner and a long soak in a hot tub, followed by a few yoga exercises.

Idly she looked down at the packages she had carried all over Hong Kong: Cyrus' tie and the ivory Buddha; and on impulse she unwrapped the Buddha, eager to see its superb carving again.

Drawing it from its wrappings, she noticed a thin slip of rice

29

paper taped across the Buddha's right hand, and frowning, she tore it loose. She was about to toss it into the wind when she noticed words written in tiny script on the paper: "If you want to see Sheng Ti he sleeps at 40 Dragon Alley in shed at back, after 10 p.m."

In a state of astonishment Mrs. Pollifax slipped her feet into her shoes and boarded the next tram to the city.

How? she asked herself. And then, Who?

As the tram descended she recalled the scene. Mr. Detwiler had taken the Buddha from her and summoned the girl, Lotus; it was not likely the message had come from him after his refusal to produce Sheng Ti. "Take this to Mr. Feng," he'd told Lotus, but Mrs. Pollifax could not conceive of Mr. Feng's adding the message, either, when he'd not even admitted Sheng Ti's existence.

The tram reached the bottom terminal, and Mrs. Pollifax limped wearily toward the Hong Kong Hilton. Her reasoning had eliminated all but the girl, Lotus, in which case she must have been eavesdropping and heard everything said in the back room.

The man with the attaché case was still behind her as she reached the hotel. She wondered if he would be waiting when she ventured out at ten o'clock to find Sheng Ti. She slipped into a side entrance and found herself at the Hilton's lower level, in a mall of shops. Hurrying along, eager to get to her room, she passed a store featuring *objets d'art*, with a Buddha in its window very similar to her own. Mrs. Pollifax walked over to the window to examine both the Buddha and its price tag. She found the Buddha definitely inferior to hers, and yet—she did some hasty calculations—it cost almost seven hundred American dollars.

She thought crossly, I think I need that hot bath now, because I am receiving too many jolts. Mr. Detwiler—who is suspected by Carstairs of being a traitor—has just presented me with a carved Buddha worth a great deal of money. No one at Feng Imports will tell me a thing about Sheng Ti, and yet his address turns up in a package like the message in a fortune cookie. I'm being followed and I don't know why. . . .

With her surveillant trailing despondently behind her, Mrs. Pollifax rode wearily up the escalator to the main lobby and entered the elevator. Her last glimpse of the man with the attaché case was of him sinking gratefully into a soft chair.

By nine o'clock, however, Mrs. Pollifax had thoroughly revived. Having treated herself to dinner in her own room, she was ready for her nocturnal adventure. No garden-of-roses hat tonight. She tied a dark kerchief around her head to match her slacks and open-necked blouse, and after tucking map and flashlight into her purse, she proceeded to plot a zigzag exit from the hotel, taking elevator, staircase and escalator to the mall at the lower level. There she browsed through the shops that were still open, spent a few minutes watching two giggling young women take their blood pressure at a machine placed in the mall for that purpose, and marveled at such an invention. Certain at last that she wasn't being followed, she walked out into the street, hailed a taxi and was driven through streets ablaze with gaudy reds, golds and glittering white neon.

Dragon Alley was distressingly dark, its windows shuttered and barred for the night. She discreetly shone her flashlight at number 40's gate, and then opened it. A narrow walkway led around to the backyard. It was brighter there than on the street, for lights as well as music spilled over from the rear of a nightclub in the next building. In the reflected radiance she could see a small shed and a slim figure seated on a bench outside it. Mrs. Pollifax moved toward the figure.

"*Oh!*" gasped the figure and jumped up. It was Lotus, her pale skin gleaming like porcelain in the dim light.

"So it was you," whispered Mrs. Pollifax.

Lotus whispered back, "Follow me—it's not safe here!"

Mrs. Pollifax obediently followed her to the rear of the night-club that adjoined the yard. A door was opened, and she was led into a dark hall and then into a room that was illuminated by a solitary oil lamp on a table. Sitting nervously beside the table, looking ready to bolt at any moment, was Sheng Ti.

"My friend!" he cried, springing up. "I could not believe!"

Mrs. Pollifax, laughing, grasped his outstretched hands. "It's me—I mean it's I, Sheng Ti. Isn't this wonderful?" But even as she greeted him she was shocked by his appearance. He was a young man whose attractive round face was made to be cheerful, but that face was haggard now, the eyes dulled by worry. "Sheng Ti," she said, "they wouldn't let me see you. Why?"

He burst into a torrent of Chinese until the girl placed a steadying hand on his arm. "Please—sit down," she said, indicating three chairs neatly arranged at the table.

It was like meeting in a cave, thought Mrs. Pollifax. A blanket had been hung over the only window, and the oil lamp cast flickering shadows over them and turned their faces a dull gold. "Why didn't they want me to see you?" she repeated.

Sheng Ti sucked in his breath. "If they know I see you now— they would *kill*."

Startled, Mrs. Pollifax turned to Lotus. "You believe this?"

"Oh yes," the girl said simply. "Something is very wrong at 31 Dragon Alley. It was a small thing at first, just a whisper for me, until I began to speak with Sheng Ti and we became friends—"

"We love," put in Sheng Ti.

Lotus blushed. "Yes, we love each other—this is very beautiful—but we have to meet secretly. And when I learn what they ask of him . . ." She shook her head. "Something is wrong."

"What do they ask of him?" demanded Mrs. Pollifax.

Sheng Ti began haltingly. "I come here before Lantern Carnival—"

"September," put in Lotus.

"Yes. And worked in shop, very okay. But near new year"—he frowned—"everything change. Many fights have Mr. Feng and Mr. Detwiler. I hear them behind door. And then they give me new job." Frustrated by his English, he turned and spoke to Lotus in Chinese.

"He says," continued Lotus, "that he stole in China to keep alive, but he hoped here he could go to school to learn."

Mrs. Pollifax nodded. "Yes, and what is his new job?"

"Stealing," Lotus said. "He was taught to pick pockets, and now they have put him to work stealing from people's pockets."

"They—what?" gasped Mrs. Pollifax.

Sheng Ti nodded. "Everything awful now, bloody awful. Mr. Detwiler hit me. Very nasty all the time. Mr. Feng has to run things more, and nasty too. Mr. Detwiler take heroin now," he said. "I see once—the long needle and white powder. He hit me again when I see."

"Oh, dear!" murmured Mrs. Pollifax with feeling. "But what do they have you stealing?"

"Passports," he told her.

This was unexpected. "Passports?" she repeated. "Not money?"

He shook his head, and fumbling for the rationale behind this, she said, "What kinds? From whom?"

Lotus answered. "They send him to the Government House or to the airport, and twice I have seen the passports he stole. One was Bulgarian, one Canadian." Sheng Ti spoke, and she translated. "He says he's stolen eleven of them for Mr. Detwiler."

"Eleven," murmured Mrs. Pollifax, frowning over this.

Lotus nodded. "Sheng Ti would like to run away, but they've taken all his papers."

Mrs. Pollifax said earnestly, "Ask him please to stay and help. The people who sent him to Feng Imports know something is wrong—it's why I'm here. And they will help you," she added, turning to Sheng Ti, "if you help them." She was remembering what Bishop had told her on the way to the airport: "We're prepared to offer him immigration to the United States, but it has to be earned."

"Could you learn more of Mr. Detwiler?" she asked Sheng Ti. "I promise you'll have your papers back, and a new job, and schooling. But first we must find out what's happening."

Sheng Ti looked at Lotus, his eyes questioning, and then he gave a bitter laugh. "Why do I stop to think? I would do anything to get away, anything. And you give me hope."

"He will do this," Lotus added. "And I too, if I can."

"Good. I don't think they suspect me, but they did have me followed this morning after I left the shop."

Immediately Sheng Ti leaped to his feet, looking terrified. "You were followed? Followed here?" he cried.

"No. This morning, after leaving the shop. I promise you no one followed me here tonight," she told him.

"But they may still—I must go," he said desperately.

"Do sit down," begged Mrs. Pollifax.

"No—let him go," Lotus said. "Go back to number 40, Sheng. Get some sleep. I will tell you later what she says."

He managed a wan smile, but he left, nevertheless, after one anguished look of entreaty at Mrs. Pollifax.

"They have not frightened you?" she asked Lotus.

"No, but I am frightened for Sheng Ti," the girl said. "He is afraid of being sent back to mainland China, where he'd certainly be placed in a labor camp. It is very serious to have no papers."

Someone knocked on the door, and Mrs. Pollifax turned a startled face to Lotus. The girl went to the door and opened it an inch, speaking in Chinese to whoever was in the hall. When she returned she said, "I sleep here with two other girls. I had to pay them to stay away, but now they want to go to their beds." She said anxiously, "You must go, but what am I to tell Sheng Ti?"

Mrs. Pollifax brought out her memo pad and wrote in it, tore out the sheet and handed it to Lotus. "This is my name, and this is where I'm staying," she told her. "Both you and Sheng Ti had better memorize this and burn it." She shook her head. "We simply must find some other way to meet. Could one of you phone me tomorrow night at ten o'clock at my hotel?"

Lotus nodded and said shyly, "I'm glad you are here. It has been so lonely. He will work hard for you now—you will see." She opened the door and peered out. "Come," she whispered.

Once out on the street Mrs. Pollifax's first reaction was to draw a sigh of relief and to admit how glad she was to leave the small, dim room that had been filled with fear. Her garden club, she decided grimly, was definitely going to have to sponsor Sheng Ti—she would insist on it—and Lotus too. Meanwhile she had to make sure that he survived physically. It was possible that heroin was the explanation for Mr. Detwiler's sloppy reports to Carstairs over the past two months, but she did not like the sound of those eleven stolen passports. She shook her head over it; no, she did not like the sound of that at *all*.

Flagging down a taxi, Mrs. Pollifax went back to the hotel and entered boldly by the front entrance. Once she reached room 614, she went to the telephone and dictated a cable to Carstairs: FRIENDSHIP RENEWED, WEATHER CLOUDY, EMILY POLLIFAX. When she replaced the receiver she saw by her travel clock that it was half past eleven, and reflecting on what a long day it had been, she crossed the room to her suitcase.

Drawing out pajamas and cold cream, she suddenly stiffened as something hit her door with a violent thud.

With a frown she dropped the pajamas and moved to the door. "Who is it?" she called.

There was no answer.

Cautiously she released the lock, and the door flew open, almost knocking her over, as a man fell into her arms, blood streaming down his face. As she instinctively recoiled he slid to the floor and sprawled at her feet.

She stared down at him, appalled: it was Mr. Hitchens.

MRS. Pollifax's initial reaction was astonishment. One talked with people on planes; one might even share a casual breakfast with them; but following this, one certainly did not expect to see them late at night, bleeding on the floor at one's feet. Accepting reality, however—for definitely Mr. Hitchens was here—she pushed the door closed and knelt beside him, one hand reaching out to gingerly explore what lay beneath his blood-matted hair.

Wincing, she sped into the bathroom and returned with a towel, which she applied to the deep gash in his scalp.

His eyes were closed, but his lips had begun to move. "Something terribly wrong," he whispered. "How . . . *how* . . ."

"Don't talk," she said. "I'll call a doctor."

"No," he gasped, suddenly opening those strange silver eyes. "Not safe. After me. How . . . must find how . . ."

His eyes closed, and he lapsed into unconsciousness. Mrs. Pollifax stared at him and considered his words. She did not believe that he would die from the blow, but he might very well die from infection if unattended. His panic, however, she implicitly believed in; his very presence here proved that he was terrified, for this was, after all, the Hong Kong Hilton, where every amenity was available, yet he'd chosen to come to her.

It must have happened in his room, she thought, and— "Not safe," he'd said. Did he mean that he might have been followed?

She had closed the door but not locked it; now she jumped up to snap the lock, but as it slammed into place she heard a movement in the hall. Her eyes fell to the doorknob, and to her horror she saw it turn slowly, to the left and then the right, accompanied by a subtle sound of metal probing metal.

Mrs. Pollifax forced down a scream.

The door opened, and Robin Burke-Jones, the ex–cat burglar masquerading as the world's third richest man, stepped into the room. "I do hope I'm not interrupting anything," he said cheerfully. "I saw you cross the lobby a few minutes ago and—" His glance fell to the man lying at her feet. "My word!" he exclaimed. "Been at your karate again? Who on earth—"

Thoroughly shaken, Mrs. Pollifax stammered, "N-not karate. It's Mr. H-H-Hitchens. He just sort of f-fell into my room, terrified of being f-f-followed, and then you—"

Robin whistled. "And you thought— I say, I'm frightfully sorry. The thing is, I'm being followed too, and I simply couldn't afford to knock on your door and wait for it to open." Regarding Mr. Hitchens intently, he said, "Chap needs a doctor, doesn't he?"

She'd forgotten Robin's crisp British accent. "He begged me not to call one."

"You know him, of course."

"Scarcely this well," she told him. "That is, we flew in on the same plane. He's a psychic, you see. He's come here to find a missing person—and we had breakfast together this morning."

Robin knelt beside Mr. Hitchens. "Nasty bash, this. How exactly did he explain his—er—impetuous arrival?"

Mrs. Pollifax closed her eyes and thought about it. "First he whispered, 'Something terribly wrong. . . . How . . . how,' and then when I told him I'd call a doctor he gasped, 'Not safe. After me. How . . . must find how.' "

Robin stood up and gave her a thoroughly startled look. "Would you mind repeating that, word for word?"

Obligingly she repeated it. "Why?"

Robin's eyes had narrowed. "And you say he's here to find a missing person?"

She nodded. "What is it, Robin?"

Ignoring this, he said thoughtfully, "I can provide a doctor who won't ask questions, and I think I'd like to stick around and hear what else your friend Mr. Hitchens has to say when he regains consciousness." He walked over to the phone and dialed a number. "And to think," he told her, "that I stopped in just to say hello. Chiang?" he said into the phone. "Three oh one here. I'm at the Hilton. Can you come to room 614? Chap with possible concussion, probably needs stitching. Good." He hung up. "He'll be here in a few minutes. Are you on a job for Carstairs?"

She smiled. "A very small one. Reconnaissance, you might say. Robin, what startled you when I quoted Mr. Hitchens' words?"

Robin perched on the arm of a chair. "What startled me, my dear Mrs. P., is that for the past two days I've been looking for a missing man, who happens to be named Hao."

It was her turn to be startled. "Named . . . You mean—you mean 'must find how' could refer to a name?"

He smiled. "In Hong Kong, yes. Hong Kong is filled with Haos. It could, of course, be coincidence."

"And I understand your name for this occasion is Lars Pettersen."

"Oh, you know that, do you?" He looked surprised.

"Actually it was Mr. Hitchens who told me, at breakfast. He'd just seen you on Hong Kong television." She looked at him with amusement. "Third richest man in the *world*, Robin?"

"Mmmm," he murmured, grinning. "It was hoped that it might bring just the right kind of attention—or the wrong kind—my arriving with great fanfare and lots of money to invest."

"And now you're being followed?"

"Only since I began looking for the missing Mr. Hao, which is interesting, don't you think?"

Before she could reply, there were three staccato knocks on the door. "That will be Chiang," Robin said. "Let me open it."

Dr. Chiang hurried into the room, a diminutive man in a nearly threadbare suit. He gave Mrs. Pollifax one quick, curious glance before he opened up his medical kit and knelt beside Mr. Hitchens, who stirred and groaned.

They carried him to the chaise longue, where the doctor began to clean his wound, applying a local anesthetic and then eight stitches. "He'll be all right," Dr. Chiang said at last. "No concussion, although he's going to have a terrible headache. I'll give him an antibiotic and something to relax him. If he's still restless in an hour, try a little brandy, but nothing else until morning."

"Thanks, Chiang," said Robin.

The doctor gave Mrs. Pollifax a second glance. "Husband?"

She shook her head. "Oh no."

Dr. Chiang looked amused. "I see. Well, call if you need me."

"Nice," said Mrs. Pollifax when he'd gone. "It's just that he doesn't *look* like a doctor somehow."

Robin laughed. "In about four years' time he just may find a free hour to shop for a new suit. A good man, Chiang—does a great deal of work with the boat people over in Aberdeen. Harvard Medical School, actually. By the way, he did mention brandy, didn't he? Frankly I could use some fortifying myself."

Mrs. Pollifax hurried to the refrigerator and brought back a

sample bottle of brandy and a glass to Robin, after which they sat
and looked expectantly at Mr. Hitchens, who had regained consciousness and was now staring at them in bewilderment.

"I'm Mrs. Pollifax," she reminded him, speaking clearly. "We
flew into Hong Kong together and shared breakfast, remember?
And this is—uh—Mr. Pettersen, who happens to be looking for a
man named Mr. Hao."

Mr. Hitchens turned his silver eyes on Robin. If he recognized
him as the world's third richest man, he gave no sign. He said,
"Damien Hao?"

Mrs. Pollifax heard Robin's quick intake of breath, but his voice
when he spoke was calm. "Damien Hao, yes. I believe you've
been looking for him too?"

Mr. Hitchens made the mistake of nodding, promptly groaned
and clutched his head. "Got hit—in my room," he explained. His
voice turned urgent. "Alec, where's Alec?"

Robin said quietly, "Inspector Hao's son, Alec?"

"Yes! He was with me this afternoon."

Mrs. Pollifax said eagerly, "He told me that one of his former
students begged him to come here to find a missing relative.
Robin, who is Damien Hao?"

"He was the head of Hong Kong's specially formed police unit
to investigate drugs, crime and corruption, until he suddenly
resigned three weeks ago in the midst of rumors that he'd been
found in some sort of compromising situation. He resigned, he
said, to clear his name and to continue his own private investigations. It was headline news, because he's known for his rocklike
integrity, and the governor, whom I interviewed, feels that Hao
was framed. And then ten days ago he disappeared."

Mrs. Pollifax turned to Mr. Hitchens. "Did you find him?"

The silver eyes closed. "No . . . used a map. . . . Saw . . .
visioned . . . place he'd been." Mr. Hitchens sighed. "Hut or barn,
green fields, waterwheel in distance. We drove, Alec and I . . .
place called New Territories."

"Go on," Robin urged, nodding.

"Growing dark . . . saw it."

"Saw the hut and the waterwheel?" prompted Mrs. Pollifax.

Mr. Hitchens opened his eyes. "Yes. And walked . . . searched
it. Very small, earth floor, and then . . . a man—a farmer, we

thought—came, and . . . when I woke up Alec was gone." His voice ended in a sob. "So I walked . . . too woozy for Alec's car . . . a taxi . . . and then my hotel room. Someone there. Pow."

Puzzled, Mrs. Pollifax said, "This farmer . . . You went to *sleep?*"

"Something . . . Chloroform, I think, but they took Alec. Planned to come back for me. Nightmare," he added miserably.

"One more question," said Mrs. Pollifax firmly. "When you used the map for your visioning, Mr. Hitchens, did you feel that Inspector Hao was still alive?"

"Yes," he murmured, and then, "Bloody awful nightmare."

"Hang in, old chap," said Robin. "We'll find them."

Mr. Hitchens blinked at him. "We?"

Robin nodded. "First thing tomorrow, if you feel up to it."

"Must sleep now," said Hitchens, closing his eyes.

"Looks as if you'll have a roommate for the night," said Robin to Mrs. Pollifax. "Can you manage?"

"I'd manage better if you told me what brought you here."

Robin glanced at Mr. Hitchens. "Let's try the bathroom. I'd just as soon he not hear this, and I can't be sure he's asleep." Entering first, he said, "You can have the edge of the tub."

She laughed and sat down. "All right, I'm perched. Now talk."

"In capsule form?" He glanced at his watch. "Definitely in capsule form. It's well past midnight. Try picturing a map with arrows converging on Hong Kong—arrows from Europe, the Middle East and the United States."

Mrs. Pollifax said crisply, "The arrows denoting what?"

With equal crispness Robin replied, "Puzzling rumors, coincidences, tips, thefts, the possibility of smuggling."

"Involving *Hong Kong?*" she said incredulously.

"I know," he said, nodding. "A tight little British island, the commercial hub of the East. Yet there is an active criminal element here dealing heavily in narcotics—it's called the Triad—and lately there have been rumors of police corruption. Inspector Hao may have learned more than was healthy for him. All we know for certain is that Hong Kong has become a magnet that's pulling together a number of unrelated incidents in the criminal world, which spells out something violent being planned here."

Frowning, Mrs. Pollifax said, "Yet as evidence none of this sounds very substantial."

Robin laughed. "My dear Mrs. P., if it were, Interpol would have an army of men here, instead of just Marko and myself."

"Marko?"

He grinned. "You don't think the third richest man in the world travels without a social secretary, do you? He's Marko Constantine, one of Interpol's best, but for the moment he does remarkably well answering my phone and taking messages."

"So you're sort of on reconnaissance too," she said almost absently. "But those arrows, Robin. I mean, how—"

"Diamonds."

"Diamonds?"

He nodded. "Interpol's principal job is narcotics control, but the drug syndicates often use diamonds to make their payments, so we keep an eye on that too. Diamonds are easy to smuggle, and far more convenient than currency. Three months ago there was a rash of diamond thefts: two in New York, three in Antwerp and four in London. Quite extraordinary, actually."

"Why so extraordinary?"

"Because the incidence of such thefts has been practically nonexistent in the past; yet inside of six weeks eight couriers were murdered—and nearly eight million dollars' worth of diamonds were stolen."

"Good heavens," said Mrs. Pollifax. "That's certainly a lot of tax-free money! You feel the thefts were linked?"

Robin nodded. "There were similarities between the New York incidents, and a link with Hong Kong too. In March three packages of those stolen diamonds were found in a shipment of narcotics being smuggled into Hong Kong."

"How much were they worth?"

"Nearly two million. One package came from an Antwerp murder and two from New York."

Mrs. Pollifax smiled faintly. "Your evidence grows a shade more substantial."

"That's what shifted our attention to Southeast Asia, where we heard an alarming rumor that some very fancy guns are due to arrive in Macao—only forty miles from Hong Kong."

"Guns!" echoed Mrs. Pollifax, startled. "But that changes the picture considerably, Robin!"

He said grimly, "Especially where one of them is rumored to

be a multiple-rocket launcher, which is very portable, small enough to be carried on the roof of a minibus and its rockets launched from there."

Mrs. Pollifax drew in her breath sharply. "You haven't learned their destination?"

He shook his head. "The silence on that score is astonishing; there are almost no leaks, and that's *highly* unusual. Our usual informants have gone mum."

Mrs. Pollifax studied him. "You mean it's the kind of silence that only eight million dollars' worth of diamonds can buy?"

He gave her an appreciative glance. "You see that. Yes, it would take something like that to accomplish this kind of secrecy. Bribes here, bribes there. But what keeps me awake nights is the feeling that this whole thing is far more advanced than my superiors believe. Which is why I want very much to locate Inspector Hao, who just may have stumbled across whatever's being planned." He glanced at his watch. "It's nearly one o'clock. I think we'd better continue this tomorrow. I'm hoping your Mr. Hitchens will feel well enough for a trip to the New Territories. I hate to let Alec Hao's trail grow cold." He stopped and grinned. "What are your plans for tomorrow?"

"I thought you'd never ask," said Mrs. Pollifax, beaming.

"Bless you for that," he said. "I don't know what it is about you, but I seem to recall a certain élan that entered the picture once we joined forces in Switzerland. Interpol can be so deadly serious."

As they left the bathroom he added, "Sorry I can't carry Mr. Hitchens off, but I'm afraid if I were seen, it would be more difficult to explain than his spending the night here."

"So long as he doesn't snore," she said.

Robin grinned. He opened the door to the hall and peered out. "Looks clear," he said, and left, closing the door behind him.

Tuesday

IF MR. Hitchens snored during the night, Mrs. Pollifax remained blissfully unaware. She was too busy sleeping to notice. When she awoke at eight it was to find Mr. Hitchens staring at her from the chaise longue across the room.

He said with dignity, "I am not accustomed to travel, as you

41

know, or to being hit over the head, or to being chloroformed, either, for that matter."

"No," she said, regarding him with interest.

"I have never in my life had such a headache," he went on shakily, "and I have the most dreadful feeling I am going to cry."

"Yes," she said, and nodded sympathetically. "What I would suggest, Mr. Hitchens, is that you get up—very slowly—and take a hot shower. While you're doing this, I'll dress and call room service and order you some *very* strong coffee."

"Thank you," he said miserably, and allowed her to help him to his feet and lead him into the bathroom.

By the time Robin joined them, letting himself in as easily as he had the previous night, she and Mr. Hitchens were sitting companionably by the window, with breakfast trays, and Mr. Hitchens had attempted an egg.

"He's much better," she told Robin. "He's been telling me that being psychic is of no help at all in his own life. He can't tell his own future, or—quite naturally—he would never have come to Hong Kong."

"Ah, but we're glad you did," Robin said warmly. "Do you feel up to showing us that waterwheel and hut where you lost Alec?"

Mr. Hitchens had obviously recovered, because he said dryly, "I won't ask how you came through that door without using a key, or why Lars Pettersen should want to—"

Robin interrupted him. "Actually I'm an ex–cat burglar working for Interpol. I'm not Lars Pettersen at all."

Mr. Hitchens nodded matter-of-factly. "I can see that this entire trip is meant to be a learning experience for me. Absolutely nothing has made sense so far, and probably nothing will. But yes, I'm ready to show you where the hut is."

"Good chap," said Robin. "Let's go, then, shall we? I've got Marko in uniform and a rented limousine waiting at the front entrance for us. We, however, will make our exit by the freight elevator and drive away in an inconspicuous Renault. We'll need directions from you."

Mr. Hitchens pointed to his jacket and climbed carefully to his feet. "You'll find a map in the inside pocket—the same map I used for Alec, with the general area circled in pencil."

"You mean you simply looked at a map and said, *'There'?*"

Mr. Hitchens smiled. "It's a little like dowsing, if you're familiar with the word."

Robin nodded. "Yes, indeed. Our neighbor in France had a man come in—a water dowser—and he located a missing well on the property by using a divining rod."

"Well, there you are," said Mr. Hitchens. "I seem to be feeling much better now. Shall we go?"

Mrs. Pollifax decided with some amusement that Mr. Hitchens had dimensions that were surprising even himself. Certainly it was a different Albert Hitchens whose eyes shone with delight as they crept down the hall, and found their way out to the car. "What a remarkable experience," he said. "I feel just like a spy."

Robin brought out a visored cap and dark glasses, and took the driver's seat. "I suggest you crouch down in back, Mr. Hitchens," he told him. "Mrs. Pollifax is the only one of us who's of no possible interest to surveillants, which is why she can wear brilliant red and pink roses on her hat."

"On the contrary," said Mrs. Pollifax, hastily removing the hat and placing it in her lap. "I was followed all yesterday afternoon after my visit to a curio shop called Feng Imports."

"Heavens, you too?" gasped Mr. Hitchens from the back seat. "My three wives—if they could only know!"

"Three?" echoed Robin.

"Who all assumed that psychics lived exciting lives, and were deeply disappointed," Mrs. Pollifax explained.

"Except for Ruthie," called Mr. Hitchens from the floor behind them. "She didn't mind my being a dull chap."

"Ruthie we must hear more about," Robin called back to him, "but Hong Kong traffic is fiendish, so save it for later."

Mrs. Pollifax occupied herself now with tracing their route on Mr. Hitchens' map as Robin negotiated the traffic. "Do you think," she asked him, "that your friend Marko is still waiting at the front entrance with the limousine?"

Robin smiled. "No. By now he will have telephoned up to our suite—after which, swearing noisily at the idle rich, he will return the car to the garage."

"Poor Marko," she murmured.

"Don't you believe it," said Robin as they sped into the tunnel leading to Kowloon. "Not too long ago I swabbed decks on a fishing boat in the Mediterranean while Marko did nothing but sit on deck with binoculars, keeping an eye on drug smugglers nosing along the coast. My blisters were monstrous." They emerged from the tunnel, and he called over his shoulder, "You can come out now, Mr. Hitchens, and see Hong Kong's newest triumph, Tsim Sha Tsui East, most of it built on land reclaimed from the harbor."

Mr. Hitchens surfaced, and both he and Mrs. Pollifax stared at the enormous complex of hotels, offices and restaurants before they swung into Kowloon's Chong Wan Road.

"Now that you're visible," Robin said to Mr. Hitchens, "what exactly did Alec tell you about his father? I tried to contact Alec, but he was never at home."

"He was probably out searching for his father," said Mr. Hitchens. "He told me very little, only that Inspector Hao had suddenly resigned to investigate something important, but he didn't confide in Alec what it was. Then one morning his bed hadn't been slept in, and no one could find him. Three days later Alec phoned me."

"Keep an eye out for Boundary Street," Robin told Mrs. Pollifax. "And do the police know you're here?" he asked Mr. Hitchens.

"I don't know. Alec didn't say. We didn't have much time together," Mr. Hitchens answered.

"There's Boundary Street," put in Mrs. Pollifax. "We leave Kowloon now?"

Robin nodded. "Full speed ahead into the New Territories. Find it on your map?"

"Got it," said Mrs. Pollifax.

Their route lay along a coast road that skirted island-dappled bays on their left and steep mountains on their right, until at last they swung north to meet with Hong Kong's farmland. How lovely, thought Mrs. Pollifax, her eyes feasting on lush green fields laid out in tidy squares as far as the eye could see. To her delight she began to glimpse duck ponds, the ducks so brilliant a white in the sunshine they looked as if they'd been freshly laundered before being dropped beside their dazzling blue ponds. It was difficult to remember that violence had been done in such a radiant and wholesome setting.

Mr. Hitchens cried, "There it is—over there! The waterwheel!"

"Right," said Robin, and braked to a stop.

It lay a quarter of a mile from the road, a charming wheel set near the edge of a narrow stream, surrounded by fields and not far from a copse of green trees. "The hut's behind the trees," said Mr. Hitchens. "There's no road in, we have to walk."

"So be it," said Robin, and turned off the ignition.

As they climbed out of the car Mrs. Pollifax gave Mr. Hitchens an inquiring glance. "Head hurting?" she asked, for she thought he looked decidedly pale.

"No," he said. "No, I just feel—uneasy, that's all."

A slender path edged the fields, and they entered on it, walking single file. Reaching the waterwheel, they found a rough bridge tossed across the stream; Mrs. Pollifax took the lead and headed for the trees that sheltered the hut, its outlines discernible now.

"That's the place," Mr. Hitchens said, looking more unhappy.

The hut was small, roughly twelve feet by fifteen. The door creaked as Mrs. Pollifax pushed it open, and she blinked at the sudden darkness inside. The room was empty, or so she thought until her eyes saw something huddled on the floor.

"Oh, dear God," she said in a strangled voice.

Robin was just behind her. "Don't look," he said sharply, and bringing out a pocket flashlight, he knelt beside a crumpled body.

But of course she looked, thinking how strange death was and how it ought to be honored, not turned from in dismay just because it was a mystery, an unknown that could never be solved by human beings bent on solving every unknown.

The light shone on the face of a middle-aged Chinese male, his eyes open in astonishment at something unseen beyond them. He wore a gray silk suit and a white shirt, both smudged with dirt. There was a neat bullet hole over his left eyebrow, with powder marks radiating from it. His right hand gripped a gun.

"It's Inspector Hao," Robin said grimly. "And he's dead."

Behind him Mr. Hitchens said, "When?"

Robin touched the face. "Not long ago. He *was* alive yesterday; you were right about that."

Abruptly Mrs. Pollifax said, "Keep the light on, Robin. There's something, a piece of paper. . . ." She leaned over, removed a slip of white paper from Hao's left hand and read aloud, " 'I despair. To be thought guilty—' " She lowered it thoughtfully. "Suicide

45

note?" she suggested with skepticism. "After he's been missing for ten days?" She handed it to Robin.

Robin studied the note. "I don't believe this," he said at last. "A torn fragment addressed to no one, no signature, and the gun placed in his hand. This has been set up to look like a suicide."

Mr. Hitchens said, "But if that's his handwriting—"

"Could have been torn from a letter," said Robin.

Mrs. Pollifax, looking curiously around her, said, "I wonder if he was killed here at all, Robin. If he was shot this morning in such close quarters, shouldn't there be a lingering smell of gunpowder? And look at the floor."

Robin whistled. "The only footprints are ours—you're right."

The three of them examined the earthen floor in the light of Robin's flash. "These tiny swirls in the dust are the marks of a broom," Robin said. "He has to have been killed somewhere else and brought here."

Mr. Hitchens shivered. "I don't like this."

Mrs. Pollifax asked tartly, "The police can't possibly overlook there being no footprints, can they? I mean, Inspector Hao didn't simply drop through the roof. How can they possibly buy the suicide theory?"

Robin shrugged. "It depends on just who among the police Damien Hao didn't trust—and who *wants* it to be a suicide."

Mrs. Pollifax nodded. "Then it's up to me, Robin, since you're Interpol." She knelt beside the body and pried loose the gun from Hao's fingers. "Beretta nine millimeter," she announced, and dropped it into her purse. Removing the suicide note from Robin's hand with equal dispatch, she dropped it too into her purse. "I think," she said in a firm voice, "that in this situation it's kinder to remove all doubt about its being anything but murder."

"Good girl," said Robin.

Mr. Hitchens looked at her with admiration. "You dared—just like that! But you're right, you know. I feel it."

Robin said soberly, "What I don't like is feeling that someone's way ahead of us. I think someone knew you'd come back here this morning, Mr. Hitchens, giving them an opportunity to arrange Inspector Hao's body here for you to discover and report."

"Then, what do you suggest?" asked Hitchens alertly.

"That you very obediently discover and report the body. Yes, I think this is where you go public, Mr. Hitchens: U.S. Psychic in Hong Kong Finds Missing Police Inspector—that sort of thing. Just leave us out of it, Mrs. Pollifax and me. You woke up this morning in your own hotel room—after being hit over the head yesterday—and you returned to this hut to look for Alec."

Mr. Hitchens nodded. "I can do that, yes."

Mrs. Pollifax, watching Robin, said, "You have something in mind for us, I'm thinking?"

He grinned. "You bet. I'll wipe away our footprints now. Dragging my jacket across them should do it. After Mr. Hitchens has established his footprints on the floor, we'll all go back to the car and take him to a telephone. After that he'll be on his own."

"How did he get here?" put in Mrs. Pollifax quickly.

"Taxi," said Robin, ushering them out into the sunlight and removing his jacket. He walked back into the hut then, and a few moments later he emerged. "Your turn," he said to Mr. Hitchens. "Walk inside, discover the body, do a little pacing back and forth, and walk out."

Once Mr. Hitchens had complied, they prepared to leave. But Mrs. Pollifax remained for a moment on the threshold of the hut and looked back at the huddled body of Inspector Hao. "God bless," she whispered to whatever spirit might be lingering, and silently pledged to find his killer.

THEY left Mr. Hitchens at the first small settlement they came to, where he practiced his new role by thanking them loudly for giving him a ride. "But you will be looking for Alec now?" he asked in a lower voice, anxiously.

"Yes," promised Robin. "But it's better you not know how or where, because you might let it slip."

As Robin gunned the motor Mrs. Pollifax said, "Oh, dear, he does look lonely." Then they headed back toward Hong Kong, leaving Mr. Hitchens standing beside a stall heaped with vegetables.

"He won't be lonely for long," Robin told her. "This is going to be very big news on the island."

"And you and I?"

"We are going to burgle the Hao residence. The important thing is to get there before the police."

She laughed. "How smoothly things go when one knows a cat

burglar! But won't there be any people in the house, Robin?"

"He and Alec lived alone," explained Robin. "The house is off Lion Rock Road in Kowloon. I visited it once—when no one was at home. I seem to recall a lavish amount of shrubbery for concealing nefarious people like myself."

When they reached the Haos' neighborhood Mrs. Pollifax saw that Robin was right about the shrubbery. There was a six-foot wall around the house, and they could see the outline of a tile roof nearly hidden by trees. Robin parked across the street, and they quickly approached a gate in the wall. Four minutes later, owing to Robin's lock-picking expertise, they were inside the house.

It was dim, the matchstick shades at each window sending alternating lines of sun and shadow across the tile floors. It looked like any suburban house in America to Mrs. Pollifax, except for a niche in the living room that contained a large gilt Buddha smiling serenely down at their feeble worldly struggles.

A moment later they entered Inspector Hao's study and stared at a room swept by chaos: at a steel file cabinet battered apart, at a desk whose drawers stood open, with half their contents strewn across the floor.

"I was afraid of this," growled Robin.

"Well," said Mrs. Pollifax, "whoever did this was certainly in a hurry. This must be where they found that slip of paper to use for the suicide note. What are we looking for?"

"Anything with words written on it," said Robin. "You take the desk, I'll take the filing cabinet."

"Treasure hunt," murmured Mrs. Pollifax, and sat down at the desk to sift through what remained in the drawers: a bottle of ink, an abacus, a snapshot album and a stack of white typing paper.

"Nothing," Robin said angrily, slamming shut the last drawer of the file cabinet. "They took everything of any importance."

Mrs. Pollifax had carefully exhumed the pile of typing paper from its drawer; now she gripped the sheets firmly at one corner and waved them back and forth to see if anything had been caught among them. A newspaper fragment fluttered to the rug, and putting down the sheaf of papers, she picked it up.

"Good heavens!" she said in a startled voice.

Robin was at her side at once. "What is it?"

It was a photograph of a man, torn from a newspaper some time ago, for the newsprint was yellowed with age, and across the top of the clipping someone—probably Damien Hao—had scrawled, "When?" The man in the picture faced the camera squarely, as was the custom in prison photos, and there was an identifying prison number across his chest, but no name. Mrs. Pollifax, however, recognized him at once. "Robin," she said, "I know this man. I keep running into him."

"Running into him?" Robin gripped her arm, his voice incredulous. "What do you mean, running into him? Where?"

She stared at him in astonishment. "Why, he was on the plane with me from San Francisco to Hong Kong, and yesterday morning I saw him coming out of Feng Imports when I was watching for the young man I was to contact there."

Robin said in a strangled voice, "Plane . . . Feng Imports. Mrs. Pollifax, I think it's time you tell me exactly what your job is here in Hong Kong. This photo—this man—*this is Eric the Red.*"

A chilly finger of shock touched the base of Mrs. Pollifax's spine. "The terrorist? The head of the Liberation '80s Group?" Her shock quickly moved into horror as she remembered the brutality of these men. She vividly recalled their last debacle—the French hostage affair—those endless, agonizing days, the miscalculations that culminated in the escape of the Liberation '80s Group, and the bloody massacre they left behind.

"Let's get out of here and *talk*," said Robin fiercely. "Mrs. Pollifax, if Eric the Red is in Hong Kong—"

He scarcely needed to complete the thought, for she was already reaching for her purse. They got into the car just in time, for as they drove away a police car turned into the street. Glancing back, Mrs. Pollifax saw it stop in front of Damien Hao's home: the inspector's death was now official.

ROBIN drove quickly toward Hong Kong, his face set in grim lines and his mind obviously occupied. Mrs. Pollifax was grateful for the silence. If Robin was considering all the ramifications of Eric the Red's being in Hong Kong, she in turn was considering the ramifications of a dangerous terrorist's making his first stop at Feng Imports. It was possible, she thought, that her assignment and Robin's were dovetailing, and that a great deal more was going on at that establishment than anyone had guessed.

Robin said abruptly, "We'll go to my suite; it's time you met Marko." He leaned over and switched on the car radio, and they listened to a crisp voice announcing the death of Inspector Hao.

"Discovered by Albert Hitchens, an American psychic brought to Hong Kong by Inspector Hao's son, Alec, to find his missing father. Mr. Hitchens had visited the shed yesterday afternoon with Alec Hao, and police are looking into his story that he was assaulted there and Alec Hao kidnapped, leaving Hitchens to find his way back to his hotel alone last evening."

"A new learning experience for him," quoted Mrs. Pollifax.

"This morning," continued the voice, "Hitchens took a taxi back to the shed to look for Alec Hao and found the body of the missing inspector. Police estimate that death occurred between five and seven this morning. Hao was shot at close range with a nine-millimeter gun. There is no suggestion of suicide."

"Good. That should startle his killers," put in Robin, snapping off the radio. "But Alec is still missing! If it's the Liberation '80s Group that has him—"

"In general," said Mrs. Pollifax in a kind voice, "I think it wiser not to allow the imagination to take over at moments like this. Much better to use our energy looking for Alec."

"Point well taken," said Robin as he edged the car into a parking space at the rear of the hotel.

Ten minutes later, in the sumptuous suite provided for Lars Pettersen, Mrs. Pollifax was meeting Marko Constantine.

"So you are the fantastic Emily Pollifax of whom I hear," he said, gravely studying her face. "The look of innocence and of the great earth mother, and the spirit of a boy shinnying down ropes and knowing the karate. *Saluté!*" he murmured, kissing her hand.

Mrs. Pollifax laughed. "I didn't expect such charm. I wasn't warned! How do you do, Marko."

"The charm is natural, for I am both French and Greek," he answered. "But I think now we get down to very serious business. I have heard the news, Robin. You found the body?"

"Yes, we found Hao dead—and much more," Robin said grimly.

Mrs. Pollifax sat down. Despite Marko's charm, she sensed in him the underlying toughness of steel. Outwardly he was a battered little man in his thirties, with a radiant smile, and a scar on his left cheekbone. His skin was swarthy, his hair black, and his dark eyes had the wisdom of an old soul. He moved into a chair and tucked his feet under him.

Robin chose the couch, saying, "We tell you what we found in Damien Hao's house, and then we hear from Mrs. Pollifax about Feng Imports."

"Feng what?"

Robin pointed to Mrs. Pollifax. "Her assignment, Marko, which seems to be wandering into ours, because Eric the Red—"

"Eric the Red!" interrupted Marko. *"Mon Dieu!"*

"Exactly," Robin agreed, and opening his wallet, he removed the torn news clipping and handed it to Marko, describing how it was found. "At which point," he said, "Mrs. Pollifax shocked me by casually announcing that whoever this man was, she'd flown into Hong Kong on the same plane with him and had seen him yesterday morning coming out of Feng Imports."

Marko whistled. "You are sure this is the same man?"

"Yes," she said. "I had the misfortune to step on his foot, and later Mr. Hitchens scrutinized him—you can show him the photo when he gets back. The man was traveling on a Canadian passport, by the way."

"You know that also!"

Mrs. Pollifax smiled faintly. "If he had been polite—but he made the mistake of calling attention to himself, a cardinal mistake, I believe, in anyone traveling incognito."

"A leopard and his spots," murmured Marko. "It was believed he was hiding in Germany, but lately rumors have surfaced that he had moved on to Italy. He broke out of prison ten years ago, and, of course, following that . . ." He shrugged. "You know the rest. He has left terror behind him in many countries. But please, tell us of this Feng Import shop and why you went there."

Mrs. Pollifax drew a deep breath and plunged into her explanation of why she had come to Hong Kong. She described Carstairs' alarm about Detwiler, how Sheng Ti happened to be known to her and why he was important; she described her meeting with Mr. Detwiler and how she was followed afterward; and she concluded with her interview of the previous evening with Lotus and a very frightened Sheng Ti.

"Eleven passports—one of them Canadian," murmured Robin. "Sheng Ti did say eleven?" When Mrs. Pollifax nodded he said, "And he or Lotus will be contacting you again tonight?"

"Yes. At least I assume so. If they can."

Robin and Marko exchanged glances. Marko said, "I think we must see this place, don't you? And also bring some men in to watch it in case Eric the Red returns. But until we have more help, I am thinking you will have to lose your secretary." His eyes twinkled at Robin. "Shall you phone Paris, or shall I?"

Robin said, "I will." He rose and walked into another room and closed the door.

Marko and Mrs. Pollifax talked quietly until Robin reappeared.

"There'll be two men here by nine tonight—Krugg and Upshot," he told them. "And a third man—Witkowski—before morning. It's all they can spare, but at least they understand that things are beginning to happen here."

Marko nodded. "Good. I will go and pack my knapsack, then. I'll take the surveillance until nine."

"Interpol, but still no local police?" commented Mrs. Pollifax as she placed her hat on her head and skewered it with a hatpin.

"I have to remind you that Damien Hao avoided them," Robin said dryly. "And don't forget all those stolen diamonds, which—if they went into bribes—bought off a lot of people. If Hao was murdered for what he learned, just how do we find which of the police can be trusted? It's too chancy right now. My superiors are sending in men from Tokyo and Bangkok."

"And what is Marko packing?" she asked quietly.

"Food, radio transmitter, camera and probably a gun. We hope we can find a hiding place for him in your Dragon Alley."

Mrs. Pollifax felt a stir of excitement; her watch told her that it was almost two o'clock in the afternoon and once again she would be missing lunch, as she had yesterday; but it was a small price to pay to watch two professionals at work. "I'm ready," she said as Marko emerged from the next room with his knapsack.

The first lesson that Mrs. Pollifax learned in the art of reconnaissance was that there would be no setting foot in Dragon Alley at all. First they researched the street in back of Feng Imports, stumbling over piles of junk, until Mrs. Pollifax spotted the large window in Mr. Detwiler's rear workroom, whereupon Robin jotted down its location and eyed the top floor of an empty warehouse nearby.

They next scouted the lane on the other side of Dragon Alley until they located a building with a good view of Feng Imports. This proved to be a ramshackle rooming house, listing subtly toward the street below. The proprietor was not on the premises, and Mrs. Pollifax was enchanted by the dispatch with which Marko and Robin dealt with this problem: they simply entered the building by the back door and knocked on doors until they found someone at home.

It was a man named Pi, who had been sleeping, he said, because he had lost his job a week ago. And who were they? Over his shoulder Mrs. Pollifax looked into his cubicle and saw that it had a window that looked directly down at the front door of Feng Imports. Twenty minutes later Pi had bundled up his belongings and had sublet his cubicle to them for a week; Robin and Marko had their stakeout. Once Pi had gone, Mrs. Pollifax gave Marko descriptions of the people working at Feng Imports; then she and Robin helped Marko set up his radio. Then they too left.

"What now?" she asked.

"Now I'll drop you off at the hotel," Robin said deflatingly. "I've got to go back and see about renting the top floor of that warehouse overlooking the rear of Feng Imports. After that I'll set up a radio in my hotel suite and establish contact with Marko. What I hope you'll do is arrange an appointment for me with Mr. Hitchens. I'd like very much to have him verify the photo of Eric the Red, but also"—Robin gave her a sheepish glance—"also . . ."

She smiled. "You want to borrow his psychic talents."

Robin parked at the mall entrance to the hotel. "There's a very real possibility that a terrorist or two is planning something in the area. I'm praying that Mr. Hitchens can answer Inspector Hao's 'When?' We desperately need a date . . . a week, a month, a day."

"That's a tall order," pointed out Mrs. Pollifax.

"All orders are tall in this business," said Robin, "and at the moment I'm feeling very short. Perhaps we'd better offer Mr. Hitchens breakfast with us in my suite tomorrow morning at eight o'clock. He's mislaid his employer, and he could be wondering where his next meal's coming from."

"I wish I'd thought of that," she said warmly.

He grinned. "If anything comes up, I'll be manning the radio until it's time to meet my men at the airport. See you!" He saluted and drove away, and Mrs. Pollifax entered the hotel to begin a search for Mr. Hitchens.

But she was thinking as she walked through the mall that she would still have no news of Alec to give Mr. Hitchens, and this would be the first question he would ask. After all, Alec was his reason for being in Hong Kong, just as Detwiler was hers.

She paused to glance idly over the magazines in one of the shops. Suddenly a thought came to her: If there's a connection between Mr. Detwiler and Eric the Red—and Alec is still mysteriously missing—isn't it possible that Detwiler might be hiding Alec in his home, wherever it might be? She wondered where she could find the nearest phone directory to see if he was listed. Leaving the magazines behind, she headed for the escalator to the lobby.

She had just found Detwiler's address and was copying it into her memo pad when she felt a tap on her shoulder.

Mrs. Pollifax turned to find herself face to face with a Mr. Hitchens whose face had almost vanished under a huge hat that looked like a cross between a Panama and a Stetson. Repressing an urge to laugh, she said, "Are you in disguise, Mr. Hitchens?"

He said reproachfully, "No. I've an ice pack on my head, and it didn't seem quite the thing to wear in the lobby, so the manager very kindly loaned me his hat. I've been looking for you. Shall we sit down?"

"Yes, do let's," she said heartily, and they moved toward the nearest couch and established themselves there.

"I can't tell you how wonderful they've been to me in this hotel," he confided. "Apparently I put up quite a fight last night with that—that *thug*, and my room was a shambles this morning. I'm in room 302 now, and"—he paused for breath, beaming happily—"and I'm going to be on the television news tonight. It's already taped, and just look—" He held out his newspaper to her.

Mrs. Pollifax unfurled the paper to gaze at a photograph of Mr. Hitchens, and a headline that read NOTED AMERICAN PSYCHIC IN HONG KONG.

"I'm noted," said Mr. Hitchens happily.

"What fun," she said. "But how are you feeling?"

His hands groped toward his head. "The ice seems to have melted now, and my head has begun to throb." He removed the hat, and the ice bag dropped into his lap. Picking it up, he said, "You wouldn't have room for this in your purse, would you?"

"No," she said calmly. "I'm already carrying a Beretta pistol and a suicide note, and there's no room for an ice bag."

Nodding philosophically, he tucked it into his pocket. "You've not found Alec?"

"Unfortunately, not yet," she said. "But we found a number of clues, and Robin wants us both to have breakfast with him tomorrow at eight o'clock to talk about possibilities. His suite."

Mr. Hitchens looked pleased.

"He also wants you to look at a photograph, and to—" She paused, for Mr. Hitchens was now staring in astonishment at a group of Americans who had entered the lobby.

"I don't believe it," he said. A smile spread slowly across his face. "It's Ruthie." He stood up and called out her name.

A woman in the group turned, saw Mr. Hitchens and looked as astonished as he had looked a moment ago. Detaching herself from the others, she took a few hesitant steps toward him, stopped, then hurried on to be met in mid lobby by Mr. Hitchens, who gave her a shy embrace. Their approaches implied a difficult parting long ago and an uncertainty about meeting again.

Mrs. Pollifax smiled as she watched. Ruthie, she remembered, was the wife who had never expected Mr. Hitchens to live an exciting life. His first wife, he had said, was a kindergarten teacher, his second an aspiring actress, and his third an aspiring magician. Ruthie, she felt instinctively, was the first wife. No show-business aspirant would ever conceal her personality so firmly behind character. She was small and at first glance plain, but at second glance there was an arresting quality about her plainness; her nose was upturned, her chin stubborn and her brown eyes almost too large for her face. She was wearing a practical suit and sensible shoes. A little brown sparrow of a woman, thought Mrs. Pollifax.

"But I don't understand," Mrs. Pollifax heard her saying. "What are you doing in Hong Kong, of all places?"

Mr. Hitchens turned eagerly toward Mrs. Pollifax. "She's here on a tour," he called. "It's Ruthie!"

Ruthie quickly followed his glance, and Mrs. Pollifax recognized the sudden fear in the woman's eyes as she searched for the person to whom Mr. Hitchens was speaking. She still loves him, thought Mrs. Pollifax. Is she expecting another young actress?

Ruthie's glance softened as she saw Mrs. Pollifax. "Oh," she said. "Oh!"

Mrs. Pollifax smiled at her. "The reasons for Mr. Hitchens' being here," she said, leaving the couch to join them, "are very intricate. I'm Emily Pollifax, by the way. Why don't you just show her the newspaper, Mr. Hitchens?"

Ruthie's face flushed as he showed her the front page. "Police business," he explained. "Ruthie, you look absolutely lovely!"

"And I," said Mrs. Pollifax firmly, "have an errand to do, so I will excuse myself and leave you both to enjoy the afternoon."

Ruthie said breathlessly, "Oh no—that is, you mustn't think—I'm on a tour, you know, and we're kept very busy. For instance, tonight we visit Hong Kong's nightclubs and—"

Mr. Hitchens, regarding her with pleasure, said, "But why not see Hong Kong's nightlife with me tonight, Ruthie?"

At this point Mrs. Pollifax withdrew, leaving them to the pitfalls and delights of reunion, and escaped on a reconnaissance trip all her own.

First she visited the mall and bought paper and a professional-looking clipboard. Then she headed for the main exit, where she hailed a taxi and gave the driver the name of the street on which Mr. Detwiler lived, but not the precise number.

A surprise soon awaited her: Mr. Detwiler lived at the base of Victoria Peak, in what was obviously a prime residential area. Mrs. Pollifax paid her fare and stood looking around her. Casually she strolled up the street past number 3216, with its discreet sign planted among the shrubs: 3216—DETWILER—JASMINE HOUSE.

"Small but elegant," she murmured. Comparing it with his shop, so modest in size and placed in such an out-of-the-way corner, she reminded herself that he did, after all, deal in diamonds. With a sigh she thought, In for a penny, in for a pound, Emily. Courage! And continuing past his house, she turned in at number 3218: THE FINCH-BERTRAMS—THE BEECHES.

A Chinese maid answered her ring. "Good afternoon," said Mrs. Pollifax pleasantly. "I'm taking an advertising survey on how many hours of television you watch each day."

The woman looked blank. Behind her, a clipped English voice called, "Who is it, Ming?" and a chic young woman appeared.

She looked Mrs. Pollifax over, shrugged and invited her inside. "Why not?" she said. "My husband won't be home for hours, and it gets so boring in this place."

Some thirty-five minutes later Mrs. Pollifax wrenched herself free, having learned rather too much about Mrs. Finch-Bertram, her bridge games and her shopping. The woman's attention apparently did not include her neighbor at number 3216, but she did watch soap operas to "see what clothes they're wearing these days." The problem with being a listener, thought Mrs. Pollifax, was that one became such a repository of unsolicited information.

She had better luck across the street at the Wongs'. The door was opened by a stunning Chinese woman in blue jeans, whose three children giggled behind her through the entire interview. "Television? Oh, it's my baby-sitter," Mrs. Wong said with a laugh. "It's on constantly."

After scribbling down her answers to the mythical survey, Mrs. Pollifax asked brightly, "And the house across the street, are there children at number 3216?"

Mrs. Wong shook her head. "Oh no. That's Tom Detwiler. He's a bachelor. Haven't seen him around for ages, but his housekeeper watches TV, I'm sure."

A bachelor . . . a housekeeper. Mrs. Pollifax thanked her profusely and proceeded directly to Detwiler's house. Crossing the road, she looked at the house with an eye for convenient corners in which to hide the son of a murdered police inspector. She rang and waited, hoping that Mr. Detwiler hadn't been seized by an overwhelming impulse to dash back home at this hour and that his housekeeper might be cherishing many grievances to pour into a listening ear.

As it turned out, his housekeeper had only one grievance, and a very unexpected one; but for another voice and a listening ear she had a real need. Mrs. Pollifax had no sooner announced her survey than she was urged to come in for a good cup of tea.

"I get lonesome," the housekeeper told Mrs. Pollifax with a shake of her head. "O'Malley's my name, by the way, Jane O'Malley. And if it wasn't for me soaps, I'd hand in me notice, even though Mr. Detwiler pays me the moon." She led the way into the kitchen, poured tea for Mrs. Pollifax and sat opposite her at the table. "Mr. Detwiler's not been to home for two months."

"Not been to—" Mrs. Pollifax stopped, and began again. "Oh, you *must* get lonesome." Was she serious? Mrs. Pollifax wondered. Not home for two months?

Mrs. O'Malley nodded. "Yes, and being here twenty-four hours a day too. There's some as would say, 'Oh, what an easy time for you,' but who's to cook for? Mr. Detwiler, he's ever so pleased with my dinner parties, when he gives 'em."

"Away on a business trip, is he?"

A puzzled expression came over Mrs. O'Malley's honest face. "Some sort of business," she said. "Although once a week comes his laundry, brought by a delivery boy, without a word of where he is; and back I send his clean shirts. It's downright depressing. Lively place this was, until two months ago. Now there's only the errand boy once a week, and me TV for company."

Two months, Mrs. Pollifax was repeating to herself dazedly. How very extraordinary. Hadn't Bishop told her that it was two months ago that Detwiler's reports to the department had become misleading? Aloud she said warmly, "Like Mrs. Wong across the street, who tells me that she too has her—uh—telly on all day."

Mrs. O'Malley's face softened. "She's a dear little thing, and so much happier now her father-in-law's dead." She shook her head. "Such a Nationalist he was—talk, talk—and she so patient!"

"Nationalist?"

"You know—what China was before the Reds took over. That general—Chiang Kai-shek—who moved his government to Taiwan and always schemed to get back to the mainland." Seeing Mrs. Pollifax's surprise, she explained, "No doubt it seems a long time ago to you, dear, but not here in Hong Kong. Most of the refugees came here running away from the Communists, so there's still feelings about it. Now, what was you going to ask me?"

Mrs. Pollifax began the survey, Mrs. O'Malley giving a running commentary on each of her preferred shows. Conscientiously Mrs. Pollifax recorded the dawn-to-midnight viewing.

"Widow too?" asked Mrs. O'Malley, watching her put away her clipboard and pen.

Mrs. Pollifax temporarily erased Cyrus from her thoughts and said that yes, she'd been a widow for many years.

Mrs. O'Malley nodded. "And this 'ere inflation—what it does to pensions! Where you living, dear?"

"Off Lion Rock Road," said Mrs. Pollifax, adopting Inspector Hao's house; and then, with a glance at her watch, she rose. "I really must be running along now. I've so many people to see."

"Well, stop in tomorrow if you're doing any surveying in the neighborhood," said Mrs. O'Malley as they reached the front door. "What did you say your name was, dear?"

Mrs. Pollifax felt her mind go blank. "Blank—Irma Blank," she stammered, and fled.

Her visit to Mr. Detwiler's house had produced a shock that she wrestled with strenuously all the way back to the hotel. Certainly Mr. Detwiler was not away from Hong Kong on a business trip when she'd seen him only yesterday at Feng Imports. Yet he'd not been home for two months, and the nagging question to which she found no answer was, *Why?*

I'm missing something here, she thought. I expected something sinister, and I found nothing of the kind. I've got to stop writing scenarios and free my thoughts for what I've not seen yet.

JUST after ten o'clock that evening Mrs. Pollifax was once again riding through the streets of Hong Kong for a second clandestine meeting with Sheng Ti, but this time Robin was with her.

"You've been to the airport?" she had asked when they met.

He had steered her to his Renault and opened the door for her. "Yes, and delivered both Interpol men to Marko. Krugg will take over in the rooming house from Marko, and then Marko will deliver Upshot to the warehouse behind Feng Imports, after which he'll be returning to the hotel to eat and sleep. According to Marko, nothing's happened, except that a man he assumed from your description to be Sheng Ti left the shop around five thirty, carrying two packages, and came back empty-handed at seven. I wouldn't mind at all finding out what he was delivering."

"And I," said Mrs. Pollifax, "intend to ask Sheng Ti where Mr. Detwiler is living." She proceeded to tell him of her afternoon.

"You have been busy," he said with an appreciative glance.

She smiled. "I have also seen Mr. Hitchens on the evening TV newscast. I thought he did a very sophisticated job. There wasn't the faintest suggestion of his knowing anyone in Hong Kong except Alec Hao."

"Good for him. I'm relieved."

"And in the late edition of the newspaper there's a photo of Alec Hao on the first page, with the headline Has Anyone Seen Him? I'm carrying it with me to show Lotus and Sheng Ti."

"I marvel," said Robin with a twinkle. "You insist with rare talent on sticking to the basics."

She said frankly, "Well, I don't want you to forget Alec. I understand how you might, what with Eric the Red entering the picture, but Mr. Hitchens is very concerned about him. I spoke to Mr. Hitchens, by the way, and he'll join us for breakfast tomorrow. He had another adventure this afternoon." And she told him about Ruthie.

"The manifestations of fate!" Robin exclaimed. "And she's on one of those awesome tours? I'd like to meet her."

Mrs. Pollifax nodded. "I think you'd like her. She's not a beauty like your wife, Court—"

"No one's like Court," said Robin firmly.

Amused, Mrs. Pollifax said, "No, of course not—for you at least." She added quickly, "There's a parking space up ahead."

Robin slid the Renault into it with skill, and they walked two blocks to Dragon Alley. Entering the tiny compound at number 40, they found Lotus already waiting in the shadows. When she saw two people the girl stood up, ready to flee, her face distressed.

"A friend," Mrs. Pollifax said. "It's all right."

Lotus gave Robin a doubtful glance, but she led them into the dim room that Mrs. Pollifax had visited before.

"Looks like an opium den," murmured Robin.

To Mrs. Pollifax's surprise, Sheng Ti accepted Robin's presence at once, which she found touching until she realized that it implied an alarming trust in her. "Friend," said Sheng Ti, shaking Robin's hand and beaming. "New friend. Pliss—a seat."

They sat down under the smoking lamp, their faces orange in its weird light, and Mrs. Pollifax began their conference by unwrapping a napkin full of sweet buns and placing them on the table. Beside them she laid twenty Hong Kong dollars. "For renting the room for half an hour," she told Lotus. "Now to business! Did you do errands today for Mr. Detwiler, Sheng Ti?"

He nodded. "Yes. Two packages diamonds: one to Donald Chang, Nga Tsin Wai Road, apartment near airport Kowloon, and other to post office, insured, Gem Mart, Bombay, India."

"The Hong Kong address particularly interests me," said Robin. "Can you fill in the address of Donald Chang?"

Sheng Ti nodded, and bringing out a slip of paper read off the numbers of both the street and the apartment. "I work good?" he asked Mrs. Pollifax eagerly.

She smiled. "Yes." She brought out Alec Hao's newspaper picture. "Now, have you seen this man at Feng Imports?"

"No, never," he said, shaking his head.

"Then what about this man?" she asked, bringing out the worn photo of Eric the Red. "Do either you or Lotus recognize him?"

"No," said Lotus, and Mrs. Pollifax remembered that the girl had not yet arrived at the shop when Eric made his exit.

Sheng Ti, however, narrowed his eyes as he studied the picture, and suddenly nodded. "Yes, I see him. He had—funny marks on—" He touched his cheek with his fingers. "He come very early yesterday, and I am sent away fast to buy *qishui*."

"Soft drinks," put in Lotus.

Sheng Ti nodded impatiently. "But I see him anyway as I go."

Robin leaned forward. "Have you seen him again?"

Sheng Ti sadly shook his head.

"One other question," said Mrs. Pollifax, "and do have a sweet bun."

"Su-eet boon?"

"Yes. Where does Mr. Detwiler sleep? Does he stay at the shop? Does he live there now?"

Sheng Ti looked at her blankly. "I leave eight, nine, ten o'clock, him still there."

"Lotus?" asked Mrs. Pollifax.

The girl frowned, puzzled. "I hadn't thought of it before, but for weeks now Mr. Detwiler's been at the shop when I leave at six. This is not usual. He always used to leave at five or half past, for he has a house—"

"Yes," said Mrs. Pollifax. "And where does Mr. Feng live?"

Her brow cleared. "Oh, he has rooms over the shop."

Mrs. Pollifax met Robin's questioning glance with triumph. Detwiler could be staying with Feng, then, to remain in charge. So Mrs. O'Malley would not be seeing Detwiler until whatever he planned was completed.

"Something wrong?" Sheng Ti asked anxiously.

Mrs. Pollifax glanced at Robin, who shook his head. "It's better you don't know," she told them both, "but this man"—she pointed to the picture of Eric the Red—"this man is very dangerous. If he comes again to Feng Imports, let us know at once."

Robin was jotting down his number. "Someone will be at this telephone if you can't reach Mrs. Pollifax."

"Or come to the hotel," said Mrs. Pollifax, removing another twenty Hong Kong dollars from her purse. "For taxi."

"So much money," murmured Sheng Ti in awe.

Robin stood up then, and Mrs. Pollifax rose also to shake hands warmly with Sheng Ti and Lotus. "Thank you both," she said.

"I LIKE your young man," Robin said as they drove back to the hotel. "He's badly frightened, though."

"Yes," she said, and then, "I am too. Aren't you?"

At the hotel, Robin went directly to his room. Mrs. Pollifax, wondering if there were any cables from Carstairs, stopped in the lobby to inquire. There was indeed a cable for Mrs. Reed-Pollifax. As she carried it upstairs she thought what a long day it had been. No wonder she was tired.

She placed her purse next to the figure of the Buddha that stood on the bureau, its expression one of such serenity that at this moment Mrs. Pollifax envied it with all her heart. With a sigh she slit open the envelope of the cable to discover that it was not from Carstairs, but from Cyrus. She read: RAINED OUT STOP RETURNED EARLY STOP CATCHING FIRST PLANE TO JOIN YOU THURSDAY NIGHT STOP MISS YOU SEE YOU LOVE YOU CYRUS STOP.

Mrs. Pollifax read it over a second time, feeling her tiredness drop away like an outworn coat. Cyrus was coming. *Cyrus!*

She laughed with delight, and catching the eye of the Buddha, she thought for a moment that it smiled back at her.

MRS. Pollifax drifted in and out of an uneasy dream, wondering why there persisted a feeling of something wrong. With her eyes still closed, she sent her mind's antenna out to probe. It wasn't Cyrus, who was on his way to Hong Kong, nor was it— Her thoughts froze as she heard a faint sound nearby. What was wrong, she realized, was here and now, and in this room.

She was not alone.

Mrs. Pollifax opened her eyes and cautiously turned her head. It was still night. The draperies had not been completely drawn, and an eerie light from the street spilled across the floor. In the center of the room was a man, standing very still, his outline clearly discernible against the lighter patch of window.

As her intruder turned away Mrs. Pollifax slid one leg over the side of the bed, and when her foot met the floor she slowly followed it until she was free of the covers and standing.

Her intruder had now arrived at the luggage rack, and suddenly a pencil-thin ray of light shone down on her open suitcase. As he leaned over it Mrs. Pollifax moved up behind him, thinking this was going to be no challenge at all. She had just reached him when he stiffened, but it was too late. Mrs. Pollifax was already assuming her stance and turning her hand into a coiled spring that abruptly shot out to hit him at the base of his skull. He gasped and started to whirl toward her, at which point Mrs. Pollifax followed through with a heavier karate slash to his neck, the first blow confusing him, the second sending him to the floor.

Flicking on the light, Mrs. Pollifax was astonished to find that it was the man who had followed her from Feng Imports, the man with the attaché case, now lying unconscious at her feet. She felt his pulse, went to the phone and dialed Robin's suite.

"Robin, there's a man in my room," she told him.

"*Again?*" he said incredulously. "Another?"

"He's unconscious now, but he's the man who followed me on Monday afternoon. *He comes from Feng Imports.*"

"I'll be right there," Robin told her, and hung up.

She was waiting at the door for him when he arrived, and she noticed that even at one o'clock in the morning, wearing blue jeans, he looked impossibly handsome and Savile Row.

"Where—ah," he said, entering and seeing the figure sprawled on the rug. "Definitely karate this time."

She nodded. "I woke up and he was—there. He simply mustn't regain consciousness in my room, Robin."

"Absolutely not," he agreed.

"The horror of this," she went on, "is that whatever we do with him, he'll remember that I hit him, and Detwiler will be told, and it will completely destroy my amateur status."

"Completely," he agreed again.

"Unless," she added, "we could somehow discredit him. After all, he didn't actually see me, you know."

Robin's eyes took on a mischievous glint. "*That*," he said, "begins to have infinite possibilities. He entered a dark room—"

She said excitedly, "The *wrong* room?"

"Exactly! In fact, if we carry him off to just the right place, he could be accused of imagining the whole thing. Who would believe that you could level a burglar with a karate chop?"

Mrs. Pollifax beamed at him happily, thinking how invigorating it was to work with someone whose mind moved in the same orbit as her own. "Of course we've not even considered why Detwiler sent him here, or for what—"

"Later," he said. "Let's get him safely out first. We can carry him between us to the freight elevator, and it will be assumed he's had too much to drink. But where can we dump him?"

"Somewhere in the hotel," said Mrs. Pollifax. And then, "No, wait. The mall will be open, won't it?"

"The shops will be closed, but it's still an entrance to the hotel, with probably a guard making his rounds."

"Perfect," she told him. "Let me get dressed now. Trust me!"

When Mrs. Pollifax emerged from the bathroom, fully clothed, Robin was tucking a wallet back into the burglar's jacket. "He does have a name. It's Allan Chen."

"I rather liked calling him the man with the attaché case," she admitted. "Shall we take Mr. Chen away now?"

They staggered down the hall, with Mr. Chen sagging between them, and were fortunate in meeting no one. The elevator descended, and as the doors slid open Mrs. Pollifax peered out.

"I'll reconnoiter," she said, and vanished around a corner. Returning, she signaled to Robin. "It's to the right. Hurry!"

"Nothing would delight me more. He's getting heavy." Robin peeled Mr. Chen from the wall, where he'd been propping him up. "What are we heading toward?"

"A machine . . . there it is."

Robin stared in astonishment. "What on earth is it?"

"You haven't seen one before? It measures blood pressure. You sit on that bench and place that strap around your wrist, and then you drop money into the slot and your blood pressure lights up on the screen, just like a pinball machine."

"How very amazing." Gently Robin lowered Mr. Chen to the bench, and Mrs. Pollifax secured the strap around the man's wrist. Then, consulting the machine's directions, Robin dropped four Hong Kong coins into the slot.

"Robin!" she protested.

"Blood pressure's a bit high," he murmured, standing back to observe the flashing numbers.

"I doubt mine's exactly normal at this moment, either," she said crossly. "I hear footsteps—hurry!"

"Just look at our handiwork," said Robin, retreating with her.

Mrs. Pollifax turned and looked, and her last glimpse of Mr. Chen was of him slumped over the console as if nearsightedly studying its directions, while the screen above him continued to flash 150/72 . . . 150/72 . . . 150/72 . . . in bright red lights.

"This," said Robin, ushering her into the elevator, "has been a very educational interlude, which I think calls for a drink."

They made their way back to the sixth floor, and Robin led her into her room and poured them each a brandy. "All right, let's do a quick probe here," he said. "Just what do you think has drawn Detwiler's attention to you?"

She shook her head. "I'd have a better idea if I knew what Mr. Chen was looking for. I'm sure that I wasn't followed today, and I'd swear that Detwiler had concluded that I'm harmless."

"Then what's in the suitcase that Mr. Chen was about to search? Or your purse, for instance, or—"

He stopped, and he and Mrs. Pollifax stared at each other. "The Beretta. The gun I removed from poor Inspector Hao," she said. "I'd forgotten all about it. Do you think he was after it?"

Robin frowned, looking puzzled. "If Detwiler was after the gun, then he must be tied to the inspector's murder."

"But why would he think I'd have it?" protested Mrs. Pollifax. "It should be Mr. Hitchens. And why would he want it back *now*, when the only fingerprints on it are mine? It doesn't feel right to me."

"Nor to me," he said. "But you'd better get rid of the blasted thing anyway." He sighed. "I think some sleep is in order, don't you? Court tells me that one of the integral sayings of Zen Buddhism is, Do the best you can and then walk on. Well, we've done the best we can tonight, so let's walk on. Think you can sleep?"

She aborted a yawn and smiled. "Yes, I can sleep—after I've propped a chair against my door, dragged the night table in front of it and laid a few other ambushes."

He kissed the top of her head. "See you at eight, then!"

He made his exit, leaving Mrs. Pollifax not only to rearrange furniture, but to ponder again what she might have done to arouse Mr. Detwiler's suspicions of her.

Wednesday

WHEN Mrs. Pollifax arrived at Robin's suite the next morning Mr. Hitchens was already there. "Sh," counseled Robin, opening the door and pointing to Mr. Hitchens, who sat upright on the couch with his eyes closed.

Mrs. Pollifax tiptoed in and sat down, seeing that Mr. Hitchens was holding the newspaper fragment bearing Eric the Red's photo.

He said now, his eyes remaining closed, "You gave me this slip of paper without showing it to me, and the impression I get very strongly is that it is the picture of a man, and—it's really strange— I feel that I've seen this man before. Someone wrote a word on this paper in a very heavy scrawl, and I can only tell you that the word was written in anger and frustration." He opened his eyes and saw Mrs. Pollifax. "Good morning!"

"Good morning," she said cheerfully.

"You can look now," Robin told him. "The word written there is 'when,' as you can see. You've absolutely no answer to it?"

"No, because whoever wrote it didn't know the answer, and I can only pick up what he or she knew at the time." Glancing down at the picture, Mr. Hitchens said in astonishment, "But this is the man we saw on the plane!" He looked at Mrs. Pollifax. "You pointed him out to me!"

She beamed at him happily. "So you recognize him too. We found it yesterday in Inspector Hao's house—which we burgled after leaving you. It's the inspector who scrawled that 'when.' "

"Good heavens!" said Mr. Hitchens.

Robin nodded. "Yes, and having jeopardized my job by insisting on three men being flown in last night, on the strength of Mrs. Pollifax recognizing him, I can't tell you how relieved I am to hear you confirm its being the same man."

"Three men?" put in Mrs. Pollifax. "Your third man has arrived?"

Robin flashed her a satisfied smile. "Yes. Witkowski made his way here from the airport while I slept blissfully on. He'll be spelling Marko and Krugg in the rooming house. And we've still got Upshot staked out at the warehouse. If anything moves in Dragon Alley, we'll know about it."

"Staked out for what?" asked Mr. Hitchens, puzzled. "And you've not found Alec. What have you discovered? Who is the man in the picture?"

Robin turned to Mrs. Pollifax. "Care to take this on?"

Mrs. Pollifax nodded. "It's much bigger than a missing man and a murder now, Mr. Hitchens; we think we know what Alec's father discovered that led to his death. The man we saw on the plane is the same terrorist who directed the French hostage affair."

Mr. Hitchens looked appalled. "But he's the man no one can find. He— Wait a minute. Eric the Red they call him, the Liberation '80s leader."

Robin picked up the story. "Yes, and on Monday morning Mrs. Pollifax saw him coming out of an obscure little shop called Feng Imports. We've put a watch on the place, hoping he may return there, but whether he does or not, he's here in Hong Kong, where it would seem that *something* is due to happen—"

A knock at the door interrupted him.

"That will be our breakfast," Robin said as he strode to the door. "While the waiter brings it in, I suggest we turn on the television and see if there've been any developments on Hao's murder—but softly, because Marko's still sleeping."

The police, according to the newscast, were still looking for Alec Hao and were distributing flyers with his photograph—it was shown on the screen—and searching for the murder weapon. The glances of both Robin and Mr. Hitchens flew to Mrs. Pollifax's purse on the couch, and she made a face and nodded. There was no further news, and to wrap it up Mr. Hitchens appeared again on the screen in a replay of his earlier interview.

"Well done!" said Robin, snapping off the set. "Now, I refuse all shoptalk; my digestion demands it. We speak of cabbages and kings, please, and myriad other things."

Mrs. Pollifax smiled. "All right—Cyrus is coming," she announced. "He expects to be here by tomorrow evening."

"Marvelous," said Robin. "I shall meet him at last. And how was your night on the town, Mr. Hitchens?"

He said almost shyly, "It was wonderful. Ruthie and I did a little dancing, but mostly we talked and talked. Her tour's here until Saturday." He turned to Mrs. Pollifax. "We're meeting later for a cruise of the harbor. Would you care to join us?"

Mrs. Pollifax, interrupting a breakfast of ham and eggs, bean curd, papaya, watermelon, orange juice, toast and coffee, said that she would be delighted. "Tell us more about Ruthie, Mr. Hitchens," she added. "The wife who didn't mind your being dull, as you phrased it."

Awkwardly then, Mr. Hitchens began to speak of Ruthie. They'd been high school sweethearts and had married young. She'd been the only woman he'd looked at for ten years.

"But then," Mr. Hitchens said with a scowl, "my first book on psychic phenomena was published. I was interviewed on a Boston talk show and met Sophie Simms."

"Sophie was an actress?" prompted Mrs. Pollifax.

Mr. Hitchens nodded, looking acutely miserable. "Trying to be, yes—with the longest eyelashes I'd ever seen. She'd been doing improvisations in a small nightclub. I think I've told you that being psychic is of no help when my own life is involved."

Robin asked gently, "And how long did it last?"

"It was horrible for Ruthie," Mr. Hitchens went on, his eyes fixed blindly on his plate of food. "I was completely hypnotized, really. Sophie was so—so—well, it was all so *glamorous*." His glance lifted from his plate. "To answer your question, there was one good year, but only because I was so dazzled, and then two more years before she wandered off with a third-rate producer who she hoped would be of more use to her career than I had been." He added sadly, "He wasn't."

"No, they never are," said Robin. "I believe you mentioned a third—er—"

"Misadventure?" Mr. Hitchens' laugh was bitter. "Oh yes. Sophie had a friend. Rosalie, also in show business. I'd given Rosalie readings—without charge, of course—and she was very sympathetic over everything that happened with Sophie, and didn't realize that being married to a psychic wouldn't advance *her* career, either. I have been—I scarcely need say—very naïve."

Robin said lightly, "I had no idea the life of a professional psychic could be so hazardous, but I can agree with you on glamour becoming addictive. It certainly seduced me for a long time, and I went to great lengths to enter the world of beautiful people—however illicitly."

Mr. Hitchens shook his head. "I appreciate your sympathy, but I have felt, since that third divorce a year ago, so ashamed. I always wanted to live a life of the spirit—I hope that doesn't sound pretentious?—and all I've learned is how shallow I am."

"Nonsense," said Mrs. Pollifax sturdily. "We all betray ourselves from time to time. It's where you are now that matters."

"What do you mean?" he asked.

"Well, Mr. Hitchens, you wouldn't be in Hong Kong this morning, attempting to solve a murder and meeting Ruthie again, if two women hadn't spun you dizzily off balance and left you open to coming here, now would you? If living is a process, then how does one arrive anywhere except by just such painful routes?"

Mr. Hitchens looked at her with interest. "You too?"

She laughed. "Of course! It wasn't *that* long ago that I felt my life was totally useless. Actually a doctor found me depressed enough to urge that I look for work I'd always wanted to do—and off I went to apply for a job as a spy! Which I must say changed my life considerably," she added humorously. "But this is not finding Alec, is it, or using your considerable talent."

"Amazing," Mr. Hitchens said, staring at her.

"Nothing less," Robin told him with a quick, warm smile.

"Last night I felt quite strongly that Alec's still alive," Mr. Hitchens put in quietly.

Robin said, "Is there some way you could find out—psychically— exactly where Eric the Red plans his drama?"

"Drama!" repeated Mr. Hitchens.

Robin shrugged. "That's what terrorism is, basically—pure theater. Nothing is ever accomplished by it, other than focusing attention on a small group of people who seize absolute power by threatening everything that holds civilization together."

"Like monstrous children," mused Mrs. Pollifax, "thumbing their noses at adults who live by codes and laws and scruples."

Robin said in a hard voice, "Terrorists are the parasites of the century. They want to make a statement, they simply toss a bomb, or hold innocent people hostage. If they need money, they rob a bank. Their only passion is to destroy."

Mr. Hitchens said abruptly, "Get me a map. As many maps as you have."

Robin brought him street maps of Hong Kong, Kowloon, New Territories and Macao. Mr. Hitchens laid them out flat, side by side, on the table, and asked for silence.

"You've got it," said Robin.

Mr. Hitchens closed his eyes and sat quietly for a long time, until the ticking of a nearby clock seemed to fill the room. At last he lifted one hand and began slowly moving it across the surface of the maps, sometimes in a circular motion, sometimes up and down, several times lingering briefly in one place. Five minutes passed, and then quickly he dropped his hand to one of the maps and opened his eyes. "This area," he said, and removing a pen from his pocket, he drew a circle. "This brings very uncomfortable feelings, a sense of violence, and very disturbing vibrations."

"Central Hong Kong," murmured Mrs. Pollifax.

"Your circle takes in a large area," Robin said in a troubled voice, "and it doesn't even include Feng Imports."

Mr. Hitchens shrugged. "There are guns somewhere inside this circle, and one looks like this. Paper, anyone?"

Mrs. Pollifax handed him a paper napkin and watched his nimble fingers block out lines. "Like this," he said.

Robin said in horror, "But you've just drawn the outline of a multiple-rocket launcher!"

"Have I?" said Mr. Hitchens indifferently. "I don't know what it is. I've only sketched what I saw."

Robin sat back and frankly gaped—his mouth was actually open in shock—and Mrs. Pollifax wondered if he had really grasped Mr. Hitchens' possibilities before this moment.

"Then they have to have a radio," Robin said suddenly, closing his mouth. "The circle doesn't include Feng Imports. If that circle is accurate, and if the eleven members of the Liberation '80s for whom the passports were stolen are hiding inside that circle, and Detwiler is the mastermind of this project, there would have to be communication between them. My guess would be a high-powered radio." He nodded. "I think it's time I visit the governor. It's time we risk some of Hong Kong's police being

brought into this. We should have radio-detection vans cruising the streets, checking for high-power transmissions." He reached for the napkin with a wry smile. "I hope you don't mind if I take this along with me as evidence?"

Mr. Hitchens smiled. "By all means, take it."

Robin had just pocketed the napkin when the telephone rang; he snatched it up on the first ring. "Yes?"

He listened, made a note on the pad in front of him and said, "Thanks." Hanging up, he turned to Mrs. Pollifax. "That Donald Chang, to whom Sheng Ti delivered a packet of diamonds . . . I phoned my superiors in Paris last night, with an inquiry about the chap. That was Paris calling back: Donald Chang works in the baggage room at Kai Tak Airport."

"Aha," said Mrs. Pollifax.

Robin nodded. "Exactly. What better place for anyone engaged in a smuggling racket for which the payoff could be a packet of diamonds? Another tidbit for the governor." Smiling, he saluted them. "I'm off. I wish you a delightful cruise—see you later!"

THE harbor and the sky were sunless this morning, and a curtain of mist had swept over the mountains. A choppy wind blew across the water, and once aboard the launch, Mrs. Pollifax shivered.

She had joined Ruthie and Mr. Hitchens not merely to sightsee for two hours; she had a more practical purpose. She was in possession of a murder weapon, and she considered the harbor an excellent place in which to drop it. But she admitted also to a curiosity about seeing Ruthie and Mr. Hitchens together; something so unusual as two people accidentally meeting again thousands of miles from home thoroughly charmed her.

It had obviously charmed Ruthie too, for she looked transformed, as most women do when they feel courted. She called Mr. Hitchens "Hitch," to which Mrs. Pollifax reacted with amusement, for she couldn't imagine calling him anything but Mr. Hitchens. She tried to picture him in high school, and smiled as she set to work enlarging on his boyishness and removing five pounds and the hint of gray at his temples.

"What are you smiling at?" asked Ruthie, shouting above the wind and the sound of the engines.

They had taken places in the stern, away from the spray, as the launch headed out. But before Mrs. Pollifax could reply, Mr. Hitchens shouted, "Coffee? They've opened the snack counter!"

"Oh *yes*," said Mrs. Pollifax, and as he moved away she said to Ruthie, "I was wondering what he was like in high school."

Ruthie laughed. "Oh—very serious, and feeling that being psychic couldn't possibly equal playing on the football team."

"And you loved him."

Ruthie gave her a quick, startled glance. "Yes." She hesitated, looking embarrassed, and then said with a controlled lightness, "Do you think that—well—old fires can be rekindled?"

Mrs. Pollifax smiled. "I don't see why on earth they should be. I think it far more interesting—and a great deal more fun—to simply begin all fresh and new."

Ruthie looked surprised. "You mean—not try again with Hitch, but look for someone else fresh and new?"

Mrs. Pollifax touched her hand. "Not at all. I mean that whatever drew you and Mr. Hitchens together once can certainly draw you together again, but I think it a great mistake to look at it as a continuation. After all, you're different people now."

Ruthie seemed relieved. "That's refreshing. You almost make my doubts disappear."

Mrs. Pollifax looked at Ruthie with a twinkle in her eye. "Doubts—or fears? You know," she said, "I really think he's seeing you with fresh eyes, which leaves it entirely up to you. Did you make a very *good* new life? Oh, thank you," she said to Mr. Hitchens, who had returned with their coffee.

Ruthie said with pride, "Yes, I did. I moved into a charming apartment in Boston, I began teaching a fifth grade instead of kindergarten, and I started traveling."

"And has she traveled!" exclaimed Mr. Hitchens. "She leaves Saturday for Bangkok, can you imagine?"

Mrs. Pollifax sipped her coffee and listened to them talk of travel, and then of Boston, and she decided that all was well between them. She made her way to the railing, opened her purse and casually dropped overboard the gun that had killed Inspector Hao. Then she settled down to enjoy the glimpses of white beaches at Repulse Bay and the city of sampans at Aberdeen, but her thoughts began to wander back to Mr. Detwiler. Why hadn't he visited his home for two months?

"WHY, IRMA BLANK!" EXCLAIMED Mrs. O'Malley, a huge smile enveloping her face. "You've come back! How nice."

"Hello," said Mrs. Pollifax. "I found myself doing surveys on the next street and thought I'd stop in."

"And just in time for a spot of tea," said Mrs. O'Malley.

Mrs. Pollifax followed the housekeeper into the kitchen, and as she sat down she placed her newspaper on the table, carefully arranged so that Alec Hao's photograph was prominent.

"Oh, that dear boy," said Mrs. O'Malley, catching sight of the newspaper as she poured tea. "The only son too!"

"Oh?" said Mrs. Pollifax. "Have your paths ever crossed?"

Seating herself across the table, Mrs. O'Malley said, "Oh no, dear, for he's been in college in the United States. It's his father I knew, may God rest his soul."

"His father," echoed Mrs. Pollifax. "You knew his father? The man found dead yesterday?"

She nodded. "Oh, many's the night he's been here for dinner, he and Mr. Detwiler being friends. Such a nice man he was too, the inspector, and how he loved my beggar's chicken! It's baked eight hours in a clay pot, you know."

Mrs. Pollifax sat stunned. Mr. Detwiler and Inspector Hao friends? The two men had not only known each other, but were *friends?* She felt herself reeling as she allowed Mrs. O'Malley's words to flow over her.

"Chicken stuffed with chestnuts, herbs and shredded cabbage, and then wrapped in lotus leaves . . ."

The circle was growing smaller, she thought. Two men in this strange confusion of clues had been in contact. They had even been friends. Had the inspector confided to Detwiler, then, his growing suspicions of briberies and stolen passports, never realizing that Detwiler was heavily involved in both, and that it would lead to the inspector's death? Or could Detwiler have inadvertently dropped the clue for Inspector Hao that had begun the search that eventually killed him?

They continued their gossip for another half hour, and when Mrs. Pollifax at last excused herself, she felt drained. At the door she said, "It's been a real pleasure, Mrs. O'Malley. No news yet, I suppose, of your employer's return?"

Mrs. O'Malley's eyes brightened. "Would you believe it? He

sent word this morning that he hopes to be home late next week."

"Late next week," repeated Mrs. Pollifax, blinking at this second staggering piece of news. Thanking her again, Mrs. Pollifax walked to the street, feeling that she had come here to fish for a minnow and had instead pulled in two whales.

Mrs. Pollifax found Marko alone in Robin's suite when she reached it, and she told him her news. "So," he mused, "it is possible that late next week whatever it is will all be over. We have arrived for the conclusion, not the beginning."

"Where is Robin?" she asked.

"He spent the morning with the governor," Marko said, "and he's meeting now with Duncan, the head of Hong Kong's special police unit, to arrange for a radio-detection van—"

"Tell me about those vans," said Mrs. Pollifax.

Marko perched on the edge of the couch. "Gladly, but I will have to make it brief because soon it is my turn to watch for Eric the Red. I have the four-thirty-to-midnight shift at Dragon Alley. The van is a closed unit, bristling with aerials inside that are operated by two men. Once there is action, they plot the course of the signals they are picking up, turning those aerials until they cross and pinpoint the location of secret radio transmitters."

"I see. And then they have found the hiding place!"

Marko smiled wryly. "Only if they are quick, because anyone who wishes to remain hidden transmits for a very short time. After two and a half minutes they are vulnerable to anyone who might wish to find them."

"That's not very helpful," she said indignantly.

Marko laughed and pinched her cheek. "In this game, nothing is easy, and one mistake . . ." He ran a finger from left to right across his throat. "Finis."

"Yes," said Mrs. Pollifax, watching him slip a gun into his holster. "Any news from the men watching Feng Imports?"

"Nothing. I don't think we'll see Eric the Red there again. I'd give my right arm to know where he is."

"Surely not your right arm," she protested.

"I do not like terrorists," Marko said simply, picking up his knapsack. "Now, I am ready. And you—you are maybe a little excited about your Cyrus on his way?"

She nodded.

"Enjoy!" And blowing her a kiss, he went out, leaving her to contemplate dinner and a welcome early bedtime.

BUT her day had not ended once she settled herself in that evening, for she finally had the time to consider the happenings of the past three days and to try to place the pieces of the puzzle in juxtaposition. There were a number of discrepancies, not to mention pieces that refused to fit as they should.

Should. Ought. Scenarios again, she thought crossly, which was how the mind persistently worked, using facts and assumptions left over from the past to draw conclusions that were frequently in error.

What was needed, she decided firmly, was to empty her mind and to begin freshly, with nothing preconceived.

She began to think of all that had occurred since she had arrived in Hong Kong. Of her visit to Feng Imports, of Detwiler and his gift of the Buddha . . . of Mr. Feng, who looked like an ivory figurine himself. Of Sheng Ti and Lotus and the missing Alec Hao . . . of Mrs. O'Malley. And then she erased all impressions from her mind and waited.

When—sometime later—she opened her eyes, it was to whisper, "But of course, how *blind* of me!"

She understood now why Detwiler hadn't visited his home for two months, and she guessed why he had given her the Buddha. Picking up the phone, she dictated a cable to Carstairs, and when she had completed this she turned off the light, and before long she slipped into a tranquil sleep.

Thursday

MRS. Pollifax awoke to an urgent ringing in her ears. She opened one eye, reached for the phone and said sleepily, "Hello."

"Is this Mrs. Pollifax?" inquired a suave male voice.

At once she sat up, suddenly alert, and assured the voice that yes, she was Mrs. Pollifax.

"This is Mr. Detwiler from Feng Imports, whom you may remember meeting several days ago?"

She did not mention that she had immediately recognized his

voice. "Yes, indeed," she said warmly. "And I have certainly been enjoying the Buddha you were so kind as to give me."

There was the briefest of silences, and then he said, "Which makes it difficult, for it is about the Buddha I am calling."

Mrs. Pollifax said merely, "Oh?" while her eyes moved to the serenely glowing Buddha across the room.

"Yes. For it seems that I did Mr. Feng a great disservice when I chose that particular one for you, Mrs. Pollifax. It was carved specially for a monastery in Kyoto, Japan. This is most embarrassing for me, but I must ask if you will return it. I will, of course, present you with another, as well as with my deepest apologies."

"How very unfortunate," she murmured, as her mind raced over the implications of this, and she began to feel pleased.

"Yes, it is. I cannot tell you how sorry I am, but I must ask if it can be returned to me here this morning. You could do this?"

Mrs. Pollifax had already reached her decision. "Yes, I can," she told him cordially. "But as I've only just waked up, I couldn't possibly return it before eleven."

"Apology must be heaped upon apology," he said, but she heard relief in his voice. "If I may expect you, then, at eleven?"

"At eleven, yes," she told him, and hung up. She sat still for several minutes, going over his words and nodding as she saw the pieces of the puzzle slip into place. She did not question why Mr. Detwiler had made no offer to retrieve the Buddha personally. She had not expected him to.

Dialing Robin's suite, she was relieved when he answered promptly. "I've just had a telephone call from Mr. Detwiler. Can you and Marko come to my room?"

"Be there at once!" he exclaimed.

Some minutes later, after ordering breakfast for one and coffee for three from room service and dressing in jumper and blouse, Mrs. Pollifax opened the door to Robin and Marko.

"Good morning," she said cheerfully. "Please sit down, both of you, because I've rather much to say. I need both your help and your witnessing of something I must do before going to visit Feng Imports this morning—at Mr. Detwiler's invitation."

"*What?*" thundered Robin. "Are you out of your mind?"

"It seems there has been a slight error with the Buddhas," she said without expression, "and he wants the one he gave me back.

Apparently it was designed especially for a monastery in Kyoto."

"You don't believe him, do you?" asked Robin.

Before Mrs. Pollifax could respond, there was a knock on her door. The waiter wheeled in her breakfast, bowed and went out. Pouring coffee, she handed each man a cup and took a bite of her egg. "What I have to say will be in some detail, because the details are important to what I came to understand last night."

"We give you attention," said Marko, sipping his coffee.

"Detail one," she said, holding up a finger. "On my visit to Feng Imports on Monday, I wondered why Detwiler invited me into his workshop when Mr. Feng had already told me that he'd never heard of Sheng Ti. Mr. Detwiler was insistent that I join him in the rear, and there was a sharp exchange with Mr. Feng about this. And two," she added, holding up a second finger. "Detwiler insisted on giving me a very exquisite Buddha."

Their eyes moved to the Buddha standing on the bureau. "A remarkably lovely one, yes," said Marko, nodding.

"Three," she continued. "He asked to see the paper on which Bishop had scribbled the address of Feng Imports. Looking at it, he said, 'You could have received this from only one source. No one else could possibly know of Sheng Ti's presence here.' "

"So why not?" asked Robin. "He's worked for Carstairs for years. He could very well have recognized Bishop's handwriting."

"Yes, he did recognize Bishop's writing—and then he gave me the Buddha. I've come to the conclusion," she said crisply, "that Detwiler is innocent of betraying Carstairs and the department."

"What?"

She nodded. "I think he deliberately sent wild reports during these past two months to draw attention to himself. I believe he desperately hoped someone would be sent to investigate."

"You're kidding," said Robin.

She shook her head. "When I arrived, he knew—from my asking for Sheng Ti and from the memo with Bishop's writing on it—that I'd been sent by Carstairs."

Robin, frowning, said, "Then what—"

"I think Detwiler is in very grave trouble," she said simply. "I wondered why I was followed only one afternoon by the man with the attaché case. I think now he wanted only to learn at what hotel I was staying, because he *didn't dare be heard asking that.*

The man with the attaché case was Detwiler's man, and it was he whom Detwiler sent to burglarize my room."

"But why?" asked Robin.

"For the Buddha," she said. "He had to get it back, and when the burglary failed he was reduced to this morning's phone call. Nothing made sense until I began to juggle all the facts: the fact that Detwiler hadn't been home for months, the strangeness of my visit to the shop, that ridiculous burglary attempt, the fact that he and Inspector Hao had been friends. Once I stopped viewing Detwiler as a traitor, I realized the trouble he's in. Detwiler's virtually a prisoner at Feng Imports."

Marko said, "Are you suggesting—"

She nodded. "Who but Mr. Feng? A little blackmail applied to Detwiler about his spying activities, the introduction of drugs to weaken his will and gain control. He couldn't afford to kill Detwiler until later, it might have attracted attention to him. It was important that Detwiler give me the Buddha openly, as an apparent act of generosity, but I believe that under duress he's now been forced into admitting to Feng what he really did, and he's been told to get the Buddha back."

"By Mr. Feng," Robin said in astonishment.

She nodded. "Yes. What, after all, do any of us know of Mr. Feng? He's a shadow figure. A man who runs a shop that's been a convenient cover for Detwiler's intelligence activities. A man who gives the impression of being defeated by life, yet by the time I left the shop, I thought him cold and manipulative— hostile too."

"But to be mixed up with terrorists?"

Mrs. Pollifax shrugged. "We don't know yet, but—why not?"

Robin whistled. "Obviously immediate inquiries about Mr. Feng are in order. But where does the Buddha fit in?"

"Very firmly," said Mrs. Pollifax. Walking over to the statue, she picked it up and carried it to Robin. "There has to be something important about it for Detwiler to have gone to such lengths to give it to me. I hope it needn't be broken, it's so *very* lovely. . . ."

Leaning forward, Marko said, "If it has secrets—" He joined Robin on the couch and moved his fingers lightly over the figurine. "I would guess the headpiece, wouldn't you? It is the only part of the Buddha that does not look to have been carved out of the same piece of ivory." Drawing a pocketknife from his pocket, he said, "Permit me."

Mrs. Pollifax winced as he inserted the knife at the base of the lacy headpiece. He applied pressure to the left side and then to the right. Abruptly the headpiece was released from the figure, and it flew to the floor. Robin picked it up.

"And there," Mrs. Pollifax said proudly, pointing to the cavity carved into the head, "is Detwiler's hiding place. He *is* a friend."

"Yes," said Robin, extracting two slips of tightly rolled paper. "The gods are smiling," he said as he flattened out the first one. "Marko—listen! Eric Johansen—that's Eric the Red. Xian Pi—he's new. Charles Szabo—oh, we know him. Jan von Damm. John Yonomoto. Hoban Holloway—he's a killer. Miguel Valentos, John D'Eon, Carl Eberhardt, Henri Duval and Angelo Gregorio."

"Eleven," said Mrs. Pollifax, nodding, "to match those eleven stolen passports."

"The roster of the Liberation '8os Group!" exclaimed Marko.

"But there's more—this is unbelievable," said Robin, unfurling the second slip of paper. Over his shoulder they peered at the words scrawled on the sheet. It was a list, short but telling:

1. The Tower/Peak: Command Center
2. Government House?
3. Radio station
4. Power station

"It has to be notes on their plan of attack," Marko whispered. "So now we know. What a find, Mrs. P.!"

"But still no mention of *when*," pointed out Mrs. Pollifax. "We're assuming the terrorists are planning some kind of take-over in Hong Kong by late next week, but only because Detwiler's housekeeper expects him home by then, and that's very tenuous."

"We'll take no chances," said Robin. "I'll alert the governor to their *modus operandi*." He went to the phone and began dialing.

Marko, smiling at Mrs. Pollifax, said, "So we now have a busy day finding out about this Mr. Feng of yours, among other matters. And . . . what is this decision to walk into the lion's den? You know the risk."

From across the room, phone in hand, Robin said, "Risk? It's suicidal! You're thinking of delivering an empty Buddha to Feng Imports, and you expect them to let you return here?"

"I'm not even considering the Buddha that Mr. Detwiler gave me," she said. "There's a similar one down in the mall in a gift shop, inferior in workmanship, but otherwise the same size. Mr. Detwiler will see at once that it's not the same Buddha, but I doubt that Mr. Feng will notice."

"Nonsense," growled Robin. His call went through and he turned away, to speak quietly of what they'd just learned.

Marko pointed out gently, "Mr. Feng will know the difference once he attempts to open it."

"There are no terrorists at Feng Imports," she reminded him.

Robin, hanging up the phone, returned to them. "You've got to put this dangerous idea out of your head," he said flatly. "If Mr. Feng is behind this, he'll be waiting for you!"

"Of course," Mrs. Pollifax said, wondering if he would ever understand. "But if I don't go, I think it quite possible that Detwiler will be killed for giving me the Buddha. Detwiler is my assignment. His call was an appeal for help, and if I go, I just may learn from him the day and hour the terrorists plan to strike."

Robin was incredulous. "And you expect Feng to let you leave?"

"You have your men Krugg and Upshot nearby to defend me, and Sheng Ti and Lotus already on the premises."

"If they all *stay* there," said Robin darkly.

Mrs. Pollifax stood up. "Robin, you're sounding more and more like an overprotective parent. You know there are no guarantees in this business." She glanced at her watch. "I'll go down and buy the other Buddha now. It's already ten fifteen, and I promised to be at Feng Imports at eleven." With a smile for Robin, she waved and left.

When she returned twenty minutes later, only Marko was in her room, sipping another cup of coffee. He took the Buddha from her, and holding it up next to the original, he nodded. "Not bad!"

"Where's Robin?"

"Robin is speaking by radio to our men in Dragon Alley. They say no one has left Feng Imports this morning. He's giving orders that at any sign of disturbance inside the shop after you've arrived, they are to act at once. For you he has much fondness."

Mrs. Pollifax nodded.

"He has been persuaded to let you go," continued Marko, "but only because of this." He brought from his pocket an object somewhat smaller in size than the eraser at the end of a pencil. "You will cut open the hem of your skirt and insert it," he said. "It is a device to tell us where you are at all times. A—what do you say in English?—homing signal. We call it an ackameter."

"All right," said Mrs. Pollifax, and went to her suitcase for needle and thread and scissors. When the device had been sewn into her skirt she carefully wrapped the second Buddha in the original's wrappings. With a glance at her watch, she made a face. "I'll just make it, if I hurry."

Marko nodded and clasped her hand warmly. "If ever I am in Detwiler's situation, I shall fervently hope for a Mrs. Pollifax to ride to my rescue. Take care, Mrs. P.!"

"Thank you," she said, and picked up the Buddha and left.

At the front entrance, the sun was in her eyes as she emerged from under the hotel's canopy, and she held up a hand to signal for a cab. One of them pulled out of line and stopped in front of her, a door was opened and she had climbed inside before she saw that the cab already held a passenger.

"Oh—so sorry," she murmured, making a move to withdraw, and then, recognizing the occupant of the cab, she realized something had gone dismally and horribly wrong.

"You are most punctual," said Mr. Feng with a faint, dry smile. "Drive on, Carl—quickly, before we are noticed."

ROBIN was in their suite, sitting by the radio, when Marko joined him. "She's gone?" asked Robin.

"She has just left, yes," confirmed Marko, and then, very gently, "Detwiler is her job, Robin. She had to do this."

Robin shook his head. "I still don't like it," he said, flicking on the transmitter switch. "Raven here, are you reading me?"

Krugg's hearty voice replied, "Loud and clear, old chap."

"Our friend has just left the hotel. Start the alert, and let me know as soon as she arrives."

"Got you, Raven. Over and out."

After calling in Upshot at the warehouse, Robin glanced at Marko and then at his watch. "Fifteen minutes to eleven. She's wearing the ackameter?"

Marko nodded, and drew from his pocket a disk slightly larger than the one he'd given Mrs. Pollifax. He attached it by suction cup to the wall, where it gave out a steady hum. "Working," he said. "Has Duncan of the special unit reported yet on that radio-detection van?"

Robin nodded. "The unit took to the streets at six this morning. The governor says Duncan's the best in the business. If we can trust anyone in the Hong Kong police, it's him."

"Excellent," murmured Marko. "Now, which of us hunts out facts about Mr. Feng?"

Robin gave him a quick smile. "I've already discussed this with Duncan, and he promises a report on Mr. Feng by midafternoon. But once Mrs. Pollifax completes her visit, there's no reason why we can't do a bit of investigating ourselves."

Marko nodded. "She ought to be at Feng Imports in what, twenty minutes at the outside?"

Robin reached for a map and traced out the route. "Let's see, it's almost eleven now. Figuring a short wait for a taxi and even the worst of traffic, eleven twenty should do it." Looking up a call number on his memo pad, Robin now contacted the radio-detection van cruising the streets. "Radio One, Blue Dragon," he said, using the password. "We've sent out a party wearing an ackameter, heading for the vicinity of Lower Lascar Row. If by chance you pick it up, ignore it. We've a line on it here."

A relieved voice said, "Thanks. We're sure picking it up. It's been driving us bats."

"Very good. Over and out." Robin switched to Krugg's channel. "Raven here. I'm changing to receiving now and leaving the line open for you."

Krugg said, "Roger. Nothing yet, all quiet."

Marko carried a chair closer to the radio and sat, relaxed and waiting. Robin envied his calm but conceded that he found such calm impossible. He was too involved. It was Mrs. Pollifax, his friend, whom he had to worry about, and he felt ruffled and cross.

The ackameter continued its steady drone, and Robin's tension began to infect the room. At eleven ten he began to pace the floor.

At eleven fifteen he went to the radio, switched it to transmitting and barked, "What's happening?"

"Nothing," replied Krugg.

"I'm switching you off, but I'll be back." Robin quickly called the radio-detection van again. "That homing signal," he said. "I want a reading on it at once. Something may have gone wrong." He turned to Marko with a wan smile. "What do you think—traffic jam, accident, flat tire or trouble?"

Without replying, Marko moved to the radio and switched to Krugg's channel. "Don't take your eyes off the target," he said, "but give us a rundown on who's left the shop. Read me everything in your report."

"Let's see," Krugg's voice answered. "When I came on duty the old Chinese chap, Mr. Feng, was entering the shop. At eight the young man, Sheng Ti, entered, and forty minutes later the girl—Lotus, is it? And then—"

"Wait a minute, go back," said Marko. "Feng lives over the shop. If he entered this morning, when did he leave?"

There was a silence, and then Krugg said, "I don't know! I just looked over Witkowski's list from last night. He went off duty at six thirty, and there's no mention of the chap leaving—"

Stunned, Robin broke in to say furiously, "Did Witkowski fall asleep? Feng had to leave the building, if he returned to it."

Krugg said flatly, "I've worked with Witkowski before, and Witkowski doesn't fall asleep on the job."

Robin drew in his breath sharply. "Oh no," he said. "Do you suppose there's another way out, another exit we missed?"

"Gently," said Marko, and calling the radio-detection van, he said, "This is Radio One, Blue Dragon. Anything on the homing signal yet?"

"It appears to be stationary in the Man Mo Temple area," the man reported. "We should be able to zero in on it in ten minutes."

"Thanks," said Marko. And turning to Robin, "That's reassuring. She's still in the Western District."

"I'm going," announced Robin, reaching for his jacket. "I can get there as fast as the van, maybe even faster."

"Take your gun," said Marko quietly, as he handed him the ackameter's miniaturized detector. "I'll stay with the radio, and I'll double-check Upshot on the rear exit of Feng Imports."

Robin stopped and said in a strangled voice, "Detwiler and Feng are both supposed to be inside the shop, Marko, waiting for Mrs. Pollifax. If one of them left without our knowing . . ." He turned, opened the door and went out, slamming it behind him.

Moments later he was speeding in the Renault, swearing at every traffic light and blowing his horn at every slow car. Soon he was in one of the oldest, most crowded sections of Hong Kong, where the narrow streets gave him a dozen new frustrations. Spotting a rare parking space, he inched the car into it, jumped out and began to run. The ackameter detector hummed confidently in his hand, and the distance meter set into it clicked quietly, measuring the distance between it and the mate sewn into Mrs. Pollifax's skirt. As he turned a corner and saw the façade of the Man Mo Temple, the ackameter's hum rose to a nearly hysterical pitch. Robin paused in confusion. There was no sign of Mrs. Pollifax. As he stood there an unmarked gray van pulled up to the temple, and when a man in coveralls stepped out Robin crossed over to say quietly, "Special unit?"

The man gave him a level stare. "ID?"

"Radio One," he said. "Blue Dragon."

The man visibly relaxed. "We've pinned down the location of the homing device to either inside or in back of the temple. I'm Harold Lei, by the way, and that's Jim Bai, who'll take the rear. Shall we go?"

They hurried into the temple, where Robin became aware of extraordinary beauty—brasses gleaming against clear, bright scarlets and incense coils suspended from the ceiling like delicate hooded canopies. It would have soothed him if he'd not been feverishly looking for Mrs. Pollifax. And she was not here.

"Damn," he said aloud, eliciting a startled glance from the temple keeper reading a newspaper in the corner.

They met outside again, the three of them.

"Nothing in the rear," reported Jim Bai. "What's happening with that detector of yours?"

Robin glanced down at the distance meter and groaned. "Oh no," he said. *"It registers zero."*

"Then it has to be here," said Harold Lei, frowning.

"You don't understand—" began Robin, but he abandoned his protest when he saw Harold Lei bend down and pick up what looked to be a pebble at their feet.

"This it?" he said.

As it was dropped into the palm of his hand Robin felt an acute

86

sense of despair. "So they've got her," he said bitterly. "What an insult to deliberately leave this here for us. Except—" But he didn't finish his thought. He didn't want to remember that the disk had been sewn into Mrs. Pollifax's skirt, which meant there would have been a threat of violence, or violence itself, to separate it from her. "I need a phone," he said.

"In the van," Lei told him.

Briefly Robin delivered the news of Mrs. Pollifax's abduction to Duncan, head of the special unit, the man the governor had introduced with every assurance of his probity.

"Awkward, this," Duncan said calmly. "Blows everything sky-high if they apply pressure and she tells them all we know. Where are you now?"

"Man Mo Temple, about to head back to the hotel."

"Good. Tell my men to get back on the job, and I'll talk with you later. And—steady, old chap!"

"Yes," was all that Robin managed to say, while inside he raged with his fears for Mrs. Pollifax, and at himself for not having absolutely forbidden her to go. Which, he conceded miserably, would never have succeeded anyway, not with Mrs. Pollifax.

Cutting the connection, he exchanged a few words with the two men in the radio van and then drove somberly back to the hotel. He could hardly believe it. They'd been outmaneuvered, and Mrs. Pollifax captured.

As he reached the lobby an elevator opened its doors, and Mr. Hitchens and Ruthie walked out.

"Robin!" cried Mr. Hitchens happily. "Oh, do meet Ruthie. This is— *Something's wrong*," he said.

Robin nodded. "They've got Mrs. Pollifax."

"Oh no!" exclaimed Mr. Hitchens.

Ruthie said, "But I saw her only an hour or so ago."

"Where?" Robin said, turning to her in surprise.

"She was getting into a taxi at the front entrance."

Robin laid a hand on her shoulder. "Let's try that couch over there," he said grimly. "I want to hear this."

Once seated, Ruthie began. "I was strolling toward the entrance when I saw her walk through the doors. The sun must have been in her eyes, because she shielded them, and then she waved at the waiting cabs, and when one moved up she climbed in."

"All right. Now let me ask you, Ruthie, was it a bona fide taxi?"

Ruthie looked startled. "Oh, dear, let me think. Well—that's funny. As I walked up the drive there were three taxis waiting for passengers, but it was another one, coming from where I don't know, that suddenly pulled up to Mrs. Pollifax."

"Was there anyone inside it but the driver?"

Ruthie closed her eyes. "Yes," she said. "Yes, I could see the silhouette of a person sitting in the rear, and then Mrs. Pollifax's head too as she climbed inside, and then—yes, I saw her head jerk back, as if she'd just noticed the occupant and was going to back out. But the taxi drove away with her in it." Ruthie opened her eyes. "Will she be all right?" she asked anxiously.

"That," said Robin, "is something I can't answer."

KRUGG came off duty at four p.m. and fell into a bed in Robin's suite to sleep for a few hours. Witkowski had left his bed to replace him until midnight.

A taxi reported stolen in the Causeway Bay area at ten o'clock that morning had been found abandoned at three o'clock.

Even more important, reports began to filter in during the afternoon on Mr. Charles Yuan Feng, the owner of Feng Imports, and all were extremely interesting.

According to his police dossier, he had come to Hong Kong from Shanghai after serving in the Nationalist Army under Generalissimo Chiang Kai-shek; and he had been accompanied by a brother, Weng Feng. At this time—it was in the 1950s—both brothers were suspected of having connections with the notorious "14-K" Triad, which the Nationalists had brought to Hong Kong for the purpose of overthrowing Mao and returning the Nationalists to mainland China.

In 1967 the brother, Weng Feng, had been arrested in Hong Kong as a Nationalist spy and saboteur, the police having found an arsenal of weapons in his apartment. He had been quietly deported to Taiwan, where he still lived, and it had been assumed that he was the troublemaker of the family. Following this, interest in Mr. Charles Yuan Feng had lessened considerably.

Robin scowled over the report unhappily. "Does it mean anything, or doesn't it? I mean, Hong Kong is full of Nationalist refugees, and amateur conspiracies still surface occasionally."

"But this is no amateur conspiracy," pointed out Marko. "Not if the Liberation '8os Group is involved."

Robin nodded. "It seems inconceivable, and yet Britain and Peking are meeting right now, again—it's in today's paper— negotiating the terms under which Hong Kong will be returned to the Chinese in 1997." He frowned. "And it's to Red China the colony's to be returned, not to the Nationalists, as once envisioned." His frown deepened. "I daresay it could make for a bit of rage, seeing Hong Kong, the capitalist center of the Orient, being turned over to the Communists."

There *was* one footnote in the dossier that dangled possibilities of a Nationalist connection. Mr. Feng's brother, the deported Nationalist spy, had been married to a woman named Xian Su-tsung, and the list in the Buddha had included a Xian Pi.

Nephew? wondered Robin as he went downstairs for an early dinner, leaving Marko behind to man the radio until his return.

It seemed an aeon ago that Chiang Kai-shek and the Nationalists had been routed out of mainland China to set up a new government on Taiwan. Chiang Kai-shek was long since dead; Mao too had come and gone, yet Robin knew how old conflicts could linger. And certainly Taiwan was still insisting—decades later—that it was the only true government of China.

Robin, feeling drained by the events of the day, couldn't even remember when he'd last eaten. He headed for a table in the corner, and seated himself.

Three tables away he saw the flutter of a hand. Ruthie and Mr. Hitchens were trying to catch his attention.

Ruthie leaned forward and called, "Has Mrs. Pollifax been found yet?"

Fortunately, there were few diners at this hour to hear her indiscretion. Robin shook his head.

At the table next to him along the wall a man glanced from Robin to Ruthie and rose from his chair: a large man in a somewhat rumpled suit, with an intelligent face, sleepy eyes and a thatch of white hair. To Robin's astonishment, he walked over to his table, pulled out a chair and sat down.

"Believe I just heard my wife's name," he said, giving Robin a searching scrutiny. "Flew in two hours ago, and nobody can find her. Emily Pollifax?"

"Heavens!" cried Robin, shocked out of his lethargy. "You're Cyrus Reed, and it's Thursday!"

"Yes to both," he said. And added calmly, "Take it Emily's gone and put herself in the thick of things again. Always does. Don't know who you are, but it looks as if I've arrived just in the nick of time. Now, what are you doing about locating my wife?"

MRS. Pollifax, finding herself in the taxi with Mr. Feng, decided that discretion was the better part of valor. Holding back the dismay that gripped her, she forced her lips into a polite smile, as if Detwiler had very graciously sent a cab for her and had included Mr. Feng as a special treat. Actually, she could think of nothing to say that wouldn't incriminate her, such as how had he managed to leave Feng Imports without Robin and Marko knowing?

"I do try to be punctual," she told Mr. Feng, repressing every normal reaction. "I feel it's a courtesy to others, don't you?"

This conversational gambit was ignored, as she had supposed it would be. They were now turning into a narrow street, and as the taxi slowed, Mr. Feng leaned forward and pointed. The car halted in front of a shop displaying the sign TAILOR.

It was at this point that Mr. Feng chose to remove a small gun from his sleeve, and at the sight of it Mrs. Pollifax gave him a reproachful glance. She would have much preferred to go on avoiding reality for a little longer.

"Out—quickly," he told her in a quiet voice. "Leave the Buddha. We have five minutes, no more."

Five minutes for what? Mrs. Pollifax wondered, but she placed the package on the seat and walked into the shop. It was a small shop, with a man at a steam iron, four women seated at sewing machines, and two curtained dressing rooms. Without a word one of the women rose from her bench and went to stand beside one of the dressing rooms. She had a sullen, hard face.

"You will strip," said the woman.

"I will *what?*" said Mrs. Pollifax incredulously.

"Quickly," she said. "Everything."

Obviously, if she demurred, Mr. Feng's gun would be pressing into her back. Bleakly Mrs. Pollifax went into the stall and stripped, handing out her clothing piece by piece.

In a few minutes it was all over. Her clothes were handed back to her, and without surprise Mrs. Pollifax found the homing device in her skirt gone. It was for this, then, that they'd made their stop, and as she was herded back into the car she thought of Robin and Marko still listening for the sound of her ackameter, which would now be sending out signals from a tailor shop.

But in this she was wrong, as she discovered when the taxi came to a stop in front of the Man Mo Temple and Mr. Feng drew out the ackameter. He gave it to Carl, the driver, who then deposited it at the entrance to the temple.

At last Mrs. Pollifax opened herself up to the monstrous reality of her situation, namely that she was now in the hands of the terrorists, with all earthly help in the guise of Robin, Marko, Carstairs and the police denied her. She was on her own. I have to stay aware, she thought. I have to keep my wits about me.

They had been negotiating narrow, congested streets, sometimes forced to halt for crowds of pedestrians, hawkers and trucks. Once she thought they might be close to Dragon Alley. They were certainly in a very old section of Hong Kong, where only Chinese lived.

Abruptly Carl turned into a tiny lane and stopped. A minute later Mr. Feng, still with gun, motioned Mrs. Pollifax out of the car. She glanced at the creped parchment of his skin, the hooded eyes set too close together, and she wondered what passion behind those inscrutable eyes had led him to this.

She climbed out of the car to face a battered faded-blue wooden door. The taxi backed out of the lane, Mr. Feng held open the door, and even as she moved toward him she was calculating strike possibilities. But he was too clever for her, moving adroitly out of reach as she passed him. With the gun behind her, Mrs. Pollifax began climbing the dark, narrow stairs inside. When she reached the top floor of the building a door opened and light spilled into the dim hall, nearly blinding her.

"Take her," Mr. Feng told the man who opened the door. Then he turned and went back down the stairs.

Blinking, Mrs. Pollifax stared at the face of the man confronting her and decided that she didn't like it, resenting especially his blond wholesomeness. He looked like any Hong Kong vacationer in his jeans and sandals, except that he was leveling a gun at her. She was pulled inside a room crammed with people and objects, illuminated by fluorescent lighting. Windows had been covered with newspapers, sleeping bags lay everywhere, and piles of cable lay on the floor like coiled snakes. Along one wall she saw rows of bottles and jars, aisles of wooden crates. At the far end of the room two men were using welding torches, their goggles turning them into Martians, the sparks flying to the ceiling. Three others were mixing something in a metal drum, while two men leaned over a radio. The heat in the room was stifling; her nose wrinkled at the smells of hot grease, sweat and something pungent that she thought might be gasoline.

The gun prodded her along the left wall; she moved past a crate and abruptly stopped. Two other guests were sitting on the floor, their wrists tightly bound together in front of them. It was Detwiler, and a young man whose face she recognized at once from the newspapers: Alec Hao.

Detwiler lifted his head and gave her a wan, rueful smile.

"Good morning—or afternoon," she said politely, and while she suffered her wrists to be bound with ropes—so tightly that tears came to her eyes—she kept her gaze resolutely on Alec Hao.

Once she was bound, the blond young man shoved her to the floor, and she fell between Alec Hao and Detwiler. Turning away with contempt, the man strode off to another section of the room, where she could see his head over the tops of the crates.

Detwiler looked at her. She said nothing—her bound hands were throbbing—and it was not until she noticed the tears in his eyes that she spoke. "I'm sorry," she told him softly.

"I can't think why," he said shakily, struggling for dignity. "After all, I'm the one who made the phone call. You brought the Buddha? Feng has it now?"

Mrs. Pollifax temporized by saying, "A Buddha, yes."

He groaned. "They'll kill me now. You couldn't know, but it has a compartment inside, with plans, papers and—and—"

"Just why did you want me to have the Buddha?"

He shook his head. "I really thought that—at the right moment— I would telephone you at your hotel and tell you what I'd hidden inside. I thought . . ." Tears returned to his eyes; with his tied wrists he dabbed ineffectually at them.

Beside her Alec Hao said in a tired voice, "He's running out of dope. They gave him some more last night to keep him quiet—he was screaming his head off—but that's a long time ago now."

She had been right about the drugs, then. She realized abruptly, too, that in removing the papers from Mr. Detwiler's Buddha she had given herself a great deal of trouble, for when it was discovered that her Buddha didn't contain Detwiler's papers, attention would at once shift from him to her. It was not a pleasant thought, not when it would be terrorists who would question her. . . .

She said to him, "You know why I was sent here?"

Detwiler nodded miserably.

"Does Mr. Feng know this too?"

A sob escaped him. "Probably. I don't know *what* I've told him. I think he began putting small amounts of drugs in my food—at the shop, at lunch—months ago. And then, after a while, he told me—told me—" He lifted his bound hands to his face and wept. "Told me I was part of his plan, and that's when he brought out the needles and said I couldn't go home." He drew up his knees and leaned his head forward, gulping down sobs and shivering.

Mrs. Pollifax tried to remember the suave Detwiler she'd met on Monday, only three days ago, the man who had asserted himself with Mr. Feng. For weeks he must have been drifting back and forth between that man and this one. There were no gold cuff links or black silk suit today; his sandals were torn, and his cotton pants and shirt were wrinkled. She thought of his elegant house and the dinner parties that Mrs. O'Malley had described, and she felt a stab of compassion for the wreck of a man beside her.

Alec Hao now leaned forward to say, "Who are you, anyway?"

With a sense of relief she turned from Detwiler. "I'm Emily Pollifax, and I believe you're Alec Hao?"

He looked at her with astonishment. "How did you—"

"From your picture in the newspapers. Mr. Hitchens has been very worried about you."

"Hitchens! You know him? Has he found my father yet?" His voice was eager, but suspicion lingered in his eyes.

His left cheekbone was purple and his lips were swollen, but he was young and resilient, and he merely looked like a college boy after a boxing match. But there was also anger in Alec Hao, the kind that Detwiler had been incapable of sustaining, she thought, and this had preserved him, so that she felt he could deal with the truth. She said gently, "Your father's dead, Alec."

He drew a long sigh and nodded. "I guess I'm not surprised. Not now. I stopped hoping three days ago. Did they— Was it fast?"

"Fast, and I think unexpected," she told him. "It was a bullet in the temple. They made it look like suicide. There was a note, and a gun in his hand, but I removed them."

"You *saw* him?" he said.

She nodded. "Mr. Hitchens and I found him in the hut where you were captured. Mr. Hitchens and I flew in on the same plane from San Francisco," she explained. "He came to me for help."

"Then you're a—a friend," he said in surprise.

"Yes."

"He used to be," Alec said bitterly, with a jerk of his head toward Detwiler. "He knew my father, and they were friends until these people got to him. You mustn't trust him."

"In the shape he's in now, no one could," she said. "They've been rough on you here?"

"Sort of," Alec replied. "They plan to take over Hong Kong, did you know that? I laughed when I heard it, but I'm not laughing anymore. Know what they're mixing over there?"

She shook her head.

"Potash and diesel fuel. It makes bombs. Last night they went out and planted a few somewhere in the city. From what I overheard, they'll go off at different times over the next two or three days. They lower things down from those two windows over there, to a van they've hidden in the alley below. The windows are built so they can be lifted out easily. Who are they anyway?"

"They're the Liberation '8os Group."

"What?" He looked staggered. "You mean that's what my dad stumbled onto? Good Lord, no wonder—" He shuddered.

"But Mr. Feng's the headman, isn't he?"

Alec looked at her in surprise. "That old man who wanders in and out? I've seen him dole out money once or twice, but what would Liberation '8os want with *him?*"

There was no ready answer to that, and Mrs. Pollifax turned back to Detwiler. She leaned close. "Mr. Detwiler?"

He looked up, his eyes glazed, lips trembling.

"Mr. Feng," she said. "What does he want?"

With an effort Detwiler steadied himself, but his words came out in broken gasps. "Worked—slaved—for years, he said. A bloody f-f-fanatic, and I never knew. One big kamikaze. Because Peking government—not legal. Only Taiwan. *Nationalists.*"

She looked at him in amazement and then turned back to Alec. "Do you have any idea when they plan this takeover?"

"Oh yes," he said. "Tomorrow morning. Around seven."

"Tomorrow?" she gasped, stunned by this news. "Tomorrow morning . . . but that leaves us no time!"

"For what?" he asked in surprise.

"For stopping them. For getting out of here."

He looked at her incredulously. "Are you mad? There's nothing we can do. Look at us. Look at them."

She was looking, and hearing too. Funny sounds of static were coming from the terrorists' radio, which was sitting some ten or twelve feet away from her down an aisle of crates. One of the welders strolled over to it, and when he removed his goggles she saw that it was Eric the Red. She watched him flick on a switch, pick up a pair of earphones, and as he listened he turned and stared at Mrs. Pollifax.

She did not appreciate his singling her out with those cold, empty eyes, and she felt a chill of foreboding.

Abruptly he put down the headpiece, flicked off the switch and walked down the aisle to her. Stopping in front of her, he stared down and then slapped her hard across the right cheek. "The Buddha was the wrong one," he said harshly.

Beside her, Detwiler had turned his head to stare at Mrs. Pollifax in astonishment, and with a dawning hope for himself.

Eric the Red seized her by the blouse. "We will see how much you know and what you did with the papers inside that statue."

Mrs. Pollifax prayed for strength as he dragged her away.

IT WAS half past seven when Robin and Marko had finished describing to Cyrus the sequence of events that had led to this hour. They were a somber trio as they sat near the radio in Robin's suite, surrounded by empty coffee cups. There had been a moment, Robin noticed, when Cyrus turned white, but he'd rallied and remained calm, continuing to weigh facts as they were presented to him and questioning them as judiciously as if he still occupied his judge's bench. Cyrus was going to be a rock, thought Robin dryly, a very *large* rock, for it had not taken him long to see that Cyrus' six feet four inches of bulk held no fat, and that his air of drowsiness, his economical manner of speaking, concealed a quick mind.

"So this takeover of the colony appears to have been painstakingly plotted over a long period of time," concluded Robin reluctantly. "Mrs. Pollifax disappeared at eleven this morning, and we guess now that it was Mr. Feng who occupied the taxi she entered, because he walked back into his shop at twelve fifteen."

Cyrus nodded. "And you've not discovered how this Mr. Feng originally left the shop without your knowing of it?"

Robin hesitated. "We think he may have access to one or two adjacent buildings and have set up an escape route between them. We've sent out a query as to who owns the building near the shop. We're in touch now, you see, with a handpicked group of men from Hong Kong's special unit, but—"

"How many?" interrupted Cyrus.

"Seven," put in Marko. "Plus Duncan, the headman."

"But tracing landlords in Hong Kong is a very complicated business," finished Robin, "and we dare not publicize the situation. We're afraid the Liberation '8os Group would then escape and surface somewhere else." He shook his head. "We want to not only recover Mrs. Pollifax, but to abort the group's mission and put them out of action forever."

"Do they know of your involvement?" pressed Cyrus.

Marko said gently, "If Mrs. Pollifax was right, they would have known nothing until Detwiler confessed to Feng about the Buddha. Then they would have understood that Mrs. Pollifax had—er—connections with Detwiler's intelligence activities."

"And now?" Cyrus' voice was even.

Marko shook his head. "We do not know."

"You mean it will be up to Emily."

Robin suddenly found it comfortable to avoid Cyrus' eyes.

"You understand it's my wife they've captured," Cyrus pointed out quietly. "My impression is you're not doing enough. Walking on eggs. Tied up in knots. You need more men."

"Agreed," said Robin.

"Then if you can't trust the police, call in the army. The British have soldiers stationed here, haven't they? Not likely *they've* been bribed."

Robin whistled. "If it could be done!" he said with longing. "It can scarcely help Mrs. Pollifax, though."

Cyrus gave him a steady look. "Don't know what can help Emily, do we? Best hope is the terrorists'll save her for a hostage."

Robin thought that if that was their best hope, it was a pretty feeble one, because there was no knowing *what* might happen to Mrs. Pollifax in the meantime.

Suddenly Marko spoke up. "I am stricken with apologies. Robin and I have been feeling sorry for ourselves here in our dismay at this event, and it is you who go at once to the heart and return us to action. Robin, go ask His Excellency for soldiers."

"Right," said Robin, and springing to his feet, he strode into the next room to call the governor.

Half an hour later, when he returned to the living room, he found Marko introducing Cyrus to Mr. Hitchens and Ruthie. "We just couldn't enjoy ourselves," Mr. Hitchens was earnestly explaining to Cyrus. "Not while your wife's still missing."

Marko turned to Robin. "You reached the governor?"

Robin made a face. "Yes, but it took ages. He's at a dinner party, and the connection was ghastly, but I think he caught the message. He's phoning us back later. Seems the calling out of even a handful of army men has to go through channels."

"And what does that mean?" inquired Cyrus testily.

"I believe there's an executive council," said Marko. "Of course it's an awkward hour to contact anyone." With a wry smile he said, "Why don't we all sit down? At least we can be comfortable."

As the others moved away Marko took Mr. Hitchens aside to ask quietly, "Could you use your talents to reassure Cyrus?"

"Oh no," blurted out Mr. Hitchens. "I've tried—I really tried. She's in a small, dark room, and there's a man—" His voice trembled. "I couldn't continue. It's terribly unprofessional of me, but you see I know her, which makes such a difference. But things are not going well for her."

"I understand," Marko said.

At ten o'clock Sheng Ti telephoned Robin, having been unable to reach Mrs. Pollifax. "You still have that taxi money?" asked Robin. "Come to the hotel's front entrance. I'll meet you there."

When Sheng Ti was brought into the suite he was in shock from hearing of Mrs. Pollifax's disappearance. Learning that Cyrus was

Mrs. Pollifax's husband, he went at once to him, shook his hand and sat down beside him on the couch, as if Cyrus were the closest connection to Mrs. Pollifax that he could find.

But Sheng Ti had little to report, except that Detwiler had not been in the shop all day—which had never happened before—and Mr. Feng had mysteriously vanished from the building. Sheng Ti and Lotus had been working so hard all day on backlog orders that Lotus had gone early to bed.

"I stay," he announced. "I want you find Mrs. Poll'fax, please. She my friend from Turfan—from *China*."

Cyrus reached over and patted his hand. "You stay," he said.

At eleven o'clock a call came through from Duncan in the special unit, reporting that Donald Chang, to whom Sheng Ti had delivered diamonds, had been arrested at the airport. Chang appeared to know nothing of any terrorist plans; he'd been bribed to remove certain packages that arrived by air, thus circumventing their inspection by customs. He had believed them to be diamonds on which Mr. Feng preferred not to pay duty.

Shortly after midnight Krugg—fresh from his rest in Robin's bedroom, where Witkowski would soon be sleeping—reported no activity at Feng Imports; and at quarter past, the special unit's radio-detection van reported no transmitting.

By one o'clock the suite had begun to acquire the look of an encampment. Cyrus had abandoned the couch, to prowl anxiously around the room, whereupon Sheng Ti had taken over the couch and was sound asleep. Ruthie nodded sleepily in her chair. Mr. Hitchens idly turned the pages of a magazine.

Yet no one considered leaving. They remained incapable of exchanging this place for their own quiet, empty rooms, knowing that if anything happened, it would happen here.

When the phone rang at half past one it was Robin who grabbed it. "Oh—Your Excellency," he said. Cyrus stopped pacing, Marko turned from the radio and Mr. Hitchens put down his magazine.

"No, nothing yet on our missing agent," Robin was saying. "What about the army, sir?" He paused, listening. "That's certainly good news, sir, but when—" He broke off. "Not until then? Yes, but— The only information we have is that it will probably take place inside of the week. . . . All right, sir. Very good, sir. Thank you."

He hung up and said flatly, "Tomorrow afternoon at three p.m. details from the army, in plain clothes, will begin patrolling Victoria Peak and the tower there, the power station, radio station and Government House on a round-the-clock basis."

"And why not sooner?" demanded Cyrus.

Robin said grimly, "He reminded me that terrorists inevitably time their attacks to coincide with the prime-time evening news, to get the fullest coverage, so we needn't be too impatient while he goes through proper channels."

"Not good enough," Cyrus said flatly.

"No, my friend," said Marko. "But it is something. Please—sit down. You will wear yourself out."

At half past two Duncan phoned with a report on the landlords of Dragon Alley, and Marko took it, scribbling notes furiously. Turning to Cyrus and Robin, he said, "Just listen: Under the name Crystal Enterprises, Feng owns half of Dragon Alley— numbers 31½, 30 and 28—and there is your explanation of how he can come and go without being seen. Under the name of Green Jade Associates, he owns a tailor shop. There may be more." Turning back to the telephone, he said to Duncan, "Try the tailor shop."

During the next hour there was only silence from both radio and telephone, and they waited at various levels of wakefulness.

It was shortly after three a.m. that Cyrus suddenly said, "I've had enough of this. Marko, call in your surveillants from Dragon Alley. Robin, wake up that third Interpol chap asleep in the bedroom, Witkowski. You may lose your jobs for this, but I could be losing my wife. This is what I suggest," he said, and then he shook his head and said, "No, this is what we *do*."

And quietly but firmly he told them all what could be done while they waited for the wheels of bureaucracy to turn.

Friday

THERE had been darkness, and then a dim, small light. There had been a hook in the ceiling, from which she had hung by her bound wrists while the man with the pockmarked face asked questions, a great many questions. And then the nightmare had begun.

She hadn't dreamed it, had she?

She stirred, groaned and opened her eyes. Something had

changed. The dark room was gone, and she was lying on the floor of a room that was so brightly lighted it hurt her eyes, and she closed them, becoming aware now of searing hot flames running down her back. What was she doing here? she wondered. And where was she? There was too much for her to understand, and she sank back into oblivion.

When she opened her eyes again it was to the pain of remembering where she was, and why. She was in Hong Kong, and she'd been questioned and then beaten so that she would tell Eric the Red what she knew. Why he hadn't killed her, she didn't know, but that would probably happen next, and in her weakness she began to cry. She remembered that Cyrus was on his way to join her. Never to see him again—never see another morning, another spring . . .

Presently she grew angry at her self-pity, and she thought crossly, It's not that I expected clean sheets, but that I resent very much ending my life on a filthy floor in a Hong Kong loft.

That was better; anger was always better.

She lifted her head, ignoring the ringing in her ears, and she saw the place she had originally occupied when she was brought here, and then she saw Detwiler somberly watching her. She began to grow aware of footsteps hurrying back and forth, and— What was that creaking noise, so familiar yet odd, reminding her of clothes being hung on a clothesline? Ah yes, it was the sound of ropes moving over a pulley. The window . . . she remembered now . . . Alec Hao had said the windows could be lifted out, that there was a van parked in the alley below, to which they lowered things. The terrorists were on the move, then, and if this was so, it was time for her to be on the move too— Because, she thought, if you continue to lie here, Emily, they'll kill you. They certainly won't leave you behind.

This thought galvanized her. She must sit up, and perhaps she might next be capable of standing, and eventually be able to walk too. She drew several deep breaths and coughed, and then with one herculean movement pushed herself into a sitting position, stifling a scream of pain as her torn back met the wall. She had just lifted her bound wrists to look at her watch—it read six oh three—when a wave of dizziness swept over her.

Moments passed before she dared open her eyes. Her situation was not promising, she conceded, but now she began remembering what she had called "karate mind" in her classes back home: the mobilizing of one's energy so that it could be directed to whatever part of the body one chose. She began to apply this formula, resolutely summoning untapped reserves of strength to send to her arms, legs, feet. Illusion or not, it had an effect.

Beside her, Detwiler said wearily, "There's no hope, you know. By seven o'clock they'll have taken over the peak."

She turned to look at him. He looked haggard and gray.

He said, "They made you talk?"

She thought back to the hell she'd just gone through. "No," she said. "I told them I loved the Buddha you gave me and decided I must keep it. I told them I'd seen a similar Buddha in the hotel gift shop and I thought you wouldn't notice the difference."

He looked startled. "You did that? We could hear you scream. It was . . . terrible," he said, tears now spilling from his eyes.

This was not at all helpful. She turned away and noticed Alec, sound asleep. Her glance went beyond him to the window, and to the cluster of men standing there, looking down into the alley, calling out orders. Then her gaze fell on the radio sitting on a crate some distance down the aisle.

Her eyes focused on it dreamily . . . a radio. Marko had told her the radio-detection van was bristling with aerials inside. Once there was a signal, after two and a half minutes anyone transmitting secretly would be vulnerable.

She thought, If I could creep down this aisle to the radio, I could flick on the transmitting switch. The men wouldn't see me—not if I stayed low, crouched behind the crates. The only risky moment would come when I stood up to turn on the switch.

She glanced at her watch. It was six fifteen. Did she have the strength?

Two and a half minutes was a long time, she noticed, seeing how slowly the second hand on her watch crept around the dial.

"What is it?" asked Detwiler, seeing her frown.

She said softly, "The radio . . ." She turned her face toward him. "If I could crawl over to it and turn on the transmitter for two and a half minutes . . ."

He scowled. "What would that do? Who would hear?"

She said simply, "It would be heard. A great deal has been

101

happening. There are people hoping the radio may be used."

His eyes widened. "You mean—*others?* People know?"

"Yes—but they don't know when," she told him. "The papers you hid in the Buddha are in good hands. I must ask—if the men should move away from the window, could you create a diversion? The switch must remain open for two and a half minutes."

He was silent, his face thoughtful. "No," he said at last.

Her consternation, her sense of betrayal were like a stab opening up wounds again. "You won't help?"

"No," he said softly, "I mean that I will go to the radio, not you." A curious smile twisted his lips. "I've been of little use, and I'm quite addicted, you know. Allow me to feel—be—a human again."

"But—"

He touched her bound hands with his. "It's all right, really. It's all right. It's the switch on the left side?"

"I think so. Flip it on, and come back." Something about him worried her. "We'll time it together."

He smiled faintly and began to crawl down the aisle. The men beyond were still occupied at the window, their backs to the radio, and when one did turn to collect an additional box it was to another aisle that he went. Mr. Detwiler remained unseen.

As he came to a stop under the radio Mrs. Pollifax tensed. This was the dangerous moment when he would have to stand and lean over the crate to flick on the switch. She waited, holding her breath. Pulling himself into a kneeling position, Detwiler glanced at her, and she saw that he was asking for a signal. Backs were still turned. She nodded vigorously, watched him place his weight on one leg, stand, lean over and push on the switch.

"Beautiful— Oh, you dear man," whispered Mrs. Pollifax, and drew a breath of relief. As he sank to the floor out of sight she looked at her watch. Six twenty-nine. Oh, dear, she thought, it's going to take so long. Four seconds, she counted. Five . . .

Detwiler was not returning. Glancing at him, she saw him crouch under the radio, but she could give him no more attention, and her eyes fled back to her watch. *Fifty seconds. . . . One minute!*

One minute and three seconds. One minute and five seconds . . . eight, nine. How astonishing time was, she thought, how arduous just one second. Did people *know* this?

Two minutes . . . And now Mrs. Pollifax allowed herself to hope, to think of two men in a radio-detection van furiously turning those coordinates that Marko had described.

Two minutes and twenty seconds. "Please," she whispered. Two minutes and twenty-five seconds . . . two minutes and a half!

She felt a rush of joy and longed to call out to Detwiler that he'd done it, that the radio had remained on for two and a half minutes . . . almost three.

A sudden shout interrupted her vigil. "Oh no," she gasped. A man stood over Detwiler; she saw comprehension dawn on the man's face, saw the switch furiously snapped off and others come to stand over Detwiler, and then a gun was drawn.

She closed her eyes as they shot him. When she opened them Detwiler was dead, his eyes staring sightlessly down the aisle toward her.

Looking at Detwiler's body sprawled across the floor, Mrs. Pollifax thought dazedly, He knew this could happen. It's what he was trying to tell me—that he couldn't find a future for himself; there was no going back. It was an incredible act of gallantry on Detwiler's part.

Beside her, Alec Hao suddenly sat up, jarred out of his sleep. "What happened?" he said sharply.

She nodded toward Detwiler. "They've shot him."

He glanced down the aisle and then turned to her. "It's you I thought they'd killed. I didn't expect—"

"I know," she said.

Alec shivered. "Are we next? Doesn't this ever end?"

She braced herself now as Eric the Red strode down the aisle and said to them curtly, "On your feet. We're leaving."

She thought, Well, Emily, this is when you find out what all those years of vitamin pills can do for you. What you may want is a soft bed and a great deal of nurturing, but what you're stuck with is leaving this wonderful floor and walking downstairs.

Stumbling a little, she found that if she concentrated on Detwiler's final act of courage, she could ignore the pain of her tender back. Step by step she followed Eric the Red down the stairs, and when she faltered Alec steadied her from behind.

The door was open, and she saw the terrorists' van waiting in

the alley. It was a surprisingly innocent-looking van, a shabby Volkswagen camper, with what looked like baggage strapped on its roof and covered with a tarpaulin, and—Oh, what a clever touch, she thought bitterly—two bicycles mounted at the back. Only the two rear windows were curtained, the others open to the world as if to emphasize there was nothing to hide, except that as she entered the van Mrs. Pollifax noticed what was hidden in the curtained rear: piles of machine guns and crates marked AMMO.

But where was the radio-detection van?

She reminded herself that she was still alive and applied herself now to sitting down next to the uncurtained front window without letting her back touch the seat.

Beside her Alec said softly, "Sunshine. I didn't think I'd ever see it again."

"No," she said, remembering that for him it had been four days. She noticed it was six fifty-five, roughly twenty-three minutes since the signal had been cut off. Surely this was time enough? Then in a sudden panic she wondered if the men in the radio-detection van had given up—or if she herself had counted the seconds properly. Detwiler had given his life for those two and a half minutes.

Others entered the van now, six men in all, counting the driver, Carl. There should be eleven terrorists, Mrs. Pollifax thought, wondering vaguely what had happened to the others. The van backed out of the alley, and Mrs. Pollifax stared into streets filled with people going to work and barrows being wheeled along crowded sidewalks. But she could see nothing that resembled a radio-detection van. Something had gone wrong.

From the back of the camper came the sputtering of a radio, and Eric the Red speaking in a low voice. She caught the words "tower coffee shop third floor, take them to the top" and "about eight minutes now." She realized then where the other terrorists had gone; an advance party must have already seized the tower and have found hostages. Hopeless, all of it—too late, too late. . . . She closed her eyes to escape the unfeeling world and dreamily thought of home.

When she opened her eyes the van had started up the steep road to Victoria Peak. They were climbing at a moderate speed— a shabby camper, with a woman at one window, bicycles mounted on the rear, luggage on the roof. The "luggage" that would be the multiple-rocket launcher Mr. Hitchens had described. For just a moment she wondered what Robin and Marko were doing. Sleeping, of course, she thought, since it was scarcely seven a.m., and at this she felt acutely lonely and bereft.

The tower could be glimpsed now above the trees, with its circular restaurant at the top that looked like a space capsule. Then the trees and shrubs on either side of the road thinned, and she could see all of the tower, the road curving around it to embrace the parking area and the gardens of bright flowers. There was a feeling of mounting tension in the van.

Beside her, Alec said weakly, "I can't stand it, this going on and on, not knowing."

With her bound hands she reached over and touched his arm. "I think," she whispered, "that one *has* to go on."

But deep down she could feel the oppression of her own defeat, which was compounded by the abuse her body had taken, as well as by Mr. Detwiler's death, and worst of all by his radio signal gone unheard. There was no longer anything she could do, and now she was becoming incapable even of thinking. Something's happening to my mind, she thought.

The van was now pulling into the parking lot near the tower. There were several cars parked there, but the grounds were deserted except for a solitary gardener in the distance, a young Chinese, patiently pruning rosebushes. She could hear the terrorists murmuring over the weapons they were collecting from the rear, and then, "Out," said Carl, and she looked up to see him with a machine gun slung over one shoulder, grenades hanging from his belt and a pistol in his hand.

Drearily Mrs. Pollifax rose, and she and Alec stumbled down from the van to begin the walk to the tower, the men behind them relaxed and chatting. An abrupt movement off to her left startled her, but it was only the gardener. She wanted to scream at him, Can't you see the guns? Don't you realize all of Hong Kong's about to be taken hostage? But she remembered the world had its own way of going on, and there would always be gardeners trimming shrubbery.

Except . . . except it was strange, she thought, how very closely the gardener resembled Sheng Ti.

I'm hallucinating, of course, she thought, because Sheng Ti is down in the city and Sheng Ti is not a gardener. Horrified at what was happening to her increasingly blurred mind, she looked away.

They entered the tower now. A bank of elevators lay to their right, where she stoically turned, following the terrorist in the lead. Ahead of them a man was standing in the hall, waiting for an elevator. It did not surprise her at all that he looked exactly like Cyrus, because this had to be what madness was like, this peopling the world with familiar faces.

This man who looked like Cyrus regarded them all with interest, his gaze coming to rest at last on Mrs. Pollifax. "Good morning," this person said cheerfully. "Elevator's rather slow today."

"Oh?" said Eric the Red curtly.

His eyes were so kind, she thought—just like Cyrus'—and his voice sounded so much like Cyrus' that tears came to her eyes. But Cyrus was a world away. He wasn't even in Hong Kong yet, was he? She stared at him suspiciously.

"Ah—coming down now," said this man who was impersonating Cyrus so deftly. "Army maneuvers?" he asked in a kindly voice, with a nod toward their weapons.

"Mmmm," grunted Carl.

Heads turned toward the arriving elevator, but Mrs. Pollifax was stealing a second glance at the man. He had managed to move closer until he stood beside her, and she now looked up at him wonderingly, turning away only when she heard the elevator jar to a halt at their floor.

She had assumed that the elevator would be empty.

The doors opened, and she screamed, confronted by an elevator crammed full of men and guns. They had to be Liberation '80s men cradling submachine guns pointed directly at them. It was to be a massacre after all, and this was the end. . . . And then, with a beautiful rush of reality, she saw the faces of Marko and Robin and their men, and understood at last. These were *not* the terrorists, and she had *not* been hallucinating. It had really been Sheng Ti outside, and it was truly Cyrus standing beside her now.

"Down, Emily!" shouted Cyrus, and hurling himself at Mrs. Pollifax and Alec, he carried them both to the floor as the machine guns began spewing out their deadly fire.

"OUTWITTED BY A BUNCH of amateurs," Marko was saying with a smile and a shake of his head. "Interpol is incredulous, and the governor is still in shock."

Robin turned to Mrs. Pollifax and said, "It was Cyrus—entirely Cyrus, you know. If it hadn't been for him . . ."

They were seated around a table in the Golden Lotus room— where it had all begun, remembered Mrs. Pollifax, thinking back to Monday's breakfast with Mr. Hitchens. And now it was Friday evening, and she was astonished at all that had happened in five days, and even more astonished at being alive and here at all.

Yet only partially here, she conceded, aware that she still hovered between two worlds, the darker, violent world holding her back from this one, whose language she had misplaced for the moment. Nevertheless, she had insisted on coming, because at midnight Robin and Marko would be flying off to Rome.

"From what we've learned," said Marko quietly, "it would have been a terrible bloodbath. That position on the peak is nearly impregnable. The government could have brought in helicopters, police, army, navy. . . ." He shook his head. "But at the slightest sign of activity the terrorists would have launched their rockets into the city below and killed crowds of innocent people. The terrorists could have held out for days, leveling whole sections of Hong Kong and leaving thousands homeless or dead."

Yes, that would have happened, she thought. She had no doubts about this, because she had experienced—however briefly—the minds and the psyches of the men involved.

For herself there had been X rays, but she had refused to be hospitalized, wanting to stay with Cyrus. Instead, she had placed herself in the capable hands of Dr. Chiang, who had anointed her back with herbal salves and given her a sedative. The fiery pain had now diminished to smoldering embers, and six hours of sleep had restored her spirit, so that she could say, "Tell me more, Robin. I want to hear all about it."

He smiled at her. "All right, but first you have to picture us sitting around in frustration, waiting for news of you, waiting for the army to send in its men.

"It was Cyrus who very suddenly announced around four a.m. that we were behaving like bloody fools, that we had six able-bodied people present in the room at that moment, plus Witkowski asleep in the bedroom and Krugg and Upshot at their Dragon Alley posts, and seven men from Duncan's special unit—if Duncan could be sold on the idea of enthusiastic volunteers."

"He refused the word volunteers," put in Mr. Hitchens.

"All right, amateurs," conceded Robin with a flash of a smile. "Amateurs like Cyrus and Mr. Hitchens and Sheng Ti and Ruthie, who could help fill in before the army arrived."

Ruthie said cheerfully, "Cyrus pointed out that at least we'd feel we were doing something, and there was always the possibility that the terrorists might act sooner than we expected."

"As they certainly did," said Mr. Hitchens. "When I think what would have happened if we'd not been there—"

"Mercifully, Duncan embraced the idea," continued Marko. "And so we decided to concentrate on the tower at Victoria Peak, due to the words 'Tower/Peak: Command Center' on the list inside Mrs. Pollifax's Buddha."

Robin nodded. "We had Duncan's seven men posted in the restaurant at the top of the tower, fully armed—"

"The restaurant doesn't open until noon, you see," put in Ruthie. "Only the coffee shop on the third floor was open."

"Yes," said Marko. "And Ruthie and Mr. Hitchens were given walkie-talkies and concealed themselves behind the roadside shrubbery, with orders to report every vehicle that passed. Sheng Ti became a gardener outside, with a gun in his sack."

Sheng Ti beamed. "With walkie-talkie too. Not bad!"

Robin smiled. "But I must admit we were shocked when we began to understand that terrorists were actually *arriving*, and that this was to be the day. And the hour."

Sheng Ti said proudly, "I was first to see."

Ruthie nodded. "Hitch and I did report a car on its way to the peak, but it was Sheng Ti who watched five men park the car and leave it, carrying guns and heading for the coffee shop."

The advance party, Mrs. Pollifax thought.

"There were eight customers in the coffee shop, plus Krugg and Upshot," pointed out Mr. Hitchens. "All ten were herded together by the Liberation '80s men and taken up to the tower."

"Where we were waiting for them," said Cyrus. "Myself, Robin, Marko, that third Interpol chap, Witkowski, and Duncan's seven men."

"After which," added Marko, "there came the glorious news from Ruthie and Mr. Hitchens that a van was on its way up the peak. We figured it was the main group of terrorists—especially since you, Mrs. Pollifax, had been seen at one of the windows."

Startled, Mrs. Pollifax remembered that lonely ride up to the peak and contrasted it with the triumphant scenario being described to her now. She still felt anchored in the estrangement that came from returning to life after an unshareable ordeal. And then two things happened: across the table she met Alec Hao's gaze, saw the same grief in his eyes and shared it with him, smiling at him reassuringly; and sensing her withdrawal from them all, Cyrus reached for her hand and pressed it.

Suddenly the darkness lifted from her, and she felt connected again to these warm and wonderful people. It was like stepping out of a tomb to be met with sunlight and a flood of tenderness.

"So Cyrus came down to ground level," Robin explained. "To wait for you, hoping that his standing so innocently by the elevators would let you know that something was going to happen."

Mrs. Pollifax smiled ruefully as she remembered. "I thought I was hallucinating. That it couldn't possibly be Sheng Ti outside pruning rosebushes, or Cyrus waiting for an elevator at the tower!"

"But you were in shock," Ruthie reminded her. "From being beaten," she added gently. "From seeing Mr. Detwiler killed."

From being beaten, from seeing Detwiler killed. Mrs. Pollifax thought that someday, perhaps on a summer's day among her flowers, she would try to make sense out of a world that could produce trips to the moon and silicon chips, yet never touch the impoverished hearts that could torture, terrorize and kill without mercy or feeling. But not now, not yet.

She would think about Detwiler instead. Detwiler, who had been abused and tricked, and who had fluctuated between weakness and strength until he had determined at last to act, even to die rather than to submit any longer.

She saw that they were all staring at her anxiously. She asked them, "When Detwiler sacrificed himself to turn on the radio signal, it wasn't entirely in vain, was it?"

Marko shook his head. "No, my dear Mrs. P. The signal was heard and the building found. The men in the radio van had to call for reinforcements, at which time Duncan instructed them to follow you in a car to the peak, keeping their distance. No. Detwiler's act was not wasted."

Mrs. Pollifax's glance went to Alec Hao. "You can perhaps forgive him now?"

"Forgive, but not forget," Alec said. "At least he didn't actually kill my father. It's Mr. Feng who—who—" His voice broke.

Marko said curtly, "Feng's dead. He grabbed a gun from a guard and shot himself after being questioned."

Alec said, "Then, for Pete's sake tell me what was behind this hell he created!"

Marko sighed. "Once the terrorists had taken over Hong Kong, they were to demand—Feng's words—that all talks between Peking and Great Britain be suspended until the Nationalist Chinese on Taiwan could be included in the 1997 restoration of Hong Kong to China."

"Was the man insane?" exploded Alec.

Marko's voice was dry. "All fanatics are more or less insane. He'd been working for years to undermine Communist China, and—failing that—he was determined to prevent Hong Kong from being given to them. He spoke of years of planning, of acquiring property where arms could be hidden. We think there must have been help from his brother and other sympathizers in Taiwan on this. Then came the first contact with the Liberation '80s Group through his nephew, Xian Pi, followed by the theft of diamonds to finance the operation, and the methodical distribution of those diamonds to buy guns and silence."

"But in the end," Marko added sadly, "I think he wanted to bring Hong Kong down in ruins and to express his rage to the world. He must have known that his dream of a Nationalist government returning to mainland China was impossible."

Robin broke in. "That was Feng's passion. The Liberation '80s Group, on the other hand, were going to demand ten million in gold for themselves and safe passage out of Hong Kong."

Mrs. Pollifax shook her head. "And Eric the Red?"

"Dead," Robin told her without expression. "He and two others were killed at the elevator. The remaining terrorists have been showing the police where their homemade bombs were planted, thereby hoping for reduced prison sentences, which is unlikely."

"But of course," said Marko quietly, "the main purpose of the Liberation '80s Group was to achieve power. Another strike against law and order, sitting up in the tower with their guns and hostages and looking down at the rest of us with contempt."

There was silence, and then Cyrus said, "But it didn't happen."

"Not this time, no," said Marko.

They reflected on these words until Mr. Hitchens lifted a glass of champagne and said, "Then I suggest we drink a toast to what didn't happen, and perhaps Mrs. Pollifax would care to add something to that?"

She smiled at him. "Yes—yes, I think I'd like to," she said, and thought about this while her gaze moved from one person to the next at the table around her: to Marko, with his wise old-soul eyes; to Robin, with whom she'd shared another adventure; to Sheng Ti, who would soon enter the United States with Lotus— Carstairs had assured her of this only an hour ago; and to Alec Hao, who had lost a father but regained a future.

Her glance moved to Mr. Hitchens, diligently collecting his learning experiences, and to Ruthie, who had apparently collected *him*. She thought too of the cable she'd received from Bishop:

DON'T EVER EVER DO THIS TO US AGAIN STOP CARSTAIRS APPLYING ICE PACKS AND TAKING SEDATIVES STOP CABLE ARRIVAL TIME NEW YORK AND WARN CYRUS OF LARGE AFFECTIONATE DEMONSTRA- TIONS STOP ALL LOVE BISHOP

Her eyes met Cyrus' last—Cyrus, with whom she was to continue living after all, savoring these small, exquisite joys of sharing.

Lifting her glass, she gave him a radiant smile and said with feeling, "To amateurs—angry, determined, caring amateurs. And to what almost—but didn't—happen in Hong Kong."

When Dorothy Gilman moved to New Mexico recently, it was for the same reason she had moved to Nova Scotia twelve years earlier: "I needed an adventure."

Why New Mexico? "Because it's a lot like Nova Scotia—it is visually dramatic, and the life-style is very relaxed and easygoing."

For someone who travels as much as Miss Gilman has, such geographic comparisons come easily. She has been to virtually every corner of the world, usually with an eye toward creating another escapade for Emily Pollifax. In fact, the setting of Miss Gilman's new home, a small, very old town not far from Albuquerque, reminds her of the locale of one of her recent books, *Mrs. Pollifax on the China Station* (a Condensed Books selection in 1983). "It is very much like China here," she says. "The dusty deserts and the sudden high mountains."

Dorothy Gilman

Born and raised in New Brunswick, New Jersey, Dorothy Gilman first began writing when she was a child. However, she didn't launch herself into her global jaunts until her two sons were grown and in college. *Mrs. Pollifax and the Hong Kong Buddha* is the sixth novel featuring that endearing gadabout to appear in Condensed Books.

When not writing novels, Miss Gilman teaches a course in creative writing at an Indian school near her home. "It's a wonderful experience," she remarks. "The people here are very accessible. There's a nice balance in this part of the country between nature and intellectual life, especially for a writer or artist."

While Dorothy Gilman is enjoying her new life in the desert, her alter ego is, as usual, casting about for a mystery to solve. "I always look for trouble spots first," she says when asked how she chooses her novels' settings. So Emily Pollifax may be turning up next in Kuwait or Southern Yemen.

For Mrs. Pollifax, like her creator, also needs an adventure.

Wildfire

A CONDENSATION OF THE NOVEL BY

Richard Martin Stern

ILLUSTRATED BY HODGES SOILEAU

*JL Harmon is worried. For weeks
no rain has fallen in the vast New
Mexican forest it is his job to protect.
The towering stands of pine, the aspens,
the woodland floor—all are tinder dry,
waiting for a spark.*

*Unfortunately, there are people who
don't recognize the warning signs. Like
Stacy Cummings, the glamorous owner of
a ranch near the forest's edge—too near for
JL's comfort. And the Lawry family, camped out
deep in the wilderness—deeper than they have
any right to be. And Don and Elsie Edwards,
honeymooners blissfully unaware of the
threat that surrounds them.*

*For soon they, and others, find themselves
in the path of a rampaging blaze, a blaze
that threatens homes, lives, an entire town.
And to stop the conflagration, JL must
literally fight fire with fire in a terrifying
war that can have no truce. Dramatic,
authentic adventure from one of
America's master storytellers.*

Prologue

THE wildland fire that came to be known as Backslope—the name Jay Paul gave it only because every large fire must have a name—began at six twelve p.m. Mountain Daylight Time on Sunday, June 19, when a single bolt of dry lightning struck a towering ponderosa pine tree deep in New Mexico's Sanrio National Forest.

The electrical charge, following the tree's living inner wood as the most direct path to the ground, easily overcame the tree's resistance, in the process generating unbelievably high temperatures and overheating sap to the point of explosion. The force of this reaction, bursting outward like a bomb, opened a great, ugly gash through the tree's heavy, platelike bark.

Smoldering pieces of bark were flung from the tree's wound like shrapnel to the forest floor. Some fell harmlessly on bare ground, but some fell on twigs, dry grass or trampled brush. Match-size flames appeared, and like matches, some flared briefly, consuming what fuel was at hand before dying away.

But one large piece lodged in the snug shelter of a recently fallen and thoroughly dry dead branch, and there, patiently, began to urge its host closer and closer to combustion.

There was no telltale smoke, and no witness to sound the alarm.

Chapter One

UNTIL midafternoon it was a lovely, clear summer Sunday in 1983: a day for swimming in the lakes of the Sanrio National Forest, for fishing the forest streams, for hiking or horseback riding on the mountain trails, for home cookouts in the city of Sanrio, for tennis and leisurely drinks at the country club.

In a shallow, glaciated bowl beneath the summit of Sierra Grande's fourteen-thousand-foot peak, which rises within the forest just north of the city, there was still snow—a reminder of the skiing that had been excellent that season. Elsewhere on the mountain slopes, in isolated meadows above the timberline, tiny blue forget-me-nots and yellow cinquefoil clung to rock and soil, defying wind and temperature extremes to bloom in profusion— and welcome hikers staunch enough to reach their elevation.

On the Sanrio side of the mountain there had been no precipitation for weeks, but with the heavy runoff from the winter snowpack, reservoirs were full, and this year water was no worry even in this semiarid land.

Jasper Lightfoot (JL) Harmon saw it differently, but then as fire management officer for the forest, that was his job.

"The brow furrowed with concern," Stacy Cummings said rhetorically, running into him that morning at the Sanrio newsstand. "Problems?" Between them these days there was no longer the kind of wariness that had been present only a few weeks before.

"Lack of rain," JL said briefly. "Six weeks without it."

Stacy studied him. "Now why is that so important?" Her quick smile flashed. "Assume I really want to know."

JL tried not to sound like a textbook. "All the stuff on the floor of the forest—the deadfalls, the fallen needles and twigs—all that, we call fuel. And we classify it ten-hour, hundred-hour, thousand-hour, which means how long it will take to dry out. The light stuff dries first, of course, but after about a thousand hours, everything is ready to burn."

"And six weeks is more than a thousand hours," Stacy said. She nodded thoughtfully. "Luck, Ranger. We'll pray for rain."

JL watched her go, and had an idea that she was aware of it. She wore tight faded jeans, handmade boots and a tooled belt with silver-and-turquoise buckle, along with a light challis shirt.

They had only met how many times—three? But you didn't tend to forget her. Especially not after that first meeting.

That day, eight weeks ago, JL had driven the green Forest Service pickup in from the county road and past the mailbox that read CUMMINGS. The gravel drive, nearly half a mile long, wound in through carefully pruned piñon and juniper. The map JL had seen showed a full section, six hundred and forty acres of Cummings property. Even before he came to the big, sprawling house, with its superb view of Sierra Grande, JL had decided that these Cummings folks had money, pots of it.

Conscious that his Forest Service uniform presented a picture of authority, he told the Spanish maid who answered the door that he wished to speak with the head of the house. The maid hesitated only a moment and then led him inside.

The floor was gleaming terra-cotta tile. From the entrance hall he could see into a living room—a huge room, with heavy, polished furniture, and oil paintings on the whitewashed adobe walls, but warm somehow, even intimate. Taste, as well as money, JL thought.

"In here, senor, *por favor*," the maid said, indicating a small office-library. Then she turned away and walked across the living room toward muffled sounds of talk and laughter. She opened a frosted sliding-glass door.

JL caught a glimpse of water churning in a small tiled pool, of glistening bodies and unrecognizable faces. Suddenly feeling very much out of place, he turned away to wait uncomfortably in the office-library.

After a bit came Stacy Cummings, cool and poised in a white terry robe, her short dark hair still damp, and her brown eyes watching him. He had expected a male head of the house.

"I am Stacy Cummings," she said. "This is my house. What do you want, Ranger?" Probably no more than in her late twenties, he thought, but with the kind of assurance she hadn't any right to for another ten or fifteen years.

JL gathered himself. "I make it a point to get acquainted with new property owners whose land abuts the forest." The words sounded stilted even to his own ears. "But I didn't intend to interrupt."

Stacy's smile was amused, mocking. "Surprised, Ranger? It is called a spa. It is considered therapeutic."

"I know." He allowed annoyance to show. "They're very big in southern California."

"You do get around, don't you?"

"I just wasn't aware," JL said, "that the hot-tub culture had come to Sanrio along with all the beautiful people." He bore down on that last adjective.

Stacy looked at him, the mocking smile no longer showing. "Was that all?"

"Anything else," JL said, "can wait. Have a good spa—or whatever it's called." Exit line, end of their first meeting.

Now, remembering that scene, JL watched Stacy until she turned the corner out of sight. A strange, prickly female, with far more to her than first appeared. Out of curiosity he had asked around and had been astonished to find out that Stacy Cummings was a world champion cowgirl, in addition to having a lot of Texas oil money.

"She's a many-faceted chick," Ken Delacorte, a friend of both, had told him. "Don't sell her short. You don't get to be world champion anything if you've got soft spots."

A little forbidding in a woman, JL thought now, but there it was. He walked out to his pickup and got in, tossing the Sunday paper to the seat beside him. He thought of going home, but except for the unfinished oil painting on the easel, home had little appeal. Nor had it ever drawn him irresistibly, even when Madge was still there.

"Another woman I could understand," Madge had said. "But how can I compete with mountains and pine trees? And at your age still jumping out of airplanes!"

"I was a smoke jumper for ten years."

"But you're not a kid anymore. Or maybe you are. You don't even want a better job."

"There aren't any."

"Then stay here and grow moss like your trees. I'm leaving."

And so on this Sunday morning, instead of going home, he drove the pickup through the quiet town, into the forest and along deserted roads until he reached the boundary of the wilderness area, a tract in the heart of the forest set aside for special preservation. Here, no cars, structures or roads were permitted. Man was intended to be a transient visitor, one who disturbed nature as little as possible. To reinforce that point, there was a large sign that said No MOTORIZED VEHICLES ALLOWED.

JL stopped and got out just to hear the silence. Automatically his thoughts went to the flight he had made a while ago, his last real overview of the forest.

With smoke jumper Andy McIlvain as the pilot and JL as copilot, they had taken off in a light plane from the Forest Service airport. JL sat quietly and let his eyes wander over the terrain below.

Three-million-plus acres of forest lay beneath them, five thousand square miles. An area almost as large as Connecticut and Rhode Island together, with a thousand square miles of wilderness area in its center—all of it his to care for, to protect.

He knew the forest as he knew the contours of the face he shaved every morning. From the lakes, the creek bottoms and the dry arroyos to the pinnacle peak of Sierra Grande itself, he had walked, ridden or flown over every foot of this vast terrain.

The lower elevations of the land were in the piñon-juniper stratum, with isolated cholla cactus here and there. Scrub oak grew on the sharply contoured hillsides. The big trees, the ponderosa pines, came next in the ascending order and with them, beginning at eight hundred feet, the aspens.

Above timberline were open talus slopes and bare rock faces—a barren, desolate terrain, hostile, even dangerous, to man. Snow-covered, as they had been that morning, the upper elevations seemed silent and at peace. It was illusion.

JL had glanced at Andy, who was pointing down to their left at a minute clear area beside an open lake. Across the lake a glaciated cliff rose sheer three hundred or four hundred feet. Miraculously, large pine trees clung to the upper slope even at the cliff's edge.

"You'll get wind currents off that cliff face," JL said.

"Yep." Andy seemed delighted. "Show you what my new parachute will do. Downwind, crosswind, upwind. Like a modern sailboat. You still want to try it?" he went on. "After all this time, and with all those chair-seat calluses? What'll Madge say?"

Madge had still been with him then. "She won't know until after."

"And Jefferson'll know afterward too, and he'll be hopping mad." George Jefferson was JL's boss, the supervisor of Sanrio National Forest.

"Could be."

Andy flew for a time in silence. He said at last, "Then why?"

"I want to see for myself how good your new chute is so I can know what kind of terrain I can send your smoke jumpers into. I don't aim to lose people."

Andy nodded. "Okay," he said. "We'll go up in a month or so, and you'll jump. I'll be your jump mate."

Funny he should think of that now, JL thought, because that morning had been back in the *safe* time, when the snow-covered forest was more or less fireproof. Today it was different. The forest was one large tinderbox.

THE family's name was Lawry—Les, Cindy Lou and young Tad—and they had driven jolting into the heart of the wilderness area, where no vehicles were allowed, as far as a narrow stretch of the upper Sanrio River, where they had stashed their jeep amid some big rocks, covering it with piny boughs.

"This is how you do it, son," Les told the boy, proud to show off his army knowledge of camouflage. "We always covered our vehicles like this when we bivouacked. You never knew when— There! See?" He pointed suddenly upward as two low-flying air force planes roared past, following the course of the river. "They won't catch your old dad as easy as that."

Cindy Lou said, "Old Dad hasn't bothered to tell us yet, hon, why we couldn't have walked in like ordinary folks."

"Because most folks don't come this far into the wilderness," Les said, "so it stands to reason the fishing's better here."

Cindy Lou said, "I didn't even know we had a fishing license."

"We don't. If anybody comes, we'll say we tried to get one in town but they said they were fresh out."

"Do you always have to behave like a wheeler-dealer?" Cindy Lou said. "What kind of example is that for the kid?"

"He could do a lot worse than copying his old man," Les said. "I haven't done so bad. Now, you two set up the tent and I'll catch us some trout for dinner. Set it under that tree yonder so it won't be seen from the air."

IN ANOTHER PART OF THE WILDERNESS on this Sunday, Elsie Edwards undid the belt of her backpack and gratefully lowered the pack's full weight to the ground. The back of her short-sleeved khaki shirt was wet through with sweat. She stood in silence for a few moments, studying the blue nylon tent pitched beneath the high ponderosa pine. She looked at Don.

"It's not exactly what I had in mind," she said, smiling. "I was thinking more along the lines of the bridal suite in, say, one of those big hotels in Nice, or perhaps the Dorchester in London."

"We'll get to that kind of thing," Don said. "Maybe for our twenty-fifth anniversary. Or our fiftieth."

Elsie pulled out her shirttails and flapped them vigorously to create a small breeze. "That illustrates one of the differences between us," she said, smiling still. "You're the patient type."

She was a strong young woman in a hurry, this bride of his, Don thought, but he was content. By her very eagerness, she brought a sense of adventure he had lacked. "And for now?" he said.

Elsie stopped flapping the loose shirt, and the quality of her smile changed. "For now," she said, "I suggest you get out of your backpack. I'd say we have all the privacy we need."

THEIR names were Frank Orwell and Felipe Vigil. And what they had in common was that both had simply walked away from the minimum security facility at nearby Los Ojos. Then they had stolen a car, walked into a sporting goods store, subdued the proprietor and walked out again with two hunting knives, a back-pack each and $161.11 from the till.

At a convenience store they bought supplies, then drove to the edge of the wilderness, left the car and headed into the wildland on foot.

"You a real fool, man," Felipe said as they walked. "You got one year left, and you walk out. Now you'll get three more. Maybe more than that."

"They got to catch us first. And in the woods there ain't nobody going to catch me. So walk, man, walk."

JL COULD almost have predicted the weather progression that Sunday afternoon. First came a faint thickening of haze behind Sierra Grande's lofty peak. Then a cloud began to form, rising

higher and higher, darkening, glowering, gradually emerging as
an anvil-shaped thunderhead.

But there was no rain. JL, by now back in his studio at home,
brush in hand, swore softly to himself and hoped that all mountain lookouts in this part of the Southwest were also watching.
Suddenly a jagged lightning streak appeared and seemed to hang
quivering, its multiple tendrils reaching down to the forested
slopes. Seconds later the thunder reached his ears.

JL waited, and searched the trees, but no telltale smoke appeared. That, he thought, would be too easy. He made himself
relax as he turned away from the window to face his easel again.

The scene of the half-finished painting was of the forest, of
course: towering ponderosa pines, an aspen touched by autumn
gold. Off center on the canvas was a patch of deep sky. No more
than a small craggy outcropping of the big mountain was visible,
but a sense of its immense presence filled the picture.

JL picked up his palette and then set it down again. The heck
with it. With a lightning storm going on right over his forest, it
would take a superman to be able to concentrate. He left the
studio and headed for the kitchen and a cold beer.

STACY Cummings watched the lightning storm too and thought
of JL Harmon, that oddly complicated ranger. After their first
meeting she had asked Ken Delacorte about JL. Ken was a friend
from college days who sold real estate in Sanrio now and knew all
the gossip. Once, not long ago, he had played football for the
Houston Oilers; Stacy felt a kind of athletic kinship with him.

"JL?" Ken said. "He's all right. He's the honcho on what they
call wildfire suppression in the whole Sanrio forest. Quite a job.
And when they get in big trouble other places, he's the head of
the team of experts they send out to take over. Quite a guy. Used
to jump out of airplanes to put out fires."

He still jumps out of airplanes, Stacy thought now, remembering.

Some weeks after JL's visit to her house, she had been riding in
the heart of the forest on Sam, her big cutting horse, enjoying the
coolness, the almost cathedral hush that surrounded her. As she
rode through a clearing in the trees, she came to a stream that
emptied into a small glaciated lake beneath a three-hundred-foot
cliff. In the lake's placid surface the great mountain was faithfully

reflected. A picture postcard, Stacy thought, smiling; and then the smile turned to a frown of annoyance as the growing sound of an aircraft broke the mountain hush.

It came down the valley, well beneath Sierra Grande's peak, a high-wing, high-tail twin-engine plane that swept over a tiny meadow among the pine trees on the lake's shore. But her annoyance turned to curiosity as three streamers of weighted yellow-and-orange crepe paper dropped from the open doorway of the aircraft and fluttered toward the center of the meadow.

The aircraft banked sharply and made a tight circle, and this time, out came one human figure and then a second, and almost instantaneously two multicolored parachutes blossomed and drifted downward.

Sam snorted at the sight and pawed the ground. "Easy, boy," Stacy said. "You're no more baffled than I am."

The lead parachute fluttered in the air, seemed to veer off to one side and then dipped slanting back to its original path. The second chute fluttered and veered in almost exactly the same spot, caught apparently by wind currents coming from the cliff face. It too recovered but with a jerky movement that left the man swinging like a pendulum.

The first man landed and rolled easily on the ground. The second man hit hard and rose on only one leg, the other held free as he collapsed his parachute. Across the water the two voices came clearly.

"Not bad for an old guy," one of the men said. "You okay?"

"I overcontrolled." It was JL's voice. He lowered the one foot, put a little weight on it and lifted it again. "Clumsy," he said.

"I'll walk out," the other man said, "and send for a chopper."

Stacy touched Sam's flanks with her heels. They trotted around the edge of the lake to the meadow, and she reined Sam in. "We keep running into each other," she said to JL. "You won't need a chopper. Sam can carry two. Come on up."

The other man grinned as he helped JL up behind the saddle.

They rode for a time in silence, Sam holding to his steady, easy walk. At last Stacy said, "Ankle bad?"

"Sprained. Plain clumsiness." JL didn't know what to do with his hands, so he kept them on his thighs.

"You came out to the house that day for a reason," Stacy said

unexpectedly, her voice coming to him over her shoulder. "Were you going to explain the facts of life near the forest?"

"Would you have listened?"

"Probably not very well. Anyway, it's my property."

"True."

"I've observed all zoning."

"True again. And you've done a lot of things right. No cedar shake roof to catch fire from sparks. No undergrowth right up against the buildings."

"I raise horses. I don't want them tangled up in brush."

"But no road out. Only the one-way gravel drive. If there was another car in there, you couldn't move."

"And you want an escape route." JL didn't bother to answer. Stacy wished she could see his face, but she refused to turn in the saddle. "I thought fire people were supposed to put fires out, not run away from them," she said.

With no change of tone JL said, "Is Stacy your real name, like it says on the map?"

"It's my name. It was my daddy's."

"Your daddy's? He named you after himself?"

Caught off balance by the swift change of subject, Stacy chose to smile. "He wanted a boy. But he took what he got. Me."

"I've heard that you're a world champion cowgirl. Barrel racer. Calf roper. Even tried your hand at bronc riding."

Stacy frowned faintly. "What is this? *This Is Your Life?*"

"I try to know my neighbors."

"*Your* neighbors?"

"In a manner of speaking. This is my forest."

"I thought it belonged to the government."

"I care for it."

"And," Stacy said, "on its behalf you resent me, us, with our houses on its fringe. Tell me why." But it was beginning to dawn on her that she already knew the answer. "We're your responsibility, is that it? Fire, flash flood, any kind of trouble, and you're the one to bail us out?" She nodded solemnly. "I hadn't thought of it that way before."

Few do, JL thought but did not say aloud.

"I think, Ranger," she said, "that I'd like to know more about what you do. And why you do it."

"It's a job."

This time her dark head shook in emphatic denial. "I'm beginning to think it's a great deal more than that." Maybe commitment was the word, she thought, and how many did she know who were really committed to anything?

As EVENING came on that Backslope Sunday, cool dense air began to flow down the flanks of Sierra Grande. Encountering little resistance, it gathered speed, first merely a faint stirring, then a noticeable current, at last becoming a downhill breeze soughing through the evergreens, setting the aspen leaves to whispering as they danced.

Around the base of the lightning-struck ponderosa pine, in response to the moving air, embers again began to glow, some of them rekindling to reach out for more fuel: dry needles, fallen twigs, small branches, a partially rotted log, which, heated, began to smolder. The large piece of bark beneath the log burst into flame. That was all that was needed to ignite the log.

At first, one man could have stamped out all the flames with ease and, with a single green branch as a broom, swept the smoldering fuel into a harmless pile in a patch of bare dirt. Even by full darkness, that same man working quickly could have contained the threat and snuffed it out with shovelfuls of earth.

Chapter Two

KEN Delacorte came to dinner at Stacy's that Sunday evening.

"I heard the Brown place next door was for sale," Stacy said. "Next door" was a figure of speech; the properties were contiguous, but the two main houses were more than a mile apart.

"Sold," Ken said. He smiled. "Character who bought it has renamed it El Rancho Costa Mucho, and it did too. The certified check he brought to the closing was well up in seven figures. Fellow named Jones, Bartlemy Jones. Goes around in a fancy electric wheelchair." He stopped, watching the sudden change in Stacy's face. "Something I said?"

"The roof just fell in, is all," she said. Her smile was wan. "You couldn't know. An old flame. We parted on something less than a romantic note. Fix yourself another drink."

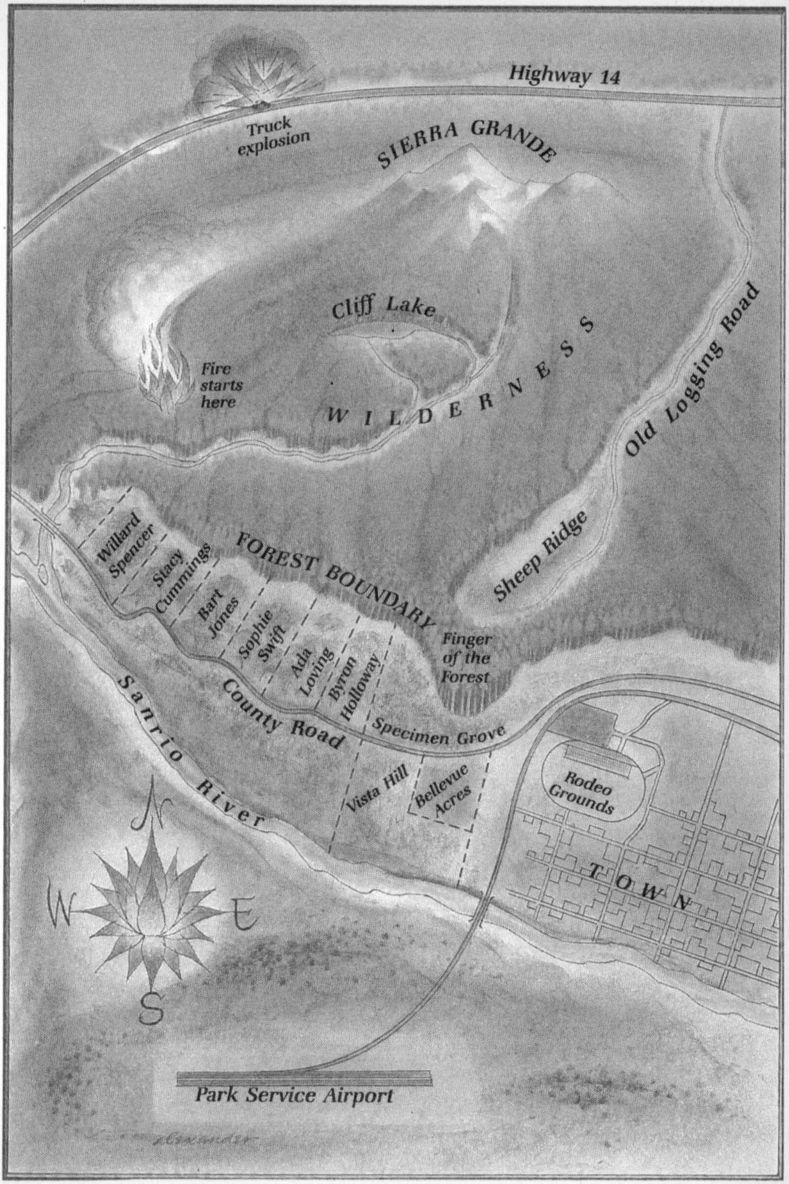

Highway 14
Truck explosion
SIERRA GRANDE
Cliff Lake
Fire starts here
WILDERNESS
Old Logging Road
Sheep Ridge
FOREST BOUNDARY
Willard Spencer
Stacy Cummings
Bart Jones
Sophie Swift
Ada Loving
Byron Holloway
Finger of the Forest
County Road
Specimen Grove
Sanrio River
Vista Hill
Bellevue Acres
Rodeo Grounds
TOWN
N
W
E
S
Park Service Airport

Ken came back from the bar in a thoughtful mood. He sat down slowly. "Jones," he said. "You don't like him? Or maybe you don't trust him? Which?"

"Why?"

"Well, aside from buying the Brown place, he's asking too many questions about Bellevue Acres, my development. It's not much, but it's all I could afford to build. It's where I've bet my shirt." He smiled crookedly. "By your standards it's not a very expensive shirt, I'll admit."

"I'll ignore that," Stacy said.

Long after Ken had left that evening, Stacy sat on in the office-library, staring. One wall of the room was floor-to-ceiling book-cases. On the remaining walls were photographs of horses, some with Stacy, some by themselves. She could name each animal and give the place and date of the photo. There were times when it seemed as though her life were there on those walls.

Stacy was then, as JL had guessed closely that first day, twenty-nine, a woman of medium height, smoothly muscled, with boyish hips, slim waist and straight legs. Of her glossy dark hair and brown eyes, her father had often said, "Most likely some Indian in us somewhere, but by golly, not enough to claim a share in any tribe's oil properties, so I've darn well had to find our own."

And he had. He liked to claim that he had tramped and dowsed every square foot of Texas, Oklahoma and eastern New Mexico, relying on a God-given gift to know where oil was to be found.

Young Stacy never knew her mother. "I was out in the middle of nowhere. . . ." Her father had told her the tale often enough, flagellating himself with the memory. "And that damn well blew in just about the time you began to put in an appearance. I was busier than a bird dog in a stubble field, and your mother said she was all right." He spread his huge hands in helplessness. "You came through it all right. Your mother didn't. Me, I got another oil well." The last sentence was said in bitter self-accusation.

It was a strange relationship, father-daughter, no woman in the house other than hired help. There were women who tried to take over; the increasing Cummings oil wealth was irresistible. But her father refused to be trapped.

Stacy did not remember when she had first been on a horse, but some early incidents remained vivid. There was, for example, the colt she called Boots, her own, hand-raised from a foal back on the old home ranch in central Texas. She was not quite fifteen when she slapped her saddle on him and climbed aboard.

Boots was no longer a foal, and his reactions to the saddle were anything but friendly. Stacy landed hard in the packed corral dirt. She got to her feet, dusted herself off and started toward Boots, who was standing docilely enough, reins hanging.

The ranch foreman walked into the corral. "Better let me take a little of the edge off him, girl," he said.

Stacy's reaction was immediate. "You," she said in a voice that shook, "keep you hands off him, you hear? He's my horse, and nobody but me's going to break him."

There was silence. Then the foreman said slowly, "Now, look here, young lady. That's no kind of way—"

"You heard her." This was Stacy the father. He climbed the corral fence and perched comfortably on the top rail. "Well now," he said, "let the show commence."

It took two more falls, and with each one, young Stacy's chin grew firmer. She limped back for the fourth try, got stiffly into the saddle and this time stayed there until Boots, tossing his head occasionally, walked obediently twice around the corral.

Stacy bent down to pat the sweating neck. "Good boy." Her voice was gentle.

"Good girl," her father said.

Schooling presented problems resulting in an inevitable clash of wills. "Your mother," her father said, "was well educated in the East. Why she married me, I'm hanged if I know. But she did, and you're the result, and I'll see that you turn out to be a lady too."

"I'm not interested."

"I didn't ask what you thought. I'm telling you. I'm not going to see you grow up to be a stable hand."

Not all of what young Stacy considered unnecessary airs and graces took, but the product that emerged after three years in Miss Walker's school in Boston was a different article indeed from the one her father had first put on the plane in Dallas.

"Each time you've come back on vacation," he said when he met her final homecoming plane, "you've looked a little better. You've turned into a real good-looking filly and quite a lady. Now, what do you want to do?"

131

"The university's got a good rodeo team."

"And you're fixing to be a part of it?" Her father nodded. "I guess you've earned it."

At the university there were boys and horses, sometimes in one order, sometimes the other. There were also books, running a poor third except in courses having to do with animal husbandry.

"Some folks," her father said, "like animals better than people. That the way you see it too?"

"People have their uses."

"I don't pretend to understand women," he went on. "But I'm beginning to believe that you're like the man said, a riddle wrapped in a mystery inside an enigma. What do you want, anyway, honey?"

"I'm still looking for it," Stacy said. Simple truth.

She was twenty-two when her father died—as he had lived, violently, his neck broken by a falling length of drill pipe.

Stacy showed no tears in public or in private, but the death left an emptiness she doubted would ever be filled.

To friends there was no noticeable change. "She's a tough one," they would say, in the admiring way that one spoke of an athlete who insisted on playing even when hurt. The result was that no one managed to penetrate the façade.

Bartlemy Jones had assumed a certain importance during this period. He was a big man, as Stacy's father had been big, and solid, but with a strong macho streak that made him as different from her father as different could be.

Stacy Cummings the father had always been willing to go for broke—but only when circumstances demanded it. Bart Jones would take chances merely to be doing what no one else would dare. To Stacy the daughter there was a vast difference.

"You don't have to show off," she once told him. "Not to me, not to anybody."

"You've been alone too much, my girl," he answered. "You get lonely, bitter."

It was a moment of relaxed candor. "Lonely? I've never been lonely in my life. I like some people, but I don't need them."

"Is that supposed to put me in my place?"

"Oh, come off it," Stacy said. "To you, I'm good for a few laughs. Other people don't really matter that much to you."

After what happened on what she still thought of as *that night*, she would have given the world to be able to retract those words. Try as she might, she could never entirely shake the sense of guilt they left her with.

The party that night was like so many others back in Texas: big houses, expensive cars in the floodlighted parking area. Inside, and out around the pool, white-coated waiters filled drink orders, and maids in Mexican skirts silently passed canapés. A mariachi band played.

Bart Jones was drunk, and there was a dangerous gleam in his eye. They had come to the party together, and now he wanted to leave. The stage was set for trouble and Stacy had known it—that was the part that would not go away.

"Suit yourself, sweetie pie," Bart told her, "but I'm headed back to town and a thick steak."

"I'll go," Stacy said. "If you'll let me drive."

"No dice. You don't always get your way, you know."

"Look," she said. "Will you for once in your life be sensible?"

Nothing changed in his face, but a new note came into his voice. "No point in starting now," he said with finality.

She watched him go, smiling and nodding as he made his way through the guests. "Old Bart can really hold his liquor." How often had Stacy heard that? Too often, she thought, and was tempted to go after him for one more try. But she didn't.

AT LEAST it was a one-car accident and nobody else was involved. "He must have tried to take that turn at well over a hundred," one of the state cops said, watching the emergency crew working to cut Bart out of the wreck.

Stacy visited the hospital as soon as she heard the news, but it was days before she was able to see Bart, and her reception then was less than warm.

"Come to say 'I told you so'?" were his first words.

Stacy swallowed hard and managed to hold back what was in her mind. "Anything you need? Books? Magazines?"

"A new spinal cord. Got one?"

It was the first she knew of the seriousness of his injury, and how she managed to hold back the sudden, unexpected tears that stung her eyelids, she would never know.

Texas soured for Stacy after that, with her father gone and now this thing with Bart. Eventually he was shipped off somewhere for physical therapy to help him adjust to his new condition. By that time Stacy's college friend Ken Delacorte, having retired from football and finished an unsuccessful ex-jock assault on Hollywood, was living in Sanrio, selling real estate. And Sanrio, which held no memories, seemed as good a place to settle down as any.

Not, she told herself, that she needed Ken or anyone else, because she was complete within herself, and if, as she knew, that was not wholly true for anybody, it was close enough.

To Sophie Swift, her Sanrio lawyer, she said one day, as she had said to Bart, "I'm never lonely. Not really." And then she had shown the brilliant smile that somehow seemed to mock herself. "I talk to my horses. And they talk back. But don't tell anyone."

"The confidentiality of the lawyer-client relationship," Sophie said, nodding solemnly, and smiled back.

And so here she was, on this quiet Sunday, hundreds of miles distant from Texas and its memories. And here was Bart again, right next door. Too much. Just too much, she thought as she got up and began to turn out lights on her way to bed. One thing was sure: Bart's buying El Rancho Costa Mucho was no accident, no coincidence. That she knew.

BY EARLY morning moonset, urged on by the night breeze, the growing flames had run downslope and fanned out. Hidden in the deep folds of the foothills and the stands of the forest itself, the fire gathered its strength and force. At last it was large and strong enough to dare the open. Like a monster roaring out of its hiding place, the fire burst into view. In the darkness it threw its lights and contorting shadows into the sky. Bellowing and roaring defiance, it was suddenly alive, and loose.

AARON Swift, attorney-at-law, and, out of a deep sense of public duty, also federal magistrate, was not sleeping well these nights. At three o'clock on this Monday morning, Debby slept beside him relaxed as a kitten. Indeed, Aaron thought, she resembled a cuddly, purring kitten—wide eyes, softness and all.

Debby was a small-town girl from west Texas who had grown

up knowing how to run a house, how to sew a fine seam and how to bake buttermilk biscuits that would almost float off the plate. Debby was, in short, the kind of girl who married dear old dad before women's liberation came along.

Aaron's first wife, Sophie, on the other hand, was strictly one of a kind. Aaron saw her every day in the office they shared, of course, and he had lived with her as her husband for twenty-five years, but he was still not sure that he understood her. His thoughts kept going back to a night he would just as soon forget.

"Mr. Bumble said that the law is an ass—an idiot," she'd said when he'd told her about Debby. "The law is also a tyrant and a slave master. I have followed its bidding. My fault. That is our problem." As clear and concise as if she were addressing the bench.

"Soph, there isn't any fault. It's one of those things."

"No fault? As in insurance? The dispassionate view? But passion is precisely what we're talking about. You have a passion for young Debby Winslow."

"You make it sound like a—brief."

"That's my failing, Aaron. I don't know how to use the words that demonstrate emotion. They embarrass me. But, believe me, I do have feelings."

"I know."

"Yes. You do. And that is what makes this all the more difficult for both of us. What should I do, try to argue you out of this situation? That would be ridiculous and, even if it succeeded, self-defeating. Our relationship would never be the same again. I can't compete with Debby Winslow. And I know it."

In the end he had left her the ranch and taken an apartment in town. After the divorce they retained their joint practice of law, and through it all Sophie maintained her calm, quiet, decisive presence. It was almost as if she and Aaron had never been more than partners and good friends.

"The quail are back at the ranch," Sophie had told him one recent morning. "And this year they've brought their chicks."

"I'd like to see them."

"You will be welcome anytime. Debby too, of course."

And another time, "We have a new foal. Stacy Cummings says he already looks like a quarter horse."

"Stacy knows horses. How's your water this year?"

"Sufficient. But we could use a good, soaking rain."

Now, what kind of conversation was that to be remembering in detail at three o'clock in the morning? Aaron demanded of himself, and heard no answer. Was there some kind of guilt involved, that his mind should keep going over scenes with Sophie?

Beside him, Debby, kittenlike, slept on peacefully.

WILLARD P. Spencer, also awake early this Backslope Monday morning, felt no sense of guilt, merely annoyance that he should find himself involved in minor financial details. Added to his annoyance was a growing dislike of Sanrio.

The area had been represented to him as an idyllic combination of the grandeur of the Swiss Alps, the charm of Old Mexico and the unhurried restfulness of the Greek islands. An impulsive man, Spencer had taken immediate steps to make a part of this dreamland his own. But the fact of the matter was that Sanrio was merely on the verge of becoming the kind of Palm Springs–Sun Valley locale Spencer had assumed it already was.

By best guess, Sanrio was a town of about twenty-five thousand, with a burgeoning ski industry, a few large and expensive estates like Spencer's and a long tradition of southwestern informality.

"Backward, ignorant and lazy" would have been Spencer's summation. A place where no one gave any thought to breeding or background. Spencer had even been called by his given name on first meeting. Intolerable. Two telephone conversations last Friday had brought it all into focus, and he had brooded unhappily all through the weekend.

The first call was from Aaron Swift. "A couple of things have come up, Willard. Although I'm darned if I know why they were referred to me instead of to you direct."

"Because you are my legal representative here in Sanrio."

"All right." There was resignation in the voice. "Bud Lewis wants to know if you're going to pay the quarterly premium on your homeowner's insurance before the grace period expires."

"Of course I am. The question is ridiculous."

There was a short silence. Then Aaron Swift said, "The second thing is a call from the manager of the bank."

"And what does he want?"

"The last two months' installments on your personal loan—"

"I am quite aware of that. You may tell him that I intend to see that my loan is renegotiated."

The silence this time was a little longer. Aaron Swift said at last in a conversational tone, "You know, Willard, when you really put your mind to it, you can be just about as obnoxious as anyone I know." The line went dead.

Spencer placed the second call himself, to John Walters, his real estate agent. "What is our situation, Walters?"

"One or two possible leads, Mr. Spencer," he said, "but nothing definite yet. I'm afraid we have to be patient." They were talking about a property with an asking price of a million five, Walters thought, seventy-odd private acres abutting the forest, with a four-bedroom main house, an exceptional water supply and stunning views of the mountain range. It was not the sort of property you sold over the telephone.

"Look," said Spencer, "I'm tired of this place, and I want to unload it. It's as simple as that. And you should be thinking of the fat commission you will get if and when. Keep me posted."

Now, lying fully awake in the early morning, Spencer found that he could recall each of the conversations word for word.

From the other bed, in the dawning light, Angela said, as if they had been talking for some time, "I've been thinking. I've heard both good and not so good about the new Orient-Express, London to Venice. I think we should try it out, Will. Fly over Concorde, of course. We haven't been to Venice in ages." There was no immediate response, and Angela raised her voice slightly. "Will! Did you hear me, Will?"

"We'll think about it," Spencer said.

JL's ringing telephone brought him instantly awake. "JL here."

"We've got one, JL." It was the dispatcher's voice, professionally calm, speaking from forest headquarters. "It's for real. I sent out two men, and they report it's already out of hand."

"On my way," JL replied. "I'll head for the airport. Have a chopper ready, and a forest map. How close can you get a crew in by vehicle?"

"Within about a mile," the man said. "A crew is on the way."

"Roger," JL answered, satisfied.

In no more than five minutes he was out of the house and starting up the Forest Service pickup. He drove fast, expecting and encountering no other vehicles. He felt keyed up, eager. With a wildland fire, time was the critical factor. What could be handled immediately by a single crew of twenty men might in only a few minutes require half a dozen crews to dig in, establish a fire line and begin their counterassault. Wildfire was the enemy, and sensible men treated it with respect.

The chopper was already rolled out and waiting at the Forest Service airport. A single-engine lead plane stood off to one side, near the high-wing Twin Otter from which Andy McIlvain's smoke jumpers operated. In the distance a vintage World War II twin-engine transport stood ready. The illusion, JL thought, was of an airfield in wartime. Well, in a sense it was.

"Ready to roll," the chopper pilot said. "Map and clipboard on your seat."

They swung up over the still sleeping city toward the flanks of Sierra Grande. The big mountain's top was now in morning sunlight, its snowcap a deep pink in the low-slanting rays.

"There she is," the pilot said, and pointed off to their left. The glow among the trees was unmistakable.

The fire area—already about five hundred acres—was midway between the south boundary of the forest, with the large estates adjoining it, and the edge of the wilderness. A breeze coming out of the west-northwest was elongating the burning area eastward.

"Take her down for a good look," said JL. He folded the map to show the pertinent area and tucked it into the clipboard. He noted date and time, then began to sketch in the fire's outlines.

The ride was bumpy. Currents of heated air rose from the ground, tossing the helicopter like a small boat in a choppy sea. JL ignored the jostling and, with frequent ground sightings to make sure of his points of reference, completed his sketching, applying quick shading to spots of heavy flames.

"Take her up now," he told the pilot. "I want an overview to see if anything else is affected."

Nothing else was—at the moment. But that condition, JL thought grimly, was only temporary.

Movement caught his eye, and through the piñon and juniper growth he could see the crew the dispatcher had already sent out:

twenty men in yellow shirts and hard hats, walking single file, far enough apart to avoid accidents from the tools they carried— McLeod hoes, Pulaski axes, chain saws, shovels, brush hooks.

"Okay," JL told the pilot, "let's take her home."

His mind was made up. He knew what was going to be needed.

WHETHER his call got George Jefferson out of bed or not was a matter of complete indifference to JL when he phoned from the airport. "It's going to be a big one," he told Jefferson, the forest supervisor and JL's immediate superior. "I think we'd better not fool around with a few isolated crews, but put in a full team right away."

This was as far as his recommendation would properly go. A fire team consisted of a complete organization of supervisory personnel and designated specialists, their ranks and responsibilities as specific as those of a military regiment. The overall commander of a fire team was called the fire boss.

There were two levels of fire teams constantly available. The Sanrio team operated only within Sanrio forest. Its designated boss was a man named Jay Paul, newly transferred to the area. The regional class A team, which JL commanded, operated on massive fires throughout the country whenever and wherever it was needed. The choice of which team was up to Jefferson.

"How's your ankle?" George Jefferson said. "Still limping?"

"It's fine."

"That was a fool thing, jumping with McIlvain. You know, you're not a kid anymore. You're forty-one."

"George," JL said, "this really is going to be big. We need a fire team. Now."

"Aren't you supposed to be going to Idaho?"

JL had totally forgotten. He was signed up for a seminar at the Boise Interagency Fire Center (BIFC—pronounced biff-see), the nerve center and information clearinghouse of the nation's fire-suppression efforts. "I was."

"You still are," Jefferson said. "Call the dispatcher. Tell him to get on it. Jay Paul's team can cope."

"Jay Paul's new to the area, George."

"Then he'll have to learn fast."

JL took a deep breath. "George—"

"You want to handle it yourself, is that it?"

"Yes."

"The answer is no. Now call the dispatcher and get the Sanrio team into action." The line went dead.

JL stood for a moment, indecisive, still holding the phone in his hand. Then slowly he hung it up, walked into the radio room and called the dispatcher.

The system worked and worked well—how often had he told himself, and others, that? The lines of authority were established, guidelines in place, all mechanisms ready to go. You took orders from above and saw to it that your own orders were followed on down the line. Period. Into the microphone, to the dispatcher he said, "Call the Sanrio team. I'm bringing in a map."

"Ten four, JL."

He put the mike down very gently. It would work, he told himself, because it had to. Jay Paul as fire boss would have immediately available to him a team of specialists and staff, including an air attack boss, a plans chief, and a fire behavior officer to advise on the probable directions the fire would take. There would be a weatherman brought in to forecast climatic conditions, and even a special aircraft carrying equipment for infrared photography. From ten thousand feet, infrared photos could show a spot on the ground one foot square that was smoldering.

At the bottom of it all, the foundation would be crews of twenty on the ground, the troops who would fight the fire face to face in shifts—an army to be fed, transported, provided with sleeping space and rudimentary sanitary facilities. There would be smoke jumpers and hotshot crews—specially trained teams that followed up the first attack forces.

The dispatcher summoning all this was, properly, the nerve center of fire-suppression efforts. The Sanrio dispatcher had his office in the forest headquarters, located east of the wilderness and north of the town. He was a carefully screened and trained man, accustomed to what was called the hot seat, coping during extreme burning conditions with as many as two hundred fires a day within the vast area he was responsible for.

But the plain truth, JL told himself, was that he would rather have kept it all in his own hands, which was ridiculous. Or was it? He had seen the fire; others had not.

JL suspected that George Jefferson, who had never in his life jumped out of an airplane, still harbored a grudge because of the test jump with Andy McIlvain. In Jefferson's, and Madge's, view, it had been merely a dangerous and unnecessary exercise in sheer juvenile romanticism.

Well, maybe it was, but still JL would do it again, because now he knew firsthand just what Andy's new parachute would do. And for that, in JL's opinion, there simply was no substitute.

Suddenly he realized they were going to need Andy and his smoke jumpers on this fire very soon.

On impulse he trotted up the steel stairs to the airport tower for the latest weather readouts. They indicated afternoon thunderstorm activity, but no rain.

"McIlvain's already reported here this morning," the man on duty said. "He's probably called the dispatcher too. He says his guys are tired of sitting on their duffs. You going to use them?"

"Not my decision," JL said, and went back down the stairs, remembering the keyed-up, eager feelings of his own smoke-jumping days.

The jumpers were an elite group, mostly in their twenties or early thirties, although a few, like Andy, who was forty, kept on until they could no longer handle the rigors of the job. They were all experienced wildland fire fighters, and all in superb physical condition. Their function was to parachute into terrain too rough for vehicles or helicopter landings, and to stay as long as necessary to subdue whatever fire they had been sent in to attack. Then, with luck, they would walk out.

That Andy and his crew were already out at the airport, ready to go, was one more indication of the soundness of the planned routine, the *system*, JL reflected as he drove back into town. Still.

He had one more try at George Jefferson, by telephone from his house. "I've seen this fire, George," he said, "and I don't like it. Maybe we don't need the whole regional fire team, but somebody had better be here to look over Jay Paul's shoulder when things start to get rough."

"Namely you," Jefferson said. His voice was heavy with irony and suppressed anger. "Forget it, JL. Now I'm going to tell you just one more time to get on up to Boise, where you're scheduled to be, and stop thinking you're the only one around here who knows anything about fire suppression. Do you understand me?"

JL opened his mouth and closed it again. "I hear you," he said. "And take your bad ankle with you."

BY MIDMORNING, at the fire command post Jay Paul had chosen— east of the fire's center and below the wilderness—communications were still being set up, phone lines strung, radio antennae raised into treetops and trucks constantly arriving with supplies. Already the fire lines had been established by crews fanned out in accordance with JL's sketch map.

Out on the line the heat was intense. And the crackling of flames, punctuated by firecrackerlike sounds as pine-pitch knots exploded, heightened the illusion of battle.

Because of the grueling demands of the job, there are not many women within fire-fighter ranks. But Bessie Wingate, crew chief, big as a big man and as brawny, was a jarring exception. Her crew was one of six ground crews already deployed. Her position was east of the fire's center, on Sierra Grande's slopes.

"Maybe I ought to take up mud wrestling instead," she was fond of saying, "but, heck, it wouldn't be near as much fun."

On this day she wielded her shovel with grim power and efficiency. The job of the nineteen men under Bessie's command, working with chain saws, axes, brush hooks and shovels, was to maintain a line beyond which their small sector of fire could not pass and, if at all possible, drive the flames back upon themselves; it was hot, dirty, backbreaking and dangerous work.

When the fire began a hundred-and-eighty-degree fishhook turn, Bessie's warning came instantly. "Watch that one! Gus, Joe, get after it! But watch that arroyo! There's brush in there!"

Feeding on the tangled clutter of brush and driven by the upslope wind, the fire tore into an area of scrub oak, consumed it with a crackling roar and raced on.

Bessie grabbed the walkie-talkie from her belt. "We've lost our line!" she shouted into it after identifying herself. "That monster is going up the arroyo right into the big trees!"

JAY Paul had spent fifteen years in fire suppression but was, as JL had said, new to the Sanrio forest. And right from the start he had an uncomfortable feeling about this fire.

"Get some aerial tankers in to douse that arroyo with slurry," he told his air attack boss. Slurry is a liquid combination of fire-extinguishing chemicals, far more effective than water, used where ground crews cannot reach. "If we can't cut it off there, we're going to have the whole stand of ponderosas on fire."

Despite himself, some of Bessie's excitement had gotten to him, and he found it impossible to keep his voice calm. JL, now, wouldn't even have batted an eye or raised his voice in the slightest. But, as everybody knew, JL had ice water in his veins.

AT THE BIFC complex on the outskirts of Boise, JL's first stop was the situation room, where teletyped reports from each area of the United States clacked in constantly. Here was his own Region 3 and the latest situation reports on the fire named Backslope. JL read them quickly. The conflagration seemed to be worse than he had feared; its estimated area was now two thousand acres.

One of the men at the large horseshoe desk recognized him and said, "You've got one going down your way, no?"

JL nodded. "Seems so." His voice was mild, apparently unconcerned. He walked down the hall to the weather room.

Here detailed information from the Weather Service was received, digested and passed along to regional and forest commands. To one of the meteorologists he knew JL said, "Sanrio. What's our forecast?"

"Tourist weather." The meteorologist was smiling. "There's a lovely high sitting right down there, and no nasty storm is going to move in on that. Dry lightning, but no rain."

JL smiled his thanks and walked out and back to the situation room. "What's been committed to Backslope?" he asked the man at the horseshoe desk.

The information was on the wall chart in the form of lighted different-colored pins. "Six crews," the man said, looking over his shoulder at the chart. "Two helitack crews, two air tankers and a lead plane."

"Smoke jumpers?"

"No."

Jay was going to need them just for starters, JL thought. Six crews—a hundred and twenty troops on the line—was not going to be enough; even from here he could tell them that.

"Are you JL Harmon, from Sanrio?" A girl, in neat Forest Service uniform.

JL nodded. Recall? George Jefferson wanted him back?

Instead, "They're waiting for you," the girl said. "The seminar is about to begin."

Chapter Three

YOUNG Tad Lawry was first out of the tent on Monday morning, leaving his father and mother still in their sleeping bag. Back home in Texas he was a Boy Scout and had done considerable hiking and some camping, but he had never seen big trees like these, nor a mountain anywhere near the size of Sierra Grande.

And the air tasted strange too, smelling like the trees and the pitch that had rubbed off on his hand last night while he was helping his mother put up the tent. And despite what his father had said about their being all alone in here, there had to be somebody nearby because he could smell campfire smoke.

His father was a funny guy, and Tad wondered why, after all the years they had been married, his mother had never seemed to realize it. "Nobody pushes your old man around," Les Lawry had told the boy once. "And don't let them push you, either."

What that meant was that if you told Pop to do something, he'd turn right around and do the opposite, simple as that. "Don't drive so fast, Les." And down went the accelerator, almost through the floor. That kind of thing.

Tad studied the nearby stream. It was clear and fast-running. He followed it a few hundred yards, pleased by its gurgling. Around a turn that opened to a view, he stopped. Two deer were drinking, oblivious to his presence. He stood quietly, watching.

A new sound obtruded, the staccato chatter of a helicopter overhead. Both deer raised their heads, then bounded away as if on springs. Tad, remembering his father's caution last night, froze until the sound passed.

ELSIE Edwards was up before Don. She peeked out of the blue nylon tent and looked around at the empty forest. She saw only a Canada jay, industriously scratching through the dead campfire. He stopped and cocked his head at her. Pulling on her shirt and shorts, Elsie stepped out into the bright but hazy morning. Don followed.

The smell of smoke was faint against the scent of the pines. A campfire? No matter. Elsie breathed deep. "You remember my mentioning the bridal suite in the Dorchester?" she said. "Forget it. This is much better." She smiled. "I think it may be the company."

"I'm flattered."

"You should be." Elsie was silent for a moment, the fond smile still on her lips. "For the record, I don't think I've ever felt so happy in my whole life."

"Wasn't that the idea?"

FRANK Orwell waited impatiently for Felipe Vigil, who had wandered off saying he'd be right back. That was half an hour ago. It was broad daylight now, and high time they got on their way. Orwell was anxious to put as much distance between himself and Los Ojos as he could.

"Hey, man!" Felipe suddenly appeared, breathless, grinning. "You know what I got? A chick, man! A beautiful chick. Wait'll you see her!" He stopped, studying Orwell's expression. "You dig, man? We got a real live woman out here in these woods!"

Orwell stood indecisive. His mind said to split just as fast as they could. But his loins, after two years of incarceration, refused to listen. He licked his lips. "She alone?"

"There's a guy with her. He doesn't look like much. We can take him easy."

Orwell shook his head. "I don't like it."

"You chicken? Nothing to it. Ten, fifteen minutes, then we on our way. It's been too long, man, too long."

STACY saw and smelled the smoke when she awakened, and noted that the sun had taken on a strange metallic-orange tinge. The seven a.m. radio news mentioned fire in the Sanrio forest, but reported it was under control. *"No hay problema,"* Stacy told Juanita, her housekeeper, who agreed that those in charge undoubtedly had matters well in hand, and would the senorita be home for lunch?

And that, of course, brought up the subject Stacy had been

trying to avoid ever since yesterday—Bart Jones and just what she was going to do about him. In the end, characteristically, she faced the problem head-on and telephoned El Rancho Costa Mucho.

A maid answered, and a few moments later Bart himself was on the line. "I wondered when you'd call." He sounded casual and without guile.

"I didn't know until last night that I had a new neighbor."

"I hoped you'd be surprised. When do I see you? Here, I hope. I don't get around much anymore."

"I have work to do this morning," she said.

"Lunch, then? I have a good cook."

"Lunch it is. One o'clock?"

Stacy hung up and sat for a little time motionless, staring unseeing across her office. Unreal, she thought; unreal that he's here; unreal that he can still get to me.

AARON Swift came into the office early as usual that morning. There was already a telephone message from Sophie on his desk, saying that she would be in late, if at all. It was unlike her, and Aaron called the familiar ranch number at once. Her voice sounded all right, and he was conscious of a sharp feeling of relief. "You're okay, then?" he asked.

"I'm fine. It's the fire."

"In the forest? It's way in, deep. Not to worry."

"We're getting ash."

"It's just that the wind is blowing that way."

"Yes. That's what concerns me." Always there was reason, careful logic behind her words.

Aaron said, "You want me to come out, Soph?"

"I don't think so. Someone has to mind the store. Besides, what could you do if you came? There isn't anything I can do, either, but I'll feel better just staying here. You can understand that."

Aaron could. More than twenty years of living had gone into that ranch, he thought, both hers and his.

"Will you call me, Soph, if you want me? Promise me that?"

"You didn't have to ask." Her voice was gentle.

The moment Aaron hung up, the switchboard operator buzzed his phone. "Mr. Willard Spencer is on line two."

Aaron sighed and punched the button. "You are up early, Willard. I was under the impression that you liked to sleep in."

Spencer did not like to be teased. "When there is a fire . . ." he began portentously.

"Oh, come now, it's miles away."

"Nevertheless, I don't like it."

"There's nothing I can do about it, Willard."

"On the contrary, you can find out at once precisely when the grace period of my homeowner's insurance lapses."

Aaron wore his courtroom face. "I have a better suggestion, Willard." He paused for emphasis. "It is that you write a check for your quarterly premium and carry it into Bud Lewis' office. Then there can be no confusion. Now, if you will excuse me—"

He hung up, and instantly the buzzer sounded again.

"Mrs. Swift is on line one."

"Debby, honey . . ." Aaron's voice now held mild protest. The last time he had seen her she had been curled up in a tangle of bedclothes, sound asleep.

"There's a fire, A. I smell the smoke. I'm terrified of fire."

"Tell you what, honey," he said. "You go over to the club for breakfast, and then stay by the pool in the sun. If the fire comes close, you can always dive in."

"I thought maybe you and I could drive somewhere. Maybe up to Santa Fe. We haven't been there for ages."

"Sorry." Aaron's voice was gentle but firm. "I've got work to do. You know Sanrio would grind to a halt without me."

"Oh, you!" There was a smile in Debby's voice. "All right. I'll be at the club."

Being married to Aaron was not exactly what Debby had imagined it might be, even though the sense of financial ease and the status as wife of one of Sanrio's—and the state's—leading citizens was even greater than she had anticipated.

But what she sometimes missed was *spontaneity*, the willingness at a moment's notice to drop everything and rush into some innocuous pleasure like a picnic or an unplanned trip. To be honest, she supposed that that kind of freedom could only be a part of irresponsible youth, that the kind of stability Aaron represented came only with the acceptance of duties and obligations. So it all balanced out. Still.

AT THE FIRE COMMAND POST within the forest, plans chief Phil Sommers ran his forefinger along the topographical map. "Getting close to the wilderness," he said, "and unless it's stopped pretty soon, we're going to have quite a mess on our hands. Once it reaches this line, it can fan out."

Jay Paul squinted at the map. In places, he had long thought, this country seemed to stand on edge, and coming as he did from the rolling hills and piney woods of Georgia, it was a wonder to him that any kind of vegetation, let alone big trees, could gain a foothold in such steep terrain. But there they were, right where Phil's finger was pointing, and they had to be protected. "No road in?" he said.

"The kind of country it is out there," Sommers said, "McIlvain's smoke jumpers are about the only choice."

Jay shook his head decisively. "It's too rough for them. I've been there, practically on all fours. You can't ask somebody to parachute into that."

Phil Sommers hesitated. "I'm no smoke jumper, but those characters seem to think they can go in just about anywhere."

"No. I won't risk them. I'll see if I can get a slurry drop in there."

Sommers shrugged. "You're the boss. They're predicting wind by noon, by the way."

"I can't help that, either."

Sommers nodded and turned away.

FELIPE Vigil said, whispering, "There they are, see?"

It was impossible not to see, Frank Orwell thought. At that moment in all the world there was only that beautiful girl in his vision—big, but not overweight, with the kind of figure you could drool over in a *Playboy* centerfold.

"What'd I tell you?" Felipe whispered.

"Okay," Orwell said. "But we make it fast, you hear me?"

"You got it," Vigil said. He looked around, picked up a large, lethal-looking rock. Then they began their short, savage charge.

MRS. Tyler Wayne came down to her beloved gardens this Monday morning as usual. Manuel and his assistant, Hilario, were already at work, Hilario on hands and knees weeding one of the rose beds, Manuel with careful skill manicuring the privet hedge that lined the flagstone walk from the big house.

"A lovely morning," Mrs. Wayne said. She was small and slim, with pure white hair beneath the sunshade hat and eyes of intense blue in her still smooth face. "You do such a lovely trimming job, Manuel. And Hilario doesn't miss a single weed. I am very grateful to you both."

In Manuel's experience, Anglos did not behave in this graceful manner. He and Hilario had discussed it often as they ate their lunches, sitting on the grounds in the shade of one of the great Dutch elms the late Senator had planted long ago in the sweeping lawns. But then, Mrs. Wayne in many ways was wholly different from all other Anglos either man had ever encountered.

"There is *humo*—smoke—senora," Manuel said. "There is a fire in the forest. It was caused by lightning."

Mrs. Wayne smiled. "That nice Mr. Harmon will attend to it, I'm sure. Now do you think we might spray the roses, Manuel?"

These days it was more important than ever, Mrs. Wayne felt, that the property be kept in flawless condition, because she was in effect a trustee. Vista Hill, her home for nearly fifty years, and Tyler's for a little more than forty, now technically belonged to the state—Mrs. Wayne's gift in her husband's name, and hers to live in and care for during her lifetime.

"Spraying is good," Manuel said. "With so many beds is maybe a little expensive, senora—"

"That is not important, Manuel. If you think it is good, we will do it. You always know best."

BELLEVUE Acres, Ken Delacorte was perfectly willing to concede, did not have classy connotations, nor was it intended to. Ken thoroughly approved of the Tyler Wayne estate, as well as Stacy Cummings' pad and all the other homes in that well-heeled category. In fact, after considerable looking around in the Southwest, Ken had picked Sanrio as a coming place, a potential Tucson, say, for growth, a place to attract eastern retired wealth. He would have loved to build luxury condominiums, but his finances were simply not up to it—hence Bellevue Acres, a hundred and thirty-six houses, eight to the acre. After all, ordinary folks needed places to live too, as Ken could well remember from his

149

wrong-side-of-town Waco beginnings, before football gave him a hand up.

The houses were not exactly flung together, but they were frame and plywood, with a skin of stucco rather than hand-laid adobe. They were crowded together too, and it was easy to hear your neighbor's TV program or family arguments. There were lots of kids, and dogs, and bicycles and roller skates.

Ken had no definite idea yet what there was about Bellevue Acres that seemed to be attracting the interest of Bartlemy Jones, who had rolled his fancy wheelchair into the closing when he bought the Brown place and produced a certified check for seven figures as if it were something he did every afternoon.

So he did what many folks in Sanrio did when they were in doubt: on this Monday morning he went to see Aaron Swift.

"This Jones dude," Ken began. "You know him, A?"

"I know him."

"Anything wrong with him?"

"I don't know him well." Then Aaron produced one of his cryptic statements. "He banks at the First."

"So?" Ken, puzzled, thought about it. Slowly comprehension dawned, and he began to nod. "They hold our note on the Bellevue Acres property, is that what you're thinking?"

"I haven't said a word, Ken."

Ken thought about it some more. "If they decided to discount it for cash," he said, "to Jones, say . . ."

"Happens that way sometimes. Banks these days do like cash."

There was no need to explain. With interest rates rising, many financial institutions were delighted to sell off older, relatively unprofitable mortgages—even at a discount—for cash, which could then be lent at far higher rates.

"A sharpie in a wheelchair," Ken said. "Is that it?"

"There are slander laws, Ken," Aaron said mildly. He looked out the window. "Seems the smoke's getting heavier."

Ken stood up. "I hadn't noticed." He nodded. "Thanks, A."

Leaving Aaron's office, Ken went outside into the bright but hazy day. The smoke really was thickening, he decided, but he had other matters to worry about.

In the off-seasons during his professional football years, Ken had put himself through Stanford University's business school, emerging with an M.B.A. and a considerable knowledge of business shenanigans. If you had capital, he knew, the possibilities for shady and profitable capers were almost endless.

The bank, the First, where Bart Jones had his no doubt considerable account, held the underlying note on the Bellevue Corporation. When Ken had run out of money for the development, the bank had loaned him enough to go on. Because of that, he and the bank were, in effect, partners. And whoever held that note controlled Bellevue's destiny, and that of the mortgaged homeowners living there.

Being a local organization, the bank had established a reputation for fair dealing if not downright compassion. It tended to view occasional late mortgage payments with understanding, and it had never been known to invoke the due-on-sale clause in each contract, which called for immediate full payment of the outstanding mortgage balance if a house was sold. Rather it had, as was its privilege, allowed a straight mortgage transfer without renegotiation when one of the Bellevue Acres residents sold out; and it had never taken full advantage of fluctuations in the interest standards upon which flexible-rate mortgages are based.

The bank had, in short, consistently behaved like a small-town institution rather than like the big-city giants. In the hands of the First, the underlying note had never represented a threat to the economic well-being of Bellevue Acres residents. But in the hands of a stranger, matters might change drastically.

Ken was not by nature a crusader. Blessed with both brains and a splendid physique, he had managed to haul himself up by the pulls of his boots to a comfortable position in society. But he knew that the world was filled with those who had not been blessed with more than average intelligence and whose physiques were no bargain, either. The best they could do was struggle through life and consider themselves lucky if they somehow acquired a house of their own in a development like Bellevue Acres. These were natural prey for the sharpies and, despite Ken's basic laissez-faire philosophy, letting the cats loose among the penned pigeons did not appeal to him.

He marched into the manager's office at the First and sat down. "A dude named Bart Jones," he said, and studied the man's face. "Making his presence felt in Sanrio, isn't he?"

"You have a point you're working up to, Ken?"

"Our Bellevue Acres note. Are you thinking of selling it? Maybe to Jones?"

The manager considered. "Who told you that?"

"I figured it out for myself."

The manager considered some more. "That's really bank business, Ken, and we don't—"

"Look." Ken's voice was soft, yet somehow ominous. "I'm asking a simple question and I'd like a simple answer. Are you thinking of selling the note to Jones? Yes, or no?"

The manager swallowed hard. "We're . . . thinking about it." He watched uneasily as Ken got out of the chair and straightened to his full, impressive height. "Was that all you wanted to know?"

"For now," Ken said, and walked out.

Chapter Four

*F*IGHTING wildland fires these days is an organized, technical business, with machines and electronic marvels of all kinds. But when you get right down to it, fires are still conquered by the people on the ground, working with hand tools, shovels, axes, brush hooks and chain saws. Fire lines are established by grunting, cursing, aching troops, breathing smoke and hearing the frightful roaring of flames and the crackling of trees and brush as they perish.

They had chosen to make their stand on top of a low ridge. Two crews—one southwest area crew, the other, Bessie Wingate's boys—were spread in a thin line, clearing back everything that would burn, leaving a swath of bare dirt and three-inch stumps as a fire line.

The sun was high and hot, and the fire fighters' yellow Forest Service shirts and hard hats were heavy and uncomfortable. But sparks were flying, and the shirts and hats were protection, so they sweated, and they cursed, and they chopped, their breath coming in short gasps because they were seven thousand feet up, where oxygen was scarce.

The fire had roared up a narrow break in the rocks to a somewhat level area, spread out and slowed its headlong progress.

Behind the fire line, and above it, a thick grove of big trees, the beginning of the forest's heart, waited helplessly. Birds had long since left, and every other species of forest folk was fleeing now in panic.

One of the southwest crew, Spanish American, swarthy, wiry, with sharp features, waved his McLeod hoe at Bessie. "Hey, *guapa*," he said, and showed intensely white teeth in a broad grin at his joke. The word connotes cuteness, sexiness, and could not have been more inappropriately applied.

"Cut the baloney," Bessie said without rancor.

"Okay. How about a beer? Ice cold? How about that?"

"Now," Bessie said, "you're talking." She glanced down the slope at the spreading flames. "But it'll have to wait. That thing's coming straight at us."

"Some like it hot, baby. It comes too close, I got my shelter."

The shelter was simply a sheet of metallic, fire-retardant cloth, with hand- and footholds on its underside. In a last-resort emergency, the fire fighter swept a patch of ground bare, lay down and drew the sheet over him, holding the edges of the cloth against the ground and hoping the flames would sweep harmlessly past.

"Me," Bessie said, "I don't aim to get into a fix where I have to use a shelter. And neither will my crew."

Her shovel had not been still a moment. With her strength she uprooted whole plants and even small trees and heaved them back from the area they were clearing. She squinted downhill at the flames. "I don't like it," she said, "not one little bit. Those big trees are too close. I can feel them against my back." She cocked her head toward the fire below them. "Hear that baby roaring at us. It thinks we're meat for the cooking."

ELSIE Edwards had pulled on trousers and a shirt. The need to cover herself was overwhelming, dominating all else.

Don was not dead, as she had feared at first, but he was unconscious. His breathing was steady, and his pulse, as nearly as she could tell by fumbling at his wrist, was regular and strong.

She supposed she ought to be doing something for him, for herself or about the smoke that was heavier now. But she couldn't seem to get her thoughts in order. She guessed she was in a state of shock, and she was sure she would never lose the sense of shame and degradation that possessed her.

She knelt now beside Don, and her hands made stroking motions on his forehead. Maybe he would die; the blow to his head with the rock had made a dull, ugly thud and he had dropped to the ground without a sound.

Dear Lord, what if he did die? Here in this wilderness?

Don's eyelids fluttered. His eyes opened briefly, unfocused, frightened, and then closed again.

"Don!" Elsie said. "Don, darling. Please!"

His eyes opened again. He stirred. "What's burning?" he said.

"Nothing, darling. It's all right."

It was not all right. That realization was slow in coming, but it burst upon her with impact at last. The smoke was heavy now, too heavy, choking. And as she strained to listen she could hear crackling sounds. She got to her feet and looked around. There— yes—she could see flames sweeping through the lower branches of a big ponderosa. The sight was terrifying.

"Don! Don!" Her voice was almost out of control.

"Help me up!" His voice was stronger now, and with her aid he struggled to his feet and stood muttering angrily to himself.

Elsie said, "The tent. Shall I take it down?"

"Never mind that." He was standing straight now. "Give me your hand. Let's go."

"But our things!"

His head ached and throbbed. He had neither memory nor knowledge of what had happened, and his vision was still blurred, but his mind was clear enough to realize that there was danger, present and unmistakable. Flight was their only course.

"Never mind our things." He could even smile weakly. "We're what counts."

HALF a mile away, Felipe Vigil was still babbling happily. "Hey, man, that was some chick, no? She was really built!"

"Drop it, stupid," Frank Orwell said. "Get your mind off that." His voice was harsh. "From here out we're going to need all the thinking both of us can do. Of all the stinking luck!"

"You clicking your teeth, man, but what you saying?"

They had topped a low, almost bare rise. Orwell stopped and looked back. "See that?" He pointed to dark, angry smudges against the hazy sky. "Smoke."

Felipe looked. "So?"

Orwell turned and pointed in the direction they had been walking. "More smoke. See it? What we got is a forest fire, and I've seen a couple and I don't never, *never* want to see another one up close."

Comprehension came slowly. Felipe looked both ways. "So what we do? You big Anglo hotshot thinker, what we do?"

Orwell waved one hand toward Sierra Grande's lofty peak. "We haul our butts up that mountain just as fast as we can."

MRS. Tyler Wayne frowned at the whitish flecks that drifted down around her.

"Ash, senora," Manuel said. "From the fire in the forest."

"They should not allow it to come so close," she said. Tyler had known how to deal with such things. He would have spoken to someone in authority. Well, Mrs. Wayne had always found that nice Mr. Harmon to be most agreeable. She thought it would be quite in order if she went to see him about this falling ash.

A short time later her chauffeur drove Mrs. Wayne up to the Forest Service headquarters in an ageless shiny black limousine. Mrs. Wayne, in hat, white gloves and a summer frock, went inside to call upon JL and ended up in George Jefferson's office. Jefferson got up promptly to greet her.

"My gardener," Mrs. Wayne said, "tells me that there is a fire in the forest."

"Yes, ma'am."

"The young lady down the hall tells me that Mr. Harmon is in Idaho."

"Yes, ma'am."

"Mr. Harmon's card, which he was good enough to give me, says that he is fire management officer for the forest."

"Yes, ma'am."

"Then," Mrs. Wayne said, "I fail to understand why he is not here, managing this fire. Ash is falling in my gardens."

WILLARD Spencer's first inclination was to ignore Aaron Swift's suggestion about paying his insurance. He was not accustomed to running errands such as carrying checks to someone's office.

A second look outside, however, at the strange copperish tinge of the sky had convinced him to set his pride aside for this occasion only. Accordingly, check in pocket, he presented himself at the Lewis Insurance Agency and demanded attention.

Bud Lewis himself appeared. "Here," Spencer said, and held out the check.

Lewis made no move to take it. "The due date on your invoice was May eighteenth, Mr. Spencer. The grace period ended Friday, June seventeenth. Today is June twentieth. Your homeowner's policy has lapsed."

"You joke, of course," Spencer said.

Nothing changed in Bud Lewis' face.

With determined calm Spencer said, "Very well," and held out the check again. "Reinstate the policy."

Still nothing changed in Lewis' face. "There is a fire in the forest, Mr. Spencer. This is hardly the time to issue, or reinstate, a homeowner's policy."

There was silence. Spencer said, "Do you realize what you are doing? You are leaving my property unprotected."

"I am saving my underwriters a possible considerable loss," Lewis said. "That is my prime consideration."

Les Lawry said, "It's a rotten nuisance. We go to all the trouble to come into this wilderness, and now they let a fire get started. We'd better pack up and drive back out."

Cindy Lou said, "A fire means a lot of people. Suppose they see us driving out? That sign said no motor vehicles allowed."

"Doesn't mean a thing. Anybody asks, we say we didn't see it."

Tad said, "Pop, if there really is a fire, a big one, I mean . . . well, here's this stream. If the fire gets bad, we could all get in the water. I've read about that."

"You just stick with your old man," Les said. "We'll be fine. It's just a nuisance. If the rangers had been on their toes, it wouldn't have happened. We pay our taxes, and this is what we get. Now, let's start packing the jeep."

Bart had mellowed, not much, but some; that was Stacy's early reaction when she arrived at his house for lunch. Maybe adversity had given him a touch of humility, although the word seemed a strange one to use in connection with Bart Jones.

The lines of his face had somehow softened and lost a bit of their harsh arrogance, but his eyes had retained what she had always thought of as the kind of cold fierceness one found in the eyes of a bird of prey. What did I ever see in him? she asked herself.

"I must say," Bart exclaimed as he showed her into the broad living room, handling his electric wheelchair with skillful ease, "that you chose nice country for your retreat."

"No retreat," Stacy said.

"New life, then?"

"Something like that."

"Breeding horses? That's too tame for you, Stacy. A little wine?"

She accepted the glass. Then, as usual, her impulse was to come straight to the point. "Why are you here?"

She had almost forgotten his lopsided grin, the expression of a boy caught with his hand in the cookie jar. "You," he said.

"Come off it, Bart. Nobody ever meant that much to you."

"You underestimate yourself."

She had forgotten too how infuriating he could be sometimes. "All right," she said, "let's talk about something else."

"Like what?"

Remembering Ken Delacorte's visit the night before, she said, "Bellevue Acres, for starters."

"Real estate's a little out of your line, isn't it?"

"Ken Delacorte's an old friend."

Bart sipped his martini. "Good football player."

"But no businessman, is that what you're saying?"

"Bellevue Acres is a nickel-and-dime operation."

"And you're used to big deals, is that it?"

"There aren't too many things I can still do, and I need some fun out of life. You'll grant me that?"

"I don't know if I'll grant you much of anything," Stacy said.

IN HER logical, analytical way, Sophie Swift on this Backslope Monday occupied herself as if she were organizing a law case about to go to trial. One prepared for the worst, she had always believed, and then one could allow hope for the best. Sitting in the June sunlight on the patio, a legal pad on her lap, she listed steps to take if the fire threatened her home.

157

First and foremost, the horses. The mare, Impatient, and her foal would go together in the horse trailer. The other two horses could be tethered behind the trailer and led slowly to safety. Her favorite paintings would go in the rear of the station wagon. The silverware she would put into pillowcases and carefully lower to the deepest part of the swimming pool. Certain file drawers containing her own and Aaron's records over the years also should be loaded into the station wagon.

Surveying the list, she smiled ruefully when she discovered that she had made no provision for clothing. No doubt Debby, if she had thought to make any list of priorities, would have included clothing first. Sophie decided there was a message for her in that realization.

The wind had shifted, Sophie noticed, and ash was no longer falling around her on the patio. She studied the big mountain and noted the usual summer afternoon clouds beginning to take shape.

Sophie and Aaron had met at Stanford law school and had carried on a courtship that by most standards, Sophie conceded, would have been unexciting in the extreme. They married the evening they graduated and spent their honeymoon studying for bar examinations.

Their marriage, she supposed, had been more intellectual than romantic, and in her unworldliness Sophie had assumed that was sufficient. Obviously it was not, and she had had no idea that the pain of that discovery would be so intense.

With a final appraising look at Sierra Grande, she got up and carried her list inside. A cup of tea while she waited for further developments, she thought, would help to pass the time.

She was leaning against the kitchen sink, sipping her tea, when Aaron walked in, wearing a strained, sheepish grin. "Just thought I'd check to see that everything was okay," he said.

Sophie turned so that her back was to him and set her teacup carefully in the sink. She wanted suddenly to laugh aloud, to squeal, to sing, to do all manner of girlish things she had seen female television contestants do when a winner was announced. Instead, turning again and smiling faintly, she said, "That was good of you, Aaron. But I think everything is under control. Would you like a cup of tea?"

THERE ARE FEW SIGHTS ON EARTH as terrifying as a wildfire on the loose when faced close up from ground level, which is the view fire fighters customarily have. Jay Paul, at his command post within the forest, was far removed from the fire perimeter, and guiltily happy to be where he was.

On the other hand, as fire boss there was no avoiding the responsibilities that came with the job, and by noon of this first day he was close to despair. It seemed to him that everything that could go wrong, had.

North of the fire's center, wind-driven flames had attacked Sierra Grande's west flank. They had overpowered the crews there, and were now racing toward the east-west line of highway 14, which had once seemed too distant to worry about.

To the south, toward the estates adjoining the forest, the flames coming downslope were advancing slowly but with apparent steadiness. And to the east of the spot where the fire had started, the monster was well into the wilderness. A good share of the problem, of course, was the presence of that great mountain Sierra Grande. Around its mass winds twisted and swirled in no immediately discernible pattern. At ground level, miniature whirlwinds picked up burning brush and fallen debris, flinging them across open ground to ignite the lower branches of big trees. Dry pine needles flared like tiny torches, creating their own updrafts of hot air, which spread the fire.

Another worry: the pilot of the chopper that had taken in one of the crews reported catching glimpses of maybe half a dozen persons in the wilderness. If the report was accurate, it was up to Jay Paul to see that the people were found and rescued.

And now came word that a new area, over near a small lake that lay within the wilderness, had somehow ignited and was burning furiously.

"Andy McIlvain's still waiting," Phil Sommers told Jay Paul. "You want him to go in with a few of his people?"

"I'm saving the smoke jumpers. All of them."

For what? Phil Sommers thought. Christmas?

ON THE phone from Santa Fe, the regional supervisor, George Jefferson's boss, said, "Looks like you've got a bad one, George."

"This time of year, no rain. You know how it goes."

"I see you've got your Sanrio team on it. What about JL's regional team? Think you'll need him?"

"Could. The weather's against us. And I'm beginning to get civilian complaints."

"So am I. Some expensive real estate is threatened, George. Expensive people own it. Fellow named Spencer, Willard P. Know him?"

"As much as I want to." In a reassuring voice Jefferson added, "We'll get it whipped."

"I'm sure you will."

For that last comment, Jefferson thought as he hung up, read: "You'd better!" He called to his secretary in the outer office. "Get off a message to BIFC. We want JL back here."

IN PLACES, the fire advanced slowly; in other places, wind-driven, it rushed forward in quantum leaps from a piñon here to a juniper there, to a scrub oak farther upslope already brought to the point of combustion by the rising currents of heated air.

Bessie Wingate, still working in tandem with the southwest crew, swore at the flames and at her men. With her, fighting a fire was a personal vendetta, no quarter asked or given. "Had me a house once," she had been heard to say one night at a bar called The Antlers. "Wasn't much, but I'd built it, me and Ted, and it was mine." She never explained who Ted was, and no one had the temerity to ask.

"A fire come busting over the ridge. There went the house. And Ted. The darn fool let himself get burned to death. What the heck, long time ago. Let's have another beer."

Now, moving into a new area of the fire line, Bessie was all business. "Gus, you and Pete take that chain saw over yonder and take down that stand of piñon. The rest of you fan out and get hacking and scraping. I want this ground slicker than a baby's behind; nothing left for that beast down there to feed on."

To a neighboring crewman, the wiry Hispanic from the southwest crew, Bessie said, "You're doing a good job with that McLeod." The tool was a modified, highly efficient hoe. "What's your name?"

"Eloy Jaramillo."

"Tell you what, Eloy. After this is all over, I'll buy you a beer at

The Antlers. You know where that is?" Bessie's shovel continued to move as she spoke. "In fact, you keep on working like that, maybe two beers. How about that?"

"*Muchas gracias.*"

"That's okay," Bessie said. "A job like this separates out the men from the boys."

THE team that later sifted carefully through the situation reports and listened to direct testimony decided that at this point, late afternoon of that first day, Backslope, estimated at something over ten thousand acres, could have been contained by quick, decisive action.

Jay Paul had his troops deployed, his communications in place and his air attack organized and operating. But Andy McIlvain's smoke jumpers remained on the ground; two hotshot crews were in the wrong places, doing routine line work; and although ground tankers were available within striking distance, none had been summoned because of Jay Paul's exaggerated respect for the rugged terrain.

As dusk gathered, the air tanker slurry drops slowed and then stopped altogether, and the wind and temperature conditions that had nurtured the fire's beginnings the night before resumed their encouraging effects.

Chapter Five

*T*HE moon that Monday night was almost full and hung low over the eastern plains. To Frank Orwell, leading the way up Sierra Grande's flank, it resembled a gigantic eye, fixed on them, spotlighting their progress. Here, above timberline, there was no place to hide from its scrutiny, and he felt naked, exposed.

Felipe Vigil, panting along behind in the thin, cooling air, said, "*Basta!* Enough! What we trying to do, set some kind of record?"

They stopped. Orwell was breathing deeply. "With that fire," he said, "this mountain's going to be crawling with people. You got that?"

"So what are we? *Brujos?* Spirits?"

"We," Orwell said with heavy scorn, "are escaped convicts."

"And we wear signs that say so? Or these men here to fire-fight,

161

they carry pictures of us? You crazy, man! All they care about is fire. They not interested in us."

Orwell thought about it. The guy had a point, he told himself in surprise, and almost said so. But instead of speaking, he merely nodded agreement.

"So what we do now?" Felipe said.

"We'll work around the mountain, spend the night up here and then early in the morning go down and see how things look on that side of the forest."

"Going to be cold."

"Yeah." Orwell wondered if there would be resistance.

Instead, "Okay," Felipe said. "I just keep thinking about that chick. She here, she'd make me warm."

Don and Elsie too had stopped climbing and running, Don at the limit of his endurance. His headache remained, throbbing unbelievably with each heartbeat, blurring his vision.

"I think we're above it now," he said, panting, sitting exhausted on the ground.

The snapping of flames and the crashing of falling branches reached them clearly from down the slope. The rising smoke was heavy, choking.

"Are we safe here?" Elsie said. She was two selves, she thought, and felt hysteria was near. One of her recognized the danger and worried about Don's condition. The other still could neither believe nor comprehend what had happened to her.

"I don't know what happened," Don said, his voice weak. "I can't remember anything except your saying that you'd never been happier." He looked at Elsie then.

Suddenly she was crying without sound—no sobs, no gasps of breath, merely her face screwed up and tears running down the sides of her nose from eyes that were wide open.

"Elsie!" Don said. "Baby!" He reached for her weakly.

"I'm all right," Elsie said. "All right. Honest."

Don closed his eyes, took a deep breath, then willed himself to focus on the girl's face. "What happened?"

Elsie shook her head. She fought back tears and wiped her cheeks with the backs of her hands. She shook her head again in stubborn silence.

"Baby," Don said, his voice patient now, "you have to tell me. We promised to share, remember? Whatever happened to you happened to me too, but I can't remember. . . . Something, somebody . . ." He shook his head in exasperation. "It won't come to me."

"You were hit on the head," Elsie said. "Two men . . ." She too closed her eyes and opened them. It was somehow easier now. "Yes"—the words came slowly—"you have a right to know what happened." She told him.

IF MOM hadn't told Pop to slow down, Tad thought, Pop wouldn't have done just the opposite and, as always, driven faster, and they wouldn't now be stuck.

"Of all the luck," Les Lawry said, and swung his legs out to stand up and have a look.

Cindy Lou got out and stood unmoving, almost rigid. "I'm scared, Les. The smoke is heavier. There's fire, and it's close. I can almost feel it! We never should have come here!"

"Oh, shut up! Tad, come here. Let's see what we can do."

With one wheel off the ground and the jeep's frame resting solidly on a big, half-buried rock, there wasn't anything they could do, Tad decided, but he did not say so aloud—that would only make it worse.

"Maybe we can lift it off," Les said.

It took two futile tries, and it was Les who called a halt. "No dice," he said. He was red in the face and puffing. "These old jeeps are heavy. That's why they stand up. In the army—"

"Les!" Cindy Lou's voice was rising. "Over there! Look! I can see the fire!"

So could they all. In the gathering dusk, first the brightening glow, and then the flames themselves were suddenly visible through the trees, angry orange-red in color, the fire's voice a crackling roar.

"Oh, Lord!" Les said. "Let's get out of here!"

Cindy Lou said, "Our things!"

"Forget the things, Cindy Lou. Just get out of that jeep and come on! Tad, you lead!"

"Which direction?"

"How do I know? Just away!"

JL CAUGHT A COMMERCIAL FLIGHT out of Boise, and landed in Albuquerque, where a Forest Service aircraft waited to take him to Sanrio. Along the way he ordered the pilot to fly low over the fire.

At first glimpse, it was just a red glow in the distance, as harmless-seeming as the comfortable glow in a fireplace on a winter evening. But as they flew closer, JL could almost hear the roaring sounds of conflagration—the crackling of huge trees, the rushing of winds. On the ground, he knew, strange, threatening shadows would be leaping and cavorting against shifting curtains of thick smoke. Around the flaming area, men and machines would be fighting to create a perimeter of containment, a firebreak across which the fire could not travel.

"Offhand," the pilot said, "I'd say you had your work cut out for you."

JL's eyes remained on the fire. "We'll whip it," he said. Because we have to, he thought. There is no other way.

Late as it was, George Jefferson was waiting in his office at headquarters when JL arrived.

"How's your ankle?" Jefferson said.

"It's fine, George." JL said, "Just fine. When I'm sitting on my butt, it doesn't bother me a bit."

"Did you make smart remarks like that at BIFC?"

"I just sat and listened."

Jefferson closed his eyes for a few moments. When he opened them again, he said, "Okay, it's been a long day. Albuquerque called, regional office; and Mrs. Tyler Wayne came in." He looked curiously at JL. "She a friend of yours?"

"I like her. When she has questions, I answer them. She's out of touch, but—"

"If she wanted to pick up the phone and complain to three, four people, old senatorial cronies of Tyler's, the Secretary of Agriculture would be down on us inside the hour. That's how out of touch she is. Ashes were falling on her roses, and that is definitely not allowed."

JL nodded as patiently as he could. "I'll bear it in mind."

"You do that. Now, how does it look out there?"

"Bad. And it's going to get worse."

Jefferson leaned back in his chair and gestured toward the map of the forest on the wall. "Show me."

At last. JL walked over to the map. With his forefinger he traced an irregular elliptical outline, its major axis running east–west, with a horn-shaped projection in the northwest, where the flames had worked their way around Sierra Grande's flank and were headed for the highway. "This is roughly the area of the open fire—"

"How many acres? At a guess?"

JL shrugged. "Must be close to fifteen thousand. I haven't seen the infrared photos, but I'd guess that here and here—between the south boundary of the wilderness and the line of large estates—there are probably other areas already smoldering and ready to combust."

He moved his finger to the big mountain's eastern flank. "When the morning sun begins to heat up the ground and starts to create air currents, the upslope wind will enlarge this area. Lots of timber up there."

"Can you stop it?"

"We'll try." He moved his finger again, to the south. "But here's the big problem. Too close to houses, that development—"

"Bellevue Acres?"

"Right." JL paused. "All those houses, all those kids. And then, if we aren't careful, the town itself."

Jefferson nodded. "And the Wayne place—Vista Hill," he said, "and all those other big estates abutting the forest?"

"They'll get the deluxe treatment." They wouldn't really, and both men knew it. The fire-suppression effort JL would direct would try to protect all property; whatever favoritism might be shown would be based on general, not specific, good.

"All right," Jefferson said, "it's all yours. Have the dispatcher call in what you need."

As JL walked outside to his pickup he felt unshackled, finally turned loose on the job he knew and liked best. He glanced up into the sky to see the reflected glow of the fire—his enemy. Preliminaries over, he thought; now to the main event.

JAY Paul was sitting at a folding table staring glumly at a map. Electric lights had been strung from the portable generator here at the command post in the forest. Radio antennas had been mounted high in nearby trees. From a catering truck not far away, cooking smells blended with the smell of smoke. In the deep shadows men were sacked out on the ground, blanket-wrapped against the chill of this high-country June night.

Jay Paul looked up, saw JL, automatically began to smile in relief, and then, as full realization came, suddenly looked less than happy. "They called you back. . . . You're taking over."

JL pulled up a chair and sat. This was the hard part. "Look," he said, "for near twenty-four hours you've been working your tail off—"

"And getting nowhere."

"Well, maybe we can change that. Let's see your last situation reports. Then you go off and have yourself a cup of coffee. You might have somebody bring me one too."

Taking over like this was never easy, either for those doing the taking or for those being superseded, and sometimes it could be downright destructive to general morale. But there was no help for it.

JL began reading Jay Paul's latest reports, which showed clearly a deteriorating situation. As he read and considered his options he glanced from time to time at his watch. On major fires, briefings for supervisory personnel were held on a strict schedule: twice daily, at 0430 and at 1630. The predawn briefing time was approaching fast.

Once, young in the fire-suppression business, he had found it incongruous that a fire boss would sit quietly, apparently doing nothing, while the world was going up in flames and troops on the lines were breaking their necks to hold what territory they had. But he had long since learned that the fire boss, like the commanding general of an army, performed best when he had the time to study and think.

It was close to briefing time when Jay Paul reappeared. His face was set and sullen. "Orders, boss?"

JL deliberately gathered together the papers he had been reading and got out of the chair before he answered. "Yes," he said. "The first one is to get that chip off your shoulder. You're not going to do me any good in that frame of mind." He waited a moment and watched a subtle change in Jay's face. "Now," JL said, "let's go find out where we stand."

To JL, the twice-daily briefings were valuable in ensuring that all supervisory personnel knew what was going on throughout the entire effort. In this instance, he was particularly interested in the people themselves and their attitudes.

First came the roll call. JL, with Jay Paul slightly behind him, sat off to one side, watching as each hand was raised, identifying the face that went with it. Next, from Phil Sommers, plans chief, came a background brief of fire-suppression progress to date.

Somewhere behind JL a low-pitched voice said, "Pitiful little, with good movement backward."

JL recognized the voice as Andy McIlvain's. Stifling the temptation to look around, JL faced resolutely forward. At his shoulder Jay Paul muttered to himself.

The fire behavior officer came next, followed by the meteorologist. The line boss, second in tactical command, followed, and JL attended him carefully. A bright boy, in JL's opinion, marked to go far. His name was Ben Hastings, college educated, a forestry major specializing in plant biology. Trim, neat, he handed out assignments that were as neat as himself.

Again Andy's voice behind JL. "And what about us? We're lepers?" This time the voice was not low-pitched.

JL, without turning his head, said, "I'll talk with you later, Andy. Simmer down." Then he rose.

He spoke to them all, deliberately keeping his voice calm. "You've held the lines for twenty-four hours," he said. Not true; they had lost their lines in a dozen places, but his voice held no hint of criticism. "Now we've seen how it's developing, we'll see what we can do to make sure that it doesn't get out of hand."

His voice altered subtly. "They brought me back from Boise because I wasn't learning anything. It wasn't that I knew it all, I just wasn't listening. I was back here instead of there, so they said, 'Might as well send him home, he's no good to us here.' "

There were smiles, and a general sense of relaxation. JL's voice changed again, to a brisker tone. "All right, let's get at it." He pointed at Andy McIlvain, Jay Paul, Phil Sommers and Ben Hastings. "I want you four, Andy first. Alone."

JL could have written Andy McIlvain's résumé from memory: A degree from Cal Tech in aeronautical engineering; forty years old; unmarried; winter-season ski instructor; thirteen years as a smoke jumper, the last eight as crew foreman; department commendation for a new parachute design; impatient.

"What's your beef?" JL said.

"You've got a fire. I've got a crew of smoke jumpers, good ones—"

"The best." JL nodded.

"And we've been sitting on our behinds, pitching cards into a helmet. I told Phil Sommers we could go into that terrain! Duck soup! With the new chute, even you could make it!"

"Thanks."

"But Jay Paul says he won't risk us. You've lost a whole square-mile section because he wouldn't let us go in at the start."

"All right," JL said. "You've make your point. Now I'm here, and we'll use you. That's a promise. You're loaded up?"

"Gear lashed down, men ready to suit up."

"Back to the airport," JL said. "I'll call you."

Chapter Six

IN FULL daylight on Tuesday, this second day, the scene was wholly different from what it had been twenty-four hours earlier. Sierra Grande's towering peak was still plain against the limitless sky as winds above the ten-thousand-foot level swept it clean, but lower, the pall of smoke hung like smog, ugly and threatening.

From the town no flames were visible, and even from the big houses abutting the forest, like Vista Hill and Willard P. Spencer's now uninsured estate, stands of ponderosa pines screened the actual conflagration from view. But fire was there, and it made its presence felt in the smoke it generated, thick, in places choking, seeping through closed windows and doors, leaving its distinctive smudgy prints on whitewashed walls and garden trellises.

Overhead in the forest there was an almost constant din as air tankers swept past at near treetop height to discharge their loads of slurry in ragged clouds. On the forest's fringe, where terrain permitted, bulldozers carved firebreaks and ground tankers pumped water by the ton. But in rougher, steeper country sweating, cursing line crews dug and chopped and scraped the ground clean by hand, hoping their lines would hold and that no errant wind gust might catch a burning branch and carry it across the cleared area into a fresh stand of trees.

Andy McIlvain was in the spotter's seat of the Twin Otter this Tuesday morning, abaft the open fuselage door. Headset and mike in place, and his head well out the open window, he scanned the forest below. On the wooden bench that lined the starboard side of the bare cabin, eleven smoke jumpers sat, suited up and wearing their two parachutes each.

One thing, Andy was thinking. When old JL got into the act, things began to happen.

"We can handle these two quadrants," JL had said on the phone. Both men, though miles apart, were studying copies of a reference map as they talked. "But up in that northwest corner, I can't get trucks or choppers in."

"We can go in," Andy said.

"Yes, I think you can." JL did not hesitate. "I just want that line held so it can't fishhook and cause us trouble. Got it?"

"Duck soup."

"Okay. Get on it. But save part of your crew in case we need you somewhere else as well."

"Charge!" Andy said, and hung up.

AGAIN Aaron Swift had not slept well, and vague guilt feelings continued to run through his mind. The previous afternoon at the ranch, after finishing the tea Sophie had made for him and listening to her plans and preparations, all logical and sensible, Aaron had gone back to his office. There was a call from Debby at the club, and as he went about returning it he could picture her, young and shapely in one of her scant bikinis, stretched out beside the pool.

"A," Debby's breathless voice had said on the phone, "would you feel like having dinner here tonight? Everyone says the new piano player is super."

"Why not?" Aaron said. "I'll bring along my fiddle and we can watch Rome burn from there."

"You say the funniest things sometimes," Debby said. "I never know when you're teasing."

That night, lying awake in the predawn blackness, Aaron was not at all sure that he knew, either.

At his office that second day of Backslope, he heard, as usual, pretty much all that was going on in Sanrio.

JL was back in town and in charge of the fire, which was all to the good. But it seemed to Aaron that during the night the fire had spread, and that was all to the bad.

Around midmorning the film star Ada Loving, Sanrio's resident celebrity, arrived at Aaron's office unannounced. Reports of her impressive figure, Aaron decided, had not been exaggerated.

Ada Loving had purchased a home in Sanrio—or it had been purchased for her; details were unclear. In an interview with the local newspapers she had said she was enchanted by the climate and the scenery and the friendliness of the folks who lived in Sanrio. The area would burgeon and prosper mightily as soon as its charms became more widely known—something she was going to help happen.

"My business manager," she told Aaron, "advised me that in any kind of emergency, you were the person to depend on."

There was shrewdness behind this careful façade, Aaron decided. Ada Loving was obviously of the opinion that sexy actresses were not supposed to be intelligent, and behaved accordingly, but glimpses of her real self showed through. "Flattering of him," Aaron said. "Do you have an emergency?"

"I don't know. Does this fire count? In Malibu it would."

"Happily," Aaron said, "this is not Malibu yet. And so far, the fire is merely a fire, no threat to life or property."

"But it could be?"

"With bad luck, very bad luck, it could be."

"You kid me not. Thank you for that." The celebrated blue eyes were steady. "Who is in charge? And how do I meet him?"

"To make sure a little extra care is taken of your property?"

Nothing changed in Ada Loving's friendly smile. "Why not?"

"Matter of viewpoint." Aaron wore his courtroom manner. "The forest supervisor is named George Jefferson. He's the top of the local totem pole."

As Ada Loving left his office, Aaron decided that the view from the rear precisely balanced the view from the front, a miracle of anatomical engineering.

JL GLANCED at the note Jay Paul handed him. "A burned-out jeep? In the wilderness?"

Jay Paul nodded. "One of the smoke jumpers found it."

"No people?"

Jay Paul shook his head.

"Get a chopper in. See if it can spot them." JL's voice was doubtful. "If they know they're not supposed to have driven in, they may not want to be seen. If they have a choice, that is. One thing about a fire: it smokes out a lot of things, including people."

ELSIE Edwards came cautiously back into the uppermost fringe of the big trees, where Don sat on the ground, resting, eyes closed, against one of the massive trunks. There was a purple bruise behind his right ear, where he had been struck, but the continuing throbbing ache included his entire head. The fact that he was conscious indicated that it was probably no more than a mild concussion. But, oh, how his head ached!

He opened his eyes as Elsie approached, and what he saw in her face took his attention away from his own condition.

"What is it? You look as if you'd seen—"

"I have. I—did!" Elsie was holding herself as tightly in control as she could manage. "They're—there! Above us! They're still on the mountain!"

"The same two men?"

Elsie caught her lower lip in her teeth and nodded.

"Did they see you?"

Her head moved sideways, a jerky, mechanical motion.

"Then we're all right here," Don said, "unless the fire comes up the slope."

"It—does, doesn't it? Move upward, I mean?"

"Sometimes. Maybe. We'll just have to wait and see."

REPORTS and photographs were all very well, but in JL's opinion there was no substitute for looking at the situation yourself. Sitting now in the Forest Service helicopter, he studied the fiery battlefield below with an appraising eye. The situation, he decided, was less than good.

By giant leaps in terrain too steep for bulldozers, one front of the fire was advancing up Sierra Grande's slopes, in its savagery obliterating all low growth and leaving the big pines as naked and blackened skeletons. Farther on, in an area of dense underbrush, ominous smoke tendrils were rising, testimony to the hidden buildup of temperatures that, unopposed, could rise steadily until the entire area suddenly took flame.

Even ground crews were useless here because of the impenetrability of the tangled growth. In a situation like this, you gambled on what appeared to be the lesser of two bad choices.

The aircraft's radio crackled and Andy's voice came through. "Northwest corner here. Eleven men with gear on the ground taking positions. They'll be in touch. I'm heading home."

JL plucked the hand microphone from the control panel bracket. "Roger," he said. "Stand by."

Still holding the microphone, he glanced out the window at the smoking undergrowth, then called Ben Hastings, the line boss. He read off a set of coordinates from the map he kept in a clipboard on his lap. "That area we wanted to clean out with controlled, prescribed burning," he said, "got it?"

"Got it."

"It's smoking now. Before it reaches flash point, I want it opened up so ground crews can get at it."

"Roger," Ben Hastings said. "Spaced explosives—will do. I'll take care of it."

JL was pleased by Ben's immediate understanding of the problem and the solution. "Any word from the people with that jeep?"

"Negative," said Ben. "The chopper is still sweeping the area. My guess is they're keeping undercover."

"Then they're making the wrong choice. Over and out."

He signaled to the pilot, who nodded and took the helicopter off in a new direction. Soon they came over the tiny opening in the trees where Andy's smoke jumpers had gone in. The pilot stared at it in awe. "You mean they went in there? By parachute?"

"Good men," JL said. He pointed. "There they are."

The jumpers were spread out in a thin, spaced line, with saws and hand tools, cutting a wide, clean firebreak. One of the men on the ground looked up and waved, thumb and forefinger held in a circle. JL waved the clipboard in reply.

They flew farther north, and JL, pointing down, said mildly, "Our one real bright spot—that highway. Natural firebreak."

The highway was two full lanes wide, with a mowed verge supporting only low grass and cactus insufficient to feed fire.

"We won't have to worry about containing the fire there," JL said. Be thankful for small blessings, he told himself, and resumed study of the map he had been marking as they flew.

Containment, that was the key: surround the monster; force it to exhaust its fuel and burn itself out. It sounded simple enough, but JL had often thought that the process of containment, particularly in mountainous terrain and with swirling wind currents, was a great deal like trying to pin down a blob of mercury on a flat surface. You applied pressure, and immediately what you were trying to contain separated into parts that skittered off in new directions. Here, in country too steep for machines, you fought the beast hand to hand, constantly aware that it might at any time outflank you, or leapfrog your position.

The pilot said suddenly, "You ever feel you've got a fire you can't whip?"

"No," JL said, and mentally crossed his fingers at the lie. "You whip them all eventually."

"Tonight," the pilot said, "I'm going to pray for rain."

JL nodded. "We'll take whatever help we can get."

RIGHT after breakfast Stacy went out to the corrals surrounding her big barn. Pancho, her stable hand, immediately appeared, to follow on her rounds. Pancho was fifteen, small and wiry, with strong, horse-sensitive hands. He wanted to be a jockey, and his postage-stamp racing saddle, a present from Stacy, rested proudly on its own rack in the tack room, bright and polished.

"The smoke's not bad yet," she said to him, "and if it doesn't get any worse, we won't have anything to worry about. But I want you to stay out here, Pancho, and if the horses start getting spooked, let me know immediately." She studied the boy. "Big responsibility. Can you handle it?"

"*Sí, señorita, con gusto*—with pleasure."

Stacy smiled, and reached through the corral fence to snap her fingers in summons to Sam, who walked over and presented a velvety nose to be stroked.

"You help keep track of things too, Sam," Stacy said. "If there's any problem, we'll get you all out in plenty of time."

As she walked back toward the big house she reflected that they were all treating what was happening in the forest as something distant, remote, as if it were not real. She wondered if civilian populations looked on war in the same way—until it actually descended upon them and shattered their lives.

She realized that she had been aware for some time of the staccato sounds of a helicopter, and she looked up now as the sounds suddenly increased in volume and the craft swept overhead. Automatically she waved, and saw an answering wave, and a face looking down. Looked like JL, she thought. Funny, but since she'd heard he had come back to take charge, she could feel a definite strengthening of her sense of security.

Soon afterward she heard the explosions, muffled, deep sounds, as of large doors being shut on distant, empty closets. She looked toward the forest, saw the columns of smoke rising and felt her first real intimations of unease.

As JL and Ben Hastings had anticipated, the spaced explosives, lowered by helicopter and detonated by remote control, had blown a rough but open path through the tangle of brush and ground clutter. They had also spread tendrils of fire and smoldering fuel in all directions. The two hotshot crews that attacked the area, one from either side, had their hands full.

Gordy Walker, chief of the closest hotshot crew, inevitably approached a new assignment with extreme caution, thereby causing suppressed snickers among his men, who knew that within minutes old Gordy would be furiously charging their objective. It was suggested that Gordy's mother had been frightened by a burning bush, and that she had passed along to her child a hatred of anything that caught fire.

Now, muttering to himself between commands, he spread his crew around in pairs to douse whatever was already on fire and to widen and clean out the pathway break the explosives had left. "Slow and easy," he told them. "There's still smoke coming out of some of that brush." To an experienced crew like his, totally unnecessary advice.

Terry Young, the crew's free spirit, said, "Yes, *sir!* Will do, sir!"

"Same to you, mister," Gordy said without rancor.

BEN Hastings took a deep breath and approached the table that was serving as JL's desk. "Yes, Ben?" JL said.

"We've lost our north fire line."

JL leaned back in his chair. He forced his face to remain calm. The one sector he had considered secure, he thought, was now just one more danger point, with no further barriers like the highway to contain the monster. "The fire jumped the road?"

Ben shook his head. "Not exactly. A trucker apparently panicked, had an accident and spread a tanker loaded with gasoline across the highway. It blew up, of course."

JL blinked, but that was all. A freak accident, happens one time in a million, maybe. No matter. It was done. "And the trucker?"

"They may find pieces of him, and they may not."

Still JL showed no emotion. Slowly he nodded. "All right, Ben. Get dug in on a new line as best you can." Dismissal.

Ben opened his mouth and then closed it again. In silence he turned away. The man was not human, he thought, totally without feelings. Unbelievable.

JL picked up the latest situation report in front of him, and found that he could not concentrate. How many more dead would there be? he wondered, and then he told himself, We're at war, and in a war there are casualties. It was scant comfort.

There was a new sense of urgency at the 1630 briefing. Phil Sommers, plans chief, spoke somberly of the fire's progress during the previous twelve hours, and neither the meteorologist nor the fire behavior officer could add any word of cheer.

"And it's not going to get any easier," JL said, addressing the group. "No rain in the forecasts, probable wind, the usual afternoon thunderstorms with dry lightning." His manner, he knew, appeared almost unconcerned. But would it have helped to present a face of gloom? "All right, let's get on with it." As he turned away he beckoned Ben Hastings and Jay Paul.

The two men followed him in silence back to his desk. "Ben and I are going for a little jeep ride," JL told Jay. "You take over here. We'll be in touch on the radio."

Ben drove; JL, map and clipboard on his lap, hung on with his free hand. "More than twenty thousand acres so far," JL said. Despite himself, a little of his worry sounded in his tone. "If we get strong winds out of the east . . ." He shook his head.

"There's a lot of forest west of here," Ben said, nodding. "It could burn all the way across Arizona if it really got out of hand. Do we want more line troops?"

"Think it would help?" JL, the teacher, was making the pupil think for himself.

Ben's answer came slowly. "Not really. Not now."

"Neither do I." There was approbation in JL's voice. "Turn here. Uphill. Let's have a good look at this sector."

They were approaching the lower slopes of Sierra Grande now. Bessie Wingate, leading her crew down the trail, stopped at JL's signal and walked over to the jeep.

"How's it look?" JL said.

Bessie was dirty and tired and unwilling to make small talk. "Stinks," she said. "That thing has pushed us halfway up the mountain, whipping us every foot of the way. I told Jim McColl—his crew relieved us—that as far as I can see, we've lost this whole sector and we might as well admit it and cut our losses." Beneath her yellow hard hat the belligerence on her face was plain. "And just what do you think of that?"

JL listened, his face expressionless. He knew such anger would be gnawing at the innards of every man in the crew; fire becomes a personal enemy, capable of arousing sheer hatred.

"Another two hundred yards, maybe," Bessie went on, "and it'll run out of fuel anyway. Timberline. We're wasting manpower fighting for that last little bit."

JL agreed. "Send one of your men back up to tell McColl to let that sector go and pull his crew over to protect against the fire fishhooking into fresh timber when the downslope breeze begins near sundown."

"I," Bessie said, "will be thoroughly skinned. Whoever heard of anybody listening to the poor slobs on the fire line?"

"And you," JL said, "catch some food and some rest."

"Aw . . ." Bessie said. "We could go on all night, if we had to."

JL smiled. "We'll need you tomorrow. Let's head down, Ben."

Ben drove in silence for a time, his face thoughtful. "Sacrificing a little timber for morale, is that it?"

"A good trade-off," JL said. "And her idea does have merit." He pointed in the direction of the estates. "Let's see what the situation is over by Vista Hill. I want to reassure Mrs. Wayne."

A short time later they were out of the forest, driving along the county road. As they pulled into the Wayne estate they saw two gardeners hard at work. They watched the jeep curiously, saw JL

177

and waved. JL waved back. "Right up to the big house," he said.

As he drove Ben thought, On the lines were hundreds of men—and a few women—in a battle against the destroyer, fire. And here he and JL were, the top command in this war, driving up to a big house to speak with an old lady. Unreal.

"It's her forest too," JL said, as if he had been reading Ben's thoughts.

Mrs. Wayne came to greet them as they got out of the jeep. "How thoughtful of you to stop by, Mr. Harmon," she said, "just to reassure me, I know. Tea? Sherry?"

"Thank you, no, ma'am, I'm afraid we're a little pressed for time," JL said as he and Ben sat down in the chairs offered.

"I quite understand. And I do want to say how much safer I feel now that you are back from—was it Idaho?" Her manner was thoughtful. "Tell me, Mr. Harmon, is this fire the result of what I believe you call prescribed burning? I recall my husband once had occasion to take that up with the Secretary of Agriculture."

"No, ma'am," JL said. "Prescribed burning had nothing to do with this fire." He was his usual calm, pleasant self, and yet Ben could sense now a new feeling of urgency. "As a matter of fact, ma'am," JL said, "if we had been allowed prescribed burning, this fire might well not have become what it has."

Mrs. Wayne thought about it. "I'm afraid I don't understand."

JL explained about the fuel that accumulated on the ground in the forest, and about the uncontrolled second growth they had had to open with explosives, all of it contributing to the threat of a large conflagration if and when, as had happened, dry lightning struck or someone was careless with a campfire. With prescribed burning, that dangerous ground clutter would have been taken out long before any threat of fire was imminent. But the Forest Service had repeatedly been forbidden to conduct prescribed burning in the Sanrio forest. Too many citizens like Senator Tyler Wayne were frightened by it.

Mrs. Wayne remained thoughtful, and when JL was done she said, "I see. I was not aware of all the ramifications, Mr. Harmon, and I thank you for informing me."

JL stood up. Ben rose with him. "We just wanted to make sure that everything was all right here, ma'am," JL said guilelessly.

"And I do appreciate it," Mrs. Wayne said.

Back in the jeep, going down the long drive, Ben said, "You were making a pitch. Will it do any good?"

"If George Jefferson's right," JL said, "she can pick up the phone and call a couple or three Senators, and they'll listen."

"And maybe, just maybe," Ben said, "we'll be allowed to care for this forest the way it ought to be cared for."

"Worth a try," JL said. And he added, "Who's this?"

A large station wagon was pulling alongside them on the county road, the driver obviously wanting to talk. "Humor him," JL said.

Ben pulled over and stopped, and they waited while the driver climbed importantly from the station wagon and approached them.

"I am Willard P. Spencer," the man said. "You are approaching my property."

JL smiled noncommittally.

"I wish to have a crew of your men," Spencer said, "patrolling the perimeter of my land to see to it that this inexcusable fire does not damage my property. I have been in touch with your regional office in Albuquerque, and they assure me that everything possible will be done to protect my holdings."

"It most certainly will, Mr. Spencer," JL said.

Ben sat quiet, expressionless.

"And now if you will excuse us," JL added, "we'll get on with seeing that it's done." He waved as they drove away.

They rode for a little time in silence. "Good Lord," Ben said. "Is he real?"

"Not only real," JL said, "but there are lots more like him."

As they rounded a curve JL pointed ahead. "Stop here," he said, and wondered at the sense of urgency he felt.

Stacy, in her customary jeans and boots, was standing beside the Cummings mailbox, a bundle of mail in her hands. "I heard you were back," she said, and added without embarrassment, "I felt better knowing that you were in charge."

JL tried and failed to think of a reply. He was conscious that Ben was watching him closely.

Stacy glanced toward the forest. "Am I shying at shadows, or is it worse?"

"I'm afraid it's worse. But still not to worry."

"My horses."

"I've thought of that."

"We'll cope." She studied his face with a strange intensity, and it was as if Ben were not even there. "And after it's all done," she said, "you can come over one night and tell me about it."

"I'd like that."

Stacy said then, as if suddenly embarrassed, "Clouds over there." She pointed her finger. "Rain?"

JL shook his head. "Unhappily, no."

"So," she said, "all you can do is hope."

JL's faint smile appeared. "That's about the size of it. We have a lot of practice at hoping. Ben, let's get back to work."

"Luck," Stacy said, and watched them drive off.

In the jeep the radio came alive with Jay Paul's voice from the command post, saying, "Come in, JL. Come in." There were undertones of hysteria behind the words.

JL picked up the microphone and spoke his name. "Over."

"We've got a new breakout," Jay Paul said. "Beyond highway fourteen. Isolated. It's either spontaneous or incendiary. And Los Ojos prison reports two convicts missing." The words were coming faster and faster. "Maybe they're responsible. Maybe they—"

"Slow down," JL said, breaking in. "You're racing your motor. Have the convicts been spotted? Over."

"Negative."

"Then they could be anywhere. Have you sent an attack crew into the new area?"

"Not yet. I wanted to—"

"Then send one in. Now. And forget the convicts under the bed. Over and out." JL hung the mike on its dashboard hook and leaned back in his seat. "You heard," he said to Ben. "Do you think we have an arsonist at work?"

"Not likely. I don't have too much faith in statistics, but very few fires in the West are incendiary." JL knew the facts as well as he did, Ben was thinking, but JL didn't ask questions without reasons. Suddenly Ben's voice altered. "Oh," he said. "I see what you mean. Jay comes from the southern piney woods, and there they have up to fifty-five percent incendiary fires."

"And habit dies hard," JL said. A bright boy, Ben, he thought.

The other man shook his head slowly. The sky was darkened by smoke, the taste of conflagration was in the air, and JL could go from detail to detail and yet still keep the big picture in mind. "You don't miss much, do you?" Ben said. There was admiration behind his words. After a moment he added, "Why don't I drop you off at your house? Jay and I can take the night shift and you can catch some sleep. Anything urgent comes up, we'll phone."

JL thought about it. "How do you and Jay get along?"

"Well enough."

"Who's your relief man?"

"Jerry Weinstock."

JL knew him. He was reliable. "Turn your line boss duties over to him," JL said, "and you hold Jay's hand. I don't want to replace him unless I have to." It was a ticklish situation he was creating, he knew, because Jay was technically Ben's superior. On the other hand, in merely this one day, JL had learned who was the better man. He glanced at Ben. "Any argument between you and Jay on something you think can't wait," JL said, "I want you to call me pronto."

"Will do."

But sleep did not come easily for JL that night, which was unusual, because he had trained himself to sleep just about anywhere anytime. He could not shake the memory of Stacy Cummings saying that she felt better because he was in charge, nor the warmth in her voice when she said that after it was all done they would talk. He tried not to read meaning into her words, and instead found all manner of ridiculous possibilities running around in his mind.

He also tried not to think that if George Jefferson had allowed him to handle the fire from the start, the crews on the line would now be simply cold-trailing—patrolling the perimeter to make sure that nothing started up again out of the near-dead ashes—instead of still fighting step by step in the sharp, acrid, choking smoke, facing terrifying nighttime flames.

On the mountain, near the timberline, the evening breeze coming off the snow probed the trees and set aspen leaves to whispering. It was cold.

"So now we stuck up here on this mountain," Felipe Vigil said. "How long we stay here?"

Frank Orwell resented the implication that it was all his fault.

"You saw the fuzz when we tried to go down. State fuzz too. Not just local yokels."

"So now they know we here."

"Not necessarily. If we stay out of sight, they may think we got off the mountain ahead of them and are halfway to Arizona."

"Yeah, and we freeze tonight for sure. How about a fire?"

"No way. Those fire-fighting crews maybe could care less whether or not we're up here, but they spot a fire and they'll be up here fast to put it out. Then what do we do?"

"You big-shot Anglo brain, you tell me."

"Walk, and try to stay warm. Think about the Anglo chick." Orwell smiled. "Matter of fact, I could do some of that myself."

Les Lawry was more exasperated than usual. He and his family had been tramping through the forest for hours, darting for cover each time they heard the whine of the searching helicopters. No one was going to put Les Lawry in the slammer if he could help it.

"Come on, Cindy Lou," he said. "Why can't you watch where you're going? I look around and there you are, either on your face—"

"Mom's hurt her ankle, Pop," Tad said. He dropped the branch he was using as a walking staff and knelt beside his mother in the moonlight, trying to remember his first aid.

"Damn it!" Les said. "Can you walk, Cindy Lou? Tell me that. Can you walk?"

"I think we're going to need help, Pop," Tad said. "I don't think she'd better even try to walk."

"Well, she can't just sit here!"

"I'm sorry, Les," Cindy Lou said. "I didn't mean to twist it."

"Okay, okay. Let me think." Les looked at the boy. "You're the Boy Scout. You got any ideas?"

Tad had been thinking about their situation for a long time. He said now in a hesitant voice, "I think we're safe enough here."

"What makes you think that? Speak up, boy. How come out here in the middle of a forest fire we're all of a sudden safe?"

Tad looked around at the blackened desolation. "It's all burned over. There's nothing left to catch fire."

"He's right, Les," Cindy Lou said.

Les too looked around. "Okay, maybe we're better off here than I thought." Grudging admission. "What now?"

"Maybe we'd better just stay here," Tad said, "until it gets light."

"Then what?"

"We can lay out a signal for a helicopter to see."

"Oh, Les!" Cindy Lou said. "Then they can help us."

"Yeah." Les thought about it. "But they'll want to know about the jeep." His face brightened suddenly. "Got it! We'll say we were trying to get away from the fire, and that's why we drove in here. To save our necks. How about that? True, isn't it?"

Tad looked at his mother. Cindy Lou looked at the ground. Neither spoke.

"Okay," Les said, in command once more. "Now Tad, you see about getting a nice level place and sweep it clean of ashes. Use a branch. A tidy camp, that's what we want. And we'll just stay here until morning. That's the way I see it."

"I'M NOT being logical," Elsie Edwards said. "I know that. And I'm not being brave, either. I'm being just what I've always hated—stupidly, helplessly female."

"You're doing fine," Don said. "Just fine." Words were so painfully inadequate, he thought. He tried to smile.

"How's your poor head?" Elsie asked. Her voice was calmer now.

"Better. Really. I can focus now." Almost true. The terrible throbbing had subsided to a constant, lesser ache, and his mind felt clearer. He tried to sound calm, competently objective. "We're very close to timberline," he said. "Above it, we're safe from fire, but not from those—rapists." It was difficult to say the word aloud.

Elsie sat silent, for the moment unable to speak.

"The problem is," Don continued, "the only place we can be completely safe is below the fire. And"—he attempted a lighter touch, accompanied by a wry smile—"the trouble is that I don't see quite how we're going to get there from here."

Elsie took a deep breath. Her eyes searched Don's face. "We can't go up or down. That's what you're saying, isn't it?"

Don said slowly, "Pretty much."

"We can't go up," Elsie said, "because you're thinking of me. So am I. But I'm thinking of you too. They'll do again what they did to me. But they'll kill you. They're that kind of animal. One of them almost used his knife on you before. This time they'd do it."

Don closed his eyes briefly. "The evening breeze blows downhill," he said. "That's how it happens in these mountains. It may hold the fire, at least temporarily. And there's a moon. We can move farther on around the mountain, just below the timberline, as we are here."

"But how far? There's that lake you've told me about. And the cliff above it. We'll have to go up when we reach that."

Don nodded in silence.

Elsie tilted her head toward the fringe of trees and the open mountainside above them. "What will *they* be doing?"

"Probably the same thing."

"So we'll meet?"

"We'll try not to." Don shook his head angrily. "That's the best I can give you at the moment, baby."

AARON Swift was having another bad night, lying awake in the darkness. At last Debby turned to him and said, "You're worried, A. I've been watching. Is it the fire?"

"Imagination," Aaron said. "Yours."

"No." Debby's voice was definite. "Yesterday you said that funny thing about bringing your fiddle and watching Rome burn. You were talking about that emperor with the funny name, weren't you? The Roman one?"

Aaron was silent, vaguely shamed. He had no business teasing her with references she would only partly comprehend. She deserved better than that.

"And you haven't been sleeping," Debby said. "I've been listening, and I know. I can always tell."

Aaron said gently, "That means you've been awake too. Why?"

"I don't like the smoke. And I'm worried about you."

Aaron thought of the absurdity of himself, a middle-aged man, trying to cope with a young woman's unease and having not the faintest idea how to go about it. He said, "At least you have reasons. I don't."

"Honest? There isn't anything bothering you? Anything I've done? Or maybe haven't done?"

"Nothing. I'm just being difficult, honey. Forgive me."

"It's all right, A. Honest. You know I love you. And I depend on you too. That sounds funny, doesn't it, but it's so."

There was a new note in Debby's voice now, an urgency arising from Aaron knew not what source. And the words she spoke were strange and puzzling too.

"You've been . . . funny lately. Not, you know, funny ha-ha, but funny different."

"How? In what way?"

"I don't know. I'm not a big brain, A. You know that already. I . . . feel things even when I don't understand them."

True enough; her almost extrasensory perception was sometimes startling. "I know," he said. Smiling in the darkness, he added, "In other times, you might have been burned as a witch."

Debby giggled. "You say the funniest things. I don't always understand them, A, but I can tell when you're laughing at me. Like now." She snuggled warmly against him. "Thank you for talking to me."

"I didn't say anything."

"Yes, you did. You said a lot. Good night, A."

In no time at all she was asleep, curled as always in her kitten position, her breathing deep, untroubled. It was almost dawn before Aaron himself found sleep.

Chapter Seven

BACKSLOPE made the local TV7 news early that Wednesday morning, with spectacular air shots taken from the TV chopper and caustic commentary from the station's ace newsman, Carter Norris. "TV Seven has attempted to contact JL Harmon, Forest Service fire management officer," Norris' solemn voice said, "but all efforts have failed. And the fire is no closer to being controlled now than it was at this time yesterday. Sanrio residents are beginning to wonder if the town itself is in danger."

By this time, JL was back at the command post. And within minutes of the telecast George Jefferson was on the phone.

"Is it?" Jefferson asked.

JL, with the reports from the 0430 briefing in the forefront of his mind, said, "Is it what?"

"TV Seven is beginning to wonder if the town is in danger."

"Carter Norris reporting?"

"He has a big following, JL. Folks believe him."

"They believed Chicken Little too. The town is not in danger unless . . ." He left it hanging.

"Unless." Jefferson said the word musingly, fully understanding its implications. He said, "Unexpected, violent wind shift?"

"That could make things difficult."

"What's your weather forecast?"

"More of the same. No precipitation in sight."

"Injuries?"

"It's all in the status reports, George."

"I've read them. Between the lines too. Do you want to replace Jay Paul? If you do, go ahead. I made a mistake. I admit it."

"I'm keeping him on a tether. He may be all right yet."

There was a silence. Jefferson said at last, "I'm getting pressure, JL. All the way from the governor in Santa Fe."

"Do you want to replace *me*, George? Ben Hastings is a good man."

"I won't even answer that. How's your ankle?"

"And I won't answer that, George. That all?"

JL hung up and leaned back in his chair to look up at Andy McIlvain, the smoke jumper foreman. "You've got a beef?"

"I've got thirteen men, counting myself, unassigned for today."

"I need you on standby."

"Come on. You know what it's like sitting around. Maybe we could—"

"I don't know where I'll need you," JL said, "or what I'll want you to do. But I want you in reserve, available. So go on back to the field and toss more cards into a helmet. But be ready to suit up in a hurry."

Andy let his breath out in a sigh. "George Jefferson would pass out if he knew how you run a fire, part by the book, part by the seat of your pants." He shook his head in slow wonderment.

As Andy left in his jeep, daylight scarcely begun, Stacy Cummings came up, riding her big gelding as if she and the horse were one. She stepped down from the saddle, leaving the reins dangling, and came over to the table where JL sat. She was unsmiling. "Don't get up. I'll sit for a moment." She pulled up a camp chair and sank into it, obviously ill at ease.

"I'm sorry to bother you." She hesitated. "But some things . . ."

"I'm glad you came."

There was silence between them. Stacy broke it. "I heard that pompous fool on TV," she said. "I wouldn't talk to him, either."

"But you, like everyone else, want to know how it's going." JL nodded. "I don't blame you. Well, here's the picture: We've taken a licking so far. It was bad yesterday, and we lost more ground during the night."

"And you don't like to lose," Stacy said. "Neither do I." She paused again. "Any help from the weather?"

"None. If anything . . ."

"Wind change?" Stacy caught the look of surprise that crossed his face. "I've been thinking too," Stacy said. "Best case, worst case. You know."

JL regarded her seriously. "You do look at things, don't you? Yes, we may have a sudden, strong wind change."

"How bad is that?"

"Depends what we can do between now and then. If the fire crowns—that is, if it rises into the tops of the big trees and begins spreading from treetop to treetop, above the reach of fire fighters on the ground, we'll be totally at the mercy of the wind."

"You're thinking about my side, aren't you?" Stacy said. "Mine and Bart Jones', Willard Spencer's, Sophie Swift's, Bellevue Acres, Vista Hill—and the town beyond?"

"I'm afraid I am."

"You're moving some men into that side," Stacy said. "I rode through and saw." She stood up. "Thank you. I admire honesty."

"I'll see that you have warning," JL said. "If it's necessary."

"Thank you for that too." She got up, walked to her horse and swung lightly into the saddle. She faced JL again. "That date we have"—she smiled briefly—"to talk things over when all this is done." She hesitated. "As far as I'm concerned, it's still on."

"I'm looking forward to it," JL said, and he smiled openly.

Mrs. Tyler Wayne left Hilario and Manuel working carefully in what she thought of as her English garden—primroses, foxgloves, Canterbury bells—and went back up to the house to rest.

Even without air-conditioning, which Mrs. Wayne disliked, it was cool inside. The broad porch overhang shielded the house from the high sun in summer, and the thick whitewashed adobe walls kept the inside temperature at a pleasant level day or night. In addition, Vista Hill enjoyed a cooling breeze even on days when the air down in town was still.

A maid brought Mrs. Wayne a glass of iced tea, which she sat sipping quietly. Sierra Grande, its remaining snow patch coming into view and then disappearing as smoke clouds swirled, dominated the middle foreground. Mrs. Wayne had always thought of the great mountain as guardian of the valley, and as such it held both her attention and her respect. Once, in her younger days, she and Tyler had climbed the mountain and eaten a picnic lunch just beneath its peak, while they gazed in awe at the broad land laid out before them, the horizons impossibly distant.

In the near foreground now she could clearly see Bellevue Acres with its bustle and its clutter. She had considered attending the city council meeting at which the variance allowing a higher density of homes in the development had been discussed, and had decided against it.

Tyler, she had thought many times since, would have gone, argued forcibly against change, and likely carried the evening. Perhaps she had let him down by not following suit. No matter; it was done now, and if she found the view distasteful, she could always look in another direction.

She glanced up as the maid approached carrying a telephone extension. As she handed the phone to Mrs. Wayne she said, "A Senator Bronson calling from Washington."

Mrs. Wayne was smiling as she raised the phone. "Hello, Will."

"Myra. How good to hear your voice. It's been a long time."

"I'm not one of your constituents, Will." The smile was in her voice now. "You don't need to butter me up, even though I love it. You have something in mind?"

There was hesitation. "You have a fire in the Sanrio forest," the Senator said.

"We do indeed."

"Is it being properly handled? I have had reports, complaints."

"I believe so, Will. I know the young man in charge, and I consider him eminently qualified."

"Bureaucrats become entrenched, Myra. You know that as well as anyone. They become careless, set in their ways. . . ."

"Like politicians, Will. Only some politicians, of course."

The Senator's tone changed. "Are you all right, Myra? I'm worried about you. The reports I have of this fire—"

"No doubt exaggerated, Will."

"Nevertheless," Bronson said, "I am going to call the Secretary and ask for an accounting on your behalf."

Mrs. Wayne was thinking of JL and what he had told her. "You might also tell him, Will, that if it were not for his ban on what I believe is called prescribed burning, I understand that this fire might not have reached its present proportions."

Was there hesitation? "I will mention that," the Senator said.

You do that, Mrs. Wayne thought as she hung up. Looking out at the smoke, she felt a little better.

BESSIE Wingate said to no one in particular, "If you ask me, this thing is determined to burn the mountain clean, right up to timberline. You, Pete, and Stinky, haul yourselves over yonder with that saw and take down that lone pine. It can be a stepping-stone if the wind carries a burning branch to it."

Bessie and her crew were back on the fire line on the upper slopes of Sierra Grande, after a fitful night camped out at forest headquarters.

Through the trees above which they were cutting their fire-break, a perpetual glow marked the approaching flames, with an occasional bright burst as a pitch-filled piñon went up like a torch. The sounds of the fire were constant, a roaring, crackling furnace sound, punctuated now and then by the crash of a huge tree collapsing.

The heat reached them too, carrying with it the smoke fumes that could be, as Bessie knew, all too lethal; carbon monoxide concentration in wildland fires could rise to more than eight hundred parts per million, more than enough to cause death. Taking a brief glance downhill toward the fire front, Bessie saw two figures dodging among the trees on a course parallel to, rather than away from, the flames. Her first thought was that some fire fighters had lost their marbles and, in panic, their sense of direction as well. She raised her voice in a great shout.

"Come out of there, you fools! You're too close to the front! Head uphill! Uphill!"

The running figures disappeared, and Bessie, leaning briefly on her shovel to wipe the sweat from her forehead with one dirty shirt sleeve, said, "Well, I'll be. Now who in tarnation would be wandering around down there with a fire front coming uphill at them like a mad bull in a field?"

ELSIE and Don Edwards never heard the sound of Bessie's voice; it was drowned out by the roar of the fire, and so they ran on, as close to the approaching fire line as they dared.

At this elevation, somewhere around nine thousand feet, the air seemed to contain less oxygen than smoke, and their breath came in great gasps. To Don, whose head had become again one huge aching throb, running at all was sheer torture.

For Elsie, the feeling was that of being on a treadmill in a nightmare. I'm going mad, she thought. One moment they were alone in their own tiny place in the forest. The next, the world was turned upside down.

She was aware that Don was stumbling now, close to the limit of his endurance. She was suddenly aware too that the faintly cooling breeze on her cheeks had shifted direction and was coming now from above them on the mountain, and that the flames below them were farther away than they had been.

Elsie caught Don's arm and slowed him down to a walk. "I think," she said through gasping breath, "that we're—safe. For now. Sit down. Rest." And when he had sunk to the ground like a doll unhinged, she knelt beside him and touched his cheek with great gentleness. "Poor baby," she said. "Rest. I'll—have a look."

Don sat where he was, his arms on his bent knees and his head bowed over them. He no longer had any idea where they were, or any clear picture of what had happened during the past few hours. He seemed to remember that at one point Elsie had whispered urgently, "There they are again! They're still here!" But his head throbbed so violently now that he could not be sure what was real and what mere fantasy.

Sitting unmoving, eyes closed, he tried to remember at least the contours of the mountain he had studied so carefully on the topographical map. The way they must have come, with the body of the fire on their left and below them, they were traveling clockwise around the mountain's mass. So far, so good.

They had not yet come to the cliff he remembered from the map. It had appeared to hang over a mountain lake, the edge of the cliff not far below timberline. It was possible, he thought, that the fire might have been thwarted by that cliff area, and that beyond it he and Elsie might be able to descend to safety.

Elsie was suddenly back. She was breathless again, but her expression had lost some of its tenseness. "Nothing," she said, and in the single word there was triumph. "When you're ready, we can go on." She dropped to her knees beside him. "Oh, darling, I think—"

"Well, well, well," Frank Orwell's voice, "will you look who we've got here?"

He and Felipe Vigil stepped out of the shadows. Each man held a knife. Orwell gestured menacingly with his. "If you're thinking of getting up," he said to Elsie, "just do it slow and easy. And you, buster, just stay right where you are."

Elsie put her hand on Don's shoulder. "Don't," she said. "Whatever you're thinking, don't. You . . . can't."

"You think good," Felipe said. "Real good."

Elsie took a deep breath. "What do you want?"

"Why, honey, we liked the sample." This was Orwell. "We been talking about it. You'd be real pleased if you knew."

Elsie was silent, motionless, still kneeling beside Don. She looked from man to man, studying the faces. There was, she thought, no pity, none. Her mind felt strangely analytical.

"Stand up," Orwell said.

Don said, "No. No, damn it! What kind of animals are you?"

"Hush," Elsie said. "Please hush, darling." She rose from her knees and straightened herself.

"Now move away," Orwell said, and watched Elsie obey.

"Run!" Don said.

"Better not." Orwell again. He had moved quickly and now dropped to one knee, pressing the point of his knife against the side of Don's neck. "Unless you want to see his throat cut."

Elsie closed her eyes briefly. She opened them again. "Please, darling. Don't do anything. No matter what. He'll do it."

"She catches on good," Orwell said. He made a small gesture with his free hand. "Okay," he said to Felipe, "she's all yours."

Felipe held his knife with practiced ease. He gestured with its

glittering blade. "You hear the man, chick? Is good. The shirt— take her off."

Don said, "Don't—" He stopped as Orwell's knife point broke the skin and a thin trickle of blood rolled down his neck.

"Please, darling! Please!" Elsie's voice came out almost in a scream as she started to pull the shirt from her trousers.

To the two men she said, "Just leave him alone. Please. I'll do what you say."

"You bet your sweet life you will," Orwell said. "Now, get those clothes off or—"

The sound was a blend of roar and scream, high-pitched, hoarse, filled with fury and entirely terrifying. Bessie Wingate, enormous and overpoweringly visible in yellow hard hat and grimy yellow shirt, her shovel clutched in one hand, burst out of the forest shadows on a dead run. "You bastards!" Her voice echoed through the trees. She headed toward Felipe.

Felipe was agile. He sprang back from Elsie, and the knife in his hand seemed alive as it flashed in the air. "*Qué vaya*, fat one! Beat it before I cut your gizzard out!"

Bessie did not hesitate. She swung her shovel with the full

strength of both brawny arms in a broad arc, edge forward. It nearly severed the arm Felipe flung up to protect himself, and—continuing almost unchecked—slammed into his side.

The knife fell unnoticed to the ground as Felipe staggered no more than two paces backward and collapsed.

Bessie faced Orwell, who had risen to his feet. "Now you, you little—" She advanced, the shovel held at the ready.

Orwell turned and ran.

Chapter Eight

BY EARLY afternoon, the party around Ada Loving's swimming pool was in full swing. Ada herself, tanned to smooth flawlessness, wore a stunning white bikini. Of the twenty guests at the party, all but one had been imported from Hollywood. The lone exception was a man named Leon Sturgis, who wore carefully faded jeans, ostrich-skin cowboy boots and a short-sleeved Sulka shirt.

"Tax shelter with cash flow is the name of the game," he told a group around the portable bar, "and if you can have it, and enjoy yourself in a place like Sanrio, why, that's a license to steal."

"Smog for smoke," one of the imports said. "I'm not sure you gain much. They both make you sneeze."

"Smoke's temporary," Sturgis said. "There's the difference."

Ada, despite her costume, was not insensitive to the anomaly of her poolside party-as-usual while the countryside burned. On the other hand, the charter flight and rented limousines to carry guests from the airport had been all arranged, and last-minute cancellations were bad public relations, so the decision had been made to carry on as planned. Profits from the sale of $250,000-and-up condos yet to be constructed were not to be taken lightly.

Ada had often wondered who really controlled the purse strings and made the decisions; not that it mattered as long as she was paid as agreed, and on time.

Sturgis, drink in hand, wandered over from the bar. "They've sent us a pretty dead group," he told Ada in a quiet voice. "What can we do to stir them up? A drive through the forest?"

"You've heard that there is a fire going on?" Ada's voice too was quiet, and her smile did not fade.

"Sure. We'll show it to them firsthand."

"Include me out," Ada said. "Folks here are taking it seriously. So am I."

Then Ken Delacorte arrived, looking around curiously at the strangers, nodding to Ada and giving Sturgis a cold stare.

Ken had met Ada a few times during his short stint in Hollywood, and since her move to Sanrio he had squired her around on occasion, often enough to suspect that beneath the gorgeous exterior was someone worth knowing. He had never met Sturgis, but he had encountered dozens like him, always on the fringes and on the make; human jackals, in his opinion.

Sturgis made his position clear at once. "You're in real estate too," he said, then indicated with a nod of his head the people around the pool. "But these are our pigeons."

"Pluck them clean for all I care," Ken said. "But I think you"— he spoke now directly to Ada—"would do well to think about where you might go if things get completely out of hand."

"Paul Revere," Sturgis said. "Warning us that the British are coming?"

"Are things going to get out of hand?" Ada said.

"They could. We all hope they won't, but that's a big fire."

"The Forest Service clowns screwing up as usual?" Sturgis said.

"You know," Ken said, "someday somebody is going to pick you up, Sturgis, and set you down so hard you'll find your teeth on the ground. I might even do it myself. Now go play with your Hollywood pigeons."

Ada watched Sturgis walk off, still wearing his easy smile. She said, "You're not usually that belligerent, Ken."

"I don't usually talk to toads like him."

Ada was silent for a few moments. Slowly she turned on the famous Loving smile and gestured toward the bar. "Would you like a drink? It is, after all, my house. On paper, anyway."

Ken looked across the pool area to Sturgis and the other guests. He looked again at Ada and shook his head. "Just don't let too much of them rub off on you," he said. "Wave the body around all you want. That isn't you—just something you happen to have been born with. But hang on to the real part. Keep it the way you'd like it. Do I sound like a preacher man?"

"Strangely enough," Ada said, "you don't. I'll bear it in mind."

JL WAS LEANING FORWARD IN HIS chair, staring glumly at the latest infrared photos with Ben Hastings. "Here, here and here"— JL's pencil moved quickly—"we have open flames, these black areas. We're moving in men to block their spread where we can."

"Slurry drops?" Ben said.

"Slurry drops are fine, but you can't hold a long fire front with them alone."

"That means backfire?"

JL nodded. "I think that's the answer. I've called in a chopper fitted with helitorch equipment capable of setting one along a prescribed line." He reached out and pulled over a map. "A limited backfire right here." He drew a line running southwest to northeast above the area called Sheep Ridge, a long, low rise strategically located just to the north of the town and the line of estates bordering the forest. "I want you behind the helitorch in another chopper, calling the shots. And we'll need a hotshot crew on the scene to keep it contained."

Ben studied the markings on the map and brought to mind the terrain, which was hilly, with thick brush and scattered piñons.

The logic of a backfire here was irrefutable, he thought; by preemptive burning, scorching to the ground the area JL had marked, before the actual danger arrived, they could deny the fire further fuel if it burst at last from the deep forest, and perhaps in that sector at least, stop it in its tracks.

On the other hand, there were always dangers. "If the wind shifts—" Ben began.

"The longer we wait, the more likely a wind shift becomes," JL said. "So get on it. I've got some thinking to do."

He sat quietly at the improvised desk long after Ben had gone. It grieved him that the forest hush was now constantly disturbed by the clamor of men and equipment—jeeps, trucks, ground tankers, bulldozers, and the sudden painful sounds as living trees came crashing to the forest floor.

In each major fire too, situations arose that could not have been foreseen, leaving a residue of what JL could only look upon as personal failure. Early this morning, for example, one of the chopper pilots had seen ground signals in the wilderness—rocks set out in a geometric pattern—and when he hovered to investigate, he saw a man, a woman and a boy waving frantically and motioning for him to land nearby. As machinery is forbidden in the wilderness, the pilot simply radioed a report, and eventually a rescue party was sent in on foot. JL was not told until it was too late to interfere, and the incident left a bad taste. It would, no doubt, be retold as an example of Forest Service insensitivity.

Thoughts of the situation involving Bessie Wingate, the honeymoon couple and the two escaped convicts continued to bother him too, although by no conceivable standards could he or any of his people be considered even vaguely culpable.

"Clear case of self-defense," the state police lieutenant had reported, after talking to all the witnesses. He shook his head slowly. "What kind of a woman is this, anyway? A runaway truck couldn't have done more damage to that guy Felipe."

"She's been on the fire line almost four days now," JL had explained, "and when you've been at it that long, you work up a pretty fair head of steam. You don't fool around anymore."

Felipe was now in intensive care in the hospital. The other convict was still on the loose and was bound to turn up again with his knife; he had to be considered dangerous.

JL shrugged and sat up straight to study the map again. The backfire he had sent Ben to set up was a gamble. That could not be denied. Wind change was coming: the high-pressure ridge that had sat over them these last few days was stirring itself and beginning to move east. But *if* the wind direction held steady for only a little time, the odds in favor of the gamble were high.

It was how these things were done, he thought—little by little and bit by bit, precariously establishing a bastion beyond which the flames could not spread, holding that area securely and at the same time throwing men and equipment into a new sector, there to fight for fresh ground from which to launch new attacks. On a minor fire simultaneous assaults on all fronts were possible. But piecemeal attack was the only way to fight Backslope.

He remembered trying once to explain that to Madge. It had been a waste of time. And here came thoughts of Stacy again, because she would have understood. Suddenly he realized that his image of Madge was fading. The picture of her in his mind, like a dream upon awakening, had lost much of its form and color. She belonged in another world.

So be it.

STACY STRIPPED, BUNDLED UP HER clothes and tossed them into the hamper. Much as she loved horses, she detested folks who always smelled as if they had just come from the stables. She remembered that it had not always been so.

"We have a house," her father had told her one evening long ago, "and we have a horse barn. They aren't the same. When you come to the dinner table, by golly, I won't have you stinking of horse sweat!"

Sometimes, she thought as she headed for the shower, the sound of his voice came back to her so vividly it hurt. And once the memories began, they were difficult to shut off.

She remembered another evening now, much later but also dinnertime. The two of them had sat alone at the big polished table with lighted candles and silver candlesticks. "Why haven't you ever married again?" Stacy had asked.

"I'm too ornery," her father had said, and showed his fond, crooked smile.

"I'm serious."

Her father studied her across the table. "Trying to find a clue to something in yourself, honey?"

"Maybe. I don't know."

"I'm luckier than most," her father said then. "I found one woman, the right one. Darn few do. Darn few like me, that is. I'm a loner, I suppose. I like folks, but I want a little distance between us. There's something of that in you too."

Stacy smiled sheepishly. "I know."

Her father took his time before going on. "Horses aren't a substitute for people, honey," he said gently, "and winning prize saddles isn't the be-all and end-all. Maybe you're beginning to find that out too."

Of course, Stacy thought now, there usually was a connection between remembered conversations and the present. In this instance, the connection was her lawyer and neighbor, Sophie Swift.

On the telephone earlier, Sophie had said, "I wonder if it would be convenient for you to meet me this afternoon, Stacy? Say five thirty. I realize that with this fire—your worry about your horses, I mean—I am troubling you, and I'm sorry. I don't usually impose."

Stacy had never heard Sophie this close to incoherence. "Of course I'll meet you. Where?"

"I thought maybe the lounge of the inn. It's quiet there."

"Fine," Stacy said. "We can talk."

SOPHIE was waiting at a table for two in one corner of the lounge, sitting very straight in the upholstered wing chair. She could not remember when she had felt like this—so helpless and indecisive. Nor until now had she realized how alone she was in this wide world. Her invitation to Stacy was a cry for help.

Looking up, making herself smile, she said, "Thank you for coming" as Stacy approached.

"It's good to see you. Even as neighbors we don't—"

"And thank you for not asking if anything is wrong. Of course it is. You already understand that."

The waiter arrived. Stacy ordered a glass of white wine. The interruption was welcome. "You and Aaron?" she asked.

"Of course."

"I'm not very good at these things, Soph, not very good at all."

The other woman sighed. "I'm supposed to be good at it," she said. "Lawyers are very good at telling clients what to do, how to run their lives. Now it's a case of *Physician, heal thyself.* And I don't know how to cope."

Through the large windows across the lounge the mountain rose grandly, shrouded in smoke. Stacy stared at it. "When things get out of hand," she said, "they seem to do it all at once, don't they?" She looked again at Sophie. "I wish I had wise advice, Soph, I really do. But I don't."

"I like Debby," Sophie said. "She's good for Aaron."

"You are generous."

A faint smile appeared and was quickly gone. "The fact is that I hate her too. Isn't that an ignoble confession?"

"I didn't even hear it," Stacy said.

It was as if she had not spoken. Sophie's thoughts would run their course unhindered, as if words too long forcibly contained had finally burst free.

"You take for granted what you have," she said, "until one day you lose it. That is trite but true. I have seen it with clients to whom the prospect of losing liberty exists merely as an abstraction until the verdict is handed down and they are led away. Then, all at once, realization takes place, and it is shattering."

It was embarrassing to listen to, Stacy thought, and yet in a strange way she was glad that it was she whom Sophie had chosen for her confidences. Her reactions astonished her too. Instead of detachment or even slight amusement, what she felt was pure compassion for another being in pain. It was a feeling she had previously reserved almost entirely for horses.

"I think another glass of wine, Soph," Stacy said when at last the spate of words slowed. "And then why don't we have dinner here? I've heard that the food is good."

DROPPING fire from the sky is always a risky business, Ben Hastings thought as he surveyed the forest below from his seat in the helicopter. Too many variables. A hundred and fifty yards ahead flew the helicopter-helitorch that would drop flaming gelled gasoline on Sheep Ridge, the scene of the backfire that JL had planned. Ben wore a headset and mike attachment, leaving both hands free.

He spoke into the mike now. "You're right on course," he said to the leading helicopter. "Start your fire on the far side of that next low ridge, and hold it steady as you go. Do you read me? Over."

"Roger. Over."

"The backfire line we want is a little more than a quarter of a mile long," Ben added, "terminating well before the heavy tree growth begins. I'll give you ample warning."

"Roger. A piece of cake. Over."

I hope so, Ben thought.

When they were able to look over the low ridge ahead, Ben saw the hotshot crew standing on the ground ready as ordered— spaced along the line of fire and well below it for safety's sake. Gordy Walker was in charge of the crew, which was something of a comfort, because if anything were to go wrong, Gordy would see that his men busted a puckering string to cope.

And then the first stream of flame dropped from the flexible hose that trailed beneath the helitorch, and Ben watched the hanging fire reach the ground. Instantly a clump of brush was ablaze. As the line of flaming gelled gasoline moved on, the men on the ground moved closer to the fire line to attack scattered flames that had been started downslope.

So far, so good, Ben thought, and resisted the impulse to cross his fingers. Into the mike he said, "You're bang on target."

JL's chosen front for the backfire was strategic: far enough downslope from the heavy stands of big trees that windblown sparks would not easily reach them, yet far enough above the large private holdings that they too would be well protected.

As the helitorch approached the end of the backfire line, Ben spoke again into his mike. "On the rise of that next ridge," he said, "cut off your fire. We want to give the ground troops plenty of room to get around the end and keep it from spreading into those big trees."

"The rise of the next ridge—will do."

Ben let out his breath in a long sigh. He had not realized how tense he had been. Watching the helitorch approach the rise, he whispered to himself, "Okay, cut it off, and we can go home."

But the string of fire continued, and through Ben's headset the pilot's voice came clearly, "Shut off, damn you. Shut off!"

"You're too far!" Ben said into the mike in sudden alarm.

"I know it! The valve's stuck! It should—"

"Then turn back! Stay away from those big trees!"

The helicopter was now right on the edge of the big trees, at an elevation of perhaps forty feet, and trying to turn back, but it was losing altitude at an alarming rate.

"Pick up!" This was the helitorch pilot's voice coming loud and clear in Ben's headset. "Up, up, up, damn—" The words were his last. Suddenly where the helitorch had been there was only a ball of fire, rising incredibly.

The blast of rushing air rocked Ben's own chopper. Three of the big trees instantly burst into flame. More followed. On the ground, Gordy Walker led his hotshot crew at a dead run toward the inferno.

Ben's pilot took their chopper up and, banking, headed away from the scene. "We can't do anything here," he said.

Speechless, Ben nodded in agreement and closed his eyes.

IT WAS still light, and the sun low in the western sky had turned a copper color by the time Stacy drove home from the inn. Along the way she paused on the county road to stare at what seemed to be a new area of fire—in the base of the stand of big trees that extended down toward the town and the large property holdings.

It was while she sat there studying the heavy smoke that the green Forest Service pickup came slowly by. She waved, and the truck stopped. JL was behind the wheel. "Yes, it's a new outbreak," he said. "Something we could have done without."

He was bone tired; that was Stacy's first judgment. There were deep lines around his eyes, and his shoulders did not seem quite as erect as usual. "Are you off duty?" she asked.

"For a while. I was having a look around here on my way home."

"Come with me," Stacy said, "and I'll give you a drink."

They sat in Stacy's living room at opposite ends of the big leather sofa. JL sipped his drink gratefully. "What happened?" she said, and listened quietly to the tale of the abortive backfire.

"The pilot's shutoff valve stuck, he fussed with it and flew too close to a stand of big trees," he said in summation. "We swung and we missed, and killed a man in the process."

"And you blame yourself?"

JL shook his head. "Blame," he said, "is for hearings and investigations. What I have is the responsibility. I'm the fire boss, and it happened on my fire."

"Do you resent that?" Stacy asked curiously.

JL thought about it. "Not exactly resent. I'd rather just answer for my own performance. But somebody has to run the show"—a small, self-deprecating smile appeared—"and I seem to be out there leading the parade and making the decisions."

"But you'd really rather be alone?"

"Yes," he answered truthfully.

The beeper on JL's belt gave out its sudden shrill signal. He silenced it as he stood up. "I'll use your phone, if I may."

Stacy waved him toward the office-library. Another loner, she thought, watching him go. Like her father, like herself.

"There's more to JL," Ken Delacorte had once told her, "than you may think on first meeting."

"You know him well?" Stacy had asked.

"I don't think anybody does. I've hunted and fished with him, played poker with him—I've even seen his paintings, but I don't know him well."

It was the first Stacy had heard of JL's painting, and she asked Ken more about it. "Watercolors? That kind of thing?"

"Not on your life. Oils. Big canvases. I'm no connoisseur, but I've wandered through a gallery or two and I've seen a heck of a lot of forest scenes hanging in them that didn't give me half the jolt in the belly that one or two of his do."

"Does he exhibit?"

"Nope. Fighting fires is his bag. Madge—that was his wife— didn't like his painting *or* his fire fighting. So she left."

It was the first Stacy had heard of Madge.

JL came back from the office-library. "I'm afraid I have to get back. We've been expecting a front and it's moving in."

"Fronts," Stacy said, "sometimes bring rain."

"This one won't. It's warm, dry air, wrung out by passing over the Arizona high country. No moisture left. Just wind and pressure change." He finished his drink. "I am grateful for the little time of relaxation. And the drink."

"*De nada.*"

JL shook his head in slow wonder. "Funny," he said. "We used to strike sparks, you and I. We don't seem to anymore."

"I've noticed that too."

"I wonder why."

"Maybe it's just that the fire's more important."

The slow smile appeared. "Maybe that's it."

IN THE tower of the Forest Service airport, Andy McIlvain had just listened to the latest weather forecast. He pondered it as he went back down the stairs to the main hangar.

The men he had parachuted in over thirty hours ago were back now, having held their sector until danger of fire had swept past. Then, gathering their gear and hoisting it to their shoulders, they had hiked out. They were now repacking their chutes and reloading fire boxes against the certainty of another drop.

Unable to sit still any longer, Andy called to one of his crewmen. "The front's coming," he said. "I've seen the infrared photos, so I have an idea what it'll mean, but I want to see the actual scene. I'll be gone maybe thirty, forty minutes."

He walked out to the field, where his own single-engine aircraft was parked. Once airborne, he felt free and loose and easy, sharing with the ravens and eagles the ability to look down on the world and see its true dimensions.

Dominating the earthbound scene, of course, was the big mountain, still proudly thrusting its rocky peak above the smoke. In one section below timberline, even as he watched, the flames spread inexorably upward, and no fire-fighting crews attempted to stop, or even slow, their progress. JL had obviously written off that fringe of trees as not worth the effort.

Andy flew over the cliff in front of which he and JL had jumped, and noted, as he had expected, that the vegetation-free rocky face had been a natural barrier beyond which the fire could not pass.

He took the aircraft up in a wide, swinging turn until his view was from a position above the mountain's peak, and the full extent of the fire called Backslope was spread beneath him.

The total fire area was roughly elliptical in shape, its major axis extending east–west, its minor axis running almost due north–south. Airborne estimates were mere guesses, but it looked to him as if the fire had grown to cover an area about fifteen miles long and perhaps ten miles deep: a hundred and fifty square miles, or—he did quick mental calculations—in the neighborhood of ninety-six thousand acres!

North of highway 14, where the gasoline tanker had exploded, the fire had established a bulge, against which Andy could see ground crews fighting a desperate holding action. At the moment, the wind was against the crews, driving the open flames farther north.

The southern line of the fire was almost straight, except for an expanding area of flames at the base of a finger of the forest that pointed toward the Bellevue Acres development and the town beyond. Along that southern line, the wind aided the efforts at suppression, although, as Andy could clearly see from his eagle-eye view, the crash of that helitorch had been a near thing indeed, and only immediate action by the hotshot crew on the spot had kept the fire from spreading out of control among the big trees. So far, then, the eastern flank of Sierra Grande was secure; the fire's penetration from its starting point had not proceeded east or northeast beyond the Sheep Ridge area.

But as he began a second, larger circle, one more item caught

Andy's attention, and at this he stared long and unhappily.

To the northwest there was no smoke, which was momentarily puzzling, since the fire beyond highway 14 was being pushed by a southerly wind. A trail of smoke from that fire should by now have stretched north and northwest.

There was, of course, only one explanation: the anticipated wind shift had arrived, and the smoke arising from the bulge beyond highway 14 was being blown back upon itself; so everything was about to be reversed, and what had been.secure to the south would soon be in jeopardy.

Andy reached for the mike and called the tower at the airfield. "Can you patch me through to JL?"

The tower could. JL's voice came through loud and clear.

"I'm up here at fifteen thousand," Andy said, "and if you want to chew me out for leaving the field, at least wait till I report. There is no smoke, repeat, no smoke beyond the fire line in the northwest quadrant. Got it?"

JL's weary voice conveyed instant comprehension. "I think I can work it out. A major wind shift." He added, almost to himself, "Just what we don't need."

FRANK Orwell, up on the mountain, was not lost; on the contrary, he knew all too well where he was—between a rock and a hard place. Below him, and coming closer, were flames. Above him he could hear the voices of a fire-fighting crew cutting a break, grunting with their efforts. And from time to time, almost as if calculated to torment him, the voice of that wild woman with the shovel sounded off, echoing through the trees and drowning out even the crackling sounds of the approaching flames.

The heat and the smoke were both increasing, and try as he might, Orwell could stifle neither the urge to cough nor the growing terror that was gnawing at his guts. Again and again he thought about what had happened to Vigil. Incredible! That woman had swung the shovel right from her heels, like Reggie Jackson swinging for the fence, and if Orwell lived to be a hundred, he would never forget the sound when the shovel blade made contact.

And so, hating himself for refusing to dare the open, he crouched like a rabbit and took one cautious step backward after another in the growing darkness, while the flames came closer and the heat and the smoke became almost unbearable. Sooner or later, he told himself, he would reach the point of daring to stop, of advancing and showing himself. But not yet.

He wiped the sweat from his eyes with the back of his wrist. Just a little farther, and then he would make his stand.

He took one more step backward. It was his last.

Rock crumbled beneath his weight. He tried to throw himself forward, but he felt himself falling, where and into what he had no idea. And then he was in free-fall, cartwheeling into space over the cliff above the small lake. The scream he heard was his own.

THEY found the body within the hour. One of the southwest area crewmen, a Chiricahua Apache, spotted it lying on the rocks at the edge of the small lake. The crew chief radioed in the information, and two men—one of them a state policeman—worked their way with a packhorse through burned-over forest to the site.

The policeman squatted on his heels for a closer look. "At a guess," he said, "I'd say we've got the second one who walked away from Los Ojos. Fellow named Orwell." He stood up and squinted at the cliff wall. "Long fall," he said.

The other man said, "Did he fall, or was he pushed?"

"You know," the policeman said, "as far as I'm concerned he fell, and that's where I'm leaving it. Couldn't have happened to a nicer guy. Let's get him on the horse."

"THE wind change will work to our advantage here and here," JL said to Ben Hastings. Bent over the table, JL indicated on the map the north and northwest sectors of the fire. "It will push the flames right back to burned-over territory, where they'll die for lack of fuel. We can pull crews out of there and bring them down here, where the new danger will be." His finger indicated the southern fire boundary, near Sheep Ridge. "We've asked Albuquerque to send in another helitorch, just in case."

Ben closed his eyes. He could still see that sudden fireball as the helitorch-chopper slammed into the ground and exploded. He could still hear the pilot's voice, cut off in midsentence. He said, "Another backfire?"

"If we have to." JL studied Ben carefully. "You'd rather someone else flew in the following chopper and called the shots?"

Ben shook his head. "I'll do it." He took a deep breath. "And I'll get some trucks to start moving crews down that old logging road through the wilderness area."

JL permitted himself the faintest hint of an approving smile. He nodded. "Get to it, then. And keep me informed."

Jay Paul came up as Ben left. Jay said, "I'm pretty much extra baggage around here. If you—"

"We don't keep extra baggage around," JL said. "So you're going to work. Have a look at this sector." He tapped the map and waited until Jay bent over it reluctantly. "Sudden wind shift. Northwest," JL said then. "What will that do down here?"

Jay straightened. "Push the fire down toward those big houses. But you've already figured on that." His voice was resentful, that of a small boy being asked the obvious.

"And over here to the east?" JL asked.

Jay Paul glanced at the map. JL's finger pointed to wooded terrain on the big mountain's flank. "I don't know," Jay said.

"And neither do I for sure. But suppose the wind bringing sparks around starts the fire moving east to south? What about the crews working that southern quadrant?"

Jay Paul looked again at the map, with careful interest now. He said, "They'd be caught. They wouldn't stand a chance."

"So," JL said, "we want to see that that doesn't happen. You go out to the airfield. Show Andy McIlvain what we've got, and let him pick a spot where he can put in a crew to guard against that kind of encirclement. I want you to fly along with them, and once they're on the ground, give them instructions for placement. From the air you'll have the whole picture, and they'll be down among the trees and rocks, working almost blind."

JL sat quietly for a little time after Jay Paul, still doubtful but now determined to try, had headed for the airfield. Jay was a good man, JL told himself, or he wouldn't be here. How good a man, they would find out.

BESSIE Wingate herded her crew into the back of the first truck, giving the last man a helping shove on the rump that almost carried him the length of the truck bed. Then Bessie heaved herself mightily over the tailgate and took a quick look around.

"We got room for one more!" she bawled. She spotted a familiar face. "Come on, Eloy!"

Eloy Jaramillo, the little fire fighter from the southwest crew, had become separated from his team and was standing nearby. Bessie caught his arm and hoisted him up bodily as by a crane. Then she hammered with her fist on the cab's top. "Let's go! We got a full load!" The truck lurched off.

One of Bessie's crew said, "Sure beats walking. But where we going?"

"Wind change, jughead," Bessie explained, "so we go down to see that those rich dudes sitting around their swimming pools don't get singed."

Bessie settled herself comfortably in the truck. "Funny stuff, wind," she said meditatively. "You can't see it, but you can sure as heck see what it does. I've watched it grab up a burning branch, carry it halfway to hell and gone and drop it in the middle of some area you thought was secure and—bang! You've got a new fire front, just like that."

Bessie was warming to her subject now. "I seen wind come out of nowhere too," she went on, "just when the fire you're fighting is whipping you good, and all of a sudden it's like somebody dropped an asbestos curtain, and the fire stops, tries to go back but can't and then dies down for lack of fuel.

"There's just no figuring it. But one thing that's for sure: whenever you get wind and a fire together, you'd better watch your step every minute."

THE front-running gusts that heralded the wind change were welcome to the crews still manning the fire line in the north, beyond highway 14. The flames they faced now wavered and lessened in force; here and there they even withdrew over areas already burned and faded for want of fresh fuel.

In the sky to the northwest, high, thin cirrus clouds, like the banners of an approaching army, announced the main front. The wind picked up; gusts became stronger. Down on the southern front, JL knew, those gusts would be carrying sparks and burning fuel into fresh, untouched areas. And down there it was not only trees but houses as well that would be threatened.

Chapter Nine

*E*ARLY Thursday morning Jay Paul climbed up behind Andy McIlvain into the Twin Otter. In the almost bare fuselage, now crowded with the jumping crew, there was only a single wooden bench and the spotter's place for seating. They put Jay on the floor next to the open doorway and, using a cargo sling, attached him to one of the fuselage stringers. He tried not to be obvious about grabbing another stringer for support. By the time they were airborne, Jay's hand holding the stringer was numb from the pressure of his grip.

He watched Jake, Andy's number two man, in the spotter's seat and Andy McIlvain in the open doorway as they searched the ground for a drop site. Craning his neck, Jay looked down too and saw only treetops and rocks, and was sure that a drop was not possible.

But it was Andy, pointing, who said, "Over there! We can circle and come upwind to it! Duck soup!"

Jake nodded and spoke into his mike, directing the pilot.

Jay Paul swallowed hard as Andy, paired with another jumper, took his place at the open doorway. Almost casually the spotter tapped Andy's shoulder, and Andy launched himself from the aircraft. Moments later his partner followed. Jay closed his eyes in relief when the two chutes deployed and the men began their guided descent to the chosen spot.

When, two by two, all the jumpers were gone, Jake left his spotter's seat to begin wrestling boxes toward the fuselage door. As the aircraft repeated its careful circling, he pushed them out two at a time. With difficulty, Jay unsnapped his cargo sling from the stringer and began giving Jake a hand. And when all the boxes were gone, Jay took another cautious look out the doorway. It was then that the two air force fighters appeared out of nowhere and swept past beneath them.

"WE WERE at twelve hundred feet," Jake reported later to JL, "and none of us saw a thing when those two came under us. I thought we'd hit something. Their turbulence bounced us like a cork in a heavy sea. I saw Jay Paul make a grab for a stringer, miss, start to slide for the doorway, make another grab and this time catch hold and hang on so tight his hand was all bloody when he finally hauled himself back. He was scared witless and so was I. Just fun and games for the fighter boys."

JL permitted himself the briefest of smiles. Then he turned to Ben Hastings, who was standing nearby, listening.

"All right, tell me about Sheep Ridge," JL said. "Did you get your crews in place?" He sat back in his chair to wait.

Ben told him. The trucks, using an old, abandoned logging road through the wilderness, had reached the Sheep Ridge area, discharged their human loads and made a fast run back to pick up more.

"We spread the men thin at first," Ben told JL, "but as more and more came down, we thickened up the line, and began to make a solid stand. By then, the wind had swung completely around and the fire was coming right down the ridge at us." He watched JL nod with understanding, and knew that he was remembering fires when he had been the one to watch the flames coming at them.

"You know what it's like. The fire's got the wind behind it. But we've got plenty of troops to man the line," Ben said. "Right now, it's a standoff." He extended both hands, fingers crossed. "I almost hate to say it, but I think we can bring it under control."

JL nodded. He hoped Ben was right. But until they were cold-trailing the embers, he'd reserve judgment.

"Well, you'd better get back there," he said. "And keep the pressure on the crew chiefs. Keep me posted." He watched Ben turn away, and stopped him. "One more thing," JL said.

Ben stood quiet, waiting.

"It's a standoff now," JL said finally, "but you could lose that line."

"Yes, sir. Depends on the wind."

"I think," JL said slowly, "that you'd better start thinking about evacuating Bellevue Acres, just in case. All those kids, pets . . ." He shook his head. "With the big places, you tell them to get in their cars and drive off. With that development, you'll have a roundup problem on your hands. Got it?"

"Got it," Ben said.

JL nodded once again. "Good man," he said, and immediately seemed embarrassed that he had uttered such praise.

Aaron Swift, in his role as federal magistrate, considered the case in his office. Les Lawry was standing before him, with a uniformed man from the county sheriff's office waiting nearby.

"The jeep in the wilderness is yours?" Aaron said.

"Well," Les said, "I guess you could say that. I mean, it was." He tried to smile. "What's the big deal?"

"We'll talk about that in a moment," Aaron said. "Right now I'd like to know what you were doing in the wilderness."

"Well," Les began, "there was this fire. It was really burning up a storm, and I thought, Les, you'd better get the family the heck out of this. So we hightailed it away from those flames just as fast as we could. Why, there wasn't time to think about it at all, you see what I mean?"

"Not quite," Aaron said quietly. "As I understand it, there was the entire night to think about it. The first night, when you camped well inside the wilderness. What about that?"

"You mean," Les said slowly, "we were where we shouldn't of been? I mean, we didn't see—"

"The tracks of your jeep, Mr. Lawry, lead immediately past a very legible sign forbidding any kind of machinery within the wilderness area. As a matter of fact, you had to take down part of a fence in order to drive through."

"Why, that couldn't of been me, Judge. It had to be somebody else. As a matter of fact, we saw—"

"I am not really amused, Mr. Lawry," Aaron said. "Blatant lies tend to have quite an opposite effect on me."

"Why," Les said, "you can ask Cindy Lou and Tad—"

"Would you ask them to perjure themselves too?" Aaron leaned back in his chair while the question hung unanswered in the air. "You see," he went on, "I can refer this case to a U.S. district court. That could turn out to be a great deal more than you may have bargained for. Perjury, for example, is a criminal offense. Or, I can deal with the matter myself. Do you have a preference?"

Les hesitated. "Well now," he said at last, "I don't see why we can't work this out right here, Judge. The jeep's totaled, no good to anybody. So why don't we just leave it lay, and forget the whole thing? Now wouldn't that be the sensible thing to do?"

Aaron's voice took on an edge. "No, Mr. Lawry, it would not. Totaled or whole, your jeep is a piece of machinery. It is within the wilderness, and you caused it to enter quite unlawfully. You will now remove the jeep, all of it."

"But Judge, that would mean having a truck go in, and that would break the rules again, wouldn't it?" Les, having scored a debating point, was smiling now. "So why don't we—"

"No one but you mentioned a truck, Mr. Lawry."

Les was frowning now. "But you want the jeep out of your woods, don't you?"

"That is correct. You will remove it. At your expense."

"What am I supposed to do, carry it on my back?"

"Precisely how you do it, Mr. Lawry, is a matter of complete indifference to me—as long as it does not involve taking more machinery into the wilderness area. The last transgressors had their jeep hauled out by mule team."

Les said, "Hire a wagon and a mule team and enough men to pick a jeep up and haul it out? Do you realize what that would cost, Judge?"

"You might have thought of that beforehand. You may go now, Mr. Lawry. The sheriff will accompany you."

ADA Loving drove a leased sky-blue Mercedes 380 SL, top down. In sandals, skintight slacks and a crisp white short-sleeved blouse, she parked behind Ken Delacorte's aged Ford and went into the real estate office.

Ken was at his desk staring at a map. He stood up to acknowledge her presence, and then sat down again as Ada sank gracefully into a visitor's chair. She was unsmiling.

"I'm scared, Ken," Ada said, the words coming out too fast. "The fire's gotten too big and too close. And everybody else seems to be pretending it doesn't mean a thing. That's the scary part."

Ken smiled. They had not seen each other since the brief time at Ada's pool. "Did you come to have your hand held?" he asked.

"It would be a welcome relief from the hands I usually have to contend with." Again the words came too fast, tumbling over themselves. "Are we safe, Ken? Can they control that—monster?"

Monster was the right word, Ken thought, then said, "You do have it bad, don't you, baby?"

Ada said in a slower, calmer voice that nonetheless seemed to emphasize her fright, "I was in a fire once. I was five. The fire department didn't arrive until it was too late, and I can still close my eyes and remember standing with my mother, watching the whole house go up—with my crippled aunt inside screaming. I've been terrified of fire ever since."

Ken was silent.

"I'm afraid to be alone," Ada said. "I want a man on the scene."

"What about Sturgis?"

"Be serious, Ken. He isn't a man. He's a piece of typecasting."

"And the Hollywood pigeons?"

"They decided to cut their losses. They sent them back in the chartered plane this afternoon."

"They?"

"Whoever backs the show. I'm hired help, not part of the management."

Ken said slowly, "There's a dude in town name of Bart Jones, goes around in an electric wheelchair. This sounds like his kind of operation."

"I've met him," Ada said. "But whether it's his bankroll or not, I don't know. I'm paid in cash for showing up, and that's an end to it." The famous eyes watched Ken steadily. "And if you think it's a pretty sleazy way of making a buck, why, I agree."

Ken took his time. "What do you want me to do, tell you everything is going to be okay?"

Ada said, "Coming from you, it would help. You're real. You're not make-believe, like the ones I spend my time with. . . . Can I stay here?" She gestured around the small office. "I don't know how to type. I don't know how to file things, either, but I do know the alphabet and maybe I could figure it out."

Ken studied her carefully. "You're serious," he said.

"I told you, I'm scared to death. I'd run, but I wouldn't know where, and besides, then I'd be alone again. Please, Ken. Let me stay. That's all I ask."

BART Jones' voice on the phone, Stacy thought, was hardly subdued, but there was a quality of restraint in it she had not heard before.

"It's short notice, I know," Bart said, "but it was just sprung on me too. Duane Semple—name mean anything?"

"It rings a very faint bell. Why?"

"Oil," Bart said. "Gypsum. Uranium, back when it was worth something, and a couple of up-and-coming high-tech industries."

"What about him?"

"I'm invited for dinner," Bart said, "and I'd take it kindly if you'd keep me company."

Stacy paused. This was unexpected. "Why me?" she said. "Don't you know anybody else?"

Nothing changed in Bart's voice. "For one thing, Duane knew your daddy, and liked him. So being with you puts me in good company."

"I'm flattered."

"For another, I thought you might want to get in a word for Ken Delacorte's nickel-and-dime housing operation before Duane takes it over. Or I do."

Stacy was silent, thoughtful. "When is this dinner?"

"Tonight. Black tie. It's a thirty-minute drive to Semple's spread. I'll pick you up a little before seven. Of course, if you'd like to give me a drink first . . ." He left the sentence hanging.

"Oh, all right," Stacy said.

"That's my gracious girl."

JL STUDIED the latest infrared photographs while Ben Hastings sat close by watching. The 1630 briefing was well behind them, but JL had given no sign that he was planning to rest.

"You had maybe two hours' sleep last night," Ben said. "Are you thinking of knocking off sometime tonight? You look beat."

"I don't like it," JL said, ignoring the question, "and that's the truth." The photos were setting off alarm bells in his mind. Things seemed to be improving to the north, but in the south the situation was still in doubt. And the most recent weather report wasn't helping JL's peace of mind.

"There's a storm in the Gulf of Mexico now. They're calling it Charley," he said, "and it's beginning to flex its muscles. They say we're probably in for another wind shift. And stronger winds." He tapped the topographic map also spread on the table. "If that happens, I think we'd better buy some insurance."

Ben looked where JL's finger rested on the map. "Sheep Ridge?" He was frowning.

"Below. Between the ridge and these houses."

"Are you still thinking of another backfire?"

"If we get a wind shift away from town. Not otherwise."

Ben was silent, thoughtful. He said at last, "You don't trust our Sheep Ridge fire line?"

"I don't trust anything in this whole fire." JL looked again at the infrared photos. "These pictures can tell us where some small spot is smoldering on the ground. Fine. I'm glad to know it. But they can't tell us if it's going to become open flame, because that depends on what the air on the ground is doing, on the humidity, on the kind of fuel that's being heated, on a dozen other factors." He paused. "What it boils down to is my judgment that Sheep Ridge is too tricky in these conditions to take chances with—any chances. This"—he drew his finger across the infrared photograph between Sheep Ridge and the houses to the south of it—"is our best defensive line. It's also almost our last before we get into the housing development and then the town. I want that line held, and a well-placed backfire will give us the chance to take out that insurance I mentioned." He looked up at Ben. "Unless you have a better idea."

Ben spread his hands helplessly. "I don't, but—" He stopped.

"Go on," JL said. "But what?"

"You're playing a hunch, aren't you? That something more will go wrong and we won't be able to hold the line we already have?"

"I am. I admit it. So I want to hedge my bet with another hundred acres deliberately sacrificed. It's not the kind of thing that's in the book, but this is my best judgment."

Ben nodded, suddenly easier than he had been for some time. "I'll go along," he said. "But I've got a suggestion. Let me call in Jerry Weinstock, my night man, to back me up here while you go home and get some rest. We'll shout if we need you." He watched JL's hesitation, and then his slow nod of assent. "We won't let you down," Ben said.

On the phone from the Sanrio Volunteer Fire Department a voice said to the Forest Service dispatcher: "We've got a roof afire at grid number A8-B6. Our pumper's on the way."

"A8-B6. Roger." A very brief pause. "Byron Holloway? Off the county road?"

"That's it. He just called it in."

"Damn!" the dispatcher said. The Holloway place, one of the large houses adjoining the southern boundary of the forest, was the closest to the Sheep Ridge fire line. "That means the fire's jumped our line. Much obliged, Sanrio. Your people will have company."

BEN Hastings took the news over the phone while he was sitting in for JL. "Okay. We'll get on it," he said after listening quietly. As he replaced the receiver two thoughts crossed his mind. The first was that JL had to be psychic, and the second was that, with the fire in this position, the proposed backfire was now out of the question.

He was just about to phone JL when a second call came through from the Sanrio dispatcher. Ben listened with growing incredulity. "You're sure you have the coordinates right?"

The dispatcher's voice was calm and unhurried. "Commercial aircraft usually know where they are. This one spotted flames and took bearings to check himself."

"Roger! Thanks." Ben hung up and instantly dialed JL, who came out of a deep sleep to answer the telephone. But he seemed to take in what Ben repeated about the two new outbreaks.

"Send a car for me," he said. "I'm too groggy to drive."

"It's on the way."

Ben hung up. He sat back in his chair to stare at the area map and ponder. The wind had shifted again, as predicted. From almost dead out of the northwest, it had swung to the northeast, with occasional gusts from the east. The new fire reported by the commercial aircraft was east by northeast of Andy McIlvain's position. And headed in his direction. It just didn't seem possible that sparks from the fire line they were already holding could have blown so far to start fresh trouble. But there it was.

Ben had the uneasy feeling that even though he didn't know the answers, he ought to be taking action anyway. It occurred to him to wonder if this was the kind of dilemma the man in ultimate command was constantly facing—to move or not to move and, if so, in which direction? He felt a guilty sense of relief when the car he had sent for JL arrived, and JL himself came to pull out a chair at the table and sit down wearily.

"You were right," Ben said. "About Sheep Ridge, I mean. Somehow it did get past us to the Holloway house. We're trying to hold it there."

"It can happen, sometimes in funny ways. How about the other houses?"

Ben moved the map closer so they both could see. "So far, we're okay. But Andy's sector could cause trouble." His pencil indicated the area reported on fire by the commercial aircraft. "The other outbreak is clear over here."

JL shook his head. "Could be anything. A lit cigarette tossed away, a campfire not completely dead." He spread his hands. "Get on the radio to Andy and warn him. If this new fire isn't too big, he can handle it. But tell him to be careful. He could get caught in it." JL looked again at the map. "What exactly is his position? Your last fix?" He watched Ben's pencil touch the contour lines on the map that encircled heavily wooded terrain above Sheep Ridge. "And the nearest ground crew?" The pencil touched paper again.

JL made a rough measurement between the two marks. "Well over a mile," he said, "a darned rough mile." He paused reflectively. "Whose is the nearest crew?"

"Gordy Walker."

JL nodded approval. "Throw your next best crew in with them. Who would that be?"

"Big Bertha. We brought her down from the north yesterday."

"Bessie Wingate?" JL smiled. "Move her in. We want to get to Andy if we can."

ADA Loving's Mercedes followed Ken's Ford into the drive of his house. Ada got out and walked with him in silence to the front door. As she watched him put his key in the lock she said, "Think of me as a stray cat that followed you home because it had no place else to go."

"It's okay," Ken answered. "I can smell the smoke too."

Ada, searching refrigerator and cupboards, found eggs and bacon, a can of chopped chilies, some onions and tomatoes. The full, dazzling smile appeared.

"A feast," Ada said. "Stand back. *Huevos rancheros*, or a reasonable facsimile, coming up."

Her hands were deft and sure, and there was no hesitation in her manner.

"You know your way around a kitchen," Ken said.

"Where I grew up," Ada said, "there weren't any restaurants, or supermarkets with frozen food. Mom worked all day. So did Pop. So I did the cooking. The glamour bit came later."

Over their meal, Ada told him more about herself. "I taught myself to dance," she said, "by sitting through Ginger Rogers movies three and four times and then practicing like mad. I stole a baton from the local high school. I gave it back eventually, but by then I was good enough to win a couple of competitions and a college scholarship. Lucky for me, baton twirling was real big then." She smiled suddenly. "I didn't have it so tough. Not really."

"Tough enough," Ken said.

"You got your brains beat out playing football so you could make it to college, and then business school."

"I got paid for it."

"Let's say we're about even. I'll clean up these things."

"We'll both do it."

"No," Ada said. "Every night after dinner, Pop would offer to help and Mom would say, 'No thanks.' That's the way I like it."

She stacked the dishes neatly and carried them to the kitchen. Ken was pushing his chair back from the table when he heard the crash. He reacted instantly, crossing the room in two long strides. In the kitchen doorway he stopped.

Ada was standing quite still, the wreckage of the dishes on the floor around her. Her eyes were wide and seemingly unfocused. "I'm—sorry," she said in a distant, automatic voice.

"What scared you?" Ken said.

Her eyes closed, and slowly opened again, back in focus now. "Look out the window."

Ken walked over to where she stood. Outside, against the black of the sky, not too distant flames were plain, flaring. Ken stared at them for a few silent moments, then turned back to Ada. "A shame. But it has nothing to do with us. They'll get it under control."

Ada gathered herself with visible effort. "I'm all right. Honest. Where's the broom?"

When she'd cleaned up the mess, she came into the living room

and sank gracefully down on the sofa. "Silly," she said. "Some people are afraid of cats. Did you know that? Ailurophobes, they're called. I guess I'm a pyrophobe. I'm sorry."

"Nothing to be sorry for. And talk about it as much as you need to. I can stand it."

"Yes," Ada said. "You can stand a lot. That's obvious. I plant myself on your doorstep like a kitten nobody wants, and you take me in as if it happens all the time. You're a nice, sweet guy."

"The world is full of guys who would give their right arm to have Ada Loving knock on the door."

"But you don't make passes, either."

"Magnificent self-control, not lack of interest."

"If you'll let me," Ada said, "I'm going to stay here tonight. Maybe even—who knows?—a number of nights." Her eyes watched him steadily.

"You're welcome to stay as long as you like."

BESSIE Wingate herded her men into position alongside Gordy Walker's crew. "All right," she told them, "this is where we start earning our C rations! Let's get the lead out!" To Gordy she said quietly, "What gives? We were told to get up here on the double."

Bessie was half again as large as Gordy, and a woman besides, but between them there was a strict sense of equality. Gordy explained about the new fire that had broken out near Andy McIlvain's position.

When he was done, Bessie was already at work with her shovel, grunting as she dug and heaved. "That Andy's a heck of a good man. They're all good men."

Gordy too was hard at work. "You can say that again."

"So all we got to do is move this old mountain," Bessie said, "or at least this hunk of it, cut down a few trees, clear out some low growth and put out a few fires on the way, right?"

"You've got it," Gordy said. Bessie loved to exaggerate, but the funny thing was, she tended to come up with performances to match. In Gordy's book, Bessie was a real pistol.

"Eloy," Bessie shouted to the fire fighter from the southwest crew, who was standing nearby. "We still don't know where the rest of your guys are, so you just stick with us."

Eloy grinned and nodded, conserving his breath for his labor.

"Real good little man," Bessie confided to Gordy. "Kind of a mascot I guess I sort of adopted!" She raised her voice again. "All right, you lazy jugheads, let's see some action! We got folks waiting for us!"

STACY rode home from dinner at Duane Semple's house in the big chauffeur-driven car Bart Jones kept for such occasions. She was in a thoughtful mood that—for a wonder, she thought—Bart acknowledged by keeping silent until she chose to speak.

"I don't like him," Stacy said at last, and turned in her seat to study as best she could Bart's face in the late evening light. "But you expected that, didn't you?"

"The dinner wasn't intended to be a lovefest."

"Semple wants to see Ken about Bellevue Acres. Why? And why try to use me as an intermediary?"

"Because Ken believes you. He might not believe me, and he doesn't know Duane."

It had the ring of truth. After a pause Stacy said, "Why does he want to see him? What shenanigans does he have in mind?"

"Don't make it too complicated," Bart answered. "Duane just wants to size him up. It helps to know the man you're going to tangle with."

"So he wants Ken to come to him."

"Because he doesn't get around even as well as I do."

True enough. Stacy had been shocked to find that Duane Semple was an obviously sick man, moving from room to room in the huge house only with enormous effort. He made her think of a great, bloated spider, waiting for its prey.

"Your daddy and Duane went around and around a couple of times," Bart said, as if reading her mind. "It pretty much was a standoff. I think that's why Duane liked him. He never met many he had to deal with on even terms." His voice changed. "How about it? You'll deliver Ken?"

"I'll leave it up to him."

Later she sat alone, still in her long dress, at the desk in her office-library, strangely hesitant to pick up the telephone and call Ken with this odd invitation.

She told herself that she disliked the feeling of being maneuvered into the position of—face it—Judas goat, in a sense leading

Ken up the ramp to slaughter. It was, of course, a ridiculous concept, because Ken was a grown man, well able to fend for himself. She picked up the telephone and placed the call.

Ken was a long time answering, and when he did his voice was a trifle breathless.

"I've interrupted something?" Stacy asked, then quickly added, "Strike that. None of my business. Look, Ken, do you know a man named Duane Semple?"

There was a short silence. "I know *of* him," Ken said then. "I've never met him. He plays in the big leagues."

"He wants to meet you."

There was another silence.

"Bart Jones took me to Semple's for dinner," Stacy explained. "They want me as go-between. What they're after is . . ."

"Bellevue Acres," Ken said. "It figures. Milk it dry, raise the mortgage rates until the people are driven out, then tear the houses down to build their fancy condos." His voice was quiet, with anger in its depths.

"That doesn't make much sense," Stacy said.

"It does, because that land already has a zoning variance, and they won't face any hassle with the city council about whether and what they can build. That's worth quite a bit to them."

Stacy was thoughtful. She said at last, "What will it do to you?"

"Personally? Nothing I can logically object to. It will put money in my pocket when they buy me out, as they'll have to. Or cut me into their project."

"And never mind the folks with all the kids and the dogs being pushed out?"

"That's about it. When does Semple want to see me?"

"Tomorrow night. Dinner. He dresses. Will you go?"

"I'll be there."

AT THE command post early on Friday morning, JL studied the latest radar-enhanced satellite photographs handed him by the Weather Service meteorologist assigned to Backslope. It was evident that the tropical storm named Charley had gone past the simple muscle-flexing stage and now, packing winds close to a hundred miles an hour, was a full-blown hurricane. The problem was to figure out which direction the storm was going to go.

Charley could decide to stay offshore well out in the Gulf, in a sense just spinning his wheels but causing winds far inland to back and veer insanely. Or he could come romping ashore and break up into smaller wind systems. He might even be obliging enough to bring some moisture with him. Meantime, we'll simply have to try to cope, JL thought.

His telephone rang, and he reached for it. It was Ben Hastings, who was out patrolling the fire line. "We've had a bad accident," Ben said. "A southwest crewman, name of Eloy Jaramillo. Been working with Bessie Wingate's crew since the truck lift down from the north line—" His voice stopped.

JL said, "And?"

Ben said slowly, "He thought he'd better get back, find his own people. He got—cut off. Used his portable shelter and the fire went over him, but he's burned. Bad."

JL closed his eyes briefly. He nodded. "Okay," he said, carefully keeping all pain from his voice. "I want to be kept informed."

"Right." Ben's voice changed. "Gordy Walker and Bessie— they're tearing that mountain apart. That's the good news."

JL said, "There's more bad?"

"Andy McIlvain and his people. They're fighting a rearguard action uphill toward timberline—"

"If there's any doubt at all, I want them to cut and run. Tell Andy I said so."

Chapter Ten

IT WAS the last ironic twist Sophie Swift would have imagined, and confronting it taxed her self-control to its limits. The situation was compounded by the fact that, as she had told Stacy, she liked young Debby, Aaron's wife, who appeared unannounced at her door.

"A doesn't know I'm here," Debby said, "but I had to talk to someone, and you're the wisest person I know. May I come in?" Young and vulnerable and obviously in over her head.

They sat in the study, where Sophie and Aaron had sat so many evenings, reading, talking or just listening to music.

"I had no idea where he was," Debby said, "until he walked up to me at the club and said hi. Can you imagine my shock?"

Sophie said in a kindly tone, "I'm not sure I understand. Whom are you talking about?"

"Johnny Joe Ames. We went to high school together. He was my date for our senior dance. He gave me a corsage."

The girl's mind, perhaps under strain, Sophie thought, jumped about aimlessly. Sophie kept her face as expressionless as she could. "And after that?"

"He went off to college and then joined the navy. Men do." As if that explained all.

"And now he's here in Sanrio?"

"Well, not exactly. He just came to see me. That isn't wrong, is it? I mean, it isn't as if I was seeing him on the sly. It was right there at the club, with lots of folks around."

"It sounds quite innocent to me."

"I wouldn't want A to think I was going behind his back. I *like* A. I really do. He's awful good to me."

Sophie knew that Debby had probably married Aaron for the things she had never had: financial security and comfort, the wisdom and easy decisiveness of an older man willing to relieve her of all responsibilities.

But the youthful fire had been missing, and until Johnny Joe suddenly reappeared, she had not realized how much she had missed it. It was as simple as that.

As if to underline Sophie's thoughts, Debby said, "Johnny Joe is . . . well, Johnny Joe, if you see what I mean."

Sophie said slowly, wanting no misunderstanding, "Perhaps you'd best tell me."

Debby took a deep breath. "I'm not very good with words, but, well, you see a person you haven't seen in a long time, and all of a sudden you start remembering things you thought you'd forgotten." Her eyes clung to Sophie's face, pleading for sympathy.

"Like the senior dance and the corsage?"

"You do understand, don't you? I was sure you would."

Sophie kept her face carefully composed. She said, "Sometimes things or events from long ago seem more important at first remembrance than they actually are, Debby."

"I know. And I've thought about it a lot. That's why I came to you." Debby's smile was hesitant. "I mean, you're a lawyer."

"True."

"You represent people, and, well, I've thought about it a lot. If Johnny Joe asks me to go with him . . ."

"Where, Debby?"

"I don't care. Anywhere. I'll go." There was finality in the words and the tone.

Sophie blinked. It was the only expression of emotion she allowed herself. "And what is it you want me to do?"

"Explain to A for me. I'm not good with words like he is. I feel things, but I don't know how to talk about them."

There was silence. Out in the front hall the grandfather clock that had belonged to Sophie's grandparents chimed the hour. Sophie listened until the last echoes had died; then she said, "Has Johnny Joe asked you to go with him, Debby?"

"No, but he will. I know it." Her smile this time was confident, brilliant. "You can tell."

"I would rather you asked someone else to speak for you."

"No. Please. I know you. And you know A. And I wouldn't know who else to go to."

"I could suggest someone."

"Please," Debby said. "Don't do it for me. Do it for A. I wouldn't want to . . . hurt him."

BESSIE got word of Eloy's burns by walkie-talkie, as did Gordy Walker. "Poor little stinker," was Bessie's immediate comment. "I didn't even know he'd gone!" Gordy, telling about it later, swore that the stout handle of Bessie's shovel bent like a toothpick beneath the sudden force of her emotion. "Blast it, Gordy," Bessie said, "I told him to stay with us!"

"He's in the hospital," Gordy said. "You want to go see him, I'll cover for you."

"You talk like a man with a paper head," Bessie said almost savagely. "We got folks waiting for us over yonder. Let's stop clicking our teeth and get to them." She worked in furious silence for a time before she spoke again. "This damn fire," she said.

AT SIXTEEN thousand feet, well above Sierra Grande's rocky peak, the reconnaissance plane bucked and jumped in heat-produced updrafts. "That," the pilot said, looking down, "is quite a little bonfire. Can you take it all in with your wide-angle lens?"

"Just about," the photographer said. "JL won't get the detail we usually give him—"

"Detail is the last thing JL's worried about now. He's thinking in miles, not acres. Look over yonder. Another house. . . ."

In point of fact, it was not a house that had suddenly erupted in flames, but the cabana at the end of Ada Loving's swimming pool.

"Look at that baby go," the pilot said, "and I'll bet that won't be the last of them. In the meantime, we've got ringside seats."

KEN Delacorte got the word by phone from one of the local volunteer firemen. "Thanks," he said, and turned to Ada. "Sorry, baby," he said. "Your cabana—"

"I don't care. Feed the whole house to the monster. Maybe it will keep some other house from going up."

"I'll go over—"

"No. *Things* aren't important. Only people matter."

Ken said gently, "It's okay. You're—"

"I'm not being hysterical, Ken. I mean it. I've been broke. Stony. It's uncomfortable, but it doesn't really matter. But when you lose somebody who counts—a friend, maybe a part of the family—then you see what really is important. That's why I don't want you going near the place. It's . . . unlucky. It's nothing but a joint to attract suckers for their money." She smiled suddenly, the full, brilliant smile. "Think I could go back to baton twirling?"

"I think," Ken said slowly, "that you could do anything you put your mind to, baby, and do it superlatively well."

STACY walked past the spa on the way to her bedroom to dress for the second dinner at Duane Semple's place. She had not been in the spa for a long time now, and it passed through her mind that the day JL had come to talk to her and interrupted the party was indeed a while ago, and much had changed, of which the fire and, to a lesser extent, the spa had become only symbols.

Showered, bath-powdered and perfumed, Stacy padded to her closet to decide which evening dress to wear for this occasion. How long had it been since she had dressed two nights in a row for dinner? That too was somehow a symbol of change, and she could imagine how her father would have teased her.

"When you put your mind to it, honey," he would have said,

"you really can turn into an eastern dude. I'm proud of you."

And if she had explained the situation to him, he would have told her to follow her instincts. Well, she had a pretty fair idea that this evening Ken was going to put his concern for the folks who lived in Bellevue Acres ahead of his own best interests and, in effect, spit in Duane Semple and Bart Jones' collective eye, by his own admission stepping into competition he couldn't really hope to match. So that left her own choice pretty plain, didn't it?

She could stay strictly on the sidelines. It was, after all, none of her concern; she bred and trained horses, nothing more.

Or she could declare herself into the game by offering Ken the financial backing he needed. She'd probably lose a bundle, but the more she thought about what Bart and Semple were trying to do, the more she got her dander up.

By the time Bart's car and driver arrived, and Bart himself wheeled up the walk to her front door, Stacy was keyed up, as she always was before competition, and smiling as if she hadn't a care in the world. "We've time for a drink, I think," she said, and stood aside for the wheelchair.

Glass of wine in hand, and the smile still holding steady, Stacy said, "I heard on the radio that the fire got Ada Loving's place."

"So I understand. Pity." Bart's eyes watched her warily.

"Your house, wasn't it?" A guess, pure and simple, but, Stacy thought, on the basis of what she knew from Ken, a good guess.

"Why do you say that?" Bart's face showed nothing.

"Part of the long-range operation, wasn't it? Famous movie star picks Sanrio for her hideaway. And, of course, acts as magnet to draw in potential investors? Bellevue Acres with zoning variance already approved, the ideal site for new, fancy condos? You aren't going to tell me it's coincidental. Daddy taught me to look at a horse's teeth before I accepted the age as represented."

Bart's eyes did not leave her face. He lowered his glass slowly. "Your daddy had a lot of moxie. He had a lot of business sense too. You inherited the first. Did you get the second as well?"

"I've never had to find out. Things have always been pretty easy for me."

Bart smiled at that. "A few busted ribs, dislocated shoulder, a broken wrist—"

"They don't count. It's the big things that have always been easy. For most folks they never are. They're always trying to get out from under, and never can."

"Look, lady, don't quote Thoreau at me about 'lives of quiet desperation.' He never knew what desperation was."

"Have you?" Instantly she wished she could recall the question.

Bart now wore his crooked smile. "I've had my moments," he said. "Of wishing. And hating."

He finished his drink. "We should go, if you're ready."

KEN Delacorte tied his black tie and turned to find Ada holding out his dinner jacket. Smiling, he shook his head slowly. "How many men would believe this scene?"

"I not only believe it, I like it. I just don't like your going."

"You know where I'll be. And you know it's important."

Ada helped him into the jacket and smoothed the shoulders fondly. "I believe what you say." She waited until he had turned again to face her. Idly she brushed a nonexistent speck from his lapel. "You don't even know this Semple character, do you?"

"Only by reputation."

"I've heard of him too. Big bucks."

Ken said, "You're making a point?"

Ada nodded slowly. "In a funny way," she said, "I'm talking about you and me. I don't mean any ties or commitments. It's just that you and I are one kind of people, and, well, the Semples are another. I'm probably talking out of turn. I learned a long time ago that men don't like to be told what they aren't, so I'll shut up if you want."

"No. That's the last thing I want."

The blue eyes searched his face. "Okay," Ada said then and took a deep breath. "You're a decent person, and there aren't very many of those. You're not out to cheat anybody, because you wouldn't want to be cheated yourself. Isn't that what the Golden Rule says? Do unto others . . ."

"I guess that's one way to put it." Ken was smiling.

"But the Semples of the world don't work that way. They figure everybody's out to get them, so they just do it first, and hardest. That's why I say we're one kind of people and they're another. We can't compete with them, because the only way would be by behaving as they do. And I've stopped trying, because even if I made it, I wouldn't like it. That's all."

There was a short, understanding silence between them.

"I'll remember it, baby," Ken said. "And . . . thanks."

IT WAS a single tall lodgepole pine tree clinging precariously to one of Sierra Grande's steep upper slopes that did it. Higher on the mountain a rock slipped beneath the boot of one of Andy McIlvain's smoke jumpers. The rock rolled, starting a minor slide. The slide loosened the pine's already frail grip on the mountainside, and slowly, almost majestically, its topmost needles already blazing from contact with a flying burning branch, the tree began its fall.

By the time it crashed to the rocky ground, breaking apart as it hit, its lower branches too were ablaze, and what had been an open if hazardous escape route for Andy and his people was now closed. Instantly the entire area was ablaze.

"Make like mountain goats!" Andy shouted. "Head for timberline! Move it!" Already scrambling up the slope himself, he poured information into his walkie-talkie. "Tell JL we're hightailing it out of here. You'll find us up top with the goats. I hope. Over and out."

GORDY Walker held his walkie-talkie at an angle so Bessie too could hear Ben Hastings' report.

"That area's cut off," Ben's voice said. "Chopper observation reports Andy and his people above the fire area and for the present safe. Break off your operation as it goes now, and start establishing a north–south line to seal off where the jumpers were working. We'll let it burn itself out to timberline. Over."

Gordy looked up at Bessie's sweat- and smoke-stained face. "Blast it," Bessie said, and shrugged in resignation.

Gordy suppressed a smile. "Roger," he said into the walkie-talkie. "North–south it is. Let her burn. Over and out." He looked at Bessie again. "Now do you want to knock off and go see Eloy?"

Bessie shook her head. "I'll wait till change of shift. Way I probably look now, I'd scare him into a coma. Let's turn these raggedy troops around and get them going."

FROM THE BROAD TERRACE OF Vista Hill, Mrs. Tyler Wayne
looked out at the great mountain across her favorite grove of
specimen trees so modestly begun so long ago. A black walnut
had been the first planting, she remembered, a gift from a now
forgotten visitor from Nebraska. It had arrived by truck, neatly
balled, and Mrs. Wayne and Tyler had discussed at length where
to have it put, never guessing that it would be the beginning of
what became almost a private forest of carefully tended exotic
plantings. Eucalypti from California, rhododendrons from Scotland,
locusts, ashes, ginkgoes and others had delighted visitors for years.

It was a pity the development had been built so close to the
grove. Tyler would no doubt have seen to it that such a thing
would not occur, but there it was. On the other side the finger of
the forest offered protection against any encroachment. When
they made their first plantings, Mrs. Wayne often thought, there
had been only open land where Bellevue Acres now was, and
who could have dreamed that such change might take place?

But it was Sierra Grande that held her attention now. As she
saw the forest destroyed before her, she wished there were something she could do about those facing devastation if the fire
spread farther. All those people in Bellevue Acres, all those
children— What would happen to them if the fire came all the
way down?

She closed her eyes in sudden pain, and opened them again
only with reluctance. For a long time she stood quite still, staring
at reality, knowing that it would not go away. At last, slowly, she
turned and walked back into the big house. There she seated
herself at a table in the library and picked up the telephone.

"This is Mrs. Tyler Wayne," she said in a steady voice to the
young woman at Forest Service headquarters. "I wish to speak
with Mr. J. L. Harmon, if you please."

JL's voice on the line was polite, but there was obvious fatigue
and faint impatience in its depths. "Yes, Mrs. Wayne?"

"I have been watching the progress of the fire down what I
believe is referred to as the finger of the forest. Can you stop that
fire, Mr. Harmon? I should like an honest answer."

"We're doing all we can, Mrs. Wayne. But these winds . . ."

"The answer then is no? I was afraid it would be."

"Mrs. Wayne—"

"Please. I did not call with a plea but rather with a suggestion. If that finger of the forest is lost, then the grove of specimen tree plantings you have been kind enough to admire in the past will also be destroyed. It is inevitable."

"I'm sorry—"

"Please, Mr. Harmon, I am not finished. That grove, as you know, abuts the development. If the grove is destroyed because the finger of the forest is lost, the development is certain to go as well. No doubt you have already considered this?"

"I'm afraid we have."

There was a picture of Tyler Wayne in a silver frame on the table. Mrs. Wayne looked at it now, expressionless. She said, "If you were to burn my grove now, Mr. Harmon, before it is in immediate danger, could you control the blaze and keep it from reaching those houses?"

JL sat unmoving. He said slowly, in a gentle voice, "The answer, Mrs. Wayne, is probably yes. But I can't promise."

Mrs. Wayne's eyes had not left the picture. "Then burn the grove, Mr. Harmon. You have my permission." She hung up. "I'm sorry, Tyler." It was no more than a whisper.

BEN Hastings, summoned, said, "Good Lord! You mean it? When I was a kid, we used to make field trips to that grove. There're two trees from the Himalayas, and a specimen from way up the Amazon."

"There's no other way," JL said. "Just make it a good, clean burn, as successful as possible. That's the least we can do."

He sat for long moments after Ben drove off. Fires, JL thought, brought out the best and the worst in people. Correction: in some people. Right now, for example, although nothing would show on the surface, Mrs. Tyler Wayne was crying inside. And when the blaze actually began, which would be momentarily, she would be standing at a window watching, compelled by the same motive that would make her hold an old, loved pet dog's paw while he was put to sleep—so he would not die alone.

And then there were the Willard Spencers and the Les Lawrys, very different types indeed.

JL looked at his watch: evening was coming on fast, and there was still too much unfinished business.

"I ASKED YOU TO COME OUT HERE, Aaron," Sophie said, "because the office is something less than . . . neutral ground. Also, I knew that we would want privacy."

"Mysteriouser and mysteriouser," Aaron said. He glanced at his watch. "It is after hours. Is a drink in order?"

"Please," Sophie said. "I'd prefer that you waited."

Aaron settled back in his chair and sat quiet but alert.

"I have a client, Aaron," Sophie said. "This client is not of my choosing. You must believe that. I tried to avoid the engagement and in conscience was unable to. Have you guessed already that my client is Debby?"

"I was beginning to see the light, Counselor." It was his dry courtroom voice, agreeing to a stipulation in order that matters might proceed.

"There is a young man," Sophie said, "who has turned up unexpectedly. His name is Johnny Joe Ames."

"Someone out of the past, no doubt."

"They were high school sweethearts."

"How romantic."

Sophie's lips tightened, and there was sudden color in her cheeks, but her voice remained calm. She said, "They are romantic, and young, as once upon a time we were. We have, I suppose the phrase is, grown up, become mature. I don't believe they have. Debby still retains—"

"If you're saying that in many ways Debby is immature," Aaron said, "I shall so stipulate. And the swain?"

"I haven't met him, but . . ." Sophie spread her hands.

Aaron forced himself to relax a trifle. He shook his head. "I think we can read between the lines. Go on."

"Debby is not carrying on an affair, Aaron. She tells me that she has behaved . . . honorably, and I believe her. But if Johnny Joe asks her to go away with him, as she is sure he will, she will go."

Aaron was silent and still. He said at last, "She wants out?"

"Just that. Nothing more."

There was a longer silence. In the hallway the grandfather clock ticked loudly. "You may tell your client, Counselor," Aaron said at last, "that she is welcome to an uncontested divorce. Is that satisfactory?"

Sophie closed her eyes. She opened them again and nodded.

"Thank you, Aaron." She drew a deep breath. "Now would you like that drink?"

It was as if the question had not been heard. "Oh, Soph!" Aaron said suddenly. "Why did it have to be you?"

BESSIE Wingate, silent and ponderously graceful, came into the hospital room almost on tiptoe, and stood quietly looking down at Eloy, motionless beneath his bandages.

Eloy had been caught virtually in the middle of a raging inferno, Bessie had been told. He had tried to use his fire shelter, but it had split as he tugged it over himself, or he hadn't stretched it taut, or maybe some other blasted thing. Anyway, what difference did that make now? This was all that was important.

Eloy's eyes opened and came slowly into focus. What showed of his mouth began to spread in a weak smile. "Hi, big mama." It occurred to him in a dreamlike way that this was the first time he had called Bessie to her face by the name he had carried in his mind for days, but it didn't matter now. "I screwed up, didn't I?"

"You want argument?" Bessie said, and shook her head. "I'm real sorry, Eloy." She reached into one of her jacket pockets. "I didn't think you'd go for flowers or anything like that, so I brought you a beer." She took out a can of cold beer and set it on the table beside the bed.

The weak smile reappeared. "When I get out," Eloy said, "and we go to The Antlers, I'm going to do the buying. Okay?"

"You got a deal."

"You get to them smoke jumpers?"

Bessie shook her head. "But they're okay," she said, hoping it was true. "They hauled it for timberline when things got too hot."

Eloy's eyes closed. He opened them with effort. "They shoot me full of, you know, all kind of stuff." He waggled his head gently toward the intravenous tube. "You know?" he said.

"Sure. Makes you sleepy. That's good. You sleep, Eloy." Bessie's big hand touched his arm gently. "Hang in there."

His eyes were already closed as she let herself out of the room and walked down the hallway to the nurse's station. There she stopped and stood, large and motionless. "How about it?" she said, looking down at the seated nurse.

"Patient Jaramillo?" the nurse said. "He's doing quite well."

233

"Cut the bull." The words hung in the air like a growl.

The nurse took a deep, uneasy breath. It was as if suddenly she faced a mother bear, a grizzly maybe, asking about one of her cubs and wanting a straight answer. *Now.*

"I'm not the doctor," the nurse began. She stopped. Wrong approach. "I don't know. He may make it," she said. "He may not."

Slowly Bessie seemed to relax in acceptance. "Okay," she said. "If that's the way it is." She turned away, then immediately turned back. "Thanks," she said, and turned away again to walk massively and expressionlessly down the corridor.

IN BELLEVUE Acres a small crowd gathered to stare at the fire in Mrs. Wayne's grove of specimen plantings. "Lord," one man said. "They might have warned us if it's that close."

Ben Hastings drove up, braked to a stop and did not even get out of his jeep. Immediately he was the center of the small crowd's attention. "I just wanted to tell you that we've set that fire. For your protection. It's a firebreak, to try to make you safe."

The man who had spoken up said, "To *try* to make us safe! That sure is poor reassurance."

"We're doing our best for all of you, but just in case—"

"Here it comes," the man said. "Can't you people do anything right?"

"Just in case," Ben repeated flatly, "you might start thinking about what you'll want to take *if* we have to evacuate you. I don't think we will." Mentally he crossed his fingers. "But we can't control the winds."

A pregnant woman said, "Oh, no! You can't mean it! Everything we have is right here! We—"

"I wish," Ben said, "that I could tell you different."

Chapter Eleven

DUANE Semple's property was enclosed by a well-maintained four-strand barbed-wire fence. A high masonry wall surrounded the house itself. "If he has a coat of arms," Stacy told Bart, "it ought to show paranoia rampant, don't you think?"

"You've got your spurs with the big rowels on tonight, haven't you?" Bart said.

Stacy patted herself. "No gun," she said. "No knife. Just me."

The car drew smoothly to a stop at the entrance to the big house. Behind them Ken's car swung into a parking place, and Ken got out. "Okay," Stacy said, "let the festivities commence."

Semple was not a big man, and he was obviously in frail health, but there was no mistaking his air of authority. His greetings were easy and gracious.

"Delighted to see you again, Miss Cummings." He smiled at Ken Delacorte. "I spent a large part of one afternoon in Texas Stadium, Mr. Delacorte, admiring your abilities on the football field. My pleasure was dampened, though, by the fact that I was sitting in the owner's box, and the Dallas Cowboys do not enjoy losing."

"I didn't think anybody did," Ken said. "I know I don't."

Semple's nod was almost imperceptible. He waved a hand toward the waiting butler. "What will you have to drink, Miss Cummings?"

Her father, Stacy thought, would probably have understood the ground rules of this meeting, as Ken and Bart seemed to, and she did not. Men were supposed to be direct and to the point. Somebody had turned conventional wisdom inside out.

Before dinner there was talk of the Sanrio fire, the current baseball standings and New Orleans restaurants. Bellevue Acres was not mentioned. Over soup the talk turned to a new television series, the national-budget deficits and the Santa Fe Opera.

"Anyone interested in what we came here for?" Stacy asked as the main course—beef Wellington—was served.

"Her daddy didn't have much patience, either," Bart said.

"Humor me, please, Miss Cummings," Semple said. "My digestion is somewhat delicate, and I try to avoid controversial subjects at mealtimes."

Stacy was aware that Ken was watching her, expressionless, and that Bart Jones wore an amused smile, which annoyed her. She took a sip of wine and tried to think of something bright to say. "Good beef," she came up with finally. "Well hung and from first-rate stock. Hard to come by these days."

Without looking directly, she saw that Bart's amused smile had faded and that Ken wore an expression of approval. "Crossbreeding experiments," she went on, "genetic engineering . . ." She shook her head. "Hard to keep up with."

Semple said, "You are against interference with nature, Miss Cummings?"

"I breed horses," Stacy said. "I go after the results I want, so the answer is no, I am not against changing things. As long as the change benefits instead of hurting people." She smiled suddenly. "You see, I'm really a very simple person."

"I am beginning to doubt it very much," Semple said. "A touch more wine, perhaps?"

In the large living room after dinner there were coffee, cognac and, for Duane Semple, a cigar as well.

"Now to business," Semple said. "Undoubtedly you have a price in mind, Mr. Delacorte?"

Stacy noted Ken's alert expression. The contest had begun.

"A price for exactly what?" Ken said.

"For your interest in Bellevue Acres, of course," Semple said.

"The property," Ken said, "the houses, the people, including the kids and the dogs? The home-built barbecues that smoke and that funny-looking badminton court? My share of all of it?"

"Oh, come on," Bart said from his wheelchair. "Let's not be mawkish. This is a business proposition."

"For you, yes," Ken said. "I see it differently."

Semple said, "I think that is understandable. The project was your idea in the first place, and you worked to bring it to fruition, which involved surmounting a number of obstacles, I am sure."

"Such as getting a zoning variance," Ken said. "That's really what you're interested in, isn't it?"

"Having the zoning variance in place is helpful," Semple said. "There is no question about that."

"Getting the people out," Ken said, "won't present much of a problem, will it? Jack up the interest rates as high as you can, which means increasing the mortgage payments. Make a few extra bucks in the process, and all of a sudden the peasants have gone and you have nice empty land where you can put up your fancy condos. Then the real profits begin."

Semple, wholly unperturbed, admired the long, even ash on the end of his cigar. "Your business school studies were not in vain, Mr. Delacorte," he said at last. "I return to my original question. Undoubtedly you have a price in mind?"

"My interest in Bellevue Acres," Ken said, "is not for sale."

"Indeed?" Semple's tone contained no indication of surprise. "You are already skating on rather thin financial ice, Mr. Delacorte," he said. "We took the trouble to ascertain that. A few obstacles placed in your way, perhaps litigation of some sort or the sudden discovery that certain building codes had not been properly adhered to—expenses arising from matters such as these might cause that thin financial ice to collapse."

"I don't think so," Stacy said.

Ken said sharply, "Stay out of this."

"I think freshman year was the last time you tried to tell me what to do," Stacy said. "It didn't work then, and it's not going to work now." Her glance included them all. "Daddy used to say that it was pretty hard to sit by and watch a bully, in this case apparently two bullies, picking on folks who couldn't fight back. I feel the same way. So—"

The butler, a cordless telephone in hand, coughed politely and said, "Excuse me, sir, but there is a call for Mr. Delacorte."

Semple said, "If you would rather take the call in my library, Mr. Delacorte, please feel free."

Ken merely shook his head and reached for the telephone.

It was Ada. Her voice, under tight control, came clearly. "The fire's broken loose," she said. "I'm not being hysterical. It's on the radio. It's blowing like mad and—"

"On my way." Ken handed the phone back to the butler. "Sorry," he said to Semple, and looked at Stacy as he stood up.

"Right with you." Stacy was already on her feet. Her eyes swept Semple and Bart Jones. "You get the message," she said.

BILLY Bob Barker, the mayor of Sanrio, was neither a bold nor a profane man. He was a pharmacist by trade, and a peaceable soul by nature. But he felt that crisis demanded extraordinary emphasis. "Damn it, George," he told the forest supervisor on the telephone, "I knew this was going to happen. JL is a nice fellow and all that, but apparently he's over the hill, and now we've got a real mess on our hands. Pete Trujillo's market is about to go, they tell me, and if it does, you know what's next?"

George Jefferson's mind was on a number of other matters. "You tell me, Billy Bob."

"The Sanrio Propane Company, that's what. What we'd have

left of downtown would be nothing but a big hole in the ground."

The second light on George Jefferson's phone was blinking. "I've got another call now, Billy Bob. I hope it's JL. I'll get back to you."

It was JL. "We've got a mess down here, George. No question about that. Our airport tower is measuring heavy wind gusts shifting through an arc that takes in a good share of the town. Willard Spencer's house is going. We can't save it. The Cummings place is probably next—"

Jefferson said, "What about that propane storage tank?"

"The city's going to have to take care of that. We're throwing everything we have in a curved line from Sheep Ridge and the Vista Hill grove around to the estates."

"All right," Jefferson said. "Keep at it and keep me posted. Anything you need . . ."

"I'll shout." There was a short pause. "And, George, if you're thinking of replacing me . . ."

"You keep at it. It's still your baby."

Jefferson broke the connection, then dialed Billy Bob's number. "It was JL," Jefferson said, "and things are not good."

"You're replacing him, George?"

"I am not. He's the best we have. Now, here's what you do."

Billy Bob listened. He said at last, "That propane tank—"

"It's a nasty situation," Jefferson said. "No argument. But we have our hands full. Your people can do the job as well as we can."

"And if the fire jumps your line?"

"Then you'd better give thought to dynamiting some houses near the city limits to protect the rest of Sanrio."

"George!"

"I know," Jefferson said. "That's where my house is too."

WILLARD P. Spencer was close to apoplexy. "The governor will hear of this outrage," he told Ben Hastings. "Washington will hear of it! I demand that my house and property be protected!"

"Fine," Ben said. He beckoned one of the crew chiefs. "Get that hose hooked up to the swimming pool, and see that the well pump keeps running until it sucks air."

"That well," Spencer said, "cost fifteen dollars a foot to drill. And if you burn out the pump—"

"Move it, amigo," the crew chief said. "We got work to do and you're in the way." He squinted through sooty eyes at Spencer's immaculate polo shirt, blazer and flannels. "Was I you, I'd be hauling out the family silver and heading for far places."

Angela Spencer took her husband's arm and urged him to one side. "They won't listen to you, Will," she said. "I believe we'd do well to take some things and move to the inn temporarily."

"You don't understand, Angy."

"Quite possibly not. But I can't see that you are accomplishing anything by staying here. The house is obviously threatened, and we may lose it, insurance or not, so—"

"What do you know about insurance?"

"We have none. Isn't that correct?" There was no answer. Angela had expected none. "So," she said, "I think we might well go to the inn. We'll need night things, at least, and you'll want your toilet kit and shaver. We'd best get them while we can."

SOPHIE Swift had the station wagon packed in accordance with the list she had made. With some difficulty she had hooked the horse trailer to the station wagon and urged the mare inside. The foal had followed. The other two horses were tethered behind the trailer, already restive in the gathering smoke.

Sophie did not consider herself an emotional female, and perhaps this was merely one more flaw in her makeup; but now, faced with the logical necessity of abandoning the house she and Aaron had built together and filled with memories, she found herself very close to tears. It was beginning to seem that the life she had once considered so organized and well balanced, so securely built, was now crumbling.

Inside the horse trailer the mare whinnied and stamped a nervous hoof. The two tethered geldings stirred anxiously.

"Easy, boys," Sophie said, but she too was conscious that time was running out and that the sensible thing to do was get into the station wagon and drive away. Still she hesitated.

Through the trees at the forest's edge, she could see flames and hear their crackling menace. The mare in the trailer whinnied again and stamped angrily. The tethered geldings tugged at their ropes.

"All right," Sophie said at last. "You're right. Time to go."

AARON SWIFT WALKED OUT OF the home he and Debby had shared into the eerie near darkness flickeringly lighted by the flames of Backslope. It occurred to him to hope that since things had been bad for so long, the chances were that any change would almost have to be for the better.

And things had been bad. First there had been and still was the fire. Raised in this country, Aaron knew what an agonizingly long time it would take for the forest to replenish itself.

Then of course there was Debby, who had already packed, wept sincerely in their farewells and gone off with her Johnny Joe. Aaron had long approved of the ease with which the laws of New Mexico allowed a husband and wife to decide jointly that they had made a mistake, and almost without further ado to go their separate ways. But now that it had happened to him, and not as a result of his own decision, he saw matters a little differently.

Foremost, of course, Debby's leaving was a blow to his ego. He was honest enough to admit this, and to admit as well that he had done precisely the same thing to Sophie, which left him ruefully contemplating Aaron Swift as a man who deserved sympathy from no one, including himself.

And now, as the final blow, there was the news on the radio that Backslope was out of control here, on its southern end, had just destroyed Willard Spencer's property and was probably fast closing in on the ranch he and Sophie had built together.

Sophie was still at the ranch. Aaron could bet on that. She would be prepared for flight, but she would not have driven away unless the danger had become too imminent, and Aaron did not think it had quite yet.

And here he was, nursing his wounded pride and pretending to mourn the departure of a young wife whom he had teased for her shortcomings.

"You," he told himself aloud, "had better put your priorities in order, Counselor." And with that he walked quickly to his car, got in and set out for Sophie's.

SITTING at the command post table was no longer possible. JL pushed back his chair and stood up. To Ben he said, "You stay here. I've got to get out there and see for myself." He started for the jeep. "I'll keep in touch."

"Take somebody with you," Ben said. But JL was already gone.

As he drove JL studied the map in his mind, setting against it the reports that had continued to flow in. Sheep Ridge first, he decided. He'd give a lot to be able to put Ben in charge of that sector, but Ben was needed right where he was. Then who?

He took the microphone from its bracket on the dashboard. "Find Jay Paul. Tell him to get over to Sheep Ridge. I want him there. Over."

Ben's voice was comfortingly calm. "Roger."

"And get your relief man, Weinstock, and give him the sector to the west, where the estates are."

Again the comforting "Roger."

"Over and out for now." JL hung up the mike and concentrated on driving.

KEN and Stacy were speeding along the county road near the Holloway place. By the furious glare of the fire they could make out what was left of the house: two standing walls pierced by a gaping doorway and a large hole where a window had been.

Stacy said unexpectedly, "Serves us right. All of us. Building that close to the wildland."

"JL's tub-thumping has got to you, has it?"

"Now hold on," Stacy began automatically, and stopped. "Okay," she said in a different tone. "The answer is yes."

There was a long silence, unbroken until they rounded the last bend in the road and approached Stacy's drive. Then, "Ken, look!" she called.

It was the Spencer house, still in flames. And in a scene from hell, the moving figures of fire fighters threw enormous shadows against the curtain of smoke rising from the forest trees.

"Ada was right," Ken said. "The wind—look there, that shower of sparks and burning branches!"

"Let me out at the end of my drive," Stacy said, remembering JL's dislike of the long, curving one-way entrance. "I don't want you stuck up by the house not able to get turned around."

"Okay." Ken looked at her gravely. "I'm not going to try to tell you what to do," he said, "but if it comes to a choice between you and your horses . . ."

"I'll take care of it."

"I know you will, but what I'm trying to tell you is to take care of yourself as well, you hear?"

"I hear." Stacy's voice was unexpectedly soft. She put her hand on his arm. "Stop worrying."

"Fat chance. You're—" He stood on the brakes as a car burst out of the entrance to Stacy's drive and almost rammed them. Ken could see that a woman was driving. "Juanita!" Stacy was already out of the car, racing to the other. When she reached it she bent to the window.

"The fire!" Juanita's words almost ran together. "And Pancho. That *chico!* He thinks of nothing but the horses. He is letting them out of their stalls. . . ."

Stacy half turned to wave at Ken. "Beat it! You too, Juanita!"

She turned then and began to run up the curving drive, uncertain on the high-heeled sandals, holding the long skirt above her knees. At last she burst into the parking area and found the house still intact. She swerved and ran toward the horse barns.

She saw Pancho. He was bareback on a big gray gelding, clinging like a burr, controlling the animal with a hackamore rope instead of a bridle. He saw Stacy, and his face split wide in a white-toothed grin. "*Vámonos, señorita!* Let's go! There is a hackamore on Sam! And the horses are loose!" He gestured to them milling in the shadows.

Good boy, Stacy thought, and ran toward Sam, who stood patiently, the rope hanging to the ground. The smell of smoke was thick now, choking. The milling horses whinnied in panic.

Stacy seized the hackamore rope, and then looked down in disgust at the long, impossible dress she wore. "Hold it, Sam," she said, and dropped the rope. With both hands she tore the dress up to the waist, and let the bottom half drop to the ground.

She seized the rope again, and a handful of Sam's mane. "Move it, boy! Let's go!" And as the big horse took his first jump forward Stacy vaulted to his back. "Get them moving, Pancho!" She pursed her lips, whistled shrilly and waved her free arm. "*Yeeeeay!*" And another whistle.

"Not the drive!" she shouted to Pancho. "Down the hill, away from the road!" There would be cars, maybe fire trucks, too much chance of collision. "Take them past Mr. Jones' house, toward the Swift property!"

Sophie Swift opened the door of the station wagon and started to get in. In the trailer the mare whinnied and stamped loudly again. "Easy!" Sophie said automatically, but hesitating there in the darkness, she too was conscious of something she could not comprehend. She searched the trees for the cause.

It was a sound, but it was also a feeling, as if the earth itself were shaking beneath her feet. And suddenly, amid the shadows, there was a running horse, and another, and then a bunched mass and a thunder of hoofs. A shrill whistle cut through the sounds without warning, and a voice raised above the din shouted, "You go on, Pancho! Take them toward Vista Hill!"

Sophie, only partially comprehending, could see then a big gray gelding, and on his back, hunched forward like a jockey, a small human shape that shouted, *"Aaaiiie! Arriba! Vámonos!"* A thin brown arm waved a coiled rope as the gray leaned obediently into his turn, forcing the mass of horses to the new direction. They galloped off into the darkness.

And here, on Sam, came Stacy, to rein the big horse to a skittering stop as she surveyed the situation: Sophie beside the station wagon, with the horse trailer behind and the geldings in tow.

"Turn the geldings loose," Stacy ordered. "I'll take care of them. You have the mare and the foal in the trailer? Good. Get going. Luck." She half turned on Sam's back to stare at headlights coming up the drive. "Who's this?"

Sophie too was staring at the headlights, as if mesmerized. She could make out the shape of the vehicle behind the lights only dimly, but somehow she *knew*—

"Turn the geldings loose!" Stacy commanded sharply, and Sophie stumbled to the rear of the horse trailer to obey.

She heard Stacy say then, "Oh, it's you! Good. About time. Get that wagon and trailer out of here! Pronto!" And again the shrill whistle sounded as the two geldings moved free and Stacy disappeared into the darkness.

Sophie hurried back to the station wagon. Inside the trailer the mare was whinnying in terror. "We're going!" Sophie almost screamed, and toward the now stopped headlights she called, "Is it you? Is it?"

"You lead," Aaron's calm voice said. "I'll follow. It's going to be all right, Soph."

"Oh, thank God!" As she scrambled into the car seat and switched on the engine, Sophie had no idea whether she had said the words aloud, or only in her mind.

From his vantage point well above timberline on the great mountain, Andy McIlvain could look down almost as if from the cabin of his plane, with a broad view of Backslope's vast area. He could watch the surging flames as wind gusts buffeted them, and although the distance was too great to hear any sounds, he could imagine the tumult on the fire lines.

It seemed the war was being won; that much was clear. In the northwest the first wind shift had driven flames back across highway 14 into territory already burned. There the flames were expiring from lack of fuel. In the northeast and east Gordy's and Bessie's crews had cut a fire line that was holding. By now, Gordy and Bessie and their people had probably been brought down to the one remaining area of great danger—Sheep Ridge and into the finger of the forest—where fire threatened the big estates, the housing development and the town itself.

It was the way these things worked, Andy thought; gradually you got one part of the area under control, then another, and yet a third; and as these conquered territories became joined, the fire shrank until at last, as now, you were in a position to throw everything you had into the last breach in your line.

His eyes still on the scene before him, he lifted his radio and called the dispatcher. "Patch me through to JL," he said. When the familiar voice acknowledged, Andy said, "Call me your eye in the sky. I've got a clear view of the entire battlefield."

JL, driving with one hand and manipulating the jeep's mike with the other, felt an immediate surge of hope. Andy with a view of the whole area—nothing could be better. Were they beginning to get the breaks at last? "I'm in a jeep," he said, "trying to cover the entire line. Mrs. Wayne's grove that we backfired—is it holding as a break?"

"As of now. Bellevue Acres is still intact."

"And down the finger area?"

"Troops fighting a rearguard action. And I suggest that if you're thinking of another backfire to protect the town, you'd better get to it quick. There's that empty parking lot by the rodeo grandstand,

and if you set your backfire with that lot behind you . . ."

"Got it. And Andy . . . stay right where you are."

"Aye, aye, sir."

ADA was waiting in front of the house when Ken drove up. She greeted him with an unsteady, welcoming smile. "I'm sorry," she said, taking his arm. "I—"

"You did just right. It's bad."

"What do we do now?"

"I get out of this soup and fish and into jeans and go over to Bellevue Acres."

"To do what? And why? That's so close to the fire line!"

"Slow down, baby. Those are my houses. In a sense, they're my people too, and—"

"But what can you do?"

Ken had taken off his dinner jacket and was undoing his tie. He stopped and looked at Ada. "Not a thing—except be there."

Ada shook her head, as if to drive a bad dream away. "Okay," she said then. "But I go too."

"Now look—"

"You look," Ada said, and her voice was firm. "I know the place. It's full of kids. Kids worry. I'm good with kids." She smiled. "I used to be one. Maybe I still am. Where you go, buster, I'm tagging right along."

COMING back from Duane Semple's house, alone in the rear seat of the big car, Bart Jones switched on the radio, tuned to the local station and immediately wished he hadn't.

"And while it is not yet known how many thousands of acres the fire has consumed," an announcer's voice said, "it is now apparent that Sanrio itself is threatened, and desperate measures are being taken in the town's defense."

Desperate measures unspecified, Bart thought, and switched off the sound. He doubted if he would get a more coherent account, and in any event he was about to see for himself just how serious the problem had become.

In the front seat the driver reacted as if the thoughts had been spoken aloud. Without turning his head, he said, "Do you think it's safe, sir? To drive to the house, I mean?" It was a mistake.

"We'll find out, won't we?" Bart said. Always he reacted instantly at the first hint of a challenge. "Just keep driving. I'll tell you when or if we're going to stop."

JL BRAKED the jeep to a sliding stop on a dirt road that overlooked the town. The air was filled with flying sparks and ash and acrid smoke. He surveyed the area swiftly but carefully, wanting no oversight to turn into a mistake.

There was the parking area, acres in extent, that Andy had mentioned, bare dirt and patches of grama grass, which would amount to nothing as supporting fuel. Next to the parking area was the ancient wooden rodeo grandstand.

Beyond the rodeo grounds the town itself began, only scattered houses at first, but farther on, more houses crowded together, divided by narrow streets as old as Sanrio itself. Once flames reached those houses, there would be no stopping the conflagration. On the other hand, JL thought, if they could hold it here, it just might spell the beginning of the end for his voracious enemy.

He plucked the microphone from its bracket, identified himself and his position, sent out another call for Jay Paul, ordering him from Sheep Ridge "on the double," and hung up.

While he waited he reviewed the situation in his mind. He had no panacea, he thought; indeed, with the winds what they were, he could be sure of absolutely nothing.

A short time later Jay Paul drove up and got out of his own jeep. Immediately JL pointed to the finger of the forest. "We're fighting a losing battle there. All we're doing is slowing the fire's progress. But we *are* doing that, and that gives us a little time."

Jay Paul listened in silence. Since flying with the jumpers, JL thought, Jay had seemed to mature. It was strange how quickly it could happen. No matter. JL pointed again, in the direction of the town this time. "Those two parallel roads," he said, "thick piñon and juniper growth between." Jay Paul nodded.

"Below the lower road," JL went on, "there's that parking area and the grandstand. Then the town begins." He paused. "And it's all downwind." He waited.

"So we burn out the piñon and juniper between the roads," Jay said. "If we do it fast enough, it will give us a firebreak as wide as the space between the roads, *plus* the parking area to protect the town." He paused. "And the grandstand?"

"Explosives," JL said. "Take it right down flat. Lumber lying on the ground we can handle if it starts to burn. Flying sparks from a standing grandstand can go right over our heads and start setting roofs afire in town."

Jay Paul thought about it briefly before he nodded. JL liked that moment of contemplation instead of blind obedience.

"You're in charge," JL said. "I want to see the rest of the line firsthand. You can reach me on the radio."

KEN was surrounded as soon as he got to Bellevue Acres. Head and shoulders above the group, he was easy, friendly, in the face of what looked like incipient hysteria. "How's it going? Okay?"

The man who had complained previously to Ben Hastings said now, "No, it's not okay! Look at all those burning branches flying around! You call that okay?"

Behind him two or three men had their garden hoses out and were spraying the roofs of their houses. "I think," Ken said in a voice that had altered subtly, "that you'd better get off your duff, mister, and hitch up your hose and fall to with the rest of them. Let the women pack up, just in case."

"And just how will we know when to run? Tell me that!"

"The Forest Service people will get word to you."

"I wouldn't trust those clowns to do anything. That's—"

"Mister," Ken said, his voice very quiet now, "I'm trying to be friendly, but you're making it hard. If you keep stirring these people up, you're going to have real trouble on your hands, starting with me." He paused. "Is that clear?"

The man hesitated. Slowly he nodded. "Okay." He turned away and said to the woman behind him, "Where's our hose?"

Ken looked around at the group. "Any more questions?"

Ada, standing a small distance away, took a deep breath. To a nine-year-old boy she said, "Hi. What's your name? Jimmy? Okay, Jimmy, how's about you get a bucket. Fill it with water. Then get a couple of tin cans, and you and I will set up an auxiliary fire brigade."

"You nuts or something? What can we do?"

"What we can do," Ada said, "is keep our eyes open for burning twigs, like that one over there. And when we see one, we dip up water in our tin can and douse the twig. Okay?"

"Where'll you be?"

Ada tried to keep her eyes from the flames in the finger of the forest beyond Mrs. Wayne's blackened grove. "I'll be right here, Jimmy." She took another deep breath. "Promise."

ON THE map in his mind JL visualized the fire line as beginning somewhere in the forest above Stacy's section of land and stretching east–southeast through a part of the Swifts' property and Ada Loving's, dipping down to include the Holloways' and Mrs. Wayne's specimen grove, then rising northeast across the finger area and above the county road.

"Give or take a half mile," he said aloud to himself, and called for Andy McIlvain.

From the timberline Andy's voice came in loud and clear.

"Your end position is near that El Rancho Costa Mucho place— and then, you're right, it runs pretty much the way you thought, staying above the county road. On the western side, by the big houses, they've got a job on their hands, but it looks as if they may contain it."

"I'll have a look-see," JL said. "Over and out."

The shortcut he took was no more than a deer path, but in low transmission and four-wheel drive the jeep bounced and hammered its way through the low brush.

Suddenly, there was the end of the fire line, ground crews at work with hand tools, and two bulldozers pushing loose debris out of the fire's way. JL stopped and got out. As far as he could see in the smoky murk and dust, men were working almost shoulder to shoulder, cutting their firebreak. JL caught sight of Jerry Weinstock, whom he had told Ben to put in charge of this sector, and made his way toward him.

Jerry was tall, cadaverous, all whipcord and spring steel, now filthy, smoke grimed and obviously near exhaustion. But he waited quietly in his reserved way, his eyes steady on JL's face.

"Can you hold the line?" JL said.

"We'll hold it." No hesitation, no doubt.

JL nodded, then turned away, and with no further words made his way back to his jeep. The radio was crackling as he got in.

"Jay Paul here." There was anger in the voice. "The mayor objects to the backfire. And to blowing the grandstand."

A new voice came on the radio. "Look here, JL. If they blow up that grandstand, how do we stage a rodeo this year? Answer me that. All that tourist trade and traffic—"

JL pressed his microphone switch, shutting off reception. "Jay?"

"Jay here." JL could picture the mike suddenly plucked from the mayor's hand.

"Carry on with that backfire," JL said. "I'm on my way." He started up the jeep's engine with a roar. Pushing the vehicle as fast as it would go through the brush, he thought of all kinds of things he might say to His Honor the Mayor.

And then all at once in his headlights, in the dimness of the forest growth, he saw what he could not for an instant really believe—Stacy, in the shreds of an evening dress, bent low on Sam's withers, herding two other horses ahead of her and running straight toward what JL knew was an area aflame.

He blew the jeep's horn and shouted, but the apparition was already gone into the gathering gloom.

JL, reacting automatically, spun the wheel, bore down hard on the throttle and set off in pursuit. The mayor, the backfire—both would have to wait.

THE horses sensed the flames ahead before Stacy saw them, and without warning one of the Swift geldings screamed, turned suddenly and ran headlong through a solid mass of piñon and juniper branches without slowing. The other gelding followed.

Sam at full gallop spun as only a cutting horse can, and tore off in a new direction, heading instinctively for the county road. Stacy had no saddle horn to grab, so she settled for a firm handful of Sam's mane, which she almost pulled out by its roots as she struggled to retain her balance. "Sam! Ho, boy!" Wasted breath. With no bit in Sam's mouth to control his flight Stacy was helpless, clinging as best she could as they crashed through low branches and across the bottom of a dry arroyo.

Up the far side without slowing the mad pace, and there in the darkness a low, solid pine branch scraped Stacy from Sam's back as cleanly as one scrapes snow from a boot sole.

She hit the ground and, rolling limply, fetched up against a dumped pile of debris by the side of the road. She lay motionless as Sam thundered off into the night.

A STATE policeman flagged down Bart's car. "Sorry," he said, leaning in the lowered rear window. "It isn't safe to go on."

"I live in there."

"Maybe you did," the cop said, "but it's a fair bet there isn't anything left to live in now."

"That I'll see for myself. And I'll take full responsibility."

"Look, mister, my orders are to—"

The radio in the police car across the road came alive with a hollow sound, and a voice spoke in police radio jargon. The cop turned away and walked quickly to the vehicle.

"Let's go!" Bart said, and when the driver hesitated, "You heard me!"

The big car rolled down the county road.

It was a scene of desolation, and even Bart, not customarily sensitive to his surroundings, was shocked by the smoking destruction of what had been a green, living forest.

"*Madre de Díos,*" the driver implored. "*Señor—*"

"Just keep going," Bart said.

They rounded a broad curve and, astonishingly, came upon a stand of tall, still living trees, flames now attacking their helpless perimeter. Wind gusts rocked the treetops, and a burning branch flew across the road and narrowly missed the car.

"*Señor—*" the driver said again.

"Shut up!" Automatic response. And then in a louder, far more urgent tone, "Stop! Stop the car, hear?"

The body by the side of the road showed clearly in the headlights, naked legs white in the glare.

"Good Lord!" Bart said. And then, "Don't just sit there, damn it! Get out and fetch her here! Jump!"

The driver set the brake and opened the door. Reluctantly he stepped out. The woman looked dead, he told himself; and he had no desire to touch her. Around him the wind wailed and shrieked with the sounds of souls in torment.

From the car Bart's voice bellowed, "Get going!"

One careful step, and then another, trying to look in all direc-

251

tions at once; and so it was that the driver saw and avoided the large burning branch that flew toward him and crashed into the car, starring the windshield as if from a hammerblow. Suddenly the car was engulfed in flames.

Without even looking back, the driver turned and fled.

IN ROUGH wooded country a jeep was no match for a western-bred horse. JL, having lost the trail, was pursuing Stacy merely by guesswork now. He plunged on, ignoring the brush and the small branches that snapped against the windshield.

There was fire to the right of him and fire ahead, so close he could feel its heat. He came to the dry arroyo Stacy had crossed, took its steep bank at an angle that almost overturned the jeep and, all four wheels churning, scrambled up the far side. Brush ahead suddenly burst into flame, and he floored the accelerator.

For a moment the heat of the flames seemed to sear his flesh, but the moment passed, and he was through and clear, bouncing out onto the county road, where Bart's automobile stood burning. He stopped then, jumped out and ran as close as he could.

Bart had managed to get the rear door open. Now, dragging himself by his hands, his clothing afire, he was making his tortured way toward the verge of the road. He saw JL, and instantly his expression of grim determination changed to triumph.

"Get her!" His words came out as a croaking scream as he lifted one hand to point. "Get her out of here! Never mind me!"

JL glanced toward the side of the road where Stacy's body lay motionless, seemingly lifeless. Stunned, he moved toward the body, slowly at first, and then broke into a trot. He scooped her up, finding her limp in his arms as he ran back to the jeep and sat her gently in the front bucket seat. Then he turned back to Bart.

Bart's head was down, but it came up again, still wearing that expression of triumph. "Now get out of here!" Bart said, gesturing at the trees. "Look!"

Near the edge of the stand a stately pine, aflame from trunk to top, was beginning a slow, inexorable death fall toward the road.

"Go!" Bart croaked. His head collapsed on the dirt.

JL ran to the jeep and jumped in. A few yards to a safer spot, he told himself, and then he could go back. He was starting away when a crackling, tearing sound announced that the last of the big tree's restraining roots had torn loose. In the jeep's mirror JL could see the tree itself, gathering speed as it fell.

He floored the accelerator, and even at the surging speed felt the heat of the burning branches as they crashed across the road behind him. He looked in the mirror again and saw no Bart, no car, only the rising flames of a funeral pyre filling the road.

He drove on, his mind numb.

BESSIE Wingate, summoned to the Jeep by JL's waving arm, her shovel still in her hand, stared at the limp body in the front seat. She took in JL's stricken expression and nodded decisively.

"I'll take care of her. You tend to your backfire." She tossed the shovel into the rear seat as she squeezed herself beneath the jeep's steering wheel. She added angrily, "Will this slaughter ever stop?" and thought of Eloy Jaramillo, poor little guy.

The jeep roared off into the night.

Chapter Twelve

JL MOVED like a man in a dream toward the spot where his boss, George Jefferson, Mayor Billy Bob Barker and Jay Paul stood waiting. On his way he noticed automatically that the backfire had been set between the two parallel roads, burning upwind from the parking area and the grandstand, and that the towering fire in the finger of the forest had progressed.

"We're wiring charges under the grandstand," Jay Paul said.

"Good." JL spoke in a normal, calm tone, as if they were merely discussing the baseball pennant races.

"You okay?" Jefferson said. "You look skinned up."

JL shrugged, indicating that what had gone before was unimportant. "Jerry Weinstock has his end anchored, secure. This is what we have to worry about." His broad gesture included the finger area, the burning backfire, the town. He looked at Jay Paul. "Who's setting the charges?"

"I called down Gordy Walker and one of his crew, Terry Young."

Jefferson watched a burning branch flying through the air in the direction of the grandstand. "Better get them out of there."

JL held out his hand for Jay's walkie-talkie. He pressed the mike button. "JL here. Come in, Gordy. Over."

It was Terry who answered. "Hi, boss."

"How much longer?" JL said.

In the background Gordy's voice said, "Tell the man ten minutes. Maybe a little more."

"You're catching sparks," JL said.

Again Gordy's voice. "Ten minutes. We want a complete job."

JL closed his eyes and nodded. "You got it." He handed the walkie-talkie back to Jay Paul. "Ten men," he said, "with pack pumps. Douse whatever lands on or near the structure." He turned to Billy Bob. "Get your city fire pumper at the far edge of the parking area. When she blows, there'll be sparks flying."

"I'm against this," the mayor said. "I want to go on record—"

"Noted," JL said. "So now get your pumper in place."

FROM his mountain perch Andy McIlvain studied the situation with experienced eyes. At last he raised his walkie-talkie.

"It's blowing merry hell up here," Andy reported to JL. "And I imagine it is down there too. Your west flank is holding. Whoever's in charge there—"

"Jerry Weinstock," JL said.

"He looks in fair shape. Bellevue Acres looks reasonably safe too. The backfire by the parking area—"

"That's where I am."

"Figured." Andy's voice took on a new, warning note. "There's more wind coming at you, pappy. I can see the smoke north of you lying out flat. You'd better blow that grandstand quick."

"Got it," JL said. "Over and out." He handed Jay Paul the radio and looked at Jefferson. "You heard? Okay." He jerked his head sideways at Billy Bob Barker but spoke still to Jefferson. "Kick his backside if you have to, but get that town pumper in position. Those homes are going to need all the protection they can get."

Then JL turned away and was gone, headed at a brisk trot for the grandstand. Bending low, he ran in under it.

Beneath the grandstand JL switched on his helmet light and made his way as quickly as he could toward the lights farther in that marked Gordy and Terry Young's location. Reaching them, he found Terry wiring a charge to one of the uprights.

Gordy said, "We'll bring her down, not blow her up. Take out these supports and she'll collapse like a house of cards."

One of Gordy's crewmen scrambled in toward them. "You're still clear overhead. The structure hasn't caught yet. But pack pumps won't hold what's flying around. That wind is *blowing!*"

Gordy moved quickly to the next upright to wire his charge.

JL followed him. "You've got a reel of wire? Good. You, Terry, take it on out and hook it up. We'll hook onto it here when we've got the charges set. Now beat it."

And then JL and Gordy were alone, working with careful haste. Gordy said, "Old guy I knew once drove a nitroglycerin truck in the oil fields back in the '30s. Got a dollar a mile, big wages then. Got paid every night. Spent it every night too. Man has to be crazy to take a job like that, no?" He threw a quick glance at JL, and in the light of his helmet lamp his face showed a faint smile.

JEFFERSON said to Billy Bob, "I'm not going to tell you again. Get that pumper in place!" He watched a burning juniper branch fly through the air and land almost lazily among the darkened grandstand seats. He waited, but no flames appeared.

Billy Bob said, "We can post more men in the grandstand, can't we? I mean, to put out any fires that could start?"

"We could not!" Jefferson's voice was sharp now. "If that firetrap ever begins to go—" He stopped, his eyes still fixed on the spot where the juniper branch had disappeared. "Oh, Lord!" he said softly. "There she goes!"

One moment there was a small column of smoke; then, incredibly, the smoke turned into flame that ran along a wooden seat and jumped to the next row. Within moments an entire section of seats was ablaze.

Jefferson turned, grabbed a walkie-talkie from a man in a yellow hard hat and pressed the microphone button. "Jefferson here," he said. "The stands are on fire. Get out. Repeat, get out!"

Terry, outside on his knees attaching the detonator to the wire he had carried with him, said, "They're coming as fast as they can."

"Damn it—" Jefferson began.

And here came Gordy on a dead run, to slide to a stop in the gravel and hunker down to inspect Terry's connections. "Okay." He nodded judiciously. "That ought to do her."

"Look at JL," Terry said. "For an old man, he motors pretty good."

JL was running toward them awkwardly, holding one arm with the other hand. His voice was raised in a shout that reached them clearly. "All set! Blow it!"

Terry pressed the detonator handle. There was a dull harrumphing sound. For a moment nothing happened, and then the whole flaming grandstand structure seemed to shudder, and with slow dignity collapsed inward upon itself in a fiery mass. All that remained when it had settled was a low-lying pile of shattered lumber, burning as a fire burns in a grate.

Out of breath, JL ran up to Jefferson, whose eyes were on the burning debris. "Town pumper on the way," Jefferson said. "It can handle that." He looked at JL. "What happened to your arm?"

JL made a sharp gesture, dismissing the question, and turned to survey the scene. The burned-over area between the two roads was still glowing, still throwing wind-driven sparks and burning branches into the air, but with the grandstand no longer there the threat was gone. Beyond the upper road, in the finger of the forest, the force and fury of the fire were slowly diminishing for want of fresh fuel. The town pumper arrived, clanging noisily, and firemen set about subduing what was left of the burning grandstand.

Jefferson watched JL. He was still holding his arm. Jefferson turned to Gordy Walker. "What's wrong with him?"

"A timber burned loose and fell on his shoulder as we were wrapping up."

Jefferson blinked. "It was that close?"

Gordy's face and voice were expressionless. "Let's say we didn't have a lot of leeway."

Reaching into the jeep with his good hand, JL switched on the radio and took up the mike. "Patch me through to Jerry Weinstock." And when the connection was made, "Still holding?"

No hesitation. "We'll hold it," Weinstock said.

"Good man." JL's voice held its customary calm. He switched back to the dispatcher and said, "Now get me Andy McIlvain up on the mountain."

It was not over yet, he thought, not quite, but despite everything they had the upper hand now, and unless Andy had bad news the outcome was no longer in doubt.

Andy's voice said, "That was quite a cliff-hanger, but never mind. You pulled it off. The town looks good from here."

"And the rest of the way around?"

"You're under control. Little flare-ups here and there, but what the heck, you'll have those to contend with for days."

True enough. But it was still good news. "Over and out," JL said, and called the dispatcher again. "Now Ben Hastings." And when Ben's voice came on, "How are we at the development?"

"So far, okay. They're packed up, ready to get out if they have to." Ben hesitated. "Your friend Delacorte wants somebody official there, but . . ."

"Yes," JL said in sudden understanding. In the end, he thought, it all came down to people, individuals—not forests or trees or paintings on canvas—individual persons. Like Stacy. "Tell Ken I'm on the way," he said. "You can reach me there."

As JL pulled up in the jeep, Ken Delacorte was easily visible, towering above the householders, directing hoses here and there, smiling, encouraging, praising. Nearby, Ada Loving was totally occupied with the kids, who scurried to and fro at her direction.

"Breaking her to harness?" JL asked when Ken joined him.

"That'll be the day." Ken's smile disappeared. His eyes studied JL's face intently. "What's the word?"

JL could savor the moment. Once again they had fought the beast and won. They had lost a great deal, but they had learned some things too, and in the process had prepared some good young people, like Ben Hastings and Jay Paul, to take over. So it was no standoff; it was victory, and he could say it with pride. "You're safe. We've got it whipped. You can tell them that."

BESSIE Wingate, now cramped into store clothes and scrubbed until she shone, was coming out of a room at the hospital as JL, his arm in a sling, walked down the corridor. Bessie stopped. "What happened to you?" She shook her head. "Never mind. You look like you'll live."

JL was smiling faintly. "I expect to."

"Somebody," Bessie said, "said they heard you were quitting. I said, 'That's a lot of baloney.' You get a taste for smoke, and like a drunk, you can't give it up." She flipped one large hand in a parting gesture. "See you at the next one," she said, and rolled off down the corridor.

JL watched her go. Bessie was about as subtle as a fist in the mouth, and nothing was going to change her, ever.

He glanced up at the number of the room Bessie had been visiting, knocked on the partially open door and went in.

Stacy was propped up in bed, her left arm in a cast, but her face reflected no pain and her eyes watched him steadily.

JL looked around the room at the vases of flowers. "I guess I ought to have brought something."

"You know better. You're the reason I'm still here at all."

"Your friend is. Was. Jones."

Stacy shook her head gently, as if to drive that thought away.

"I just wanted to see how you were," JL said.

Stacy was smiling faintly, almost certainly reading his thoughts. "You whipped it," she said. "I knew you would."

"We were lucky."

"Yes." The faint smile was gone, but amusement remained in her eyes, and something else. "The harder you fight," she said, "the luckier you get. I've noticed that too. Shall we add that to the list of things we have to talk about?"

"That list," JL said, "is getting pretty long." He took a deep breath. "What I mean is—"

"That it's going to keep on growing," Stacy said. "Yes. I've been thinking that too. It's going to take a very long time to talk our way through it."

From sparks that had flown between them, JL thought suddenly, to—this. Hard to believe. But also more pleasant to think about than he would have thought possible. He said slowly, "Maybe we won't ever reach the end of it."

Stacy's smile had returned, but its amusement was replaced by pure warmth. "We'll have fun finding out," she said. "Together."

Firsthand experience is a trademark of Richard Martin Stern's intensely realistic fiction. *Wildfire*, his seventh novel to appear in Condensed Books, is a case in point, for the veteran storyteller himself battled forest fires as a teenager in California. "My family had a place near the Angeles National Forest," he explains, "and whenever there was a fire, the ranger would come and ask for volunteers. Once you've seen a forest fire close up," he adds, "you don't forget it!"

Richard Martin Stern

A stickler for authenticity, Stern also familiarized himself with the latest fire-containment methods, and even flew with a team of smoke jumpers over New Mexico's vast Gila National Forest. "Quite an experience," he says. "I was sitting on the floor right next to the open doorway—there is no door—and watched the first two men go out, and my stomach went with them! They were jumping from twelve hundred feet into a place that looked no bigger than my hand. And they did it!"

The starkly beautiful countryside of New Mexico is something else the author knows intimately. For twenty years he and his wife, Dorothy, have lived in the hills of Santa Fe in a house they designed themselves, "with lots of glass and a view of three mountain ranges." Though both Sterns are native Californians, they are clearly devoted to their adopted home in the Southwest. "There's a sense of space out here which we love," he explains. "Some days you can sit on the portico and feel as if you're looking forever."

For recreation the author and his wife, who have been married for nearly fifty years, enjoy walking and traveling. Over the years Mrs. Stern has learned to keep a detailed journal of their trips, which her husband refers to when he needs facts and figures on faraway places. However, when Dick Stern went up with the smoke jumpers, Dorothy remained with her feet planted firmly on the ground!

Arnie

and
a house
full
of company

A CONDENSATION OF THE BOOK BY

Margarete Sigl Corbo
and
Diane Marie Barras

ILLUSTRATED BY MARK SCHULER

For Margarete Corbo, it is an uncertain homecoming. Returning to her family home on Cape Cod after an absence of seven years, she finds the house filled with echoes of the past and memories of relatives long gone.

But almost at once she discovers a larger and more varied family. It includes friends and neighbors, as well as a host of animals that march, fly or waddle their way into her yard. And greeting them all is Arnie, the pet starling she rescued from a daisy patch years before.

Here, as in her first book, Arnie, the Darling Starling, Mrs. Corbo recounts the true story of that remarkable bird and his uncanny knack for bolstering the spirits of all those around him. And though the Corbo household may get just a wee bit crowded from time to time, it is a house full of warmth and love, in which the reader too will find a welcome place.

CHAPTER ONE

SINGING at the top of my lungs, I swung the Blazer into the driveway, slammed on the brakes, and gasped. "Where's the house? Somebody's stolen my house!"

Aghast, I tumbled from the car and looked around. The modest Cape Cod ranch in which I had lived for more than twenty years was nowhere in sight. The quarter-acre lot upon which it should be so clearly evident was a dense miniforest surrounded by a thicket of tall hedges. And amid it all stood I—cold, tired, hungry, and feeling permanently attached to the behemoth of a trailer I'd just hauled two thousand miles, from Texas to Falmouth, Massachusetts.

I leaned my head back, closed my eyes, and shouted with frustration. "Is there an idle jinni around? My three wishes are simple: a hot shower, a crackling fire, and a bowl of steaming clam chowder!" It was one of those raw autumn days that call for such wishes: gusty, misty, chilly—the kind of weather that chases away the last remnants of tourists and summer residents, leaving Cape Cod to its small, permanent off-season population. Aside from the wind and the occasional lowing of a distant foghorn, there were no sounds about me, no signs of activity to lessen the desolation I felt.

Taking a few steps to the side, I searched for the sidewalk that had to be somewhere beneath the sweeping spruce branches. Then I spotted the silvery sheen of well-weathered cedar shingles peeping through evergreen needles. A drainpipe wobbled stiffly within the loosened grasp of a metal strap binding it. Nature had stolen my house from view and begun to ravage it, but it was there, within the trees, waiting for me to reclaim it.

Stepping onto the front stoop, I slipped the key my brother had mailed to me into the doorknob. The lock clicked quietly, and the door opened a tiny crack. I drew in a deep breath, gave the door a push, and went in. Immediately a spiderweb engulfed the right side of my face, and I leaped backward and teetered on the edge of the stoop.

"No way will I go inside alone," I muttered. I stepped down and broke into a trot, not slowing until I reached the car. Glancing over my shoulder, I could see one window, its shutters askew and broken. Through it shone a light. Yet the house had been unoccupied for years. Jittery with wild imaginings, I yanked open the car door and was barraged by a cacophony of mournful yowls.

"Keep your complaints to yourselves, cats," I said. "My nerves can't take your nonsense today." Reaching into the back seat, I wrestled out two of the four travel cages, rushed with them to the house, and shoved them inside the door. "Yell all you want now," I said. "In fact, sound ferocious! If there's an intruder here, let him know I'm not alone." But my two black-furred felines, Samantha and her son, Vagabond, just stared at me—silently.

The screech of brakes from a faded orange Volkswagen shattered the quiet. "Maa-gret, Maa-gret," called a voice with a hearty Boston accent. "It's really you! I couldn't believe it when I heard your voice on the phone."

"You didn't have to rush over so fast, M.A.," I said as my old friend strode toward me with a welcoming smile. Mary Alice hadn't changed a bit in the twenty years since my daughter, Hannelore, had introduced us. Her long, strong-featured face was framed by light auburn hair that spilled over her wool plaid poncho, and her every gesture was flamboyant.

"Looks like the place has reverted to jungle." She looked around, tsk-tsking in sympathy at the dilapidated condition of the house and yard. "Don't worry," she said, "you'll have it shaped up in no time."

"I'm not so sure I'll bother. I thought I was finally ready to come back, but now that I'm here . . ." I shrugged. "I don't know if I'll be able to stay. I feel like a displaced person."

"You're tired, that's all," she said.

"And cranky. And cold. Let's get into the house."

After another trip to the car I led the way, carrying the third cat, Mitzi, and the birdcage. As I paused in the doorway, M.A. said, "I see you still have the bird and the cat."

"Same cat, plus two others—different bird." I took a cautious step through the door. The lamp beside my mother's chair was on, as was the light in the kitchen. I took another step and felt the warmth of the house embracing me, the nurturing warmth of home. It was as if I had just been down the road to the grocery store, instead of absent for seven years, as if the life and love and laughter of so many friends and family were still housed within these four walls.

"It's strange having this house empty," I said. "I wrote ahead to have the electricity turned on, but it was eerie to see light shining through the window. Guess my brother forgot to turn them off when he locked up." I put the birdcage down on the living-room coffee table and whisked off its cover, then opened the doors that confined the cats. Cautiously, they stepped out of their cages into the room and began a sniffing exploration that would undoubtedly keep them busy for hours.

Close on my heels, M.A. kept up a running chatter as I flipped on lights and inspected the other rooms. Though the beds were neatly made, vacant closets gaped open and crooked drawers gave evidence of a hasty emptying in the two bedrooms where my parents had spent their last days. In each, fallen tree branches protruded through broken windows. I closed the doors behind us; tomorrow was soon enough to cope with the realities of those unoccupied rooms.

"Help me settle in for the night, will you?" I said. "There are a few things I need from the store. I don't have the energy to struggle with that trailer again today."

Clutching my hastily scribbled list, M.A. backed the Volkswagen out of the drive, waving as she drove off. I grabbed a suitcase and the overnight bag from the car. Something brushed my ankle, scurried past, and stopped a few steps down the walkway. Looking up at me, a gray squirrel stood tall on its hind legs, its eyes brightly curious, its nose twitching. "Well, hello," I said. "Guess you and I are going to be neighbors." It cocked its head to one side, gave me three brisk tail waggles, and bounced away to join two other squirrels nearby. Like an audience, they watched as I struggled with my bags up the steps and through the door.

"Is that you, Mrs. Corbo? Margarete?" someone called.

"Huh? Yes," I said. I turned and smiled at the middle-aged blond woman standing in the doorway. "How are you, April?"

"Welcome home, my dear. Welcome home." She stepped forward to hug me. "I saw the trailer when I got home from work and rushed right over. Oh, it's so good to see you!"

"Hi there," Arnie said from his cage. "Hi there. C'mere, gimme a kiss."

"Oh!" April cried, startled. "I had forgotten about your parrot. He talks so clearly now!"

"The parrot died years ago, I'm afraid. Arnie's just a common wild bird."

"But . . . but didn't I just hear him talk?" She walked over to the coffee table and looked into the cage.

"Peekaboo. How are you?" Arnie said.

April put her hand over her open mouth and leaned closer.

"You're no more astonished than I was when he first talked," I said. "He was just a baby when I found him. He'd fallen from his nest into my daisies—didn't even have a feather on his body. I was certain he would die, but I brought him into the house and fed him, and, well, before I knew what was happening, he'd twisted me right around his little talon."

"I love you, yes I do," Arnie said. "C'mere, kiss Arnie. He's a little bitty baby boy, yes he is."

"He's adorable!" April said. "I can't wait to tell the kids. Speaking of which, I'd better get dinner on the table for them. Remember, my dear, if there's anything you need, we're right next door."

As she disappeared through the hedges between our houses, I listened to the silence. Oh, Mama, Papa, I thought. You're really gone, aren't you? Hanna's grown and on her own. And it's a cinch that Frank and I will never patch up our marriage. It's painful being here with all the reminders of the way things were. I feel as lost and lonely as I did when I landed in New York as a young

German immigrant. What am I going to do with the rest of my life?

The Volkswagen screeched to a halt outside. "I'm going to quit feeling sorry for myself for starters," I mumbled as I spotted Mary Alice. "I have faithful friends and nice neighbors and my animal companions, and I'm going to spend the winter here if it kills me, that's what I'm going to do!"

"It'll probably freeze tonight," M.A. said as she banged through the door, laden with groceries and an electric heater. "You won't have heat until your water's turned on, so I thought this would come in handy. You should be snug for the night, Maa-gret."

I poured water from a bottle into the electric coffee maker while she got acquainted with the animals. "Ahhhh, what a darlin'," I heard her saying. When I looked around the corner from the kitchen, Arnie was watching her as intently as she was him. She moved to one side of the cage to see him better, and he scooted along his perch to be near her. "I've never seen a bird like him before," she said over her shoulder. "Does he sing?"

"You've probably seen more birds like Arnie than any other kind you can imagine," I said. "He's a starling."

"Really? You mean those pesky things that are always pecking around in the yard? He can't be one of them. They're black and homely. Arnie has brown and white specks, and he's so cute!"

"The others have specks, too. You've just never really paid attention to starlings. No one does, because they're so common."

"If they're so common, why are you bothering with this one?"

"Arnie's special, M.A., very special," I said. "Sit down and drink your coffee. I have a long, very interesting story to tell you."

She was on her third cup of coffee when I finished telling her an elaborate version of the same tale I'd told April. Looking intently at Arnie in his cage, she began to shake her head. Then she started to laugh.

"You almost had me, Maa-gret. Only you could get away with convincing me that you'd taught a wild bird to talk."

"He can, M.A., really. Say something, Arnie. Oh, never mind. I know from experience that he won't utter a sound right now. Just wait, though. When you're least expecting it, he'll talk."

"Well," she said, smiling broadly, "I should get home now."

"Thanks for coming over," I said. "I really needed a friend today."

"You know, I don't think I could stay here if I were you. Why don't you come home with me?"

"Don't be silly. Why?"

"Well . . ." She hesitated, glanced over her shoulder, and lowered her voice. "Your father died right here in the house, didn't he? Maybe his spirit is still here."

I laughed. "M.A., I don't believe in ghosts."

She laughed, too, but nervously. "You're right, of course. Still, it's almost Halloween. If there are spirits, this is the time of year they're supposed to be restless and roaming."

I shrugged off her words as nonsense, but they came vividly to mind some hours later, when I was jarred from a sound sleep by noises in the night.

Ka-thump! Flutter, flutter. Thud! Flap!

"Mmmph! What's that?" I sat upright on my makeshift bed before the fireplace and stared into the darkness. Vagabond, my husky male cat, slept with his head on the pillow next to mine. I listened intently for a while, then muttered, "Must have been a dream," and lay back down.

Flap, flap, flutter. Ka-thud!

So much for wishful thinking. The noises were real. That was Arnie flying around in his cage, bumping about in the dark. I jumped to my feet.

There was just enough moonlight filtering into the room to allow me to make out his shadowy form clinging now to the cage door. Rapid, loud panting sounds told me of his extreme fright.

I switched on a lamp. "There, that's better, isn't it?" Uttering agitated little *trrrpppping* sounds, Arnie pried at the door with his mandibles. I opened the cage and reached down so he could hop onto my hand. With a brief flutter of wings, he moved to my shoulder, softly whistled the first few notes of Beethoven's Fifth Symphony into my ear, and snuggled against my neck.

"*Maaaaaoooww*," Samantha said in the shrill voice she'd inherited from her few drops of Siamese blood. She crept to the fireplace and peered around the corner and down the hallway. Her tail whipped from side to side. Deep in her throat she began to growl.

With a ferocious feline at my feet and a savage starling on my shoulder, I was inspired to act more bravely than I felt as I opened the doors and peeked into the bedrooms. Curtains flapped from the wind gusting through the broken windows. Outside, something banged loudly against the side of the house. My heart skipped a beat as Samantha made a sudden spurting run past me and down the hallway. I slammed both bedroom doors shut. In the living room, Sammie scuttled from one window to another, crouching below the sills as she looked out.

With trembling hands, I switched on the outside lights and looked into the yard. Tree branches and bushes bent and bobbed, buffeted by the wind, but nothing else was there.

Behind my father's bedroom door, a floorboard squeaked. Mitzi, my calico cat, and Vagabond snapped awake. Side by side the three felines crouched, their widened eyes fixed on that door. Arnie pressed tightly against my neck. I gulped, suddenly feeling very cold.

"If there are spirits, this is the time of year they're supposed to be restless and roaming," M.A. had said.

Then the sound of a loud crash froze me into immobility. The crash had come from the bedroom in which my father had slept—and died.

At the sound of the crash Mitzi spurted to a far corner and crouched, ready to defend herself if necessary. Vagabond, for whom the term scaredy-cat was invented, hugged the ground so tightly as he ran that he looked like a bug scurrying for cover. Sammie nudged him to greater speed, and together they disappeared beneath a chair. Proving that birds are no dummies either, Arnie took to the heights and claimed the safety of a curtain rod.

Unfortunately, curiosity compelled me to check out the bedroom and find out what had caused the noises. Step by careful step, lamp in hand as a weapon, I crept down the hallway toward my father's old room. The broken window in there provided a likely explanation. How simple for someone to reach through that hole in the glass, quietly turn the lock and lift the window, then climb surreptitiously through. Well, whoever it was, was wasting his time: there were no family jewels here, and most of the household silver was monogrammed "stainless steel."

As I reached for the doorknob with my left hand, I hefted the lamp in my right. Slowly, ever so quietly, I turned the knob and eased the door open. It was pitch-black inside. I flipped the wall switch; the room was bathed in brightness.

The covers on the bed were in disarray. A lamp lay on the floor. My father's radio, which I'd turned around earlier so I could hear it better, had been moved from the spot where I'd left it.

Otherwise, the room was empty.

I would have shrugged and rationalized an explanation if not for one fact. I remembered vividly where I had put that radio. Now it was right back on the exact same spot it had always occupied when Papa was alive.

"Coo-coo," Arnie said into my ear the next day. He settled onto my shoulder, tucked his beak into his wing feathers, and went to sleep. I didn't blame him for being tired; he'd kept me company through the rest of my night's vigil and consented to being put back into the cage only after the sun came up.

"There, you heard him that time, didn't you?" I said to M.A. as we sat over coffee. "Didn't you hear him say coo-coo?"

She looked at me over the rim of her cup, which did little to hide the obvious mirth on her face. "Sure I did, Maa-gret."

"M.A., why won't you believe me about Arnie? How could you not believe me? Just for that, I'm going to put you to work again."

She knew I was teasing but stood up and stubbed out her cigarette anyway. We still had a long way to go before the rental trailer was empty.

"Back into the cage with you, Arnie," I said, opening his door and nudging him toward the top perch.

We worked at unpacking the trailer until late afternoon, when we ran out of objects we could handle unassisted. Things like the refrigerator and the six-foot-long freezer with six hundred pounds of good Texas meat in it, all packed in dry ice.

"Maa-gret! It'll take you years to eat it all!"

"It's not just for me. I love to cook, you know, and this will be the first time in ages that I'll have my brother and his wife and kids around to make it worth doing. I'll have big Sunday dinners, the way my mother used to do. We'll be a real family again."

Knock. Knock. Knock. Knock.

"Sounds like someone's come for dinner already, Maa-gret."

I opened the front door and looked into the bright eyes of a chipmunk. Sitting on top of the mailbox next to the door, he paused to acknowledge my presence, then calmly resumed munching the acorn clutched between his upper paws. "Hello," I said. "Are you selling encyclopedias or vacuum cleaners?" He twitched his nose, stared at me, then dropped the acorn, ran down the side of the house, and scampered away. "Just a friendly neighbor," I said as I closed the door, "but I really don't think he's the one who knocked."

Thud! Thud! Thud! Thud!

M.A. snapped to alert erectness in her chair. "It's coming from the bedroom!" she whispered loudly.

"Maaaaoooooooowww." Ka-thunk. Ka-thunk!

"It's coming from the basement stairs." I laughed. "I closed the cats down there so they'd be out of the way while we worked." I opened the hallway door and three miffed felines paraded through it, ignoring me as though I didn't exist.

And then, "He talks! He really does talk!" M.A.'s brown eyes sparkled with excitement as she leaned over the birdcage. Arnie was in the middle of his favorite monologue.

"He's a little bitty baby boy. Yes he is. Kiiiissss Arnie. He's a love. C'mere, gimme a kiss."

"He'll keep that up for a while now that he's started," I said smugly. "You might as well sit back and be comfortable."

We had a glass of wine and talked over old times while waiting for clam chowder and stuffed quahogs to heat on the makeshift grill I'd rigged over smoldering coals in the fireplace. This was roughing it in luxury. Once I put my things away I'd be set for the winter, for a nice long visit with my past while I considered my future.

"You know, Maa-gret," M.A. said as she was leaving that evening, "it's strange how warm this house is after all these years. I mean, houses usually get cold and forlorn when they're vacant, but your house . . . well, it feels like someone has been living in it all along."

"She's right," I commented later as Arnie and I stared out the kitchen window. Lunar light filtered through thinning leaves; a tiny breeze ruffled them with the tenderness of a mother stroking a sleeping child's hair. It was a dry, snapping cold night; without a doubt, frost would glisten on the pumpkins in the morning. "Just between the two of us, Arnie, I think the house is warm because it was always so full of love, and somehow those feelings lingered, waiting for me to come back. Well, here I am." I sighed. "Here I am."

Arnie reached up with one foot and scratched the top of his head. "What are you doing?" he said. "I love you. Sing me a song. Sing it!" Then he began to whistle "Mary Had a Little Lamb."

Something moved out in the yard, so far off to one side that I almost missed seeing it at all. At first there was just a white blur that shimmered in the moonlight, appearing to float several inches above the ground. As I strained my eyes, trying to make it out, it began to move slowly toward me. Inch by inch it bobbed along, stopping every few seconds; then abruptly it turned and waddled off toward a nearby clump of bushes.

I'd had enough of mysteries in the bedroom the night before; quickly, I turned on the porch light.

Blinded by the sudden glare, a pair of beady eyes squinted at me past a diamond-shaped white patch on the forehead. The little, pointy face that peered backward over a fuzzy shoulder held a clearly exasperated expression. A white tail marked with just a touch of black stood straight as a flagpole behind an arched, solid-white back.

"Edelweiss!" I shouted. "Arnie, it's Edelweiss. He's an old friend of the family."

And indeed he was. I've no idea how long skunks live, so maybe this one was a descendant of the original Edelweiss, but it seemed he had inhabited this neighborhood since we'd first arrived here so many years ago. He was three times larger than most of his kind, and his stripe was so wide and unbroken that I'd thought him an albino until he allowed me to get close enough for a really good look. My father had called him Edelweiss after the velvety white alpine flower his coat brought to mind.

He seemed to stare directly at me, then lowered his tail and ambled off, stopping every few feet to sniff at the ground.

"Looks like we'll have plenty of company outdoors, Arnie," I said. "This yard was always a naturalist's paradise. I'd almost forgotten how much I'd enjoyed that. C'mon. It's time for us to go to bed now."

I put him into his cage and pulled the cover around it, then lowered myself to the mattress that still occupied the floor in front of the fireplace. "Night-night. You go to sleep," he said as I crawled beneath the warm electric blanket.

"You go to sleep yourself, silly," I retorted. Five minutes later I was sound asleep.

Five hours after that I was rudely awakened by the sound of Arnie's fluttering. "Not again," I grumbled, getting to my feet. A series of little thumps sounded from behind the closed door of my father's bedroom. Mitzi ran toward it, and Sammie trotted the few steps necessary to join her. I tagged along.

"Tonight we're going to get to the bottom of this mystery," I said, flinging the door open and instantly hitting the light switch.

The bedcovers were again in disarray, and the lampshade tilted. And though I had once more turned the radio so I could hear it better as I worked, it was back in its original position now.

"All right, Papa, it's time for the game to end. You're scaring Arnie and the cats." I laughed nervously. "I know there's a perfectly logical explanation to all this."

I took one last look around the room and turned to leave. Then something caught my eye, sending a chill up my spine. A bright red object lay on the floor. I bent over and picked it up. It was a slipper—a man's red plaid slipper. Papa's slipper.

CHAPTER TWO

"AND SO, Dieter, it seems I've come home to live in a haunted house," I said.

My brother was silent for a while as he stared at me through glasses that framed his version of our father's eyes. Then he began to laugh. "You've come home with a wild bird that talks . . . to a house that's haunted by our father." He slouched down in the chair across the room from me and grinned.

I glared at him for a moment, then laughed, too. "Okay, so I'm nervous about being back. Arnie does talk, though. You'll see."

Suddenly Dieter stood up, looking pointedly at his watch. "Well, I haven't been home yet, and it's late. I just wanted to say hello and show you where that broken radiator pipe is so you can get it fixed."

On his way to the door he stopped in front of Arnie's cage and looked him over thoroughly. "Hi, bird," he said, and whistled.

Arnie yanked his beak out of his wing feathers. "Night-night," he said. "You go to sleep. Night-night."

"I think that's a hint," I said. I tried to control the smug grin on my face as Dieter's eyebrows climbed higher on his forehead.

"Wait . . . un-til . . . I . . . tell . . . Mar-tha," he said. "Is that all he knows?"

Arnie had pulled his head into his shoulders and closed his eyes again. I was certain he wouldn't talk anymore that night. "You bring Martha and the kids over for roast beef and bread balls when I'm settled, and you'll find out how much he says."

"That's a deal! Make it soon, Gretel."

My heart was full as I watched him go. Gretel, he'd called me and, with two simple syllables, revitalized the closeness we'd shared in youth. No one had called me Gretel in years. I doubted if I'd ever be able to verbalize it, and I was certain my brother would be disconcerted if I did, but fear that I might never see him again was part of the reason I'd come back to Cape Cod. His serious heart attack the previous year had jarred me into remembering how isolated I'd felt in the years when my family was still in Germany—a vast ocean and another culture away—before they had decided to join me in the United States.

Cooking Dieter's favorite meal now would be a pleasure, but I couldn't handle a family gathering until I'd finished putting the house in order. As I reassembled Arnie's permanent home, a telephone booth–size aviary, I looked around with dismay at the old furniture, the threadbare rug, and the ten-year-old paint on the walls. I ticked off the list of needed repairs I'd discovered with only a cursory survey of the house. "What am I doing here?" I groaned.

"Sell the house and come to Florida so you can be near us, Mumma," my daughter, Hanna, had urged when I'd announced I was moving back here. "There's nothing for you there anymore."

Maybe she was right, but I had to be sure before I burned the bridge behind me. This was my house, the one I'd planned and had built after it became obvious that I could no longer live with my husband. He'd remained for a while in the big house that had been our home, then rented it to my parents and moved to a larger

274

city. My life was full as I finished raising Hanna, but the inevitable day arrived when she was grown and gone. Feeling suddenly adrift, I began to look around for a cure for empty-nest syndrome. That's when my husband sold the big old family home and I invited my parents to live with me.

To give us all breathing space, I built my own small apartment in the basement and settled in. I suppose I had a glorified image of myself as the dutiful daughter taking care of her elderly parents, while they saw themselves as the loving parents once again caring for their little girl. Alas, we were too many parents in a home without children. The years we shared this house were warmly close ones—often fun, usually happy, yet always trying! One day I decided we all needed a break from one another, so I packed up and started off on the long drive down to Florida to visit my daughter. When I pulled into Hanna's driveway several days later, she greeted me with tears and the news that my father had died the night before, less than an hour after I had last spoken to him on the telephone.

Afterward, I gathered my grief into a little ball, stuffed it into a deep subconscious well, and moved restlessly from one state to another, ending up in Texas. Before my mother died, she had visited me, and we'd finally become friends rather than merely mother and daughter. But I'd never returned home again—until now. Tired of running at last, I needed to belong somewhere.

Let it be here, was my last thought as I fell asleep the third night.

For a change, my sleep was uninterrupted. Refreshed, I awoke early next morning and walked from room to room, making decisions. I went to the carpet store, selected new floor coverings, and took them home. Then I turned my attention to the ruptured radiator pipe in the living room that Dieter had pointed out. As usual, I had plenty of supervision to make certain I did everything right. Arnie perched on my shoulder and Vagabond sat at my knee; both watched my every move so intently it seemed they were trying to learn how to do the task themselves. "Pay close attention, boys," I said, digging out the pipe cutter that had long been part of my homeowner's basic self-defense kit. "You're going to see an expert at work."

It would not take long to cut out the ruptured section and add a new piece between two fittings. "Nothing to it at all," I bragged to the animals. "I'll have hot running water and heat by tonight."

My cockiness lasted about thirty seconds. The pipe was so close to the wall that I couldn't swing the tool full circle to make a severing cut.

With a sigh, I stared at the problem, while Arnie hopped into the toolbox and began rummaging around in search of a toy.

I tugged experimentally at the pipe. If only I could think of a way to get through that little tiny bit of copper at the back. . . .

Clink, clink. Clink, clink. Clink, clink, clink.

"Arnie, what are you doing?" I said. He looked up at me, his expression innocent behind the piece of flat metal he clutched in his beak; then he turned his attention back to the reggae rhythm he was tapping on the copper pipe. "What is that thing you have, Arnie? Let me see it."

When I reached for him, though, he ran away from me, trotting across the carpet with the gait of a jogger on stilts. "Arnold! I don't have time to play games now. That looks like something you could hurt yourself on; give it here!" I lunged toward him, and he dropped the object, *trrrppping* with annoyance. I snatched it up, saw that it was a broken piece of hacksaw blade, and tossed it into the trash can.

"You're as troublesome as a baby that's just learning to walk, Arnie," I scolded. "I have to keep an eye on you constantly."

"He's a little bitty baby boy, yes he is," Arnie said.

"Hacksaw blade! Of course!" I whirled around, retraced my steps, and dug through the trash can. An entire hacksaw would never fit into those close quarters, but the broken piece of blade would. Using two pairs of pliers to hold it by either end, I whizzed through the rest of the pipe. A few minutes later, the replacement pieces had been fitted and I had soldered everything together.

I'd just leaned back to admire my handiwork when there was a knock at the front door. I opened it to greet the man I'd asked to check out the furnace and get it going. While he went about his job, I went outside and replaced the broken windowpanes in the two bedrooms.

It was a brisk autumn day, the chill wind forewarning that it would again be a cold night. This night, though, I would finally be all set in the house. The heat would be turned on, and I could take a long, hot shower before retiring to the room that had originally been mine. I carried the tools and ladder down to the basement, then checked on progress with the furnace.

"Almost finished," the man said. "I'll fill 'er now, and we'll know for sure how she's held out." He reached up and twisted the valve that would divert part of the house's cold-water supply to the furnace, then stood back to wait for the water to heat up and start circulating through the baseboard pipes. The needles on the temperature and pressure gauges of the old furnace climbed steadily.

"There she rips!" the furnace man said.

Gurgle, gurgle, burp, bup. The water signaled its progress as it began to run into the pipes serving the heating system. *Tick, tick, pop, crack.* The cold copper tubing protested as it expanded with the heat. The water sounds changed from joyful to disastrous. *Drip, drip, drip, trickle, splash, ka-shoooossh.* "Oh, oh," the furnace man said. All around, water cascaded in great, gushing torrents from the basement ceiling.

"Er, I guess there was more than one ruptured pipe that needed fixing," I said.

"Yup. Looks like it," he replied as he turned off the water. He picked up his equipment, and I walked with him up the stairs. The man paused at the door. "Give me a call again when you think you have it all set to go, lady."

"How about tomorrow? Can you come back first thing in the morning? Please!"

"Yup. But no way you can have it fixed that soon."

"Yes, I can. I know I can." And I hoped I could. A quick walk around the house confirmed my fear that there were ruptured pipes in almost every radiator. So I cut, fitted, fluxed, and soldered my way through the bathroom and both bedrooms. It was hours before I shut off the blowtorch for the last time, satisfied that I had ferreted out and repaired all the damage. By then it was late. Arnie had retired long ago; his cage was covered for the night. And there wasn't a cat in sight.

Almost midnight—the witching hour, I thought, and smiled to myself, remembering M.A.'s theory that my father's ghost was roaming about. "Barbaric nonsense," I said, chuckling.

I lit a cigarette and looked through the window. Edelweiss was waddling across the lawn, his head down, as though disappointed that he was finding no tasty morsels worth digging up.

Over in one corner of my kitchen, however, was an entire night's worth of tasty morsels. I scraped leftover cat food into an old margarine tub, turned on the outside lights, and slipped out the kitchen door. "Edelweiss, come. Come, Edelweiss," I called softly. He stopped and looked at me. I set the dish on the grass at the edge of the light's reach. He stood as still as a statue, watching me, until I went back inside the house, when he ambled over and began to eat.

Suddenly his head jerked up. He stared toward the corner of the house, seeming to see something I could not. Then he turned and broke into a funny, rolling run.

Yooowwwwlllooooowwwlllllll! Hiisssssssss!

"What on earth . . . ? Vagabond, if you're picking on Mitzi again, you stop it right now, you hear? Vagabond! Samantha!" I ran toward the chilling sounds of cat hysteria somewhere inside the house.

The felines almost bowled me off my feet as they exploded out of one of the bedrooms and pounded past me down the hallway, spitting, hissing, and bumping one another as they ran.

Suddenly my steps faltered; my blood went cold.

It was from my father's old bedroom that the cats, all three of them, had departed in such great haste. Yet, inside the room, I could still hear little bumps and shuffles, the sounds of someone— or something—moving around. It was just past midnight, on All Saints' Day, I realized now. And something very strange was going on in the room where my father's body and spirit had parted company.

Swimming within the darkness framed by the doorway, two brightly glistening eyes glared out at me. Instinct urged me to turn and run. But I stared hard into the darkness. The eyes still gleamed out at me. "You are simply a product of my overactive imagination," I told them timorously. "Go on, get out of this house!" The eyes disappeared. I waited. The darkness within the room remained, simply, darkness.

My pent-up breath exploded in a relieved sigh. *"It was imag-i-na-tion, I know,"* I sang to myself as I stepped toward the room, flipped on the light switch, turned, and ran down the hallway.

"Good morning?" Arnie said from beneath his cage cover.

"Sh. You go back to sleep, Arnie. It's not morning yet." Though I sure am going to be happy when it is, I thought.

I stood at the end of the hallway. There were no sounds, no signs of movement from my father's bedroom. I could see the dresser and part of the bed; everything looked perfectly normal. By now I was feeling quite foolish. With growing confidence, I strode the few steps into the bedroom, reached to turn out the light while glancing briefly around—then banged my head on the door as I reeled backward in surprise.

There was a burglar in the room! He stood in the far corner, his eyes glistening through a black mask. His tail was ringed in black, too. And he stood less than two feet tall. My dangerous burglar, my fearsome ghost, was packaged in the not particularly imposing body of a raccoon!

"Well, hello there," I said softly. Very slowly, keeping my eyes on the raccoon every second, I reached behind me and closed the door. He looked friendly enough, but I knew he might be skittish, and the last thing I wanted was for him to run out of the room and force me to chase him through the house. "So . . . how long have you been living here?" My tone was conversational as I crept toward the window. "I guess you've come to think of this room as your home, haven't you?" I unlocked the window and began to inch it open. The raccoon's eyes never left mine. "And I'll bet you were pretty upset to find you'd been locked inside when I replaced the broken glass today." The intruder sniffed at the crisp outdoor air that blew in. "Sorry, but you're going to have to find another home after tonight. I'm certain you're too set in your ways to fit into my family. I'm sure you understand."

I stepped backward as cautiously as I'd advanced. When the doorknob nudged my hip, I turned it and squeezed out of the room. Closing the door, I put my ear to it. Within seconds, a series of thumps marked the raccoon's progress across the room; he'd taken the graceful exit offered.

I went back into the bedroom and closed the window. Silhouetted in the moonlight, the raccoon sat on top of the fence outside and looked at me. His eyes sparked, his tail swished, and suddenly he was gone.

"*Auf Wiedersehen,* ghost of Papa," I said, experiencing a pang of regret.

The feeling surprised me, but it explained why I had, for a time, almost believed a ghost was haunting the house. I would have liked seeing Papa—and Mama, too, for that matter—one more time, in whatever form. Just to say all the things I'd never said while they were alive, and maybe to take back some of the things I had said. To brag a little about my accomplishments since they'd gone, and to say how disappointed I was that neither had stayed around to witness everything I'd done with my life.

WHEN the first snow began to fall, I declared my chores finished for the year. All I wanted was to settle in enough so that I could relax and see some old friends, perhaps do a bit of baking for the holidays, pace my days to a normal routine. With Arnie on my shoulder, I stirred steaming cider with a cinnamon stick and stared out the picture window at the lightest, most enormous flakes I'd ever seen. Large as leaves, they floated on the air, biding time patiently until the slightest breeze invited them to dance; then, with the spirit of a fandango and the grace of a waltz, they whirled and twirled before curtsying gently to the ground.

"Isn't it beautiful, Arnie?" I said. "Doesn't the very sight of snow make you want to run outside and play?"

He fluttered from my shoulder to the windowsill. Then he pecked at the glass, opening and closing his mandibles as though trying to reach out and catch a flake on his tongue. A lone ray of sunshine lanced through the leaden skies, penetrated the window, and struck Arnie full blast. Brightly illuminated, his black plumage took on an iridescent blue-and-purple sheen. He blinked languidly, shook himself several times, tilted his head up, and slowly unfurled his wings. His beak gaped wide. My thoughts might be fixed on snow, but Arnie's attention had been diverted to his greatest delight—basking in the sun.

Leaving him to his pleasure, I went to the telephone and made the call I had most wanted to place since my arrival. "Hi, Dieter," I said into the receiver. "Why don't you bring the family over for dinner on Sunday. I'm finally ready for company."

When I hung up, I dug through my bountiful meat supply until I found the largest, most select roast. On Sunday morning I whistled merrily as I seasoned the meat with a Cajun herb-and-spice blend, poured an onion-mushroom soup mix into the pan, and slid it onto the cooking rack. "Mama never did it quite like this," I confided to Arnie, "but just between you and me, my roast and gravy are better than hers."

"*Bradddttt!*" he commented.

"Who asked for your opinion? Can I help it if you've sworn off meat lately? You're probably the only vegetarian starling in the world. No taste, that's what you have. Absolutely no taste!"

"Yes I do," he said. "I love you."

I stared at him, then shook my head. "Coincidence," I muttered. "The words are just sounds to him; he has no idea what they mean." Still, sometimes the things he said seemed so appropriate to the occasion.

He kept me company throughout my preparations, tapping around on the counter while I kneaded the bread-ball mixture, stealing tidbits of onion and endive as I chopped them for the potato salad, bursting into spontaneous words and whistles from time to time. The kitchen was warmed as much by my joy as by the oven's heat while I prepared that meal, and he seemed to sense it. "It'll be the best feast I've made in years," I said. "Matter of fact, it'll be the first full-fledged meal I've cooked in years. I'm so excited!"

Two hours later Dieter's family of five sat at the dinner table as I pulled the roast from the oven. Despite their cheerful faces and happy conversation, from my standpoint they looked like a jury waiting to pass judgment on my meal. As they ate, I chattered inanely, wishing I hadn't boasted so much beforehand about my cooking. So intent was I on diverting their attention, however, that I almost missed noticing the only legitimate accolade for a cook: second helpings.

"Please pass the potato salad over here when you're done," fourteen-year-old David said to his mother, Martha, as she plopped two spoonfuls onto her plate. College junior Linda and older sister Christine split another bread ball and reached for the gravy boat. I stared at the empty platter, then got up and carved more beef from the roast.

Humming, I returned the platter to the table. Chrissie reached for a piece of meat and said, "You know, Aunt Margarete, I'm

281

surprised you haven't even mentioned your bird yet." That big birdcage dominating my tiny living room obviously required some explanation.

"Dad says he can talk," David said.

"Dad loves to tease us," Linda explained.

"He does talk," I stated adamantly, and I told Arnie's tale. Carried away with enthusiasm, I walked to the aviary and opened the door. Arnie catapulted from his perch and flew out. "See how friendly he is?" I said. With the pride of a doting mother, I watched him swoop through the acrobatic turns and circles he usually made around the living room. When he'd had enough exercise, he flew toward the table to check out our guests.

That's when I noticed the expressions on Martha's and Linda's faces, expressions that progressed from surprise to distress to terror as Arnie flew closer to them. My niece squealed and ducked. Martha made a weak little cry and threw her hands in front of her face. Realizing that he wasn't exactly being greeted with enthusiasm, Arnie slammed on his brakes in midair and dropped like a rock, landing on top of Martha's head. She shuddered, and her hands fluttered up and down as though she couldn't decide whether to brush him off or protect her face.

Moving quickly, I scooped him off her head. Sounding his starling scold, Arnie flew to his cage and cowered for some time after I closed the door.

"I'm so sorry," Martha said. "Much as I love birds, it terrifies me when they fly nearby."

"My fault." I sighed. "I shouldn't have let him out without saying something first." I wondered at the strangeness of human nature, that any creature as large and powerful as we are could fear something as small and harmless as a bird.

Despite her reaction to Arnie, after dinner Martha stood in front of the aviary, studying his every gesture, talking sweetly to him. "Generally speaking, Arnie, I dislike starlings; they're always robbing my feeders. But you're kinda cute. Say something for me, hmmmm?" Exhausted by his ordeal, Arnie only stared sleepy-eyed at her, then tucked his beak into his wing to take a siesta. "Aw, Arnie, I meant no offense. I think he's insulted," she said, turning to me. He replied with a little hiss of annoyance and snuggled his beak deeper into his feathers.

CHAPTER THREE

"I HATE December," I said to the empty room. I sat there, fingering my mother's wedding band. It felt strange on my hand, weighty, yet worn from fifty years of contact with her flesh. Of course, the fact that it was on my finger at all, just as my father's matching band was now on my brother's, was part of the reason I hated December. The trouble with close families is that the realities of life don't permit them to remain intact forever. And the trouble with memories is that they can be so downright intrusive during the holiday season.

This year was particularly bad. Being back in the house was proving far worse than I'd expected when I was down south and dreaming of a white Christmas at home. Like cobwebs, visions of Mama and Papa, of my daughter as a child, of a whole and happy family lurked in each nook and cranny of every room. Echoes of laughter—Papa's deep chuckle, Mama's coquettish titter, Hanna's contagious giggle—were elusively just beyond the range of hearing. The imaginary scent of fruit breads baking would waft through the air at any moment if I would but allow my mind to wander at will.

Thank goodness that a knock on the door signaled the arrival of one of the few human beings to whom I could speak unabashedly when I was in this kind of mood. Responding to that knock, I stood gawking at the unexpected apparition with the familiar voice that said, "I'm a bone-weary traveler seeking refuge from the storm. Is there room at your inn, madame?" Sleet whipped at the snugged-down beret and upturned coat collar of the person huddled at my door.

"Patsy?" I said uncertainly. "What a surprise! What on earth are you doing out in this weather?"

"I had an appointment in town," she said as she stepped inside and removed her coat and hat. "Of course, I never dreamed the weather would turn so; the sun was peeping through this morning when I left home."

We embraced like two old friends meeting for the first time in years—which we were. Almost thirty years old our friendship was, dating to our daughters' grammar school days together. And, just as Hanna and Kitzi had stayed best friends since then, so had we mothers. But Patsy had been out of town when I arrived, and we'd only made contact recently.

Dear Patsy. How close we'd always been. How many difficult times she'd seen me through. Yet, though she knew most of my intimate secrets, Patsy's private life was like a newspaper shorn down to bare-bones headlines. An attentive, empathic listener, she never talked about things that troubled her.

Thus it was that I'd burbled halfway through our first telephone conversation since my return before she said, "By the way, Riki's dead. Last March. He'd gone back to school in Florida. He was on his bicycle. A car hit him." Stunned, I'd been unable to say a word. Riki was one of her two sons, the one perpetually in search of himself. "There, now you know," she'd said. "Let's not speak of it." And though we'd conversed on the phone at least twice a day since, she'd never again so much as said his name. I had a feeling she was out in this storm today because she couldn't stand being in the house during the holiday season.

But I respected her too much to violate her deep sense of privacy. Today we'd speak of trivialities. So in my usual tactful manner, I blurted, "I hate December."

"Let me guess," Patsy said with a twinkle. "You've heard from Hanna. They've changed their minds about coming for Christmas, right?"

I sighed. "Right. Travie's father won't let him come. The court says Christmas Eve is Travie's holiday with him, and that's that. Guess I shouldn't complain. At least he wants to spend time with his son, which is more than many fathers do in these divorce cases. Still, I can't help wishing that grandparents had some rights in these things, too."

"But you've spent the holidays without Hanna and Travie before, Margarete. What else is it?"

"It's being in this house right now," I admitted. "I should have sold it and never come back. The memories are killing me!"

"No, they're not." Patsy's mouth twitched with a sad little smile. She was a widow, a woman who sorely missed her adored husband, and yet she'd carried on with the rearing and support of their children. She'd been essentially alone for years, alone with her houseful of memories. It was a knowing and humbling smile that preceded her softly spoken observation. "Memories may hurt, but they don't kill. Healing doesn't begin until the memories can flow; it's about time for you. Don't fight it, Margarete. You're starting to heal."

"Healing shouldn't hurt so much, if that's what it is," I mumbled later, after Patsy had gone. I stared at the Christmas goose platter Mama had given to me one wedding anniversary. Her own mother had passed it on to her, just as I would someday present it to Hanna. A daughter's rite-of-passage symbol, that platter. Too bad it was going to remain unused this year, again.

"I'm just not going to have a Christmas this year!" I shouted. In a fit of pique, I stomped out of the kitchen and glared through the window at the thickly falling snow that was beginning to cover the ground. Looked like it was going to be a white Christmas, just as I'd wanted—for those celebrating it anyway. In the view from my window, the world seemed limited to the first few feet of my front yard. I was isolated, with only my morbid thoughts for company.

"Peekaboo. Hi there, coo-coo," said a raspy voice near my ear.

Correction. I was isolated with only my thoughts, the cats, and, of course, Arnie for company. And he was the greatest cure for melancholy I'd run across in many a year. "Come out here and help me get rid of my December blues, Arnie," I said, opening the aviary door. "I'm feeling so sorry for myself. Do you think you could give me a good swift kick to bring me to my senses?"

"Kissy, kissy," that silly starling said. He flew from his perch and landed on my shoulder. "C'mere, you gimme a kiss."

"No, no, not a kiss, a kick," I said.

"You're a baboon," he scolded, and took a nip at my earlobe. "Peekaboo. I love you, yes I do!"

I sighed. "If you love me, little rascal, I must have some redeeming qualities, huh?"

That night I dreamed of the Decembers of my youth, back in Munich. How bright and shining the city had been with all its merry lights. Our parents had saved all the year long to be certain the *Christkindel* would bring many wonderful gifts for Dieter and me. While my brother and I sipped punch and nibbled cookies in the kitchen on Christmas Eve, the tree would be decorated and presents laid out in our large dining room. When all was in readiness, my parents turned out the lights and jingled a bell. In response to the signal, we children lit candles to guide our way down the long hallway. Step by slow step, we walked hand in hand to that transformed room—transformed because of the wondrous tree, all aglow with tiny lit candles and bright, spitting sparklers. Even in the worst of times, my parents always found some way to celebrate what they regarded as *the* family holiday.

As I would do this year, too, I realized the next day. How could I not, after a night like that, with memories more acutely haunting than any nightmare could possibly be?

I went to the phone and called Dieter's wife. "I know you've been doing things differently in recent years, but don't you think it would be nice if we go back to the old tradition of a family Christmas Eve here?"

"Thank goodness!" Martha said. "We were beginning to worry that you weren't going to ask us. Of course! It'll be Christmas Eve at your place, Margarete. Will you make your potato salad for us? You can spend Christmas night over here. This is going to be the best holiday we've had in years!"

"Sure hope Patsy's right about memories being part of the process of healing grief," I said several days later as the animals helped me decorate the tree and wrap gifts, "because I'm certainly having more than my share of them this month."

"Good!" Arnie said, diverting his attention from the bow he was trying to rip off one package. Sammie watched his efforts, occasionally nudging with her nose at the unyielding ribbon, which I pulled off and tossed into the middle of the floor. While Sammie and Vagabond attacked it, Arnie flew to a window and whistled "Mary Had a Little Lamb."

When I'd finished with the packages, the telephone rang. "Mumma," Hanna said when I picked it up, "I've been thinking. . . . Since we're not coming for Christmas, suppose I send Travie to you for spring vacation? And Ronnie and I are planning to be married this time next year. Then we'll all come home for a long summer vacation."

Ronnie was Hanna's longtime boyfriend. Ah well, life does have a way of working out if we simply allow it to. Families change as people come and go within them, but without change, there would be no life.

On Christmas night at my new extended family's house, my nephew squeezed my right hand while my brother embraced me from the left. In their dining room, a group of wonderful people stood in a circle around the table, holding hands and singing *"Silent night, holy night. All is calm, all is bright . . ."* That is, everyone but two—my brother and I belted out the words *"Stille Nacht, heilige Nacht. Alles schläft, einsam wacht . . ."* to the same tune.

OoooooooHHHHHOOOOOwwwwwwwLL!
Oooohhoooooooowwwwlll!
I shivered, put down the paint roller I was using on the living-room ceiling, and pulled my sweater closer around me. When the wind whistled down the chimney that way, the cold cut right to the marrow of my bones. This was a winter Mother Nature had fabricated to try everyone's endurance.

Yet, in his cage, Arnie was singing so happily that I had to wonder if he thought it was spring. Considering the fact that I had dragged him north for the winter, a move so contrary to a bird's nature, I wouldn't be the least bit surprised if he did have his seasons all mixed up. On the other hand, there was a great deal about which he should be happy. After all, he wasn't outside, having to endure the effects of that winter.

Each time I watched his fellows, I felt like inviting them all in for a visit. The weather was brutalizing the birds. After each new temperature plunge, there were obviously fewer of them.

"I'm really glad you don't have to be out there, Arnie," I said as I looked out the window. "I wish none of the other birds had to be, either. If I were rich, I'd turn my entire backyard into a solar-heated aviary so the birds could fly in and out to warm up during the winter months."

"Coo-coo," Arnie said.

"Now you be nice! If not for you, I wouldn't be noticing the birds as much as I do."

On top of the television set beside me, Vagabond and Mitzi stood with whiskers twitching as they pushed their noses against the glass panes. I shivered again. The old, familiar scenes to which I was long accustomed resembled alien landscapes carved from ice. It was a bright winter, but something about the extreme low temperatures changed the very character of the light outside. A large but pale sun climbed the horizon each day, illuminating the earth with a strange blue light but not warming it.

Among the needles of the spruce tree flanking the driveway, a chickadee hung upside down from the thistle-stocking feeder, his black-capped head bobbing rapidly as he pecked at the last seeds in the bottom. Most of the tiny seeds lay scattered on the ground, shiny specks glistening like black sequins on top of the frozen snow.

House sparrows nibbled at them, though in a desultory manner. Lying on their bellies in the snow, they looked as though they were eating only because the food was right under their beaks, not because they were particularly hungry. Well, who invited them to the party anyway? I'd never intended to feed so many common birds when I put up my feeders. I was more interested in the tiny titmice, finches, nuthatches, and such that were less numerous and more difficult to attract.

"Bad boy, bad, bad boy," Arnie said as there suddenly came a loud banging and clattering noise from outside. I rapped on the window.

About six inches from Vagabond's nose, a large ebony grackle clung to the wire rim of a feeder designed to accommodate birds one quarter his size. He looked at me unflinchingly with tiny yellow eyes that seemed to acknowledge my rapping as a greeting rather than a signal that he was unwelcome. He blinked once, then leaned back, flapped his wings for balance, and proceeded to empty the feeder with great, gobbling mouthfuls, not leaving until he'd had his fill.

"Darn grackles," I grumbled. "They're as bad as the sparrows and starlings about emptying my feeders! No offense to you, Arnie. It's just that they waste so much food that might otherwise keep the pretty little birds from starving to death this time of year."

As the grackle disappeared over a neighbor's roof, my attention turned to the half dozen starlings sitting on a pile of brush. How cold they looked! They sat with their heads drawn tightly down into their necks, the capricious, icy wind ruffling their plumped feathers. As I watched, one of the birds suddenly lurched and fell to the ground, where it lay on its back—unmoving.

Without thinking to grab coat or boots, I ran outside. Every bird in the yard scattered at my approach—every bird except the fallen starling. I scooped him up and carried him into the house. Cupping him with both hands, I thought of how I would revive him, give him a nice meal, then let him go so he could rejoin his family outdoors. I blew gently into the space between my thumbs, hoping that the warmth of my breath would help thaw him. Maybe I wouldn't send him back outside after all; maybe I'd adopt him until spring; maybe he and Arnie would strike up a friendship. That was it. I would save his life, just as I had done with Arnie, and then I'd make him, too, a part of my little family.

"C'mon, little starling, wake up. It's nice and warm in here, feel it? Arnie, say something to him, to let him know he's among friends. Wake up, little starling."

Again and again I blew into my hands. Softly, I whistled between my teeth in tones to which Arnie had always responded. And I rubbed the tiny body ever so gently, trying to restore circulation.

Shocked, I realized on close examination that the bird was nothing but bones and feathers held together by the thinnest covering of skin imaginable. His eyes remained open and glazed. I was too late to save him. The horrible truth slowly dawned on me—he had starved to death, and that was something I could have prevented.

"Aw-w-w. See what I mean, Arnie? It's really a cruel world out there. And here I've been begrudging the birdseed he managed to steal. Poor baby. He deserved a chance to live as much as the other birds I chose to feed."

Arnie stared through his screening at me. He cocked his head first to one side, then the other, and uttered uncharacteristic little peeping noises. Then he hopped down to the bottom of the cage and began gobbling corn as though it was going to be yanked from beneath his beak at any moment.

Once more the feeder banged and clattered against the side of the house. It was a grackle again. But this time I didn't try to chase him away. On the ground, mourning doves and juncos and blue jays and the dead starling's relatives vied for every crumb they could snatch of the seeds the grackle spilled.

Seeming heavier by the moment, the tiny dead bird lay like a lump of guilty conscience in the palm of my hand. I wrapped him in a paper towel, but it was impossible to bury him in the frozen ground. "I'll start throwing out bread for your relatives, little starling," I promised as I placed him, with utmost tenderness, in my garbage can. I paused for a moment and looked at the tiny body in the blue-flowered paper shroud. Scattered about it were the corn kernels and cat food and table scraps that Arnie and the cats and I invariably left behind after we'd eaten our fill.

I went back to painting the living-room ceiling and settled in to some deep thinking. I had put out the feeders strictly for my own entertainment, hadn't I? I had determined to feed a few select kinds of birds without regard for the genuine needs of any of them, hadn't I? Did that really make me a bird lover?

I finished early with that day's work and put away my tools and paint as quickly as possible. Then I went down to the basement storage room and dug out a flowerpot and a bag of potting soil. At the kitchen sink, I filled the pot half full with soil. I reached down into the garbage can, removed the body of the dead starling, laid it on top of the dirt, and finished filling the pot. It was a bit unorthodox to inter a bird in a flowerpot, I suppose, but it would have to do for now. I carried the pot outside. When the ground thawed enough to be shoveled, I'd give him a proper burial. Silly or not, it would make me feel better.

Returning to the warmth of the house, I closed the kitchen door. Now all three cats were sitting in front of dishes that still held the substantial but dried-out remnants of that morning's feeding. "It's obscene how much food is wasted here when there are starving creatures all around us," I grumbled. I took a covered dish from the cupboard, snapped off the plastic lid with a flourish, and emptied the leftover cat food into the container. "There will be no more waste in this household, not ever again." I glared at the cats and opened a fresh can of food. "There are going to be some changes made around here, starting today! From now on, every crumb will be eaten. Every crumb!"

"Da-da-da-dum!" Arnie whistled.

I dished out the food. "Anyone who wants to eat, better start now," I said. "And I do mean now!" Three pairs of widened feline eyes stared at me with bewilderment. "Eat!" I commanded. The three furry heads ducked down quickly. Loud smacking noises assured me that I was the boss of the household—for now.

I went to Arnie's cage, opened the door, and walked to the bookcase. Arnie fluttered after me, landed on my shoulder, then hopped to the nearest shelf, looking at each book in turn as though searching for a title to his liking.

"It's time for me to do some homework, Arnie," I said. "If I expect the birds to entertain me, the least I can do is establish a proper feeding program for them."

The book I was looking for had been my favorite Christmas present this year. I found it and pulled it from the shelf.

Arnie followed me to my easy chair and paraded up and down the chair's arm until I was settled. Then he perched on my wrist and used his beak to help me turn the pages as I began to leaf through *A Complete Guide to Bird Feeding*.

The book was wonderfully detailed. I quickly learned that I could feed the several varieties of "trash" birds—including grackles and house sparrows—enough to help them through the brutal winter months without causing any hardship to the more favored little birds, and that in all probability, once the weather broke, most of the "nuisance" birds would return to their natural food sources with no urging from me.

"Do you see that long list of starling favorite foods, Arnie?" I said. "Things like rice and potatoes, cheese and bread and corn. Why, basically it's all table scraps!"

"*Bradddddtttt!*" Arnie said.

"No one asked you. Your canned corn and eggs are on the list, too, but generally I'd say you're just too particular—very unstarling-like of you."

Mentally, I started to tick off some of the things I could have been doing all along. Why, many of the birds resorted to the birdseed only out of desperation, because there simply was nothing else on which they could survive. They were freezing and starving out there while we were so snug and well fed in here.

"I meant what I said," I announced to my animals. "Every crumb will be eaten from now on. Because whatever we don't eat is going out onto the ground for the birds."

For I would tolerate no more hungry birds around my house. Trash birds or not, pretty birds or not, all were welcome at Margarete's "soup line."

CHAPTER FOUR

FOOTSTEPS galloped on the roof as boy squirrel chased girl squirrel for the umpteenth time that day. I smiled, welcoming the sound and its significance. The severe cold had broken, most of the snow was melted, and the animals had begun mating rituals. With its new coat of paint and all the repairs I'd done, the house sparkled, and my spirits were bright. Already, I had decided to remain in Falmouth through the summer, and I was beginning to admit I was going to stay. Despite so many changes, this was still home, and I was part of a family.

As I cleared lunch dishes from the table, Arnie pranced around on Travie's head, parting my eight-year-old grandson's hair with that incessantly busy beak of his. Ignoring this self-appointed hairstylist, Travie knelt on the couch, leaning against its back. His hands were clasped together, his eyes closed, his face upturned.

"What are you doing?" I asked.

He giggled. "I'm imagining what it will feel like to have snow fall on my face."

Ugh! I had promised him snow when we'd talked on the telephone before he left home. And he'd been so excited at the prospect of spending his spring vacation watching a snowstorm. Travie had been glued to the window for days, but the closest thing to snow he'd seen was a drizzling, icy rain. Florida born and reared, he'd never seen so much as a flake of the real thing and often asked what it felt like to be hit by a snowball.

"The cartoons should be on now," I said. "Do you want me to turn on the TV set?"

"Uh-uh."

"How about putting together a jigsaw puzzle, then?"

"Uh-uh."

He stared steadily out the window, his chin resting on the backs of his folded hands, his fine-featured, freckled face just a few inches from Vagabond's black furry one. Arnie lost interest in hairstyling, squatted down as though nesting in Travie's hair, and whistled "Mary Had a Little Lamb." I always thought of them as "my three boys" when they were together like that, which was often. Sammie and Mitzi loved Travie, too, but there was a special bond linking him and Arnie and Vagabond.

"I know," I said. "Why don't you build something with your Lego set? That's one game that Arnie and Vagabond always liked to play with you."

He made a face. "Can't I just look out the window, Margarete? You have different kinds of animals here than we do in Florida. See, there's Manx!" he added, excited now. "He's hanging from the tree and looking right at me!"

Manx was a gray squirrel, not a cat, but I thought Travie had named him quite appropriately. His tail, though incongruously bushy, was only a bit longer than a nub. Manx was king of the neighborhood acorn pile these days. He swung from the tree branch and sailed about four feet to a landing on the sill outside the window, ran along it until he was in front of Travie, stood tall and straight on his hind legs, and peered into the living room through forepaws braced against the glass. Vagabond reached up a paw and gently placed it on the glass in the middle of Manx's face. The squirrel stretched himself a bit higher so he could see over it and worked his mouth in a chewing motion.

"I think he's ordering dinner, Travie," I said. "Do you want to wait on him today, or shall I?"

"I will, Margarete. Remember, I'm here to help you."

He hadn't reached the ripe old age of eight without learning a great deal about chivalry and gentlemanly behavior. In fact, he was being so very solicitous that I'd begun to examine my image in the mirror with some degree of anxiety, looking for a sudden burgeoning of wrinkles or gray hair, telltale signs of frailty. No matter how I reassured myself, though, he continued to act as though he thought I might break if I lifted anything heavier than Arnie. Probably just a stage he's going through, I decided.

"Get the can and dip out some sunflower seeds," I told him. "Remember, though, no more than half a can. I'm trying to wean the little beasties so they'll start looking for their natural foods."

Actually, it was more that I was trying to wean myself from the soup-line habits I had developed during the winter. Once I had established a spot on my countertop for the birds' scrap dish and had begun automatically emptying leftovers into that container, it was almost impossible to stop. And while I was caring for the omnivorous birds, I couldn't very well neglect the squirrels, could I? Or Edelweiss and the raccoon I'd chased from my father's bedroom, both of whom had begun making nocturnal appearances again.

I felt responsible for them all. In fact, it had become almost a sacred obligation for me to extend hospitality to the wild animals that frequented my yard, maybe partly because it hit me one day that it had been their yard long before it became mine.

I had no idea if my grandson would understand why I fed them, but I was grateful to realize that he found simple joy in the act for his own reasons. That Travie felt so much for animals gave me a comforting sense of continuity; like one season following another, my grandson would carry something of my spirit into the future long after I had gone.

"It's quit raining, Margarete." Travie's voice snapped me out of my thoughts. "The sun's even coming out. Could we walk to the beach?"

"Oh, well, sure, darling, if you want to. Bundle up real good, though, you hear? It's still pretty cold out there."

"You, too," he yelled as he ran to get his coat. When he came back, he struggled into it, zipped it up, and reached for his gloves and ski cap. "I don't want you to catch a cold."

"Bye-bye. See you later," Arnie said from his aviary as we opened the front door. "Bye-bye. See you later. Bye-bye."

"Bye-bye, Arnie," Travie replied. "See you later, alligator." He went skipping off up the street, laughing gleefully.

Walking was a gait with which he seemed totally unfamiliar; hopping, skipping, jumping, and running were his styles of locomotion. Though he never stopped for an instant, he never went far from me, either, constantly coming back to share one observation after another. "The houses sure are built different here. . . . This kind of cold air really feels good. . . . There was a raccoon in the trees over there, but he ran away. . . . Did you know the trees are all waking up after their winter's sleep?"

After he'd skipped stones across the gently lapping waves, tested the water temperature with a tentative forefinger, and run along the beach until his shoes were filled with cold sand, he was ready for a leisurely stroll home. By the time we arrived there, he was happy to curl up in front of the TV set.

"How about a cup of hot chocolate?" I asked. He nodded with enthusiasm.

As I reached for cups in the kitchen, I heard a scream—shrill, penetrating, panic-stricken. I'd heard that particular sound before—twice before, in fact. Once when Arnie had become entangled in a string and once when he'd flown to a landing on top of a hot pot lid. The scream was repeated three times; then there was silence. Arnie was in trouble!

In bounding leaps I was out of the kitchen and into the living room. Breathlessly, I looked toward the aviary. Arnie sat on the middle perch, nonchalantly looking about with total unconcern.

"You scared the wits out of me, Arnie," I said. "Don't you dare screech like that again unless you're in real trouble. You—"

EAEAEEEeeeeeeeeeeeeeeeeeeeeeeeeeeEEEAEhhh!

Arnie's neck stretched a good three inches as he looked around, his head swiveling right to left. The scream had come from the yard. It was a starling distress call.

I hurried to the window and looked out. There were no signs of a bird in trouble. I opened the door and checked again. Nothing. It was so still out there, so silent, that it seemed every living creature had suddenly vacated the neighborhood.

EEEEeeeeeeeeeeeeeee!

This time I had it pinpointed for sure. I ran to my bedroom window and froze in my tracks.

On the ground, not more than three feet away from the house, was a very large, light gray bird. A mourning dove? Uttering starling distress calls? How little I still knew! My grossly mistaken impression lasted for only the few seconds it took the bird to lift his head majestically and look at me with imperious disdain. His amber eyes fixed upon me from behind the hooked beak of a predator. He was magnificent! And he was much too busy at his calling to be concerned with a mere human who didn't even know a gentle dove from a hawk.

Lying on its back, completely imprisoned by the larger bird's strong talons and exposed to that efficient beak, was a starling. It could easily have passed for Arnie. Leisurely, as though he had all the time in the world, the hawk reached down, nuzzled the starling's chest with a gesture of apparent gentleness, then came up with a beak full of feathers. The starling didn't twitch a muscle. The hawk arched his neck, opened his beak, and stretched toward the smaller bird's chest once again.

"Nooo!" I cried, and banged on the window glass. "No you don't, you beast. Get away from here. Go away!"

Slowly, ever so slowly, the hawk lifted his head again, swiveled his beak to point in my direction, and glared so fiercely that I quit my frenzied pounding. Those eyes locked onto mine, and my breath stopped in my throat. The effect was so mesmerizing that I understood to the depth of my being why the starling was not resisting. It couldn't. The hawk nuzzled it again. Abruptly, the starling's head slumped to the side and it looked toward me. Its eyes gleamed, then glazed over.

With a knot in my throat so large I thought I would choke, I banged on the window glass again. The hawk unfurled his wings, gave me a final look of contempt, and took to the air, carrying his dinner with effortless grace. I watched until he disappeared from sight beyond the trees.

I sighed, realizing I'd been foolish to try changing the natural order of things. After all, the hawk had to eat, too. I turned away from the window. And bumped into Travie, who was standing at my elbow. Seeing the look of horror on his face, I didn't have to ask how much he had seen. Great tears coursed down his cheeks.

I put my arm around his shoulders and led him to the kitchen table. His eyes were downcast the whole time; he didn't utter a sound. I made hot chocolate, poured it into two cups, and put a plateful of chocolate chip cookies between us. He bit into a cookie and sipped at the chocolate without much enthusiasm.

"It hurt me, too," I said.

He shrugged, sipped, nibbled at the cookie. "I've seen dead things before," he said slowly, "but I never saw anything die. I mean, one minute the bird was looking at me; then all of a sudden he wasn't a he anymore; he was just a dead . . . thing."

"That's what death is, you know. No matter how it happens, death is just a matter of the life force leaving the body. Without the life force, a body is just a thing."

"Is Arnie going to die someday?"

"Yes, but not for a long, long time, I hope. No hawks are going to get to him in here. He should live for about fifteen years, maybe even longer. You'll be a grown man by then."

Travie was quiet for a while. Sipping chocolate and nibbling another cookie, he stared at the tabletop, avoiding my eyes.

"When are you going to die, Margarete?" he said at last.

The words were like a kick in the stomach. I'd been prepared for "Are you . . . ?" Not for "When . . . ?" So I laughed. "I haven't the slightest idea, darling."

His words came out in a torrent now. "My friend's grandmother was always laughing and happy and having a good time with him. Then, one day, she got sick and went to the hospital, and they wouldn't let him see her. They just told him she died one night. And that's what I'm afraid you're going to do to me."

It was my turn to sip chocolate and be quiet. Finally I said, "Well, Travie, all I can tell you is that I'll live as long as I can. And I promise, if I ever get so sick that I think I'll die, I'll send for you so you can see me one last time, hospital rules or no hospital rules. I understand exactly how you feel."

"You do?"

"Of course. I know how I'd feel if you went home to Florida without saying good-bye to me. I'll bet the part that hurt your friend the most was that he didn't get to say good-bye to his grandmother before she left him."

"Yeah, I guess you're right, Margarete."

"I'll tell you what we can do. We can say our final good-byes now. I'll go out the door, and then we won't have to worry about whether or not we'll have the chance later on."

"Huh?"

"Let's pretend. Let's pretend that I'm going to live forever, but I'm going to have to move to another planet to do it. Of course, that means you and I will never, ever, see or hear from each other again. Naturally, you'll come to the spaceport to say good-bye to me, won't you?"

"Sure."

"Okay. I'm going to the departure gate in the other room to wait for you. And you pretend you just came in on the space shuttle from the moon. Then I want you to do and say whatever you would want to the last time we see each other." I walked into the living room.

"Grandmother, Grandmother." He ran into the room and threw his arms around my waist. "Don't go away and leave me."

"You've always called me Margarete; don't stop now. Travie, no one can live on earth forever. You know I have to leave you no

298

matter how much I want to stay. As long as you love me, though, a part of me will always be with you. Having you for my grandson has been one of the best parts of my whole life. I'm so glad I was able to stay around long enough to watch you grow up and become a professional jet jockey."

He giggled but continued with his role. "And I'm so glad I had you for a grandmother. I love you, Margarete, so I guess you will always be with me. Do you have to take Arnie and Vagabond and Sammie and Mitzi with you, though? They won't like Pluto." He giggled again, though a bit nervously.

"You're right, Travie, they can't go with me. So I've decided to leave them all with you. You will take good care of them and love them, won't you?"

"Sure!"

"Well, I guess that's it, then. Good-bye, Travie. I love you. Thanks for being my grandson."

"And I love you, Margarete. Good-bye. Thanks for being my grandmother."

We hugged. Very tightly. His eyes glistened suspiciously as I walked out the front door.

I strolled around the block before going back into the house. He was sitting in my easy chair watching television when I came in. Vagabond was on one side of him, Sammie on the other, and Arnie was perched on his head. He lifted Vagabond to the arm of the chair, put Sammie into his lap, moved way over to one side, and patted the cushion next to him. I sat and put my arm around his shoulders.

"Feel better?" I asked.

He gave me a long kiss on the cheek and said, "Uh-huh."

"You realize, of course, that I fully intend to be around for another twenty or thirty years or more. I have to finish watching you grow up. And I have to teach your children all about loving animals. By the time we really have to say good-bye, we might think of a few more things we want to say."

"Uh-uh," he said adamantly. "We've said it all."

SPRING was here! And what a spring it was. If awards were given to the seasons, this one would certainly take the prize. Each day now, the sky was a rich, velvety blue with just enough wispy white clouds to adorn it like tasteful touches of lace. Though the nights were still cold, the days were warm and filled with the promise of summer. Forsythia bushes, ablaze with yellow blossoms, were downright ostentatious in contrast to the last clinging dinginess of winter. Rhododendron and azalea buds had fattened to their utmost and were simply awaiting their turn to burst open and spray the world with vivid hues. And the color green, in all its varied shades, was being reborn to the landscape.

All that vibrancy of life reawakening, combined with the crisp salt tanginess of Cape Cod air, was enough to make me want to climb mountains and sing operettas and run the Boston Marathon all at the same time. I settled for humming and hammering away at my number one project for the season, repairing any cat-size holes in the backyard fence.

As I worked, Arnie's voice joined mine, resounding clearly from inside the house with snatches of Beethoven's Fifth Symphony, "Mary Had a Little Lamb," and an assortment of his own unique tunes. I wondered if he was as happy as he sounded, cooped up indoors as he was. Sunshine and fresh air and the stimulation of watching nature's normal activities would be good for him, I was certain. This year he was going to get daily outings while I worked in the yard, just as the cats would.

Indeed, if I didn't let Mitzi join me soon, one of the two of us was going to have a nervous breakdown. She was the reason the fence was a top priority. She'd spent most of the winter on the fireplace hearth, contentedly purring in a state bordering on hibernation. Now, though, she was too restless to sleep and so anxious to be outside that I felt like a terrible troll holding her free spirit imprisoned.

I blamed her newfound discontent on Manx, the squirrel, who teased her unmercifully. When Mitzi lay sunning herself upon the windowsill, he made good use of his acrobatic skills to hang by his toes from the shutter so he could bang the screen in front of her face. When she was at the door looking out, that mischief-making squirrel would charge across the lawn and up the porch steps, take a flying leap that landed him in a belly flop against the glass of the storm door, and look back over his shoulder at her as he sauntered away. I couldn't help thinking that he was telling her to come out and play.

But that was something I would not permit until I had cat-proofed the entire fence line surrounding the backyard. The measure was for my own protection, of course; pets that wander all too often have shortened life-spans and owners with prematurely gray hair.

Mitzi danced over when I came in and sat down to lunch. She jumped onto my lap, put her front paws on my shoulders, and licked my face, then meowed and nuzzled my chin with hers. On the table right behind her, Arnie reached out, grabbed her tail, and gave it a good tweak. She looked at him, snorted, and jumped to the floor, positioning herself at the door. "*Meeeoooooowww?*" she said, looking yearningly at me.

Manx bounced up the porch steps, put his paws against the storm door, and peered inside. Mitzi pressed her face to the glass so that they were nose to nose, my cat and that troublesome squirrel, making cow eyes at each other like two lovers.

"That is completely unnatural behavior," I told them between bites of my sandwich. "I hope you have the good sense to keep your distance when she goes out, Manx. She is a cat, you know."

"Coo-coo, peekaboo, Mitzi loves the boo," Arnie said.

"Maybe Mitzi loves the boo, but if she goes kissy, kissy, it could mean bye-bye for Manx. Never trust a cat's friendship all the way, Arnie, never."

I took another bite of my sandwich while Arnie picked at the lettuce that had fallen onto my plate. As I chewed, Mitzi and Manx stared at me, and stared, and stared. "Look, Mip-Mip," I said at last. "The fence is all finished except for the gate. I can't hang that until I get some help. I'm going to take a chance and let you come out with me after lunch. But if you go anywhere near the opening in the fence, you'll be back inside so fast your head will spin."

Finished with lunch, I carried my dishes back to the sink and gave them a quick wash. Then I let Mitzi out, and I sat on the back porch to rest for a while. She moved warily out onto the patio, chewing blades of grass and sniffing at every centimeter of ground. To my relief, Manx had disappeared, probably because I hadn't thrown out sunflower seeds on demand. He didn't fool me one bit—he came to the doors and windows for handouts, not friendship. I certainly hoped Mitzi could see through him,

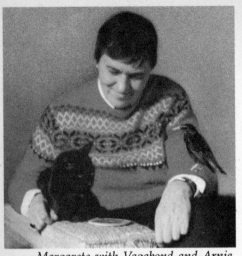

Margarete with Vagabond and Arnie, above. Right, Arnie alights on a lampshade, and below, the starling finds a handy perch on Mitzi.

Above, the proud starling shows off his brown and white speckles. Margarete's grandson, Travie, below left, enjoys a day at the playground with a chum.

too. I wouldn't want her heart broken by a mangy squirrel.

Oh no, I'd spoken too soon. Manx was still around. Intent on the acorn he was munching in a corner of the yard, he hadn't even seen us. But Mitzi had seen him! I opened my mouth and shouted a warning. He looked up, dropped his acorn, and seemed to dance a little jig in front of her.

Then the chase was on. Round and round a tree they ran, Mitzi never more than two inches away from Manx's stub of a tail—though she never seemed to get an iota closer than that, either. Manx suddenly came to a screeching halt, stood, turned around, and looked up at her. She braked, sat, and looked down at him, her mouth open, and panting from the unaccustomed exertion.

The prey waited for the predator to catch her breath; then they were off and running again, zigging and zagging, crissing and crossing with such synchronous movements that it could have been an energetic ballet they'd carefully choreographed.

When he became bored with the game, Manx ran up an oak, stood on a lower branch long enough to wave his tail in farewell, then lunged to an overhanging limb of a neighbor's hickory tree on his way to other parts of town. Mitzi watched him until he'd disappeared, cleaned her paws on the bark, and pranced to the patio with the expression of Alice's Cheshire. She lay down next to my chair and licked my hand.

"Do you feel better now?" I asked. "As I remember it, you used to chase all of the squirrels exactly the way you chased Manx. Funny how they seem to know you'd never harm them."

Behind us, Vagabond meowed long and plaintively. I looked over my shoulder and saw him with his nose and front paws pressed to the door glass. Well, if Mitzi deserved an outing, I supposed Vagabond did, too.

I opened the door, not realizing that Samantha was right behind Vagabond. Like bursts from a Roman candle, the two cats erupted through the door, separated, and shot in different directions. Vagabond wobbled no farther than the patio, where he crouched cautiously and looked about suspiciously. Sammie stampeded to the far corner of the yard, found the fence, and clambered over it. Inside I could hear Arnie crashing about in his cage, squawking and *trrrpping* his protest at all this fuss.

Suddenly Manx reappeared. He bounced across the lawn, and

Vagabond was instantly just inches away from him, sprinting after the squirrel with obvious determination. Manx gave a defiant flip of his tail remnant and stretched out into a series of flying leaps that took him to the nearest oak well ahead of Vagabond. Up the tree scampered the squirrel. Up the tree clambered the cat. Higher and higher they climbed, then farther and farther out a limb, until it began to bend beneath Vagabond's bulk. Manx stopped, turned with a triumphant look, and *chukka-chukka-chukka-cheeeeed* over and over again, announcing to the entire neighborhood that he had a cat treed.

At that point, Vagabond noticed where he was. The pupils of his eyes grew larger as he stared down at the ground, tried to turn around on the branch, and realized he could not. *"Ow?"* he said very quietly. A twig snapped from beneath one of his paws, throwing him off balance. With an *ooomph*, he landed on his belly, astraddle the branch. Both sets of paws locked in place, hugging that meager piece of tree as though it were the dearest thing in the world. He looked down at me with a wretched, pleading, trusting, terrified expression.

"Bye-bye, see you later," Arnie shrilled.

"Margarete, your cat's over here," a neighbor shouted across the fence. In her arms was Mitzi, wiggling and squirming.

"I think this is yours, too," a man's voice said behind me. The neighbor on the other side of me reached across the fence from his yard, a wriggling bundle of black fur in one hand as he held Samantha toward me. "I have a stepladder you can use to rescue the one in the tree."

"Nothing like a fun family outing." I sighed and set about gathering the clan.

CHAPTER FIVE

"You're a murderer, Arnie."

He cocked his head to the side and looked at me with beady brown eyes glowing softly, sweetly, innocently. No cherub could have looked more hurt than he did at that moment.

"And you can quit giving me that look, too. How can you pretend innocence when the victim is dangling from your beak?"

The mangled remains of the latest fatality hung in shreds from

both sides of his mouth. This one looked as if it was—had been—
a sweet pepper. Nothing green and growing was safe in this
house. If the culprit wasn't Arnie, it was the cats, eating my
garden seedlings before I could get them into the ground.

Arnie gave the tattered plant a final brutal blow against the
tabletop, swallowed a bite, and dropped the remains. I watched,
waiting to see if there would be some indication of remorse in his
starling soul. But he merely wiped his beak on a napkin. Looked
at me. And glibly snatched another seedling.

"Not that one, Arnie!" I grabbed at the plant. He sidestepped.
"Those tomato leaves are poisonous!"

Like a toddling human, Arnie put everything new and different
into his mouth. Straight pins, staples, splinters of wood—he
found them all in cracks and crevices in the floor and furniture or
buried in the pile of the rug. He knew by now that the most
certain way to persuade me to play with him was to find a poten-
tially dangerous toy and threaten to swallow it. When I grabbed
again, he ran to the other side of the table.

"I'll get it, Margarete," Travie said from behind me. "I know a
trick." He tore a corner from a magazine cover, rattled the paper
loudly, then stuck it between his fingers and put his hand palm
down on the corner of the table. Travie wiggled the piece of
paper. Arnie cocked his head, looking at my grandson's hand with
a mingling of interest and suspicion. Again the paper moved, ever
so enticingly. Arnie galloped across the table, thrust his beak
between Travie's fingers, and pried them open, dropping the
plant. I snatched it.

"Clever thinking," I said.

"I just thought the way Arnie would think," Travie said with a
modest shrug. Then he grinned. "But you do have to be clever to
outthink him! When is David coming?"

David, my fifteen-year-old nephew, was scheduled to spend
the day with Travie. But he had called earlier to cancel. I hadn't
had the heart to tell Travie that David wasn't exactly eager to play
games with someone so young.

"He's not," I said reluctantly. "Teenagers have very busy
schedules, especially at the end of the school year."

"Oh. Well, c'mon, Arnie. C'mon, Vagabond. Let's watch cartoons. I guess you're the only friends I have here." The way he

walked, you'd have thought he had a barbell on his shoulder instead of a four-ounce starling.

Travie was visiting me again, on his summer holiday. He needed playmates, of course, but there was no one around yet to fill the bill. And in a few weeks he would be leaving for his half summer with his father, right when the Cape Cod season was just beginning.

Still, I was determined that he would have a wonderful time. As he grew, I wanted him to feel that this was the location of our family roots, one place he could always call home. He'd never feel that way, though, if he didn't have fond memories to look back on from his visits.

"C'mon, Travie," I said. "You can watch cartoons another time. Right now the fish are biting off the jetties."

His face brightened. "I'll get the gear out of the shed," he said, and he was off and running, like a horse leaving the starting gate.

"Wait! Be careful! You still have Arnie on your shoulder!"

Too late. In his excitement, Travie was out the door and off the porch before I finished speaking. The door swung wide, then started arcing back to its place within the frame. Arnie, who had to be carefully coaxed and cosseted before he would go outside, looked around in surprise. Then he flattened himself against Travie's neck, squawked loudly, and flung himself into the air.

His body assumed the shape of a dart as he hurled himself back toward the house. But with horror I realized that he and the rapidly closing door were in a dead-heat race for the same space. It was a nightmare scene: the door was going to close on him and there was nothing I could do about it.

Inches short of the jamb, the safety feature of the door's automatic closer engaged. The door jerked to a stop, leaving a crack of an opening—toward which Arnie hurtled. Then the automatic closer released the door. Arnie streaked through the narrow space just as the aluminum edge of the door surged at him. He screeched loudly, his eyes reflecting panic. The door closed. And he hung, pinioned between door and jamb.

Travie's eyes bulged as they stared through the door glass. He was paralyzed by shock, unable to move.

Arnie, it seemed, was the only one of us capable of action. With a mighty flapping of his wings, he struggled free and shot across the room, *trrrppping* angrily as he careered into the aviary.

Protruding from the crack between the tightly closed door and its frame was a clump of feathers.

"Bad, bad, bad, badbadbadbadbadbadbadbadbad," Arnie sputtered. He fluffed, shook himself, looked over his shoulder. And stared. Then gently combed the two remaining feathers where his handsome tail had been.

"Maybe we could poke them back into place, Margarete, like a hair transplant," said Travie as he stared at the detached feathers.

"Awwwwwwwwwww. He's a little bitty baby boy. C'mere, gimme a kiss," Arnie said plaintively. Then he hopped down to the bottom of his cage, took a long drink of water, and began to eat.

"I think he'll be okay," I said. "He's due for a molt soon and would have lost them anyway. He'll probably have a whole set of new ones before you leave."

"Can we wait and go fishing tomorrow, Margarete?" Travie asked. "Arnie might need us today."

"Fine with me," I agreed with a relieved sigh. All things considered, Arnie seemed little the worse for wear, but I'd just lost ten years off my life and could do with a chance to recuperate.

In the days that followed, we more than made up for that one lost excursion, going to our favorite spot at each tide's turning, the salt spray nibbling amiably at our shoes. With uncanny instinct, Travie hooked everything that so much as bumped his bait, while I bemoaned my propensity for simply feeding the fish. Of course, it's a time-honored tradition that the one who doesn't catch the fish must clean and cook them, so I wasn't totally useless.

And then there was Travie's tree. He was so proud of it. A week after his arrival, the UPS truck had delivered the fruit and nut trees I'd ordered. While we planted them, I told Travie my favorite tree story. In 1973 I'd gone to my native Germany for a visit, a good part of which I spent with my friend Anni in Brannenburg, a Bavarian village. Each day we'd taken long walks through dark spruce forests, trudged up gently ascending mountains, and meandered back to Brannenburg through well-tended farmland. Along the way, I noticed many trees laden with little round balls growing at the ends of long stems. I asked Anni what kind they were. She looked, laughed, and said, *"Kirschkernbaum."* Cherry pit tree? I thought, perplexed. Anni explained that the amsel, a European blackbird, always stripped the fruit and left the pits dangling. No one begrudged the amsel its cherries, regarding them as fair payment for the bird's exceptionally beautiful song.

"Cherry pit tree!" Travie laughed. "I wish I could have seen that. If I had a cherry tree, I'd leave the fruit for the birds so I could have a *Kirschkernbaum*, too."

"This is a cherry tree we're planting now," I said.

"It is?" He gave me his most beguiling smile. "Can I have it? Can this one be my special tree? Not to take back to Florida, to have here. This is my home away from home, you know. I'll take very good care of it, I promise."

So now he had his own tree, just as he had his own tomato, watermelon, cucumber, and bean plants. Together, he and I were learning about gardening. But despite the watering and weeding and fertilizing, that poor garden was one sorry sight, except for Travie's plants, all of which were thriving.

"He has to be bored, though," I said to my friend Patsy in one of our phone conversations. "He won't admit it, but I'm sure he is."

"Maybe he's happy to be bored for a change, Margarete," she replied. "Don't worry so much. How many little boys have a talking bird for a playmate?"

"He needs human companions his own age," I fretted.

"He'll have them soon," she said. "My grandsons are coming from Maryland next week. Joshua's just a baby, of course, but Christopher is nine and Michael is seven. They'll get along wonderfully with Travie."

"You're a liar!"

"No I'm not."

"You are so. My brother wouldn't call you names for nothing!"

"So much for the boys getting along wonderfully, Patsy," I said. The heat of the argument out on the water carried their voices to us even over the lapping of the waves, the screeching of sea gulls, and the boisterous yelling of dozens of other children playing at the beach near Patsy's home.

"They're just being boys. They'll be laughing together anytime now," Patsy assured me.

"Margarete! Margarete, please tell them I'm not lying," Travie called as the three boys splashed through the water toward us.

"He's not lying," I said. "Now, what are you not lying about, Travie?"

"They don't believe me about Arnie, that he's a wild bird and that he can talk. Tell them, Margarete, tell them what a real super bird he is."

"Buuurd," young Joshua echoed, pointing at a wheeling sea gull with his sand shovel. "Come, buuurd."

"You're coming to my house for a cookout tomorrow, boys," I said. "You'll meet Arnie then and learn if Travie's lying or not."

I should have known better than to put Travie's reputation on the line, however. As Michael and Christopher stared through the screen at Arnie the next day, all that starling did was stare back at them. Not one word would he utter.

"C'mon, Arnie," Travie kept saying, desperation growing. "He's a little bitty baby boy. See you soon, baboon. Coo-coo, peekaboo."

"Peekaboo," little Joshua said, putting his hands over his eyes and staring through his fingers. He toddled to the aviary and turned his face up to Arnie. "Peekaboo, buuurd, peekaboo."

"Peekaboo," Arnie said. "Peekaboo, I see you, I love you, yes I do. C'mere, gimme a kiss." He hopped to a lower perch, where he was at eyeball level with Joshua.

"Peekaboo, buuurd," Joshua chortled, tugging at Patsy's dress and pointing. "Peekaboo. Buuurd!"

"He's a little bitty baby boy, yes he is," Arnie said, and whistled a few notes from Beethoven's Fifth.

Christopher and Michael were convinced and a bit impressed, but they were also busy building a new friendship, and Travie hadn't even begun to show them around his territory. While the three of them checked out the video game and Legos and books in Travie's play area, Joshua sat on the floor on his diapered bottom and stared at Arnie. Who stared back at him. I'm not sure who was more enthralled—Joshua, who'd never seen a bird so close before and certainly never dreamed that birds could talk, or Arnie, who'd never seen a baby before and undoubtedly never dreamed that humans came in such tiny sizes. When Arnie started to peck on his screening, there was no doubt in my mind what that inquisitive bird wanted.

"You want to come outside, Arnie?" I asked.

"Let him out, Margarete," Patsy said. "Joshua's very gentle with animals."

I opened the aviary door, and Arnie hopped to the floor, marched to Joshua's foot, inserted his beak between two chunky baby toes, and pried them apart. The owner of the toes screwed up his face, then pointed at Arnie. "Buuurd. Buuurd tickles!" he said, and giggled.

The "buuurd" looked toward the sound, jumped onto the baby's foot, fluttered to Joshua's head, and launched into a song. After another peal of giggles, Joshua settled back and listened with a smile.

"I think it's love at first sight," Patsy said.

Indeed, it proved to be. "My buuurd?" Joshua asked as they left that afternoon. It took some doing to convince him that Arnie would be happier staying with me than going with him.

That day was the high point of Arnie's summer, too. His molt set in just as temperatures shot to unusual highs for the Cape. The only thing that took his mind off the heat was the irritating itch of new feathers emerging all over his body. In his misery he became mute, except for the trrrpps, hisses, and queeks with which he expressed annoyance.

"Maybe we could train Vagabond to chase him," Travie said with a twinkle in his eye. "That would take his mind off his feathers."

I didn't find this joke very funny. "Vagabond is already doing entirely too much chasing, thank you."

And he was. As if squirrels weren't enough, Vagabond had discovered rabbits, too. Between the trees and the brush piles and the thorny tangle of wild raspberry canes I was allowing to cover one corner of the yard, Vagabond was repeatedly trapped somewhere that summer, and Travie was constantly crawling or climbing to his rescue.

"You're going to have to learn, Vagabond," I scolded at least a thousand times. "Travie will leave soon, and I may not help you."

Travie wrinkled his nose, said, "Sh," and put his hands over his ears at the mention of his departure. It wasn't that he didn't want to go home; he just didn't want to have to leave to do it. "I wish we could all live in the same place," I overheard him confide to Arnie. "You're lucky—you don't always have to go someplace and change your whole routine so you can be with everyone you love. Being a kid is the pits."

Ah well, partings can be eased with plans for the next get-together, and they give us perfect excuses for parties. Naturally, we had to have one so Travie could bid farewell to his new friends.

While he and Christopher and Michael crammed in every single "last chance to . . ." imaginable, and Joshua played with Arnie, Patsy was quiet, her face reflecting troubled thoughts. I'd noticed her pensive mood, but we hadn't discussed it yet. Wanting to cheer her up, I decided a change of scenery was in order.

"Let's sit on the patio," I said. "It's too nice to stay indoors."

Outside, we settled into chairs and surveyed the puny results of my novice attempt at gardening. "Wait until next year," I said. "It's a new challenge, and I don't give up easily."

Patsy sighed. "I don't either, usually. But . . . I've been doing something lately that I'm tempted to give up on—sometimes, anyway. It's so discouraging." She paused, and I waited for her to search out the right words. "I've been visiting a bedridden woman, trying to cheer her up. Terminal cancer. Her vision's going, so she can't read or watch TV. She's so . . . so angry, so bitter. Understandable, of course. I wish I could think of something to take her mind off herself."

"Is it anyone I know?" I asked. "Maybe—"

"No, no one you know, though you have things in common. She's from Europe, for one. Her name is Ekaterina."

Ekaterina? Surely there couldn't be more than one Ekaterina in a small town like Falmouth. "Why, I know—"

The boys ran out the back door. "Margarete, can we have something to drink?" Travie asked. "We sure are thirsty!"

Patsy and I dropped the subject. This was, after all, the boys' day. By the time we'd crammed in a last chance to walk to the beach and skip rocks over the waves and feed the swans at the pond and visit the ice cream parlor, it was time for the good-byes.

"You'll be back next year, won't you?" Christopher asked Travie as they shook hands like the young gentlemen they were growing to be.

"Of course he'll be back," Michael answered for him. "Cape Cod is the only place worth being for the summer."

"Michael's right, Margarete," Travie said as we hugged inside the airplane the next day. "I'm really glad you moved here."

"Me, too." I smiled with trembling lips as I checked his seat belt.

When the stewardess asked me to leave the plane, we said our farewells through the tears we'd promised each other we wouldn't shed. I watched the plane take off and disappear into the sky over Massachusetts Bay. Then I headed for home.

It's a long drive from Boston's Logan Airport to Cape Cod, and driving is the kind of activity that encourages the mind to wander. By the time I crossed the Cape bridge, I had exhausted the memories of summer. That left me face to face with the intruding, troubling thoughts of Ekaterina.

I THINK she was a countess but maybe not; perhaps that was just the way I preferred to perceive her. I'd been a very young woman when we met, and Ekaterina was entirely too enigmatic, too glamorous, too haughty to be anything less than nobility, I had decided.

It was her accent that drew me to her that long-ago day in Appell's Pharmacy in Falmouth. Low-pitched, almost husky, her voice filtered through cabinets lined with aspirins and cold remedies and liniments and bandages. Though English, her muffled words sang in my ears with the familiar inflections and cadences of my native German language.

I was at the newsstand, leafing through magazine pages in search of something with a great many pictures. Just beginning my struggles with the language of my newly adopted country, I was following my husband's advice about reading things that would challenge me to turn each page, then force me to struggle with the words in order to learn the ending. As I stood and looked at photographs of a prospector and his mule, I became enmeshed in the excitement of panning for gold in California. Normal voices would not have interrupted my fantasy, but hers was no normal voice.

"Today I vill have a cup of that terrible stuff you Americans accept as coffee," she said from the other side of the store.

The regal tone made me wonder if she also expected it to be served in a china cup and poured from a silver urn. This, then, must be the "other German lady" I'd heard mentioned as a frequent Appell's customer. I had looked forward to meeting her, to the opportunity for a conversation uninhibited by my usual struggle to find the right combination of words among so many unfamiliar ones. Hastily, I returned the magazine to the rack.

I forced myself to take slow, normal steps as I walked around the sundries counter and headed toward the soda fountain. Words lay on my tongue, German words so deliciously familiar. I hadn't had the opportunity to speak any of them in months.

"*Guten Tag, gnädige Frau,*" I said heartily, extending my hand. "*Ich habe—*"

The rest of the sentence stuck in my throat as she whirled on me, her finely honed, aristocratic features contorted by fury. With controlled grace, she raised her chin until she was peering down her nose, surveying me from toes to head with deliberate scrutiny. For the first time in my life, I felt the heat of a blush on my cheeks.

"Speak English," she commanded. Then her face softened. "Come. Sit here." She patted the stuffed red leather seat of the stool beside her, then turned her attention to the steaming cup on the counter. "A cherry Coke for the child," she said without looking up.

This twenty-one-year-old "child" with a husband and baby at home stood glaring at her, daring her to issue another command. Who did she think she was, telling me to speak English in that manner?

"Sit," she said again. "Perhaps ve have things to say to each other." Her voice was low but compelling. Beneath her icy exterior, she hid emotions that I sensed she would never utter. To say them would be beneath her, but I could feel her need as surely as though she were pouring out her heart to me. She was lonely!

I sat down beside her. Unable to think of anything to say, I sipped the cherry Coke. "It is good, yes?" she said. I nodded. We were silent for a few minutes, then she spoke as though to herself. "It is not a good time to be German. Do not remind people that you are. Speak English. I myself vas born Russian, but my family fled to Germany vhen I vas a baby. Then I fled back to Russia vhen my husband became more Nazi than man. And I fled to America vhen all of Europe seemed to be going crazy. So remember, be as American as you can learn to be. Chameleons vill alvays survive; tigers, maybe not."

Between sips of coffee, she counseled me as though she had been my mentor for years, and I listened. How could I not? I was mesmerized. As she dropped the tidbits of history that had marked her lifetime, I realized that she had to be as old as my mother. I saw the fine lines of age around her mouth, at the corners of her eyes, beneath her proud chin.

"Do not forget," she said when we parted. She stared into my eyes then, as though trying to burn her lessons into my soul. "Speak English."

I mumbled something—in English—then walked home, sifting through the advice she'd given me. And as time went on, I followed it. I took up softball. Developed a taste for apple pie almost as strong as the one I'd always had for strudel. Began to read newspapers instead of picture-laden magazines. Learned English. And proceeded with the building of my new life.

I ran into her often after that, but neither of us mentioned that day. I never saw her speak to anyone at any great length, never knew of anyone with whom she became intimate; that would have been contrary to her philosophy for survival.

We never became friends.

I did, however, have one glimpse of her private life. Quite without intention, I walked into her home one evening as the guest of someone who'd been invited to a dinner party. I had accepted the invitation without knowing who my hostess was to be.

As it turned out, she was wonderfully hospitable, and the evening became one I would long remember. Not so much for the excellence of the dinner gathering, though, as for the special piece of her life she chose to share with me.

"Come," she said to me after the meal. Her hand, at my elbow, was already nudging me through her fine home. "There is something I vould show you."

Puzzled, I followed her down a long hallway to the back of the house. She turned through a doorway, and we entered a huge room that I guessed was a closed-in porch. In the middle of its flagstone floor was a seven-tier marble fountain. Water bubbled gently from its top. A single wooden rocking chair and a small marble table beside it were the only accommodations for human comfort. The remainder of the room was devoted to plants and birds. Cages of every size and description were arranged everywhere.

"This is my refuge," she said. "This is my joy." Her face showed it; for once she looked serene.

She lifted the curtains of each cage to show me the occupants. Her charges included robins, sparrows, blue jays, quail, house finches, a mockingbird, a crow, and a cardinal. All had been either injured or orphaned, and consequently they had been hand raised by a human being. Ekaterina cooed and spoke softly to each bird before enclosing it for the night again. Some responded with soft chirps or peeps.

"So now you see," she said. "It vill be our secret, yes?" With a gesture of her hand, she led me back to the dinner guests.

Just as we never spoke of our first meeting, we never discussed her secret. The existence of that room and its contents, of its place in her heart, faded slowly from my memory. Memories do that over the course of twenty-five years. And just as surely as my life blossomed with ever expanding horizons during that period of time, Ekaterina's shriveled. She left her house less and less, eventually becoming a total recluse. Now, on her deathbed, she existed within the very void she had created to safeguard her life.

I suppose I never would have thought of her again if not for Patsy. Despite her thoroughly modern outlook on most matters, when it comes to the meaning of charity, Patsy's as old-fashioned as people come. You do what you can for others for the simple reason that you're a person yourself. So she visited with that lonely, bitter, dying woman, trying to touch her empty hours with a bit of simple human warmth. Certainly I understood the problem when Patsy said, "I only wish I could think of something to take her mind off her predicament." And, at a later date, "What would you talk about in my place?"

That's when the memory of that secret room full of birds came back with stunning clarity. I smiled. "Arnie," I said. "What else? I talk to everyone about him, and no one's been bored yet. Tell her about Arnie, Patsy, and I'll bet you have her looking forward to more of the same each time you go to see her."

She laughed. "Of course! I should have thought of that sooner. You'll keep me supplied with stories, I know."

"And you'll keep me supplied with material to build my stories around, won't you, Arnie?" I said to him that evening.

No longer driven to scratch and clean his body all day, he was once again a polite and charming companion. He still wasn't talking, but his annual molt was almost completed, and if he followed last year's pattern, he'd soon be chattering away again, possibly with a few new words added to his vocabulary.

At least I hoped so. As summer's heat cooled and he remained mute, I began to worry. Though I loved Arnie and found him entertaining whatever he did, I wanted to make a tape recording of him talking—for Ekaterina.

"You won't let us down, will you, Arnie?" I pleaded as he helped me bag the tomatoes I had stewed the day before.

"You wanna go outside, Sammie, Mitzi? You wanna go outside?" After the long silence, Arnie's scratchy voice startled me. I ran out of the kitchen, grabbed the tape recorder, and hurried back, hoping he would continue to talk. "You wanna go outside, Sammie, Mitzi?" Arnie repeated, looking pointedly in my direction.

"They can't go outside, it's raining," I said as I reached for the telephone and punched a number. "Hello, Patsy? Tell Ekaterina I'll have a tape for her in a couple of days."

I made the recording and sent it along with Patsy. "You should have heard her laugh!" my friend reported to me a few days later. "I can't believe what an interest she's taken in Arnie. She tells me she plays the tape over and over, remembering all the stories I've told her as she listens."

One day I happened across a cassette recording I'd made when Arnie first started to talk, and sent it, too. "I thought she'd never stop laughing when she heard his squeaky baby voice," Patsy told me afterward. "Her entire disposition has changed lately. If there's a healing power to laughter . . ."

"Is there any chance?" I asked.

"Not at her age, with her kind of cancer. It's spreading fast."

It was only a matter of weeks before Patsy handed the tapes back to me. One of them had been in the cassette player next to Ekaterina when her ordeal ended.

"She sent a message she said you would understand," Patsy said. "She asked me to tell you that Arnie is enough joy to fill an entire room."

CHAPTER SIX

A TERRIBLE, strong, obnoxiously offensive odor assailed me when I stepped outside. I sniffed tentatively and immediately wished I hadn't. Then I noticed Vagabond near the back hedges. His forehead was creased with deep frown lines, his eyes were tightly shut, his nose twitched.

A few feet in front of him was one of Edelweiss's youngsters, its black-and-white-striped back turned to Vagabond, its bushy tail standing straight as a flagpole.

"Come, Vagabond," I called. Even with his eyes shut, the poor cat ran right over to me.

Nearby, Samantha wiggled her nose and belly-crawled under the patio table when he drew near. Vagabond slunk to my feet and licked my ankle. Tears streamed down his facial fur as he peered imploringly up at me.

"There are limits to everything, including motherly love, Vagabond," I said. "And skunk stench stretches the limits of love for me, too." I held my breath and picked him up. On the way to the kitchen sink, I grabbed a handful of ripe tomatoes from the harvest basket on the table.

"This is messy," I warned Vagabond, "but it'll take away most of the smell." Holding him firmly by the scruff of the neck, I let water run from the sink hose into his eyes, then rubbed the juicy vegetables into his fur. He stood quietly in the sink and endured the tomato bath. I was soaked to my elbows when the telephone rang.

"Hello," Arnie said. "Hi there. How are you?"

"That's very good, Arnie. Now pick up the telephone and say it again."

I scooted Vagabond outside to rub himself clean, snatched a towel, wiped hastily at my dripping arms, and reached for the telephone. The receiver clicked and buzzed as I put it to my ear.

"They'll call back," I said, shrugging, and went outside. The days were growing shorter now, and there were chores to do. I looked around with smug satisfaction at the yard I'd planted with ornamental trees and bushes after clearing the wild growth. Bright reds and yellows and oranges blazed everywhere.

What a beautiful season autumn was! After a year back home, I realized that I'd really missed the rhythm of the seasons while down south. Of course, there are penalties to be paid for the enjoyment of each season. Fall, for instance, is a major cleanup time. Mostly because once those much admired autumn leaves have drifted past the windowpanes, they settle into a pain in the back. It's bend, rake; bend, bag; bend, lift bag. Human anatomy was not created to cope with autumn leaves.

And yet—perhaps that was exactly what I needed. Hard work eases frustration while leaving the mind free to sort out problems. And boy, did I have a decision to make, a big, tough one that might determine the course of my future for years to come. Grimly, I reached for the rake.

I'd thought myself free to create a new life when I finally came home, and confronting the ghosts of my parents and the memories within this house had started the mending of old wounds.

Now, though, I was faced with another specter, one I'd wrestled and—so I thought—defeated not long ago. The prospect of losing all the fruits of one's labors is unsettling at any stage of life. But—I had to face it—when old age approaches and poverty appears to be the condition in which it'll be endured despite years of labor to ensure it won't be so . . . Tears welled, then streamed down my cheeks.

Ashamed, fearful that I might be seen in the midst of feeling sorry for myself, I dropped the rake and ran into the house, where I could continue to cry. "We're going to lose everything!" I moaned to Arnie, my only witness. Correction, one of two witnesses; Mitzi was eyeing me sleepily from the fireplace hearth. I let Arnie out of the aviary and continued to wail my recent news to him.

"That young couple I liked so much—the ones who were leasing the house in Texas and had decided to buy it—they've skipped out on us! They left the house wide open for vandals to destroy, with an insurance policy that won't cover the damage. If only they'd let me know they were leaving, I could have taken steps. But I trusted them, and I don't know what we're going to do!"

Sobbing, I threw myself onto the couch. Arnie squatted on my head, unmoving. Mitzi jumped up, put a paw on my hand, and meowed gently, then lay down beside me. I stroked her, letting the tears and self-pity flow. "My life savings went into that place.

Now, if the bank doesn't take it over, the tax people will. We're ruined!"

I don't know how long I lay on that couch, crying. Eventually I must have dozed off, for when I opened my eyes Arnie was perched on Mitzi's haunch next to me.

He stood up and stretched when I moved my hand. "Good morning!" he said. "I love you!"

I laughed. Sad as I'd been, I felt a bit better. Tears do have emotional healing power; some scientists say they contain a chemical that the body manufactures in times of sorrow, a chemical that leaves one feeling better once drained through tears. Whatever the explanation, it can be soothing. I'd had a good cry, indulged my moment of weakness, but I must move on now.

I still had a decision to make, and it was a big one.

I could save the property in Texas, but only if I had the courage to take the risk. Mama and Papa had taught me that it's great folly to trust either paper money or property rights to endure in a changing world; one's assets must be spread as much as possible so there will always be something to fall back on in times of crisis. So, in a safe-deposit box at the bank, I had a few gold coins and a bit of silver tucked away. It wasn't much, but it was enough to pay taxes, insurance, and the mortgage for a while on the Texas house. I just didn't know if it was worth it to put my final assets at risk.

I'd often thought it was an ill-omened star that led me to Texas in the first place. Five years I'd spent there, working my heart out to build a home, a small business, and a future. Yet everything I'd touched had been doomed to failure. For me, nothing good had come out of Texas . . . except Arnie, Vagabond, and Sammie, that is. Could I expect my luck to change now?

Some strange instinct told me to hang on to the house. Or was it just plain stubbornness? I may crumble into self-pity from time to time, but I'm more inclined to be like a bulldog defending a favorite old bone when it comes to giving up on dreams. And everything I owned in Texas was part of a dream.

"We'll see," I sighed as I stroked Mitzi. "Arnie, quit pulling her whiskers. You go home now so I can check on Vagabond and Sammie. Then I have to get back to work."

"Let's go to work," Arnie said as I put him back into the aviary. "Let's go to work."

And that's just what I did—I went back to my leaves. I couldn't be bothered with answering the telephone the two or three times I heard it ring that afternoon, and when I'd finished, I was too exhausted to think another thought.

With a groan, I settled into my easy chair with the evening paper. Arnie flew to the top of it and looked at me. "You wanna go outside?" the little smart aleck said. "Let's go to work!"

"No way!" I said. "I'm not moving from this chair until it's time to go to bed. Leave me be, little pest."

He flew to the window and paced on the sill, squawking and tapping on the glass. Wondering what was holding his interest at the window for so long, I glanced up.

Manx sat on the outside ledge, looking through the glass. And standing on a nearby branch, a titmouse cocked his eye at the emptiness of the window feeder, then flew away. I had forgotten to put out bird food today, I realized. I forced myself to get up. With one coffee can full of sunflower seeds for the animals that feed on the ground, and another of mix for the suspended feeders, I made my daily rounds.

As I reached the last station, the lid of the bird feeder popped open and the startled face of a chipmunk appeared. His cheek pouches were bulging so much he couldn't even close his mouth. At the sight of me, he scurried out and away. "Monster," I muttered. As I struggled with the feeder, the telephone rang.

"Oh, drat!" I said vehemently, and ran.

I was out of breath when I hit the door, but the shrill rings were still sounding. I grabbed the receiver and panted, "Hello."

"Good evenin', ma'am. May I speak with Margarete Corbo, please?"

"This is she."

"Mrs. Corbo, I'm callin' from Houston, Texas. I've been tryin' to reach you all day, ma'am. Sorry to bother you, but I'm hopin' you can help me locate the owners of that piece of land you used to own down here."

"You're speaking to the owner," I said. "It's back on the market now, if you're interested in buying it."

"Actually, we had somethin' else in mind, ma'am. I represent Mapp Petroleum Company. How would you feel about leasin' the mineral rights to us? Our geologists say it has wonderful prospects. We want to start drillin' for gas on that tract as soon as possible."

How did I feel about leasing the mineral rights? If only the man knew! Originally, I had bought the land and invested my life savings in Texas for one reason: I'm an inveterate impossible dreamer. An oil well—that's what I'd dreamed would come of my stay in Texas! A gas well would certainly do.

"You're welcome to drill all you want," I said. "Send me the papers to sign."

It would take a while, he explained. There were permits to obtain, and no telling how long the actual drilling would take. Maybe it would be a dry hole, but if they were lucky, I could look forward to royalties as long as there was something worth pumping out of that hole. I knew all that, but it was nice to hear my thoughts come out of someone else's mouth.

"Come on over here and help me celebrate, Arnie," I said after I hung up the telephone. "Looks like we're going to get our Texas well after all. Some dreams do come true, you know. Just takes a stubborn believer to hang in until the time is right."

"I love you," he said. "C'mere, gimme a kiss. Let's go to work."

The next day I would go to the bank, then to a coin dealer, and back to the bank. With a cash deposit. Okay, so it was a risk. Maybe the well would be dry, but I didn't think so. And what's life without risk—for the sake of a dream?

Now I could get on with my life, maybe look around for a few new dreams. Even if I had to hold my breath in anticipation for a while. "My well wouldn't dare be a dry hole!" I shouted to the animals. "Would it?" I mumbled.

"Is IT true that you have a wild bird living in your home?" the voice on the telephone asked. Its owner had identified herself as a reporter for the Cape Cod *Times*, the daily newspaper published in Hyannis.

"He's not exactly wild," I said, "not after living with me and my cats for almost three years. He is a starling, though, and he was hatched in the wild."

"Er, this may sound strange, but well, I've heard that he talks."

"I still find it a bit strange myself, but yes, he does talk."

Sitting on the back of my chair, Arnie reacted as though I had given him a cue. "Hi there," he said. "Hello. How are you? He's a little bitty baby boy, he is. Yes, old boy. Sing me a song; sing it! *Da-da-da-dum, da-da-da-dum!*" After whistling a little Beethoven, he ruffled his feathers, pointed his beak up, and settled in for a long session of whistled tunes and singsong snatches of his vocabulary.

"Is that the bird?" the reporter asked.

"That's him," I answered, raising my voice over Arnie's.

"Would you mind if I came for an interview, Mrs. Corbo? I think our readers would be very interested in a story about your little bird."

I was admittedly nervous about being interviewed for a newspaper, but I could have saved myself the anxiety. Talking with young Helen Boursier was much like visiting with a new friend. And Arnie was his simple starling self, not the least bit shy in the presence of this stranger, who kept jotting notes as he walked all over her. Seeming not to notice the brightly flashing lights, he also gave me kisses and took a bath in the sink for the benefit of the camera.

I was therefore disappointed that as days, then weeks, passed, the article did not appear in print.

"I guess our story isn't as interesting to other people as I thought it would be, Arnie," I said.

I didn't dare utter my doubts to Diane Barras, the longtime family friend who'd reluctantly consented to write about Arnie's and my adventures. "Even the most ardent bird lovers hate starlings," she'd said. "No one will publish a book about one." Nevertheless, she'd sent off a proposal to several publishers. So I knocked on wood, looked through the paper each day, and hoped I was right in thinking that Arnie was unique—all the while terrified that his charm existed only in my doting eyes.

Finally, when more weeks went by—and no story appeared—I called Helen Boursier and asked her what had happened.

"Er, I'm afraid they're not going to publish the article after all," she said. "Frankly, I'm very upset. They think we're stretching the truth. They don't believe any wild bird is capable of talking."

"Well!" I huffed. "Let's see if they are willing to put their skepticism to the test. We'll just have to get someone else over here to listen to Arnie and back you up, Helen."

"A STARLING THAT TALKS? I DON'T like disbelieving my reporter, Mrs. Corbo, but this is a hard story to swallow. All I want is to hear him say one word that I can understand."

Arnie was not cooperating. The Falmouth bureau chief of the Cape Cod *Times* had been sitting in my living room, waiting to verify Helen's—and my—story about Arnie's talking abilities, and Arnie was too busy pulling Mitzi's tail to utter a sound. Finally, after more than an hour, the tall man stood. "I'm sorry," he said, "but I really do have to leave." He jingled car keys in his hand.

"Bye-bye. See you later," Arnie said.

The man stayed a while longer, listening intently to Arnie's every word, laughing over his rendition of "Michael, Row the Boat Ashore," and shaking his head with amusement over the raspy, silly sound of the starling voice. On April 27, Arnie's story made the front page of the Cape Cod *Times*, along with a photograph of the two of us making kissy-face to each other. By then the local story was anticlimactic, though. I had heard from Diane that a major Boston publisher had decided to put out an entire book about Arnie. His story was going to be read by people all over the country!

Furthermore, my daughter had just remarried, and the newly-weds were going to bring Travie for a long summer visit. The house was becoming a real home again, and the oil company was going to drill for gas on my property in Texas. My life was taking a new shape, composed of family and friends—old and new—as well as a variety of projects I really enjoyed. My animals were so gratifying, my health was good, my finances adequate to my needs; it appeared that I was going to live happily ever after!

Which always marks the end of fairy tales. Ah, but real life is not a fairy tale. And my new phase of life had only just begun.

CHAPTER SEVEN

THE red tulip trembled, waggled, then toppled over and disappeared. "What on earth . . . ?" Before I could finish wondering, a yellow tulip also trembled, waggled, then toppled over and disappeared.

Mysteriously, one after another, my tulips had been vanishing for a couple of weeks, but this was the first time I'd actually seen it happen. The young hedge roses lining the driveway provided just enough cover to hide the stems of the tulips, so I suspected my culprit had to be something quite small.

"Critters," I grumbled as I sneaked out the door. Tiptoeing down the walk, I craned my neck in an attempt to get a glimpse of the miscreant before he made his getaway.

Four bulging brown eyes stared right at me. Totally unperturbed by my presence, Manx and a female squirrel stood upright, holding their ground and waiting like statues for me to go away. When I didn't move, the female looked to Manx uncertainly. He wiggled his nose, flipped his tail, ripped a petal from the yellow tulip clutched between his front paws, and chewed it in the most leisurely manner. Reassured, she delicately munched on the tip of the red tulip.

"This is too much, Manx," I yelled. "This is entirely too much! How dare you steal my flowers? Shoo! Go on, get away from here." Clapping my hands above my head, waving my arms in the air, I stamped across the ground with malice in my heart and meanness on my face.

Both squirrels tucked tulip stems between their teeth and fled to a neighbor's yard, then up an oak tree, the flowers snuggled against their cheeks in the classic Gypsy Rose Lee pose.

"Isn't it wonderful, Margarete," Patsy laughed the next day when I told her the story. "You're never without company at your house."

"I don't know how wonderful it is." I sighed. "Sometimes I think the animal kingdom around here is too much company."

But spring fever wasn't limited to the animals outside my door. When I let Arnie out of the aviary that day, he streaked past my face, heading, as he frequently did these days, for the linen closet. Dangling from his beak were the limp remains of a seedling he'd stolen from one of the peat cubes hidden on top of the refrigerator. Puzzled, I watched as he returned to the living room, flipped aside the doily that hid the worn upholstery of my armchair, methodically ripped out a beakful of cotton stuffing, and flew to the closet with that prize—chortling. Then he flew out, grabbed a cigarette butt from my ashtray, and disappeared in the direction of the closet again.

Seedlings. Stuffing. Cigarette butts. What was going on?

Slowly something began to float out of my memory from the many bird books I'd consulted.

Nesting material! Of course! How could I have been so oblivious to the obvious? All that time Arnie had been spending in the linen closet, all the "toys" he'd been taking into it with him—he'd been following his natural springtime instincts. Building his first nest, was he? So, my little boy bird was a fully mature man bird at last!

After all, each spring since Arnie had become part of my life, I'd wondered if he was going to get yearnings to return to the wild when mating season arrived. Yet he'd never once in three years shown any indication that he even knew what mating season was all about. This year, when I hadn't even given it a thought, he was finally acting as a bird preparing for parenthood does.

"And just what do you think you're going to do about it, young bird?" I asked him. "There are no girl starlings in here."

He stared brightly at me from deep inside the closet. Eye level with me, he sat snugly in the corner he'd trampled down and staked out as his own. "I love you," he said. "C'mere, gimme a kiss." Then he flung himself out, sat on my hand, looked me in the face with soulful eyes, and whistled "Mary Had a Little Lamb" as earnestly as a troubadour singing a love song beneath a lady's balcony. Suddenly, all his behavior of the past few months made sense: in his own inept, untutored way, he'd built a love nest in the linen closet and he'd been paying court in the best way he knew how—all for me!

As he launched into his serenade again, I sighed with sympathy for his predicament and tried to explain. "This is only a young bird's crush, Arnie. You'll outgrow it in time, I promise. I wish I could persuade an older, wiser starling to tell you all about the birds and the bees, but I'm afraid this is another part of your development you're going to have to suffer through on your own."

And he did. I really don't think he suffered, though; it was all just part of another game as far as he was concerned. Periodically, I cleaned out his nesting material, an act that didn't seem to bother him in the least. He just carried in more bits of Kleenex and rug fuzz and plant seedlings.

During this phase, he remained as uninterested as ever in the outdoor world and everything remotely connected with it. Maybe he didn't even realize he was a bird. I would never know. Though his vocabulary continued to grow, Arnie hadn't learned enough for us to exchange thoughts and ideas. Or maybe it was I who wasn't learning enough. After all, I didn't know how to say a single word of starling talk, while he'd mastered more of my language than many three-year-old humans. There were times when I would wonder as I watched him what thoughts were going through his mind, just as I wondered what went through the minds of the cats, of Manx and his gang, of Edelweiss, and of the other creatures who so enriched my world.

Because Arnie so often made me feel that he knew the meanings of some of his words, I began making it a point to read articles and books on the subject of animal communication. There wasn't much on talking birds. Researchers who deal with them are concerned primarily with the question of *how* they manage to imitate human speech at all. With such tiny brains and limited vocal apparatuses, birds that vocalize with words literally fly in the face of the impossible. Yet there is no question that some of them do so. A comprehensive article on the subject appeared in *The New York Times* that spring, and two starlings were specifically mentioned as being among the birdly marvels causing scientists to scratch their heads. One of the starlings, on exhibit in New York's Museum of Natural History, said, "Hi Sam; hi kid," as he flitted about his cage; the other starling was Arnie.

"You're coming up in the world, Arnie," I said after reading the story. "Of course, most of the research states that none of you has any idea what you're saying when you speak, but still, a mention in *The New York Times*—now, that's prestige!"

My prestigious bird grabbed the newspaper by its corner, yanked heartily, and tore the story in half. Stretching his neck to look around the corner into the kitchen, he said, "You wanna go outside, kitties?" The three cats were lined up at the back door, staring at the knob with bored patience. Obviously the timing of Arnie's words was coincidental. However, unfettered by scientific strictures, I delighted in the entertainment value of my own romantic conclusions. I respect the scientists and their ways, of course, but amateurs have more fun.

"This amateur has to put aside her little studies until the quiet winter months, though," I said as I let the cats out and noted that the sun was shining for the first time in almost a week. Starlings, red-winged blackbirds, and grackles were busily probing in the yard, gathering food for their nestlings. A Baltimore oriole was singing his melodious song from a nearby tree. I noted with satisfaction that the peas and lettuce and spinach in the garden were looking quite perky. It really was going to be a super garden, one that would redeem my shame of the year before. Just wait till Travie saw what I'd accomplished!

"LADY Margarete, Lady Margarete, come hither quickly. Princess Samantha is in grave danger!"

The manner of my grandson's speech this summer reflected the fact that he had abandoned the space-age world and opted to live in medieval times, at least while playing at his new passion, a game called Dungeons and Dragons. He was cool on video games and had put away his Legos. The trappings of his amusements now were suits of armor, swords, and sorcery, and damsels in distress. Arnie had been dubbed his enchanted raven, a wizard in disguise, and the cats were renamed Queen Mitzi, Princess Samantha, and Lord Vagabond.

"Call Lord Vagabond for assistance, Sir Travis," Hanna said. "It's his duty to rescue his mother when Princess Samantha is in danger." My daughter had been exposed to the game long enough to know the proper replies without having to think about them.

"This is for real, Mom," Travie said. "You'd better hurry if you don't want Sammie smelling like a skunk. There are two of them out here. Hurry!"

We did. On the patio, less than five feet from Sammie's nose, were Edelweiss and another skunk, smaller than he and with more black to its coat. So far, neither had struck the skunk's tail-high defensive pose, and Sammie looked curious rather than hostile, but there was no point in taking chances. I gestured for Hanna and Travie to get back into the house. They were strangers to Edelweiss.

"You're out early today, little one," I said conversationally. Moving cautiously, talking soothingly as I went, I picked up Sammie and stepped slowly backward. "Is this your new wife?

I'll bet you brought her around to introduce her, didn't you? And soon I'll see the two of you parading around with a group of youngsters in tow, right?" Both skunks watched attentively without moving. I opened the door and scooted Sammie inside. "Hand me that open can of cat food, Travie," I said, "and a spoon." I refilled two of the dishes from which the cats dined on the patio, then stepped into the house. Sammie, Hanna, Travie, and I watched through the kitchen window as the two skunks daintily ate the cat food, took long drinks from the water bowl, then ambled into the garden and disappeared.

Moments later the front door opened, and a tall, bearded man wearing cutoff jeans and jogging shoes stumbled in. Perspiration flowed copiously from his body; droplets shone like pieces of glass sprinkled through his dark curly hair and beard. My new son-in-law bent over and struggled to catch his breath.

"Hills!" he yelled. "Nobody told me there were hills! Jogging five miles here is like doing fifty at home."

Hanna giggled. "The hills are why they call it the Heights, silly," she said. "I thought you'd figure that out for yourself."

"Don't laugh. I haven't gotten around to making you beneficiary of my life insurance policy yet."

Ronnie collapsed onto the couch and drank Hanna's glass of cola in one gulp. Sammie climbed into his lap and rubbed her chin on his chest. Then Arnie flew into the room, landed on Ronnie's shoulder, grabbed a lock of curly beard with his beak, and pulled. "Ouch!" Ronnie said. "Aaar-niee, please, it's attached to my face."

"C'mere, gimme a kiss," Arnie said, and stuck his beak between Ronnie's lips. In Ronnie's short visit, they'd become friends.

Looking at my son-in-law's disheveled appearance, I had to grin. When he'd arrived here, Ronnie had been in a conservative business suit, something he wore like a uniform most of the time. I was really happy that Hanna had decided to marry him. And, though it was ancient history now, I couldn't help feeling special delight at the thought of having my grandson surrogate-parented by a man who'd worked his way to an accountant's credentials by playing the role of Mickey Mouse at Disney World.

In the next few days Hanna, Ronnie, Travie, and I crammed in sights the way tourists do: Plymouth Rock and Plimoth Planta-tion, complete with realistic re-creations of what life was like for the Mayflower Pilgrims; the sand dunes at the Cape's tip; and Provincetown, where New England fisherfolk coexist with artists in a uniquely diverse atmosphere.

"I think I'll retire and become a beach bum right here," Ronnie said one evening as Arnie sipped at his wine and tugged on his beard. "Imagine being able to spend every day in cutoff jeans and sandals instead of a suit. Can I move into the linen closet with you, Arnie?"

"He's a coo-coo," Arnie said. "You be a good boy."

"Good for you, Arnie," Hanna said. "He can't retire until I do. Then we'll get a farm near here and return to the land."

"I'd go along with that," Ronnie said. "Let's do it."

"Yeeaah!" Travie cheered. "Really, can we move to the Cape? I'm already saving money to buy a house here. You could have all of it if you want to buy a farm instead."

Hanna gave him one of those looks mothers reserve for too precocious outbursts from their children. "When the mortgage is paid off, and the business loan, and all the zillion other little loans for things like the car, your braces, and a college education, and . . . probably about the year 2050."

"Awwww!" Travie's disappointment was evident, and shared by me. Well, one brief week had planted the seed. Perhaps by the time Hanna and Ronnie left, the yearning would firm up into a commitment for the future.

As we were planning a more relaxed second week, Ronnie called his office to check on a project he'd thought could run smoothly without him. The call was a mistake. Something was going wrong that required his personal touch, and Ronnie had to cut short his vacation. When we put the conservative young businessman in his conservative business suit onto a plane in Hyannis that sunny Sunday, he leaned over and whispered into my ear, "Tell Arnie to save me a place on that shelf in the closet. My body may be leaving, but my soul is staying here."

Almost as though it had stayed picture-perfect strictly for Ron-nie's benefit, the weather turned downright cold and dismal overnight. While I brushed my teeth the next morning, I could hear the mournful lowing of the foghorn at the entrance to Falmouth harbor. Beside me, Arnie's head popped from behind the towel hanging over the toilet tank top long enough for him to say, "Good! You come see me." Then he disappeared behind the towel again and whistled "Mary Had a Little Lamb." Guiltily, I acknowledged that I had been neglecting him lately, but we had planned to go into Boston that day.

"Good morning," Arnie said. "Good morning. How are you? Did you come see me? Good morning!"

"Good morning, Arnie," Hanna's voice said. She peeped around the door leading to the basement rooms she and Travie were sharing. "Good morning, Mumma. We don't have to go into Boston today, do we? Please?"

"Of course not. Did you want to do something else instead?"

"Absolutely. Sleep! I didn't get a wink last night. Either your chimney is haunted or there's a bird's nest in it. I thought I heard something moving in there when Ronnie was here, but it didn't keep me awake. Last night it did. Brrrrrr! It's cold."

"You could make a fire downstairs. But if there are birds nesting in the chimney, then they probably still have babies with them."

"No fire. I'd rather snuggle under the covers anyway. Good night."

"Night-night, you go to sleep," Arnie said. "Bye-bye. See you later."

Hanna slept until noon, and Travie quietly watched TV with the animals. After lunch I went downstairs to listen to the fireplace, curious to hear the noises that had kept Hanna awake. Though both fireplaces were vented through the same chimney, I'd been unable to detect a sound from the one upstairs.

Travie hunkered beside me as I banged the damper door back and forth. "Whosoever ye be, ye best be gone, Sir Ghost," Travie shouted up the flue.

There was a quiet rustling within the upper reaches of the chimney. A shower of soot fell onto the hearth. The rustling became louder. "Squirrels!" I said. "I guess we'd better let them stay, Travie. I don't think their babies are old enough to be moved."

The rustling noises became a frantic scrabbling sound. This time the soot fell in an avalanche that hurled a cloud of ashy dust into our faces. Dismayed, Travie and I looked at each other. His face was caked with black. "Too late," I said. "They're on the move. Let's go outside and see what's happening."

We pelted toward the back door. "What are you doing?" Hanna, now awake, asked with alarm. The cats pounded after us, leaping through the door at our heels. We ran across the patio, stopped beneath the oak tree, and looked up.

"Look, Margarete," Travie said, so excited he forgot Dungeons and Dragons. "Look at the drainpipe, the one you painted white last year. Look at it now!" I looked. The drainpipe was coated with black smudges. "And look up there," he said, pointing at the underside of the gutter. Black smudges were there, too, and three perfect imprints of a critter's paws. But they were much too large for a squirrel's.

"Let's watch a while longer, Travie," I said as Hanna joined us. We waited and watched the chimney and were soon rewarded with the cautious emergence of two fuzzy brown ears, then two black-masked eyes, a button-black nose, and a mouth clutching a squirming mass of fur. "Hello, friend raccoon," I called. "So that was you in there. Beautiful baby you've got. You can stay if you want to. Sorry for the disturbance."

She looked at us, hopped out of the chimney with a nimble bound, and walked carefully with her burden toward a front corner of the roof. Her babe dangled quietly from her jaws, eyeing us with bright curiosity.

As we watched, she carefully placed her charge in a crotch of one of the evergreen trees that brushed the roof of the house. The baby clung to the bark for dear life, waiting for his mother to climb around him to a lower branch, from which point she grabbed the scruff of his neck and lowered him to another crotch. After repeating the maneuver all the way to the ground, the mother ran across the lawn with her baby and began to clamber up one of the forty-foot spruce trees near the fence line. Her progression up that tree was marked by the bending and swaying of branches all the way to the top, where she deposited the little one and started down again.

While we watched that afternoon, she moved two more babies from the chimney to the spruce tree. For one brief instant, we were treated to the sight of four masked faces peering at us from

the end of one upper branch; then they abruptly disappeared and all movement ceased.

I regretted that we had made them move. They'd been doing no harm, after all, though I shuddered to think of the problems it would have caused had one of them fallen down the chimney and wound up inside the house. Never a summer goes by on the Cape that the papers don't carry at least one story of such a mishap, usually at a home that's empty except in the summer months. During the winter or spring, the coons move into what seems to them a ready-made, unused den, then find themselves suddenly displaced by returning human owners. And in the course of being forcibly evicted, they frequently panic and cause great damage.

As far as Travie was concerned, the raccoon incident was the most exciting thing that happened on that vacation. I think he was enjoying this summer more than any in years. His cherry pit tree shot up more than three feet, according to the careful measurements he took, and the thriving garden was a perfect setting for his perpetual quests. While the cats followed him around as though he were the Pied Piper, Arnie rode on his shoulder, pretending to be a sorcerer turned raven.

For Arnie, too, it seemed to be an extra happy summer. I wondered if he was responding to my own frame of mind. For I was practically in a state of euphoria. The last remnants of a dark cloud of misfortune that had plagued my life in recent years seemed to be leaving me with blue skies at last. Among my many prospects for the future, there was that gas well being drilled in Texas, and as the well deepened, soil samples continued to show great promise.

"I've started to count my blessings," I told Hanna. "I'm totally at home here at last, with not a trace of restlessness left in me. I've made peace with myself, you see. I have my animal kingdom, my friends, my family, company enough so I'm always busy. There's my garden and this old house to keep me challenged. And I have great hopes for Arnie's book. You know, never a day goes by that I don't listen to that silly little starling, look out my window, and feel touched by the wonder of life. I'm so happy that I bubble inside all the time!"

Hanna smiled and hugged me. "I'm so happy for you. You deserve it all, Mumma."

"I don't know that I deserve it, but I'm certainly going to bask in the sun while it's shining. Though I really don't trust absolute perfection; it's an open invitation to fatal flaws."

I should have listened to my own words. Perhaps they would have prepared me for what was to come.

CHAPTER EIGHT

"I LOVE . . . Did you . . . ? Good . . . You go to . . ."

"What's gotten into you, Arnie?" I said. "You never finish a sentence anymore."

He looked at me without comment, then flew against the door of his aviary and hung on to the screening.

"I'm sorry," I said, "but you know I go swimming with the Easter Seal kids on Tuesday, and I'm running late now. You'll just have to wait until I come back for your outing."

I was tired and tempted to use any excuse, even Arnie, for canceling out today, but people were counting on me. The one-hour-a-week swimming session sponsored by the Easter Seal Society was the only entertainment some of the special kids got, and I had volunteered to help this year. Eddie, who'd been stricken by a rare disease that left him brain damaged, was my *special* special kid, and I just couldn't disappoint him. Only a couple of years older than Travie, Eddie made me realize how fortunate most of us are that our children survive intact.

As I gathered my things that autumn day, the three cats stared at me with sad longing, while Arnie pecked at his screening. I hadn't been home much at all lately, and they were all pouting, which was probably why Arnie wasn't talking properly.

Well, it couldn't be helped. No matter how much they're loved, pets have to take a back seat to human needs sometimes. "I'm sorry," I said to mine, "but I really do have to leave you alone one more time. Tomorrow I'll be home all day, I promise." I snatched my keys off the coffee table and stopped in front of the aviary. "You be a good boy while I'm gone, Arnie. C'mere, gimme a kiss."

He hopped down a couple of perches to the one nearest my face and opened his mouth into the biggest yawn imaginable. "Am I boring you?" I laughed.

It wasn't until the next day that I saw enough of Arnie to notice that he wasn't behaving normally in several little ways. He yawned a lot, for one thing . . . or was he yawning? There was something strange about the way he opened his beak that reminded me of the way humans open their mouths for a heartfelt "Ooouchh," and he seemed to do it only when he moved from one perch to another. Come to think of it, he was mostly sliding down that ladder of perches these days instead of hopping steadily as he'd always done. And he had a new habit of pecking at his toes.

I sighed. "Arnie, I have a feeling that you've picked up a splinter, little boy. Much as we both hate it, I'm going to have to catch you so I can get a good look." I opened the door to the aviary. "C'mon out here, Arnie. Let's get this ordeal over with." He hesitated, eyeing me suspiciously.

Trying to capture Arnie was always a challenge, requiring subterfuge, speed, and downright sneakiness. The two or three times a year I'd been forced to do so in order to trim his nails and beak had always required hours, sometimes days, of elaborate game playing before I could emerge the winner.

"Well, suit yourself," I said, turning and walking away.

He flew to my shoulder and whistled his Beethoven tune, then snuggled against the hair at the nape of my neck. "Let's see what's in the news today," I said, and sat down with the newspaper in hand. As soon as I opened the pages, he hopped to my left wrist and pecked at the paper. Slowly, ever so slowly, I lowered it to my lap, raised my right hand, scratched my nose with it, then snatched—my empty left wrist.

Arnie sat on my foot and *trrrrppppped*. "You be a good boy!" he said, then took to the air with a chortle, flew down the hallway, and made a sharp right turn into the bathroom. I sat for a while, allowing him to think I'd given up. When he could stand the wait no longer, he summoned me to play with a "Peekaboo, I see you. I love you, yes I do."

I walked into the bathroom, and as nonchalantly as possible closed the door behind me and ran water from the faucet. Leaning over, I looked at Arnie crouching behind the towel. "Peekaboo," he said, and pranced cockily onto the countertop.

"Want a drink?" I asked, letting water run into my cupped

hand. Keeping one eye on me, he jumped onto my forearm, perched on my thumb, and leaned down to scoop water into his beak. I let him tilt his head back, swallow, and lean over for another scoop before my hand swooped out at him and captured—my own thumb. I sighed as he scolded me from behind the towel.

"Smart aleck bird," I said. "Don't you realize that if you have a splinter hurting your foot I can make it well again?" He smirked at me from the opposite end of the tunnel he'd trampled into shape in the towel—the perfect trap, I suddenly realized, and he'd created it for himself! Slowly, I eased my right hand, palm up, behind the towel and toward him. He charged toward my fingers. I used my left hand to grab the towel, imprisoning Arnie inside. Cupping the fingers of my right hand, I grasped him firmly, brought him out into the light, flipped him onto his back—and gasped.

This was no little splinter. The bottoms of both feet had enormous blisters covering at least three quarters of the pad. Remembering how he'd been sliding from perch to perch lately, I wondered if that was the cause of the blisters or if he'd been doing it because it was easier on his feet than hopping. No wonder his mouth flew open in a grimace of pain when he jumped from one wooden stick to another!

"Ooh, Arnie, I'm so sorry, little boy," I said with tears in my eyes. "I should have noticed you were having a problem before this." Beneath my fingers, his heart pounded.

Still holding on to him, somehow I sterilized a needle with fire, dunked it into alcohol, then pricked each blister. Applying gentle pressure, I drained them, painted both feet with Mercurochrome, blew them dry, and turned him loose.

From the safety of a curtain rod, Arnie scolded me nonstop for the next five minutes, reverting to the starling sounds he always regarded as more potent than human words for expressing anger and indignation. Then he bent over, looked at one foot and then the other, giving each the closest scrutiny imaginable—and flew to my shoulder. "I love you," he said. "C'mere, gimme a kiss."

"I love you, too, little one. Now let's make your cage more comfortable for those poor feet." As I removed the wooden dowels that were his perches, he flew to the lamp and scolded me again.

"I'm sorry," I said, "but this is necessary. I'm going to replace these hard old sticks with some nice, flat, padded perches. You'll love them."

I put his food and water on the kitchen table and allowed him to fly free while I fashioned new perches from parts of an old shutter. I padded each slat with thin foam rubber and wrapped it with a piece of thick white towel. Arnie flew to my shoulder frequently to check on what I was doing. "You go home?" he complained in my ear.

"Soon *you* can go home," I said. I positioned the new perches so far apart that he'd have to use his wings to get from one to another, thus landing more lightly on his feet than he did when jumping. Very proud of my handiwork, I walked to the aviary with Arnie on my wrist, bragging to him. "You're really, really going to love your new perches."

He took one look at them, screeched at the top of his lungs, flew into the hallway, and disappeared. No amount of enticing would persuade him to go into his aviary that day. He spent the night in the linen closet. "I think discipline around this household is slipping," I grumbled to the cats that night.

Repeating the towel trick the next morning, I checked his feet. They were festering again. So I picked up the phone and called the vet, describing the problem and explaining that Arnie was not accustomed to being handled. "Could I just come by to get some antibiotic salve?" I asked.

There was a long pause on the other end of the line, then, "You really should bring him in so we can have a look."

The examination was anticlimactic. As I held Arnie, the vet took a quick look at his feet and legs. "Your bird has gout," he said. "Stay away from those feet. Gout is a very painful disease already without putting him through any more. Sometimes oral antibiotics will clear it up for a time, but the prognosis isn't very good. You might want to consider euthanasia."

I took the antibiotics, paid the bill, and drove off in a daze. Consider euthanasia? Put Arnie to sleep—kill Arnie? No, no, the vet had to be mistaken. He had to be! I'd get a second opinion.

The second vet came up with another disease, bumblefoot, which happens when a bird lands time after time on a hard or abrasive surface. Oral antibiotics were again the prescription.

"Well, Arnie," I said as we sat together that evening, "looks as if it's up to you and me, kid. Whether you like it or not, I'm going to have to capture you twice a day for a while and somehow persuade you to open your beak long enough to get two drops of medication down your throat."

"He's a little bitty baby boy," he said desultorily. "Love Arnie."

We wrestled twice a day after that, but between our bouts, Arnie seemed to grow ever more cheerful, singing almost non-stop, cuddling up to me when I was idle, as though telling me that he wasn't holding a grudge. In my upset over his ailment, however, most of the rest of my life had come to a standstill. I couldn't even leave him alone at home without feeling guilty about it.

And my guilt had only begun to grow. As I paid my bill at the feed and grain store, I was telling the proprietors about Arnie's ordeal when one of the employees interjected, "Bet you had him sitting on those foolish sticks like you see in store-bought bird-cages, huh?" He informed me that wooden dowels are the un-healthiest perches ever invented for most birds, especially if they're unyielding and all the same size. "Just think about their natural habitat," he said. "Tree branches are all different sizes and have a lot of give to them, so a bird in nature never has a jarring landing. Then we take 'em, stick 'em in cages, and use those hard wooden sticks because they're easy for us to clean. Fine for some birds, but not for one like Arnie."

"I'll make it up to you somehow, Arnie," I promised as I struggled to pry open his beak and give him his medication that evening.

The Christmas holidays came and went without causing more than a tiny ripple in my life. The entire month of January seemed to consist of no more than a handful of days. I was consumed by worry about Arnie. Sometimes it looked as if he were healing; then the infection would flare up again. I consulted other vets, to no avail. All agreed the antibiotics were his only hope. But I was learning that most vets really don't know much about treating birds. It's not their fault. Birds have a nasty habit of dying before their owners even know they're sick, so most vets don't see sick birds enough to learn to diagnose and treat them. In desperation, I ordered my own books on bird medicine, determined to find an answer.

Then someone recommended Dr. Margaret Petrak, a veterinarian who specialized in birds, at Boston's Angell Memorial Animal Hospital. At last, an expert! I made an appointment with her. But on the morning of the appointment, the worst snowstorm of the season was in full swing, and roads to Boston were closed.

Arnie and I watched together as the snow fell. He rubbed his head against my cheek. "You're a coo-coo," he said. "I love you. Yes I do." In truth, he no longer seemed to be in pain. He chattered cheerfully from sunup to sundown, giving the house a festive air. Was it only my imagination that the color seemed to be draining from his skin, his legs, the inside of his mouth, as though he had acquired anemia?

By then, some of the medical books I'd ordered had come in, and I'd begun to read. There were little references here and there to the dangerous side effects that go hand in hand with indiscriminate use of antibiotics. Now I worried that I'd been overdosing Arnie; he had, after all, been on that medication for almost three months now. Acting on my own instinct, I stopped giving it to him and switched to a medicated salve a friend had recommended. And I made another appointment with Dr. Petrak. She had sounded so genuinely concerned and caring when I'd talked with her on the phone that I really wanted her to take a look at him. Meanwhile, for whatever reason, Arnie's feet finally began to heal. At first I thought it was my wishful imagination, but within days I was certain that the abscesses on his feet were shrinking. I crossed my fingers and kept using the medicated salve. Arnie was happier than ever, now that I had quit forcing his beak open for the antibiotics.

The day of the appointment with Dr. Petrak dawned bleak and dreary. It was snowing again, though lightly so far, and the roads were icy.

But Arnie's feet were completely healed! I was wishy-washy about putting him through that long trip to Boston. Now, though, I was worried about his anemic appearance and concerned about the damage that might have been caused by the antibiotics. When I noticed two tiny flecks of dried blood on one of his legs, I decided my peace of mind was worth the trip.

"I hope this will be the last time we have to go through this, Arnie," I said as I caught him behind the towel.

341

"You be nice! C'mere, gimme a kiss. I love you," he said.

Suddenly there was blood on my hands. "What on earth . . . ?" Fresh and warm, the blood gushed from Arnie's upper leg. Quickly I clamped my thumb over the wound, put my forefinger on the other side of his leg, and squeezed hard until the flow stopped. "Arnie, what on earth is happening here?"

His expression was one of complete bewilderment. He didn't understand what was happening any more than I did. I yelled for Diane Barras, the friend who'd agreed to make the trip to Boston with me. "Call the vet here in town and ask him to meet me at his office. Tell him Arnie's bleeding to death!" It was six twenty in the morning, but the veterinarian's answering service called him at home and he phoned us back. While I applied pressure to Arnie's leg, he talked to Diane. "Use an ice cube and give it time," he told her. "The bleeding will stop."

It slowed, but forty-five minutes later blood was still leaking gently past my thumb. Again we called the vet. "Keep the ice fresh. Keep the pressure constant. You have to give it time," he said. "If that doesn't do the trick, I'll meet you at my office."

Diane called Dr. Petrak, who was already at work. "It'll take you two hours to get here," she said gently. "If he continues to bleed . . . well, birds are small creatures. They can't afford to lose much blood." After that we drove to my vet's office.

The styptic powder the doctor sprinkled on the wound stopped the blood flow entirely. "Take him home and feed him liver to build up his strength again," the vet advised.

I shoved pieces of liver down Arnie's throat for the next hour or so. Too weak to stand, he didn't struggle, didn't make a sound. His eyes never left mine, the expression on his face changing from indignation to bewilderment to resignation as his body grew steadily colder. Finally, he couldn't even swallow. "Okay, little boy, no more torture," I said. I held him to me as tears rolled uncontrollably down my cheeks. He tilted his beak up so he could see me, then rested his head on my breast.

Numbly, I sat there for the next hour cuddling him. Gently as a feather floating on a breeze, the life force that had been Arnie ebbed from the little bird body that I clutched in my hands. Finally, he struggled to lift his head, looked up at me with love shining in his eyes, and breathed a tired sigh. It was his final breath.

The ground was frozen. As I'd done once before with another bird, I put his body in the middle of a flowerpot filled with dirt. I would bury him in the spring, when the ground thawed and his kind had begun to make new little starlings.

"I feel as though I killed him," I said to Diane as we shared a glass of wine over lunch. For the first time in weeks, I wished I had a cigarette. Almost with a sense of offering a sacrifice in exchange for his life, I had quit the nasty habit during Arnie's illness.

Diane looked at me through her own red-rimmed eyes. "You didn't kill Arnie, Margarete. Ignorance did. I ran across a reference in one of those books you ordered that said prolonged antibiotic use can destroy the blood's ability to clot. You know, Arnie was a starling. No one knows much about them. Maybe they don't respond to the same antibiotics as other birds."

She paused for a long while, then said softly, "Or maybe it was just time for him to go. Maybe Arnie has fulfilled his purpose in this world."

Snow squeaked beneath my boots as, weeks later, I trudged a path so familiar that it was no longer necessary to watch where I was going. Hands deep in my jacket pockets, collar upturned to my nose, ski cap pulled to my eyebrows, I walked with head down, watching the sparkling ice crystals crush beneath my feet.

I climbed the hill near the house and stopped to look about me, remembering that first day when I'd parked the rental trailer on this spot before driving the last few blocks, a minor pause so I could revel in being home again. The gray Atlantic had glowered then, its surface waters whipped to frothy white peaks by a stiff south wind. In the distance, ducks and gulls had bobbed near the jetties, sparrows and starlings had lined the white fence barricading the bluff drop-off.

There are times when we all come to a crossroads. At such a crisis, I'd packed the bird, the cats, and all my belongings and sought the refuge of home. Though I wasn't sure it could ever again be home to me, I had been determined to sort out my life.

"Time will tell if we stay, but at least I got us here, gang," I'd said back then as I stared through the windshield of the car.

"Good! I love you. Gimme a kiss," the raspy bird voice had retorted from the back seat.

Trust Arnie to know exactly the right words to make me feel I'd done something wonderful. It seemed we'd always been together, perhaps because he had been with me, serving as confidant, helping me to stay strong, through a difficult period of time. Friends are like that—always there when it counts.

I sighed. How I missed that little voice. I'd never walked so much in my life as I was doing these days.

With one more sweeping glance, I took in the nearness of Martha's Vineyard. The water was like a gigantic brooch this day, emerald green studded with countless sparkling sun diamonds. Changing, ever changing, that scene, the one constant being the birds to whom it all belonged. I'd found the changes I'd sought and much more, of course. Now it was up to me to keep change happening, for that's the way the human spirit grows, especially if it has roots, the constant of a home.

I bowed my head and walked down the hill, past boarded-up summer houses and hotels, along the shore, and around the curve to the pond. A lone man shooshed toward me on cross-country skis and smiled a greeting as he passed. I smiled back, welcoming his presence as a reminder that I was not alone, though I'd chosen to be these past weeks. Arnie's death might be trivial compared to the losses of others, but still, there was emptiness in all those spaces he'd occupied in my days.

Rounding the pond's shoreline, I stepped off the road into a clearing for the ritual that now filled one of those empty spaces. Within seconds, the first green-headed mallard flew toward me, honking to his fellows to follow. His wings angled down, his webbed feet spread, and hitting the ice, he skidded with flailing wings and wobbling body for several yards before sliding onto the water. Then he paddled toward me and waddled to my feet as I scattered cracked corn on the snow.

Starlings fluttered to the ground and stood nearby, waiting for the leavings. "Bet nobody feeds you guys," I said, and tossed them bread from another bag.

Starlings seemed to be everywhere these days. Probably they always had been, but I'd failed to notice them until a very special one came into my life. It made me muse about how many other little touches of wonder I'd missed along the way. Because of Arnie, I had learned to see, rather than merely look at, the world around me, and in doing so, I had gained an acuteness of vision as wondrous as the discovery of color where once had been only black and white. As I thought this, I lifted my eyes from the ground and looked to the trees, so alive with activity. Don't ever again forget to look, I chided myself. And *see*.

When I arrived home, I rushed to close the door and cross the room. Entering the house without being greeted by a "Hi there" was still difficult. I tossed my coat and cap on the couch, grabbed a book, and settled down to get lost in its pages.

Sammie bounced from the floor and curled up in the middle of my reading material. Vagabond nipped my heel, meowed, and ran to Mitzi's side. She was in the kitchen, looking pointedly at their empty food dishes. There was a tap on the window glass, and I glanced up to see Manx dangling upside down, staring at me. On a jutting branch of one evergreen, a blue jay glared in, opened his mouth, and screeched. Mourning doves stood shoulder to shoulder along the telephone line in front of the house, and the branches of the corner oak tree were laden with starlings, sparrows, crows, and the pair of ravens who'd recently joined my soup line.

I looked at them all and sighed. "I take it none of you wants me to read; I guess it must be feeding time at the zoo." Then I laughed, for I was not alone and probably never would be again as long as I lived. And, of course, it wasn't fitting that I mark Arnie's passing by going back to the depressed state of mind in which he'd found me. "Shame on you," I said for him.

I dished out double portions of cat food, sunflower seeds, and mixed birdseed for all the creatures furred and feathered, then tossed a loaf of bread into the yard. Sooner or later it would all be eaten by one creature or another. Digging in the freezer, I located a hunk of fat, ran a straightened clothes hanger through its middle, and hung it in the spruce tree for the flickers and downy woodpeckers. Then I filled the birdbath, knowing it would be well used before I had to empty it to prevent freezing. Starlings were the first to take advantage of the water, as usual.

Watching them bathe and squabble, I picked up the telephone and started to make calls I'd been neglecting. "Hi, Patsy, how about stopping by for lunch tomorrow?" "M.A., I'm going shopping later. Why don't you join me?" "Hanna, how about sending Travie for spring vacation again this year?"

The next morning I dismantled the aviary, put it into the basement, and rearranged the furniture.

I moved the birdbath closer to the house so I could see it better. In my little bit of idle time, I watched the birds more carefully than ever. Amazing how many baths starlings take in one day. How much like Arnie they all acted—regular clowns compared with the other birds. Had my home always been so quiet before he'd arrived to fill it with his song and chatter?

I sat stroking Vagabond and Sammie for a long while afterward. If Arnie could learn to talk, I mused, couldn't another starling? Wouldn't it even have the same basic personality? I'd never missed a creature so much in my life! It was almost April now. It wouldn't be long before the trees would be filled with the demanding chirps of newly hatched baby birds of all kinds.

Reaching for the phone book, I looked up a very special number and called it. "Hello, Audubon Society? Do people ever bring you orphaned starlings in the spring? I know where there's a wonderful home waiting, if you should happen to get one and don't know what to do with it."

Who knows? There are many mysteries in the universe, and undoubtedly more to the almighty plan than we mere mortals have yet discovered. Maybe there is a wheel of life included in that plan, even for the simple, insignificant little creatures that add so much wonder, so much joy, to our world. Including starlings.

One way or another, I was certain that somewhere out in the world there would be a lost, lonely, impertinent baby starling waiting to be rescued by someone who'd learned to appreciate the uniqueness of that species—someone like me. Perhaps someday there would be another Arnie for Margarete.

It is the privet hedges bordering the road the visitor sees first, standing tall and dense and hiding Margarete Corbo's small cedar-shingled house, which lies beyond. "My hedges," she says, laughing. "They are for the birds, of course."

Of course. For "The Bird Lady of Cape Cod," as one letter to her was addressed, continues to devote herself enthusiastically to her birds and other animals, both wild and domestic. In two large aviaries behind the house, several dozen sick or injured birds are currently in residence, including a grackle, a mockingbird, an oriole, assorted finches and, naturally, some starlings. The several bird feeders in the yard also attract constant attention, as do the berry bushes and the nut trees.

Margarete Sigl Corbo

The Munich-born Mrs. Corbo settled in this country with her husband when World War II ended. After she had raised her daughter, Hanna, she began to share her life with an ever widening circle of friends and family. She met her co-author and fellow animal lover, Diane Barras, while running a pet clinic in California, and the two have been good friends ever since. Miss Barras, a journalist by profession, insists she lacks her colleague's special gift with birds, but when she is not busy with her writing she too contributes time and attention to their care.

Looking to the future, Mrs. Corbo has begun to build a fourteen-by-twenty-foot "winter room" adjacent to her house to hold those birds still too weak or infirm to survive a winter on Cape Cod. Into that room may go a young female starling named Daisy, who has already learned to say "Kissy," and a year-old male starling named Oliver, whose spoken phrases include "Come here, Daisy."

One can't help wondering what will happen in the spring. Will Daisy and Oliver produce a fledgling of their own? And if so, will they speak to it in part using human words? It may require another book by Mrs. Corbo and Miss Barras before we know the answer.

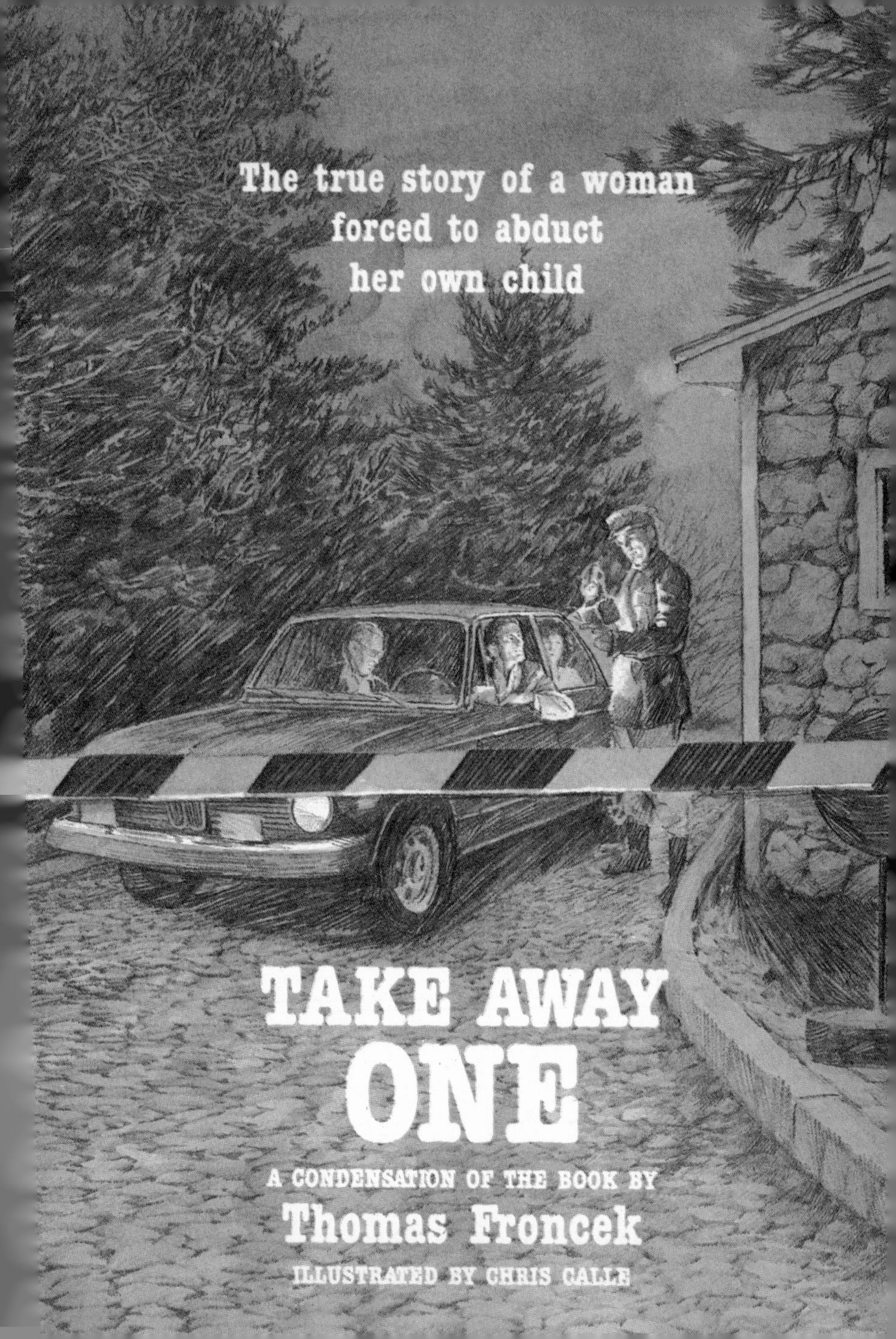

The true story of a woman
forced to abduct
her own child

TAKE AWAY
ONE

A CONDENSATION OF THE BOOK BY

Thomas Froncek

ILLUSTRATED BY CHRIS CALLE

On a quiet Friday afternoon in 1976 Sarah Stefanovic handed over her five-year-old son, Joey, to her estranged husband for one of their regular weekend visits——as dictated by a court order. By the end of that weekend it was clear that Sarah's worst nightmare had become a reality. Joey was gone. Kidnapped by his father.

Several times Jovan Stefanovic had threatened to take off with his son for his native Yugoslavia. Now he had made good on that threat. And somehow Sarah had to get her child back. But how? She is a shy, sheltered woman brought up in suburban New Jersey. And Joey is a continent away, deep in an iron curtain country.

Take Away One is the story of Sarah's desperate struggle to retrieve her son. And though it often reads like the most dramatic spy fiction, it is all true. A moving testament to a mother's love and determination.

CHECKPOINT: Saturday, April 23, 1977, 12:30 a.m.

SARAH did not realize the car was slowing down until it swerved and hit the gravel at the edge of the road. Suddenly she was wide awake.

"We there, Mum?" she heard the boy ask his mother for what must have been the hundredth time. "We in Spain?"

"I don't know, luv," the woman said.

"Then why are we stopping?"

"Shh. I told you, I don't know."

Outside in the dark Sarah could see nothing. No lights, no houses, only a mass of black mountain silhouetted against the night sky. She glanced forward at the green dial on the dashboard of the BMW. It was past midnight. Against her shoulder the window felt cold.

The driver stopped the car and cut the lights. His name was Peter Wilkes. They had been instructed to do exactly as he said.

"Where are we?" Sarah's father asked from the front seat.

Wilkes ignored him. "Still up, then, lad?" he asked over his shoulder.

"It's all the excitement," said the boy's mother apologetically. "The airplane ride and all."

"And no bloody chance for 'im to get comf'table neither," said the boy's father.

"I'm aware of the inconvenience, Mr. Hardy," said Wilkes.

They had been traveling that way for hours: five adults and a sharp-elbowed six-year-old crammed into a space intended for four. In front were Wilkes and Sarah's father, whose name was Ted Novack.* In the back Sarah sat shoulder to shoulder with the English couple, David Hardy and his wife, Sheila. Their boy, Adam, was slouched on his father's lap. He had his legs stretched across his mother's thighs. His stocking feet were jammed against Sarah's rib cage. There was luggage shoved under Sarah's legs. It was impossible to move.

"I know you could all do with a stretch," Wilkes said. "So could I. But not here. We're tired and we should look tired. When we cross over the border into Yugoslavia, I want the guards to think they're seeing a car full of sleepy tourists."

Cold and hard and wary. That had been Sarah's impression when she met Wilkes for the first time, that afternoon. And so far nothing had happened to change that impression. Good-looking, yes, with fair hair. But wintry cold behind his horn-rimmed glasses. And suspicious of everyone.

"How far is it now?" her father asked.

"We're almost to the pass. From here it's three miles to the checkpoint."

"We in Spain, then?" asked the boy.

"Not yet, lad."

Spain was a ruse, another of Wilkes's precautions. The less the boy knew about their destination the better.

Wilkes turned halfway around in his seat. In the dark, with the green dashboard lights behind him, Sarah could not see his face, but his voice commanded attention. "Now listen to me, all of you. And listen carefully. When we get to the checkpoint, I'll do the talking. None of you will say a word. Is that understood?"

"Understood," said Novack.

"Yes," said Sarah.

"Me legs," said David Hardy. "They're killin' me, all cramped up back 'ere an' no place to put 'em."

---

*The events in this story are true. However, the names of the principal characters and many of the settings have been altered to protect the privacy of those involved.

"Look, Hardy"—Wilkes's words cut like slivers of ice—"you're being paid plenty for your trouble. If you can't be counted on for a minimum of cooperation, I'm quite prepared to leave you right here and let you jolly well walk back to London."

"Aw roight, aw roight."

"Now, Adam," Wilkes said, the edge still on his voice, "we're going to play let's pretend. First, I want you to move over to Sarah's lap. Will you do that for me?"

Reluctantly the boy climbed onto Sarah's lap.

"Next, I want you to pretend that Sarah here is your mum and that you're very tired. Pretend that you're asleep in Sarah's arms."

"Me mum's arms, you mean," the boy said, snuggling against Sarah's shoulder.

"Right, lad. Exactly right. Now, turn your face toward her a little more and keep your eyes closed. That's the important part. Don't open them until I tell you that make-believe time is over."

"Yes, sir," the boy said, squeezing his eyes tight.

"Good," Wilkes said. He turned his attention to Sarah. "You know your part. You're Adam's mother and Adam is your son, Joey. He's asleep and you don't want him wakened. If the guard wants you to get out, be stubborn. Remember, you're a tired mother and you're not going to let anyone disturb your child."

She nodded. Suddenly she was beginning to be afraid. Why Wilkes should be so nervous about getting into Yugoslavia she did not understand. She knew it would be dangerous getting out again. But getting *in?* She held the boy closer.

"Now, let me have your passports, please," Wilkes was saying. When he had them all, he sorted them as carefully as a bridge player arranging his suits. He put his own passport on top, Ted Novack's under it, Sarah's and Joey's next. The Hardys' passports he put on the bottom.

"Okay," he said. "Here we go."

THE main road from Klagenfurt, in southern Austria, to Ljubljana in northwestern Yugoslavia, crosses over the craggy Karawanken mountains at Loibl Pass—or Ljubelj Pass, as it is called on the Yugoslav side of the frontier. There, a tunnel, which was dug by Nazi slave labor during World War II, cuts beneath the top of the pass, shortening the distance and making the frontier accessible even in winter. The Yugoslav checkpoint lies a little over a mile beyond the southern end of the tunnel.

At the checkpoint a pair of gatehouses stand on either side of the roadway. They are built of stone, the windows are high and wide, and each is lit inside by a single ceiling fixture. Between the two buildings a hand-winched barrier, painted in red and white candy-cane stripes, falls across the roadway.

The gatehouses reminded Sarah of some tollbooths back home in New Jersey. But the area was not nearly as well lit as the toll plazas. That surprised her, and so did the flimsy-looking crossing gate. She had expected something more formidable of an iron curtain border post. Floodlights. Barbed wire. Machine guns.

There was a car ahead of them as they approached the gatehouses. Holding Adam close, Sarah wondered if it wouldn't have been wiser to cross in daylight, when traffic was heavier. But Wilkes had insisted that in the dark the guards were less likely to notice the difference between the boy asleep on her lap and the boy in the passport photo. And that was the crucial part of the plan—getting little Adam into the country on Joey's passport.

There seemed to be only two guards on duty, one at each gatehouse. They wore baggy gray uniforms, and each had a pistol at his belt. Sarah then noticed another small building off to the left—some sort of administration building, perhaps.

The car ahead was waved through. Now it was their turn.

Wilkes rolled down his window. *"Guten abend,"* he said.

The guard said something in German. Wilkes handed over the passports. No one said anything. Sarah stopped breathing.

Suddenly the guard's face was at the window, his flashlight probing the darkness inside the car: on Wilkes's face, on Novack's, on the Hardys'. One by one he checked them against the passport photos. Then the light was in Sarah's eyes. She clutched Adam tighter, felt him burrow deeper into her shoulder.

And then it was gone. The light was gone. She breathed again. It was over. Now they could drive on.

But no. The guard was waving Wilkes over to the roadside.

"What does he want?" Sarah's father whispered.

"He means we should wait here," Wilkes said.

"Wait? Why? What for?"

"I don't know. He just wants us to wait."

The guard had turned away. Walking across to the administration building, he opened the door and disappeared inside, taking the passports with him. Five minutes passed. Then ten. With the engine turned off, the car began to get cold.

"What's keeping that guy?" Ted muttered.

Wilkes said nothing. Sitting perfectly still, he was staring straight ahead into the darkness.

"At least they should tell us why they're holding us," said Ted.

"Should?" Wilkes said, without turning his head. "You'd better understand one thing, Mr. Novack. We are in Yugoslavia now. They do things differently over here."

For a long time Wilkes's words hung like frost in the cold air.

The darkness beyond the gatehouse lights seemed darker than before. Sarah felt her legs tingling. The boy's weight on her thighs was cutting off her circulation. She shifted slightly and realized that he had fallen asleep.

"Do you think the guard noticed something?" she said quietly, so as not to wake the boy. "About Adam, I mean."

Wilkes said, "I couldn't tell."

The man was infuriating. Of course the guard had noticed. How could he *not* notice, when the difference between the two boys seemed so obvious to her. Dutifully she had been trying to imagine that the small stranger on her lap was her own son—wishing even that it were true. But there was almost nothing the same about Adam and Joey. Height and age, that was all. Adam's hair, his eyes, his voice—all were different and strange. And part of her resented Adam because of this. Resented his parents, too, because they had their son and she did not have hers.

Were they happy together, she wondered, the Hardys and their little boy? Was any family really happy together? She could not imagine so. Not after all that had happened in the last few years. How had she put up with it for so long? *Why?* It made no sense at all.

Or did it? Knowing what she knew now, it was easy to upbraid herself for getting trapped the way she did: trapped by love, by such awful need. But when she thought about it, she doubted she could have done anything very different at the time.

Not that it mattered now. Not that anything had mattered to her for months except getting back her son.

ONE

IT HAD been Jovan's turn to have Joey for that Labor Day week-end in 1976. Visiting rights. There had been nothing she could do.

Sarah had prepared as usual for Joey's visit with his father. On Friday, after lunch, she packed his suitcase with clothes, and put in crayons and paper so he'd have something to do on the train. When it was time, she called him in to wash up and change. Then she drove him to the station to meet Jovan.

Not that she had to drive him, of course. "You're always bend-ing over backward to make it easy for Jovan," her father kept reminding her. "If he wants to see Joey, let *him* make the effort." But Sarah had had enough of rancor and recriminations. If she could save Jovan time and taxi fare, she was willing. Besides, it meant she could have the boy with her until the last minute.

From her parents' house on the west side of Sommerton, New Jersey, where Sarah was living temporarily, it was a twenty-minute drive to the station. Jovan's train from New York was due at three. She headed north on Mercer Street for three blocks, then turned east, past Eberhardt's Tool and Die plant, with its great crenellated clock tower. It was twenty minutes to three. She'd be in good time.

"Please, M-Mom," Joey said. "Why do I have to g-go with Daddy again? Why can't I st-stay with you?"

She glanced over at him. Usually he liked to sit up straight so that he could see out the window. But today he was slumped morosely in the seat beside her. And his stutter was back.

"It's only for the weekend," she told him.

He was five and a half. He had Jovan's almond eyes and broad cheekbones; he had her tawny curls. She loved his curls. When the sun was behind him, his hair shone like amber: a rich brown at the center, a golden halo around the edges.

"I'll tell you what, though," Sarah said. "On Monday, when you're back, we'll do something special."

"Like what? G-go to the z-zoo?"

"Okay. Let's do that."

They were pulling into the station parking lot now. It was ten to three. Getting out, she lifted Joey's suitcase from the back seat and locked up. He was already waiting at the meter. She handed him a quarter and watched while he pushed it into the slot. It was one of their little rituals.

He turned the dial. *"Bzzzt,"* he said, mimicking the sound.

She took his hand and led him out onto the platform. They waited in their usual place, on a bench halfway along. Joey sat very still, his hands jammed into the pockets of his shorts.

"You'll have fun," Sarah said. "You'll see. I'm sure Daddy's got some nice things planned for you to do."

He shrugged, said nothing.

"Didn't you have fun the last time you saw Daddy?"

Joey shook his head. "D-Daddy just wants to w-work all the t-time," he said.

"Well, his work is very important to him," she said, then immediately wished she hadn't. She of all people should know what little comfort there was in hearing over and over again how important Jovan's work was.

Not that she'd ever begrudged Jovan his dream, his vision. It was one of the things that had attracted her to him in the first place. Science. To him there was nothing more challenging in its complexity, more beautiful in its well-ordered simplicity. He was especially fascinated by chemistry. One day, he vowed, he would make important discoveries. He would be asked to lecture at universities. He would be welcomed in his homeland as a hero. He would win a Nobel Prize!

In the beginning she had admired that dedication. Eventually, though, Jovan's dream had become an obsession. He would hurry down to the lab early in the morning and not return until seven or eight at night. Then he spent the rest of the evening at his desk, poring over his papers. If she managed to persuade him to spend a Sunday in the park with her and Joey, he would be forever glancing at his watch, worrying about the time he was wasting. The harder Sarah and Joey tried to reach him, the harder he fought them off. He could not seem to understand that as much as Sarah loved his dream, she loved him more, needed him more— to see her, to hear her, to love *her.*

Not until last December, when she'd finally taken Joey and gone home to her parents for good, did it even seem to occur to him that he, too, might need something separate from his work.

That was when he first threatened to take Joey away from her.

Now she reached for Joey's hand. "You're important to Daddy, too," she told him. "He loves you and wants to be with you."

It was five past three when the train's headlight came dancing through the distant haze. Behind it, the train took form. It swelled in size and sound and then was rushing alongside the platform. It slowed to a stop and a few people got out.

Then there was Jovan, book in hand as usual. A hank of wavy dark hair fell rakishly over his forehead, and his face was lit with that incredibly charming smile. Once upon a time Sarah had found that smile absolutely irresistible. Now it only made her wary.

"Hello, Sarah," he said.

"Hello." She let him kiss her on the cheek, then pulled away. His smile flickered out.

"Hot out here," he said. "Why didn't you wait inside where it's cool? You didn't think of that?"

The edge in his voice made her suddenly tense. Must he always make her feel small? "Please," she said. "Don't start."

He turned from her, scowled, and bent to kiss his son. "Hello, Joey. How are you?"

Joey looked at his feet. "Okay," he said so quietly they almost didn't hear.

"What's wrong with him?" Jovan asked.

"Nothing," said Sarah. "He'll be all right."

They had half an hour to wait for the train that would take Jovan and Joey back to New York. They went inside to the coffee shop, took a booth, and ordered soft drinks.

With a straw Jovan stirred the ice in his glass. He looked tired, older somehow than when Sarah had last seen him. But then, part of her still thought of him as the young man she had fallen in love with ten years ago—the suave Continental with the strange yellow-brown eyes. Tiger eyes.

He was thirty-nine now. His hair was thinning. In his eyes she rarely saw warmth anymore, only hardness. But she was used to that. What puzzled her now was why he seemed so tense. It must be his work, she decided. Had he finished his dissertation yet? Was he preparing for his orals? She wouldn't ask.

"Sarah," he said, without looking up from his glass, "come with us, will you? We could have a nice weekend together. Go to Jones Beach. Whatever you want."

Joey looked at her hopefully. "Oh, Mom, will you?"

"Will you, Sarah?"

"No. I can't. I have plans."

"A date?"

"I have plans, that's all." She said it firmly but then held her breath, waiting for the reaction she was sure would come. What would it be this time? she wondered. Icy silence? A fist slammed on the table? She was surprised when all Jovan did was shrug indifferently. Was it possible that he had finally resigned himself to the fact that it was all over between them? She hoped so.

They finished their drinks and went out to the platform. When the train came in, Sarah scooped Joey up and kissed him on both cheeks. "Good-bye," she said. "Have fun."

Joey threw his arms around her neck. "P-please, Mama, d-don't m-make me g-go," he cried into her shoulder.

"It'll be okay. You'll see." She gave him one last hug, then put him down. But Joey held onto her.

"P-please, Mama. Please."

Gently she pried his arms loose. "See you on Sunday," she said.

Straightening up, she found herself looking into Jovan's eyes. He seemed very sad just then. For a moment she thought he was going to kiss her. Or was waiting for her to kiss him. Part of her wanted to, just as part of her wished they could be a normal family, loving each other, doing things together. But she'd realized long ago that it could never be that way. "Bye," she said.

He seemed about to say something but changed his mind. He nodded. "Good-bye," he said. Then he picked up Joey's suitcase and shepherded the boy onto the train.

FROM the start, Sarah's parents, Ted and Emma Novack, had been against letting Jovan have visiting rights. Her mother had been especially adamant.

"Hasn't he threatened?" Emma warned. "Hasn't he said he would take Joey the first chance he got?"

Sarah knew her mother was right, but to battle Jovan in court? To prevent him from ever seeing Joey again? It seemed so spiteful. She'd never intended it to be that way. She had left Jovan to save herself, not to punish him. If he could see Joey whenever he wanted, maybe their separation could be amicable after all.

Besides, her parents knew as well as she did that Jovan was not about to go anywhere, with or without Joey, until his university handed him the piece of paper that would allow him to call himself *Dr.* Jovan Stefanovic. He had worked too long and hard. Nor was he about to assume the day-to-day responsibility of looking after Joey—not while he was trying to finish his thesis. If for no other reason than that, he was likely to keep bringing Joey back to her. At least for a while.

It was Bob Koenig, the Novacks' lawyer, who had clinched the argument. "Look," he'd told them, "you can't deny the man the right to see his own son. What guarantee do you have that he won't just come and grab the boy off the street? You can't watch the kid every minute. Not a five-year-old."

In the end, the county court had granted Sarah custody and, according to the decree, Jovan was permitted to have the boy every other weekend. Since the middle of June, Jovan had taken Joey for five weekends.

For Sarah the first few times had been nerve-racking. From the minute they left her at the station on those Fridays until the time Jovan brought Joey back on Sunday afternoon, she was unable to think or do anything without being distracted by fear and worry, without wondering if he would do what he had threatened to do: take Joey and never bring him back.

But the first weekend came and went, and the second, and the third. And each time, they had been there at the station on Sunday afternoon, Joey with his hair a mess and needing a bath, but home at least. Gradually the leavings had ceased to be quite so difficult. Now, when she watched Jovan and Joey's train disappear down the tracks, she could almost ignore the small nagging fear that lay curled in the pit of her stomach.

FRIDAY evening went by quickly—dinner and a movie with friends. Saturday night she would be going out again. She was enjoying herself immensely. She and Jovan had rarely gone out together. She had a lot of catching up to do.

Saturday evening she had just gotten out of the shower when

she heard the phone ringing. A moment later her mother was calling up the stairs to tell her it was Jovan. Something wrong with Joey? Sarah wondered.

"I'll take it up here," she said. She wrapped a towel around herself and went down the hall to the phone in her parents' bedroom. She picked up the receiver. "Hello."

"Just wanted to say hello," said Jovan.

"Yes," she said. "How's everything going? How's Joey?"

They were having a good time, he told her. They had been shopping and had lunch. "Oh, and I took him for a haircut."

"Oh, no, Jovan. You didn't."

"It was only a little trim. He looks much better."

She did not believe him. She had an awful picture of all those beautiful curls strewn on the tiles of the barbershop floor.

But then Joey was on the line, telling her about his new clothes and the toy truck Daddy had bought for him. What new clothes? she was about to ask, but before she had a chance he was telling her a joke that the barber had told him. "A cabbage, a faucet, and a t-tomato are having a r-race. Who's the w-winner?"

"I don't know. Who?"

"The c-cabbage is ahead, the faucet is r-running, and the tomato has to c-catch up."

It was more than the joke that made her laugh. It was her own relief at hearing him sound so happy and excited.

"That's a wonderful story, Joey. That's very funny."

When he said good-bye, it was in his father's native Serbo-Croatian. *"Do vidjenja, Mami."*

"Do vidjenja, Joey."

She was pleased. Joey sounded like he was enjoying himself. Maybe the separation would work out after all.

That evening, over dinner, she found herself thinking about Jovan and Joey only once. Her date, an architect who acted in amateur theatricals, kept her talking and laughing from the moment he picked her up. It was when she was almost through with her coffee that she happened to glance at her watch and wonder fleetingly if Jovan had gotten Joey to bed at a reasonable hour.

But that was all. Blessedly, that was all.

Not until Sunday afternoon did she begin to think that something might be wrong.

Usually Jovan telephoned her early on Sunday to let her know which train he and Joey would be taking back to Sommerton. But noon came and went, and he did not call.

Would he phone from the station? she wondered. He did that sometimes—waited until the last minute before letting her know. Most of the time it didn't matter. Today, though, she had decided to drive over to the swim club with her parents. This was the last weekend before the pool closed for the season. Besides, it was just too beautiful a day to sit around the house waiting for a phone call that might not come until two or three in the afternoon.

She finished lunch and went up to her room to change into her bathing suit and white terry jacket. Then she brushed her long dark hair and tied it back with a scarf. By now her parents were almost ready to go. She could not wait any longer. If Jovan was not going to call her, she would have to call him.

She was just starting to dial, using the wall phone in the kitchen, when her father came clopping into the room in his beach sandals. "Hey, you coming or nŏt?" he asked impatiently.

"I'm trying to reach Jovan." The phone was ringing now on the other end. Ringing in the little apartment in Yonkers she and Jovan had once shared. "I'll only be a minute," she said.

The phone kept ringing. How many times? Six? Eight? Had she missed them? Were they already on their way to the station? Or was he just playing games again? Keeping her off balance?

She wouldn't let him. She was going to have her swim.

She hung up. Turning around, she found her father still there.

"No answer," she said in reply to his unspoken question.

"Well, a nice day like this, they probably went to the beach."

"I don't know. He would have said something."

"You can always try calling from the pool. Let's go."

"Isn't Mother coming?"

"She decided she needs a nap more than a swim."

Sarah picked up her beach bag. "Good. Then she'll be here if he calls."

"Right. So stop worrying. I'm sure everything's okay."

BUT two hours later Sarah wasn't so sure. From a pay phone near the bathhouse she dialed the apartment for the fourth time, and for the fourth time listened as the phone rang and rang.

Then she dialed home. Maybe he'd called the house.

But oddly, there was no answer at home either. Why not? What if Jovan *was* trying to call? And where was her mother? Suddenly apprehensive, Sarah picked her way among the clusters of sunbathers to where she and her father had parked themselves.

Her father was stretched out in a chaise, with the Business section of *The New York Times* open in front of him and one of his long dark cigars clamped between his teeth. Big-shouldered and barrel-chested, he was a man of fifty-eight, who prided himself on keeping fit. This afternoon he had already done a fast two dozen laps in the pool.

She stood beside his chaise. "Dad, I want to go home," she said as calmly as she could. "There's still no answer at the apartment and Mother's not answering either."

He looked up at her over the top of his sunglasses. "She's probably just out in the yard."

"But if Jovan's trying to call . . ." She heard the edge of panic in her voice and tried to fight it down.

"Come on, Sarah," he said. "Take it easy. It's still early. Sit down. Relax. You're getting yourself all worked up."

Calm. Sensible. Reassuring. Was he right?

"It's a holiday weekend, too," he said. "There's going to be a lot of traffic on the roads. Chances are they'll get tied up coming back from the beach."

"We don't know they went to the beach. That's only a guess."

"They're likely to hit traffic, wherever they went. Let's give it another half hour or so. Until three thirty. Then, if there's still no answer—"

"Yes? Then what?"

Abruptly he stubbed his cigar out in the grass. "Then we'll go home and see what we can do." Suddenly it occurred to her that his assurances meant nothing, that maybe he was just as worried as she was.

WHEN they finally arrived home, Sarah found her mother on the back porch knitting. "Have fun?" she asked without looking up.

"Where have you been, Mother? I called— There was no answer."

"Oh, was that you? I was in the shower. I heard the phone ringing, but I couldn't get to it in time."

"There weren't any other calls? Didn't Jovan call?"

"Why, no, dear. I was in the house all afternoon. I would have heard. Don't worry, dear. I'm sure everything's all right."

By suppertime, however, there was still no word from Jovan. Now it *was* too late. Sarah was getting frantic.

"I want to go to Yonkers, Dad," she said. "Come with me?"

"Now just sit tight, hon. He's probably on his way down here right this minute. Tell you what, though. If it'll make you feel better, we can drive over to the station after supper. It could be there's some problem with the trains."

"You go. I want to stay near the phone."

He was gone about an hour and a half. When he got back he looked tired and drawn. "Everything's on schedule," he reported. Wearily he sank into a kitchen chair. "You know, I wonder if Jovan didn't make a mistake because of the three-day weekend. I'll bet he's planning to bring Joey back tomorrow."

Sarah shook her head. "He said today! He knows it's today."

"She's right, Ted," her mother said quietly.

He looked at his wife for a long moment, then let his gaze drop. "I know," he said. "I know."

They decided then; if Jovan did not call that evening, Ted and Sarah would drive up to the apartment first thing in the morning. Emma Novack would stay home and listen for the phone.

IT WAS just after nine thirty the next morning when Sarah and her father stepped off the elevator on the third floor of the apartment building in Yonkers. The corridor smelled of cigarettes and cat boxes and other people's cooking. Sarah had almost forgotten that smell. She hesitated.

"Go ahead," her father said behind her.

Mechanically she walked down the corridor and stopped at 3-B. The hand-lettered nameplate over the buzzer said STEFANOVIC.

She was uncertain what to do. Press the buzzer? Use the key and go right in? Her hands were shaking. She hadn't been back here since that morning in December when she'd called her father to come and take her and Joey away from this place.

Ted pressed the buzzer. "Just in case," he said.

They waited, heard nothing.

"Let's go in," he said.

Sarah fitted the key into the lock, turned it, pushed the door, and stepped inside. "Hello?" she called.

Something was different. She knew it immediately. But what? Puzzled, she scanned the living room. Home. Had this place ever really been home? she wondered. Is it possible that I lived here for six years? The pictures on the walls were the same—the garish abstracts that Jovan had promised to sell for a Belgrade artist friend. Joey's blocks and toy cars were strewn on the floor, as if he'd just gotten up from playing. But that was usual enough.

"It's stifling in here," her father said, coming in behind her. Stepping over Joey's blocks, he threw open a window.

Suddenly she realized what was different—the draperies were gone. Now, why would Jovan take the draperies down?

In the kitchen, dishes were piled in the sink. The countertop was littered with bread crumbs, an open jar of peanut butter.

She turned the corner to the bedroom. The first thing she saw were the clothes scattered on the floor: the Mets T-shirt and the pair of shorts she had dressed Joey in on Friday, the extra clothes she had packed in his suitcase. Why? It didn't make sense.

Then she noticed the bed. Stripped of sheets and blankets, it looked cold and barren. Their bed once—hers and Jovan's. Once.

It was littered with bits of paper, cellophane wrappers, pins, little paper tabs. She went closer, picked up one of the tabs. It was a Macy's price tag. The labels and wrappers were from new clothes. Boys'. Shirts, pants, socks.

Suddenly her legs felt weak. She sat down on the bed, her body trembling. "No," she whispered. "Please, no."

Her father was in the doorway. For some reason he was holding a wire clothes hanger. "I checked the closets," he was saying. "They're empty, Sarah. Both of them. Everything's gone."

And then she heard a voice screaming, her voice, screaming over and over and over, "No, no, no, no, no. . . ."

CHECKPOINT: Saturday, April 23, 1:05 a.m.

IT WAS twenty minutes since the guard had walked away with the passports and disappeared into the administration building. Since then, Wilkes had turned the engine and the heater back on. Now, instead of being too cold, the car was hot and stuffy. And little Adam had become a deadweight in Sarah's lap.

What was that guard up to? Was he suspicious? Was something wrong with the passports? Would they all be arrested?

In the front seat her father stirred impatiently. "How long do we wait before doing something?"

Wilkes shrugged. "It's their show. We wait as long as they want us to." But Sarah heard the edge on his cultured English voice. He was not as calm as he was pretending to be.

She shifted in her seat. "We can at least ask them what's going on, can't we?"

"No," Wilkes snapped. "We sit tight."

"That's ridiculous," said Ted. "It can't hurt to ask."

"I'll decide what can hurt and what can't," said Wilkes through clenched teeth. "You may be paying the bills on this trip, Mr. Novack, but I'm still giving the orders, and don't you forget it."

"Well then, do something!" Ted hissed. "We look more suspicious just sitting here than we would if we got out and talked to those guys."

Wilkes glared at the older man but said nothing. He looked over at the administration building and at the gatehouse where the lone guard sat.

"Maybe you're right," said Wilkes. He pushed open his door. "You stay here. I'll see what I can find out."

Stepping out of the car, he shut the door behind him. He stretched his arms and legs, making a show of looking nonchalant. Then, while Sarah and the others watched, he strolled across the road to the administration building.

Inside the car they waited. Minutes passed.

"Look," said David Hardy, " 'e's comin' back."

Sure enough, Wilkes was striding toward them purposefully. He swung open the car door and slid behind the wheel.

"What did they say?" Ted asked.

Instead of answering, Wilkes held up three passports. Two of them he tipped back toward Hardy. The other he kept for himself.

"But that's only three." Sarah tried to quell the alarm in her voice. "What about ours?"

"I don't know," Wilkes said grimly. "It could be nothing. Remember, American passports need a visa stamp. And apparently the man with the stamp is down in the town. Taking his break."

"I don't believe it." Sarah slumped in her seat. "You don't believe it either, do you, Mr. Wilkes?"

He did not turn around. "I don't know. The man could be telling the truth. Or he could be trying to put us off our guard."

Sarah shuddered. What would happen now? Getting Joey's passport stamped was the key to the whole operation. Without it, there was no hope of getting him out of the country.

TWO

"WE'RE going to get him back," her father said. Fierce with rage, he was driving fast down the parkway, toward New Jersey. "We're going to get him back if it's the last thing we do."

Sarah wasn't listening. Numb, dazed, she sat stroking the small pile of clothes on her lap. "Joey has nothing of his own now," she murmured. "Nothing from home. Why would Jovan do that to him?" Tears kept blurring her vision.

"I'll send him a package," she said. "I'll send him Mr. Monkey to keep him company."

Mr. Monkey was Joey's favorite stuffed "pillow friend." At home Joey went to sleep every night with his arms around Mr. Monkey. The doll's grinning red felt mouth had come unglued long ago and one of the button eyes had fallen out, but she could repair it all before she sent it to him. He'd be so happy to see Mr. Monkey. He needed a friend.

"He must be so lonely over there," she murmured.

Over there. In Belgrade.

THEY had gotten the news on the telephone, when her father called home to report what they had found. Sarah, still sitting on the bed, exhausted from weeping, had heard his voice in the next room—heard the quiet murmur turn abruptly to explosive rage, then the slamming down of the receiver.

Her father loomed in the doorway, fists clenched. "Jovan just called the house. From Belgrade. He says to tell you that Joey's safe with him. They're with his mother. He says to tell you—" He cleared his throat. "He says to tell you that if you want to be Joey's mother again, you'll have to go and live with him over there."

Sarah nodded. Belgrade. Of course. It was what she had known all along, what she had feared and turned away from—Belgrade.

You are my wife. You cannot leave me.

It's over, Jovan. I can't take any more. I won't.

We belong together. You belong to me.

You're wrong, Jovan. I belong to myself.

I'll make you sorry. I'll take Joey. I'll make you hurt. I'll take him home with me, where he belongs.

His words. His. He had been telling her all along. But how could he actually do such a thing—tear Joey away from her? It was more than she could bear.

P-please, M-Mom. Why can't I st-stay with you?

And then, remembering, she had wept and wept, burying her face in the pile of clothes and shaking with grief. Joey. Oh, Joey.

"WE'LL call Bob Koenig," her father said as they sped south down the New Jersey Turnpike. "We'll call him as soon as we get home. Koenig will know what to do."

"Jovan will never give him back." She said it coldly, matter-of-factly. It was nothing but the truth.

"I never said he'd give him back. I said we'd *get* him back. Jovan has broken the law. He's violated a court order."

"So I guess all we do now is call him up and ask him to please come back to the States so we can have him arrested."

"Of course not. But it gives us some legal recourse."

Sarah turned away. She didn't believe any of it. Not a word. Because she knew that Jovan had won. Jovan always won. It was all up to her now. Her choice. No way out: Go back and live with Jovan. Or never see Joey again.

HER father was on the telephone almost from the minute they got home, calling friends, business associates—everyone he could think of who might have some idea how to get Joey back.

Upstairs her mother listened on the extension phone, then made calls of her own.

Useless, these calls were useless, Sarah kept thinking as she wandered absently from room to room, or stood at the window looking out—yard empty, swing set empty. Useless.

The clock on the mantel struck the half hour. Eight thirty.

Joey's bedtime. She would have just finished reading him his bedtime story and would be tucking him in, kissing him good night, her nose pressed against his sweet, soft child's hair.

Joey. Joey.

Later, wandering into the kitchen, she found her father on the phone again. She sat down across from him. "Call me as soon as you get back," he was saying into the receiver.

Hanging up, he made a note on a yellow legal pad. "Still no word from Koenig," he told her as he wrote. "I left another message on his answering machine. We'll just have to wait."

Sarah shrugged. It didn't matter. It wouldn't do any good.

"What about Jovan's friend?" Ted asked her. "You know, what's his name, the doctor, Marko. Maybe he knows something."

"I don't know. I'll see."

Listlessly she began looking for her phone book among the litter that covered the table: the Sommerton and Manhattan telephone directories, the family phone book, her father's at-home directory of his business contacts. There were also assorted pens and pencils, a half-empty coffee mug. And scattered everywhere were pages torn from the yellow legal pad, scrawled with lists and notes and names.

She smiled to herself. Her father was in his element. This was the way he'd spent most evenings and weekends for as long as she could remember—telephone in one hand, cigar in the other; talking, hustling. He was a salesman. House paints and finishes, wholesale. It was what he did, what he was good at.

Unearthing her own phone book, Sarah found Marko's number and showed her father the place.

"Thanks, kitten." He picked up the phone and dialed again. "Hello, is this Marko Markovic? My name is Ted Novack. I'm Jovan's father-in-law and I'm calling because . . ."

She didn't stay to hear the rest. What was the point? There was nothing to be done. It was only a matter of her making a decision. One way or the other.

At last Ted hung up. "Liar," he muttered to himself.

"Not very helpful, was he?" Emma said when she came in from the front hall. "I heard on the extension."

He nodded wearily. "Then you know."

He took off his glasses and rubbed his eyes with his thumb and forefinger. He was tired and depressed and angry. After hours on the telephone all he had to show for his efforts were sore eyes from the glare of the overhead light. But not one lead.

"What about trying Sherwood Brice?" Emma asked. "Isn't he the one who's always bragging about his good connections? Maybe he'll have some suggestions."

Ted smiled faintly. Her description of his sometime luncheon companion and financial adviser was accurate enough. "I called him a while ago, but he wasn't home either. Not him, not Koenig, not half the people I've tried. Jovan couldn't have picked a better time to pull his lousy stunt: a holiday weekend, everyone away. Perfect. Just perfect."

"You don't think he planned it that way, do you?"

"I wouldn't put it past him, would you?"

"No, I guess not." She sighed heavily. "You know what I wish? I wish Jovan were here now, so I could wring his neck."

Ted laughed out loud. "Lady," he said, "I like your spirit."

They had just decided to call it a night when the telephone rang. Ted snatched it off the hook. "Hello?" He listened briefly, then put his hand over the mouthpiece. "It's Koenig."

"It's about time," Emma said. Hurrying from the room, she ran back up the stairs to the extension phone.

Koenig was not only Sarah's lawyer, he was also a friend—one of Ted's regular partners on the squash court. While he was full of high spirits at first, his mood changed abruptly when Ted told him what had happened. "Oh, no," he said. "I was afraid this might happen."

"You were afraid?" Emma said over the extension. "Since when were you afraid? I was the one who kept saying we shouldn't let Jovan have visiting rights. And now Joey's gone."

"Emma, I realize this is upsetting, but let me assure you—"

"We don't want assurances; we want Joey back."

"Look," Ted said, "what can we do? What about extradition? Could we get Jovan back here for violating a court order?"

"I suspect that in a case like this, where you're dealing with a foreign government and so on . . . well, it's not going to be easy. Our firm doesn't usually handle this kind of thing."

"Well then," Ted said with forced patience, "what about another firm? Is there someone you can recommend?"

"Offhand, I really can't. But in the meantime, I'll go into court and get Jovan charged with violating the consent order. That could be an important weapon in any future proceedings—"

Ted interrupted. "What kind of proceedings?"

"Oh, say you end up taking Jovan to court in Yugoslavia. Or maybe you get help from someone in the federal government—your Congressman or somebody. You'll need that kind of documentation."

Ted jotted hasty notes on his legal pad. "Okay, let's say we get that. How soon does this happen?"

"I can be in court first thing in the morning."

"Sounds good. Let me know how it goes."

"Will do. Take care now. You, too, Emma. Oh, and Ted? Tell Sarah how sorry I am that it turned out this way for her."

CHECKPOINT: Saturday, April 23, 1:20 a.m.

"THERE!" said Hardy. "Is that 'im?"

Ahead, at the bend in the road, a mist of white light shone on the fir trees. As Sarah watched, the light grew brighter, then narrowed abruptly as a pair of headlights flared into the open and a big car rounded the bend, coming fast.

"We'll know soon enough," Wilkes answered.

None of them said a word as the car came barreling on. Suddenly it veered, slowed, and came to a halt in front of the administration building. It was a large gray sedan with some sort of official-looking insignia on the driver's door. The headlights went out, the door opened, and a burly figure in a guard's uniform got out. Pausing to cast an appraising glance in the direction of the crowded BMW, he turned and shambled toward the administration building.

They watched and waited in tense silence. The boy on Sarah's lap slept on.

Then the door of the administration building burst open. The new guard stepped out and lumbered in their direction. Wilkes rolled down the window.

"*Guten abend, Mein Herr,*" the man growled. In one gloved hand he held the passports, level with the pistol on his hip. Bending to the window, he began speaking in animated German, his hands in constant motion, his head bobbing. Then, in the midst of his hand waving, he gave Wilkes the passports so casually

371

that Sarah almost missed it. Wilkes had them! He had their passports! But had they been stamped?

Abruptly the torrent of words ceased. Straightening up, the guard rapped the roof of the car and stepped back. Wilkes turned on the lights, waved once to the guard, and pulled out onto the highway. Heading south. Into Yugoslavia.

"You mean we made it?" Sarah asked. "He gave us the visas?"

Wilkes handed her the passports over his shoulder. "That's right," he said.

Sarah opened one of the little booklets. On the page after Joey's photograph, a simple rectangular impression had been stamped in purple ink, with Serbo-Croatian words around the edges.

"All right," her father said, turning to Wilkes. "Are you going to tell us what that was all about back there?"

Instead of answering right away, Wilkes took a pack of cigarettes from the pocket of his jacket, tamped one loose, and flicked open his lighter. In the mirror, in the sudden flare of light, Sarah caught a quirk playing at the corner of his mouth. It was the closest thing to a smile she'd seen yet on his stone-hard face.

"I'm afraid the poor man was rather distressed," Wilkes said, blowing smoke. "It seems the amount of time he's allowed for his break is not sufficient to permit him to get to the town and back at the appointed hour. He asked us please to accept his apologies for the delay and he hopes we enjoy our stay in Yugoslavia."

"You're kidding," Sarah's father said. "You mean that whole show back there was an apology?"

"Volatile people, these Yugoslavs," Wilkes said. "Very passionate."

Sarah took a long breath. "Well, at least it's over now."

"I'm afraid not, miss," Wilkes said, and this time there was no hint of humor in his voice. "It's only just beginning."

THREE

ALL that evening—the evening after Joey disappeared—Sarah kept hearing voices. Sometimes it was her father on the phone, sometimes her mother, telling the story over and over, while Sarah sat curled up on the sofa watching television, trying to think what the tune was that kept going through her head. A lullaby. "*Hushabye, don't you cry/ Go to sleep my little baby.*"

He would already be asleep, wouldn't he? Where he was, it was the middle of the night. What was it, six hours' difference? Over there. On the other side of the world.

Just yesterday, wasn't it? When Jovan took him away. Or was it two days ago, on Saturday? When she'd last spoken to him on the telephone. Jovan could have done it right then. Could have taken Joey and been on his way to the airport as soon as he'd hung up the phone.

The television flickered. The image on the screen showed the New York skyline at night. A disembodied voice intoned, "It's ten p.m. Do you know where your children are?"

"Oh, God," she moaned, tears flooding her eyes. Why? Why had she trusted him? He'd been lying all along. Such a fool she'd been. Right from the beginning.

Except she'd been so much younger then. And wanting so much, dreaming. In the beginning . . .

THEY'D met in Paris, at a café on the Boulevard St.-Michel. It was a warm night in the middle of July, 1966. Out on the sidewalk rivers of people swirled and eddied, soaked in the red-and-purple luster of neon. Now and then a few more strollers came spilling in through the open door, and nobody seemed to be leaving. The bar was shoulder to shoulder. Every table taken. Voices, laughter everywhere. Which was why Sarah didn't notice him at first.

She was sitting at a small table, sipping wine over the remnants of a late supper, and telling Carole Hartman what a godsend her invitation had been and how exciting it was to be in Paris and how happy she was to see her old roommate again.

Carole tossed her blond hair and laughed. "You're the godsend," she said. "And what a perfect time to arrive, on the eve of Bastille Day! There'll be dancing in the streets tonight."

Chattering away, Sarah only gradually became aware of the two young men who had been working their way up and down the crowded aisle looking for an empty table. When she finally glanced up she found herself looking into a pair of yellow-brown eyes. Odd eyes. The man had thick eyebrows, and wavy dark hair that flopped over his forehead. And he was smiling at her. Then the couple at the next table got up to leave, and the men walked over and sat down.

It was awkward at first. The tables were side by side and jammed so close together that Sarah kept bumping elbows with the dark-haired man. He turned and smiled an apology, and she wondered if he hadn't been bumping her elbow on purpose. But his smile was gentle. A little impish, too. She smiled back.

The trip was a graduation present to herself: six weeks away from home while she tried to figure out what she wanted to do with herself now that she was almost twenty-two, now that she had her degree.

Yes, Paris would be just the thing.

By sharing a room with Carole in a little pension, and living frugally, Sarah guessed she could squeak by on the money she had saved up while working summers at a department store and on the two hundred dollars her father had kicked in as a graduation present.

THE waiters were turning the chairs up on the tables when Jovan poured out the last of the cognac, careful to see that each of them got some before letting the last few drops slide into his own glass. He had been doing things like that all evening. Having pushed their two tables together, he had made himself the gracious host of their little party. While he talked and laughed and listened attentively, and lit one Gitane cigarette after another, he also made sure that the coffee and dessert arrived promptly, that the cognac was "three star," and that the check was taken care of before the rest of them were even aware that it had been presented. Sarah was impressed.

His face was broad, with Slavic cheekbones, and thick eyebrows that came together over the bridge of his nose. And those strange eyes. Still, he could be unbelievably charming and considerate. He dressed well, too! A fitted corduroy jacket, a crisp white shirt open at the neck. And he had the nicest smile.

What surprised her was how easy it was to talk to him, especially since neither of them spoke the other's language and they had to make do in French. His was marked with a guttural accent, and his syntax was sometimes confusing. Hers was stiff with textbook formality. But he was patient and kind. He was as eager as she, it seemed, to understand. And to be understood.

Leaning close, he told her about the work he did as a draftsman in an engineering firm, drawing up plans for the heating systems of new buildings.

"That sounds like interesting work," she said.

"I hate it," he said, rolling his vowels deep at the back of his throat. "There is no poetry in it; there is no passion, no art."

"And you are an artist?" She heard the awe in her voice.

He heard it, too, and grinned. "Artist of *science!*" he said proudly, raising a finger for emphasis. His passion was chemistry. It was why he had come to Paris, why he was willing to spend evenings and weekends penned up in stuffy classrooms or buried in books at the library.

"I think it must be wonderful to have a dream like that," she heard herself saying. "Something to dedicate your life to. But why Paris? Why couldn't you study chemistry in Belgrade?"

"Why Paris? Paris is everything! It is true, Petor?"

Petor interrupted his quiet conversation with Carole and paused to consider. He was thin and scholarly, with a high forehead. "In a way, perhaps, yes. Being here changes one."

"A lawyer's response," Jovan chided. "You see? I can always rely on my friend Petor to put things into perspective. Besides"—Jovan turned back to Sarah—"in Belgrade I cannot study chemistry. It is not my training. When I am thirteen, my mother enrolls me in state technical high school. My uncle tells her engineering is good profession, that I will make money and support her."

"Your father couldn't support her?"

"My father is dead."

"Oh. I'm sorry."

He dismissed her sympathy with the wave of a hand. "There is no need. It was a long time ago. During the war. He was with the Partisans. With Tito. He was fighting the Ustachi, the Chetniks."

"Who?"

"Our own Nazis."

She nodded, but still the names meant nothing. They only made her more aware than ever that he came from a place and a time so entirely different from her own as to be completely unimaginable—and absolutely fascinating.

"You must have been only a child then," Sarah said gently.

"I was seven when my father went away to the mountains. That was 1943. After that, I never see him again." He put his cigarette to his lips, inhaled deeply. "And now I am engineer and the state will let me do nothing else. The state gave me education. They have a right that I should give back in return something. For most people it is good system. But for me it is disaster! When I go back, it will be as scientist," he said with a ferocity that alarmed her. "As great scientist!"

Petor, who had given up trying to talk to Carole over Jovan's rising voice, lifted his glass in salute. "And winner of the Nobel Prize. But not for peace," he added, giving Sarah a wink.

Jovan caught the tone—and the wink. Suddenly he was out of his chair and leaning over the table, flushed with rage. "You sneer at me, eh?" he hissed in Petor's face. "You mock me?"

Sarah held her breath. Carole sat frozen.

But all at once Jovan's fury went slack. He sat down and wiped his forehead with a napkin. "No," he said sheepishly. "Not for peace." Reaching over, he gave his friend a playful punch on the shoulder. "It is a good joke, eh? Not for peace!"

Caught up in the spirit, Carole was laughing, too. So was Sarah. But when she stopped to take a last sip of cognac, the glass was shaking in her hand.

THE four of them walked on the boulevard afterward, past the cafés and the cinema marquees, and then along the river Seine, away from all the lights and the people.

It was cooler there, under the trees. Jovan was beside her, leaning close, talking, listening. Gone was the intensity that had so unnerved her half an hour before—yes, and excited her, too, strangely. He was quiet now, and attentive. It was very confusing.

Yet here she was, telling him all about herself, telling him more than she intended. Maybe it was a mistake. But she needed to. She talked about the longing she felt for—she didn't know what exactly, but for something . . . *different*, something to . . .

"Fill your life. Give it meaning. Give it a purpose, direction."

"Yes, that's right."

"So that you do not regret forever all the things you could have done if you had not been always so afraid, always so ready to settle for a handful of crumbs off the floor when the whole loaf of bread was up there on the table."

"You know, don't you? You know what it's like."

"Yes, I know. It has been also for me like that. Growing up in war, afraid, always hungry. And then, after the war, being put in state orphanage because my mother could not support me and my sister together and one of us had to go. I, I had to go. Ach." He flicked his cigarette away. "I am sorry. I speak too much."

They walked on, turned a corner, and stood facing a broad esplanade. At the far end rose a domed building, a basilica, with double tiers of columned porticos. Lit by floodlights, it lay upon the night like a jewel in a velvet case.

"Les Invalides," Jovan said. "Where Napoleon is buried."

"It is very beautiful," Sarah whispered.

"That was a man who was not afraid," Jovan said as he gazed at the monument. "Who took of life everything he could."

"Can we sit down for a minute? I feel . . . a little dizzy."

"Yes, yes. Of course. Come. Over here."

Taking her lightly by the arm, he led her to a bench in the lamplight. Leaving Carole and Petor to go on ahead, he sat down beside her.

"You're right about what you said about being afraid," she said after a while. "I've been afraid for as long as I can remember. Always holding back, always letting someone else make my decisions for me. I guess I'm not very brave."

Reaching over, Jovan touched her chin and gently turned her face toward him. "But that is changing now," he told her.

"Is it?" She was doubtful. "How? What do you mean?"

"You are here! You came to Paris because *you* wanted to."

"I guess that's true," she said. Sitting there under the trees, she savored the revelation as if it were the tastiest of chocolates. Except that the pleasure began to melt away, and she heard a small voice asking, "Then why am I still afraid?"

"You are afraid now?"

"I guess I am."

"Of me?"

"Yes. A little." She tried to laugh. "Because you tell me I don't have to be afraid. And if I don't have to be afraid, then I'll have to do all kinds of things that I've been too afraid to do."

He took her hand. "Like become in love?"

She let her hand rest in his. "It's late," she said quietly. "We

377

better go. Carole will wonder what's happened to me." She got to her feet. "I'll wonder, too."

Later they stood together in the dark street outside the pension. "I want to see you again," Jovan said.

"Yes," she said. "I'd like that."

THEY spent the Bastille Day holiday together and part of the next day and all of the next. They took a trip down the Seine in a glass-topped boat. At the Rodin Museum they took pictures of each other mimicking the poses of the nudes. For lunch they bought salami and bread and sat on a bench by the river.

One evening they went to a dark little Serbian restaurant in Montparnasse that was down a flight of steps, below the sidewalk. Jovan spoke to the waiter in what must have been Serbo-Croatian, the cadences rising and falling as if the words were being sung. They ate and talked and took their time. And all the while Sarah was amazed at how easy it was to be with him.

Afterward he invited her up to his room. It was a small room on the third floor, overlooking the Rue Rollin. There was the smell of cigarettes. There were books everywhere: biology and chemistry textbooks, engineering textbooks, volumes of French poetry.

He cleared a place at the end of the bed. "Here. Sit," he said. "One poem I would like to read to you. By a modern poet." He picked up a typewritten sheet.

The poem, in French, was about a girl with brown hair and brown eyes, a beautiful girl who laughed and dreamed of something to fill her life, and about a man who hoped he could be everything to her, as she had become everything to him.

When he was finished, she didn't know what to say. No one had ever written a poem for her before. "Thank you," was all she could manage.

"Do you like it?"

"Like it? Jovan, it's beautiful."

He came and sat next to her. "Because you are beautiful, you make my poem beautiful," he whispered.

SHE let it happen, let Jovan wrap the summer days around her like a down comforter. She neglected Carole, stopped writing to her parents. Jovan, who had promised to visit his mother in

Belgrade, decided to stay with Sarah instead. They were together constantly. But then, too quickly, the summer was almost over.

"Stay," Jovan begged her. "Don't go back. The visa you can get extended, yes? And money you could get from your father."

No matter how often she told him otherwise, Jovan could not get the idea out of his head that just because she was an American her father must be wealthy. Anyway, that was not the point. Visa or no visa, money or no money, she needed to get back home.

He did not understand. If she loved him, she would stay. No reasons, no excuses. There was never any middle ground with him. It was either all love or all hate, all loyalty or all betrayal, all his way or not at all.

She needed time to think, she said, time to catch her breath.

He shook his head. He was annoyed now. "You talk like a child," he said. "You are talking foolishness."

But she knew she wasn't. As much as she loved being swept along by his dreams, by a vision and purpose that she could not find in herself, she also felt overwhelmed by him sometimes, as if her own life could be swallowed up by his, by that voracious will.

So she held firm. Later she could come back, she told him. In the spring, perhaps, after she had had a chance to work for a while and save up some more money. Yes, in the spring.

His letters began dropping through the slot in the front door almost as soon as she got home—three and sometimes four of them a week. Letters full of longing, telling her how much she missed her. Letters with poems enclosed.

Wonderful letters. But also confusing. Sarah was having a hard enough time getting used to being home. She had taken a job with the children's program of the public library and had settled once more into her old room in her parents' house. It was a little girl's room, with frilly white curtains and a white chenille bed-spread—the room she had lived in all through high school and during semester breaks from college. The neighborhoods she drove through every morning on her way to work were the same neighborhoods she had driven through for years. No, nothing had changed. Nothing would ever change. At times, in fact, she found it hard to believe that the summer had ever happened.

Except she knew it had happened, because *she* had changed. And because here were Jovan's letters to remind her.

By November he was pleading with her to come back to Paris, and she was beginning to think it might be a good idea. At least she might be able to get things settled in her mind.

"Settled?" said her mother, pouring dressing on her salad. They were sitting at the kitchen table having supper.

Ted Novack peered at Sarah. "What do you mean, settled?"

Sarah's younger brother, Richard, a gangly nineteen-year-old, glanced quickly at each of them but continued eating.

"I think Jovan wants to get married," she said, trying to sound nonchalant.

"Married," her father repeated.

"He hasn't actually said so, but I think he does."

Then the questions began, as Sarah knew they would. What about her job? her father wanted to know. It was the first career job she had ever had. What about cultural differences? What did this Joe-vahn know of her way of life? Or she of his?

"His name is Yo-vahn," she corrected. "In Serbian the *j* is pronounced like a *y*."

"Whatever," Ted said.

It was her mother, finally, who asked the only question that made any sense at the moment: "Do *you* want to marry *him?*"

"I don't know," she said. "I really don't. That's what I have to get settled. That's why I have to go back and see him again."

Instead, he came to see her.

The visit was a compromise, her mother's idea. Rather than jeopardize her new job, Sarah could invite her friend to be a guest in their house over the Christmas holidays. That way he would have an opportunity to meet the family and to see something of what life was like in America. More to the point, of course, the family would have a chance to meet him.

Sarah wrote to Jovan that evening, to pass on her parents' invitation. His reply arrived a week later.

> Tell your mother and father for their generosity I thank them. I will like very much to be the guest in their house. But the cost of tickets is too expensive.

Fortunately, because she was living at home, Sarah had managed to keep her expenses low and to save a good portion of her take-home pay, so she was able to send him the fare.

ON THE DAY JOVAN WAS TO ARRIVE, Sarah and her parents drove to Kennedy Airport to pick him up. From the windowed gallery above the customs area she searched the lines at the customs counters. She found her gaze settling on what looked like a familiar figure, except the man seemed shorter than she remembered, the hair thinner. But then she was certain.

"There! There he is." She waved, trying to catch his eye. If only he would look her way. When at last he spotted her, he threw up a hand, grinned happily, blew her a kiss. And then he was through customs and she was in his arms.

He had brought gifts for everyone. For her father there was a fine leather wallet; for her mother, a ceramic brooch, hand-painted with tiny flowers. Her brother, Richard, got a pen-and-pencil set in a case lined with velvet. And for Sarah? For Sarah he brought not just an anthology of French poetry and a yellow-and-black Saint Laurent scarf, which she loved, but the wonder of his actually being there, of knowing for certain that the summer had been no illusion, that Jovan Stefanovic was real.

With her parents he was at his most charming: bowing slightly from the waist when he was introduced; deferring respectfully to her father, who seemed impressed; bestowing bouquets of compliments upon her mother, who blushed.

Grandma Helen—her mother's mother and Sarah's own most loyal ally—was enchanted when she finally had a chance to meet Jovan. "Oh, Sarah, he's a real gift horse," she gushed, displaying her usual talent for mangling clichés. "He's *so* charming. If you don't grab him, you're just plain crazy."

The visit soon turned awkward, however. Richard kept a shy distance and dodged quickly past Jovan whenever he met him on the stairs or in the hall. Sarah's mother tried hard to make Jovan feel welcome, but she went too far, tried too hard. At supper she served things like goulash and stuffed cabbage. The recipes, she explained, had come from Mrs. Ruschak down the street, whose parents or grandparents—she wasn't sure which—had come from somewhere in Eastern Europe. "Hungary or Romania or one of those places." Her mother's efforts at making Jovan welcome succeeded only in making him feel more like a stranger.

Nor did Sarah's father help matters, for despite his efforts to appear a generous and good-humored host, Sarah sensed that he was, in fact, struggling against a contrary impulse. She noticed it one evening at supper when he began interrogating Jovan about his background, his education, his goals. The abruptness, the hard edge on his voice, made her father sound less like a concerned parent than a TV detective grilling a burglary suspect.

Puzzled, Sarah thought at first that it might be the language barrier. But gradually she realized that the trouble was something more than language. She saw it in the skepticism with which Ted Novack greeted Jovan's fervent declaration that he would one day win a place of honor in the annals of science.

"Sounds good," her father said blandly, but it was obvious that to him Jovan's dreams of success were just that: dreams. What mattered to Ted was how this man would support himself and Sarah if the two of them decided to get married. And where would they live? And when was Jovan going to finish school?

"Come to think of it," Ted said one evening over coffee, "why is he still in school anyway? He's thirty years old. He should be out making a living by now."

Should? Whose *should?* In her father's mind there seemed to be some sort of timetable for how people were supposed to live their lives. Well, it certainly wasn't Jovan's. And Sarah did not want it to be hers either.

Years later, looking back, Sarah sometimes wondered if it wasn't her father more than Jovan who finally induced her to get married; whether it wasn't her father's insistence that security and certainty were the only things that mattered. For secretly Sarah feared those things mattered as much to her as they did to him, and that if she did not grab the chance to break free the way Jovan kept urging her to do, she might miss her chance of ever finding out all that her life could have been.

THEY were married at the end of March by a Paris magistrate. Though her parents were both convinced that she was making a mistake, they flew over with her for the wedding. Sarah was grateful to them for that.

The ceremony was a simple one. Sarah, Jovan, and her family took their places in line with a dozen other wedding parties in an ornate courtroom. Petor was there, serving as Jovan's best man, and so was Jovan's mother, who had flown in from Belgrade.

When it was their turn, Sarah and Jovan stepped forward. Only then, and then only for a moment, did Sarah feel a stab of panic. It suddenly occurred to her that maybe her parents were right, that maybe she was making a mistake, and that she had no idea who the man was to whom she was about to give the rest of her life.

Afterward her father invited everyone to an elegant restaurant for a champagne lunch, with crepes and salad, and a wedding cake festooned with bows of white frosting. Whatever his feelings about Jovan, he did not stint. And after the cake was cut, he presented Sarah and Jovan with an envelope. Inside was a check for five hundred dollars. "This is to help the two of you get started," he said.

FOUR

"SARAH? Are you up?" It was her mother, calling from downstairs.

"Yes?" What time was it? Morning? She could not remember turning off the television and getting into bed.

"It's Jovan, dear. He wants to talk to you. He's got Joey on the phone. They're at his mother's."

Her heart lurched. Joey. She jumped out of bed, rushed to her parents' room, and picked up the phone.

"Sarah?" Jovan sounded as though he were speaking through a pipe.

"I want to talk to Joey," she said. She would not get angry. She would not cry. He would not hurt her anymore.

"Yes, he wants to talk to you, too. And I wanted to—"

She cut him off. "I have nothing to say to you. Either you put Joey on right now or I'm hanging up."

"Yes, yes. All right. Don't hang up."

A murmur of voices on the other end, then, "Mama?" His small voice was somewhere between a squeal and a shriek.

"Joey. Oh, Joey." Tears flooded her eyes, but she fought them back. "How are you? Are you all right?"

"I'm o-k-kay. I'm at B-Baka's house. It's n-neat. There's an outhouse, j-just like on a f-farm. And there's a w-well where we g-g-get w-w- . . ." He could not finish the word.

"Water," she said, to relieve him of his agony. His stutter was worse than ever. He wasn't okay. He wasn't okay at all.

"Why d-didn't you c-come like D-Daddy said you would, Mama? He said you'd be c-coming on the next air-p-plane."

"I'm sorry, Joey, I . . ." She groped for words. What was Jovan trying to do to him? How could she tell him the truth: that his daddy had lied to him, that his daddy was using him to hurt her? Jovan was all he had now. He would need to trust his father more than he needed to hear the truth. "I—I got delayed. I'm sorry. I won't be able to come right away."

"I miss you, Mama. I want you to b-be here."

"I miss you, too, Joey. I miss you very, very much. And I'll see you just as soon as I possibly can."

"But when, Mama?"

"Please, Joey. I'll be there." What was she saying? "I don't know when yet, but I'll be there very soon. Okay?"

There were some scuffling sounds; then Jovan was on the line again. "You see what you are doing to him? He is crying now. He wants you here with him. You belong with us, Sarah. Sarah! Listen to me!"

He was still shouting at her when she hung up the receiver.

JUST before noon on Tuesday, September 7, Bob Koenig called Ted at his office in downtown Sommerton.

This morning, at his request, the lawyer told Ted, the family court had issued a contempt citation charging Jovan Stefanovic with violating the custody provisions of the consent decree. Accompanying the citation was a warrant for his arrest.

"That's terrific." Ted was elated. It was the first good news he had heard, the first positive step.

"Well, ah . . ." He heard Koenig clear his throat. "Ted, I'll be frank with you. There's really no way the warrant can be applied unless your son-in-law decides to return to New Jersey."

Ted felt his elation slipping away. "What about extradition?"

"Not much chance. Turns out that in New Jersey it's not a felony for a person to steal his own child. It's only a misdemeanor. Which means it's not an extraditable offense."

"I see," Ted said grimly.

"Look," Koenig was saying, "I've got calls in to several colleagues who are familiar with international law. One of them might be able to offer some suggestions. In the meantime, I've also spoken with a friend of mine who's a private investigator. He's handled a number of cases like this. Tracks the kids down."

"Wait a minute, Bob. We don't need someone to track Joey down for us. We *know* where he is."

"I know that. But you've got to be realistic. If negotiations and legal routes don't work out . . ."

Ted felt a sudden chill run through him. "Why shouldn't they work out? We've got the law on our side, don't we?"

"Yes, yes, of course. But it may not be that simple. You'll be dealing with an iron curtain government. You can't expect those people to be very sympathetic."

"Well, I'm not going to be pushed into a counterabduction or whatever it is you've got in mind. This is my family we're talking about, not some characters in a suspense thriller. Thanks, but I don't want any part of that."

The call left Ted Novack depressed and annoyed. He was still thinking what to do next when the phone rang. Business this time.

It had been a morning of constant interruptions. One minute he'd be worrying about Joey, the next he'd be answering a call from a customer or one of his district salesmen.

If only he could drop everything else. Getting Joey back, that was all that mattered now.

Joey. His beautiful boy. Gone. And with him a part of himself gone, too: the childlike, playful, loving part that he had somehow never allowed himself to share with anyone, not even his own children—the part that even he had forgotten had ever existed, until Joey came along and teased it out of hiding.

"I'M GLAD you came with me today," Ted said.

"Thank you," Joey said matter-of-factly.

They were bicycling together on the towpath that ran along the old canal down by the river. A bright summer afternoon, just a month ago. The river the blue of crystal, the shade of the trees deliciously cool. Joey, in red shorts and a T-shirt, kept racing ahead, falling back. He was growing so fast these days that he complained about his legs hurting.

"You're good company," Ted said, trying again. He longed to hear that Joey was enjoying the outing, too, that he would happily come bicycling with Grampa again and again.

"That's what I'm here for," Joey piped up cheerfully. "If I weren't here, you'd be very lonely."

Ted had to laugh—at himself as well as at Joey. "Pretty sure of yourself, aren't you?"

Joey grinned. "Yup," he said. Then he stood on his pedals and took off down the path. "Beat you to the big tree, Grampa," he called back over his shoulder.

"Probably," said Ted.

THE trouble, Ted knew, was that he had never had the same kind of time with his own children that he'd had with Joey. Always too busy earning a living. Days at a time away from home, or getting home so late the kids were already in bed. Hardware and general housewares had been his line when he was just starting out. Eventually he had begun specializing in paints. Having the answers. Helping people. Performing a service. In Ted Novack's book, these were the important things. His work was gratifying, and he had done well over the years. By living modestly, by saving and investing, he had managed to put two kids through college and could now look forward to retiring early and comfortably.

Yes, he had come a long way.

And yet during all these years they had never had a chance, Ted and his kids, to get to know each other. Which was why Joey had come as such a blessing. It was as if Ted had been given a second chance to catch up on all he had missed: the bike rides, the afternoons of swings and sandboxes, of building towers out of blocks on the living-room rug. And Joey got whatever he needed. Ted made sure of it.

Indulgent? Jovan thought so. "You are going to make him spoiled," he would growl, showing indignation.

"Sure, I'm spoiling him," Ted would reply with a wave of his cigar. "That's what grandparents are for."

If Jovan wasn't able to give Joey the things he needed, it was Jovan's own fault. With his grants and his government loans he and Sarah should have been able to manage just fine. But to Jovan, of course, managing was not living. Wine on the table every evening, that was *his* style. And a trip to Yugoslavia every year, while every other month Sarah was calling home in a panic because the power company had turned off the lights, the rent was overdue, or the car had broken down again. *Could you please help us out, Daddy? I'm sorry to be asking again, but please.*

Ted always gave in. And that, of course, was exactly what Jovan counted on. It was probably what he was counting on now. Now that he had Joey.

Now that he had a way of getting Sarah back, too.

Except this time it wasn't going to work. This time Jovan wasn't going to have it his way. Because they *were* going to get Joey back. Somehow.

BY LATE afternoon Ted was ready to call it quits for the day. His card file had yielded half a dozen new leads, but most of them were pretty tenuous. There was one plus, though. From an old contact he'd gotten the name of a New York businessman who was involved in promoting trade between Yugoslavia and the United States. The man's name was Steven Kobelec.

Ted was looking over his desk for the last time when the telephone rang. It was his stockbroker friend, Sherwood Brice, on whose answering machine he had left a message the night before.

For what must have been the hundredth time that day, Ted went through the story.

Sherwood's response was as forceful and unequivocal as ever. "What you absolutely need is a lawyer in Washington. You're talking international, right? Government pressure? Legal avenues? You need someone who knows the ins and outs of the bureaucracy, what kind of steps are feasible."

"Yeah, I get the point." Ted took a long breath. "Do you know anybody I can talk to?"

"Matter of fact, I do. Man's name is Stevenson. Colonel George Stevenson. He was a White House adviser under Eisenhower. Now he's head of one of the top law firms in Washington. He's also a close friend of my family. I'll give you his number."

When Ted hung up, he felt exhilarated. He was finally making headway: first the Yugoslav-American trade man, now this Washington lead! Of course there were no guarantees that any of it would pay off. But at least there was some hope.

He picked up the phone again and dialed the Washington area code, then the number of Colonel Stevenson.

ONCE past the gate, the road descended the mountain fast and dropped so steeply that Sarah's ears kept popping. A snowbank flashed white in the headlights as the car pitched around a sharp bend.

"Do you have to go so fast?" she asked through clenched teeth.

"You didn't imagine this was going to be a pleasure trip, did you?" Wilkes replied, and headed into another turn.

Sarah took a deep breath. The sky was filled with stars. It was somehow comforting to see them from the car, so clear and steady, when everything else in her life was in such turmoil.

I'm coming, Joey, she said to herself, sending the words up to the sky. I'm coming.

After a while the road broke out of the forest, and they found themselves driving down the main street of a small town. The town, Wilkes said, was called Kranj, a ski resort. It was apparently a prosperous and busy place in the daytime, but at two in the morning the streets were deserted.

"Any chance of stopping for coffee somewhere?" Sarah asked.

Wilkes cruised slowly down the street, peering to the right and left. "Keep your eyes open," he said.

Finally, on a back street, they came upon a café that had its lights on. Wilkes pulled up in front and turned off the engine.

The café was a drab, low-ceilinged place, with a small bar and a few tables covered with red-checked oilcloths. On one wall hung a black-and-white portrait of a glowering Marshal Tito.

As they all arranged themselves around a table, the barman came over and Wilkes began speaking to him in German. He ordered soda for Adam and his mother, coffee for the rest of them. When the man was gone, the Hardys got up and went looking for the rest rooms, taking their boy with them.

Wilkes adjusted his glasses and lit a cigarette. "Look," he said, addressing himself to Ted, "I've been thinking about what happened at the checkpoint. I don't trust it."

"You mean about the guard being on his break?"

Wilkes nodded. "I'm still not convinced that wasn't a phony story. If it was, they could be on the watch for us right now. If those chaps at the border put out an alert for us and if we get pulled in, all they have to do is start questioning the Hardys and their lad and it will be all over for us."

"What do you have in mind?" Ted asked.

Wilkes leaned closer. "I want to get the Hardys out of this as soon as we can. For their protection as well as for ours. We've got the visa stamp now; that's the main thing."

"Yes? So?" Ted said impatiently.

Wilkes blew smoke through his nostrils. "There's an airport in Zagreb. We'll be there around dawn. Instead of taking the Hardys on to Belgrade with us, we'll put them on the first flight back to the West."

"But what if we're stopped?" Sarah asked. "The police have a record now, don't they? They'll know I came in with a child."

But just then the Hardys reappeared and Wilkes was on his feet. Ignoring both Sarah and her question, he strode off toward the rest room.

FIVE

The odd thing, Sarah realized, was the way she kept expecting every minute to hear Joey or see him. As if he were just in the next room, or out playing in the yard.

Late in the morning, when she was lying in bed not wanting to get up, she'd find herself listening, waiting to hear his voice calling, "I'm back, Mama. Daddy brought me back. I'm home."

She was doing it now. Lying there. Listening. But there was nothing. Just the awful quiet permeating the house, filling every room, seeping into every corner.

Lost. She felt so utterly lost.

And always so tired. Her body so heavy. Unable to move. Always ready to sleep, terrible sleep, like falling down a well.

What made it all worse were the reminders she kept finding everywhere: one of Joey's miniature toy cars poking out from under a sofa cushion; his toothbrush in the holder over the bathroom sink; his Mets jacket hanging on the hook inside the back door, as if he'd left his shadow behind.

Sarah had finally decided to make her way downstairs and was halfway into the kitchen when the phone began ringing. During these last days the phone had become a hateful intrusion in her life. Reluctantly she edged toward the phone and lifted the receiver. "Hello?" she said tentatively.

"Well, there you are. I was just about to hang up."

To her relief, Sarah recognized the voice of Grandma Helen. "Hello, Gran."

"How are you holding up, dear?"

"Not too well, I'm afraid."

Sarah pulled out a chair from the kitchen table and sat down. There was no one else—aside from Joey—whom Sarah would rather talk to. Ever since Sarah was a child, Gran had been one of her best friends, a trusted and trusting confidante.

Grandma Helen Heilicki, who lived near Philadelphia, could be a difficult and domineering woman. Before she met her husband, Harry, she had been a dancer and a fashion model. Widowed now, she still carried herself with what Sarah's mother tactfully referred to as "flair." Although her figure reflected her total surrender to a passion for cakes and chocolates, in her own mind apparently she was still a coquette. Over her voluminous hips she wore skirts that showed off plenty of leg. And to conceal her too wide feet, she insisted on wearing shoes that were a size too small, with the result that most of the time she was hardly able to walk.

None of this mattered to Sarah, however. On the contrary, she enjoyed Gran's quirks and foibles, even admired them. For Gran always seemed to say and do exactly as she pleased, in a way that Sarah had never felt free to do. Gran, for her part, delighted in being part of Sarah's life, as if through Sarah she were somehow reliving her own youth. They shared a special bond, the two of them, and to Sarah there was never any doubt that she could always count on Gran to be there for her.

Today they talked for over an hour, Gran listening, encouraging, offering advice. Talking to Gran finally gave Sarah the strength she needed to make the call she had been putting off all morning, to Jovan's adviser at the university.

"Try and find out if he knew anything ahead of time about Jovan's intentions," Ted had instructed her. "And while you're at it, see if he knows anything about the status of Jovan's degree."

Now, buoyed by Gran's call, she dialed the university. And somehow managed to speak clearly to the professor, a Dr. Knight.

"HE WAS SURPRISED WHEN I told him that Jovan was gone," she reported to her parents that evening over dinner. "He said Jovan was supposed to have come in to see him the day after Labor Day to talk about job prospects. But he didn't show up and nobody knew where he was. The other thing Dr. Knight told me was that Jovan handed in his dissertation last month and had his orals last week. He finished his work. He's just waiting for his grade and then he'll get his diploma."

Ted set a forkful of salad down. He was suddenly alert. "You mean he doesn't have the diploma yet?"

Sarah shrugged. "No. I guess it'll be mailed to him."

"Exactly what I was thinking," Ted said. "That diploma might be just the weapon we're looking for. If we can stop the university from sending it to him, it might give us some leverage. If we can get that diploma, we can arrange it so that Jovan has to come to us for it. Then we trade. He gets his diploma if we get Joey."

Sarah exchanged glances with her mother. So it was blackmail! Her father was talking about doing the same thing to Jovan that Jovan had done to her. And the amazing thing was that Sarah realized she didn't mind a bit.

On Friday morning Ted and Sarah drove to New York, where Ted was to meet with Steven Kobelec, the head of the Yugoslav-American trade office. They left home early so that they'd have time to stop at the university on the way.

Once there, they found the office of Martin Zinkler, the university's chief counsel. He was a man of late middle age, with a gaunt face, and rimless spectacles perched on the end of his long nose.

"I doubt that there is any legal precedent for withholding a student's degree on the grounds you're suggesting," Zinkler told them after Ted had explained the situation. "As far as the university is concerned, a student's personal life really has no bearing upon his or her academic standing."

"I see," said Ted, not bothering to hide his disappointment. "But look, there is one thing maybe you could help us with."

"Yes? What's that?"

"Let us have a list of the university's board of trustees. There might be someone on the list I know."

"Going to pull a few strings, is that it?"

"Something like that."

Zinkler shook his head. "I'm sorry, but I really cannot condone that kind of intrusion into the university's affairs."

"No, of course not. It's just that—"

"The answer is no, Mr. Novack. Now, if you will excuse me . . ."

Ted let out a deep breath. Clearly there was no point in arguing. Zinkler was about to show Ted and Sarah the door when his telephone rang.

"We'll find our way out," Ted said.

They stepped into the reception area, where Zinkler's secretary was busy at her typewriter. By the lighted button on her telephone console, Ted could see that her boss was still on the phone. It gave him an idea.

"Excuse me, miss," Ted said. "Mr. Zinkler told me I could have a list of the university's board of trustees. I forgot to get it from him before I left. Would you have a copy by any chance?"

The young woman hesitated. "Well, yes, I do. But I don't know if I—"

"Oh, it's perfectly all right. Marty was going to give it to me himself, but we both got so involved, it just slipped our minds."

"Well . . . I guess if Mr. Zinkler said so. . . ."

Ted left with the list tucked inside his sport coat. As he hurried down the corridor and out into the street, Sarah had to run to keep up with him. When they were in the car, he unfolded the paper.

"Now let's see what we've got," he said. He scanned the paper's contents. Halfway down the list he stopped. "Here we are; just what I was looking for."

The name he had come to was that of Charles Kogan, a senior vice president of one of the world's largest banks. Ted had known Kogan for years, ever since the two of them had worked together on a fund-raiser for the Sommerton Lion's Club.

"What can he do?" Sarah asked.

"Put pressure on the university to withhold the diploma."

"Are you going to call him?"

"Later." He tucked away the list and started the car. "Right now we've got to get downtown."

By the time Ted negotiated the city traffic and found a place to park in the garage of the World Trade Center, he was already five minutes late for his appointment with the head of the Yugoslav-American Trade Association.

"You go ahead," Sarah said as they hurried through the lobby. "I'll wait for you down here in the coffee shop."

"Have it your way." Ted headed for the elevator.

Steven Kobelec had a corner office on the forty-sixth floor. To judge from the setting and the room's luxurious furnishings—all sleek wood and muted fabrics—trade relations between Yugoslavia and the United States were going very well indeed.

"I have grandchildren of my own," Kobelec said as he ushered Ted in and offered him a seat. "I can imagine what you must be going through and I sympathize."

A man of considerable girth, Kobelec leaned forward in his chair and folded his pudgy hands across his belly. "But Mr. Novack, allow me to be frank with you. To imagine that any business concern is going to jeopardize its profits for the sake of a purely personal matter such as this— Well, you're a businessman yourself. I'm sure you understand my position."

"Oh, yes. I understand completely. Business first, isn't that the way it goes? Well, that's not the way *I* do business. In my book it's people that come first. Always have and always will." Ted got to his feet. "Thanks for taking the time to see me." He turned and started for the door.

"Just a minute. Please." Kobelec lifted himself from his chair. "Before you go storming out, I'd like to make one suggestion."

Ted waited, his hand on the doorknob. "I'm listening."

Kobelec's grave voice was low, confidential. "I would suggest that you find yourself a lawyer in Yugoslavia. I give you this advice," he said, "because I suspect that eventually your daughter is going to have to go to Belgrade and work out some arrangement with her husband through the Yugoslav courts."

THAT evening Sarah telephoned Jovan's number in Belgrade. She couldn't help herself. She had to talk to Joey again. She had to let him know that she had not abandoned him.

"Joey? Hello, it's Mama," she said when he came to the phone.

"Hello, M-Mama." His sweet small voice sounded so strange over the six thousand miles of telephone cable.

"How are you, lovey?" She tried hard to sound calm, casual, tried to control the tremor in her voice.

"I'm f-fine, Mama. . . . M-Mama, I m-miss you."

"I miss you, too, Joey. And Gramma and Grampa send their love, too. Did you get the package I sent? Did you get Mr. Monkey?"

"Yes."

"Now you've got Mr. Monkey to keep you company. Did you notice I fixed his mouth and his eye? He's just like new."

Silence, then an odd sound—a kind of moan—and she could hear him sobbing.

"Joey, what is it? Don't cry. Tell me what's the matter."

"I want you, Mama. I don't want Mr. M-Monkey. I want you."

She felt a stone shift in her chest. "Oh, Joey. Don't cry. Please don't cry." But she was crying herself now.

"Please come, Mama. Will you c-come?"

Why did I call? she thought. Why did I stir it all up again? But I had to. He has to know I'm here. He mustn't forget.

She wiped her eyes with the back of her hand. "I don't know when I can come. I'll have to see. I'll—"

"Sarah, you are coming?" It was Jovan's voice. He must have pulled the phone away from Joey. "Are you really coming?"

"Where's Joey? I want to talk to Joey."

"He's too upset now. He's crying again, like last time. See what you do when you talk to him? You turn him into a crybaby."

"He's only five years old. Please. Bring him back."

"So he can live in America? So you can turn him against me, you and your father? No, Sarah. That is finished. Joey is going to live here now. You want to see him, you come here."

"Jovan—" she pleaded.

He cut her off. "No. You have had your turn. Now it is my turn. *Mine.* I tell you something. My father went away to fight when I was the same age as Joey is now. I told you once. You remember? He never came back and I never saw him again. Now for my son it will be different. Joey will have his father. Do you hear me, Sarah? *My son will have his father!*"

SIX

On Saturday, September 11, Sarah drove to Yonkers with her parents to close up Jovan's apartment.

"Maybe we'll find something we can use against him if we have to go to court," her father had said on the drive up the turnpike. Now he was busy at the desk, opening drawers and leafing through the papers Jovan had left behind. They had already ascertained that the photo album was gone, all those pictures of Joey that Sarah had pasted in so carefully.

"There," her mother said, folding down the flaps on a carton. "That's about it for the books." She surveyed the living room. "What about the paintings?"

"Give them to Niki," Sarah said.

Niki Djordjevic was the building superintendent. By an odd coincidence, he was another displaced Yugoslav. He was also a sharp operator when it came to making a dollar on other people's castoffs. Old furniture, appliances, rugs—everything had a way of ending up in Niki's storage area in the cellar, to be sold off to any tenant willing to pay his price.

WHEN Sarah and Jovan moved into the apartment in the spring of 1968, they had already been married for over a year. Jovan had passed his final exams at the Sorbonne in December 1967 and had agreed to try living in America, where he thought it might be easier to get a job. First they had stayed in her old bedroom in her parents' house, and within a short time Sarah had landed a job as a substitute teacher in the Sommerton public schools. But finding something for Jovan proved more difficult, especially since he seemed to be having such a hard time adapting to his new world.

When he finally did find work—as a lab technician at a small pharmaceutical company in New York City—it was far from the exciting research work he had envisioned for himself. He spent his days running tests on pills and medicines, making sure they came up to legal standards. Still, it was about as much as he could hope for without an advanced degree and a better command of English. And it was a beginning, as Sarah hastened to remind him; it enabled them to get a place of their own. And that was something!

True, the apartment in Yonkers was no more than an impersonal set of rooms in a featureless high rise. But it was cheap, it was close to the city, and it was theirs. As soon as they moved in, Sarah set about trying to give the apartment some of the homeyness it lacked. She found cheerful blue-flowered curtains for the kitchen and hung spider plants in the window over the sink. The dining-room table and chairs were a housewarming present from Gran, and to liven up the living room Sarah bought some pretty fabric and made draperies for the windows.

And yet none of her efforts added up somehow. The books on the shelves, the Serbian folk music on the stereo—most of it was Jovan's, and in a language of which she knew only fragments, as if Jovan were building himself a refuge from an alien and seemingly hostile world. The trouble was, while shutting out the world around him, Jovan was also shutting her out of his life.

One evening Sarah pleaded with him, "Don't close me out. This is Sarah. Your wife. I love you and I want you to be happy."

Suddenly misty-eyed, he put an arm around her and kissed her. "You are my only friend," he said, stroking her hair tenderly.

Yet nothing changed. The longer he was in America, the more he seemed to isolate himself. His friends—the few he had—were fellow Serbs whom he had met at the Yugoslav consulate down-town, where he sometimes went to read Serbian magazines and to attend concerts and lectures. He made it plain early on that he was not interested in spending time with her friends, who were mostly colleagues from the Yonkers high school where she was now a teaching assistant. When she did invite someone over, he would spend the evening closed up like a clam.

The single exception to this rule were the Markovics, Elena and Marko, who were welcome at any time. Elena was a teacher at Sarah's school; Marko was a doctor. Together they had emigrated from Yugoslavia and together they had achieved the kind of professional and material success that Jovan aspired to. They drove a Mercedes and owned their own apartment. But most important, they had offered their friendship at a time when Sarah and Jovan were very much in need of friends.

To Sarah, Elena was an especially rare kind of friend, because she alone understood what Sarah was up against with Jovan.

"You must only be patient," Elena told her one afternoon over tea. "We all sometimes miss the old country. But it passes. Wait. Give him time. He will become used to the life here."

Sarah hoped Elena was right.

In the spring of 1970 Sarah discovered that she was pregnant. The prospect was frightening. Most of the time it was all she could do to take care of Jovan's and her needs. Besides, they had come to rely on her paycheck as a supplement to his meager income; she wasn't sure they could get by without it. Still, she *wanted* this child. It was a new life, a part of herself. And she would love it and care for it, and maybe, just maybe, it would fill the empty longing inside her.

"A son!" Jovan rejoiced when she told him the news. "I am going to have a son!" He immediately ran to the kitchen, poured a glass of slivovitz, and made a toast. "To my son," he said, and drank it down in one gulp.

She laughed. "It might be a girl. There are no guarantees."

"No, it will be a son. I am sure of it." He came and kissed her. "Today you have made me the happiest man alive."

"I'm glad," she said.

Jovan telephoned his mother in Belgrade immediately with the news. Sarah waited until after five, when the phone rates were lower, and then called New Jersey to tell her parents. They were delighted. The baby would be their first grandchild.

Planning ahead, Sarah's parents offered to hire a nurse to help her at home during the first few weeks after the baby was born. But Jovan refused to consider any such arrangement. "I will not have a stranger in my house," he stormed. If Sarah needed help, his mother would come and stay for a few weeks.

"But that's impossible," Sarah said. "We've only got one bedroom. Where will she sleep?"

"I will talk to Niki Djordjevic. Niki always has something. Maybe an extra bed we can buy. We will manage for short time."

So it was arranged. The money Sarah's parents would have spent on a nurse would go instead to pay for bringing Jovan's mother to the States. And Niki, as hoped, came up with someone's cast-off convertible sofa.

Jovan was happier than Sarah had seen him in months. His mother would be coming, and his child, his son, was on the way! Finally something was going right for him.

SARAH's labor pains began two days early. It was the middle of the afternoon and she was home alone. She telephoned the lab, but Jovan was unavailable. She left a message for him, then called a taxi to take her to the hospital.

She was in labor for seventeen hours. And she was alone. Where was Jovan? She had no idea.

But somewhere during a lull in the cycle of pain, he appeared. He stood at the door to her room, looking frightened, as pale green as the wall. It was clear that he did not want to be there. She was about to tell him how happy she was to see him when another wave of pain engulfed her. Jovan turned white and hurried from the room.

Later, under the bright lights of the delivery room, when the baby was finally born, Sarah was too exhausted to feel anything but relief and an all-consuming desire to sleep. Except that there was an elation, too, a sense of triumph. She had done it! She had overcome fear and pain and had brought a son into the world, healthy and alive. She had found a strength she did not know she had.

The next day her parents came to the hospital to see their grandson. Jovan and his mother were already there.

And Joey. Twisting and turning, he kept wriggling out of his blankets and peering vaguely at the world around him. The hair on his head was no more than a light brown haze, and his pink fists waved in the air.

Watching him from the nursery window, unable to take her eyes off him, Sarah wanted to fix him in her mind forever, just the way he was now, so pink and healthy and new, still so full of—
possibilities.

Jovan grinned and hugged his mother.

Sarah's father smiled. "He's going to be trouble, that one."

"He's beautiful," said her mother, her eyes glistening.

She put her arms around Sarah and hugged her, and Sarah remembered later that for that brief moment they were all happier together than they had ever been.

The moment passed almost at once, for it was just then that Jovan announced that he had paid a visit to the Yugoslav consulate that very morning and had obtained a Yugoslav birth certificate for Joey. He repeated it for his mother in Serbo-Croatian and was rewarded with a shriek of delight and a kiss.

"I don't understand," said Sarah's father. "He'll have a New York birth certificate. Why does he need one from Yugoslavia?"

"Why?" Jovan looked surprised. "He is my son! He is Yugoslav!"

"Partly he is," Ted corrected with an indulgent smile.

"A birth certificate makes it official." Jovan thrust out his chin.

Sarah saw the smile fade from her father's face. "Wait a minute," he said. "Are you telling me you've made Joey a citizen of Yugoslavia?"

"Of course. Yes." Jovan said it proudly.

Ted scowled. Anxiously Sarah sought to reassure him. "I think it's supposed to be like a gift to his mother," she said.

Ted looked at her, then at Jovan's mother, then at Jovan again. "But why?" he asked.

"Why not?" Jovan shot back. "He *is* citizen. He is my son."

HER recovery was difficult. She could never seem to get enough sleep in the hospital. She couldn't wait to get home to her own room, her own bed.

But when she finally got home, the crib was set up in the living room and Jovan's mother had taken up residence in the bedroom.

"And just where are we supposed to sleep?" Sarah protested in whispers in the kitchen. "The sofa was going to be for her."

"What an idea! She is the guest. She must have the bed."

"But with the baby—"

They were interrupted by his mother's husky voice calling to him from the next room. She sang out, *"Gde ste vi,* Jovan?" (Where are you?)

He poked his head around the corner. "I am here, Mother." Jovan turned back to Sarah. "It will be all right," he said. "It is better she has her own room to be in. Now, be a good wife and make us coffee and do not talk more about this thing. The way it is, is the way it is going to be."

Sarah was able to put up with it for a total of four days. How she managed that long, she had no idea. With the crowding in the apartment, the lack of privacy, and the baby waking up every two hours in the night, she was more exhausted than ever. And Jovan's mother—or Baka, as she wanted to be called now that she was a grandmother—did little but complain of being ignored and neglected. Had she forgotten that she had been invited to help, not to be waited on?

Some nights when the baby began crying, there the old woman would be, wrapped in Jovan's bathrobe, nudging Sarah awake.

"Get up. Your baby is crying, don't you hear? Your baby is hungry. How can you lie there like that, you lazy thing, and not go to him? What kind of mother are you, eh? Get up! Get up!"

There was no relief. The old woman never went out. In the evenings, when Jovan was home, the two of them would sit huddled together on the sofa, mother and son, chattering away in Serbo-Croatian, totally ignoring Sarah and the baby. If Sarah had earlier felt like an intruder in her own house, she felt even more so now.

"Jovan, don't you see what's happening to us?" she whispered to him one night when they lay awake on the sofa bed. "I have no place here anymore. Everything is for her now. When it's not Joey, it's her I have to cook for and clean for and make room for."

"Yes? And what am I to do? Send her away?"

"Would you, Jovan? Please? For me? For us? It's you and me I care about."

"No. I will not. She is my mother. She will stay in my house as long as she wants."

"Then I will go. I mean it. If she doesn't go soon, I will."

He laughed contemptuously. "Do not talk such foolishness."

Sarah left the next morning, after Jovan went off to the lab and while Baka was still in bed. Taking Joey with her, she got in the car and drove to Sommerton.

As soon as Jovan heard she was gone, he called, full of apologies. "I love you. Please come back. I need you." Her leaving had shaken him badly. He had never imagined she would do it.

But Sarah refused to give in. Not until two days later, when he called to assure her that his mother was gone, did Sarah return.

Jovan made a big show of welcoming her and Joey back. But the damage was done. From that time on there existed between them a depth of bitterness and mistrust that was never overcome. Sarah had forced him to choose. She had forced him to plead, even to beg. And for that she would not easily be forgiven.

"Look at this!" exclaimed Sarah's father. "Here's another one. That makes two thousand six hundred and fifty-five dollars worth of parking tickets in less than a year."

The contents of Jovan's desk drawers were mostly overdue bills: telephone, electricity, and credit card. But there were also dozens of unpaid parking fines and unanswered summonses.

Her mother went to look. "That's incredible," she said. "How did he get away with it for so long?"

Sarah shrank farther into the sofa, where she had been sitting for the last two hours. Each new bill was like a slap in her face. But her father was positively gloating in triumph. To him the overdue bills and summonses would be an important advantage if they ever succeeded in taking Jovan to court. Clear evidence of a disreputable character, the lawyers would call it.

Still, a few minutes later, when he turned up a different kind of paper, Sarah herself felt a twinge of excitement. The paper was a notice of default on a student loan for twenty-five thousand dollars, issued to Jovan through the university by the National Institutes of Health.

"What if we try making a bargain with Jovan?" she offered.

"What kind of bargain?" Ted asked.

"If the university decides not to give him the diploma until his loan is paid off," she said tentatively, "maybe we could—"

"Pay off the loan if he gives Joey back?" her father interrupted.

"That's crazy," her mother said. "Where are we going to get twenty-five thousand dollars?"

"We'd pay it in installments." Ted turned to Sarah, beaming. "You know," he said, "you're one clever cookie."

Sarah smiled. "I'm glad you noticed."

ZAGREB: Saturday, April 23, 5:15 a.m.

How Wilkes was managing to stay awake, Sarah had no idea. She did not even try to keep her eyes open. Speeding toward Zagreb in the early morning hours, they had the highway almost to themselves, and Sarah drifted into a fitful sleep.

She came out of it when she felt the car rolling to a stop. It was just before dawn. In the east the sky was turning a milky gray.

"Here we are," Wilkes said.

Sarah, still half asleep, peered out the window and saw that they were in a parking lot in front of the passenger terminal of Zagreb Airport. For a moment she had to stop and think what they were doing here. But then she remembered. They'd come to put Adam Hardy and his parents on a plane.

Wilkes got out and helped the Hardys with their bags. Then he led them toward the terminal. He was back ten minutes later to get Sarah and her father.

"The coast is clear," he said. "If there is an alert out for us, it's not evident here."

As he tended to do, he addressed himself to her father exclusively. To Sarah he paid no attention whatever, except to absent-mindedly hold open the door to the terminal for her.

"I got the Hardys on a flight to Rome," he told Ted as he led the way through the lobby. "From there they'll go to Madrid for their holiday. They board their plane in forty-five minutes."

Sarah said, "Do we wait and see them off?"

Wilkes spared her hardly a glance. "That's the idea."

What was it with this man? Why did he dislike her so? Or was it just the way he treated all women? Sarah pitied whoever had married him. Someone had. He wore a wedding band.

When it was time for the Hardys' flight to begin boarding, Sarah, her father, and Wilkes were at the gate to see them off. They all shook hands warmly, as Wilkes had directed. The two women embraced. If any policemen were watching, they were getting the show that Wilkes had intended: a typical farewell among good friends.

"Aren't you coming with us?" little Adam asked Wilkes.

"I'm afraid not, son. I've got some things to do here." His voice was so tender, so full of warmth, that it took Sarah by surprise. For the first time she wondered if he had children of his own.

The boy looked up at Sarah with his big eyes, then turned back to Wilkes. "Is the nice lady coming with us?"

Sarah was touched. "I have to go with Mr. Wilkes," she said, giving him a hug. "I hope you have a nice time in Spain."

"I will."

"It was fun playing make-believe with you last night. You did a really good job."

He grinned, gave her a quick kiss, then went with his mother toward the gate. But a moment later he turned and ran back to Sarah. "I hope you get your little boy back," he said earnestly.

She felt a sudden catch in her throat. So he had known all along what the game was about. "Thank you, Adam," she said. "I hope so, too."

SEVEN

WHEN the alarm went off, Ted opened an eye, peered at the clock's glowing digits: 7:16 a.m. Time to get moving. Lots to do. Paperwork to catch up on, calls to make . . .

Still he lay there, weighted down, his temples throbbing with the beginnings of a headache. And he felt a tightness in his lower back that hadn't been there the day before. Have to watch it, he told himself. Can't afford to get sick now. Not when there was so much to do and so many people counting on him.

As soon as Ted got to his office he telephoned the dean of Jovan's university. Jovan had defaulted on his loan; surely the university would not want to send him his diploma before he had fulfilled his financial obligations. To Ted's disappointment, however, this argument cut no ice. "When was the notice dated?" the dean asked.

"August third."

"Mr. Stefanovic could very well have cleared it up since then. All that is usually required in such cases is that the student resume making payments on the loan. In certain cases a simple written statement of good faith is sufficient."

"Well, did he make such a payment? Or submit a statement?"

"I have no idea," the man replied dryly. "But even if I did, I would not be free to divulge that information. The financial status of our students is a matter of strict confidentiality."

That's what you think, Ted thought as he slammed down the phone. There were ways of prying information loose. For starters he'd have Sarah's lawyer subpoena the university's records.

First, though, he'd have to do something about the headache that was continuing to plague him. That and the tightness in his lower back. He went and took a couple of aspirin.

Later that afternoon he and Sarah drove to her old Yonkers post office. The idea had been Emma's; perhaps they could intercept the diploma in the mail. Since Sarah was still officially Mrs. Stefanovic, she might be able to have Jovan's mail forwarded to her in Sommerton.

Sarah had been doubtful. "I just hope we're not too late. He may already have had his mail forwarded."

Talking to the woman behind the post-office counter, she and Ted found that Jovan had done exactly that.

But Sarah wasn't through. "Can you tell us the forwarding address, please?" she asked the woman.

"Same address but a different apartment number."

Sarah looked at the card. She could not have been more astonished. The name was that of Niki Djordjevic, the superintendent of the building where she and Jovan had lived.

Sarah turned to her father. "I thought he told you he didn't know anything."

Ted glowered. "Obviously he was lying."

"But why?"

"That's what I'd like to find out. Come on."

Half an hour later they were winding their way through the dimly lit cellar of the apartment building. Everywhere were piles of old furniture. They found the man himself back in a corner, gluing a leg on a battered old dining-room chair.

"Jovan Stefanovic is my friend," he told them defiantly when Ted confronted him with the evidence of his deceit. "My friend asks me as favor to say I know nothing. I say I know nothing."

"I'm sure your loyalty is commendable," Ted said. "But now that you've fulfilled your obligation, maybe you can help us by answering some questions."

Niki shook his head. "I do not have time to answer questions."

But the sight of a twenty-dollar bill in Ted's hand changed his mind. Yes, he told them, he had sent Jovan some mail. Yes, there had been a large envelope from the university; Jovan had asked him to watch especially for it. "I sent it right away. It is the favor he asks of his friend Niki."

So, they were too late. The diploma was already gone. They had been robbed of their only weapon before they even had a chance to get their hands on it.

"I guess there's no point in trying to subpoena the university's records now," Emma said gloomily as she sat over coffee that evening with Ted and Sarah.

"No," Ted said. "There's no point."

"I guess Jovan's got everything he wants." Emma sighed.

Ted reached out a hand to her. "No, not quite."

She looked puzzled. "What do you mean?"

"He hasn't got Sarah." He nodded in their daughter's direction.

"That's true," Sarah said quietly. "The trouble is, Joey doesn't have me either."

WHILE phone calls and letters were going back and forth, Ted's headaches and the pain in his back were getting progressively worse. Finally one afternoon he called his doctor, Ben Larkin.

"Sounds like stress," said Larkin. "I'll phone in a prescription for a painkiller. In the meantime, try to get more rest and take it easy."

Take it easy! Ted almost laughed out loud.

The next day he went to his office early to catch up on his paperwork. He had just sat down at his desk when suddenly he felt a stab of pain in his spine. Doubled over, he managed to hobble out to the watercooler, where he downed one of Larkin's painkillers. Then, thinking to further ease the pain, he lowered himself carefully to the floor in his office and stretched out full length on his back.

The telephone rang on the desk above him, and then everything went dark.

SARAH and her mother arrived at the hospital ten minutes after the ambulance brought Ted in. They had been told only that he was unconscious and that tests were being conducted to find out what was wrong.

The wait was interminable. After what seemed like hours, Dr. Larkin finally came to see them, a surgical mask dangling from his neck. As if through a fog, Sarah heard the diagnosis: "Spinal meningitis . . . bacterial variety . . . unpredictable . . . touch and go for the next twenty-four hours. . . ."

With a low moan Emma sagged against Sarah's shoulder. Numbly Sarah put a protective arm around her.

"When can I see him?" her mother asked. "I want to see him."

The doctor did not try to discourage her. "He's still in quarantine, so I can't let you into his room. You'll have to look in from outside his door."

"Just so I can see him."

Dr. Larkin led them through a door labeled INTENSIVE CARE and down a hall. At room 317 he stopped. The door was closed, but it had a glass window in it. Inside, Ted lay as pale and still as a corpse. There was a tube running up into his nose and another taped to his wrist. A third led from a nearby machine to somewhere under the covers, chest high.

"His body signs have stabilized," the doctor was saying. "That's a good sign, but it's going to take a while before we know anything definite. The best thing you can do now is go home and get some rest. If there's any change, we'll call you immediately."

Shaken and depressed, Sarah and her mother drove back to the house, silent except for Emma's quiet weeping.

At home, Sarah helped her mother prepare a light supper and sat with her for a while before seeing her off to bed. Afterward she sat alone at the kitchen table, sipping coffee and leafing aimlessly through the piles of notes made over the last few weeks: notes scrawled on legal pads in her father's broad, confident hand; tallies of people called, leads followed. Useless now because only her father knew how all the pieces went together.

What would happen if he didn't get better? she wondered. What would happen to her? To Joey?

O God, she prayed, please help him. Please help all of us.

It was two days before Sarah's father was removed from quarantine and pronounced out of danger.

"It's a good thing we got him here when we did," Dr. Larkin told Sarah and her mother in the corridor on the way to Ted's room. "The infection was starting to move up his spine. If it had reached his brain, it would almost certainly have been fatal. Fortunately, he kept himself in good shape. That's going to help a lot in his recovery."

"How long will it take?" Sarah asked.

"It's not the kind of thing that can be hurried," Larkin replied. "Complete recovery could take four or five months."

Sarah's heart sank. Months! Not weeks but months! Her father had to get well. That was the important thing. Joey, everything, would just have to wait now. Except, how could it? How could she put Joey out of her mind for as long as that?

But Ted improved steadily, and by the end of the week he was sitting up in bed and was well enough to carry on a whispered conversation. Sarah and her mother visited him every day. Sarah's brother, Richard, flew in for a few days from California, where he was now in college; and Grandma Helen also came to pay a visit.

After Gran left, Sarah's father turned to her with a mischievous gleam in his eye. "What did Larkin say was the normal recovery time for meningitis? Four or five months, wasn't it?"

"About that."

"See if he'll stretch it to six."

"Ted!" Emma looked appalled. "What a thing to say!"

"Look, if we can stretch this thing out long enough, I'll have just that much more time to concentrate on getting Joey back without having to worry about the office, too."

Sarah felt tears of gratitude welling up. Despite everything that he had been through, he hadn't stopped thinking about Joey.

"What you need to spend time doing is getting rest and getting better," Emma told Ted.

Sarah followed her mother's lead. "That's right, Dad. The main thing is for you to get well. I've canceled all your appointments, and there's nothing for you to do now but rest and take it easy."

Suddenly he looked alarmed. "You didn't cancel the trip to Washington, did you?" he whispered hoarsely.

Sarah took his hand. "Dad, that appointment with Colonel Stevenson was for two days ago. There was no way you were going to make it. All that is just going to have to wait for now."

He gripped her hand hard. "No," he whispered. "It can't wait. I want you to make that appointment again. If I can't get there myself, then you two are going to have to go in my place."

"I'm not leaving you," said Emma.

"That's ridiculous," Ted said. "There's nothing you can do for me while I'm in the hospital."

Sarah had been struggling against doing what she knew she must do. But now she had made up her mind. "Don't worry, Dad," she said. "I'll go down there myself. I'll see Stevenson."

Both of them stared at her.

"Are you sure you're up to it, dear?" her mother asked.

She wasn't, but she lied and said she was. "Anyway, Dad, you certainly don't need both of us here to look after you. And this way we won't have to wait until you get better."

He squeezed her hand. Tears flooded the corners of his eyes. "Thank you, Sarah," he said. "You've just made me very happy."

THE OFFICES OF STEVENSON, Davis, Russell & McLean were located on the top floor of an elegant gray stone office building in downtown Washington, less than a block from the White House.

"Colonel Stevenson will see you in a few moments," the receptionist said softly. "Won't you make yourselves comfortable." With a wave of a well-manicured hand she directed Sarah and Grandma Helen toward a deep plush sofa.

Gran's loud "Thank you, dear" made Sarah wince. Although she had been fully prepared to make this trip on her own, Sarah had been relieved and grateful when Gran had offered to come along and keep her company. But amid all this muted elegance, Gran's irrepressible "flair" was decidedly out of place.

"The colonel will see you now," purred the receptionist at last.

"It's about time," Gran declared, hoisting herself to her feet.

Following the receptionist, Sarah and Gran passed along a carpeted hallway, then through a pair of massive walnut doors, which opened into a high-ceilinged room that looked like a richly paneled library in a stately home. Heavy draperies framed the rain-streaked windows. In the center of the room a polished walnut conference table gleamed softly.

Before they could take it all in, a side door swung open and through it strode a lean gray-haired man, his hand outstretched.

"Sorry to have kept you waiting, ladies. I'm George Stevenson. Welcome to Washington."

The man's voice, deep and mellow, slid mellifluously in a soft southern accent. "I'm sorry we couldn't arrange better weather for your visit," he drawled. "Early October is usually the most beautiful time of year for us. Have a seat, won't you?"

With a languid wave he indicated the leather-backed chairs around the conference table. "May I provide you with some refreshments? Coffee, perhaps?"

"Yes, thank you," said Sarah for both of them. Gran was still preoccupied with the elegant furnishings.

The colonel stepped to a side table, where he poured coffee from a gleaming silver pot into two delicate china cups. Just then a door opened behind them.

"Ah," said the colonel. "Here's Bill. Come in, Bill. Come in."

Turning to follow the colonel's gaze, Sarah found herself facing an earnest-looking man who was carrying a manila folder.

"Ladies, may I present my colleague, Bill Borden. Bill, this is Mrs. Sarah Stefanovic and her grandmother, Mrs. Helen Heilicki."

"How do you do," Borden said, giving a little bow. He had fair hair and serious gray eyes. And he was considerably younger than the colonel—probably in his late forties, Sarah guessed.

"Bill will be handling your case, if you decide to come with us," the colonel said.

Sarah was puzzled. "I'm sorry, Colonel Stevenson, but I don't understand. I thought you would be representing us."

Borden cleared his throat. "There are, ah, a number of partners in the firm, Mrs. Stefanovic," he explained patiently. "Each of us takes on different kinds of cases. However, each of us has the full services of the firm at our disposal."

"You will be in excellent hands with Bill, I can assure you," the colonel said, smiling warmly. "Now, if you'll excuse me, I'll leave you people to get acquainted."

Sarah felt disappointed to see him go. She liked his stately manner, his grandfatherly charm.

"Wonderful old gentleman," Borden said as soon as his partner had left the room. "Brilliant lawyer. Of course he takes on only a few cases himself these days, but his name still carries a good deal of weight around Washington. With the colonel's help, there isn't anyone in this town we can't reach if we have to."

"If you're trying to impress us, Mr. Borden," Gran said, "you're certainly doing a good job of it."

Borden smiled for the first time. "As a matter of fact, I'm trying to do just that. I want both of you to know that we are prepared to bring considerable resources to bear on your behalf. Besides"—he turned to Sarah—"once I began reading the background material on this heartbreaking case, I discovered that I very much wanted to do whatever I could to help you get your boy back."

Sarah felt her uneasiness melting away. Somehow this man managed to be both personal and businesslike at the same time. The combination was reassuring.

Soon she found herself telling him her story. With Borden taking notes and Gran sitting quietly at her elbow, Sarah talked at length about how she and Jovan had met and how he had courted her; about how she had finally agreed to marry him; about coming with him to live in America; and how, since that time, she could remember only one brief period when she and Jovan had been really happy.

It was 1971, the year just after Joey was born. Jovan had not forgotten that Sarah had walked out on him. But as the weeks passed, he seemed anxious to make a fresh start. He bought toys for Joey and played with him on the living-room rug. He spent more time at home and was more attentive to her. He even began writing poetry again: verses about the delights of fatherhood and about the small miracle that was his son.

There was a new calmness in him, a sense of contentment that Sarah had never seen before. And when, during that summer, he received the news that he had been accepted at graduate school, in chemistry, he was ecstatic. The brilliant scientific career that he had envisioned for himself was finally about to begin.

"Everything will be good now," he told Sarah confidently.

Indeed, that summer he and Sarah were happier together than they had been since those first days in Paris. There were picnics, sunny afternoons at the beach, walks in the park with the downy-haired boy asleep in his stroller, one chubby fist lying open on his pillow like a blossoming rosebud.

But those special days ended abruptly in September, when classes began and Jovan discovered that the work load was far more demanding than he had imagined. And the linguistic subtleties Jovan encountered in the classroom and in his textbooks made his studies all the more frustrating. Between attending classes, reading, and doing research, he had hardly a free moment. Coming home in the evening, he would rush in like a freight train, grab a bite to eat, then bury himself in his books.

Sarah's nights became as empty as her days, with the routine of child care and house care unbroken by adult conversation. And Joey, who had so recently been Jovan's darling and delight, was now little more than an irritant in his life.

"Sarah, can't you make him stop that!" Jovan would demand if Joey's crying went on too long. "How can I think with him screaming like that!"

"We live here, too," Sarah would protest. But that only made Jovan angrier. After a while she simply retreated to the bedroom with the baby and closed the door behind her.

How they made it through that first academic year, Sarah had no idea. She was proud of Jovan's efforts, nonetheless. His success was her dream, too; she wanted it for him as badly as he did.

The school year was not yet over when Jovan's sister, Myra, sent word from Belgrade that Baka was seriously ill with pneumonia.

Jovan did not hesitate. "I must go to her."

"Of course," Sarah said, seeing the anxiety in his eyes. Then, hesitantly, "But where will you get the money?" The meager grants and loans that he had managed to obtain gave them hardly enough to buy groceries, let alone a plane ticket to Belgrade.

Jovan brushed the objection aside. "We can borrow from your father. He has plenty."

"You think he's rich or something? You're wrong. Anyway, I just borrowed from him to have the car fixed. I can't ask again."

"Then I will find someone else."

"But how will we pay it back?"

He flared up. "Enough! You think I can worry about a little money when my own mother is maybe dying?" His face contorted with rage. "A year and a half I do not see her. For you I send her away. And now you wish me not to go to her. No! I will go!"

Somehow—he never told her how—he found the money for the airfare. He packed a few clothes and a suitcase full of books.

Sarah drove him to the airport, then took Joey and went to stay with her parents.

When Jovan returned ten days later, he brought word that Baka was on the mend. She had begun to improve, it seemed, almost from the moment he'd appeared at her bedside.

"My sister was not believing the change. Like a miracle, she said."

"I'm really glad," said Sarah.

In the weeks that followed, however, it became clear that the trip to Belgrade had unsettled Jovan. He was more harried than ever. He seemed unsure of himself, discontented and disagreeable in a way that Sarah had not seen for a long time. And when he finally took his exams and then did poorly on them, he began to sink back into his old isolation. He would go out for long walks by himself and not come home for hours. Soon he started talking about going to Belgrade for another visit, this time taking Sarah and Joey with him.

"If you want to go, I guess you'll find a way," Sarah told him.

"But I'm not going with you and neither is Joey. We're already too deeply in debt."

"Excuses. It is only because you do not want to visit Baka and you do not want me to visit her. Go on, admit it. It is the truth."

"No. It is not."

But it was. She did not like what happened to him when he was with his mother. His last trip had undermined his independence, his confidence. If he saw Baka again, Sarah feared that he would come back to her even more divided and confused than ever.

So he made the trip alone: a three-week excursion fare, the cheapest he could find. As before, Sarah and Joey stayed with her parents while he was gone. It was better than staying alone in the apartment. At least in Sommerton Joey had a backyard to play in. Besides, it gave Sarah a break as well. She did not realize how much she enjoyed being home until the three weeks were almost over and she found herself dreading Jovan's return.

And she had reason to dread it, as she discovered when she went to pick him up at Kennedy Airport.

"Where is Joey?" he snapped as soon as he saw her.

"Joey's home with Mom and Dad," she told him. "They want us to have supper with them before we go home."

"Oh? And why do you not ask me first if this is okay?"

"I'm sorry, Jovan. I just thought—"

"You thought what you wanted, not what I wanted."

He kept at her all the way to Sommerton. It was as if he had been storing up his grievances for days. "You spend too much time with your parents," he complained. He was driving fast, jumping lanes, cutting in and out of traffic. "I do not like it. It is going to change. You are my wife; you will do things my way, not theirs. I will not be made a fool."

They sailed onto the Verrazano-Narrows Bridge doing seventy. Sarah dug her fingers into the armrest. "All right, Jovan. All right. Just slow down, please."

When they got to Sommerton, Sarah apologized to her parents for not staying for supper, and began getting ready to leave. She packed the last of Joey's things while Jovan took her suitcase out to the driveway. She said good-bye to her parents, then carried Joey outside and began buckling him into his car seat.

Jovan was behind her now, holding the door open. "Come on,

get in," he prodded. "I want to get home. I have work to do."

He had touched the wrong nerve. Into Sarah's mind leaped a single word: *no*.

She backed out of the car and turned to him. "No," she said.

Jovan looked surprised. "What do you mean, no?"

"I mean I'm not going back with you."

"What are you talking about?"

"Your work! Your needs! What about me? What about *us*? I can't do it anymore, Jovan. I won't."

His arm flew out and he grabbed her by the wrist. "You will do what I tell you to do," he snarled.

"Let go of me."

He squeezed her wrist hard now. His mouth was twisted into an ugly slash. His eyes flared dangerously. "You think I become like American husband and let my wife tell me what to do, eh?"

"Let go. You're hurting me."

"It is them. Your parents. They turn you against me."

"You're wrong. They have nothing to do with this."

"I should never let you come here. Get in the car. Now. Go on. Or I throw you in."

Twisting her arm up behind her, he tried to force her through the open door. But she jammed her free arm against the frame. "Stop it!" she shouted. "Let me go!"

In the back seat Joey began screaming.

Then from somewhere behind her came another sound, a throaty growl. "Take Joey and get in the house."

It was her father's voice. Suddenly the pressure on her arm was released and she was falling backward, catching herself in time to see her father pulling Jovan around and away from her. Jovan's fist came up. Ted blocked it. Then his own fist shot forward: a blow to the stomach that doubled Jovan over.

"No!" Sarah ran to her father, pulling him away. "Don't hit him again, Dad. Please don't hit him."

Behind her, her mother had pulled Joey out of his car seat and was running with him toward the house.

But now Jovan was up again and stumbling after her, fighting to wrench Joey from her arms. He was yelling like a crazy man. "Give him back! You can't have him. He's mine!"

Emma screamed, and then Ted was moving again, plowing into

Jovan shoulder first, sending him sprawling. This time Jovan did not try to get up.

"Get in the house, Sarah," Ted commanded again. "Go on."

Choking on tears, torn by shock and guilt and confusion, Sarah forced her legs to carry her up the steps and into the house.

"How long ago did that happen—Jovan's fight with your father?" Bill Borden asked her.

Sarah shrugged. "I don't know. Four years ago, I guess. Joey was one and a half. Almost two."

"And it was after that that you left your husband?"

"Oh, no."

"No?" the lawyer asked.

Sarah studied her hands. "I hoped things would get better."

"Did they?"

"For a while, yes."

Jovan had been as shocked and bewildered as any of them over what had happened that afternoon. He did not resist when Ted sent him home alone to cool off. And when he reappeared the next day, he brought apologies and gifts for each of them. In the days and weeks that followed, he went out of his way to make up for it.

But with the new academic year, the pressures began mounting all over again. He got behind on his research; inflation began cutting into his grants and loans, and there wasn't enough money to pay the bills. And so it went. The rows never again reached the point of physical violence, but they were destructive enough, poisoning what was left of love and trust.

What hurt Sarah most was seeing what their quarreling was doing to Joey: the fearful silence that came over him the instant he heard his father's key in the door; his stutter, which was always worse when Jovan was home. It made Sarah want to weep every time she heard that painful groping for words.

That, if nothing else, should have forced her to make a move. But still she did nothing.

"Why not?" Borden's voice was not unkind.

Sarah squirmed. "I—was afraid of the alternative."

"Which was?"

"Being alone. Admitting it was over. That I had failed."

"When did you decide you'd finally had enough?"

"Last year. Just before Christmas. When Jovan's mother came to live with us again."

Borden looked up from his notepad. He did not bother to conceal his astonishment.

"It was supposed to be temporary." Sarah rushed on, feeling suddenly defensive. "We needed someone to look after Joey. I was going to have to start looking for a job, you see. We needed the money. And Jovan was so insistent."

"About his mother coming, you mean?"

She nodded. "And I knew that having her there would give me a chance to get out and find a job."

"You sound as if you were looking forward to going to work."

"Oh, I was. I thought that if things got bad enough and I had to leave Jovan, at least I'd be able to support Joey and myself. I didn't want to have to go running home to my parents again."

"So having Jovan's mother there was good for you, too."

"Yes. I knew I couldn't move until I had a job, and I couldn't look for a job until I had someone to take care of Joey—"

"Excuse me," Gran interrupted, laying a hand on Sarah's arm, "but something just occurred to me. Maybe Jovan wanted his mother there as a kind of insurance policy. Baka was really the only person he could trust to look out for his interests once you went to work, which meant guarding Joey to make sure you wouldn't run off with him. He knew that if Baka was with Joey, he could count on you always coming home again."

"Is that right?" Borden prompted. "Joey was their hostage even then?"

Instead of answering, Sarah told him about the day last December when she was finally driven to leave Jovan for good. She had been in the bedroom while Joey slept, and was quietly talking on the phone to her father, who was urging her to come for a visit.

"It's been weeks since we've seen you and Joey," he was saying. "How about it, hon? I'll come and pick you up."

"I'd love to, Dad. So would Joey."

But Jovan had been listening on the living-room extension, and suddenly he was shouting into the phone. "Sarah stays here. You come near here, Ted, I will kill you. I have a knife, and I will use it if you make me. Stay away from here. I warn you."

"Jovan," she heard her father saying, "listen to yourself, son. You're talking crazy."

"You come near this place, I'll show you how crazy I get."

"Sarah," Ted shouted, "are you still there?"

"I'm here, Dad." But now Joey was up and crying beside her on the bed, clinging to her in terror at the sound of Jovan's rage, which came in loud and clear from down the hall. "Look, forget about us visiting for now, Dad," she told him. She was shaking so badly that she couldn't hold the phone still.

"Sarah!" Jovan shrieked. "Shut up and get off the phone."

But Sarah did not get off the phone. Something had just snapped, and she realized with a cold certainty that she had finally reached the end, that she was not going to take any more.

"Mama, Mama," Joey cried.

"Sarah! Do what I say!"

"Dad—"

"All right, honey," said Ted. "All right. I'll talk to you later."

Sarah had no sooner hung up than she heard Jovan slam down the phone in the other room and come storming down the hall toward the bedroom.

"You—" he was yelling. "You go plotting behind my back with him, I'll take care of you—"

But she leaped for the door and had it slammed and locked before he got there.

Jovan was livid. He cursed and shouted and pounded on the door. For one terrified moment she thought he was going to break it down. But finally he backed off.

"All right, you stay there!" he bellowed. "Stay there all day. And you better not come out while I'm gone. Because if you do, Baka will be here to take care of you."

He went away then, and for a while she heard him banging around in the living room, venting his rage to his mother, whose sympathetic murmurings were clearly audible in the bedroom. At last Sarah heard him go out, slamming the door behind him. She quietly picked up the phone and dialed her father.

"I'll be there as soon as I can," Ted said when she asked him— coolly, calmly—to come and take her and Joey home.

"Be careful," she warned. "He may have given Baka the knife."

While Sarah waited, she got the suitcases down from the closet

418

and packed clothes for herself and Joey. Eventually the doorbell rang. Cautiously she turned the bedroom lock.

"You stay here," she told Joey. "I'll be right back."

She stepped out into the hall and came around the corner just in time to see Baka backing away from the front door, a hand to her mouth in fright. In her other hand, waist high, was a long carving knife, its blade thrust before her.

And then Ted was coming through the door. In the corridor behind him stood two burly Yonkers policemen. The words Yugoslavia and police state leaped into Sarah's mind, and she realized that Baka must be terrified of the police.

"Come on, Sarah," her father said. "Let's get you and Joey out of this loony bin."

Quickly then, she told Bill Borden the rest of the story: Jovan's rage when he discovered that she had fled with Joey; her blind, foolish will to believe that she could still somehow make everything all right between them. They would remain separated, but she didn't want him to hate her forever, or take some revenge.

"Is that why you went along with his having visiting rights?"

"Yes, that. And, well, I wanted Joey to have a father. I also hoped— It was stupid, but I hoped that if I let Jovan see Joey whenever he wanted, he'd be satisfied. I guess I was wrong." She paused, took a deep breath. "Can you help me, Mr. Borden? Do you think we can get Joey back?"

The question seemed to surprise him. "Why, of course we'll get him back," he said. "I won't settle for anything less."

SARAH and her mother made the financial arrangements with Bill Borden the next afternoon—three thousand dollars as a down payment, with another three thousand to follow when he got Joey back. Two days later Borden called to let them know that he was already at work on their behalf.

"I just spoke with a friend over at State," he told Sarah. "About legal precedents in cases like this. Unfortunately, under the terms of America's treaty with Yugoslavia, civil cases are not subject to extradition. However, if we can prove that Jovan committed a felony, we might have a chance."

"He hasn't committed robbery or anything," said Sarah.

"No, but what about fraud? You mentioned something about

his having defaulted on a loan from the National Institutes of Health. I'd like to pursue that. Even if we can't get him extradited, the loan default will certainly help your case if you end up having to take him to court in Yugoslavia."

"Is that a possibility? Going to court, I mean?"

"Only as a last resort. I'm hoping we can avoid it."

"Well, what do we do instead?"

"We let him know that if he doesn't want to cooperate, he faces some pretty serious consequences. Prosecution for fraud. A suit for breach of contract for violating the custody agreement he made with you. I'm sure we can come up with a few more. That's why I'll need all your documents—anything relating to your separation, to Jovan's education, and to his debts."

"Yes, all right."

"I also want you to be prepared to go to Belgrade."

His words brought her up short. So, the time had finally come, as she knew it would.

"A surprising amount can be accomplished just by getting people to talk things out," he added. "Perhaps some compromise is possible. Joint custody, say, or some arrangement that would at least allow you to see your son. You could also sit down with a Yugoslav lawyer while you're there. . . ."

Sarah had stopped listening. Her mind was in turmoil. Belgrade would mean having to face Jovan again. But it would also mean seeing Joey! And *that* would be wonderful. To hold him, to be with him . . . Did she even dare to hope?

IN THE weeks that followed, Sarah spoke with Bill Borden two and three times a day, as he confirmed facts, gathered information, reported on his progress. One day he called to say that the United States embassy in Belgrade had sent the names of three Yugoslav lawyers; one of them, a man named Dimitri Dimitrivic, had studied law at Harvard and came highly recommended. "I suggest we work with him."

The day after that, Borden called with instructions for Sarah to apply for a family passport—one that would include a recent photograph of both herself and Joey. Did she have such a photograph? No? Then she should go to a camera shop and have them prepare a composite: a single photo made up of two separate photos, so that it looked as if she and Joey had posed together.

"Is that really necessary?" Sarah asked.

"If everything goes well in Belgrade and you manage to get Joey back from your husband, it will make it easier to get him out of the country. He won't be able to travel with you unless his name and picture appear on a valid passport."

"But what if I already have a passport for myself?"

"Tell them you lost it."

"You're c-coming, Mama? You're really c-coming?"

"Yes, Joey. I'm coming to visit you and Papa."

"Just to visit?"

"We'll make it a nice long visit, okay?"

"Yes, Mama," he said, but she could hear his disappointment. "Will you b-bring me Lionel and F-Fritz when you c-come, Mama? Mr. Monkey m-misses them."

"I'm sure he does, Joey."

Lionel and Fritz were Joey's bedtime playmates and sometime "pillow friends"—a cuddly pair of hand puppets made out of felt. One of them was a round-faced orange lion with a yellow mane, and the other was a gray pussycat.

"Sarah?" It was Jovan now. "When you come, bring him warm clothes. He has not enough, and it gets cold here soon."

She said she would.

"What time do you arrive? We'll meet you at the airport."

"No. . . . I mean, I'm not sure yet."

"When you are sure, then you will let me know."

"Yes. Yes, of course."

She hung up. Borden had told her to sit down with the lawyer first, before seeing Jovan. She couldn't let him meet her at the airport. She'd have to find some way of putting him off.

EIGHT

"The name Belgrade means white town. Did you know that?" Gran asked, without lifting her eyes from the guidebook. " 'The first fortified town was built there by the Celts in the fourth century B.C.' Imagine that, a city that's almost as old as I am!"

Once again Gran had offered to come along to keep Sarah company, and she was grateful beyond words. For Gran, the trip to Belgrade had been like a holiday right from the minute their plane took off. She had never been to Europe before and she was enjoying herself immensely. And now that they were only an hour away from landing, she was getting giddy with excitement.

Sarah appreciated the distraction. Without it, there would have been no escaping her anxiety about what lay ahead.

" 'Occupied by the Romans in the first century B.C.,' " Gran went on. " 'Destroyed by the Huns . . . captured by the Turks. . . .' My Lord, what a history! Can you believe it! 'Serbian rule since 1867 . . . bombed by the Nazis in 1941 . . . rose phoenixlike from the ashes to become the modern European city we see today. . . .' "

The city they saw when they were finally on the ground and speeding by bus toward their hotel was a city whose streets and buildings were blurred by a cold November drizzle. The trees lining the broad avenues were bare of leaves. In the gray light the rows of modern office blocks and high-rise apartments looked more desolate than Sarah remembered from the first time she had been here. But, of course, it had been spring then. The sun was out, the trees were green, and the flowers were in bloom.

Nine years ago that was. She and Jovan had just been married, and he had brought her to Belgrade to visit his mother and to see his homeland. It was their honeymoon trip. Belgrade had been so beautiful that spring, and she had been so very much in love.

Now, nine years later, hardly anything looked the same.

THE Metropol, the hotel that she and Gran checked into, was described in the guidebook as the smartest in Belgrade. In actuality it was an impersonal white stone block that looked more like an office building than a hotel. The lobby was all polished marble, sleekly elegant and cold as ice. But the clerks were friendly enough, she thought as she and Gran followed the bellboy from the lobby. And Joey was somewhere very close now. Just a few miles from here.

Their room was on the seventh floor: double beds, a desk and an easy chair, and a window overlooking Tašmajdan Park. As soon as they were settled, Sarah picked up the telephone and called Baka's number. Jovan answered.

"Sarah, where are you? You sound so close."

"I am. I'm in Belgrade. At the Metropol."

"You are here? How does this happen? We are not expecting you until tomorrow. We were going to meet you at the airport."

"I—" She had to think of something. And quickly. "The airlines. There was a mix-up with the airlines."

Silence. Did he believe her? She had never been a good liar. She rushed on. "There was no time to call. But I'm here now. Can I come over later? I'd like to see Joey."

"Why later? Why not now?"

"I— It's four in the morning for us. We're still on New York time. I have to get some sleep." What she could not tell him was that she also had to follow Bill Borden's instructions; she had to see the lawyer first. "I'll come this evening. About five."

Sarah could hear muffled voices. He must be consulting with Baka. Finally he came back. "Yes. Good. Come at five."

DIMITRI Dimitrivic, Sarah's Yugoslav lawyer, was a small, elegant man in a neat white shirt and a blue silk tie. His English was only slightly accented, but he spoke so softly that Sarah and Gran found themselves leaning forward in their chairs to catch his words. Was he afraid of being overheard? Sarah wondered. And if so, by whom?

"Your Mr. William Borden has done a magnificent piece of work here," he told them. In his hand he held a memorandum that Borden had sent. "However, I am afraid, ah . . ."

"Yes?" Sarah asked. She did not like the note of reservation.

"Mrs. Stefanovic, permit me, please, to be candid with you. If you were a Yugoslav woman, you would have no difficulty in getting back your son. But what the judges will see when they look at you is an American woman who wants to take a Yugoslav child, a male child, out of Yugoslavia. And that . . ." He spread his hands in a gesture of hopelessness.

"But my son was born in America," Sarah said. "He spent all of his life in America until two and a half months ago."

"Yes," added Gran. "An American court granted Sarah custody. She has the documents. She can prove it."

Dimitrivic shook his head wearily. "Your husband, Mrs. Stefanovic, he has documents as well. A certificate, for instance, showing that your son was registered at birth as a Yugoslav citizen."

"That's true," said Sarah. She remembered only too well the scene in the hospital when Joey was born. "But that was only a formality, a ritual. It didn't mean anything." She stopped, hearing the emptiness of her own argument.

"Mrs. Stefanovic, you must understand. There are many people in this country who mistrust America. Citing the ruling of an American court, this will not help you here."

"Are you saying there is nothing I can do to get my son back?"

"I am saying that as far as the government is concerned, you can expect very little in the way of . . ." His voice fell away.

"Assistance?"

"Probably none at all. I am sorry. But as your attorney, it is my duty to speak realistically. I have seen too many such cases."

Sarah slumped in her chair. "You're telling me it's hopeless?"

Dimitrivic shook his head. "I am saying no such thing. Mrs. Stefanovic"—his eyes were kind, so was his voice—"go to your husband. Have your visit with your son. See how things are with them. After that, we will have a better idea of how to proceed."

THE light was already fading as Sarah's taxi sped down the Boulevard Revolucije toward Baka's house. She had come alone. On the seat beside her lay the package she had promised to bring. Inside were Joey's two hand puppets and a new winter coat. She had more clothes for him back at the hotel, as well as toys and some children's books, but at Gran's suggestion she was saving those for another visit.

Not until the taxi turned off the boulevard and up a broad tree-lined street did Sarah begin to recognize where she was: embassy row. On either side, set well back behind high walls and hedges, were the great mansions that had once been the homes of Serbian aristocrats and were now the headquarters of foreign governments. Not far away, Sarah knew, was the official residence of President Tito. Uniformed sentries with machine guns slung over their shoulders were posted at the gates of the various embassies and at regular intervals along the street. "It is not the usual Belgrade neighborhood," Jovan had told her dryly the first time he brought her here. And, indeed, it had not changed since then.

The taxi driver took a turn, passed still another sentry, and then they were in the narrow cul-de-sac that backed on the woods behind the presidential palace. Alongside a low wooden fence the driver brought the taxi to a halt. Sarah's heart began pounding. Just beyond the fence was Baka's home: the place where Joey had been living for the past ten weeks, the place where she was now about to see him again.

The house looked the way Sarah remembered it from her last visit—a rustic stone cottage set amid lawns, shrubs, and flower beds. An eighteenth-century relic, the cottage had been wrangled for Baka by a relative who had connections in the government; it came to her free, as part of her war-widow's pension. Although the amenities were primitive—the outhouse in the back and a pump down the road, from which water had to be carried by hand—the setting was gorgeous, especially in the summertime, when it was like living in the middle of a private park.

But none of that mattered now. The only thing on Sarah's mind was one small boy—and the uncertain reception that awaited her.

She opened her purse. Her hands were shaking. She paid the driver, picked up the package from the seat, and got out. The taxi did a U-turn and drove away, leaving her standing alone. She took a deep breath and pushed the gate. At the sound of it squeaking on its hinges, the door of the cottage flew open.

And there stood Joey, wide-eyed, with Baka looming in the doorway behind him. Joey—in old jeans and sneakers and a dirty sweater—taller and slimmer than she remembered, but her boy!

"Joey," she said. "Oh, Joey."

Stooping down, she opened her arms to him.

But stopped. Because something odd was happening. Instead of running to her, he was just standing there, watching her.

"Joey! Lovey! What's wrong?"

What she saw next chilled her to the very core: Joey glancing back at Baka and asking her, in her language, "May I?" Asking Baka if he could go to his own mother!

With a smile of triumph that was like a knife in Sarah's heart, the old woman nodded. She said, *"Idi naprijed. Idi svojoj mami."* (Go ahead. Go to your mother.)

And stolidly Joey came to her, not running up the path, not flying into her arms, but moving robotlike, almost dutifully, as Sarah, shocked and bewildered, thought, What have they done to you, my beautiful boy?

But then he was in her arms, and she was pressing him to her as she was weeping and saying his name. "Joey, oh Joey. I'm here. I've come to you, just like I said I would."

And then at last she felt him respond, his arms tightening around her neck as he whispered the word that sang like the most exquisite music in her ear. "Mama, Mama."

Baka was beside them now, tugging impatiently at Joey's arm. "Come inside, come inside. Do not keep him out here in the cold. Already he is coughing. Do you want to make it worse?"

Only then, rising to her feet, did Sarah see Jovan. He was leaning against the doorframe, arms folded across his chest, head tilted arrogantly to one side.

"Well, well," he said. "Look who's here."

The first thing Sarah noticed when she got inside were the draperies on the sitting-room windows. They were the ones she had made for their apartment in Yonkers.

Next she discovered that she would have no chance whatever to be alone with Joey. The cottage was tiny, consisting of the low-ceilinged sitting room, a kitchen on the other side of the fireplace, and a sleeping loft upstairs, under the eaves. The most she was able to manage was to hold Joey on her lap while she sat in a chair, huddled before the warmth of the coal fire that smoldered in the grate. While Baka bustled around in the kitchen making coffee, Jovan prodded her with questions about what she had been up to since her arrival in Belgrade.

"Up to?" she echoed. "I told you on the phone; we just got in this morning. When we got to the hotel, we went right to bed."

Avoiding Jovan's eyes, she busied herself with fussing over Joey. Setting him down in front of her, she held him at arm's length. "Let me look at you. Oh, you look so tall. You're not a baby anymore. You're a big boy now, aren't you?" Lightly, lightly. "And you just had a new haircut, didn't you?" It looked horrendous. All of his wonderful curls were gone, just as she'd feared.

"Baka cut it for me," he said flatly in Serbo-Croatian.

"Oh?" she said in surprise. "And you're learning the language, too. I'm impressed."

He beamed proudly. "I'm a Partisan now," he said. "Just like my grampa Stefan was."

"So I see."

She was forcing herself to be as cheerful as possible, but her heart was coming apart. It wasn't just the strange language that troubled her, nor the shock of how big he was. He was bigger than she'd remembered, but he was also thinner. A lot thinner. And he did not look well. He was pale, and he seemed to have no energy at all, no light in his eyes. A hacking cough came from deep inside his chest. Baka had been right to pull him in out of the cold. Yet the cottage itself was cold and drafty just a few feet from the fire.

"That doesn't sound good," she said after another coughing spell. "How long has he had this cold?" she asked Jovan.

He let out a snort of derision. "You mean you care?"

For a moment Sarah was too stunned to do anything but gape at him. "Jovan, how can you say that? Of course I care."

And then it struck her. Had Jovan put the same thought into Joey's head? Was that what Joey thought, too—that she didn't care? Was that why he had hesitated at the door? She hugged Joey to her. "I love my Joey. How could I not care?"

"Well, I'm certainly surprised to hear it," Jovan taunted. "If you did care, you would have come to see him long ago, not waited all this time. Over two months it's been."

"Jovan, my father has been sick. I—"

But Baka cut her off. "Here, here is coffee. Drink."

Sarah took the cup, then watched dumbfounded as Baka handed a cup to Joey, too. She was even more surprised when Joey sipped it without making a face.

"What did you bring?" Jovan asked, nodding toward the package.

"Oh, I almost forgot." She was annoyed, feeling flustered and off balance. "I brought a few things for Joey. Here, Joey, you open it."

He did not wait for her to ask twice. Eyes wide, he tore eagerly into the paper bag. On top he found the coat. It was of warm goose down, with a hood. Joey held it up without enthusiasm.

But then he saw what was at the bottom of the package—his cuddly puppet friends, Lionel and Fritz. "Oh," he said softly, holding them to his chest. "You remembered, Mama. You d-did remember."

The radiant look on his face filled her heart. At last she had done the right thing for him. And, perhaps, if she was lucky, it would make up somewhat for all the lost weeks.

"Say thank you," Baka coached in Serbo-Croatian.

"*Hvala vam, Mami.*"

Sarah shot the old woman a hateful glance. Baka had a thin smile on her lips.

"You should have sent him earlier this coat, or sent us money to buy one," she hissed in broken English. "We are not rich in our country like you Americans."

The remark was meant to be snide, but it was also obviously a painful understatement of their situation. Aside from the draperies on the windows—*her* draperies—the place looked shabby and run-down. Sarah did not have to ask whether Jovan had found a job. She knew he had not.

"How about a walk, Joey?" she asked him. "You can wear your new coat and tell me all about what you've been doing."

She thought she saw Joey's eyes brighten for a moment. But then, as if checking himself, he turned to Baka. "May I?"

"Only a short time. It is cold outside."

Sarah was elated. At last she would have a few moments alone with him. But then Jovan dashed her hopes. "I'll come, too," he said, moving to get his coat.

With Joey between them, the hood of his coat buttoned tight around his head, the three of them walked hand in hand past the walled gardens, past the sentries standing guard outside the baroque stone palaces of embassy row.

"Just like old times, eh, Joey? You and me and Mama walking together?"

Joey looked up at Sarah uncertainly, then at his father.

"It is, Sarah, isn't it?" pressed Jovan, grinning.

"Yes," she said. "Just like old times." She squeezed Joey's hand to reassure him, and at last he smiled back at her.

And all the while Jovan hung on to Joey's other hand. Not letting go. Not even for a minute.

SHE left the cottage that night feeling trapped and depressed and angry.

"I've got to get my son out of there," she told the lawyer the next day. "As soon as possible. The way he's living, it's awful.

The place was cold and damp. Joey looks terrible and he coughs all the time. Please tell me what I can do, Mr. Dimitrivic."

Dimitrivic gave a little shrug. "There are perhaps unofficial ways." He picked up a pencil, turned it over in his hands. "You could go back to your husband. Long enough at least to reinstate the marriage and establish residency in Yugoslavia. Then, after a certain length of time, you could take him to court and sue for divorce and custody, as one resident suing another."

"What length of time?" Sarah asked tentatively.

"A year. Perhaps two. And then, of course," he continued, "it would take more time for the case to go through the courts."

Sarah shook her head. "I just don't see how I—I could do that, go back to living with Jovan again for that long. Pretending to be happy. Living a lie."

Dimitrivic nodded sympathetically. "It would be very difficult. However, if you wanted your child back badly—"

Sarah had heard enough. She rose from her chair. "Thank you for your help, Mr. Dimitrivic. I will consider what you have said."

"Please do." He got up to escort her and Gran to the door. "And may I ask what your plans are in the meantime?"

"I don't know," Sarah said. "I'll need some time to think."

But she had already decided what she was going to do next.

AT THE front desk of the United States embassy, Sarah and Gran introduced themselves to the receptionist. The man they had come to see was the chief of the consular section, Fletcher Wethering. It was reassuring to them to see the Stars and Stripes displayed in the lobby.

After a few minutes Sarah and Gran were led to a small office on the second floor where they were greeted by a very business-like young man. He did not smile as he offered them chairs facing his desk.

Another desk, Sarah thought wearily.

Once more she heard herself going through the introductory remarks. Once more she heard in return the same protestations of helplessness.

"I wish there was something we could do," Wethering said blandly. "But I'm afraid since the boy is the child of a Yugoslav citizen, his father is protected by Yugoslav law."

"But my son is also the child of an *American* citizen," Sarah said. "Why isn't he protected by *American* law?"

"In America he would be. But possession is still nine tenths of the law, and your son is currently in his father's possession."

"Mr. Wethering, I'd like to know just whose side you're on. You sound like you're working for Yugoslavia instead of America."

Her anger left him unfazed. "We are here to protect American interests and to abide by the local laws and customs," he replied coolly. "We cannot keep watch on every American in Yugoslavia."

"I'm not interested in every American in Yugoslavia," Sarah shot back, emboldened now. "I'm only interested in one small boy. My son is the most important person in the world to me. And what I want to know is what my government is going to do to help me get him back."

Wethering shifted in his seat. This conversation was obviously beginning to make him uncomfortable. "We can offer you legal advice," he said. "And if that route proves ineffective, we can try to intercede on your behalf with the Yugoslav government. But beyond that—"

"Beyond that, Mr. Wethering?" Sarah said.

He smiled an icy, thin-lipped smile. "Mrs. Stefanovic, we're not about to go to war over this."

EVERY afternoon now Sarah went to the cottage to see Joey. Always she brought along a gift: a sweater, a pair of corduroy pants, a soccer ball. The storybooks she took him were all in English. With a little luck, they and the other gifts might help counter some of the influence that Jovan and his mother had already had on him. And if Jovan or Baka suspected her motives, they gave no indication of it. On the contrary, they seemed quite content to let her provide whatever she wished toward feeding and clothing the third member of their pathetic little household.

"It is very bad for them," Jovan's sister, Myra, told Sarah one Sunday afternoon while the two of them were cleaning up after dinner in Myra's apartment. "When Jovan appeared, we did not know what had happened. He had his son with him but no wife, no job, nothing. He was like a little lost puppy."

Myra was round-faced and chunky, like her mother. She and her husband, Branko, lived in this small apartment in the city's western suburbs. Three days ago she had telephoned Sarah at the hotel to invite her and Gran for this Sunday afternoon get-together. Baka, Jovan, Joey—everyone would be there.

"It will be a real family reunion," Myra had told her excitedly. "Please come, Sarah. It is so long since I have seen you, and we used to have such good talks together. We were like sisters."

It was true. On Sarah's first trip to Belgrade the two of them had spent hours chattering away in French outside Baka's cottage. They had gone on shopping trips together, and one afternoon Myra had even taught her how to crochet. It was with memories of that spring in mind that Sarah had consented to this visit. Maybe—just maybe—Myra might turn out to be the ally she needed, someone Jovan trusted, someone who could persuade him to give Joey back.

Welcoming Sarah and Gran at the door, Myra had been as friendly and warm as ever. And the generous meal she served— lamb with rice and cabbage and fresh-baked bread—had won Gran's approval immediately. But it was not until after dinner, at the kitchen sink, that Myra and Sarah had a few minutes alone together to talk.

"It is so insane," Myra was saying. "What is there for Jovan here? Nothing! With his degrees he could be making lots of money in America." Myra sighed. "But what can we do? 'It is for my country,' he tells us. 'I will not let America have my son.' You know how he talks."

"Yes, I know," Sarah replied, thinking, Do I ever!

Myra shook her head. "He was supposed to be our mother's hope for her old age. But now look! It is she who is supporting him. And the boy as well. What she has from her savings and her pension is hardly enough for one to live on, never mind three. And Jovan gets more unhappy all the time."

"I'm unhappy, too," Sarah said quietly. "And so is Joey. Does Jovan ever think of that?"

Myra handed over a dish to dry. "Oh, he does! But he needs you back, Sarah. When you left him, it was a terrible blow."

"He gave me no choice." Sarah did not like the way this conversation was going. Instead of sympathizing with her, Myra was expecting her to sympathize with Jovan! "You don't know what it was like living with him," she said.

"I know. I know how impossible he sometimes can be. But that does not give you the right to leave him. You took a vow. He is your husband. You are his wife."

Sarah felt her anger rising. Very carefully she set the dish and the towel down on the countertop. "You do *not* know," she said evenly. "You have no right to judge."

Myra, surprised by her tone, quickly backtracked. "Yes, yes. I am sorry. You are right. What happens between a husband and a wife no one else can know. But when I see my brother so unhappy, and the little boy, too, I cannot bear to even look at them sometimes." She wiped her hands on her apron and turned to face Sarah, a plea in her voice and in her eyes. "They need you. Both of them. They need your help."

"What are you talking about?"

"Help them. With money. If you were here, you could get a job. You could teach English. Or perhaps your father could—"

Sarah cut her off. "No," she snapped. Suddenly she knew why this friendly family get-together had been arranged. "No," she said again. "I won't listen to this. You're trying to use me just the way he is. Well, I'm through being used."

"No. It is not like that. You're wrong."

"Am I? Poor Jovan, you say; he needs help. You're right. He *does* need help. And I used to think I could be the one to give it to him. But I've found out that nobody can help him, because he doesn't want to be helped. All he wants is for somebody else to take care of him so he doesn't have to take care of himself. He's almost forty years old and he doesn't want to grow up."

Tears came to Myra's eyes. For a moment she had no words. Then slowly, sadly, she nodded her head. "Yes," she said. "Yes, what you say is true." She wiped her eyes with a corner of her apron and stood staring down at the linoleum. "But it hurts me to see him the way he is now. So mixed up. So confused."

Gently Sarah laid a hand on Myra's arm. "It hurts me, too," she said truthfully. "But I can't afford to worry about Jovan any longer. I've got to help myself now. And Joey."

"But how?" Myra looked at her. "What can you do? Jovan will never let you take Joey back to America. And how can you leave without him? So, what choice do you have? Tell me that."

"I don't know," Sarah said. "I wish I did."

NINE

"SARAH, is it true?" Jovan asked. "This is wonderful."

"Mama, do you m-mean it?" Joey's bright eyes were so full of delight that it almost hurt to look at him.

"Yes, I mean it." She bent to hug him. "We'll try it for a while and see how it works out."

It had taken her several days, but finally she had made up her mind. She would not do as Dimitrivic suggested: go back to Jovan. But she would try to find some way to stay in Belgrade on her own so that she could be near Joey. It was the only alternative. And now, walking in the park with them on this crisp fall day, it seemed as if she might even enjoy living here.

"When, Sarah? When will you be moving in?"

Careful now. "Moving in wasn't what I was thinking of."

"Ah, of course. I see. Yes. The cottage is too small. You are right. We will have to get a place of our own. That will be better."

"No. I don't think that's a good idea either."

"No? What are you trying to tell me?"

She did not answer immediately, but stopped to tie one of Joey's shoelaces, which had come undone. "Joey, why don't you go watch the ducks for a while. See them over there? In the pond? Your father and I have some things to talk about."

Joey looked from one to the other with his big eyes, then turned away. Sarah watched him go. His hands were pushed deep into his pants pockets and he kicked at a stone as he went. Poor Joey, she thought. Her heart ached for him.

She and Jovan sat on a park bench. Sarah took a breath. "I don't think it's a good idea for us to live together again. I want to get a place of my own. I want to be here, to be able to see Joey."

"But not to live with me," he said tonelessly.

"It wouldn't work. We've tried. It's just not good."

"And what about Joey? It's not good for him this way."

"It would be worse the other way. We'd be at each other all the time. You know that. This way he'd still live with you, but I could visit him. He could visit me sometimes."

Jovan said nothing for a long time. Finally he turned to her. "It's a trick, isn't it?"

"A trick? No, it's not a trick. What kind of trick would it be?"

He pinned her with those strange yellow-brown eyes of his. "I know what you'd do. The first time I'd let you out of my sight with Joey, you'd take him on a plane back to America."

"No," she protested. "It's not true. It's just not."

"I don't believe you. You're lying."

"But I'm not."

"Prove it, then." He took her hand. "Live with me again."

She tried to pull her hand back, but he held it tight. "Let go. You're hurting me."

"You want to prove to me I can trust you? Live with me. Be my wife again. And give me another child."

"What! You're crazy. Let me go."

Now he gripped her chin with his free hand, forcing her head back. His face was inches from hers. "Otherwise I don't let you near Joey. I don't care how long you stay here. You hear me?"

Had he pushed harder, Sarah was sure he could have snapped her neck. But suddenly Joey was there pulling at Jovan's arm, trying to get him to release his grip. "Daddy!" he screamed. "Stop it, Daddy! Stop it!"

Without taking his eyes off her, Jovan finally let her go. As soon as she was free she leaped up from the bench and ran, her eyes burning with tears of hate and rage. Behind her she could hear Joey's voice crying, "Mama, Mama! Come back, Mama."

But she knew now there was no turning back.

THAT night she and Gran sat in silence while the waiter cleared away the dinner dishes.

"What am I going to do?" Sarah asked when he had gone.

"I don't know. As long as he's got Joey, there doesn't seem to be anything you can do. As Mr. Wethering from the embassy said, possession is two thirds of the law."

"Nine tenths."

"Never mind. He's got Joey, so I guess that's that."

"I guess so."

But Gran's last words kept replaying themselves in her head: *that's that.* Meaning there was nothing else she could do. Or was she only making the assumptions that Jovan wanted her to make? Suddenly she had an image of him holding on to Joey's hand as

435

they walked near the cottage that first night. Holding on and not letting go. Holding on for dear life.

Jovan was afraid! The real meaning of it sank in. He was afraid of *her*. He had said it himself in the park this afternoon. He was afraid that she would do the same thing that he had done—get Joey onto a plane and take him away.

"Gran, I've got it," she said aloud.

"What are you talking about?"

"Possession, Gran. Nine tenths of the law. I'm talking about taking possession of Joey myself."

"What?"

"Why not? He took Joey from me!"

"Sarah, dear, will you calm down? What you're suggesting is just as illegal as what Jovan did to you."

"I'm aware of that."

"Are you? Then just what do you intend to do when you get Joey away from Jovan, assuming you can? Where will you go?"

"I'll do what people do when they want political asylum. I'll take him to the embassy. Then Mr. Fletcher Wethering will have to do something."

IN THE morning Sarah and Gran arrived at the American embassy just as a taxi pulled up to the curb and the tall, lean figure of Fletcher Wethering stepped out. He had his briefcase in hand.

"Mr. Wethering," Sarah said, "you're just the person we've come to see."

For an instant he looked nonplussed. "Mrs. Stefanovic, isn't it?" he said as he stepped through the gate.

"Yes, and we want to talk to you," answered Sarah, following him in. "We want to talk to you now."

"That may be, but I have other matters to attend to this morning. So, if you'll excuse me . . ."

"All right," she called after him as he started up the front steps. "But when I bring my son here and you have to figure out how to get him out of the country, don't say I didn't warn you."

Wethering stopped in midstride. Turning to face her, he studied her for a moment. It was enough. "You'd better come inside." Sarah and Gran exchanged satisfied glances.

He led them upstairs to his office and asked them to wait. He went out, closing the door behind him. A minute later he was back. "Come with me, please."

Without another word he led them down a corridor and into a spacious office. Sarah was aware of thick blue carpet underfoot, an American flag in one corner, and, coming toward her, a big, balding man in shirt sleeves.

"Sir, these are the ladies I was telling you about," Wethering said. "Mrs. Stefanovic and her grandmother, Mrs. Helen Heilicki. Ladies, I'd like you to meet Ambassador Laurence Silberman."

The ambassador stretched out a hand. "How do you do," he said. "I'm glad we've finally had a chance to get together. I've been following your case closely, Mrs. Stefanovic."

Inwardly Sarah groaned. Another smoothy, she thought.

But the ambassador surprised her. "Fuddy-duddies," he said when Wethering had left the room.

She blinked, startled, and he grinned at her reaction. "Oh, don't mind me," he said with a wave. "It's these State Department types. They're all alike." He swung around behind his sprawling desk, dropped into his high-backed leather chair, and cocked one foot on the edge of an open drawer.

"I admire your persistence, Mrs. Stefanovic," the ambassador continued genially. Putting on his glasses, he plucked a file from amid the clutter on his desk and leafed through the papers. "Why, I've got letters here from Congressman Vanderbeck, Senator Case, notes on transatlantic phone calls from your Washington attorney. You've certainly covered all the bases."

Sarah shrugged. She was determined not to be distracted from her purpose by flattery. "Most of that was my parents' doing," she said, nodding toward his folder.

"That's very loyal of you to say so, but it wasn't your parents who had Fletcher Wethering in a panic a few minutes ago."

Sarah regarded him evenly. "I meant every word I said to him. I came here to get my son back and that's what I intend to do."

"And I intend to help you in any way I can," said the ambassador, adopting a tone as serious as her own. "I've got children and grandchildren of my own, and I know how I would feel if one of them were abducted. But," he said, "it is exactly *because* I want to help you that I must tell you that bringing your son to the embassy would be the worst thing you could do."

"Just who would it be worse for, Mr. Ambassador? For you? For the American government?"

The ambassador looked pained. "Mrs. Stefanovic, let me make one thing clear. I am not especially fond of the Yugoslav government and they are not especially fond of me. What I am worried about is what happens to you if you do bring your boy here."

"That would be your problem," she said stubbornly.

He shook his head. "It's not that easy. Oh, getting him in here would be no problem. But you might never get him out again. You'd be arrested the minute you tried to leave. Would you want your son to grow up a prisoner inside these walls?"

"He's a prisoner now," she shot back. But suddenly things did not seem as certain as they had a few minutes ago.

"All right, then, what if I don't bring him here? What if I just wait for a chance to take him out of the country?"

Again the ambassador shook his head. "Bad idea. They'd nail you at the airport, and you could find yourself in jail."

"But what can I do, then?" Sarah cried out in frustration, angry at the tears she felt welling up. "What can I do?"

"Look," said the ambassador gently. "Sit tight for a few days and let me see what I can come up with. Will you do that?"

Sarah studied her hands for a moment. What alternative did she have? "Yes, all right," she murmured reluctantly.

"Good. Maybe we can work something out—unofficially, of course. For now, don't talk about any of this over the telephone. The jugs are always very interested in anyone who comes to see me. If your phone hasn't been tapped already, they'll certainly put a bug on it when they see you leaving here."

"You're not serious," said Gran, astonished.

"Oh, yes," said the ambassador. "I'm quite serious. And I'd also advise you to stay away from that lawyer of yours."

"Mr. Dimitrivic?" Sarah was puzzled. "I thought it was you people who recommended him."

"That's correct. But none of us were aware at the time of just what your case entailed. Oh, Dimi is a good man. But over here there's no such thing as confidentiality between a lawyer and his client. If the authorities questioned him about your case, he'd have to tell them everything he knows, including your intention to take your son back to America."

"Then what on earth am I supposed to do?" Sarah asked plaintively. "Can you tell me that? What am I supposed to do?"

"Come see me on Monday." Ambassador Silberman got to his feet. "I should have some answers for you by then."

Afterward Sarah and Gran stood in front of the embassy in the cold November sunlight, waiting for a taxi. As Sarah surveyed the street her eye caught a movement across the way. A man sitting on a park bench was folding his newspaper. Was he an informant? she wondered. Or was it that old man with the dog? Or that woman pushing the baby carriage?

Suddenly Sarah felt very vulnerable. It was bad enough knowing she had failed in everything she had tried to do—failed with the lawyer, with Jovan's sister, probably with the ambassador as well. But it made her feel even worse, even more isolated, to know that every move, every word she said, was most likely being monitored.

"I think you should face it," Gran told her that evening as the two of them sat over dinner in the hotel dining room. "You've done all you can."

Sarah shook her head. "There must be something else. There's got to be. I can't just give up."

"I know, dear, but we can't stay here forever looking for a wild goose in a haystack. I want to go back home. And frankly, if you'll take my advice, I think you should go back, too."

The prospect stunned her. Go back? Could she? And leave Joey behind? Would she ever see him again if she did?

"Gran, stay just a couple more days, can't you? At least through the weekend, until I see what the ambassador comes up with."

Gran sighed. Beneath the broad expanse of her silk blouse, her bosom rose like a tide, then fell back again. "All right, dear. But I won't stay any later than Tuesday. After that, if you want to stay, I'm afraid you'll be on your own."

TEN

WHEN Sarah and Gran were shown into Ambassador Silberman's office on Monday morning, the weather outside was gray and cold.

"I did some checking over the weekend," the ambassador said

after his secretary had provided them with coffee. "There might be something we can arrange. On the quiet, of course."

He leaned forward. Not far from the embassy, he explained, was a school for the children of diplomats, journalists, and other foreign nationals stationed in Belgrade. "My wife tells me there's going to be an opening for a junior high school teacher. From what I know of your background I'm sure you would qualify."

"Wait a minute," Sarah said. "What are you suggesting?"

"Just this. Once you were settled in, with a job and a place to live, you could work at gaining your husband's confidence to the point where he'd be willing to let you see your son alone. Then, when the time was right, we could arrange to distract him long enough for you to get the boy on a plane and out of the country. If you're interested, I could make the necessary arrangements."

In the courtyard outside the window the wind was blowing the last dry leaves from the trees. Sarah remembered being in the park with Jovan, and him telling her what he would demand of her in return for his trust. She shook her head.

"It wouldn't work," she said. "I could never make him trust me enough."

"She's right," said Gran.

The ambassador sat back in his chair. "Well, I hope you'll give some thought to my suggestion. It is possible we could figure something out. There is one thing I need to know, however."

"What's that?"

"A technicality, but an important one. It's the question of how your son came into this country. Was he on an American passport?"

She shook her head. "He didn't have one. Jovan got him a Yugoslav passport two or three years ago, when he was talking about bringing us over here for a visit."

"And that didn't make you suspicious?"

"No, not at the time. I didn't see that it mattered."

"Unfortunately, it matters a great deal. Without an American passport bearing a visa stamp that proves the boy was brought into Yugoslavia as an American, you won't be able to take him out of the country. In the eyes of the Yugoslavs, you'd be making off with one of their citizens. Your lawyers never told you that?"

"Mr. Borden did. He said I should get a family passport with both Joey's and my picture on it." She opened her handbag and took out the little blue booklet. "This is what I've been traveling with," she said, showing it to him.

The ambassador studied the passport. "This is dated last month," he said.

"That's right."

"And the picture was taken when?"

Her heart skipped a beat. Oh, no, she thought, he's spotted it. He knows it's a forgery. "During the summer," she lied.

"Before Joey was abducted, then."

"Yes."

"Hmm," he said noncommittally. He handed the passport back. "Joey's a handsome boy," he said.

"Thank you," Sarah murmured in relief, hastily tucking the booklet back into her purse.

"Well?" Gran asked. "Is that what Sarah needs?"

"It's possible," he said cautiously. "Under the normal procedures each of you would need to have a visa stamp, even on a family passport. But you might get lucky. It's just the kind of wrinkle that the customs men would overlook. Yes, it might just be okay."

"WELL?" Gran asked as she and Sarah rode back to the hotel. "Are you going to take the man up on his offer?"

Sarah shook her head. "You know what I'd have to go through with Jovan for him to leave Joey alone with me. I can't do it."

"Well, don't dismiss the idea out of hand. You should keep all your options in the fire."

Sarah turned to the window, to the bare trees that lined the boulevard, the people huddled in their heavy coats against the wind. "I'm afraid my options have just about run out."

When they arrived at the hotel, Sarah called the airline and confirmed reservations on the morning flight to Paris, with a connecting flight to New York. Next she telephoned Dimi Dimitrivic to thank him for his help, such as it was.

That done, she was left with only one more chore before she and Gran left Belgrade, the one she had been dreading more than any other. She had to tell Jovan and Joey she was going.

If it had been only Jovan, she would have done it over the phone. Maybe not have said anything at all. Just disappeared. No good-byes, no regrets. But there was Joey. No way could she not tell Joey.

"Would you like me to come along?" asked Gran.

"No, thanks. It's better if I go myself. You take a nap. I'll be back as soon as I can."

She went downstairs to the street to catch a bus, but first she stopped in a nearby shop to pick up some candy and fruit and a little windup toy clown for Joey. No telling when he would get such treats again, once she was gone.

Then she caught a bus on the Boulevard Revolucije. The city slid by beyond the windows, but she saw none of it. She sat as if in a daze, trying to think of what she would say to Joey, how she could possibly tell him that she was going away and did not know whether she would see him again.

The bus stopped near the Mongolian embassy. Sarah got off and walked up the street that led to Baka's cul-de-sac. Except for the sentry pacing at the corner, the little road was empty.

Sarah pulled her coat collar closer around her neck and pushed open the squeaky gate. She walked up the path and knocked on the door. It was opened by Baka.

"Oh, it's you," she said in Serbo-Croatian.

"I've come to see Joey."

"He's sleeping."

"Please wake him. I need to talk to him. It's important."

Baka eyed her warily for a moment, then stepped aside. "Close door," she said, switching to English. "We do not have money to throw away on coal."

Gracious as ever, Sarah thought. But she did as she was told.

Once inside, she glanced around the room and was relieved to see that Jovan was apparently not home. Maybe she could avoid saying good-bye to him after all.

Baka went into the kitchen and called up the stairs. "Joey, come down. Your mother is here to see you."

There was a whoop, and in an instant Joey came flying down the stairs. "Mama!" he cried, and threw himself into her arms.

As Sarah hugged him to her she could feel the warmth of his small body, the smell of sleep in his hair. She drank it all in voraciously, wanting to impress the smell and feel of him on her mind, to memorize every detail.

"Hello, sweetheart. I'm sorry I had to wake you up."

"I'm n-not. I'm g-glad," he said gleefully, hugging her again.

"Look, Joey! Look what I brought you. Here's some chocolate. And some apples. And I found this little clown. If you wind him up, he does a little dance. See?"

"Oh, Mama. He's n-nice. Thank you." He clapped his hands happily and kissed her. His exuberance filled her with pain and delight at the same time. In the last three weeks he had gotten used to seeing her again. There was no more holding back, none of the untrusting restraint with which he had first greeted her. She had become part of his life again—and that was going to make it even harder to say good-bye.

Sarah took off her coat and draped it over her shoulders. She was just sitting down by the fire when the door burst open. Jovan stood there, a bucket of coal in one hand and an armload of kindling in the other.

"Well, well. The grand lady honors us with her presence." Brushing past her, he set the bucket down and dumped the kindling. "Did you finally come to your senses, eh?"

Joey began to back away, his face shadowed by fear, but Sarah put an arm around him and held him near her. She did not want to add to Joey's fear nor provoke another argument. That wasn't the way she wanted Joey to remember her.

Despite the pounding of her heart, she managed to keep her voice calm and steady. "If you mean did I decide to move in here, the answer is still no," she said to Jovan.

"Then what are you doing here?"

"To tell you—" She took Joey's hands in hers. She spoke to him rather than to Jovan. "To tell you that Gran and I will be leaving tomorrow. We're going back home, Joey. Back to America."

Joey froze. He stared at her in disbelief, his tender, sweet face hardening into a mask of stone. She would have done anything to have avoided this moment. "It's not what I want to do," she told him, searching his eyes, beseeching him to believe her. "What I want most in the world is to be with you."

"You can't leave. I won't let you," Jovan declared. "In this country the husband makes the rules, the wife obeys."

Sarah paid no attention. It was only Joey who concerned her now. "Grampa Ted is still very sick," she explained carefully.

She would not tell him the truth. She would not turn him against his father. Now more than ever he would need Jovan to love, to lean upon. "Grampa needs me there to help him get well again. You want him to get well, don't you, Joey?"

"I will lock you in," Jovan shouted. He was pacing like a cornered animal now, and her calmness seemed to agitate him even more. She was no longer afraid of his threats.

"Gran knows I'm here," she told him evenly as she got to her feet. "If I'm not back soon, Gran will go to the embassy and they will send the police."

The word brought a shriek of dismay from Baka.

"*Policija!*" she cried, her eyes wide with the fear. "They are coming here? The *policija?*"

More distracted than ever, Jovan hurried to reassure her. "No, *Mami.* Do not worry. There are no police coming." He turned back to Sarah, pleading now, his eyes brimming. "Sarah, please do not go. I am sorry. I did not mean what I said just now. Listen to me. You can see Joey whenever you want, take your own apartment, anything. Just do not go back. We need you." He reached out an imploring hand. "*I* need you."

She knew he meant every word of it. Knew also that he was capable of saying the opposite in the next breath and believing that, too. "It's too late," she said quietly.

"Sarah—"

"No." She cut him off. "I'm going now. That's final." She turned to Joey. He stood head down, not looking at her, hands limp at his sides. Pale and cold as marble. She lowered herself to one knee. "Will you give me one last hug before I go?"

Once, slowly, he shook his head, and turned away.

"Joey, I know you're mad at me and you've got good reason to be. I want to take you home with me, but I just can't. Not now. But that's why I need a hug from you, so I can take *that* home with me. So I can have that little part of you with me always."

For another moment he stood rooted to where he was. Then he took a single step forward, into her arms. And stood there. Rigid.

"I'll be back, I promise," she whispered, her tears welling up. His hair smelled like musty leaves and coal smoke; his sweater was rough against her cheek. "I want you to be a good boy and do what your daddy and your baka tell you. Will you do that?"

A nod against her shoulder.

"I know it's hard to be good all the time, but try and do the best—" She stopped. It was all wrong. It was not what she wanted to say to him. "Joey, listen to me. Whatever happens while I'm gone, I want you always to remember that your mama loves you. Don't ever forget that, Joey. Promise you won't forget."

He nodded once. He was fighting his own tears now. Fighting them hard. He nodded again. "I promise," he whispered.

And that was all. Aside from one last *"Do vidjenja, Mami"* as she stepped out the door, that was all.

Afterward she realized that it was probably the most she could have hoped for. There were already too many good-byes in his short life. Another one was simply more than he could bear.

BELGRADE: Saturday, April 23, 11:50 a.m.

IT WAS just before noon when Wilkes, Ted, and Sarah crossed the bridge over the Sava River and found themselves skirting the edge of central Belgrade.

They had been driving steadily all morning, speeding southeast into the glare of the sun. Her eyes half closed, Sarah had been only vaguely aware of the country through which they'd been traveling—a wide, flat valley, where lush pastures and vineyards periodically gave way to factories and refineries.

Wilkes got off the highway in the newer part of town, amid rows of modern apartment blocks. A single square tower stood taller than the rest, and as he drove toward it Sarah read the sign over the entranceway: HOTEL SRBIJA.

"I'm afraid it's not as elegant as the Metropol," Wilkes told Ted as he pulled into the parking lot. "But if we went there, Sarah might be recognized. I didn't want to take any chances."

They got out, and Wilkes led the way into the hotel. Following the instructions that she had been given earlier, Sarah hung back near the entrance while Wilkes and her father stepped up to the reception desk. "Look shy and nervous," Wilkes had told her, and she had no trouble acting the part.

"Good afternoon," he greeted the desk clerk. "We have reservations for two rooms. A single for my friend here and a double for me. The name is Wilkes. Peter Wilkes."

"A double for you, sir?"

"A double, yes. I'll be, ah, having a guest." He tilted his head meaningfully in Sarah's direction.

The clerk slid her a languid glance. Sarah's cheeks burned. She looked at her feet. When she looked up again, the clerk was busy handing out forms for Wilkes and her father to complete.

The ruse had worked. Obviously the private arrangements of the hotel's guests didn't matter to the clerk at all. Which was just what Wilkes had been hoping for. He wanted to pass Sarah off as his local girlfriend—a visitor, at any rate, rather than a paying guest. That way she would not have to show her passport to the clerk, who was required to enter in a police registry the names and passport numbers of all hotel guests. Wilkes did not want to make it too easy for the police to track Sarah down later.

When the forms were filled out and the clerk was finished examining their passports, an aging bellhop in a frayed uniform lifted their suitcases onto a cart.

"Come along, love," Wilkes called to Sarah across the lobby.

Sarah flinched. This was not a role she liked playing, especially since she had the feeling that Wilkes was secretly enjoying this particular masquerade. But she set her smile and allowed him to take her by the elbow and escort her to the elevator.

They got off on the fourth floor, where the bellhop led them down a corridor. Halfway along he stopped, opened a door, and stepped back to reveal a narrow cell crammed with teak furnishings. There was hardly enough space to turn around. Still, the room was clean and bright, and the single large window had a sweeping view of the city.

Ted lifted his bag off the cart and stepped inside. For now, this would be his room; when the coast was clear, he would switch with Wilkes and share the double with Sarah.

"See you for dinner?" Ted asked through the open door. "How does seven o'clock sound?"

"Seven it is," Wilkes said with forced good cheer. And with his hand still on Sarah's arm he followed the bellhop down the hall.

Their room was only slightly larger than the one they had just seen. It had two windows instead of one, and two beds. But otherwise it was exactly the same.

"Well, here we are," Wilkes said, once he had tipped the

bellhop and closed the door behind him. He let himself drop wearily into a chair, then glanced around the room. "I trust you will be comfortable here."

"Yes."

It was awkward being alone with him . . . in a hotel room. She sat down on the bed nearer the window. She felt very tired.

"What about you and Dad being registered here?" she asked, to fill the silence. "Won't the police be able to track you down if something goes wrong?"

Wilkes shook his head. "The names won't mean anything to them. As far as they're concerned, I'm just an ordinary Englishman on a business trip."

"What kind of business? Or shouldn't I ask?"

"On the contrary, it's better that you and your father know in case you're questioned." He reached inside his tweed jacket, withdrew his passport, and handed it to her. It identified him as Peter Wilkes of Maidstone, Kent, and listed his profession as salesman.

"What are you supposed to be selling?"

"Machine tools. It's something I know a little about."

He also showed her photos of a woman and two children sitting on a park bench, and a letter from a Maidstone address. The letter was signed, "Love, Chrissy."

"Your wife?" Sarah asked. Not that it mattered, of course.

"Not mine. Somebody's, though."

She handed back the photographs. "So none of this is real?"

"Oh, yes. The passport itself is quite authentic. So is the name. And there *is* an executive at a manufacturing firm who's prepared to vouch for me." His grin was that of a small boy sharing the secrets of a clever prank. Sarah couldn't help but smile back.

"You people have taken care of everything, haven't you?"

"I certainly hope so. For your sake as well as mine." His crystalline-blue eyes rested on hers for a long moment, and their warmth surprised her. Then, as if suddenly remembering himself, he got to his feet. "We'd all better get some rest," he said. "I'll stop back here at seven to pick you two up for dinner."

And then he was gone.

Only later did she realize that she still knew nothing about Peter Wilkes except his name. And that he liked being mysterious.

THE AD CAUGHT TED NOVACK'S attention one morning in mid-November while Sarah was still in Belgrade. He was sitting in bed, leafing idly through *The Wall Street Journal*, when his eye fell on an advertisement at the bottom of an inside page.

SPECIALIZED INTERNATIONAL SERVICES
Highly trained, skilled professionals available for hazardous-type assignments. Security-conscious, confidentiality protected. Licensed, insured, and bonded.

Interested parties were invited to address inquiries to a post-office box number in Lakeland, Florida.

Carefully Ted tore the ad out of the paper and clipped it to the front cover of a manila folder labeled "Joey." The folder bulged with the notes, memos, and correspondence that Ted had accumulated in the months since Labor Day; the clipping would help him remember to get a letter off to the Florida address this afternoon. These days his health was improving steadily, but he still had to parcel out his energies.

A few weeks earlier Ted would not have even considered responding to an ad like the one in the *Journal*. He had not forgotten the righteous indignation with which he had dismissed Bob Koenig's hints about alternative measures. But things looked different now. Sarah had called him regularly from Belgrade, and her reports had grown more discouraging every day.

Then, just yesterday, Ted had had a call from Sherwood Brice, his well-connected friend in the brokerage business. Brice had been in touch with a former classmate at Princeton who now worked for the Central Intelligence Agency.

"My friend says you should forget about going through official channels," Brice reported in his prep school accent. "You won't get anywhere. He says you should hire a professional."

"A professional? What does he mean by that?" Ted asked.

"A private investigator, I assume."

Ted hesitated. The idea appealed to his sense of adventure. But that was exactly the kind of reaction that made him distrust his own motives. "No. No, thanks," he finally replied. "I guess I'd rather wait and see what else turns up."

Still, once the idea of seeking professional help had been planted in Ted's mind, it kept teasing at the corners of his consciousness.

And now here was this ad in *The Wall Street Journal.* "Highly trained, skilled professionals." Well, it certainly wouldn't hurt to inquire. He drafted a letter that very afternoon.

"I'M SORRY," said Bill Borden when Ted broached the subject to him over the telephone. "That's not the kind of thing we here at the firm like to get involved with."

"I know. I don't like it either. I wouldn't even ask such a thing if there was any other way. But nothing else is working."

For a moment there was no sound on the other end of the line. Finally the lawyer let out a long breath. "You're right."

"Well then, what about it? There must be people who would be willing to take on something like this."

"Sure there are. Lots of people. The newspapers are full of stories about private investigators who specialize in snatching kids in custody cases. It's a real growth industry. But you're talking about getting a child out of a Communist country. Not every flake in a raincoat could handle a job like that."

"I understand that. But—"

"And even if we did locate the right kind of person, there could still be problems. Even the professionals get caught. And if that happened, you could lose any chance of getting your boy back."

"The way things are going we don't have any chance anyway."

Again Borden hesitated, but this time only briefly. "Okay. Look, give me a few days. I'll see what we come up with."

Two days later Ted picked up Sarah and her grandmother at the airport and brought them back to Sommerton. Gran only stayed long enough to have dinner. Then, exhausted from the trip, she asked to be taken home. As soon as she and Emma drove off, Sarah went up to bed.

"Are you all right, kitten?" Ted called after her. He was worried. She looked terrible. Her complexion was pasty, her brown eyes dull, her face devoid of expression.

She murmured something about jet lag, but Ted knew it was more than that. The weeks in Belgrade had been an emotional roller coaster. And leaving Joey behind had been devastating.

And yet, over the next few days it became clear to both Ted and Emma that something in their daughter had changed. This time her depression did not immobilize her. As they watched her moving about the house, making calls, they sensed in her a self-assurance, a quiet determination they had not seen before. And when Bill Borden finally called back a few days later, Sarah was right there at Ted's side.

"Well?" she asked as soon as he hung up. "What did Mr. Borden say? Did he come up with anything?"

Ted allowed himself a cautious nod. "He's been in touch with an American in London, a former FBI man named Harry Lipton, who runs"—Ted consulted his notes—"Atlantic Information Services. The man specializes in 'in-depth studies' for the big multinationals—Exxon, ITT, that kind of thing."

"In-depth studies?"

"Spying," said Ted. "He also has another specialty: smuggling people out of Eastern Europe."

TED telephoned London early on Monday morning. His call was received by a woman with a perky British accent. She answered by reciting the last four digits of the phone number, followed by a polite "May I help you?" No names mentioned—not Lipton's, not the company's. Just four anonymous digits. It was, Ted noted approvingly, all very discreet.

"Mr. Lipton, please. My name is Novack. I believe he's expecting to hear from me."

Harry Lipton was cordial but businesslike. Yes, he said, Borden had filled him in on the general situation. He wanted Ted to understand that the firm did not usually handle domestic cases; as a personal favor to Bill, however, he would be willing to see the Novacks and talk in more detail. "Could you be in London during the second week of January?" Monday, the tenth, was the earliest Lipton could see them.

Reluctantly Ted agreed. He was anxious to get started; there had already been too many delays. When he thought about it later, however, he decided that having to wait several weeks might be a good thing after all. It would allow him just that much more time to regain his strength and make the necessary arrangements.

Later that day, while Ted was doing some gentle back exercises, Emma called him to the phone to take a long-distance call. "He didn't give his name, but he's got a southern accent."

Ted took the receiver. "Hello?"

"Mr. Novack? I'm Tom Carleton. I'm calling about the letter y'all sent? In answer to our ad in *The Wall Street Journal?*"

Tom Carleton identified himself as a lawyer representing a group of retired police officers, detectives, and security guards—"all professionals, you understand"—who hired themselves out for special undercover missions. They referred to themselves, Carleton said, chuckling, as the over-the-hill gang.

"Now, your kind of job would cost a good bit of money," he went on. "It could be a dangerous business, crossin' international frontiers and all. Might even be some shootin'. The higher the risk, the higher the cost, if y'all see what I mean."

"Just what kind of costs are you talking about, Mr. Carleton?"

"Well, as a ballpark figure, I'd say around seventy-five to a hundred thousand dollars, somewhere in there. If y'all would like to come down here for a little talk . . ."

Ted begged off. Not only did the fee sound outrageous, but so did the man's easy talk about gunplay. The boys in the over-the-hill gang were going to have to find someone else to supplement their pensions.

"HELLO, Joey. Happy birthday, sweetheart." Sarah fought to keep her voice steady as she spoke into the receiver.

It was Monday, December 20, 1976. Joey was six years old today.

"Hello, Mama." His voice was flat, without emotion.

"How are you, sweetheart? Are you having a nice birthday?"

"Uh-huh."

"Did you open your presents yet?"

"Uh-huh."

"I hope the clothes fit okay. Did you like the racing cars and the track that Gramma and Grampa sent?"

"*Da.*"

"Would you like to tell them that yourself? They're right here."

"Okay."

Sarah's mother got on the line and said hello and happy birthday; then her father did the same. It's so hard, Sarah thought as she waited. What could they say? How could they reach him over the phone when she herself hadn't even been able to do it in person?

"I hope you have a really nice birthday," she said when her father handed back the phone. "I miss you a lot, Joey."

When he answered, his voice was so quiet she could barely make out the words. "I m-miss you, t-too, Mama."

BELGRADE: Saturday, April 23, 7:00 p.m.

HAVING spent the afternoon catching up on their sleep, Sarah and her father had only just managed to drag themselves out of their beds when Wilkes came to collect them for dinner.

The café Wilkes took them to was in a cellar a few steps below street level. Its menu and its atmosphere had a Turkish flavor, complete with hanging lamps and waiters in fezzes. In one corner a drummer and a flute player set up a plaintive, wailing rhythm. The place was crowded with Russian tourists.

The dinner—moussaka for Sarah and Wilkes, cabbage and lamb for Ted—and beer had a soothing effect on them all. Even Wilkes began to relax and open up a little about himself.

He was, it turned out, only in his mid-thirties, which surprised Sarah, since the lines in his face and the weariness in his gray-blue eyes suggested that he was at least ten years older. He had been educated in Scotland and had planned a career as a history teacher before a stint in the army led him into intelligence work. "The pay was better," he explained laconically, taking a sip of his beer.

"And how did you come to be assigned to our case?" Ted asked. He had been listening to Wilkes with obvious fascination.

"Eastern Europe happens to be a specialty of mine. And then, of course"—he lowered his voice—"I've done this kind of thing before, helping people get out of, well, other places like this. But those were adults, not children, and the cases were political, not domestic. Still, the requirements are similar."

"Yes, I imagine they are."

"I'll be frank with you, though. This is not my favorite kind of job. I prefer to work for corporations rather than individuals."

"Oh? Why is that?" Sarah asked. "I'd imagine corporate work would be much more demanding."

"It is. But"—Wilkes took another sip of beer—"corporations don't cry."

ELEVEN

ATLANTIC Information Services was not included among the names listed on the registry in the lobby of Pemberton House. Neither was the name of Harry Lipton.

"Are you sure this is the right place?" Sarah asked.

Her father checked the letter he'd been given by the driver who had brought them from Heathrow Airport. The typewritten note bore no identifying information, only the address in the upper right-hand corner and Lipton's signature at the bottom.

"At Pemberton House," the letter instructed, "take the elevator to the top floor, then walk up one flight."

"This is it," said Ted. "Come on. Let's go up."

Getting off the elevator on five, Sarah followed her father up a flight of red-carpeted stairs to a small landing. They found themselves facing a single white door. The small brass plate over the buzzer was inscribed with only one word: "Lipton."

Ted pressed the button.

They were admitted by a prim middle-aged woman in sensible shoes, who took their coats. The place looked the way Sarah imagined a rather stodgy men's club would look, and Lipton's own office turned out to be very much the same; it had a comfortable sofa, coffee table, easy chairs, nautical prints on the walls.

"Hello, I'm Harry Lipton," said the man who was waiting to greet them. "I hope you didn't have any trouble finding us up here."

He was a big haystack of a man, with a midwestern American accent. Broad-shouldered, thick-necked, he had a head of bushy gray hair, a bushy mustache, and bushy eyebrows that flew up at the ends like feathers on a hat, giving him an oddly startled look. There was nothing odd, however, about his manner or the way he was dressed: white shirt, dark blue three-piece suit. He looked more like a bank manager, in fact, than a private investigator.

"Before we begin," Lipton said once they had all been seated, "I want you both to understand right from the start that the work we do can be very costly."

Sarah glanced anxiously at her father, who nodded soberly. "I understand. Just how much money are you talking about?"

"At this point I wouldn't even want to guess," said Lipton. "First I'll need a lot more information from both of you."

"What is it you want to know?" asked Sarah.

"Everything you can tell me about your husband and your son. What they're like, where they live, how your husband spends his days. I want to know where he goes when he goes out, how he lives, who your son plays with, where he goes to school."

"He doesn't go to school."

"Why not?"

"He's too young. He just turned six."

"What does he do all day?"

She shrugged. "If the weather's nice, he goes out and plays. There's a little boy who lives down the street. Otherwise he stays inside."

Sarah talked for she didn't know how long, while her father chewed on his cigars and Harry Lipton took notes on a yellow legal pad. It was late in the day when they finally called a halt.

"We'll pick up again in the morning," Lipton said. By then his original air of formality had softened considerably.

Sarah was glad for the break. But she would have been even happier if the interview had been over for good. How many more times was she going to have to go through this? she wondered.

But the next morning she and her father were back, this time filling Lipton in on their unsuccessful attempts to work through the lawyers and government officials. Not until well after lunch— a cold buffet of sandwiches and salad—did Lipton finally indicate that the interview might be nearing an end.

"I'll be honest with you," he began. "This is a difficult case, from what you've told me about your husband. It would certainly be a challenge. But then"—he offered a boyish grin—"I've always been a sucker for a steep hill."

He stretched and got to his feet. "I'll need a little time to think about this and to consult with a few of my colleagues. I've got several scenarios in mind, but I can't be sure which of them will work best—if, in fact, any of them will work at all—until we've had a chance to conduct a feasibility study."

"How long will that take?"

"It depends. Figure on a minimum of two to three months."

"*Months?*" Sarah was shocked. "Why so long?"

"Mrs. Stefanovic, abduction is a risky business."

Sarah flinched. There it was. Laid out in the open for the first time. The last resort.

That they had finally arrived at this point now seemed almost inevitable.

"I want to make certain," Lipton continued, "that the risks are absolutely minimal before I agree to go ahead. And that takes time. Safety has to be our paramount concern."

"Whose safety?" Ted asked warily. "Yours? Your men's?"

"The boy's, first and foremost, but everyone else's as well. If an abduction starts to look too dangerous, we wouldn't go through with it."

Ted sat back, satisfied. "I don't think we can argue with that."

Lipton nodded his shaggy head and began to explain what the feasibility study would entail. For starters, he'd need a thorough briefing from Bill Borden on the legal aspects. Then a team of operatives would be sent to Belgrade to survey the neighborhood where Joey was living. The area would be mapped and photographed, with special attention given to the timing and routes of police patrols, the proximity of neighboring houses, the location of alternative entrance and exit routes. There would be a lengthy surveillance of Joey, his father, his grandmother.

"It all sounds very thorough," Ted commented dryly.

"Oh, it is," said Lipton. "People think of this as an adventurous business, but a lot of it is just tedious legwork and attention to details. Careful preparation—that's the secret of success for us. Adventure is only the result of poor planning."

"I begin to see why this kind of thing gets so expensive," Ted said. "How much do you figure this is going to run us?"

Lipton's gaze did not waver. "To begin with, we'd need twenty thousand dollars to conduct the feasibility study."

Sarah glanced quickly at her father. He was sitting very still.

"Twenty . . . thousand," Ted said. "For just the study?"

"That's right," said Lipton. "And if we decide to go ahead with the project, you should figure on it running another forty or forty-five thousand."

Ted cleared his throat. "We'll have to give this some thought."

"Of course," said Lipton. He got to his feet. "Meantime, I'll give you the name and address of our bank. We could get started as soon as we've been notified that the initial installment has been deposited in our account."

With an effort Ted pushed himself up off the sofa. Absently he extended his hand, thanked Lipton for his help. Sarah was still too stunned to do any more than follow his lead.

Not until they were downstairs and out on the crowded sidewalk was she able to vent her outrage and bewilderment.

"I don't believe it!" she cried. "Dad, where on earth are we going to come up with that kind of money?"

Her father was barging along now like a rampaging bull, dodging around the people on the sidewalk. "I'm not sure yet. It'll . . . take a little doing."

Sarah stopped in her tracks. "You mean you *have* that much?"

Ted stopped as well. People swirled past. "There are some stocks and things," he said vaguely. "And I guess the bank will give us a good bit for the house."

She stood there absolutely dumbfounded. "You can get that kind of money and you'd be willing to use it for—"

He turned to her, his face a mask of rage and pain. "This is Joey we're talking about. Your only son. My only grandson. I told you once before that the money didn't matter and I meant it. Now forget it, will you. Just forget it."

For once she faced his anger without flinching. "No," she said, facing him straight on, her eyes misting. "I won't forget it."

"Well, you better. Because that's—"

But before he could finish she had thrown her arms around his neck and she was hugging him with all her might. "Thank you, Dad," she said. "Thank you."

TED snapped off the light over his seat and leaned back, hoping that the hum of the 747's engines would lull him to sleep. He glanced over at Sarah. Her eyes were closed, and her waves of walnut-dark hair poured lavishly over her shoulders just the way Emma's used to do before she'd taken to cutting it short. Ted smiled to himself. Sarah's relief and gratitude made it easier for him to bear the weight of what he would have to do when they got back home—made it a *little* easier anyway. Agreeing to Lipton's terms would mean giving up everything he and Emma had been planning and saving for all these years. And, yes, face it; he'd have to refinance the house, just when the mortgage was almost paid off. What was Emma going to say about that?

He outlined Lipton's terms to her the next afternoon, making an effort to break the news about the expense as easily as he could. For a long time she sat there at the kitchen table, sunk in gloomy silence. At last she nodded. She knew as well as he did what their decision was going to be.

First thing the following morning Ted telephoned Sherwood Brice with instructions to sell off all of his stock portfolio. Next he drove downtown to the bank, cashed in his and Emma's savings certificates, and transferred the funds to Lipton's bank.

That done, Ted cabled Lipton to tell him half of the down payment was on the way and that the rest would follow in a few days. Then he went home to bed. He slept for seventeen hours straight.

WITHIN a week of giving Lipton the go-ahead, the Novacks were bombarded with phone calls and cables from London: requests for information, for photos of Joey and Jovan and Jovan's family, for documents. Sarah herself was told to be prepared to travel to Belgrade in the event that the project proved feasible. To avoid raising any questions about her recent trip to Yugoslavia, which was recorded in her current passport, she was told to apply for a new one, as well as a separate passport for Joey; but as a precaution, she was also to hang on to her family passport—the one with the composite photo of herself and Joey.

IT WAS a Monday morning in April. Sarah and her parents were having breakfast when the telephone rang. Ted picked it up.

"Hello? Oh, hello, Harry. How you doing? . . . Yes, we're all here." He exchanged glances with his wife and daughter. "Yes . . . yes." He began to smile. "Wonderful! Glad to hear it."

He held a hand over the receiver. "Lipton's men have reported back." Then, into the receiver, "That's great, Harry. . . . Right, we'll let you know. . . . Good-bye. And thanks again."

He hung up. By now he was beaming.

"Well?" Emma said. "What did he say?"

"The field report looks good. They're ready to go ahead. They'll start as soon as we can get over there."

TWELVE

Now everything began happening very quickly.

On Wednesday, April 20, 1977, Sarah and her father flew to London. Sarah's mother stayed behind; if things went badly in Yugoslavia, they'd need her at home to make sure they got help.

Arriving in London on Thursday morning, they went directly to Harry Lipton's office, where he explained the intricacies of Yugoslavia's visa regulations. After weeks of research and detailed evaluations of various scenarios, Lipton and his associates had hit on a scheme that offered both a chance of success and a low risk of physical danger. The scheme, Lipton told them now, depended on a peculiar hitch in Yugoslavia's visa conventions—the fact that while Americans needed visas to enter and leave Yugoslavia, citizens of Britain and several other European countries did not.

"Which means?" asked Ted.

"Which means," Lipton said, "that a child from Britain, say, could be used to impersonate Joey long enough to cross into Yugoslavia on Joey's passport. The passport then gets stamped with the necessary visa. When our people are ready to bring Joey back across the border, they can prove that he entered the country as an American citizen and is therefore free to leave as one."

Sarah leaned forward. "And since the British boy doesn't need a visa, he can leave afterward on his own passport, is that it?"

"Exactly."

Finding a child to impersonate Joey had been the last detail.

"We lined up a boy just this past weekend," Lipton told them. "Of course we had to hire his parents, too. At any rate, the boy's likely to be a lot more cooperative if his folks are along."

Then Lipton proceeded to outline the plan. Sarah would meet the English family at Heathrow Airport in the morning and fly with them to Frankfurt. There they all would be met by a man named Peter Wilkes, who would drive them across Germany and Austria and over the mountains into Yugoslavia.

"Wait a minute," Ted interrupted. "You're only talking about Sarah going. I assumed I'd be going, too."

Lipton shook his head. "I'm sorry, Ted. Sarah needs to go along in order to help with Joey. Your going would only complicate matters. Besides, the car would be too crowded with six people."

But Ted would not be put off. "Come on, Harry. There's got to be room for one more. The boy can sit on my lap."

Sarah reached out and touched his hand. "I'll be all right, Dad," she told him. "Really. You don't have to worry about me."

"I'm not worried about you," he shot back. "I know you can handle yourself. The point is"—and here he turned to Lipton—"I really think I can be of some use if I go along. I can spell the others with the driving. And I can help Sarah with Joey."

Lipton studied Ted. "It's that important to you?"

"It is. Yes."

Lipton expelled a long breath. "All right. I'll call Wilkes tonight and let him know. But remember this. You're to follow Wilkes's orders absolutely. You may be footing the bill for this little escapade, but he's the one who'll be running the show."

Ted nodded soberly. "He'll get no argument from me."

There remained only one more piece of business: Sarah's signing of documents that gave power of attorney to Peter Wilkes, to act on her behalf, and to an agent they would meet in Belgrade, someone named Vladimir Popovic. Thus, should the agents be arrested during the abduction, they'd have some legal protection.

"Wilkes is a good man," Lipton assured them. "One of the best. And he hired Popovic. You can trust them both."

Lunch then. Toasts to the success of their mission. A restless afternoon and evening. A night of unsettled sleep.

Finally the morning came. Friday, April 22. The drive to the airport. Meeting the Hardys and their downy-haired son. And afterward, as planned, they were boarding the flight to Frankfurt. For Sarah the excitement was unbearable. At last it was happening. At last she was on her way back to Joey.

Then had come the long, cramped drive southeastward, the stop at the border crossing, the frightening uncertainty as they waited in the cold nighttime darkness until finally the guard with the visa stamp appeared and sent them on their way.

IT HAD worked! They had gotten Joey's visa. But as Peter Wilkes reminded them now, the real dangers still lay ahead.

"Once we've got the boy, that's when we'll have to worry."

They were just finishing dinner in the crowded little Turkish café in Belgrade. The rhythm of the flute and the drum music was picking up, and the place was getting much hotter and noisier.

Wilkes took a sip of the thick, sweet Turkish coffee the waiter had just set before him. For a long moment his eyes were hidden by the steam that clouded the lenses of his horn-rimmed glasses.

"If we're caught with Joey in our possession and the police are looking for his kidnappers, we could all end up in jail. That's why I don't want any slipups. I've got too much to lose."

Sarah shuddered. Maybe he gave this speech to all the people he worked with. But it worked. She was scared.

Suddenly Wilkes was on his feet and signaling toward the door. Following the direction of his gestures, Sarah saw an orange-haired man standing at the top of the steps surveying the crowd. He had on a worn sport coat and baggy trousers. With his drooping mustache and the cigarette that hung from his lower lip like a tusk, he reminded Sarah of a rumpled walrus.

"Who's that?" she asked.

"Popovic," was all Wilkes said. Having caught the man's attention, he now settled back into his seat. "Vladimir Popovic knows everyone in Belgrade and is related to at least half of them," Wilkes explained as the man sauntered in their direction. "He's been a great help these last few weeks."

Sarah recognized the name. This was the other man for whom she had signed a power of attorney in Lipton's office. But seeing him now, all swagger and self-importance, made Sarah wince. Had she really signed over Joey's welfare to this character?

The man stepped up to their table. As Wilkes introduced him, he extended his hand with stiff formality. He held his chin high and murmured, "A pleasure," in thickly accented English. But as he turned to shake hands with her father, Sarah realized that the haughty tilt of his head probably kept his carrot-colored toupee from slipping.

Wilkes now passed on some surprising news. He and Popovic had spent the afternoon delivering fertilizer to a certain old gardener that Popovic knew.

"Fertilizer?" asked Ted in bewilderment. "Are you running a garden-supply business on the side?"

Wilkes grinned. "Vlad, why don't you tell them about it?"

Popovic explained that the old man tilled a plot in a public garden across the street from Baka's cottage. "I know him now for

461

several weeks. It is very convenient arrangement. He gives me gardening advice; I bring him tea, sometimes other things. Pesticides last week. Fertilizer today. This way I am keeping the lookout on the house where your boy is living, missus."

Sarah felt her heart jump. "You saw him today? You saw Joey?"

Vlad nodded. "He was there. He was playing in the street with his small friend, a boy from the Mongolian embassy."

"Your husband was there as well," added Wilkes. "And there were other gardeners about, and strollers in the park. It was not a good time to make a move."

Ted lit up a long black cigar. "When will you try again?"

"Tomorrow morning. We'll get there early."

He and Popovic would arrive in separate cars. They would wait for Jovan to leave the house, wait for Joey to come out and play. If all went well, Wilkes would pick up Joey. Popovic would be waiting nearby in the backup car, ready to run interference if they were followed.

Wilkes turned to Sarah. "Have you got the blanket?"

"In the suitcase."

"Good. We'll take it along."

At Lipton's suggestion Sarah had brought along the Snoopy blanket from Joey's bed. It was something Joey would recognize, a familiar token to ease his fears in the first traumatic moments after he was grabbed off the street by a stranger.

"I know it's going to be hard to wait," Wilkes was saying. "But timing is critical."

Tomorrow morning, he continued, while he and Popovic were gone, Ted and Sarah were to stay in their own room in the hotel. They were to keep their bags packed at all times and be ready to go at a moment's notice.

"When it happens, it'll happen fast," he said. "So you have to be prepared to move. Keep an eye on the street. If you see us pull up with the lights flashing, it means we've got Joey. Get your bags and get out to the car—fast!"

FOR a long time that night Sarah lay awake, watching the shifting patterns made on the ceiling by the lights of cars passing in the street below.

Not two miles away was Joey. He was probably snug in his

blankets, an arm outflung, lips parted in the soft kiss of sleep. Was he warm enough? she wondered. Was he even actually in bed? He should be; it was well past his bedtime. Not that Jovan paid much attention to such things. He'd keep Joey up all night if it suited his convenience. All that concerned him was himself—his rights, his dreams, his pain.

No more, Joey. It will be over soon. Tomorrow.

EARLY the next morning Sarah and her father watched from the window of the hotel dining room as Wilkes and Popovic drove off in the blue BMW.

They finished breakfast and lingered over coffee, both of them reluctant to go back to their claustrophobic little room. But when the dining room began to empty, they knew it was time to leave before the staff began to take too much notice of them.

Once upstairs, Sarah and her father took turns at the chair by the window. One hour stretched to two. Two stretched to three. As the sun rose higher, Sarah watched the shadow of the hotel go sliding down the face of the apartment building across the way. Stabs of fear kept cutting into her. She kept thinking of what would happen if Wilkes failed, if she had to go home without Joey. Home? What kind of home could there ever be for her if she had to leave Joey behind? To never see him again, to never again be part of his life—it would be unbearable.

Wilkes had to succeed. He just had to.

The shadow was gone from the face of the building across the street and the sun was shining straight down onto the pavement below, but still there was no sign of the BMW.

"What time is it now?" Sarah asked.

Ted checked his watch. "Twenty after twelve."

"What can they be doing all this time?"

He shrugged. "Wilkes said it might take all day. They probably just haven't had a chance to make their move."

But the truth was that Ted himself was beginning to think something had gone wrong. The waiting, the unrelenting tension were working on his nerves, too.

Feeling restless, he had just gotten up from the chair by the window when the blue BMW turned into the parking lot below.

"They're here," he said.

His words brought Sarah bolting to the window as the car slid into a parking place. The headlights were not flashing.

"Are you sure it's the right car?" she asked.

"Look for yourself."

Sure enough, emerging from the the driver's side was the familiar fair-haired figure of Peter Wilkes. But no one else got out of the car with him. He was alone.

In bleak silence Sarah watched Wilkes walk toward the hotel. Minutes later there was a knock at the door. Ted went to open it.

"No luck?" he asked as Wilkes stepped into the room.

"Afraid not." Wilkes flung his jacket onto the bed.

Sarah exploded. "Luck! You mean you're relying on luck?" She heard the shrillness in her voice but couldn't control it. The man's bland acceptance of failure was infuriating.

Wilkes closed his eyes. "A figure of speech, Mrs. Stefanovic."

"Well, will you kindly tell me what you have been doing all this time, then? Where is my boy? Where is Joey?"

Her father reddened. "Sarah, please."

Wilkes raised a patient hand. "It's all right, Ted. It's been a long morning for all of us." He took out his lighter, lit a cigarette. Then in his low voice he began quietly to explain what had happened that morning.

He and Popovic had watched Baka's house from eight thirty on. They watched as the first dog walkers appeared. Then came the gardeners, with their forks and spades. Finally, just before noon, Baka and Jovan and the boy came out of the cottage together.

"They walked to the corner and got on a bus," Wilkes said. "We followed them, of course, but from the bus number we knew they were off to visit Jovan's sister. It's the only place they ever go together. They usually go on Sundays and stay all afternoon."

"Does that sound right, Sarah?" her father asked.

She nodded sullenly. She was still angry, but she had to admit that Wilkes and his men had done their research thoroughly.

"Anyway," Wilkes went on, "there didn't seem to be much point in us hanging about. Tomorrow is Monday; people will be at work. We should have a better chance then."

He turned to Sarah. "Look here," he said. "I'm sorry. I know this is frustrating. The waiting is the hardest part of this job, even for professionals. But you've got to understand. These things take time. The conditions have to be just right: the boy alone, no one in the way. And in this particular situation that's pretty difficult; with Tito's palace just around the corner that neighborhood is guarded like a military base."

But Sarah hardly heard. She had turned away, her face to the window.

WILKES was at their room early the next morning, his suitcase in hand. "Feeling better about things?" he asked Sarah.

She nodded, smiling faintly. "I guess it was just the strain. A good night's sleep helped a lot."

"Good. I'm glad to hear it." And from the way he said it, Sarah knew he meant it.

A few minutes later they were in the car and on the way to a new hotel. The move was a safety precaution. Wilkes had decided to change their base of operations.

The new hotel was the Moskva. Located near the city's center, it was an elegant old turn-of-the century building that had suffered the indignity of being modernized, complete with bright orange vinyl furniture in the lobby.

At the check-in counter Wilkes used the same ploy as before to get Sarah up to the room without showing her passport. The charade worked as well as it had the first time. Leaving Sarah and Ted to have breakfast by themselves in the hotel dining room, Wilkes drove off to meet Popovic and to once again take up their surveillance of Baka's cottage.

Sarah and her father waited in their room for the rest of the morning. From their window they watched the pale morning turn to rainy noontime.

They had a light lunch. When four o'clock came and went, there was still no sign of Wilkes or Popovic. All the fears of the day before surfaced again. What was happening? Had Wilkes been arrested? Was Joey all right?

A moment later there was a soft knock at the door.

"Open up. It's me, Peter."

Her father let him in. "We didn't see you drive up," he said. "Where did you park?"

Wilkes glanced at him distractedly. "We, uh, had to change cars. The BMW lost its clutch just after I left you this morning.

465

Piece of junk." He collapsed into an easy chair, his legs stretched out in front of him.

Sarah threw an alarmed glance at her father. It was the first time she had seen Wilkes looking so strung out, so defeated.

"Are you going to tell us what happened?" Ted asked.

Wilkes sucked in a long breath, let it out. "Nothing happened. Absolutely nothing. We waited for the boy to come out to play, but he never did. The weather must have kept him in. *Dammit*," he said, pounding his fist on the arm of the chair. "They never *go* anywhere. They just *sit* there."

Ted sighed. "All right. What do you propose we do now?"

Wilkes got to his feet, went to the window, looked down at the street. There was a sadness in his eyes that Sarah had not seen before. "Look," he said, "I hate to say this, but I think we should put off trying to get Joey. For the time being."

"But—" Sarah was appalled. She could not believe what she was hearing. After all this effort, all this waiting, to quit now!

"It would only be for a few months," Wilkes hurried on. "In the fall, when they send Joey to school, we'd have a better chance."

"No!" Sarah shouted. She would have none of it. "We're not quitting. Mr. Wilkes, I came here to get my son and I'm not going home without him. If you're too timid to do the job, I'll do it myself! We've got the visa now. We don't need you."

She looked over at her father, expecting him to try to quiet her. Instead, he said, "Sarah's right. We didn't come all this way to go home empty-handed."

Wilkes shook his head. "Look, I feel as badly as you do about the way things have worked out, but—"

"You?" Sarah steel-eyed him. "I find that hard to believe."

"Then you misjudge me," he said, his own anger rising. "I happen to have a boy of my own at home. He's just about Joey's age, and believe me, he's in my mind every time I go over there and sit outside that house and see your boy living the way he is, cut off from his mother, from his home, from everything familiar. I want to see him out of there as much as you do."

Sarah could not have been more surprised. "I—I had no idea you were even married," she stammered. "I mean, other than the marriage you made up for this trip."

"I'm divorced, actually."

"And your boy is . . ."

"I have a girl as well. They live with their mother. But I see them every chance I get and . . ." He brushed the rest away with a wave of his hand. "Look, maybe I shouldn't have taken this job. It's too close to me. Maybe that's what's making me so cautious."

"I'm sorry," said Sarah. "I didn't know."

"Well, now you do." He walked over to Sarah, stood very close to her. "The point is, I want you to know that if we leave here now, I will be back in the fall. I'll bring your boy back to you. I promise. I won't rest until I do." His eyes held hers.

"Thank you," she said. "But I still think you're giving up too soon."

"So do I," said Ted. "I'm prepared to stick it out a little longer."

Wilkes looked at them both uncertainly for a moment, then seemed to make his decision. "Right, then. We'll stay with it a few days more." He straightened up, made an effort to look authoritative. "If you'll excuse me, I'll go wash up a bit before dinner."

They agreed to meet in half an hour. Sarah showered and was just starting on her makeup when there was a sharp knocking at the door and Wilkes's voice urging her to let him in.

"We're not ready yet," she called.

"Never mind that. Just open up."

The urgency in his voice was alarming. Quickly she unlocked the door. "What is it? What's wrong?"

He was in stocking feet and his hair was still dripping from the shower. But there was a smile of triumph on his face.

"We got our break! Popovic just telephoned. Jovan boarded a plane for Paris half an hour ago. He's not due back until Thursday."

THIRTEEN

ALTHOUGH Popovic had been unable to discover the reason for Jovan's abrupt departure, there was no doubt that he was gone and that he had left Joey behind with Baka. The old woman was now the only person guarding the boy. If Wilkes was going to make a move, this was the best chance he was likely to get.

That evening over dinner Wilkes explained the plan for the next morning. He and Popovic would drive in separate cars to the cul-de-sac, as before, and await their opportunity. If the weather was fair and Joey was sent out to play—

"Joey should be in my car before the morning's over. I'll pick you two up here; then we'll head west toward Zagreb," Wilkes concluded.

"There's something I don't understand," Sarah said. "Why don't we just get a flight out of Belgrade instead of driving all the way to Zagreb? Wouldn't we get out a lot quicker?"

"It might be quicker, yes," Wilkes conceded. "Then again, it might take twenty years. As soon as Joey is reported missing, the police will start watching the airport. What we have to do is get away from Belgrade as quickly as we can by car."

THE weather was perfect the next morning. From a flower stand on the corner a warm breeze carried the sweet scent of blossoms through the window of the hotel dining room, where Sarah and her father sat with Peter Wilkes. Sunlight shimmered on the breakfast dishes.

"If Baka is ever going to send Joey out to play," said Ted, "today has got to be the day."

Wilkes glanced at his watch. "That's what we're counting on," he said. He got to his feet. "All right. Stay put, both of you. Watch for the car, and be ready to move when I get back."

He gulped a last mouthful of coffee, adjusted his glasses, then headed for the door.

"Don't forget Joey's blanket," Sarah called after him.

He smiled. "It's in the car."

"Good luck," said Ted.

"Thanks."

Wilkes turned and strode briskly out of the dining room. The car he'd gotten in exchange for the faulty BMW was a little green Volkswagen. From their table at the window Sarah and her father watched him climb into it and drive away.

HALF an hour passed. Forty-five minutes. Wilkes did not appear. Neither did Popovic.

Sarah and her father still lingered at their table by the window, watching the traffic outside. Fortunately, the restaurant was not crowded and no one hurried them to leave. The waiting, though, was hard. Sarah folded and refolded her napkin; Ted's right leg bobbed nervously.

"Dad? What if he can't get Joey back? What will we do?"

He looked away. "I've been wondering that myself. I—" But he stopped. Something out the window had caught his eye.

Following his gaze, Sarah saw it. The green VW. Wilkes was backing it into a parking space in front of the hotel. Her heart sank. The headlights were not flashing. Wilkes was alone.

"Oh, no," she moaned, her eyes suddenly stinging with tears of anger and frustration. He had failed again. Everything had been so right! Jovan was gone; the weather was perfect. And still he had come back empty-handed. What a fool she had been to have trusted him. To have trusted anyone but herself!

Overwhelmed with disappointment, she buried her head in her hands.

But now her father touched her arm. "Sarah, look."

And lifting her head, she saw that Wilkes had gone around to the passenger side of the car and was opening the door. For a moment his body blocked her view.

But then she caught a glimpse of the small figure, the tawny hair, and all at once she was on her feet.

"It's him, Dad!" she cried in disbelief. "Oh, God, it's Joey!"

He reached for her hand. "Steady," he murmured. "Steady." But his own voice was choked.

Her hands covering her mouth, her vision blurred by a mist of tears, she saw Wilkes taking Joey by the hand and leading him toward the hotel entrance.

"Steady," her father said again. But she broke free.

And then she was running. As if in a dream, she ran through the door and into the street; and he was there, Joey was there, holding on to Peter Wilkes with one hand, clutching his Snoopy blanket with the other, looking terrified and bewildered as he peered about. And then he saw her. His look changed to wonder and he was starting toward her, uncertainly at first, wide-eyed, disbelieving, until with a rush he was in her arms and she was sweeping him off his feet and hugging him to her, and murmuring, "Joey. Oh, my Joey, my beautiful boy, my beautiful Joey."

How wonderful it felt to hold him, to feel him holding her. He was here. He was hers again, with his arms around her neck, his

soft cheek against hers, the sweet music of his tiny voice in her ear, singing, "Mama, I m-missed you s-so m-much."

"I'm here now, Joey. Mama's here."

Her father came over and was hugging them both, and his own eyes were wet. But now Wilkes's urgent whispers were breaking in on them. "Come on, come on. Forget that now. We've got to get moving. If we don't get out of town fast, we won't get out at all."

Quickly Ted ran back inside to get the bags. While he was gone, Wilkes led Sarah and Joey to the car. As he was opening the door a blue sedan pulled up next to the VW, its horn blaring. Police, thought Sarah in sudden panic. We've been caught. Joey!

But then she saw the orange hair, the drooping mustache. It was Popovic. He was grinning and waving and blowing his horn as if he had arrived at a wedding just in time to cheer the bride and groom. Around them heads were turning. He's going to ruin everything, Sarah thought.

Wilkes hurried over to Popovic's car and ordered him away. "If we have to, we'll call you later. Now get out of here." Popovic shifted hard. Tires squealing, he sped off.

Five minutes later Wilkes was at the wheel of the VW, speeding through the back streets of Belgrade. Ted sat beside him in the passenger seat, clinging to the door frame. Wilkes seemed to know the city inside out, every cobbled alleyway, every one-way street. As he spun the car around corners and down alleys he did not hesitate, not even for a second. In the back seat Joey, trembling, huddled under Sarah's arm.

"It's all right," she murmured, keeping fear out of her voice.

Soon the car was sailing across the bridge over the Sava River, then speeding along the *autoput* through the western suburbs of Belgrade. Wilkes lit a cigarette. "So far, so good," he said.

Ted turned around and smiled fondly at Joey. "It's so great to see you again. I really missed you, kiddo."

Joey, still shaken, responded with a guarded smile. He huddled closer to Sarah. "Where is the m-man t-taking us?"

"Home, lovey. We're going home."

THEY followed the same route they had taken on the way into Belgrade. In the back seat Joey dozed, his small body tucked under Sarah's arm. She couldn't take her eyes off him, couldn't help touching him, as if to reassure herself that yes, he was real; yes, he was actually here with her again—not somebody else's son but her very own, her Joey. Her fingers traced the curve of his cheeks, the gentle slope of his nose, the roundness of his chin.

His eyelids fluttered open. He smiled up at her and slid her hand into his, clutching it to him, embracing it. He dozed again.

For a while they drove in silence. Then Ted turned to Wilkes. "What happened back there? When you took Joey, I mean. Did you have any trouble?"

"None at all." Wilkes glanced over his shoulder to make sure Joey was asleep. "He was out in the road with a little playmate. Baka was nowhere in sight. The setup couldn't have been better. All I did was drive down to the end of the cul-de-sac, make a quick turnabout, and pull up next to the boys. I got out, scooped Joey up in my arms, and off we went. It all happened so quickly he was too surprised to even cry out. Of course once I started driving away he did put up rather a fuss. But as soon as I told him I was taking him to his mother, he quieted down."

"What about the other boy?" Ted asked. "What did he do?"

"The last I saw of him, he was running toward the house shouting for Baka."

"And the sentry? He didn't try to stop you?"

Wilkes laughed. "It was quite incredible, really. When we drove past the fellow, Joey was still yelling bloody murder and I was trying to quiet him down. But all the sentry did was stand there watching. I expect he thought he was seeing nothing more than a frustrated parent trying to cope with an unruly child. Poor chap must be catching it from his superiors about now."

Ted laughed. "But what about the headlights?"

"Headlights?"

"They weren't flashing when you got to the hotel with Joey."

"Oh. Right. Must have slipped my mind in all the excitement."

As Sarah listened, all she could think of was the terror Joey must have felt. Her boy. Lying now with his head in her lap, his features so blessedly familiar. Yet in the last eight months he had experienced things she had not shared. A whole part of his childhood had been stolen from her. Physically she may have gotten him back, but there was a large part of his life that would be forever lost to her.

"Remember the joke you told me?" she asked him as he stirred, snuggling up once more under her arm. "About the cabbage and the faucet and the tomato that were having a race? Remember, Joey? Remember who would win?"

He looked at her blankly.

"The cabbage would be—ahead," she prompted. "The faucet?"

A light came into his eyes. "The f-faucet would b-be running?"

"Right! And the tomato?"

"Would have to c-catch up!" he declared triumphantly. And then they were both giggling and laughing, and Sarah was thinking, hopefully, that maybe so much hadn't been lost after all.

It was six in the evening before Wilkes pulled the VW into a parking spot in front of the Zagreb air terminal, where they had dropped the Hardys off for their flight to Rome. When was that? Sarah wondered. Only four days ago? It seemed like years.

"Oh, no," Ted groaned. "Look at that!"

Joey sat up and rubbed his eyes. "What's the matter, Mama?"

"Nothing's the matter, Joey. Do you feel better? You slept a long time." But something was the matter; otherwise why were all those police cars lined up at the curb outside the terminal?

"You three stay here," said Wilkes. "I'll go check it out."

He was back a short time later. Leaning in the window, he reported that the next flight to the West was to Munich. "But it's not due to leave for another three hours, and I don't want to sit around here waiting all that time. Not with all those chaps standing about." He nodded toward the police cars.

"Did you find out why they're here?" asked Ted.

"Guarding some visiting dignitaries, apparently. But I don't want to take any chances." He handed Ted the keys. "How about you driving for a while? I could use a rest."

Ted got out and went around to the driver's side. "Where to?"

"Follow the signs to Ljubljana. We'll try Loibl Pass again."

Outside of Ljubljana they stopped briefly for gas. At a nearby café they got coffee and a snack and used the rest rooms. Then they got back into the car.

"I'll take over now," said Wilkes, sliding behind the wheel.

They were on the final leg. Ahead of them rose the jagged

peaks of the Karawanken mountains. Somewhere up there was the border crossing, Loibl Pass. Once beyond it, they'd be home free.

It was after dark when they approached the checkpoint at the southern end of the pass. From a distance Sarah saw the floodlit plaza. In the pool of light were the gatehouses and lines of cars, and tiny figures moving about.

Over his shoulder Wilkes said, "We'll do it as we did before."

She got the message. "Not a word now, Joey. I want you to pretend you're asleep. Will you do that? Here, stretch out and put your head on my lap. Good. Now just keep your eyes closed. I'll tell you when it's okay to look up again."

There was more traffic at the checkpoint than there had been last time. Five or six cars were lined up, waiting to cross the border. And there were more guards on duty, too.

Wilkes coasted into line behind the other cars. In nervous silence they waited their turn. Sarah's heart was pounding.

Finally the car in front of them was waved through. The red-and-white striped gate went up and came down again, blocking their way. Wilkes edged the car forward and came to a stop.

A guard stepped up to the car. "Good evening, " he responded in English to Wilkes's greeting. He signaled Wilkes to shut off the engine.

"I'd rather not," said Wilkes reasonably. "If you don't mind. I've been having a devil of a time with the starter. And I'm afraid that if I turn it off, we won't get it going again."

The guard scowled, then shrugged. "Passports," he snapped.

Wilkes handed them over.

Using his flashlight, the guard examined them one by one. "You have had short visit," he said, eyeing the dates on the visas.

"Afraid so," said Wilkes. "Next time we hope to stay longer. It's a beautiful country, especially this time of the year."

In the back seat Sarah squirmed. Suddenly the beam of the guard's light was slashing across her face. Joey flinched in her arms. His eyes flew open. "Be still, Joey," she whispered.

Then, blessedly, the light was gone, and now the guard was turning away, taking the passports with him. In silence Sarah, Wilkes, and her father watched him step into the gatehouse.

Inside they could see the man showing the passports to his colleagues and nodding toward the VW.

They know! thought Sarah. They're going to stop us!

The guard came out again. He did not have the passports in his hand. He spoke to Wilkes. "Registration," he said. "I must see, please, the registration for the vehicle."

"Ah, yes. Of course." Wilkes reached across to the glove compartment, fumbled through the papers there, handed one of them over. The guard examined it under his flashlight, took it with him into the gatehouse.

Through clenched teeth Wilkes said very quietly, "If they try to detain us, I'm going to gun it and go through the gate. Be ready to duck. There may be shooting."

The breath caught in Sarah's throat. This couldn't be happening. Not after we've come so far. Not now, when we're almost there. "Please," she begged, "don't do it. Somebody might get hurt."

Wilkes only glanced at her distractedly.

Sarah looked down at Joey. He was lying still, but his eyes were wide open and he was clinging to her arm so hard that it hurt. She put a finger to her lips, then closed his eyes gently with her fingertips. Her beautiful boy! Whatever happened now, at least she'd had these few hours with him. These precious hours.

The guard was back. He shone his flashlight on a little metal plate on the dashboard below the windshield, comparing the number he found there with the number on the registration form.

"I think he thinks we've stolen the car," said Ted.

Carefully Wilkes eased the car into gear, his hand tightfisted on the stick, his foot on the clutch. He was getting ready to gun it.

But then the guard was at his elbow again, handing back the passports and the registration, wishing them a good trip, waving them on their way. Almost before Sarah knew what was happening, the car lurched forward and they were through the gate and speeding up the open highway toward Austria.

Then suddenly the car was filled with their cheering.

"We made it!" cried Sarah, hugging Joey fiercely.

"Whoo-eee!" Ted whooped. "Fantastic!" He grabbed Wilkes's free hand and began pumping it wildly. "Congratulations, Peter. Well done! Oh, boy! Fantastic!"

Sarah, laughing and crying at the same time, let go of Joey long enough to reach over the back of Wilkes's seat and throw her arms around his neck. She planted an exuberant kiss on his cheek.

"Hey!" He laughed as he struggled to keep the car on the road. "Keep that up and I might just go back and do it all over again."

Ted reached into his jacket pocket and pulled out one of his long black cigars. "This one's for you, Peter. I've been saving it ever since Belgrade. Take a look. It's even got your name on it."

Wilkes flicked on the overhead light and glanced at the label. And grinned from ear to ear.

The label read EL CAUDILLO. The boss. The hero.

HOME AGAIN: Sunday, July 10, 1977

REACHING up, Sarah took dinner plates down from the cupboard and carried them into the dining room. On the way she stopped to glance out the kitchen window. Although it was almost three months since Joey had been back, she still found herself checking constantly to make sure she knew where he was.

At the moment he was on his hands and knees in the sandbox by the garage, racing his Hot Wheels with Michael and Jason. The two boys lived a few houses away and had come over to make friends with Joey within the first week after Sarah's parents had moved into this new house, this new neighborhood.

Three months! It was incredible to think it had really been that long ago. It seemed like just yesterday that Peter Wilkes had driven them over the border into Austria. She could still remember her elation, her relief, her joy.

Exhausted after the hours-long drive from Belgrade, they had stopped overnight at a hotel in Klagenfurt, where Wilkes had put through a call to Harry Lipton in London.

"Harry? . . . Wilkes here. Mission accomplished."

That was all. No details, no excitement. Cool as a cucumber.

After he'd hung up, her father had gotten on the phone and placed a call to Sommerton.

"Emma?" he said. "Ted here. Mission accomplished." The smirk on his face was priceless.

While he was on the line, he left instructions for Emma to send Baka a telegram letting her know that Joey was safe with Sarah. As a precaution, Emma was to have Sarah's brother send the wire from California. It might just help to throw Jovan off the scent in case he came looking for Joey. They were not about to let Jovan near him ever again. Not if they could help it.

The next day they drove over the mountains to Munich. Wilkes had already called ahead to the airport. Sarah and Joey and her father would be on a flight back to the States that afternoon.

"Oh, Joey, Gramma Emma is going to be so happy to see you again," Sarah said as the four of them waited in the airport lounge for the flight to begin boarding. "And you'll sleep in your own bed and see your old friends again. Won't that be nice?"

"*Da*, Mama."

That word. Should she correct him? No, not yet. Give him time. He needs time.

"What about you, Peter?" Ted asked from around his own El Caudillo. "Where are you off to?"

Wilkes shrugged. "Home for a few days. Then back to work."

He said it so offhandedly that work might have been nothing more unusual than selling shoes or sitting behind a desk.

THE day after Sarah had Joey home, when she thought Jovan might be back from Paris, she put a call through to Belgrade. She wanted to let him know what had happened. It seemed only fair.

"Don't tell him where you are," her father cautioned.

When Jovan answered, she was pleased with her coolness as he poured out his rage. And as he turned to remorse, to begging for another chance, she felt not the slightest twinge of sympathy.

Quieter then, more subdued, he told her how relieved he'd been to get the cable. Baka, too. Until it arrived, the police had assumed Joey was still somewhere in Belgrade, taken where or by whom they had no idea. Baka had been sick with worry. So had Jovan when Baka had reached him in Paris to tell him the news. He had hurried home immediately.

"What were you doing in Paris?" Sarah asked.

"I was seeing some people about a job, and you know it."

"How would I have known it?" she said, taken aback.

"Because someone knew and they told you. Or they told that man who took Joey for you." His voice was rising again. "And just who was that man anyway?"

"He was . . . a friend." She smiled to herself, remembering Peter Wilkes's face, his caring. Yes, a friend.

"Who was it, Sarah? Tell me who told your friend that I would be away. You think I am stupid, eh? It was Branko, wasn't it? It was my sister's husband. I never trusted him."

"No, Jovan. It wasn't Branko."

"Then tell me who it was, Sarah. Tell me. Who was it? Who betrayed me?"

Two weeks later an envelope from the State Department dropped through the mail slot in the Novacks' front door. Inside, Sarah found cables from the American embassy in Belgrade. The cables reported that the Yugoslav newspapers were shocked that the child of a Yugoslav citizen could be kidnapped off the streets of Belgrade in broad daylight—and from under the noses of the soldiers guarding the residence of President Tito himself.

"My heart bleeds," said Ted sardonically. Meanwhile, he had been taking his own security precautions. Through Bill Borden in Washington he had petitioned the Immigration and Naturalization Service to prevent Jovan from reentering the country.

The new house was another precaution—a new address in a new town, an unlisted phone number. This house was smaller and had less property than the one in Sommerton, but most of the profit from the Sommerton sale had to be used to pay the bulk of Harry Lipton's bill. Even so, a substantial debt still remained.

Sarah, too, would soon be moving to a new place, once she started teaching again. And Ted had promised that when Joey started kindergarten in the fall, he would be sent to a private school so that if Jovan did manage to get back into the country, he was going to have a hard time tracking Joey down.

"I don't like it," Sarah's mother had said. "We're making hostages of ourselves."

But even she had to admit that the alternative was just too awful to contemplate: Jovan grabbing Joey again, all that grief and heartache. None of them could bear to go through that again.

JOEY and his playmates had grown bored with their sandbox games. As Sarah watched from the kitchen window, her hands full of dishes, the three boys ran helter-skelter for the swing set, where Joey and Michael began pushing and shoving to be the first one up the ladder of the slide.

"One at a time, boys," Sarah called through the window. "And be careful on the ladder. Hold on with both hands."

The words were hardly said when the telephone rang.

"It's for you," her mother said, holding out the receiver. "It's long distance."

Sarah's stomach lurched. Jovan, she thought. But how did he know where— "Hello?"

"Hello, Sarah? Peter Wilkes here. Remember me?"

She laughed, both with relief and delight. "Peter! Of course I remember. How could I ever forget? Where are you?"

"I'm in Rome, actually. Another assignment. But I had a few minutes and I thought I'd ring you up and see how you're getting along."

"But how—"

"Harry Lipton gave me your new number. Don't worry. It's safe with me."

Out of the corner of her eye Sarah saw that her mother was listening. She pulled the phone cord around the corner. "How are you?" she asked, lowering her voice.

"Oh, I'm still in one piece. But tell me about yourself and Joey. How are you managing?"

"Joey's just fine. Really. His stutter is almost gone. He's coming along pretty well."

"And what about you?" he asked.

She toyed with the phone cord. "Oh, I'm all right. You know, getting along. It looks like I'll be teaching in the fall. I'd like to help pay off some of these bills."

"Mine included?"

She laughed. "Yours especially."

"Yes, well, the reason I'm calling is, I'm going to be in New York next week and I was wondering if you'd like to go out to dinner with me."

"I . . ." She hesitated. In her mind's eye she saw his warm eyes behind his glasses, his impish grin that first time he sneaked her past the desk clerk at the Hotel Srbija. She felt the pressure of his hand on her arm and remembered his tenderness with Joey.

"Hello," he prompted. "You still there?"

"I'm here. I'm just a little surprised."

"Pleasantly, I hope."

"Well, yes, as a matter of fact."

"Well then?"

"I'll, uh, have to see if my parents will be free to stay with Joey. What if you call me again when you get in?"

"Come on, Sarah, you're stalling. We don't have to be coy with each other, do we?"

"I guess not. Not after all the hotels we checked into together."

This time it was his turn to laugh. "So, what about it? Will you let me take you to dinner?"

She took a deep breath. "Yes, all right. I'd like that. Yes."

SUPPER was ready by the time she hung up. She finished setting out the silverware, then went to the kitchen window to call Joey in.

He wasn't there.

Joey wasn't in the yard. He wasn't anywhere in sight.

Panic. Sarah's mouth went dry. "Joey!"

She ran to the back door.

And found him sitting on the steps, deep in conversation with his playmates. She closed her eyes. Thank God, she thought; thank God. And wondered if the time would ever come when she could bear to let Joey out of her sight again.

OUTSIDE on the steps, Joey and Michael and Jason were discussing their new spy club.

The club was Joey's idea. Joey was the boss, and Michael and Jason were his spies. Their job was to watch the street and keep an eye out for strangers or for suspicious-looking cars.

If they saw anything or anyone unusual, they were to run and tell Joey about it right away.

It has been nine years since the Novacks brought Joey home, and according to author Thomas Froncek, it took much of that time for the family to recover from its ordeal. "Joey was at first a terrified little boy who would not eat or sleep alone," Froncek explains. "His feet bothered him because the shoes he'd worn in Belgrade were two sizes too small, and he was suffering from malnutrition." With the benefit of time and love, however, Joey has grown into a healthy and active teenager. He's the star of his high school soccer team, and even his painful stutter has disappeared.

Sarah Stefanovic is also on the road to a new happiness. She is engaged to a man "Joey gets along with beautifully," says the author. (No, the man is not the mysterious Peter Wilkes.) As for Jovan, he is

Thomas Froncek

living with his second wife and their children in Europe. For a time he tried to regain visitation rights to Joey, but negotiations foundered, and father and son have not seen each other since a formal meeting in a lawyer's office in January 1984.

Thomas Froncek, a journalist by training, first learned about Sarah's experience from a business associate. "I met with the grandfather, Ted Novack, and the more he talked—about a parental kidnapping, midnight crossing of a foreign border, government contacts—the more intrigued I became." By a quirk of fate, the author's own son, Jesse, and *Take Away One*'s Joey share the same birthday. This unexpected tie helped Froncek write the book "with genuine feeling," he says, "and with the ability to connect as a parent. For example, the first time Jesse rode his bicycle down the street and out of sight, I knew the fear Sarah must have felt about losing her son. It's terrifying. Being a parent can be so perilous."

Tom and his wife, Ellen, live in the New York City area, where Tom is already at work on another suspenseful drama.

THE
TWO FARMS

One rich, one poor . . .
And a young man caught between them.

A CONDENSATION OF THE NOVEL BY

Mary E. Pearce

ILLUSTRATED BY BEN STAHL

Once, the two farms nestled together peacefully in the lush English countryside. To the east was Peele, neat and prosperous, owned by John Sutton. To the west was Godsakes, home of Morris Riddler, a man plagued by bad luck and bad judgment. Over the years, as Godsakes slips ever closer to ruin, the peace between the farms turns into a bitter contest—a contest Godsakes seems certain to lose.

Then a new player enters the drama. Jim Lundy has been raised as a gentleman, but he has a farmer's love of the soil in his blood. And when a cruel betrayal reminds him all too bluntly of his humble origins, he pits the two farms against each other as never before. It is revenge that Jim seeks. What he finds is far more precious.

An enchanting story, as warm and rich as the land it celebrates.

CHAPTER 1

THE valley ran from north to south, and the two farms, Godsakes and Peele, lay on opposite sides of it. The Suttons had been tenants at Peele for four generations, having come there in 1746, but the Riddlers had been at Godsakes only since 1821. The little valley was sheltered and warm, and the land was as rich and fertile as any land in Gloucestershire, varying from a light sandy loam in the upper part of the valley to a rich red marl in the lower parts. On the same side of the valley as Godsakes, lying in a hollow beside it, was a third farm known as Granger's, but it was only sixty acres or so, and all of it heavy clay.

Peele, on the valley's eastern slopes, was sheltered by the round green hill known locally as Luton Camp, while Godsakes, on the western side, had its back to the twin humps of Hogden Hill and Derritt Hill. On both these farms the fields sloped gently down to the flat green valley floor, where the Timmy Brook, with many a twist, made its way through the meadows to join the little river Cran outside the hamlet of Abbot's Lyall.

In summertime the Timmy Brook flowed sedately between its banks, but every winter without fail it would flood out over the meadows. This flooding was welcomed by the valley farmers, for it left the meadows so enriched that in spring they gave new grass for the cows before it grew elsewhere. These meadows were common land, and stock from all three farms grazed there together, crossing and recrossing the brook by a number of little bridges.

John Sutton of Peele Farm, with four generations of breeding behind him, was a vigorous man of some education and polish who farmed his land by modern ideas. Isaac Riddler, on the other hand, was a near illiterate cattle dealer who had taken the tenancy of Godsakes with more courage than capital. His son, Morris, had succeeded him, but farmed in the same haphazard way and was almost always behind with his work. It was inevitable, therefore, that the educated John Sutton, successfully farming three hundred acres, should feel himself superior to the uncouth Morris Riddler, muddling along on his hundred and ten.

Still, they were good enough neighbors until, in 1842, their landlord, James Goodwin of Allern Hall, decided to sell the three valley farms and offered the tenants first refusal. The estate agent, Mr. Maule, called on John Sutton first, and he stated the exact terms of the offer and gave him a week to think it over.

Sutton did not need to think. He knew his own mind; already he saw the fields as his own. And the purchase presented no problem, because an uncle had recently died and left Sutton a tidy fortune. The chance of buying Peele so accorded with his ambitions that it came like the answer to a half-formed prayer.

For Riddler, however, it was a different matter.

"Buy Godsakes? How much?" he asked the agent.

"Mr. Goodwin would accept eighteen pounds per acre for the farm itself and fifty shillings per acre for the hill pastures."

"But that would be over two thousand pounds! I haven't got it!"

"It would fetch more than that if it went for auction, and I'm sure the bank would advance whatever you need."

"Yes, at an interest of four percent!"

"Does that mean you do not wish to buy?"

"Don't I get time to think?"

"Yes," Mr. Maule said. "You have until a week today. Then I would like you to call on me and let me know your decision."

But although he wanted time to think, Riddler had also made up his mind, for he saw that the chance was too good to miss. He talked about it to his wife, Agnes.

"Well, for one thing, we don't want to leave here, do we, when we've been here twenty-one years and put so much work into the place, eh?" He was also thinking of his son, Eddy, at that time nine years old. "What a wonderful thing that'll be for him—taking over his own farm! We shall never have such a chance again."

"How much will you have to borrow?"

"I reckon about six hundred pounds."

"You'll see Mr. Maule, then?"

"Be sure I shall!"

But the whole week went by, and Riddler, behindhand as usual, was still at work in the meadows. Mr. Maule would have to wait. There was no great hurry.

JOHN Sutton's purchase of his farm was already under way by this time. An agreement had been signed between the two parties, and ten percent of the price had been deposited with the estate lawyers.

"What about Hessey at Granger's? Have you had his answer?"

"He's decided not to buy. Would you be interested? Mr. Goodwin would accept fifteen pounds the acre."

"I am willing to pay that."

"Excellent. I thought you might."

"What about Riddler at Godsakes? Will he be buying?"

"He hasn't given his answer yet, but it seems very doubtful," the agent said. "Not much capital there, I think."

"Well, if he doesn't, you know where to come. I'll have it off you like a shot."

"That would give you quite a substantial holding," the agent said with a little smile.

"It would mean the whole valley was mine," Sutton said. "The idea has taken hold of me. Riddler is a good enough chap, but he's forty years behind the times. A glance over Godsakes shows you that. I could farm it a lot better than he does."

"Well, I'll give Riddler another few days; then I'll go over and chivy him up. But I would say Godsakes is as good as yours."

Sutton nodded, satisfied. "If Godsakes went to auction, how much do you think it would fetch?"

"I would think, perhaps, three thousand pounds."

"Yes, well," Sutton said. "Certainly, if I were there, I would be willing to bid that high."

The agent smiled understandingly. "I'll see Riddler soon."

"WHAT DO YOU MEAN, SUTTON's made you a better offer? Tenants had first option, you said, and I'm the tenant here."

"You seemed doubtful about buying," the agent replied. "I asked for your answer within a week, and it is now eleven days since we talked."

"I don't sit around here, you know! I have my day's work—"

"And I have mine."

"Yesterday I went into the town and had a talk with Mr. Forester at the bank. I was getting it all fixed up. Finding out how I was placed. You've got no right to welsh on me."

"If you had come when I asked you to, the matter would have been settled by now, but in view of Mr. Sutton's offer—"

"What *is* his offer? Thirty pieces of silver, is it?"

"Three thousand pounds," the agent said.

"And what if I say I'll pay that? Will you go running over to Peele to see if Sutton will bid higher still?"

"If you're prepared to pay three thousand pounds—"

"I've said so, haven't I?" Riddler snarled.

"I can't make any promises, of course, but if I advise my employer to accept, he will most probably do so."

"Then get on with it," Riddler said.

In due course the transaction was made, and Morris Riddler became the owner of Godsakes Farm. But to do so he had to borrow fourteen hundred pounds, more than twice what he'd bargained for, and he never forgave John Sutton for that. The old neighborliness was gone, and a bitter hatred took its place. He tried to avoid Sutton now, but in the Corn Hall one market day they came face to face by accident. The story of their quarrel was well known all around, and Riddler, aware of this, stood foursquare in front of Sutton.

In a loud voice he said, "I would turn my back on this man—except that he'd stick a knife in it!"

John Sutton looked at him with a mixture of tolerance and contempt. "You don't seem to understand—farming is a business, like any other, and in business there's always competition."

"Well, in this competition you lost, didn't you?"

"Just for the present, yes, perhaps. But farming is not quite the same as it was. Things are progressing. And you will have to work a sight more efficiently than you have done till now if you are to keep abreast of the times and pay off the mortgage you've been foolish enough to saddle yourself with."

"I'll pay it off; be sure of that!"

"Well, we shall see," Sutton said.

IN THE summer of 1843 the well in the farmyard at Godsakes ran dry. This had never happened before, and Riddler knew who was to blame: John Sutton, taking over Granger's Farm in the hollow just below, had had the land drained, and this had drawn off the underground springs that fed the well at Godsakes.

Riddler got on his horse at once and rode into Missenham to seek his solicitor's advice. But it was a question, Mr. Nicholson said, of *damnum absque injuria*, or damage without wrong.

"In other words, Mr. Riddler, your neighbor has a perfect right to drain his own land if he so wishes, and if it causes damage to some other party, I'm afraid there is no redress for it."

A piece of legal information that cost Riddler half a guinea.

"Why is it that the blasted law is always on the side of the scoundrels?" he asked his wife when he got home.

The shortage of water was acute, and Riddler had no choice but to sink a deeper well. This was yet another expense he could ill afford, yet another setback to be laid at John Sutton's door. And in its wake, over the years, one misfortune succeeded another until, as Agnes Riddler said, it seemed that the farm had a curse on it. First it was a bout of blackleg, which took three cows; then it was the failure of the grain harvest; and then, in 1844, winter gales tore the roof from one of the older cattle sheds.

None of these misfortunes was ever visited on Peele. There everything prospered, and Sutton, now that he owned the farm, was making improvements everywhere. New farm buildings had been built to store the most modern machinery, and more grassland was being plowed to grow more grain. He had also built himself a new house, up on a gentle slope of land just below some beechwoods, set at a slight angle to give a view south along the valley. It was a fine square-built home, in front of which lay a gravel drive, a garden laid out with trees and shrubs, and a lawn running down to a small lake. The old farmhouse was occupied by the bailiff now.

Certainly, the handsome new residence at Peele drew the

attention of anyone traveling along the valley road. The old house at Godsakes, on the other hand, built of locally quarried stone, so merged with its background of fields that had it not been for the pale, sandy track climbing the side of the valley toward it, people would scarcely have known it was there.

RIDDLER was now working harder than ever, but often while he plowed in one field, his two men, Lovell and Smith, would be taking it easy in another. They had no respect for him, and argued with him constantly over the work that had to be done. Once they were so late sowing the spring crop that it never ripened properly, and Riddler fed it green to the stock. One heifer died of it, and a number of ewes slunk their lambs. Stock was down to a minimum, and the lack of manure showed itself in yields of sickly-looking kale and beets no bigger than a woman's fist. In the autumn of 1844 Riddler could not afford to buy seed, and some of his fields, left unplowed, tumbled down to grass and weeds.

John Sutton, across the valley, could see how bad things were at Godsakes, and one afternoon he rode over, coming straight into the field where Riddler was flattening molehills.

"It's two years since you bought this farm," Sutton said, "and if you've got any sense, you'll admit that you're just about done for. I don't care to see a good farm going to ruin like this, and I am willing to pay you exactly the sum you gave for it. No one else would pay you that. Not in the state it's in today."

Riddler, in shirt sleeves, a heavy mattock in his hands, looked up at Sutton on his horse and gave a deep-throated growl.

"Get off my land," he said savagely.

Later, at tea with his family, he talked about Sutton's visit.

"My father slaved all his life, scraping enough money together to take this farm for himself and me. He loved this place . . . the valley, the hills. I'm damned if I ever let it go."

"We are still slaving," Agnes said, "and where will it get us?"

"Things'll get better, you'll see. We've had bad luck, but things will pick up for us from now on."

"Why not sell while the price is still good? Sutton means to have this place, and he will do so sooner or later, I'm sure."

"Is that all you can say?" Riddler's voice, always loud, now rose to an angry shout. "Things've come to a pretty pass when my own wife wants to do me down. You talk about slaving? At least you slept in your bed last night! I was up with a sick cow—"

"Please don't shout at me," Agnes said. "I know how hard you have to work."

Riddler fell silent, staring at her, his anger gradually dying down. Then, as he spooned buttered beans into his mouth, he turned to look at his two children.

"Mother works just as hard as you ever do," his daughter, Kirren, said. "You've got no right to shout at her."

"All right, all right, that's enough," Riddler said.

Although she was only eight, Kirren always had more to say for herself than her brother, Eddy, who was twelve. And often, when she looked at her father, her eyes were darkly hostile.

"Mother isn't well," she said. "You ought not to make her work so hard."

"Kirren, be quiet," Agnes said.

"Not well? What's this about not being well?"

"Nothing, Morris. Nothing at all. I get a bit tired sometimes, that's all, and I worry about you working so hard. That's why I thought if you gave up the farm—"

"I'm not giving up, and you'd better make up your mind to it!"

In the yard afterward, Riddler talked to his young son. "Women don't see things the same way as us, boy. But you understand. You wouldn't want me to let the farm go, would you?"

"No, Father," Eddy said. "Especially not to Mr. Sutton, after what he did to you."

Riddler, much moved by this, gripped Eddy's shoulder.

"Sutton won't have it; I swear to that. I'm going to make a few changes here. I only need a bit of luck, and now that you are leaving school and going to do a full day's work—"

"I shall work hard, Father, cross my heart."

"I know you will. We shall soon pull the place up, shan't we, eh? Oh, we shall show them a thing or two, you and me!"

Riddler's son was his pride and joy: his hope for the future, his bright star. He saw the boy as a young man—clever, determined, vigorous, strong. In a few years' time Eddy would be making the old place hum. Riddler saw it as plain as glass.

But this dream, like so many others, was to be most cruelly shattered, for in that winter an epidemic of influenza swept through Gloucestershire, and Riddler's family went down with it. His wife and daughter soon recovered, but Eddy developed pneumonia, and in three weeks he was dead.

Riddler was beside himself with grief. For days he went about his work in an anguished trance. Once, Agnes found him in tears in the barn, and when she touched him on the shoulder, he burst out at her in a terrible howl.

"Why did it have to be the boy that died?"

Agnes turned and left him, and outside in the yard came upon Kirren, standing like a small statue, an empty bucket in each hand. The child's face was pale and stiff. Agnes saw that she had heard.

"Your father is not himself," she said. "He doesn't know what he's saying. We must both be patient with him."

Kirren said not a single word, only stared at her mother with darkened eyes and then, with the ghost of a shrug, turned away.

CHAPTER 2

JOHN Sutton was a widower, his wife having died in 1832 on giving birth to their only child, a son named Philip. Sometimes Sutton worried about his son being brought up in a household run by an elderly housekeeper without other children for company; but in the winter of 1844 this problem unexpectedly solved itself.

One black wet night in December, just after Christmas, a drover with a large flock of sheep stopped at Peele, asking if he could sleep in a barn and leave his flock to graze in the meadows before moving on in the morning. The bailiff, Warren Oakley, gave his permission, but he never learned the man's name, nor did he see his face clearly. In the morning the drover and his flock had gone.

Nothing more was thought of it then, but three days later a small boy in ragged clothes was caught stealing turnips from a field and told the bailiff that his uncle, the drover, had left him behind deliberately. Oakley brought the boy to the house, and as John Sutton questioned him Philip looked on curiously.

"Do you mean to tell me that you've been in the barn since Thursday night?"

The boy gave a nod.

"What is your name?"

"Jim," the boy said, and gave a small husky cough, partly from fear and partly from cold.

"Jim what?" Sutton asked.

This time the boy shook his head.

"Well, then, what is your uncle's name?"

Yet another shake of the head. "Uncle said not to tell. He said if I told, I should fall down dead."

"What else did your uncle say?"

"He said for me to keep out of sight for two or three days. Then to go to the nearest workhouse and ask for them to take me in."

"Have you no parents?"

"No. They're dead."

The boy was about ten years old, dirty, louse-ridden, dressed in rags, and with red scurfy sores on his face and neck. He also had a large bruise just below his left eye.

"Did your uncle do that to you?"

"Yes."

"Does he often beat you?"

"Yes, when he's drunk."

Sutton was fond of children, and the boy's condition angered him. "All right, Oakley, you can go," he said to the bailiff. "I'll keep this boy here for a day or two while I decide what to do with him. Come along with me, Jim, and we'll see if Mrs. Abelard can find you something better to eat than a raw turnip."

The housekeeper was none too pleased at having this dirty, verminous child presented to her in her clean kitchen, and she told John Sutton so in vigorous terms.

"The boy is starving," Sutton said. "Give him some good hot food to eat, then get him washed and into clean clothes."

"And what shall I do with him after that?"

"Philip can take him under his wing."

WITHIN an hour Jim had been so thoroughly scrubbed that his fair skin glowed as though lit from within, and, dressed in velveteens borrowed from Philip, with his fair hair brushed smoothly down, he looked quite presentable.

John Sutton talked about Jim with his son. "I'll see if his uncle can be traced. But unless the boy agrees to tell us his last name, I don't hold out much hope."

"Still refuses to tell his name?" Philip said. "Hah! *I'll* soon get it out of him!"

The two boys went outside and were gone until darkness fell. From then on, they were together a great deal, mostly out and about in the fields, for the farm stock, especially the sheep, drew Jim like a magnet. And Philip, during this time, would question him repeatedly, trying to make him reveal his name.

"Is it Smith? Is it Brown? Is it Murgatroyd?"

Jim shook his head, but the name Murgatroyd made him smile.

"That's it! That's it!" Philip cried. "Your name is Murgatroyd!"

"No, it isn't."

"What is it, then?"

"I told you, my uncle said not to tell."

"Well, you're not going to be called Sutton, so there, and you needn't think it!" Philip said.

AFTER three weeks at Peele, Jim was scarcely the same boy that Oakley had collared in the turnip field. The bruises and sores had vanished completely, leaving his skin a clear, healthy pink, and his fair hair, washed every day by Mrs. Abelard, was now as smooth and fine as silk. The pinched look had gone from his face, and these days his eyes were a brighter blue and often twinkled with merriment.

"All thanks to you, Mrs. Abelard, and the trouble you've taken with him," Sutton said. "But what are we going to do with him when Philip starts going to his lessons again?"

"You said you were going to see about finding his uncle."

"Where should I start? We know nothing about the man. Even if we found him, would *you* hand the boy over to him?"

"No, I would not," Mrs. Abelard said. "The bruises he had when he came here . . ."

"Exactly so, Mrs. Abelard, and therefore it seems to me that Jim had better stay with us and go with Philip to the vicarage for the parson to teach him to read and write. How would you like that, young man? Would it suit you, do you think?"

Jim gave a nod.

"He nods to everything, this boy, except when he shakes his head," Sutton said. He turned to his son. "What do you think of my idea, that we should keep Jim with us?"

"I thought we were going to anyway."

"Glad to have a brother, eh?"

"No, not a brother," Philip said. "Jim can be my servant."

Sutton, laughing, turned back to Jim.

"Do you agree to that?"

"No, I don't." The jut of Jim's chin showed Sutton that the boy had a will of his own. "I want to work on the farm."

"Well, and so you shall when you are old enough. But first a little schooling, I think, to give you a good start in life."

So every day Jim went with Philip in the dogcart to the vicarage at Lyall St. Mary's, where Mr. Bannister took his education in hand.

Jim was thus very happy at Peele, and as the months went by, bringing a sense of security, his fears gradually died away. And at last he revealed his name.

"Jim Lundy?" Philip laughed. "No wonder you kept it a secret so long. It's almost as bad as Murgatroyd."

"And where did you come from?" Sutton asked. "In what part of the country were you raised?"

"I don't know. All over the place. My parents died when I was small."

"And then your uncle took charge of you?"

"No, it was my granny at first. Then she got ill and died, and Uncle Albert came for me. He was the drover. We moved about. We came up here from Salisbury Plain. Before that we were on the Downs. And before that"—Jim spread his hands—"before that we were everywhere."

"So! You're Jim Lundy from everywhere, or nowhere—whichever you please."

Sutton eyed the boy searchingly, wondering if the story was true, but so far during his six months at Peele, Jim had never once told a lie, even to get himself out of trouble. When the boys got into mischief, like bringing hedgehogs into the kitchen or putting a number of tiny eels into the housekeeper's chamber pot, more often than not it was Jim who owned up to the pranks, while Philip denied all knowledge of them. So Sutton was inclined to believe him now.

"Anyway, true or not, it doesn't much matter, does it?" he said, speaking to Mrs. Abelard afterward. "It's all worked out pretty well on the whole. It's good for Philip to have another boy to play with, and he seems to like Jim well enough."

"What young Master Philip likes is having someone to boss about and lead into mischief at every turn."

"Ah, well," Sutton said, "you're only young once."

When he was not at the vicarage having lessons, Jim spent all his time on the farm watching the work going on in the fields and, if allowed, joining in. But Philip's favorite activities were those of the young gentleman: shooting, fishing, and riding to hounds. He soon became bored with the farm and would try to coax Jim into some more adventurous exploit. The two boys were much indulged and were given plenty of money to spend; they had the best rods and guns, and two good ponies to ride.

In winter Philip lived for the hunt. And one morning at the end of the season, when the last meet should have taken place, the boy, on being awakened by Mrs. Abelard and told that there was a hard ground frost, burst into a storm of tears.

Later that same day there was a partial thaw, and Philip, still disappointed, persuaded the groom, Charlie Clements, to let him and Jim take their ponies out for an afternoon ride.

"All right, Master Philip, but no trotting or cantering, mind. Just a gentle walk, that's all. The frost is only thawing on top, and the ground's still stone hard down below."

"I know that. I'm not a fool," Philip said peevishly.

By an odd stroke of fate, however, as the two boys rode slowly through the beechwoods, a fox emerged from the undergrowth and moved off in front of them. Philip instinctively gave chase. Just as instinctively Jim went after him.

The fox broke from the wood and went down into a deep dry ditch, ran along it a little way, then leaped out at the other side. Philip was highly excited by now and jumped his pony straight over the ditch. It was a very easy jump, but the land on the other side, lying as it did in the shade, was still iron hard with frost, and the pony, jarring his forefeet on it, stumbled and fell onto his knees, with Philip sprawling over his neck. Jim, leaping the ditch behind him, was barely able to avoid a collision, and such was the check to his own pony that he was thrown right over its head. The pony ran off, but soon slowed down to a walk, which to Jim's great distress showed him lame in one foreleg. Philip's pony was lame in both forelegs, and it was a sad, silent procession that made its way back to the stables.

For their offense Philip got a thrashing and so did Jim, and as the offense was serious, Sutton had little mercy. The boys could not sit down all day; but worse than this, for Jim at least, was the terrible feeling of guilt and shame. His pony, Sandboy, was suffering, and *he* had caused it. Worse too than Sutton's anger was Charlie Clements' quiet, perplexed reproach.

"I dunno how you could do such a thing. Those two trusting brutes, they'd go through hell and high water for you. And that's just what's happening now—they're going through hell, and all on account of your selfishness."

"They will get better, though, won't they?" Jim said in a voice he could just control. "They won't be in pain much longer, will they, now that we're looking after them?"

"We?" Charlie said sardonically.

"Yes, I want to help," Jim said.

Philip, on the other hand, was never much troubled by guilt. He blamed his misfortunes on bad luck. If only there hadn't been a frost. . . . If only that fox hadn't come along. . . . Anyway, he had been thrashed, hadn't he, so surely that was the end of it?

In the days that followed, when Jim was not in the stables helping the groom nurse the ponies, he was out searching the hedgerows, picking the fresh, succulent greenstuff just beginning to grow there. Both animals were fond of coltsfoot and cow parsley, and in a day or two Jim was able to tempt them to eat. In a week they were much improved.

"Thank goodness for that!" Philip said. "The stable's been like a morgue lately."

For him the incident was over. However, what had happened to the two ponies still weighed heavily on Jim; and when, not long afterward, Philip suggested some prank with a flavor of mischief to it, Jim refused to take part.

"Why are you so pious all of a sudden?" Philip asked.

"I don't like getting into trouble."

"You mean you don't like getting thrashed."

"It's not only the thrashing. Doing wrong makes me feel bad inside."

Philip jeered at him over this.

"Jim's a Goody Two-shoes these days," he said to Mrs. Abelard. "That thrashing made a coward out of him."

"That's not cowardly. That's common sense. It's all very well for you, Master Philip; you're the master's son. But Jim's got to make his own way in the world. That means watching his p's and q's and keeping on the right side of people."

"Well, he'd better keep on the right side of me," Philip said, "because I shall be master here one day, and that's something he seems to forget!"

Jim laughed at this. "What will you do? Turn me out?"

"I could do if I wanted! You wouldn't care for that, would you, going back to being a drover?"

"Well," Jim said deliberately, "I'd rather be a drover any day than stop in a place where I wasn't wanted."

"There, Master Philip!" Mrs. Abelard said. "I reckon we've had enough talk about turning people out of the house. And all because Jim won't go out with you."

"I never said I wouldn't go out with him, Abby. I said I wouldn't do anything that landed us in trouble again."

"Shooting rabbits won't land us in trouble!" Philip said scornfully.

"Well, so long as it's only rabbits," Jim said.

"It wouldn't be anything else, would it? Not now the breeding season's begun?"

With this assurance from Philip, Jim went willingly enough to shoot rabbits in the plantation just behind the old farmhouse. But again they were dogged by the "bad luck" that always seemed to put temptation in Philip's path. On their way home, each with a brace of rabbits in his satchel, they came upon a hen pheasant sitting on her nest in the undergrowth. Jim could sense that Philip, beside him, was itching to get a shot at her, and he moved to take hold of Philip's arm.

"No, you can't! You mustn't!" he said, speaking with quiet vehemence. "Can't you see she's on her nest?"

Philip pulled himself free of Jim's grasp and went on his way. As he went he stumbled, however—on purpose, it seemed to Jim—and the noise frightened the pheasant into flight. She went whirring off between the trees with a loud cry. In the same instant Philip swung around, bringing his gun swiftly to his shoulder. He was a very good shot and brought the pheasant down at once. With a satisfied grunt he went forward to pick up his prize.

But the pheasant, shot at such close range, was badly damaged. Philip held it up by the legs, turning it this way and that. Then, as Jim came up, he commented, "Look at her! She's all shot to bits!"

"What does it matter?" Jim said coldly. "You couldn't have taken it home anyway, or you would have got a leathering. You shot a sitting bird on her nest!"

"She wasn't sitting. She got up."

"You put her up on purpose," Jim said.

"So what if I did? It's no business of yours!"

They were near the edge of the wood, and Philip, going to the fence, hurled the dead pheasant over into the pasture beyond. He wiped his bloodstained hand on his jacket and turned back toward the woodland path. Jim, in silence, followed him.

THE incident did not end there, however, for the pheasant was picked up by one of the farm boys, Peter Gray, who hid the bird inside his jacket. But the bailiff, noticing the bulge, asked to see what was causing it and, on discovering the pheasant, took Peter to Mr. Sutton and accused him of having shot it. The taking of game by the farmhands was a serious matter at any time, but this offense in the breeding season so incensed John Sutton that he threatened to send for the constable. But Peter's story was convincing enough to give Sutton pause. He left Peter in his office and went in search of Philip and Jim.

"Have you been out shooting today?"

"Yes, Father," Philip said.

"Did you shoot a hen pheasant in the pasture?"

"No, Father. Just rabbits, that's all."

Sutton now questioned Jim. "You were with Philip in the wood today, were you not?"

"Well," Jim said evasively.

"Peter Gray has just been found with a dead hen pheasant in his possession. I was going to send for the constable, but Peter says he found the pheasant lying in the woodside pasture. Now, Jim, I ask you, did you shoot a pheasant today?"

"No. I did not."

"Did Philip shoot one?"

"Yes," Jim said.

"What became of it?" Sutton asked.

"He threw it over into the pasture."

"All right, Jim, you may go. Philip, bring me the cane."

After this second thrashing Philip came storming into the kitchen to vent his fury on Jim, who was talking to Mrs. Abelard.

"Filthy, dirty sneak, telling tales on me like that! You got me six lashes!"

"Don't blame me for what you got. If you'd spoken up in the first place instead of telling that stupid lie—"

"Oh, you never tell lies! You never do any wrong."

"Peter Gray could've gone to jail on account of that pheasant."

"That's not why you told on me! You did it to get me a thrashing, that's all! You've always been jealous of me from the start, because I am my father's son and you're nothing but dirt left by somebody on our doorstep!"

Philip went out, slamming the door, and Mrs. Abelard looked at Jim. "Master Philip's a fine one to talk about your being jealous," she said, "when the boot is on the other foot."

"Is it?" Jim said in surprise. "But why should Philip be jealous of me? I haven't got anything he wants."

"Just as well," Mrs. Abelard said, "or he'd have it off you like a shot."

"I don't think I am jealous of Philip," Jim said, still considering the matter.

"Well now, and what if you were? Master Philip's got so much, and you're a poor boy with nothing at all."

"Poor?" Jim said, surprised again. "I wouldn't say I was poor, Abby. I'd say I was very lucky indeed."

"Yes, so you are, Master Jim. After what you'd been used to, to come and live in this fine new house. But what sort of life will you have later on? That's the question that vexes me."

"I'm going to work on the farm," Jim said.

"Yes, I know," Mrs. Abelard said. "But it seems all wrong to me, somehow, when you're being raised like a gentleman, that you should later be expected to work like a laborer on the land."

"But I want to work on the land, Abby, more badly than anything else. And I'm not a gentleman, nor shall I ever be."

"No, Master Jim," Mrs. Abelard said. "You're neither flesh nor fowl nor good red herring, and that's why I feel sorry for you. Still, you'll be all right, I daresay, for you've got a good head on you and you know how to make the most of yourself. But you need to watch out for Master Philip. It's not that he's wicked, but he's got to come first in everything. So mind what I say."

Jim nodded. "I shall watch out for myself, Abby."

CHAPTER 3

Mrs. Abelard was not the only one who worried about Jim's future; the vicar, Mr. Bannister, was also concerned. And one day in the summer of 1847 he mentioned the matter to John Sutton.

"Jim's future?" Sutton said. "What do you mean?"

"Well, he's being brought up with your own son, and yet—may I ask—do you intend to make Jim equal with Philip later on?"

"Certainly not! Jim is going to work on the farm. He'll make a good bailiff one day, and a not too distant day at that."

"Ah, yes. Very suitable."

"And yet you're still worried. Doesn't he work at his lessons?"

"Yes, indeed. In fact, that is perhaps the problem. He is doing almost too well. He was almost completely illiterate when he first came to me, but now he not only reads and writes but has made such good progress with his Latin and mathematics that he has actually caught up with Philip. Jim is getting an education better suited to a gentleman than a farm bailiff, and I think if we continue with it, it may cause problems later on."

"Give him ideas above his station, you mean? Yes, well, you may be right. What do you advise me to do?"

"I think, when Philip goes away to school this autumn, Jim should stop his lessons and start work on the farm straightaway. After all, he's nearly thirteen. I shall be sorry to lose such a good pupil, but he's got to find his proper level."

In the second week in September, therefore, when Philip went off to Surpingham, Jim began work on the farm, which was where he wanted to be anyway. He was strong and energetic, and the work, far from degrading him, brought him satisfaction and joy.

John Sutton's plan was that Jim should spend two years working with the cowman, two with the carters, and two with the

shepherd, Mrs. Abelard's brother-in-law, George. This suited Jim
very well; he wanted to know everything that cowman and carter
could teach him, but his greatest friend on the farm had always
been George Abelard, and any spare moment he had was spent
helping with the flock. Because of this special interest in sheep,
he was allowed time off in the spring so that he could take a hand
in the lambing.

"You're the best helper I ever had," Abelard said to him once,
and for Jim this was high praise indeed.

JIM was not paid with the other farm employees, because he
already received an allowance, just as Philip did, and this custom
was kept up even now that he worked on the farm. Jim's allowance was ten shillings, and to him it always seemed a fortune, for
grown men on the farm received no more than that.

He spent very little, and in this he was different from Philip,
who, although he received a whole guinea, was always skint by
Wednesday and badly in debt by Saturday night. Often Philip
would ask Jim to lend him a shilling or two, and Jim would
oblige. But there came a time when Philip, home for the holidays,
borrowed half a crown from Jim and returned to school without
paying it back. So the next time he was at home and asked for a
loan, he met with a forthright refusal.

"You are a mean old stick!" said Philip. "You must have stacks
of tin put away. What are you going to do with it?"

"One of these days I intend to buy some sheep," Jim said.

"What on earth for?" Philip asked.

"For one thing, I happen to like them. For another, they'll
make a good investment."

"Well, you'll have to ask my father's permission before you
start raising sheep of your own on our land."

"Yes, of course. I intend to," Jim said.

John Sutton gave his permission without any hesitation, and at
the autumn sheep fair that year Jim bought twenty Cotswold
shearling ewes—theaves, as old Abelard called them—and a
Cotswold ram. The Peele flock consisted of Downs and Leices-
ters, and Jim chose to keep a different breed so that his twenty-
one sheep could be picked out easily from the rest.

His investment cost thirty-eight pounds, but he had only to

walk out into the pasture and see his sheep grazing there, their thick curly fleeces a rich pale gold in the autumn sunlight, to feel that they were worth every penny, even of this huge sum.

Jim's flock lambed in April, giving him twenty-six lambs, and of these he lost only two. One of the original ewes proved barren, and she was sold off with the lambs. Together with the sale of the wool, Jim's profit that year amounted to some forty pounds.

"Ah, Jim will end up richer than any of us, you mark my words," John Sutton said with a laugh. And Philip, with a look of disdain, replied, "He'll end up a miser, if you ask me."

At the sheep fair in October, Jim, again with Sutton's permission, bought twenty more ewes, so that he now had forty sheep in all. Thus, in the following spring, his flock yielded fifty-three lambs, and that year his total profits amounted to eighty-eight pounds. Once again he planned to buy another twenty ewes, but this time John Sutton was less ready with his permission.

"H'mm," Sutton said. "I think it would be better if you were to buy just ten, and keep your flock to a round fifty. That's plenty big enough for you to manage, what with your proper work as well. We don't want the land getting sheep sick, do we, eh?"

"No, sir," Jim said. But he was puzzled by Sutton's edict.

"Why does Mr. Sutton want me to keep my flock down to fifty?" he asked old Abelard.

The shepherd gave a grunt. "We underlings have got to be kept in our place, you see, and it seems that goes the same for you as it does for the rest of us."

Jim was somewhat cast down. "Had I better give up my flock altogether, d'you think? After all, I do graze them on Peele land."

Old Abelard shook his head. "You keep your little flock," he said quietly. "That's your investment, your stake in the future. As for grazing Peele land, why, they manure it at the same time, don't they? And many a flock gets its keep free for doing that."

So Jim kept his little flock and tended them with earnest care. And every year his profits were such that he added upward of eighty-five pounds to his savings.

PHILIP was scornfully amused at Jim's interest in sheep. They were poor man's stock, he said, and out of place now on a farm like Peele.

"And just what are you going to do with all this silver you've got mounting up?" he asked Jim.

"I hope one day to rent a few acres of land of my own."

"A smallholding? But you're going to be our bailiff here and take over from Oakley when he gets old."

"I can easily do both. Many a bailiff does that."

"Small farms are a thing of the past. They're uneconomic. They're suicide. You've only got to look at Godsakes going to ruin over there: fields all overgrown with brambles and thorns, stock reduced to nothing at all, house and buildings falling down."

"That's nothing to do with the size of the farm. It's good-sized, taken all round. It's just that Riddler has had bad luck and isn't very good at managing things."

"Bad luck, my eye! A man's got no business buying land when he hasn't got the money to do right by it!"

"No, but there's more to it than that, isn't there?" The story behind Riddler's misfortunes was as well known to Jim as it was to Philip himself, for it was often discussed at Peele. "It's not entirely Riddler's fault, is it, that he ran into trouble over money when he first bought his farm?"

"He blames my father. We all know that. And to judge by the way you talk, it seems as though you take Riddler's side."

"I'm sorry for Riddler, I must admit."

"Sorry for him!" Philip exclaimed. "After what he's done to that farm? Why, he only stays there to spite us and stop us from getting our hands on it. And yet you feel sorry for him!"

Philip turned and marched off, and old Abelard said to Jim, "It doesn't do to stick up for Morris Riddler. The master's been waiting a long time to get his hands on that farm, and it's a main sore subject here that he hasn't managed it so far."

"I suppose he'll have to give up in the end? Riddler, I mean."

"It's only fair amazing to me that he's hung on as long as he has. It's Riddler's wife and young daughter I feel the most sorry for, working so hard. If Riddler's got any feeling for them, he should sell up and give them the chance of a decent life."

"Yes, I suppose he should," Jim said. "But if I were Riddler and had my own farm, I reckon I'd feel the same as he does. I'd stick it out to the very end and fight for it to the last breath."

"Well, that's what he's doing, sure enough," Abelard said.

IT HAPPENED NOT LONG AFTER this that Jim had a meeting with
Morris Riddler. It was a day in early August, and he had gone
with the other Peele men to begin cutting a field of grain on that
part of the farm that had once been Granger's and which lay on
the same side of the valley as Godsakes. The men were at work
with their scythes when the warm west wind blowing down from
Godsakes brought with it a scent of hay so exceedingly sweet and
strong that the men stopped work and sniffed the air.

"Riddler's got a hot stack," said Joe Greening, the head carter,
and turned to look up at Godsakes rising in a series of gray-green
fields beyond the boundary of Granger's. "There it is. Look." And
he pointed to an ungainly haystack. "Whew!" he said. "That'll go
up in flames directly if something isn't done."

"Going to tell him about it, are you?" Arthur Slatter asked slyly,
for the Peele men, these nine years past, had kept clear of Morris
Riddler for fear of offending their employer.

"Somebody ought to," Greening said.

And Jim, putting away his scythe, volunteered.

Riddler was letting his cows out to pasture when Jim came up
the adjoining field and spoke to him over the farmyard wall.

"You've got a hot stack," he said, and pointed in its general
direction. "In the field with a hut in it, just under the hill. It'll go
up in flames, Joe Greening says, if you don't do something."

"Blast! If it isn't one thing, it's another!" Riddler came across
the yard to the wall. "Did Joe Greening send you to me?"

"He said somebody ought to come."

"That was good of him. Good of you too. Your master would
have stood and watched it burn." Riddler was eyeing Jim curiously.
"You're Jim Lundy, aren't you? The boy Sutton found in his barn
that time? I've seen you about these many years, but never close to
like this." Resting his folded arms on the wall, he looked across
the valley at Peele. "I see the lot of you, over there, coming and
going about the place. You look like a lot of puppets from here,
and no doubt we look the same to you."

"Yes," Jim said, and the thought made him smile.

He was just as curious about Riddler as Riddler was about him;
but being a boy, barely seventeen, he was rather less open about
it, and only when the man's queer, crooked face was averted did
he steal a few quick glances at him. He found himself wondering

how it was that Morris Riddler, who was not really a big man, should give an impression of bull-like solidity and strength.

"Does John Sutton treat you all right?"

"Yes. He treats me very well."

"Is he still waiting like a carrion crow to have my carcass, eh?"

"I must get back to work," Jim said then. He turned away.

"Hang on. I'll walk down with you and look at that stack."

Riddler climbed over the wall and dropped down beside Jim. Together they walked along the neglected fields. In one a dozen sheep were grazing, and Jim carefully looked away, for the sheep had not yet been shorn, although it was August and their wool hung from them in tatters.

"All a bit different from Peele, eh?" Riddler said as they walked. "Those few sheep of mine, now. Different from your little flock of Cotswold Lions, aren't they, eh?"

Jim, at a loss, said nothing, and Riddler, perceiving his surprise, laughed deep down in his throat.

"I see what goes on over there, you know. And I hear most of the gossip, especially on market days. Well, this is where we part. Did I say thanks about the stack? I'm obliged to you."

He went off with a wave of his hand, and Jim went back to join the mowers in the grainfield.

"So what are things like up there?" Joe Greening asked.

"Pretty bad," Jim said, "but Riddler seems cheerful enough."

"Yes, well, from what I hear, there's a reason for that," Greening said. "His wife's expecting a little un, but I doubt if she's pleased about it. Not at her time of life, poor soul, and with only middling health at that."

It was not the first hot stack Riddler had had at Godsakes, and probably wouldn't be the last, for Nahum Smith and Bob Lovell, the two men he employed, would sooner do a job badly than well. Whenever he grumbled at them, they always made the same reply. "If you only pay us six shillings a week, master, you only get six shillings' worth of work."

"I'd think myself lucky," Riddler would snarl, "if only you did three shillings' worth of work."

The stack had to be opened out. He told the men to do it at once, then watched as they ambled away, "trying to see how slow they could go," as Riddler often said of them. He turned back into the yard just as his daughter, Kirren, now a girl of fifteen, came out of the house with a tubful of washing.

"How's your mother?"

"Just the same," she said quietly.

"Still in bed, is she?"

"Yes."

For a moment he stood uncertainly, watching Kirren as she hung the clothes on the line, but her young face was closed against him.

"I'm going up to have a bit of a chat with her."

Kirren, without saying a word, continued her task.

"How are you feeling now, Agnes? A bit better, are you?"

"Yes, Morris. Not too bad."

"Then why aren't you up and about? Such a beautiful summer day it is, and you always did say you liked it hot."

"I come over giddy when I get up. All I want to do is sleep."

"There's three months to go yet," Riddler said. "And it's not as though it's your first. . . . You had no trouble with the other two."

"That was a long time ago, Morris, and I've lost three babies since then. I'm older too."

"Yes, but not so old as all that. You're forty-five; I don't call that old. If it was, you wouldn't be like you are now, would you?"

"Oh, I'm young enough to be having a child," Agnes said wearily, "and old enough to be dreading it."

"Don't say that, Agnes, don't say that. It'll be all right; you mark my words. Now, what about drinking some milk? It came from old Daisy—I milked her myself. It'll do you good."

Riddler, helping his wife to sit up, held a glass for her to drink. "There, that'll soon buck you up," he said. And after a pause he added huskily, "It's lonely downstairs without you, old girl. I miss you, Agnes, and that's a fact."

HE COULD not believe that his wife was ill, right up to the very last, and when she died he was drunk for three days. Hopelessly drunk, in a blind stupor, so that Kirren had to do everything.

On the morning of the funeral she went into the scullery, where her father lay on his back on the floor, and emptied a jug of cold water over him. She then went back to the kitchen, and a few minutes later he lumbered in after her and sat, groaning, in a chair at the table. Kirren put his breakfast in front of him, but he turned away from it, gray-faced and sick.

"Do you expect me to eat that when I've got to go down to Marychurch and see my wife put into the grave?"

"Eat it or not, as you please."

"First the boy, Eddy. Now her. What sort of God is it that takes away as good a wife as a man ever had?"

"It isn't God you should blame—it's yourself."

Riddler only put his head in his hands, but after a while he looked up again. "We were hoping for a son."

"*You* were hoping for a son."

"We loved each other, your mother and me."

"You may call it love if you like. I do not."

"You're only a girl; you don't understand. You will do in time, when you're married yourself. What a man feels for his wife. You've no idea what it's like."

Suddenly Kirren turned on him. "You seem to think you're the only one that's got any feelings! How do you think I feel, now that my poor mother is dead and all I've got left in the world is you?"

"It seems to me very hard that you should hold it against me for still being alive," he said.

"I don't see why it should be so hard! You've held it against *me* all these years because I'm alive and Eddy is not!"

"That's not true. That's rubbish, that is."

"I heard you say it, out there in the yard. 'Why did it have to be the boy that died?' That's what you said. I heard it myself."

Riddler, sitting slumped in his chair, made a small, helpless gesture with his hands. "Times like that, people say these things. . . . But I didn't mean it; you must know that."

"How should I know? I'm only a girl! I'm no use to you compared with a boy. You hoped all these years for another son, and you killed my poor mother trying to get one."

"I never said you were no use to me. Girls've got their place in the world just the same as boys. They become women, and us men need them, there's no doubt of that. Where should I be if I hadn't got you, Kirrie? You and the farm—that's all I've got left."

Clumsily he put out a hand, taking her arm and squeezing it.

"You're a good-sorted girl, and a better daughter than I deserve. I don't mind admitting it."

Kirren's glance was sardonic. Firmly she withdrew her arm. But her anger was gone. She spoke quietly now.

"Eat your breakfast. It's getting cold."

KIRREN had always been old for her years, and at fifteen she was almost a woman: tall and slender, yet well developed, with strong, supple arms toughened by the work of the dairy. Although Riddler might grumble at her sometimes, he depended on her, and he looked forward to the time when she would marry and produce children who would grow up to work on the farm and take over when he died.

Marriage, however, was a subject that filled Kirren with angry disgust. "After seeing the life my mother had? One stillborn child after another? All the heartbreak, all the pain! Oh, no! That is not for me!"

Kirren took after her mother in looks but was rather darker than Agnes had been, with hair so brown it was almost black, and a skin as dusky as any Gypsy's, especially in the summertime, when she worked in the fields without a hat. By the time she was sixteen, she was growing attractive. At seventeen she was comely indeed. At least she would have been, Riddler thought, if only she were a little less sullen. Certainly, the higgler, Billy Hayzell, calling once a week to buy Kirren's eggs and butter and cheese, was obviously smitten with her.

Billy was a rather smug young man, deaf in one ear, and he used this as an excuse for coming right up to Kirren and putting his face close to hers, and once, catching her unawares, he succeeded in touching her cheek with a moist, thick-lipped kiss.

Kirren, twisting away from him, let him have the full force of her wrath. "If you ever try that again, I'll fetch you such a mighty clout that you'll end up deaf in both your ears!"

Billy, calling at outlying farms, was apt to cheat his women customers, paying them prices well below those their produce would have fetched in the market, knowing only too well that they could not get there easily themselves. Once, when Kirren was grumbling to her father about the price Billy paid for her cheese, he said it was all her own fault.

"If you weren't so hoity-toity with him, you could get good prices enough, I daresay."

"You mean I should let him maul me about and fumble at me with his hot, sticky hands? I'm not having that!"

"No, you'd sooner lose us the farm!" Riddler said with great bitterness. "God knows we've come desperate close to it for want of some ready cash sometimes."

"If we are in danger of losing the farm, it's you that's to blame for it, not me!" Kirren exclaimed. "You with your drinking on market days!"

"You call that drinking?" Riddler said. "Just a few glasses of ale once a week after doing business?" Then, eyeing her critically, he gave a shake of his head. "You'll never get a husband, the way you go on."

"A husband is the last thing I want."

"And who's going to take over the farm when I die, if you don't give me a grandson?"

"The farm, in all probability, will have gone under the auctioneer's hammer long before then," Kirren said.

Riddler, swearing, went off to the fields, and Kirren, studying her account book, tried to work out what profit, if any, she had made from the sale of her produce that day. The conclusion she came to so angered her that when Billy Hayzell called again, she told him in no uncertain terms that she would not deal with him anymore, and she sent him away empty-handed.

Thereafter, to her father's disgust, she went into the market herself, walking the three miles there and back. "You must want seeing to," Riddler said, "traipsing all that way with those heavy baskets instead of dealing with Billy Hayzell at your own door."

"I make nearly half as much again on my produce as I did when I sold it to him. And I pay less for the groceries I buy than when he used to get them for me."

"Yes, and you're gone all day, when you're needed here."

"Going into Missenham is the one and only break I get. The one and only day in the week when I see a few fresh faces instead of just yours and Lovell's and Smith's."

"Yes, well," Riddler said, suddenly growing rather reflective. "I suppose it is pretty dull for you, stuck out here. At the market you meet all sorts of people."

Kirren saw the track his thoughts were taking. "You mean I might find a husband there?"

"Well, you've got to look somewhere, haven't you?" Riddler said cheerfully.

CHAPTER 4

IN THE autumn of 1855 Warren Oakley retired, and Jim took over his duties as bailiff. Jim now earned eighteen shillings a week, which, for a young man of twenty-one, was riches indeed.

In spite of his extreme youth the men on the farm respected Jim, knowing that whatever job they were doing, he could do it as well as they. But he rarely took his coat off now, for the post of bailiff, on a farm such as Peele, carried with it a certain amount of prestige. He wore a good suit of Cotswold tweed and rode a smart dapple-gray horse. He was not expected to sweat, but to organize the work of the farm and see that it was carried out. He took pleasure and pride in his position.

There was plenty of variety in his duties, and in winter, when there were guests in the house, most of whom came for the shooting, it was his job to make sure that the party got a good day's sport. These guests were all farmers from neighboring counties whom John Sutton knew through the farming clubs.

Sometimes the Suttons, father and son, went on return visits to these friends, hunting with famous packs and shooting over great estates of three thousand acres or more. At other times Philip went alone, and often he would be absent for months at a time. John Sutton was not best pleased at this, and once he took Philip to task about it.

"I don't want to spoil your fun, my boy, but I think it's time you settled down and found yourself a wife instead of gadding about all over the country."

"You seem to forget," Philip replied, "that there are three pretty girls at Langley."

"Ah," Sutton said, much mollified. "So that's how the wind blows, is it, eh? And which of the trio do you favor?"

"The youngest, Caroline," Philip said. "And when I go on my next visit there, I intend to propose to her."

"Splendid! Splendid! I couldn't have chosen better myself!"

IT WAS IN THE SPRING OF 1858 THAT Jim met and fell in love with Jane Reynolds. Her father, who owned a glass manufactory in Birmingham, had recently rented Hide House Farm, near Abbot's Lyall, and John Sutton, as a good neighbor should, had soon called there, taking Jim with him.

Alec Reynolds had moved to Hide House so that he and his wife and daughter should have all the benefits of living in the country, and the farm, of about a hundred acres, was to be his hobby. He confessed he knew nothing of farming as yet.

"Jim will soon tell you how to get the best out of your land," Sutton said. "You can't do better than listen to him."

"That's uncommonly good of you."

"Not at all," Sutton said.

And that was how Jim, in the month of April, came to spend so much of his time at Hide House Farm, and in doing so met Jane Reynolds. He was now twenty-four; Jane was eighteen. And all through the spring and early summer their friendship grew and blossomed, with Jane's easygoing parents looking on indulgently and, so it seemed, with approval.

John Sutton also watched the progress of Jim's courtship with interest and, on the whole, approved. "Jane Reynolds is the prettiest thing I've seen for many a long day," he said. "Intelligent too. But will she make a good wife for a workingman?"

This was a difficult question for Jim to answer. Being in love with Jane, he naturally assumed that she would make him a perfect wife, but he *was* only a workingman, and Jane was accustomed to a style of living he could not afford. Still, he had certain ambitions and a fair sum of money saved, and he was by nature an optimist. If Jane was willing to trust him, he knew he could do great things for her.

On an evening in late July, therefore, Jim and Jane walked alone together in the hayfields at Peele. Jane had been to the Sutton farm many times but never to these outlying fields, and Jim pointed out the lonely barn where, thirteen years before, he had been abandoned by his uncle. Jane stood staring at the place with intensely blue eyes.

"Weren't you frightened there by yourself, only a little boy?"

"I liked the owls. They were company in the dark. But yes, I was frightened—of what would become of me."

"Your uncle was a wicked man."

"He did me a very good turn, however, for I have had a better life in Mr. Sutton's care than I could have had otherwise."

"I know Mr. Sutton's been good to you, but he says you have more than repaid him by working so hard for him on the farm."

They had been walking side by side, but now Jim stopped and looked at her, and she met his gaze without any shyness.

"Does it make any difference to you, knowing that I am a foundling?" he asked.

"Difference? What do you mean?"

"I think you must know—I'm sure you do—that I love you and want to marry you. But—"

"Oh, there are buts!" she said, pretending to be downcast.

"It's all a question of whether I am good enough for you."

"Silly," she said, her voice soft, and reached up to kiss him on the mouth. His arms went around her, holding her close, and she leaned against him with a little sigh, which he felt gentle and warm upon his lips. It was the first time they had kissed.

"Does that mean you love me?" he asked when they drew apart.

"I think it must."

"Enough to say you'll marry me?"

"Goodness! You are in a hurry!" she said.

"No, no, I'm not! That is, there are certain things I must tell you first. What money I earn. What my prospects are."

"Practical things."

"Yes, that's right."

As they walked together over the fields he did his best to tell her all about himself. "I've got about twelve hundred pounds in the bank, and I've got a flock of fifty sheep worth, say, another eighty pounds. I earn eighteen shillings a week—"

"Eighteen shillings! Is that all?"

"Eighteen shillings is very good. Most bailiffs get fifteen. If my wages seem little to you, I want you to know that I've got plans to rent a bit of land of my own. Only about thirty acres or so to begin with, where I can raise a few cattle and sheep and maybe fatten a pig or two. And one day I shall take a really good-sized farm and set up in style as an independent farmer."

"And how long do you think that will take?"

"Ten years, perhaps. Do you think you could put up with being just a bailiff's wife for that long?"

"A lot depends," Jane said gravely, "on what a bailiff's wife has to do."

They were now close to the old Peele farmhouse, looking down on it from above, with its casement windows and its porch overgrown with rambler roses. The house looked directly toward the west, and now, in the evening, reflected a pink sunset glow.

"That is the house," Jim said, "where the bailiff's wife, if she be what she ought, will spend her time looking after the bailiff."

"Can we go inside?"

"Well, yes, of course." Hand in hand they walked down the gently sloping fields.

"If I'm to do things properly, I ought to see your father soon and ask his permission to marry you."

"I know what he'll say. He'll say I'm too young."

"But at least he might let us get engaged."

"I don't know. I'm not so sure. But I think if I spoke to him myself, I might be able to pave the way."

"I'm afraid he'll think I'm not good enough—"

"Hush," Jane said. She leaned against him, her face upturned, and he bent to kiss her on the lips. After a while she drew away.

"Promise me this," she whispered. "No more talk about practical things. I'm more in the mood to be silly and gay."

AT THE end of July, Philip came home, lured by a letter from his father mentioning "interesting developments at Godsakes concerning our friend Riddler." And over supper that evening, with Jim also present, Sutton gave Philip the full details.

"Riddler's really done for this time. He owes money everywhere, and the collector's men were there yesterday, intending to seize his cows—he's only got two left—but he met them at the gate with a loaded shotgun. Anyway, what is more important to us is that he's fallen behind with his mortgage dues, and the bank has given him until next month to pay off the arrears."

"So the end is in sight, then?" Philip said.

"Yes, my boy," Sutton said with immense satisfaction. "It's only a matter of weeks now before Godsakes is ours at last." He looked at Jim. "We'll be farming more than five hundred acres once we've taken the place in. Surely that's something to be proud of, eh, being bailiff on such a farm?"

"For myself, yes, I can feel well pleased," Jim responded. "I just wish that your buying Godsakes didn't involve hurting a man who has struggled so hard for so many years."

"Jim is such a moral man, and of course he's always been inclined to feel sorry for Morris Riddler," Philip said tartly as he lit a cigar. "Luckily for us it isn't his business to decide."

"Quite so," Jim agreed, and rising from the table, he excused himself, having work to discuss with old Abelard.

John Sutton, left alone with Philip, pushed a bottle of port toward him. "I haven't yet heard about your latest round of visits," he said. "How is your courtship of Caroline going?"

"It's not," Philip said with a certain stiffness. "She is soon to become engaged to one of Colonel Conroy's sons."

"Oh," Sutton said, and was silent awhile, watching his son with a scrutiny that was at once sympathetic and shrewd. "Well, there are plenty of other nice girls about. But it seems rather as though Jim is going to pip you at the post when it comes to finding a wife."

"Does it, though? And who's the girl?"

"Someone you haven't met," Sutton said.

"Imagine Jim being in love!" Philip poured a glass of port and sipped it. "You must tell me all about it," he said.

HARVEST began early in August, and from then on Jim was kept fully occupied, for the acreage of grain now grown at Peele was the greatest ever. Philip, at his father's instigation, was at this time often in Missenham, collecting information about Morris Riddler's debts that might be useful to them when buying Godsakes.

One afternoon, coming back from one of these errands, Philip turned off at the crossroads just outside Abbot's Lyall and rode up the lane toward Hide House Farm. It was a day of intense heat, and when he reached the river Cran, he walked his mare down to the ford so that she could drink and be cool.

While he sat at ease in the saddle, a girl in a pale blue muslin frock, with a blue straw hat on her head, came slowly along the riverbank, picking wild tansy. She had almost reached the ford when suddenly a hot, surging wind carried her straw hat from her head. She gave a quick, clumsy grab, and then a small exclamation as the hat blew into the river.

Philip, having dismounted quickly, was just in time to reach the hat as it floated across the ford. He fished it out and gave it a shake. The girl had now come to the top of the slip, and Philip, with the hat in his hand, stood looking up at her.

"No need to ask who you are," he said. "I know you from my father's description."

"Your father?" She studied him with her head to one side.

Leading his mare by the bridle, he splashed his way across the ford and walked up to where the girl stood.

"I'm Philip Sutton of Peele Farm." He bowed to her and proffered her hat. "I'm afraid it's rather wet," he said.

ALL through August, whenever Jim could spare the time from superintending the harvest, he walked over to Hide House in the hope of seeing Jane, but each time he was disappointed. She had "gone into town," or "gone on a picnic with some friends." Once when he called in the evening, she was "lying down with a headache, quite unable to see anyone," but when he called to inquire the next morning, she had recovered sufficiently to have gone for a ride by the river, "with a party from Allern Hall."

Jim thought it strange that never once in all this time had she strolled over to see him, as she had often done before, but "really her life is in a whirl these days," Mrs. Reynolds said to him, "and she seems to be such a favorite, you know, with all our nice neighbors round about."

"Yes, it would seem so," Jim replied. "I'm glad she is better, at any rate."

As he walked away, thinking of what Mrs. Reynolds had said, he became more and more aware that her manner to him had been evasive, had even smacked of embarrassment.

The feeling became so strong that instead of going back to Peele he went down to the river and along the bank, and there, about a mile downstream, where the willows formed a shady grove, he saw Jane and Philip together. They were walking along arm in arm, absorbed in each other, plainly lovers. Their two horses were tethered nearby. There was no party from Allern Hall. Philip and Jane were quite alone.

They did not see Jim, and he stole away without showing himself. Seeing them together was a shock, and it filled him with an anger that weakened him. He felt too hurt, too vulnerable, to face them at that moment. He needed time to be alone, to absorb the pain, to think things out.

AN HOUR was enough. By then, instead of weakening him, his anger gave him a kind of strength. True, some faint hope lingered in his heart; after all, there might be some innocent explanation of what he had seen. He had to know for sure. So he walked back to the narrow lane leading up to Hide House and was standing in the shade of an oak tree there when Jane returned home.

As he stepped out into the lane she went rather pale. He took hold of her horse's bridle, and she gave a small, nervous laugh.

"Jim! Just imagine seeing you! I thought you were harvesting."

"I've called at the house any number of times. Surely they must have told you that?"

"Oh, yes. But I have been out a lot just lately. . . ."

"I must tell you, Jane," he said, "that I saw you about an hour ago with Philip Sutton at Dunton Reach."

"Do you mean you were spying on me?"

"You can call it that if you like. But I wanted to know how I stood with you. You said you loved me."

"Yes. Well . . ."

"You also said you would marry me."

"No, I didn't. I never said any such thing."

"But, you were going to speak to your father about it."

"Yes. I was. But I didn't say when."

"You mean," he said with some irony, "that you may still speak to him, even now?"

"No. Not now."

"Because something better has come along."

"Jim, I'm truly sorry. I didn't mean to hurt you."

"Are you going to marry him?"

"Yes."

"In that case there's nothing more to be said—except for one or two things I shall have to say to Philip himself."

"What things?" Jane asked.

But Jim was already walking away, impatient to return to Peele.

PHILIP STOOD IN THE STABLE doorway talking to the groom. As Jim came into the yard Philip turned and sauntered toward him, tapping his boot with his riding crop. "My father is out looking for you. Nobody seemed to know where you were."

"I've just come from seeing Jane."

"Ah," Philip said, and his gaze sharpened, becoming wary.

"She tells me she's going to marry you."

"Then, of course, it must be true."

"You haven't wasted much time," Jim said. "You've only been home a month, and never once have you even mentioned her."

"There was a good reason for that. I was trying to spare your feelings, you see, because right from the very start I loved the girl and she loved me."

"Loving people," Jim said, "is something she seems to find easy to do."

"That is not a very gentlemanly remark."

"I'm not feeling gentlemanly. But then, I am not a gentleman, nor have I ever laid claim to be."

"No?" Philip said with a lift of his brows. "And yet you expected to marry Jane, a girl of superior breeding." He spread his hands in disbelief. "You, a farm bailiff earning eighteen shillings a week, hoping to lure the girl into marriage with your few paltry hundreds in the bank and your talk of a little farm—"

Philip, though watching so warily, was nevertheless taken by surprise when Jim suddenly lashed out and caught him a stinging backhanded blow on the mouth. Until this moment Jim's feelings had been kept under control, but now, as he learned that his cherished ambitions had been made the subject of ridicule, he allowed his anger a free rein. When Philip, with a muttered exclamation, cut at him with his riding crop, Jim struck out straight and hard with his fist and sent Philip sprawling.

John Sutton suddenly walked into the yard. "What the devil's going on?"

Philip slowly got to his feet. "Jim," he said, nursing his jaw, "has just found out that I am going to marry Jane Reynolds."

"You are going to do what? When did all this happen?"

Philip stood brushing the dust from his clothes. "You have said often enough it was time I married. It just happens that the girl in question is one Jim thought he had a lien on."

"Well, it can't be settled by fighting like stableboys." Sutton glanced at Jim. "If the girl has made her choice—"

"Oh, yes, she's made her choice," Jim said with great bitterness, "but you mustn't be surprised if I'm not very ready in offering my felicitations. Anyway, there's work to be done, as your bailiff, earning my eighteen shillings a week!"

He strode out of the yard, and Sutton turned to his son. "Come indoors," he said. "I've got a few things to say to you!"

LATER that morning Jim received word that he was wanted up in Mr. Sutton's study. He found the man alone there.

"This is a bad business, Jim, and I am more sorry than I can say. I've had it out with Philip, and I've told him what I think of him. But it seems he's perfectly serious about wanting to marry Jane."

Jim said nothing. Sutton motioned him to a chair, but he refused and continued to stand.

"Philip tells me," Sutton went on, "that they intend to marry quite soon. In fact, they talk of an autumn wedding. Early October, perhaps. It all seems very quick to me, but there it is. . . . You will have to consider what to do."

"Do?" Jim queried. "Why, what would I do?"

"Well, you can't very well stay on, with Philip and Jane living here and such bad blood between you and him. The ideal solution, it seems to me, is for you to go out to Canada and join my cousin Tom on his farm."

"Canada," Jim said hollowly. "Is that quite far enough away, do you think?"

"It will mean a new life for you, my boy. A challenge, an adventure! Tom farms five thousand acres in Ontario. Miles and miles of nothing but corn! It will be a splendid chance for you, and better for everyone if you were gone clean away before the wedding takes place. It'll spare your own feelings and theirs."

"Whatever I do, it will not be to spare Philip's feelings."

"I understand how you feel, but—he is my son, remember."

"And I am nobody's son. I've got no family, no land, no home."

Sutton gave a small sympathetic sigh. But he was anxious to have Jim's answer. "Well? What do you say to my idea?"

Jim suddenly turned to the door.

"I'll think about it and let you know."

CHAPTER 5

Once again Jim needed to think, and this time, driven by some primitive instinct, he climbed the gently sweeping slopes of Luton Camp. When he got to the top, he sat on a low grassy mound underneath a hawthorn tree and looked down on the valley below. Everything he saw was dear to him, so that the thought of leaving it caused an angry ache in his heart.

Of course, John Sutton was right: Jim would certainly not want to stay at Peele. But his lack of choice induced a fierce rebelliousness in him, and it was this—the fact that the whole of his future life was being thus decided out of hand—that made him reject Sutton's plan for sending him to Ontario.

His life was his own to direct. And as he sat looking down on the valley, comparing the rich, productive lands of Peele with the rough, neglected sprawl of Godsakes, he saw that he could use his life in a way that would not only further his own ambitions but defeat the Suttons in one of theirs.

The idea brought with it such a sense of purpose that his pain and anger were transmuted at once into strength and energy. He felt the stirrings of a fierce impatience, and he got to his feet and set off quickly down the hill toward Godsakes Farm.

Morris Riddler had been served with an official county court notice three days before, informing him that the property known as Godsakes Farm, in default of payment of certain debts and dues, would be put up for sale by public auction on Monday, September 27, 1858.

Riddler had read the notice and then torn it up, telling the officer who had delivered it that "anyone who comes here trying to put my farm up for sale will get a skitter of shot in his backside."

He had seen Jim coming along the path and was at his gate waiting for him, shotgun nestled in the crook of his arm.

"What do you want?" he asked with a growl.

"I've got a proposition to put to you."

"If the Suttons sent you, I'm not interested."

"This is nothing to do with the Suttons. This is business of my own. They don't know I've come."

Riddler cocked an eyebrow at him, giving him a long, hard look. "Something wrong between you and them?"

"Yes."

"Maybe I can guess what it is. I've heard the gossip that you and Philip Sutton were both after the same girl."

"In that case you knew before I did myself."

Riddler opened the ramshackle gate. "You'd better come into the house," he said.

The farmhouse kitchen was very bare. A table, three chairs, and a Welsh dresser were the only furniture in it. Every salable thing at Godsakes had gone to pay Riddler's debts.

Kirren, who was sweeping the stone-flagged floor, looked up in surprise at seeing Riddler enter with Jim. She leaned on her broom, frowning at him, sharing her father's first suspicions. Riddler sat down at the table, motioning Jim to do the same.

"You know my daughter, Kirren?" he said, and over his shoulder to Kirren herself, "This is Jim Lundy from Peele."

"I know perfectly well who he is."

"You needn't take that tone with me. He hasn't come to turn us out." Riddler looked at Jim sitting opposite. "A proposition, I think you said?"

"Yes, and I'll make no bones about it," Jim began. "You're done for here. We both know that. Your loan at the bank still stands at a little over six hundred pounds, but it is your payments on the loan, and a few other debts elsewhere, that are causing your most pressing problem."

"Two hundred pounds! That's all I need, and because I can't find it they'll sell me up!" Riddler exclaimed bitterly. But in his small, narrowed eyes there was already a gleam of hope. "But maybe you've come along with some miraculous solution?"

"I've come to offer to pay your debts."

"Have you?" Riddler breathed. Kirren stood in silence nearby. "And in return—what do you want?"

"A share in the farm. A partnership. Half and half."

"Just for paying off my debts?"

"No, there's more to it than that," Jim said. "I've got twelve hundred pounds in the bank, my savings over thirteen years. I've also got my flock, worth perhaps eighty pounds. I propose using my money to pay off your debts, restock the farm, and cover the running expenses. We then work together to build it up, and when that is achieved, a half share of the farm will be mine."

"You don't expect much, do you, in exchange for your twelve hundred pounds? Have you any idea, I wonder, how much it cost me to buy this place?"

"Yes, three thousand pounds. But you wouldn't get half that sum for it now, it being so run down. Anyway, I propose *earning* the rest of my share by putting the farm to rights, and—"

"All right, you've made your point! But I don't fancy sharing a farm that I've had to myself all these years."

"In that case you'll lose it altogether," Jim said. "When the sale takes place, the farm will go to the highest bidder. And that, as you know, will be John Sutton."

"Yes, you've got me there, haven't you? I'd do just about anything rather than see him get my farm. But there's one or two things to account for yet. What happens, for instance, when I die? My share of the farm will be Kirren's then. Do you propose being partners with *her?*"

"By that time, all being well, the farm will be on its feet again, and I shall be able to buy her out."

Riddler twisted around in his chair to look at Kirren. "What do you think about it?" he asked.

Kirren shrugged. "It seems a good enough plan," she said, "up to the point where I get turned out."

"Bought out, not turned out," Jim said.

"It means the same thing. I still lose my home."

Her words surprised him. Until today he had never met the girl. But he knew what her life had been like on this farm, and he had assumed that she would welcome a chance to escape.

"Does the place mean so much to you, then?" he asked her.

"I've never thought about it till now. But this is the only home I've ever known, and God knows I've worked hard enough for it."

"You'll be repaid for that work in the end, because when I buy your share of the farm, you'll be able to rent a cottage somewhere and have enough money to make you independent for life."

"On the other hand," she said, "if everything goes as well as you think, I could in the end buy you out instead."

"Oh, no, I wouldn't want that!" Jim said emphatically. "I would want the farm for myself."

Riddler now spoke again. "Why should you want the farm so much? To spite the Suttons and that girl from Hide House?"

"I don't think my reasons matter," Jim said. "But certainly I would want the farm."

"Seems we all want it," Riddler said. "We are united in that, at least. But supposing I was to drop dead before the farm was paying its way. You'd both have to stick it out here together, and that wouldn't do at all. It wouldn't be decent. Folks would talk."

Jim became silent. It seemed to him unbelievable that such an irrelevant problem should threaten his plan. But before he could frame any kind of answer, Morris Riddler was speaking again.

"Your plan is fine, but you haven't thought it through. I reckon the best way of making it work is for you and Kirren to get married. That way you get hold of the farm without having to turn her out, and there's no need for complicated legal arrangements."

Jim and Kirren both stared at him.

"You're surely not serious?" Jim said finally. "Marriage doesn't come into my plans at all."

"Nor mine," Kirren said. "I'm not going to marry this man just to please you and keep the farm."

"It's you I'm thinking of, Kirrie, not myself," Riddler said. "I'm talking about the future now—when I'm dead and in my grave and you're left with no one to take care of you. I doubt if you'll get another chance of a husband falling into your lap—"

"How many times do I have to tell you that a husband is the last thing I want?" Kirren, with angry impatience, began sweeping the flagstones again. "To saddle myself with the kind of life my mother endured with you? Oh dear me no! I'd sooner be dead!"

The violence of Kirren's outburst had a strange effect on Jim. It enhanced his own dark disillusionment, and looking at her more closely now, he saw her as though for the first time. Riddler, catching this, guessed the nature of the young man's thoughts.

"Well," he said shrewdly, "seeing you're both so set against marriage, it seems to me you're ideally suited. The perfect match! So why not look on it as a business arrangement, without any strings on either side? If you bought Kirren out, Jim, you'd only have to get someone else to cook and keep house for you. And one thing about a wife is you don't have to pay her a wage."

"Ah," Kirren said, "and there we come to the heart of it!"

But she had stopped sweeping again and was now looking directly at Jim. Their eyes met in a steady stare with a curious kind of hostile reserve, but this hostility somehow formed a bond between them. They were strangers, and both understood that strangers was how they wished to remain.

Quietly, cautiously, Jim spoke to her. "Purely as a business arrangement, exactly as your father suggests, would you be willing to consider it? It would simplify matters when it comes to joint ownership of the farm."

"Oh, it would simplify matters beautifully," Kirren said in a dry tone, "for a wife has almost no rights in property matters."

"Yes, but a wife does have rights of a kind. She is entitled to expect that her husband will always do well by her. And that is a duty I would certainly fulfill."

"No strings attached, as my father suggests?"

"None whatever," Jim said. "I would make no demands on you as a husband."

Kirren, it seemed, still had her doubts. "How do I know I can trust you?"

"You don't," he said bluntly, meeting her gaze. "But it is scarcely the kind of matter on which I can swear an affidavit."

Riddler gave a cynical laugh. "You can always lock your door, girl. That's simple enough. And if Jim is worried on the same score, he can lock his!"

"Your daughter needs time to think," Jim said, "and so, for that matter, do I."

"All right," Riddler said. "But that's my condition—no marriage, no deal. Now come with me. I'll show you what you'll be taking on, and Kirren will have time to think."

IT WAS seven years since Jim had set foot on Godsakes land, and in those years its ruination had been complete. In every field it was the same: a wilderness of rank grass and weeds, with clumps of thorn and brier here and there. Riddler's plows, unused in recent years, lay under a heap of junk in a corner of the crumbling barn. All the farm buildings were in disrepair and, like the land itself, infested with vermin.

"A sight for sore eyes, eh?" Riddler said. "And all Sutton's fault. This was a good farm once, but when I was given the chance to buy, and Sutton ran up the price like that—that big loan has dragged me down. It's as if I was stuck in the mire. The more I struggled, the deeper I sank."

After a while the two men came to a halt. Their tour had brought them back to the yard, and they leaned together over the gate, watching the few scrawny hens pecking about in the dust.

"Well," Riddler said, "think you can pull the farm back on its feet?"

"Yes, if you let me have a free hand to run things my way."

"Oh, so you're to have all the say, are you?"

"We should discuss things together, of course, as any business partners would. But you've made the decisions up to now, and as a result the farm has failed. And as it will be my money—"

"All right, all right, don't rub it in!" Riddler said with an angry scowl. "Who pays the piper calls the tune. And I know you can work—you wouldn't be Sutton's bailiff else." He turned his head away, then looked at Jim again. "It seems from the way you're talking, you've made up your mind to accept my condition."

"Yes, I accept it," Jim said.

"So," Riddler said quietly, "it all depends on Kirren, then. Let's go and see what she says."

Kirren was standing on the back porch waiting for them.

"Well, miss? Have you made up your mind?"

"Yes." She looked at Jim. "If he agrees to it, so do I."

Riddler could scarcely contain himself. Boisterously he turned to Jim and clapped one heavy hand on his back, at the same time taking Kirren's arm and giving it a long, hard squeeze.

"Come indoors, the pair of you! If there's anything left in the bottle, we'll drink damnation to the Suttons!"

Just after two o'clock Jim returned to Peele House, quietly mounted the stairs to his room, and put his clothes and other belongings into an old canvas satchel. With this slung over his shoulder he went downstairs, knocked on the door to John Sutton's study, and, without waiting for a reply, let himself in.

"What's this?" Sutton asked with a frown, eyeing the satchel on Jim's back.

"I thought, since you wanted me to leave, I might as well go straightaway—but not Ontario. I'm going to Godsakes instead."

"Godsakes?" Sutton said blankly, and then, with quickly growing suspicion, "What the devil do you mean?"

"I'm going to pay Riddler's debts. We shall be partners, he and I, and we'll work together to pull up the farm. I've just been over there bargaining with him, and now I'm going back—for good."

"You would do that to me?" Sutton was crimson in the face. "You know I've always wanted that farm! I've waited years!"

"Yes, I know it well, just as Philip knew I wanted Jane."

"All this fuss over a girl! Jim, just look at yourself! You've got enough about you to take your pick from a dozen girls. You'll have no trouble finding another wife."

"I've already found one. I'm going to marry Kirren Riddler."

"Riddler's daughter? But you don't even know the girl!"

"It would seem I didn't know Jane either."

Sutton was now thunderous. "Do you mean you are marrying her just to get hold of Godsakes Farm? After what I've done for you, giving you a home all these years! Bringing you up and caring for you almost as though you were my son!"

"You've always been good to me, and I thank you for it," Jim said. "But now, although I've done nothing wrong, you would send me to a place where I have no wish to be, and no doubt, if you had the power, you would rub me clean off the face of the earth. Well, common nobody I may be, but I still have the right to run my own life."

Following these words, Jim became silent, looking straight into Sutton's eyes and seeing there a burning reflection of his own anger and bitterness. Then, with some awkwardness, he said, "I'm sorry it's ending like this. I know that my going to Godsakes will put paid to our friendship once and for all."

"I suppose it's your idea of revenge."

"Whatever it is, Philip is the one to blame for it."

A few minutes later, with his long shepherding stick in his hand and his dog, Jess, close at his heels, Jim made his way into the pastures to fetch his flock. Sutton came out of the house and stood in the open doorway staring grimly after him.

FROM the top of the main farm track that led into Godsakes land, Riddler and Kirren stood watching as the neatly bunched flock of sheep came slowly up the sloping fields with the young man and the dog behind. The sight of these golden-fleeced sheep affected Morris Riddler deeply, and the surge of emotion was so strong in him that when he turned to Kirren, his queer, crooked face was wet with tears.

"Look at them, Kirrie! Just look at them! Did you ever see anything so beautiful in all your born days? That little flock of Cotswold Lions means that this farm is in business again!"

Even Kirren herself was affected; there was a smile on her lips and a gleam of living hope in her eyes. For once she and her father were in accord, and he, aware of this, suddenly clasped her in his arms. Then just as suddenly he released her, and with his lumbering gait he set off down the track to meet Jim.

AT FOUR o'clock three people instead of two sat down to eat their first meal together at Godsakes.

"You won't find us delicate here," Riddler said. "Plain boiled bacon and cabbage and taters, that's what we live on. You will find it a bit of a change after the way you've lived at Peele."

"Plain food is good enough for me," Jim said.

But the boiled bacon was terrible stuff. The smell of it told him what to expect, and it required an effort of will to swallow the first mouthful of tainted meat. Kirren was watching him.

"You don't have to eat it," she said. "It can go back in the pot."

"If you can eat it, so can I."

It was with a sense of relief that Jim at last finished the meal and laid down his knife and fork. He rose and pushed in his chair. "I'm going for another walk round the farm."

"Hang on a minute," Riddler said. "I'll come with you."

"Thanks, but I'd sooner be alone. I've got some thinking to do."

Looking around the farm again, noting things that had to be done, Jim could scarcely wait to begin. But his first task in the morning would be to go into town with Riddler and arrange for the payment of his debts and to buy new stock for the farm.

But all the time, as he laid his plans, other thoughts were troubling him, and the source of these was Kirren. He was fretted by feelings of guilt. Was he doing wrong, marrying someone he cared nothing about? Had he taken advantage of Kirren's poverty merely to further his own ends? When he returned to the house, he found her alone and broached the subject immediately.

She heard him out, looking at him searchingly. When he had finished, she asked bluntly, "Are you having second thoughts?"

"For myself—no. For you—yes, perhaps. I feel you've been thrust into this thing without having enough time to think."

"I'm not a fool. I know what I'm doing. You said you didn't want a proper marriage, and I said I felt the same."

"Most women want children. Don't you?"

"No. I do not. When women marry, they generally have children whether they like it or not. They just have to make the best of it. But I wouldn't want to bring a child into the world. Another life, another soul . . . The responsibility is frightening to me."

"Frightening? But if a man and woman love one another . . ."

"Yes? What? I've heard my father say that he loved my mother, but he had a queer way of showing it, driving her into the grave."

"You have a poor opinion of men."

"They like their own way," Kirren said, "and they always make sure they get it. No, this marriage will suit me very well. My father's been nagging at me for years to find a husband. By marrying you I shall get some peace. And if you can really make the farm pay—"

"That I promise and swear to do."

"Then I shall be well satisfied."

There was no further argument after that; it only remained to see the vicar and arrange for the marriage to take place at the earliest possible date. And Jim, his last lingering doubts removed, felt free to give his mind to the farm.

CHAPTER 6

IT WAS strange for Jim, after living at Peele all those years, looking across the valley at Godsakes, to find himself now living at Godsakes, looking across the valley at Peele. It induced a queer feeling of dislocation, as though the sun itself were at fault for rising in the wrong part of the sky. But he never for an instant forgot where he was or why he was there.

The work at Godsakes was a challenge to him. His whole being rose to it, embracing it as a kind of crusade. He knew what needed to be done and the best way of doing it. For the past fourteen years of his life, he had listened to John Sutton and

Philip discuss how to put Godsakes in order again when at last it came into their hands.

And here Jim's heart always gave a leap because of the way things had fallen out—because Godsakes had come into his hands, and the Suttons would never have it now. Philip had taken Jane from him, and he in turn had taken Godsakes from them. It was a method of revenge that tasted sweet on the tongue.

But there was a moral side to it too that added an extra dimension to his satisfaction. He had always had some sympathy with Morris Riddler in his struggles; the man had been treated badly by John Sutton and much of his life had been spoiled by it. Now Jim had given him the weapons with which to fight back and win, and the two of them were working to the same end.

Not that they were always in agreement. Far from it, in fact. There were endless arguments between them in the early days: arguments over the horses Jim bought, the new machines, the new farm stock.

"Why Shorthorns?" Riddler said. "What's wrong with Old Gloucesters, I'd like to know? And what do we want with so many sheep? The place is swarming with them already."

"This farm needs the sheep," Jim said. "They'll tread the soil and make it compact, and their dung will put new heart into it. As for the cows, Shorthorns milk better than Old Gloucesters, and their milk makes better butter and cheese."

"Well, if you say so, of course. It is your money, after all. I suppose you can spend it how you like. Even waste it, paying it all out in wages!"

This was a sore point with Riddler, because Jim had engaged an extra man, thus making three hired hands in all, and was paying them eight shillings a week.

"You can't expect good work if you don't pay for it," Jim said.

"You won't get good work out of Lovell and Smith. They don't know the meaning of the word."

"I've seen well enough how they slack off in your fields. But this new man, Townsend, is first class. And as he will get eight shillings a week, so Smith and Lovell will get it too. And if they don't earn it, they'll be dismissed."

"Have you told them that?"

"Yes," Jim said. "And they will find I'm a man of my word."

JIM WANTED TO GET AS MUCH land plowed that autumn as time and the weather would allow. And so it was, on a warm misty morning in mid-September, that there were five teams at work plowing the fields at Godsakes.

Jim had not plowed for three years. It felt good to take hold of the handles again, to see the plowshare cutting the ground and the furrow slice heeling over, burying the weeds. Riddler worked in the same field as Jim, grumbling all the while, yet plowing with a certain jaunty, swaggering gusto.

"Three years since you plowed, did you say? For me it's more like five or six!" he called across to Jim.

"You've still got the knack of it, anyway." And Jim looked back at Riddler's stretch, with its furrow running clean and straight.

"I'm glad I'm still good for something!" Riddler said.

The weather that autumn was clear and mild, and the work of plowing, rolling, and harrowing went ahead without hindrance. Riddler complained endlessly about the many cultivations Jim considered necessary for the cleaning of the land, and he thought it the height of folly that Jim meant to plow up certain pastures only to sow the ground with new grass. For grass was just grass to Riddler, and he would stare in astonishment when Jim pointed out the various species, giving their scientific names and describing their respective virtues.

It was the same with the artificial fertilizers Jim had bought. "Guano?" Riddler said, sniffing the sacks. "All the way from Peru? Seems a bit farfetched to me. I've never used it in my life."

"Are you holding yourself up as an example?" Jim asked.

"All right, all right, I know I'm a failure!" Riddler said. "My only business these days is to watch you run my farm for me!"

But although he argued at every turn and was always making sarcastic remarks, Riddler's desire for Jim to succeed overrode everything. "I'd stand on my head if you told me to," he said.

"I don't want you to stand on your head. I want you to stand on your own two feet."

"Hah! And what about my corns? Am I to put guano on them?"

"Yes, if you want them to grow," Jim said.

Riddler went off with a loud guffaw. Passing Kirren in the yard, he said, "One thing about this husband of yours—at least we get a few laughs since he came."

And as autumn progressed and more and more land came under the plow, Riddler's spirits soared.

"I hope John Sutton can see what's happening here," he said one day, jerking his head toward Peele.

Jim, forking field rubbish onto a fire, paused and looked across the valley. The big square house stood without any sign of life, but out on the land the winter grain was being sown.

"He can see it all right," he said quietly. "He has no choice."

"Well, that's the whole idea, isn't it? To let that wife of Philip Sutton's know that she married the wrong man?"

Jim turned back to his work. "I understand from Abelard that Philip and Jane are still on their honeymoon."

"Seems they must be enjoying it, staying away so long as this. How long is it? Five weeks or six?"

"I haven't been keeping count," Jim said.

Riddler took a malicious delight in taunting Jim this way. Philip and Jane had been married on the second Sunday in October, a week after Jim's marriage to Kirren, and the couple, according to gossip, were honeymooning abroad.

"France and Italy!" Riddler would say. "Now, you could never have given her that. Not on a farm bailiff's wages, eh?"

Toward the end of November the young couple returned home, and a week or so afterward three large covered vans were seen driving up to Peele.

"Paintings and statues and such," old Abelard told Jim when they met down at the brook one day, "and something called a spinet, that they've brought back from Italy."

The changes being wrought at Peele these days, now that the house had a new mistress, could be seen and heard plainly enough at Godsakes. There were often parties in the evenings, and sometimes, when the wind was right, the sound of music could be heard across the valley.

"No wonder that girl jilted you," Riddler would say. "She wanted a lot more out of life than you could've given her."

"Yes, it would seem so," was all Jim said.

IN BETWEEN those times when the fallow lands were being cleaned by repeated cultivations, Jim and Riddler and the other men were busy cutting and laying the hedges. Jim also engaged a warrener to trap the rabbits infesting the farm, and during the first month or so more than two hundred rabbits were killed. As a result, rabbit stew and rabbit pie appeared regularly at the table.

"Better than reasty bacon, eh?" Riddler would say, grinning at Jim, and to Kirren, more than once, he said, "You're getting to be quite a good cook, now that you've got a husband to feed. This rabbit pie is something, like."

"Give me good meat to cook," Kirren said, "and I will give you decent meals."

Certainly, the reasty bacon had proved too much for Jim, and he had very soon asked Kirren to bring home a joint of thick fresh meat every week from the butcher's in town.

"A pretty penny that must have cost!" Riddler said when the first rib of beef was brought smoking-hot to the table.

"It's his own money he's spending, remember."

"As though I was likely to forget."

"Are you going to carve?" Kirren asked.

"No, not me." Riddler said. "Not at sixpence a pound, I'm not! He paid for it. He can carve."

Kirren, in exasperation, picked up the great dish of meat and put it down in front of Jim. "I'm sorry about my father," she said. "He's always had this childish side."

"Childish be damned!" Riddler poured himself a mug of ale. "Nice thick slices for me," he said as Jim picked up the carving knife. "And plenty of fat off the outside."

But these joints of meat, Jim knew, were heavy loads and had to be brought home by Kirren, along with all the other provisions, which meant a six-mile walk in all, sometimes in pouring rain. And so he would, in the early days, walk down to meet her at Abbot's Lyall and carry her baskets the last two miles home.

Kirren was astonished. She had never been helped before, and because she was unused to it, she was inclined to be ungracious.

"You're wasting good working time, trailing out here like this. I can manage perfectly well."

Riddler was even more astonished. "It's her own fault she has to go to the town," he said to Jim. "We used to have the higgler here, buying her butter and eggs, but she stopped him from coming. You don't need to fuss over her. She can manage a couple of baskets all right."

"Yes," Jim responded. "But I don't intend that she should for much longer. I'm going to buy her a pony and trap."

"Pony and trap!" Riddler said. "We shall end up at auction if you go on spending at this rate."

"What I spend on it will not break us, I promise you."

The trap was bought at a farm sale: rather old and shabby, with its dark blue panelwork blistered and crazed, but sound enough in all other respects; and with it a docile Welsh pony called Griff.

"Potbellied brute, isn't he?" Riddler said critically.

"He won't be, though, when he's properly fed."

"I hope he understands English," said Kirren, offering the pony a lump of sugar, "because I don't speak any Welsh."

The pony ate the lump of sugar and nuzzled her apron in search of more. She stroked his bristly mottled nose.

"He understands sugar, anyway," she said, and turned with a little smile toward Jim, who stood nearby watching her.

Riddler was also watching, and because it was such a rare thing to see her smiling in this way, with a faint flush of color on her cheeks, he could not allow it to go unremarked.

"Why, Kirrie, what a difference it makes to see you looking pleased with yourself! It's something I haven't seen for years!"

"No, well," Kirren said, "it isn't every day of the week that I am given a pony and trap."

"Seems you're like all the rest of them, then, if a man's got to dip into his pocket before he can get a smile out of you. But I must say it's worth it to see you smiling like that. You should do it more often, that's a fact."

"What for?" she said. "To please you men?"

"There, that's gratitude for you!"

"And why should I be grateful to you?"

"Because if I hadn't found you a soft husband, he wouldn't have bought you a pony and trap just to take a few paltry eggs and a bit of butter to town every week!" Riddler, pleased with his own logic, turned and walked away from them.

Kirren, blank-faced, watched him go. Then she turned to the pony again, and after a moment Jim spoke of the trap.

"Have you ever driven before?"

"No, never."

"Then you'd better have some practice," he said.

A little while later Kirren was driving around the farm, and Jim, beside her in the trap, was giving such advice as was needed. As they drove down the steep rutted lane and out onto the open track, they were watched from the middle field by Lovell and Smith, who were there digging out the lower ditch.

"I reckon they make a handsome couple, don't you, Bob?" said Nahum Smith, leaning on his trenching spade.

"Handsome enough," Lovell agreed. "And as long as Jim Lundy goes on paying me eight shillings a week, good luck to him with both the farm and the girl."

So KIRREN, now that she had her trap, could drive into town in comfort and be glad of it, for the quantity of produce she took with her was growing. There were six cows milking these days, and six more were due to calve. She had butter and cheese to sell again, and as there was more poultry on the farm—geese and ducks as well as hens—she also had many more eggs.

Riddler scorned using the trap, and even in the worst weather rode to town on his gray pony mare, who could be trusted to bring him safely home even when, "as happened sometimes," he had had a glass or two more than was wise. But Jim, if he had business in town, often drove in with Kirren. Cold-blooded partnership though theirs was, he wished the world to see that he and she were well satisfied with it.

One market day they had a brief meeting with Philip and Jane Sutton, who, driving a smart four-in-hand, came up behind them at Cooper's Bridge. Jim had got down to open the gate so that Kirren could drive through, and he was about to close it again when the four-in-hand came bowling along. He saw at once who was in it and held the gate open for them, giving a little formal nod as they crossed the bridge within a few inches of him. Jane, who was closest, smiled somewhat hesitantly at first, then with a sudden radiance, and spoke to him as she passed.

"Thank you, Jim. That was very kind."

Philip drove by without a glance, staring ahead, red-faced and tight-lipped, and Jane again turned her head to nod and say good morning to Kirren.

Jim returned to his place beside Kirren, and they drove on along the road, watching the carriage in front as it rapidly drew

away from them. Then Kirren spoke. "So that is the famous Jane Sutton? I've never seen her close to before."

"Certainly she stared at you hard enough as she passed."

"She was probably wondering what sort of creature you had married."

"Yes," he said curtly, "I daresay she was." His mind was still full of Jane's smile, full of the memories it had evoked. But with an effort he brought his thoughts back to the girl sitting beside him. "Sometimes I wonder that myself."

"Surely you must know that by now, having lived with me these three months or more."

"I know you as cook and housekeeper, yes. As dairywoman and rearer of hens. You certainly work very hard."

"So do we all. We have no choice. We are slaves to the farm, all three of us, bound to it body and soul."

"Do you resent that?" he asked.

Kirren, considering, gave a shrug. "I used to, in the old days, when everything seemed so hopeless. But that's all changed now, since you came. I don't mind hard work so long as I see some reward at the end of it."

"What reward?" Jim asked.

"To keep the farm, of course, and get it running properly."

"Is that reward enough for you?"

"What more would I want? A houseful of servants? Statues and paintings from Italy? No. The sum total of my ambitions, for today at least, is to get a shilling a pound for my butter and eightpence a dozen for my eggs."

Jim smiled. "And what about the future?" he asked. "There must be things you would like to have."

"Yes, there are, but I look to my poultry to pay for them, and as I've gone without them for so long, I can easily wait a while longer yet." She gave him a brief sideways glance and said, "I am not like your Jane Sutton. I'm prepared to work for what I want."

No, he thought as they drove on, Kirren was not like Jane. Indeed, the contrast between the two young women could not have been greater. And it seemed peculiarly right, somehow, that whereas Jane was fair and blue-eyed, with gentle manners and a bright, easy smile, Kirren should be dark-haired and dark-eyed, with a temper that, more often than not, moved between sullen reserve and a quick, dark, withering scorn. Kirren's hard life had toughened her and made her strong, physically and mentally, and now at the age of twenty-two she had no softness or gentleness, no feminine grace.

Jim took grim pleasure in this, because Jane possessed these qualities and he had been led astray by them. That would not happen with the girl he called his wife, for he expected nothing from her and therefore could never be disappointed. And although they had made certain vows in church, in private the only vow they had made was to work together for the good of the farm. Nothing else mattered to them. Only Godsakes, first and last.

SOMETIMES when Jim was working down in the meadows, he would pause and look up at the farm and note the improvements made so far: the three plowed fields that were still bare, showing up a rich red-brown between other fields already sown, where the winter grain was like a green mist creeping softly over the soil; the new leas, a darker green, already growing thick and close.

But these improvements were only a beginning. And on cold winter evenings beside the fire with Riddler and Kirren, Jim would discuss his plans for the future.

"In five or six years, if all goes well, every acre we possess will have been cleaned and put in good heart again. I hope to start work on the buildings soon—I've ordered timber and tiles for the roofs. In time everything on the farm will be in tip-top order."

"In other words," Kirren said, "you want to make it like Peele."

"No! Like itself!" he said sharply. "It must have been a good place once, and it will be again. I shall see to that."

"We shall all see to it," Riddler said. "Go on with your ideas."

"I mean to have every inch of land producing its maximum yield," Jim continued. "The grain we grow on this land will not fetch top prices till fertility's been restored. And that will only come about if we stock the land to capacity. All of which means growing crops we can feed directly to the stock. Turnips, kale, carrots, and beans. And dredge corn."

"But at present you're buying feed for them," Riddler said. "I don't see any profit in that. There's plenty of grass here, if nothing else. And as for this notion of feeding the ewes—"

"Ewes should always be given extra, coming up to breeding time, just as they get shortly before they are due to lamb."

"And what about the rams? Don't they deserve extra feed too? Something sweet and tasty, like asparagus?"

Just as Riddler jeered at Jim on the subject of artificial manures, so too did he jeer when Jim quoted from certain agricultural pamphlets.

"You can't learn farming out of books!"

"I didn't. I learned it on the land. But books are written by men who have tried things out for themselves, and we should be willing to learn from them."

Riddler picked up a small book that Jim had left lying about. Opening it, he stared at the printed page in disgust. "Latin!" he exclaimed. "Lawyers' language! The language of rogues!"

"This book is a poem about farming, written by a man called Virgil, who lived and farmed in Italy about two thousand years ago."

"Two thousand years ago?" Riddler tossed the book across to him. "Well, read us a bit. In English, so's we understand."

Jim found a suitable passage, studied it for a moment or two, and rendered it aloud in English. *"There comes a time when the corn is blighted; when thistles spring up everywhere; when no crops grow but wild tares and wild oats, beggarweed and spiky caltrops. You must, therefore, wage war on the weeds unceasingly; cut down the trees that darken your land; shout the birds away from your crops and, in the summer, pray for rain. Otherwise, though your neighbor's granary be full, you will have to shake the acorns from the oak to stay your own hunger."*

Jim, as he put the book away, found that both Kirren and Riddler had been listening as he read, and that both were looking at him intently.

"You chose well, didn't you, reading that bit to us?" Riddler said. "It might have been Godsakes he was writing about, except that we never came so low that we had to eat acorns to keep alive."

"No, just reasty bacon, that's all."

Riddler threw back his head and laughed. He enjoyed these exchanges he had with Jim. And he was more than just a little impressed by Jim's superior learning.

"Kirrie, you've married a Latin scholar. What do you think of that, eh?"

Kirren, turning to her needlework, snipped off a length of cotton. "I must try not to let it go to my head," she said.

CHAPTER 7

DURING the worst winter frosts, when all work on the land was stopped, Jim worked on the house instead, replacing tiles that had slid from the roof and repairing and painting the big kitchen. He then turned to the outbuildings. With help from Riddler and the other men, the most urgent jobs were done in three weeks, and by then the frost had gone, making field work possible again.

With a kitchen that was fresh and clean, Kirren began adding improvements of her own. She had made new curtains in a pattern of rusty reds and browns, and these gave the room a look of warmth. She was often buying new things because the poultry money was hers to spend now as she pleased, and gradually the big room became more homely and comfortable. There was new brown-and-white china on the dresser, and a new set of earthenware jugs stood on a shelf of their own.

One day, having been into town alone, she returned wearing a new dress of dark green worsted, ribbed in black, with a double cape of the same material, and a black beaver hat with a curled brim. As she drove into the yard Riddler and Jim were standing there, and both men stopped talking to stare at her.

"Why, Kirrie," Riddler said, "I hardly recognized you, all dressed up to the nines like that! I thought it was some fine lady or other coming to call on us out of the blue."

With a satirical glance Kirren turned to take from the trap a large rectangular parcel bulkily wrapped in paper and sacking. She handled it with great care.

"What've you got there?" her father asked.

"You'll see when we get indoors," she said.

Jim now went to the trap and took out the two heavy baskets of shopping. Riddler touched him on the arm.

"What do you think of your wife's finery?"

"Stylish and elegant, I would say."

"Do you know," Riddler said as they followed Kirren into the house, "I never noticed until today what a fine, handsome figure she's got on her. She must've caused quite a stir in the town."

Kirren, although she had colored a little, bore their comments with composure, walking before them into the house. "Whatever stir I caused in the town was nothing to the stir I seem to be causing here at home."

"Well, open your parcel, girl," Riddler said, "and let us see what it is you've bought."

What Kirren had bought was a fine clock, old but in excellent working order, in a case of polished mahogany and with a brass face. Jim hung the clock on the wall straightaway, wound it up, and cautiously set it to the correct hour.

"Nice to have a clock in the place again," Riddler said approvingly. "This room is beginning to look more cheerful, like. How much did you pay for it?"

"Why, what business is that of yours?"

"I was just thinking to myself that if ever we fall on hard times again, at least we'll have something worthwhile to sell, eh?"

Kirren's face became darkly flushed. "You will not sell that clock," she said with angry emphasis, "nor any of the other things in this room, because *I* bought them and they are *mine!*"

"Can't you take a joke, girl?" Riddler said.

"It is no joke to me," Kirren said, "that you've stripped the house bare over the years."

"I needed the money to pay the bills!"

"And how much of it went on drink?"

"I've had enough of this!" Riddler went out, slamming the door, and Kirren began gathering up the sheets of brown wrapping paper, folding them with quick, angry movements. Jim turned to the door, but paused a moment and looked at her.

"It was only a joke, after all. Surely you must know that."

"Oh, I know it well enough," Kirren said. "But I've never cared for my father's jokes, and I doubt if I shall learn to now."

ANGER was always close to the surface in all Kirren's dealings with her father, and it was easy to see why. The man was so rough and insensitive; everything he did was clumsy and ill-judged.

One morning in early March a polecat got in among the poultry, and the commotion was such that Jim and Riddler, who were in the barn, ran out to the yard immediately, followed by Kirren, who came hurrying out of the house. The polecat, laying about him in murderous fashion, quickly made off when the two men shouted at him, leaving behind the mangled remains of three pullets, one of which still shuddered and twitched.

Riddler, cursing at the top of his voice, threw a stone at the fleeing polecat, then picked up the three mangled pullets and ran with them to the pig run, hurling them over to the pigs, who gobbled them up at once. As he came lumbering back, wiping his hands on his corduroys, Kirren confronted him in a rage.

"Why did you do that?" she cried. "One of those pullets wasn't properly dead!"

"Well, it will be by now!" Riddler said.

Kirren, with a little exclamation, walked quickly away from him. Riddler scowled after her, but when he turned and met Jim's glance, it was with a certain sheepishness.

"Women!" he said defensively as they walked back to the barn together. "The bird's head was half hanging off! So what was I supposed to do? Get the doctor out to it?"

"You should have wrung its neck," Jim said, "quickly, in the proper way. Women are sensitive about such things."

"Oh, Kirrie can be hard enough when she likes."

"Yes, well, she's had a hard time of it. There can't have been much joy in her life, slaving away here with you."

"As for the joy in Kirren's life, it's up to you to give her that, and the sooner you get around to it the better, because then perhaps she'll have something to do besides fussing over a bloody fowl!"

Riddler strode into the barn, but Jim followed him. "You know the terms of my marriage to Kirren," he said. "A business arrangement. Nothing more."

"Yes, yes!" Riddler said. "But that was agreed all of six months ago. I thought you'd have seen some sense by now."

"You mean you expected things to change?"

"Of course I did! You're a man, aren't you? A man needs a woman to be a proper wife to him. And as for Kirren, well, I know she's got queer ideas about marriage and men, but she'll get over that in time, especially if you manage her right. But don't take too long over it. I want to see a few children running around on this farm before I join my wife in the churchyard."

Riddler took up a shovel and began shoveling turnips into a wheelbarrow. Jim watched him, half vexed, half amused. "I think you should put these ideas of yours clean out of your mind," he said, "for nothing will ever come of them."

Riddler, still shoveling, shot him a glance.

"Yes, well, we shall see," he said.

UNDER the brisk March winds, which blew hard and cold along the valley, the land was drying out nicely, and Jim, preparing for his first batch of lambs at Godsakes, chose a field known as the Browse, which lay up behind the house and was sheltered from the north by a belt of trees. He placed shallow troughs in the field and into them the ewes' extra feed, which was measured out twice every day. Here and there about the field he placed a number of straw bundles so that the ewes and their lambs would have warm "cooches," as Abelard called them, against which to shelter from wind and rain.

The early lambing went well and was all over in three weeks. Jim's fifty ewes produced sixty-four lambs, and of these, sixty-two were raised. One ewe died giving birth to twins, and these were kept in a pen in the barn, where Kirren tended them, giving them milk from a newly calved cow. The twin lambs were sickly and delicate, so small that when she fed them she held them easily under one arm, letting them suck in turn at the bottle.

Even Riddler was pleased with the results of this lambing, but disapproved of Kirren's efforts to care for the orphaned lambs.

"It's nothing but a waste of time, rearing lambs by hand," he said. "Even if they pull through, they never amount to much."

"What would you have me do? Throw them to the pigs?"

"Lord Almighty! Listen to this," Riddler said. "Aren't I ever going to be let to forget what I did with those poor pullets?"

He went off muttering, and ten minutes later was mounting his mare. It was a Friday, and he was going into the town to draw money from the bank for the men's wages.

He was gone all day, and when he returned after dark, he was very drunk. He rode right up to the porch and hammered on the door. When Kirren, who was alone in the house, reluctantly went out to him, he leaned forward in the saddle and dropped a closed basket at her feet. He had brought her three new pullets.

In leaning so far forward, however, he lost his balance and pitch-rolled head over heels to the ground. An effort to scramble up proved too much for him; he gave a feeble groan, rolled himself over onto his back, and lay stretched out, insensible.

It was not the first time that Kirren had had to take charge of the mare, bedding her down for the night. Nor was it the first time Riddler had lain out in the yard, covered by a horse blanket thrown over him. Kirren performed these ministrations without a second thought. She then went to the poultry yard and put the pullets into a coop, and by the time she returned, Jim had come in from the sheepfold and was standing over Riddler.

"Surely you don't mean to leave him like this?" he said.

"Yes, I do. He's used to it."

She picked up her father's saddlebags, heavy with coins, and went indoors. It was past nine o'clock, and she began making up the fire for the night. While she was doing this, Jim came in the door, carrying her father's limp body over his shoulder.

"I'm taking him up to his bed," he said.

He went out into the hall; she heard his tread on the stairs. The moment Jim reentered the room, she said, "Perhaps you think I should have carried him up to his bed?"

"No, I do not. But I think you could have done something more than leave him lying out in the yard."

"That was where he chose to fall."

"You are very hard on him," Jim said. "He is your father, your own flesh and blood. Don't you care anything for him at all?"

"No, why should I?" Kirren said. "He's never cared anything for me. He's never been able to forgive me, because I pulled through the flu years ago and my brother did not."

"How can you say that? I'm sure it's not true."

"I heard it plain," Kirren said. " 'Why did it have to be the boy that died?' That's what he said."

"Did he say that?" Jim was shocked. "That was a terrible thing to say. But people speak cruel things in moments of stress, things they don't mean at all. I think you should try to forgive him now, if only for your own sake. It's wrong to store up bitterness."

"Yes, well," Kirren said, "you should know about that, shouldn't you? What was it that brought you here if it wasn't bitterness against the Suttons?"

Jim was taken aback. He had not expected such a counter-stroke. What she said was perfectly true. But it was not the whole truth.

"You choose to overlook the fact that part of my reason for coming here was to help your father keep the farm."

"It was part of your reason, perhaps. But you don't have to justify yourself to me, because your coming here was the best thing that ever happened to us."

"I'm glad you can give me some credit, at least."

"A moment ago you were lecturing me for my lack of tenderness toward my father out in the yard. But at least I covered him with a blanket. Perhaps you will give me credit for that."

"If I did lecture you, I have been repaid in full," Jim said. "It seems we are quits, then, so I'll take myself off to bed before we begin wrangling again."

The atmosphere had eased between them. There was humor in the glance they exchanged. But afterward, when she had gone and he stood for a while alone in the kitchen, he was filled with an irksome restlessness, a sense of something left unresolved.

AT FIVE o'clock the following morning Jim was out in the lambing pen attending to his sheep. And he found himself brooding on what Kirren had said about his bitterness against the Suttons. He still felt immense satisfaction at having taken Godsakes from them. So why, when the fruits of his revenge were still sweet to him, should he feel irked?

Slowly he realized that it was because the element of revenge was no longer of prime importance. He had been at Godsakes more than six months now, and lately he had scarcely thought of the Suttons at all. He had been too busy, too absorbed. He saw now with great clarity that what he was doing at Godsakes had become more important to him than his original reason for doing it—important because it was good in itself.

This realization gave him a jolt of pleasure, a sense of release, because the bitterness was gone. With this discovery he returned to the house, where Kirren was laying the table for breakfast. Jim was glad to find her alone, and he came to the point immediately.

"I've been thinking over what you said, about my feeling bitter against the Suttons. It's not quite true."

Kirren stood looking at him in surprise. "I told you last night that you don't have to justify yourself to me."

"No. I just want you to understand," Jim said. "What I felt about the Suttons doesn't matter anymore. What I am doing on this farm is more worthwhile than anything else I could ever have done with my life. Or to put it another way, the fact that I no longer hate the Suttons somehow makes my revenge complete."

He went outside to wash at the pump then, and thoughtfully Kirren went back to preparing the breakfast. After a while Riddler came in. He stood at one side of the hearth, watching her.

"Somebody put me to bed last night."

"Yes, I know."

"Seems I've got a better son-in-law than I have a daughter."

"By that same token," Kirren replied steadily, "I've got a better husband than I have a father."

"I don't see that that follows at all."

"At least he doesn't come home drunk."

"Did you see after the fowls I brought you?"

"Yes. I shut them up last night, and this morning I let them out with the rest."

"Don't I get any thanks for them?"

"I'll thank you when they begin to lay."

"And when will that be?" Riddler asked.

"It will never be, I'm afraid."

"Why, what the devil's wrong with them?"

"They are all cockerels," Kirren said.

CHAPTER 8

Soon the second batch of ewes began lambing, and again all went well. The lamb harvest altogether numbered a hundred and eighty-eight, including the orphaned twins fostered by Kirren. By early May, too, the six heifers had all calved and were milking well, which meant so much more work for Kirren that Willie Townsend's wife, Prue, came every day to help in the dairy.

The old silent fields had been transformed, and in the evenings, especially, the gentle clamor of the ewes and lambs constantly calling to one another was heard from one end of the farm to the other and, indeed, all over the valley.

"I hope they can hear it," Riddler would say, jerking his head toward Peele.

Jim turned his flock out onto the hills at the end of May, thus giving the home pastures a chance to grow a fresh green bite. And all through May and part of June, in those fields that had been plowed and harrowed to a fine tilth, the teams went steadily to and fro, drilling in the turnip seed, the kale, and the peas.

On a warm sunny day in late June, Jim brought his flock down from the hills onto the meadowland by the brook, where the ewes were herded into a long pen that led steeply down to the edge of the wash pool. The upper sluice had been opened wide, the lower one almost closed, and as soon as the ewes were all penned, Jim and the new shepherd, Billy Smith, lowered themselves into the pool. Riddler, in the pen with the sheep, seized one in his great clumsy hands and swung it over into the pool, where Jim in turn took hold of it, dunking it three or four times in the water before sending it down to Billy, who guided it onto the stone-paved slip that led up the bank and out onto the meadow.

The sluice gates in the Timmy Brook had been put in recently by John Sutton, who at that time was the only farmer using the pool. Neither Jim nor Riddler, therefore, felt any great surprise when they looked up from their work to find that they were being watched from the other side of the brook by two men on horseback. One, Jim saw, was Philip Sutton, and the other, he could guess, was Dick Bowcott, who had taken his place as bailiff at Peele. Some way behind them, under an oak tree, Abelard leaned on his shepherding stick, his dogs lying peacefully at his feet.

"Aye, you can watch," Riddler muttered as he flung a ewe into the pool. "And think what thoughts you please!"

Riddler and Jim and Billy Smith went on working without pause, but after a while the man Bowcott, obviously acting on Philip's orders, rode across the meadow to the pool's edge.

"How long are you going to be? Our shepherd is waiting to use this pool."

"It's a funny thing," Riddler said, "that you should want to use the pool just when we are using it."

Philip Sutton now rode to the edge of the water. "You people have no business here at all, seeing that we put these sluice gates in without a penny piece from you."

"Sluice gates or no sluice gates, it's all as one to me," Riddler said. "The rights of washing our sheep in this pool are written into the deeds of my farm, just as they are in yours."

Philip, defeated in argument, hit back at Riddler with a sneer. "*Your* farm? It seems to me it is more Lundy's than yours."

"At least it'll never be yours," Riddler said evenly.

"As to that, we shall see!" Philip said. "You've got a long way to go yet before you've paid off that mortgage."

He and Bowcott rode away. Riddler stood looking down at Jim. "I don't know which I hate most, John Sutton or his son."

"Take no notice of Philip. He'll never take the farm from us."

The sheep washing was resumed, and while this was going on, old Abelard came and spoke to Jim.

"That there fuss of Mr. Philip's—I didn't have no part of it."

"I didn't think you had," Jim said.

"Just thought I'd mention it," Abelard said.

The summer sheep sales at Dunton Payne came at the end of July, and here Jim's lambs were sold, together with a number of ewes, for a total of four hundred pounds. Riddler was up on stilts at this. He could scarcely believe his ears. That sheep from his farm should fetch such a sum!

In all, it was a good summer that year, and the crops were flourishing. Turnips were bulging nicely in the ground. The kale was doing well, as were the beans; and—most beautiful of all in Riddler's eyes—the eighteen acres of dredge corn—oats and barley growing together—were ripening splendidly in the sun.

This was the first successful grain crop grown at Godsakes for ten years, and Riddler could not keep away from it. No oats ever danced so merrily, no barley ever bowed so low, and when the day came to begin cutting, Riddler was the first man in the fields, wielding his scythe with such strokes that the grain went down in front of him as though laid low by a fierce, rasping wind.

"Can't you keep up with me?" he roared, pausing once and looking back to where Jim and the other men worked together.

"The question is, master," said Willie Townsend, "can you keep up with yourself?"

But although as the morning progressed, Riddler was indeed obliged to slacken his pace, he worked in a fever all that day and the following days, until the last of the grain was cut.

Behind the men, as they cut the grain, came the women and children, binding the sheaves. There was much chatter and laughter then, especially from Willie Townsend's wife, Prue, for she could make a joke out of anything. When the last sheaf was bound, Prue tied her red-and-white neckerchief around it, held it up for all to see, and placed it in Riddler's arms.

"There you are, master! There's the neck and my neckerchief round it. What'll you give me in return?"

Amid a burst of applause from the watchers, loudest of all from Prue's own children, Riddler gave her a smacking kiss and pressed a coin into her hand. He then carried the "neck" aloft and placed it on top of some nearby sheaves. A warm southeasterly wind was blowing slantwise across the valley; the oat seeds dangled and danced 'in it, and the red-and-white kerchief fluttered gaily. And all over the harvest field, every way you looked, the rows of sheaves stood in regular columns, up and down.

"One thing about it," said Nahum Smith, looking across the valley at Peele, "we shall get our harvest in before them!"

This was a sly joke on Smith's part, made at Riddler's expense, for against the eighteen acres of grain grown at Godsakes the acreage at Peele was immense. Field upon field of pale ripening wheat and bronze ripening barley glowed on the opposite slopes of the valley, and day after day the reaping machines clackered and whirred, and swarms of dark figures moved busily to and fro, toiling in the wake of the reaper.

AT THE sheep sales toward the end of August, Jim bought fifty ewes to make up his flock, and four new Cotswold rams. And at the Missenham cattle sale soon afterward, he bought a four-year-old Shorthorn bull, a handsome blue roan.

"Purebred, every inch of them, and don't they know it!" Riddler said. He enjoyed attending these sales: the outing, the gossip, and the company; but more important than this was the fact that he and Jim were there not merely as spectators but as buyers bidding along with the best. After the bleak, empty years it was pure balm to him to hear the auctioneer bring down his hammer with the words "Sold to Messrs. Riddler and Lundy of Godsakes Farm." And if it happened that the Suttons were there too, as they were occasionally, then Riddler's joy was complete.

IN MID-SEPTEMBER THE GREEN rye was mowed. Jim had been at Godsakes almost a year by this time. Much had been done, but much remained still to be done.

"You'll get at it, all right," Riddler said as they walked over the farm one evening. "You're twenty-five; you've got time on your side. Though in certain respects I wish you would show a bit more dispatch." Receiving no response to this, he suddenly burst out in a passion, "For pity's sake, man, don't you want a son?"

Jim looked away over the fields. The question had caught him unawares. Yes, he would have liked a son. Every man wanted that. And when he had hoped to marry Jane Sutton, he had taken it for granted that he and she would raise a healthy family. But his plans had gone astray, and he had committed himself to a life in which love and the joys of fatherhood would never have any part.

Riddler broke in on Jim's thoughts. "It's no good moping over what might have been. It's the future you've got to think about. Look at this farm. When I'm dead, you and Kirrie will carry it on—but what about when you and she die? What will happen to Godsakes then if you've got no sons to come after you?"

"I can't answer that," Jim said. "But the future is a long way off, and I have enough to do thinking of more immediate things."

But although he seemed to dismiss the future, he found himself thinking about it in the following days, and he was filled with a kind of restlessness. A strange loneliness came over him, bringing back memories not only of Jane, who had jilted him, but of his uncle, who had treated him brutally as a boy and then abandoned him. He thought how very sad it was that he, who had never known a father, should be fated never to know a son.

Sometimes, as he worked in the fields, he would see Kirren in the distance, shooing hens from the barn, and he would think, That girl, that stranger, is my wife. And the thought, framed in words like this, brought a sense of amazement.

She was not such a stranger now, of course, for he had lived in the same house with her for nearly a year. In some respects he knew her well: what her capabilities were, something of her history, and what to expect of her when her temper was roused.

But what of her innermost feelings? Her woman's heart? Was she so hard, so self-complete, as she chose to appear? Sometimes he wished they could talk together, quietly, without Riddler chipping in with his sly remarks. There were few opportunities for this, but one day when he was up on the hill, looking for sheep that had broken out of the upper pasture, he came upon her quite by chance, picking blackberries in a sunny hollow.

At first she was unaware of him, and as she rose on tiptoe, with arms upstretched, trying to reach a high bramble, it afforded him a certain amusement to observe the slender shape of her body stretched to its uttermost, strong and lithe. But then his two dogs, Jess and Sam, went running down the slope to her, wagging their tails, and she turned to make a fuss of them, giving each a few blackberries from one of her baskets. Jim too went down the slope, and when he got close to her, he reached up with his shepherd's long stick to hook the high bramble down to her. With a little laugh she picked the fruit, and he let the bramble spring back again.

"Why are the best blackberries always out of reach?" she asked, putting the fruit in one of her baskets.

"What's out of reach always seems the best," he said.

He hooked down another high bramble and watched her pick the fruit from it. Then he laid his stick on the grass and motioned the dogs to lie down beside it. Kirren looked on in surprise as he took up a basket and began picking blackberries.

"If you are seen doing that, it will lead to talk," she said.

"Why?"

"Because it is women's work, of course. Men do not bother with such trivial tasks as this."

"Then it seems I am not as other men."

"No, that's true, you're not," she said.

"Knowing your opinion of men in general, I suppose I may take that as kindly meant?"

"Yes," she said. "I suppose you may."

It was a perfect September day, and the blackberries, warm in the sun, filled the air with the smell of their ripeness. For a while Jim and Kirren picked in silence, moving slowly away from each other around the thicket of bramble and brier. In a grove of hawthorn trees a skylark sang, and nearby, goldfinches twittered and whirred.

"I'm glad to have met you up here like this," Jim said. "It gives us the chance of a quiet talk. I was thinking about you as I came up the hill, and it suddenly occurred to me that we have now been married a year."

"Not quite a year, surely?" she said.

"Well, all but a week or two, anyway."

"All but three weeks, to be precise. But surely, in a marriage like ours, we shall not be keeping anniversaries?"

"No, hardly that," Jim agreed. "It's just that I am looking for some sort of assurance that you do not have any regrets."

"Then you have that assurance," Kirren said. There was a pause. "Have you any regrets yourself?"

"No. None. But I have been looking back over the past and . . . thinking about certain aspects of my life."

"Have you been thinking about the Sutton girl?"

"Yes."

"Do you still love her?"

"No," he said. He thought for a while before speaking again. "Love, as I see it, is a two-way thing. It's a kind of bargain that one human being strikes with another—or fails to strike. If love is one-sided, it doesn't last long."

"Doesn't it?" Kirren said.

"Well, in very rare cases it might, I suppose—where the object is exceptionally worthy. But Jane was amusing herself with me, without any regard for my feelings, and that is not a worthy thing. However, I don't intend to let it spoil my life. We can most of us get along perfectly well without love."

"It doesn't seem to bring much happiness to those who are afflicted with it."

"Perhaps not."

For a while they gave their whole attention to the business of picking the blackberries. Then Jim spoke again.

"Certainly, there's a lot to be said in favor of a marriage like ours, based as it is on a practical footing instead of on sentimental ideas. It means we do not ask impossible things of each other, and that, in turn, means that neither of us can fall from grace. Indeed, the only person who isn't pleased with the arrangement is your father, whose idea it was."

"Ah yes, my father," Kirren said.

"We are a great disappointment to him."

"He will get over that in time."

CHAPTER 9

THE weather was very hot at that time, but after Michaelmas Day the rains came. The rest of the autumn was so wet as to stop all further work on the land, and Jim again turned his attention to repairing the farmhouse.

If anyone entered the front door at Godsakes and stood in the wide passageway, a door on the left led into the kitchen, and a door on the right, under the staircase, led into the only other ground-floor room, which Kirren called the parlor. There was no furniture in this room—it had all gone to pay Riddler's debts—and for years the place had been used only for storing sacks of grain. But it was a fine, spacious room overlooking the valley, with a fireplace and a big open hearth.

The sacks of grain were removed, the dirt and cobwebs were swept away, and the whole room was scrubbed throughout. Jim then got to work. He repaired the holes in the plaster, white-washed the ceiling, and distempered the walls a pale shell pink. The timberwork was all oak, including the board-and-batten door, and this he treated with linseed oil. The metal casements he painted white.

Kirren, meantime, had bought a dark red Wilton rug that made a cheerful splash of color in front of the hearth, and some second-hand furniture too: three Windsor armchairs with flat cushions on the seats and backs; a large, handsome oil lamp with amber-colored glass; and a bookcase to hold Jim's books. There were also some heavy curtains, old but with plenty of wear in them, of crimson-and-gold brocade.

By then it was Christmas, which fell on a Sunday that year, and Riddler stood on the threshold and marveled. For the room—with a great log fire in the hearth, with red-berried holly on the beams overhead, and the table arrayed in a white linen cloth—was a welcoming place indeed to a man coming in from feeding the beasts on a raw winter morning.

"It does you credit, Kirrie," he said, "and I only wish your mother was here to see the place made so homely again. I must go and spruce myself up before I'm fit for a room like this." And later that day, after a dinner of roast goose, followed by rich plum pudding served with thick cream, he said, "Kirrie, I reckon you've done us proud! I doubt if they've had a better Christmas dinner at Peele."

He and Jim went to sit by the fire, and when Kirren had gone, he sat back in his armchair and looked around him.

"You and Kirrie between you have made the old place into a proper home again. All it needs now to make it complete is a few children gathered round the fire with us."

Jim remained stubbornly silent, staring into the heart of the fire. Riddler, watching him, gave a sigh.

"Ah, well!" he said sadly. "You can't stop an old man from dreaming his dreams."

THE new year came in cold and wet, and although there was nothing surprising in this, it was, as it turned out, setting the pattern for the rest of the year. By the beginning of February heavy, unrelenting rain had turned the whole farm to mire. Down in the valley the Timmy Brook flooded the meadows for weeks on end. The little bridges were all submerged, and when Kirren drove to town, she had to go around by Marychurch and cross the river at Lyall Bridge.

There were a few dry days toward the middle of March, but then, just as the first batch of lambs were due, the heavy rain descended yet again out of the north. And although Jim provided all the shelter he could, conditions were so wet and cold that many ewes giving birth were too enfeebled to play their part.

"That's the trouble with sheep," Riddler said. "They give in too easy. They've got no spunk."

He and Jim were out at all hours, attending the ewes in their labor, rubbing life into weak, sickly lambs, and doing their best to get them to drink milk. But in spite of their vigilance and care, a great many lambs were lost. Kirren, bringing hot food and drink to the men at work in the lambing field, saw the heap of small dead bodies lying sodden and limp in the rain and turned away, sick at heart.

"How many have you lost?" she asked Jim.

"So far, more than half," he said, looking at her with tired eyes.

Kirren knew what his flock meant to him and was stricken anew. "What about the live lambs? Will they pull through?"

"I hope so, but it's hard to tell. A lot depends on the weather. If it goes on like this"—he gave a shrug—"we are bound to lose a few more, I'm afraid."

It was the cold and the wet together that did the flock so much damage. A ewe could easily stand the cold if only she had a dry resting place, and a lamb too could withstand the cold so long as its birthcoat had a chance to dry out. But ewes that would not lie down on wet ground remained on their feet until exhausted. Thus, many lambs were stillborn, and others, already weak at birth, died within a matter of hours.

Still, miraculously, there were survivors. Some of these needed special attention, and every available shelter had been brought into use as a nursery. There were also a few orphan lambs, kept in a separate pen in the barn, and it was Kirren who looked after these. She was good with animals. And Jim, noting her gentleness whenever she handled a sickly lamb, was deeply moved by her concern.

One cold, dark morning after breakfast Jim came into the kitchen, and partially opening the front of his jacket, showed her a newborn lamb he was carrying inside, a lamb so incredibly small that Kirren had to peer closely before she could make out its shape in the jacket's folds.

"Oh, how tiny!" she exclaimed, and gingerly put out a hand to touch its coat of tight curls. "It's scarcely as big as my two hands."

"He's one of twins," Jim said. "The ewe has turned her back on him—she hasn't enough milk for both—and he's only just barely alive. Can you look after him indoors?"

"Yes, of course," Kirren said.

Jim, opening his jacket farther, eased the lamb carefully into her hands. It was the merest morsel of life, all head and ears, its frail body nothing at all, its long legs limp and knobbly, like the legs of a rag doll. Kirren folded it into her arms and it nestled against her wearily, seeking her warmth, until, with a little sudden thrust, it buried its nose under her armpit and rested there.

"If you can manage to pull him through the first two or three days or so . . ." Jim began.

"I can but try."

"Yes, that's right." He turned toward the door. "I'll be back from the pens in half an hour."

Riddler, sitting longer than usual over his breakfast, watched with a mixture of interest and scorn as Kirren dealt with the newborn lamb, bedding it down in a shallow box lined with hay and placing it to one side of the hearth. She then put some diluted warm milk into a drinking bottle and, crouching down beside the lamb, smeared a few drops of the milk on his lips, gently persevering until at last he opened his mouth and licked at the bottle with his small pink tongue. There was a faint snuffling noise as he blew through nostrils not quite clean, a gulping sound as his throat worked. And at the end of the tiny wrinkled body lying curled in the box, a wispy tail waggled and twitched.

Riddler rose from the table. "It's high time you had a lamb of your own," he growled, and pushed past her to get his coat.

Kirren was silent, still feeding the lamb, and he stood looking down at her broodingly.

"I just don't understand you. You're a married woman, and—"

"Married at your instigation, remember, as a business arrangement, nothing more. That's what we agreed, Jim and me."

"But you must have known that I had something more in mind?"

Riddler threw on his coat and fastened the buttons up to the neck. The lamb had had enough for its first drink, and Kirren now rose to her feet, the half-empty bottle in her hands.

"Yes, I knew what was in your mind, but it wasn't in mine."

"More fool you, then!" Riddler said. "I thought I'd done pretty well by you, finding you a husband like Jim, a well set up chap, healthy and strong, with something about him more than most, and handsome enough. Of course, he's got his faults, I allow. For a start, he's inclined to think he's always right."

"So he is, more often than not."

"Seems you think pretty well of him, then?"

"I have good reason to think well of him, and so have you. Without him we should have lost the farm."

"I suppose, but he thinks well of you too. And I reckon there's more to it than just that. He feels something for you, Kirrie, I'm sure. Why, the way he looks at you sometimes—"

"You are making all this up. I have never seen Jim looking at me in any special way."

"You wouldn't, would you?" Riddler said. "You made your

views on marriage and men pretty clear from the start, and so a young man of Jim's sort needs some sign from a girl before he'll come out in the open with her. It's up to you now to let him know you've changed your mind."

"I didn't say I'd changed my mind. And I wish you would leave me alone!"

Abruptly Kirren moved to the table and began clearing the used breakfast things. Riddler, swearing under his breath, took his hat from the fireplace and jammed it down hard on his head.

"Stupid cat of a girl!" he muttered, and slammed the door.

WITHIN a few hours of being brought indoors, the lamb, thoroughly warmed, had left his bed beside the fire and was exploring the kitchen, tottering over the flagged floor on legs that were apt to crumple beneath him. In a matter of three or four days, although his legs might still let him down, he was able to right himself without help, and would follow Kirren constantly while she went about her chores.

"He's doing nicely," Jim said. "You've pulled him through the most difficult time. He's got it in him to thrive from now on."

"Do you think he will?"

"I'm sure of it."

The rest of the lambing came to an end, having lasted fifteen days. Of the seventy-six lambs born, only forty-two had survived, and with the weather still bad, a few more of these might also be lost.

On the morning that the last two ewes had lambed, Jim came into the kitchen at ten o'clock, when Riddler had just ridden off to town to pick up the money for the men's wages. Kirren was about to begin her baking, and as she moved between cupboard and table the hand-reared lamb, now eight days old, followed her faithfully to and fro.

When Jim entered the room, the lamb scampered toward him, putting up his chin to be fondled and scratched.

"I've come to take this chap off your hands," Jim remarked. "I think I've got a mother for him. It's the ewe I've just left—her lamb was stillborn."

"Can I come and watch?"

"Yes, of course."

559

They went together through the rain across the yard to the open barn. Inside, Jim led the way to a pen against the far wall. In it stood the bereaved ewe, her attitude listless and dejected. But her tightly stretched udder was full of milk, and she would make a good mother if she could be persuaded to accept the orphan.

Jim opened the front hurdle a few inches and entered the pen. From his pocket he took a bottle containing balsam of aniseed. He got astride the ewe from behind, uncorked the bottle with his teeth, and poured some of the strong-smelling oil into the palm of his left hand. He gave Kirren the bottle to hold and began to rub the oil under the ewe's chin and jaws and all around the outer rims of her nostrils. Protesting a little, she tried to break free, but Jim had her wedged firmly between his legs. In less than two minutes the job was done, and the ewe moved away, shaking herself. Then Jim took the lamb, rubbed a little of the oil on its hindquarters, and set it down.

The ewe did not see the lamb at first. She was busy moving her head up and down as though trying to escape the smell of the all-pervasive aniseed. But when the lamb began to bleat, she turned and stared at it in surprise, in a way that seemed quite clearly to say, Where did you come from? Jim put the lamb closer to her, and she leaned toward it suspiciously, sniffing it.

But her sense of smell was badly impaired by aniseed, and the lamb had the same smell anyway. In another moment or two, although still plainly mystified, she had stepped forward and was working her way down his back with a nibbling movement of her lips. The lamb gave a short, rippling shudder and turned toward her. Jim guided him to a teat, and as soon as he began to suck, so his tail began to twirl. The ewe, looking over her shoulder at him, viewed the movement indulgently, giving a little whickering cry. Ewe and lamb, so it seemed, were very well pleased with one another.

"He'll be all right now," Jim said. "They both will."

Kirren nodded. "So that's the last of the lambing for now?"

"Yes, praise be. I've never had a lambing like it before."

"You've lost a great many."

"Yes, it's been bad. Smith and Townsend are out there now, burying the last of the carcasses."

They walked out of the pen to the open doorway and stood

looking at the white shafts of rain splashing down on the ground. "It doesn't look like it's improving yet," Kirren said.

"No, it's setting in for the day. Your father will have had a wet ride to town, and he'll have a wetter one coming back. There's a good two feet of water covering the bridges over the brook, and it's rising steadily. If your father's got any sense, he'll come straight home when he's finished his business at the bank."

"But he hasn't got any sense; you know that. He'll stay chatting all day to the market folk, taking a glass with this one and that one, and won't be home until after dark. But his mare usually brings him safely home. *She* has sense, if he has not."

CHAPTER 10

THE rain continued all day, growing heavier all the time, and by afternoon it was falling in torrents, and the whole farm was awash. Jim, coming into the house at two o'clock, ate his food as fast as he could and went out again. The greater part of his flock, ninety-five ewes, were standing in water over their hooves in the home pasture.

"I'm taking them up to the pinewood," Jim said to Kirren. "It's the only place that's not flooded."

By four o'clock it was almost dark. Down in the bottom of the valley the Timmy Brook had broken its banks and was spreading out over the meadows in a great sweeping tide. At half past six Jim went down with two of his men, Townsend and Smith, to take a closer look at it and found that the swirling floodwater had covered the lower part of the track. It was completely dark now, and Jim carried a lantern.

"It's worse than I've ever known it," Smith said, "and I've been on this farm more than twenty years."

"What about the master?" Townsend asked. "Will he come round by Lyall Bridge?"

"I don't know, but I doubt it," Jim said. "He doesn't take much account of the floods."

"The bridges will all be under three or four feet of water," Smith said, "and by the way it's swirling here, I'd say the current is pretty fast."

"Yes, I think you're right. I'm going down to watch for him."

Jim looked at the two men huddled in the pouring rain. They had been working with him for fourteen hours and were soaked to the skin. "Get off to your homes, both of you, and get yourselves into dry clothes. And call at the house on your way and tell Mrs. Lundy I've gone down to the brook to wait for the master."

"We'll tell her, yes," Townsend said. "But are you sure you should go down alone, what with these floods—"

"Don't worry," Jim said. "I shall take care, be sure of that."

Leaving the main farm track, Jim went splashing across the meadow through water that reached halfway up his shins. The rain made the night as black as pitch, and in the darkness the great meadow, so familiar by day, seemed like a never-ending waste, full of unremembered dips, where thick mud sucked at his boots. His lantern was no help; it merely lit a small patch of rain and cast a will-o'-the-wisp reflection on the floodwater swirling about his feet. But at last a willow tree loomed up at him, and he knew he had found the bank of the brook.

He reached up to the tree and broke off a long, slender branch and, proceeding with even greater caution, began moving rightward along the bank, prodding the brook in search of the bridge he knew Riddler was in the habit of using.

The floodwater now reached to his knees, eddying around him with a force that told him how swift the main current must be. He felt the ground begin to dip and knew that he had arrived at the place where the bank sloped down to the bridge. The water covering it was, as Nahum Smith had predicted, between three and four feet deep.

When Jim had waited perhaps an hour, he heard the sound of hoofbeats coming across the flooded meadow on the far side of the brook. Standing on the bank above the bridge, he raised his lantern shoulder-high, swinging it gently to and fro, at the same time calling out in a great voice that would carry above the noise of the rain.

"Morris! Is that you?"

Riddler, approaching the flooded bank on his mare, heard Jim and picked out the glimmer of the lantern on the other side.

"Of course it's me!" he answered. "Who else would it be?"

"I don't think you ought to cross here—it's too dangerous," Jim called. "I think you should go round by Lyall Bridge."

"Don't tell me what to do!" Riddler bawled. "I've crossed this brook in floodwater before and never got myself drowned yet."

This answer was only what Jim had expected, and he knew it was no use arguing. "Very well!" he shouted back. "But keep a close rein as you come across. The current is running very fast."

"My mare's not afraid of the water, current or no current."

Sure enough, encouraged by Riddler, the mare picked her way through the deepening water and down onto the narrow bridge, and with the flowing brook now up to her belly, began very gingerly to cross. When she was halfway across, however, a floating log struck her a sharp blow in the ribs. She gave a high-pitched whinny and the next instant was in the water, hindquarters plunging, forefeet pawing wildly.

Riddler, half drowned, held on to her, first swearing at her and calling her names, then speaking reassuringly to her.

"Come on, old girl, you must swim for it now. That's the idea! It's only a yard or two more to the bank."

Jim, although he could see almost nothing, knew from the noise what had happened. Knowing too that the swift current must be carrying the mare downstream, he made his way along the bank to the place where mare and man struggled together in the brook.

"Morris?" he called. "Are you all right?"

Riddler shouted back, "Get out of the way! We're coming up there!"

The mare had great difficulty in mounting the steep, slippery bank, but urged on by Riddler's shouts, she made it over at last in three gallant heaves. But as she gave the final heave, bringing her shuddering hindquarters up over the edge, Riddler was thrown out of the saddle. He struck the ground sideways, while one foot remained in its stirrup, twisted in such a way that he could not pull free; and as the mare cantered away, he was dragged along beside her through the mud.

"Whoa, you fool. Would you kill me?" he roared.

Jim too shouted for the mare to stop, but she ran on, frightened and confused, making instinctively for the gate that led onto the main farm track, and Jim, splashing across the meadow, followed through the darkness.

The closed gate brought her to a stop, and she was waiting, all in a tremble, when Jim at last caught up with her. Soothing her as best he could, he hung his lantern on the saddle hook and gathered up the trailing reins. Riddler was unconscious now but still alive. Jim freed his foot from the twisted stirrup and heaved him up into the saddle, holding him there with one hand while he opened the gate with the other.

Kirren, hearing him in the yard, came out at once to the porch door. She watched him carry her father in.

"What happened?" she asked.

"Your father was thrown out of the saddle, but his foot got caught up in the stirrup. He's been dragged right across the meadow."

"Is he hurt badly?"

"I don't know, but he's unconscious and soaked to the skin. We must dry him and get him into bed."

Jim laid Riddler on the mat in front of the fire and stripped off his clothes. He gave him a good hard toweling and rubbed warm brandy into him—into his chest, his stomach, his back, even into his legs and feet. Then he wrapped a warm blanket around him and carried him upstairs to his bed. Kirren had placed a lighted candle nearby, and now she was lighting a fire in the grate.

Riddler lay flat on his back, with the bedclothes drawn up to his chin, his face as pallid as yeast, and blood oozing from a cut above one eye. Kirren came to the bed and touched his face.

"He feels very cold."

"Yes, and his pulse is weak." Jim turned toward the door. "I'm going to fetch Dr. Hoad," he said.

Kirren followed him down the stairs and into the kitchen.

"You're not going to cross the brook, I hope?"

"Yes, I am."

"After what's happened to Father tonight? Are you out of your mind?"

"Your father'd been drinking," Jim said. "I have not."

"Why not go round by the main bridge at Lyall?"

"Because, as you well know, it will add an hour to the journey."

"I see no point in saving an hour if you end up drowned," Kirren said. "And what about the mare, anyway? Will she cross again after such a fright?"

"I hope she will. Indeed, she must."

"I wish you would not go," Kirren said. "You may not have

been drinking, but when did you last have a good night's sleep? You've been out with your flock at all hours this week—" She broke off, looking at him, and her eyes were suddenly very dark. "You're just about tired unto death."

There was a silence between them, full of feeling, full of thought.

"I'm not so tired as all that, and I think it's important to get the doctor as soon as I can."

"Dr. Hoad won't cross the brook. He'll—" Once again she broke off. "Oh, it's no use talking to you! I'm wasting my breath! Go and get yourself drowned if that's what you've set your heart on doing!"

She turned away from him angrily, but he caught her arm in a firm grip and drew her around to face him again.

"I shan't drown," he said quietly. "I care too much about my life to run any risk of losing it." And, drawing her toward him, he kissed her on the mouth.

A quick glance between them, and he was gone out the door. For a moment Kirren stood stock-still, her thoughts going with him through the night. Then, with a faint flush in her cheeks, she went up the stairs to her father's room.

RAIN was still falling heavily by the time Jim reached the doctor's house, but he made the trip without misadventure. The doctor agreed to come, but by the longer route of the bridge at Lyall. Jim rode home the way he had come, again safely, and Kirren, having been listening for him, came to peer down through her father's bedroom window and raised a hand to him as he rode by on his way to the stables.

It was past ten o'clock when Dr. Hoad arrived, his temper somewhat short.

"Trust that fool Morris Riddler to bring me out on a night like this!" he said.

After making his examination, the doctor stood in front of the bedroom fire and drank the brandy Jim had brought him.

"No bones broken as far as I can tell, but I shan't know for certain until he comes to."

"When do you think that will be?" Kirren asked.

"Just don't know. He's pretty badly concussed, of course, but he's got a thick enough skull, Lord knows, and I doubt if much harm will come of it. As for the twisted foot, well, it'll be pretty sore for a while."

"What should I do for him when he comes round?"

"Keep him warm and quiet and still, that's all, and if he starts asking for food, give him something easy and light. Gruel, perhaps, or arrowroot." The doctor drained his brandy glass. "I'll come out again sometime tomorrow."

Jim, after seeing the doctor off, returned to Riddler's bedroom. Kirren was sitting by the bed, with needlework in her lap.

"I'll sit with him now while you get some sleep," he said.

"You're the one who needs to sleep," she replied.

"Don't argue with me. Just do as I say."

"No, I will not! Why should I indeed?" Her dark eyes flashed in the candlelight. "He's my father, not yours."

"I thought you hated him," Jim said.

"Yes, well, so I do sometimes. Or at least I have done, in the past." She looked at the gray-faced man in the bed. "But how can you hate anyone who lies so cold and still and quiet and looks so, so close to death?" she said. "Oh, he's a selfish, stubborn brute of a man. . . . But he's worked so hard all these years, and for this to happen to him now—"

"He's not going to die," Jim said. "Your father is as tough as oak. There's no need to worry."

"Very well," Kirren said. "But if there's nothing to worry about, you may go to your bed and sleep."

Jim, with a little smile, gave in. "You'll call if you need me?"

"Yes, I will. I promise you."

He touched her arm and left the room.

AT FIVE o'clock the following morning, refreshed after six hours' sleep, Jim was in the kitchen making tea. During the night the rain had stopped, and the outside world seemed strangely still. When he went up to Riddler's room, taking Kirren a cup of tea, she had already drawn the curtains back, and there was a cold pale light in the room.

"A short while ago he woke up," she said. "It was only for two or three seconds, that's all, but he knew me, I'm sure."

"Here, drink this while it's hot," Jim said, and gave her the tea.

He went to the bed, touched Riddler's face and tested his pulse. "He's a lot warmer than he was last night, and his pulse seems to be stronger too."

"Yes, I thought the same myself."

"Have you slept at all?"

"Yes, off and on."

Jim went down to the kitchen again and drank his own cup of hot, sweet tea. He then went out on a round of the farm.

He found the fields awash in mud. Their miry state would make extra work for all the hands. First, a young sow, heavily in pig, fell into an open drain, and it took three men to haul her out. Next, it was the hand Bob Lovell, who slipped wheeling a barrowload of muck across the yard, so that it ran into one of the pillars supporting the lean-to and brought part of the roof sagging down. Then Kirren's pony, Griff, had to be treated for colic. While Jim was giving the horse a mild draft of peppermint and laudanum, Townsend came to him with a message.

"The master's awake, and he's asking for you."

Riddler, clad in a nightshirt now, still lay flat on his back, but there was some color reviving in his face, and he was breathing more normally. Jim sat down in the chair by the bed.

"I ache in every particle," Riddler groaned hoarsely. "How's my stupid cow of a mare?"

"In better shape than you by far," Jim said.

"She doesn't deserve to be, dragging me over the lot like that. Did you bring my saddlebags in?"

"Yes."

"Money safe?"

"Yes, quite safe."

"I reckon I'd better leave it to you to pay the men their wages."

"Yes, all right," Jim said.

Kirren came into the room with a bowl of warm barley gruel. Riddler looked at it with some distaste.

"If this is all I'm getting to eat, the sooner I mend the better."

Jim, with a little smile for Kirren, quietly left the room.

At three o'clock the doctor came again, and Jim, called into the house, was climbing the stairs to Riddler's room when he heard the old man give a bellowing shout. On going in, he found

Riddler sitting on the edge of the bed, glaring ferociously at the doctor, who stood nearby.

"He said he couldn't straighten his foot, so I straightened it for him," Dr. Hoad explained, quite unmoved.

"I reckon the fool has just about crippled me for life."

"Well, we shall see, shan't we?" the doctor said cheerfully, and downstairs, as Kirren and Jim saw him off, he said, "Keep him in bed for a day or two—if you can get him to stay there."

It had begun to rain again, and by early evening, when Jim paid the men their wages, it was turning to sleet.

After the men had gone, Jim went into the barn to look over his ewes and lambs, and found Kirren there. She was with her fosterling and was letting him suck her thumb.

"It seems he still remembers me."

"So he should," Jim said. "You were his mother till yesterday."

"He likes his new mother best."

They stood for a little while in silence, watching the lamb. Then they both began speaking at once, Kirren to say what a day it had been, and Jim to ask about her father.

"How is he now?"

"Better," she said. "But still very quiet—for him."

"Make the most of it."

"Yes." She laughed.

They left the barn and went into the house, and Kirren at once became very busy, first making up the fire and swinging the kettle over it, next lighting the lamp on the table. Jim, having hung up his jacket and hat, stood quietly watching her moving to and fro. At last he spoke.

"Kirren, can't you be still for a moment?"

"What?" she said with a flickering glance. "Yes, very well, but I thought you'd be hungry for your supper."

"Supper can wait," Jim said. "I want to talk to you, and I can't talk sensibly while you keep flitting about like that."

"Behold me, then—standing still."

She stood at the opposite side of the table and placed her hands on the back of a chair, folding them there in a gesture of primness. But although she was now facing him, her glance was still evasive, unsure, and, watching her closely in the lamplight, he saw a faint tinge of color come stealing slowly into her face.

"Something's been happening to us, hasn't it, during the past few weeks?" he said. And when she failed to answer, he added, "Or perhaps it's only been happening to me. . . ."

"No," she said quickly, "it has happened to me as well."

"Then why won't you look at me properly?"

"Because you haven't yet said what it is. . . ."

"I love you," he said, "and you love me."

There was a pause as she drew a deep breath. She was looking at him directly now, letting him see what she felt for him, and although when he moved and came toward her, there was a hint of shy alarm in the sudden widening of her eyes, she went into his arms and gave herself to him in a kiss that was free of shyness, free of constraint.

In a little while, when Jim spoke again, it was in a voice very quiet and deep, and he looked at her in wonderment, touching her face, her lips, her throat delicately with his fingertips.

"When I married you, I was deceived. You allowed me to think that you had no womanly passion in you, nor any womanly tenderness."

"And now you know better?" Kirren said.

"Yes," he said in the same deep voice. "Now I know you for what you are."

There came a loud knock from the room above, making them jump. They looked at each other with laughing eyes, drawing apart reluctantly with a last lingering touch of the hands.

"That's Father," Kirren said, "just in case you didn't know. I'd better go up and see what he wants."

"I'll come with you."

"No. I don't want you with me. Not just yet. He'd know there was something. And I need time to—to gather my wits."

Another loud knock, and she hurried away. Jim stood, a faint smile on his lips, listening to the sounds overhead, of Kirren and her father talking. Then, in a moment, she reappeared.

"He's asking for something to eat," she said, "and he wants you to take it up to him."

When Jim entered the bedroom, with a bowl of gruel and milk on a tray, Riddler was sitting up in bed.

"Is this all I get? Pig slops again?" he said.

"H'mm," Jim said, surveying him. "You are better, obviously."

"Yes. If you thought to be rid of me, you'll have to wait a while longer yet." Riddler motioned him to a chair. "Meanwhile, you can sit and talk and watch me feasting myself."

LATER Jim and Kirren ate their own supper, sitting at the kitchen table in the golden circle of light from the lamp.

With the curtains drawn close over the windows against the cold wet night outside, and a good fire burning red on the hearth, they were shut in together in comfort and warmth, with a new special intimacy between them. Knowing that Riddler was now asleep, they talked in quiet voices, and everything they said to each other deepened the feeling between them.

"If we were not already married, would you marry me?"

"Yes, of course."

"Ours was a strange wedding," Jim said. "Surely no other two people can ever have married in such a way, knowing nothing about one another, caring nothing, as we did then." And after a little while he said, "When did you first find it had changed?"

"I don't know," Kirren said, "and I wouldn't tell you if I did."

"Your father said this would happen to us, that a man and a woman thrown together were bound to feel something for each other sooner or later."

"I know pretty well what my father said. But oh, Jim, is that all it is?" Kirren looked at him in laughing dismay. "Something that would have happened to us, quite regardless of who we were? Just any woman? Any man? I can't believe that."

"No more can I. Because you are not just any woman, and I am not just any man."

There was a silence. He looked at her.

"Kirren," he said.

"Yes, what?"

"Your father is much better now. I don't think it will be necessary for you to sit up with him tonight."

"No," she said. "I don't think it will." She looked at him with a dark, steady gaze. "Tonight will be our wedding night."

IN ANOTHER three days Riddler was up and about again, groaning and swearing at the pain in his joints but hobbling stubbornly everywhere, refusing all help save that of a walking stick.

The weather continued wet and cold, and the valley remained flooded for the best part of ten days, kept wet by repeated rains.

"Is there to be no end to it?" Kirren said. "Oh dear, what I wouldn't give to have a few dry days for a change!"

"You seem cheerful enough anyway, in spite of the weather," Riddler said.

"Do I?" said Kirren, on her guard.

It was one morning, after breakfast, and they were alone. Riddler was taking it easy by the fire.

"Not only cheerful," he said, "but something else besides."

Kirren, washing the dishes, glanced at him from under her lashes but made no reply.

"I can't quite fathom it out," Riddler said thoughtfully. "There's something different about you these days, and whatever it is, it suits you right well."

"Does it, now? Fancy that."

Kirren came to the hearth to fetch a cloth for drying, plucking it down from the string line that hung in a loop from the mantelpiece. Instead of turning away, however, she stood with the cloth between her hands, and Riddler, leaning back in his chair, slowly raised his face to hers.

For a little while father and daughter eyed each other unsteadily, until the amused satisfaction of one and the indulgent mockery of the other kindled a mutual gleam of warmth mixed with sardonic understanding. Riddler was the first to speak.

"I knew you'd come to it in the end."

"I suppose you think the credit's all yours?"

"Of course! If it wasn't for me, you'd still be the same crabby spinster you were before, sharp-tongued and hard as nails."

"No compliments, please," Kirren said.

"You were made for marriage, Kirrie. I always knew that, all along. And I'll tell you something else as well: you were made to be the mother of sons."

"All in good time," she said, "perhaps."

"Time!" he said. "You've already wasted a year and a half!"

A few days afterward news came to Godsakes that Philip Sutton's wife, Jane, had given birth to a baby son.

"Well," Riddler said to Jim and Kirren, "I never thought to say this about the Suttons, but, let that be an example to you."

CHAPTER 11

THE spring and summer of that year were the coldest and wettest anyone could remember, and the bad conditions brought much trouble to farmers everywhere. In the second lambing at Godsakes, losses were almost as bad as in the first, and all through the summer there was much to do to keep the flock free of sickness.

But whatever the trials and anxieties of that dismal year, it seemed as though some benign spirit were keeping watch over Godsakes and its people. There was a radiance over their lives, a sense of warm unity in everything they did together. Jim had the feeling, new every day, that his life was rather astonishing, that many great and marvelous gifts had been bestowed upon him. He saw his future laid out before him as in a vision, with a rich golden light spread over it. And at the heart of this feeling was the love that had grown between him and Kirren.

"Sometimes I feel that I don't deserve the good fortune that's come my way," he said to her once. "But I mean to deserve it, by working for it and earning it."

"You have always worked, all your life," Kirren said.

"All that is nothing," he said with a smile, "to what I shall do in future years."

At the end of August, when haymaking was finished at last, they cut their few acres of dredge corn—oats and barley—as before. But this year, due to the constant rain, the whole crop was fit only for the pigs and fowl.

The one comfort Riddler could find for the year's disappointments was that things had been much worse at Peele. There was no golden glow in the harvest fields across the valley that year, but only a somber, shadowy pall. There was no happy noise of reaping machines, for the grain was so wet and so badly flattened that it had to be cut by hand.

"Just look at them all, having to put their backs into it and do a bit of work for a change!" Riddler said to Kirren and Jim. "It makes me laugh like a spinning top, knowing they'll get no gain from it."

"Why? What good does that do us?" Kirren said.

"I don't know what it does for you, but it does me a power of good to see bad luck come to them for once."

It was a dull but dry day, and they were at work in their own harvest field, opening up the shocks soaked by days of rain and setting the sheaves out in twos so that they might dry in the wind. Kirren and Jim were working together, and Riddler, who had finished his row, was standing near them, his hands on his hips, looking across the valley at Peele.

"After what they did to me, I reckon I'm about entitled to crow over them for a change," he said.

"And do you intend," Kirren asked, "to carry your grudge right through to the end of your life?"

"Yes. Why shouldn't I?" Riddler said.

"It only seems rather childish to bear a grudge for so long. Jim doesn't feel like that. He's put his quarrel out of his mind."

"And what's so surprising about that?" Riddler said with a curl of his lip. "The harm he got at the Suttons' hands was nothing but a fleabite compared with the harm they did to me. In fact, that was a bit of good luck for him when John Sutton turned him out, for he wouldn't have come to us otherwise."

With his chin jutting pugnaciously, Riddler turned and went stumping off, to work by himself farther down the field. Jim and Kirren looked at each other across the sheaves.

"It's no good trying to change him, you know. His hatred for Sutton goes too deep."

"Yes, I know," Kirren said. "I'd do better to hold my tongue."

"Nor is it any good using me as an example, because what your father says is true. Twice in my life when someone has done me a bad turn, it has worked out to my advantage. First, when my uncle abandoned me and John Sutton took me in, and then, as your father said, when John Sutton turned me out and I came here."

"You consider yourself lucky, it seems."

"Yes, for I've not only got this far but I've got you as well."

"Riches indeed!" Kirren said.

"Oh, you may mock if you like, looking at me with those dark gypsy eyes! But what more could a man want from life?"

"Surely, there must be something more you want. . . ."

"Kirren, are you telling me something?"

"Yes. I'm going to have a child."

They stood looking at one another, and there was a quietness over them both. And a stillness in him. A growing smile.

"Well, that explains it," he said at last.

"Explains what?"

"Why you are looking so beautiful."

"Am I beautiful?"

"Yes. You are."

"My father is looking over at us. He will be shouting at us in a minute, asking why we are standing idle."

"In that case, we'd better get on."

In another few minutes, however, they stopped work again, because overhead in the gray sky the clouds parted and the sun shone out, falling on them with a gentle warmth and filling the valley with a soft bright light. They stood with their faces upturned to the sun, grateful for the light and the warmth they had seen and felt so rarely that summer, and Riddler, just a little way off, stood in exactly the same way, lifting his blunt, crooked face to the sun in a childlike gesture of gratitude.

And away on the far side of the valley, the reapers in the fields at Peele, laboring over their blighted harvest, also stopped work and stood, greeting the sun with a little cheer that was heard clearly in the fields at Godsakes. Hearing the sound of this cheer, Kirren and Jim smiled at each other, and Kirren, putting one hand to her eyes, turned to look out over the valley, softly lit by the golden sun shining through the parted clouds.

"I wonder how this valley will look, and these two farms, when our children are growing up, say in ten or twenty years' time."

"You are looking a long way ahead."

"Yes, and why not?" Kirren said.

A beautiful Gloucestershire valley of fields and farmland dotted with sheep—this pastoral nineteenth-century scene, which Mary Pearce brings to life so vividly in *The Two Farms*, is in fact the real twentieth-century countryside in western England where she lives. "For the sake of the story I made the valley a little smaller," she says, "but the actual area is much as I've described it—quite old farms, with all sorts of livestock roaming the hills." Miss Pearce's own home, with the delightful name of Owls' End, fits perfectly into this setting. "It's on a quiet lane overlooking the valley, and I do indeed have plenty of owls. For the last week or so, one especially hardy specimen has taken possession of my garden gate!"

Mary E. Pearce

After reading *The Two Farms*, one can't help wondering what the future will hold for the fictional residents of Peele and Godsakes. "Well," the author says, "the next generation would have to survive the 1870s, which was a bad time for the small farmer in England. And perhaps Godsakes would keep improving while Peele experienced greater decline. But," she adds, "some things are better left to the imagination, don't you think?"

The idea of writing as a career first took hold of Mary Pearce at the tender age of ten, while she was living in Willesden, a London borough and her birthplace. But it was not until she relocated to Cornwall that she took up the pen professionally. *The Two Farms* is her eighth book, and it shares with her other novels—among them, *Polsinney Harbour* (a Condensed Books selection in 1985)—her strong preference for rural life over city life.

It also reflects the author's intense interest in people's occupations. In addition to farming, she has written about carpentry, grain milling and fishing. "Men and women at work is something I find endlessly fascinating." Along these lines, Miss Pearce's next book will focus on England's woolen industry in the 1850s.

ACKNOWLEDGMENTS

Page 129: map by James Alexander.

Back jacket, Hemingway quote: from "Old Newsman Writes" in *By-Line: Ernest Hemingway*, edited by William White, © 1967 by Mary Hemingway. Reprinted by permission of Charles Scribner's Sons. First appeared in *Esquire*, December 1934.